ALSO BY JOYCE CAROL OATES

NOVELS

With Shuddering Fall (1964) • *A Garden of Earthly Delights* (1967) • *Expensive People* (1968) • *them* (1969) • *Wonderland* (1971) • *Do With Me What You Will* (1973) • *The Assassins* (1975) • *Childwold* (1976) • *Son of the Morning* (1978) • *Unholy Loves* (1979) • *Bellefleur* (1980) • *Angel of Light* (1981) • *A Bloodsmoor Romance* (1982) • *Mysteries of Winterthurn* (1984) • *Solstice* (1985) • *Marya: A Life* (1986) • *You Must Remember This* (1987) • *American Appetites* (1989) • *Because It Is Bitter, and Because It Is My Heart* (1990) • *Black Water* (1992) • *Foxfire: Confessions of a Girl Gang* (1993) • *What I Lived For* (1994) • *Zombie* (1995) • *We Were the Mulvaneys* (1996) • *Man Crazy* (1997) • *My Heart Laid Bare* (1998) • *Broke Heart Blues* (1999) • *Blonde* (2000)

"ROSAMOND SMITH" NOVELS

Lives of the Twins (1987) • *Soul/Mate* (1989) • *Nemesis* (1990) • *Snake Eyes* (1992) • *You Can't Catch Me* (1995) • *Double Delight* (1997) • *Starr Bright Will Be With You Soon* (1999) • *The Barrens* (2001)

SHORT STORY COLLECTIONS

By the North Gate (1963) • *Upon the Sweeping Flood and Other Stories* (1966) • *The Wheel of Love* (1970) • *Marriages and Infidelities* (1972) • *The Goddess and Other Women* (1974) • *The Poisoned Kiss* (1975) • *Crossing the Border* (1976) • *Night-Side* (1977) • *A Sentimental Education* (1980) • *Last Days* (1984) • *Raven's Wing* (1986) • *The Assignation* (1988) • *Heat and Other Stories* (1991) • *Where Is Here?* (1992) • *Where Are You Going, Where Have You Been?: Selected Early Stories* (1993) • *Haunted: Tales of the Grotesque* (1994) • *Will You Always Love Me?* (1996) • *The Collector of Hearts: New Tales of the Grotesque* (1998) • *Faithless: Tales of Transgression* (2001)

NOVELLAS

The Triumph of the Spider Monkey (1976) • *I Lock My Door Upon Myself* (1990) • *The Rise of Life on Earth* (1991) • *First Love: A Gothic Tale* (1996)

POETRY

Anonymous Sins (1969) • *Love and Its Derangements* (1970) • *Angel Fire* (1973) • *The Fabulous Beasts* (1975) • *Women Whose Lives Are Food, Men Whose Lives Are Money* (1978) • *Invisible Woman: New and Selected Poems, 1970–1982* (1982) • *The Time Traveler* (1989) • *Tenderness* (1996)

PLAYS

Miracle Play (1974) • *Three Plays* (1980) • *Twelve Plays* (1991) • *I Stand Before You Naked* (1991) • *In Darkest America (Tone Clusters and The Eclipse)* (1991) • *The Perfectionist and Other Plays* (1995) • *New Plays* (1998)

ESSAYS

The Edge of Impossibility: Tragic Forms in Literature (1972) • *New Heaven, New Earth: The Visionary Experience in Literature* (1974) • *Contraries* (1981) • *The Profane Art: Essays and Reviews* (1983) • *On Boxing* (1987) • *(Woman) Writer: Occasions and Opportunities* (1988) • *George Bellows: American Artist* (1995) • *Where I've Been, and Where I'm Going: Essays, Reviews, and Prose* (1999)

FOR CHILDREN

Come Meet Muffin! (1998)

Joyce Carol Oates

Middle Age: A Romance

Fourth Estate • *London*

This paperback edition first published in 2002
First published in Great Britain in 2001 by
Fourth Estate
A Division of HarperCollins*Publishers*
77–85 Fulham Palace Road
London W6 8JB
www.4thestate.com

7 9 10 8

In the chapter "The Fell of Dark," the quoted poetry is
Gerard Manley Hopkins's "I Wake and Feel the Fell of Dark."

Throughout the novel are scattered quotations from Plato
(primarily the *Symposium*, the *Republic*, and the *Phaedo*),
translated by W.H.D. Rouse.

A catalogue record for this book is available from the
British Library

ISBN 1-84115-642-6

Typeset by Rowland Phototypesetting Ltd,
Bury St Edmunds, Suffolk
Printed and bound in Great Britain by
Clays Ltd, St Ives plc

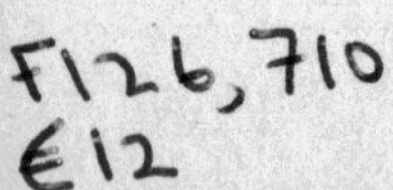

To my Princeton friends,
who are nowhere in these pages

Contents

. . . I was trying to find out the meaning of certain dreams . . .

—Socrates speaking in Plato's *Phaedo*

Life devours life, but man breaks the cycle, man has memory.

—"Adam Berendt"

Middle Age:
A Romance

Prologue: *Fourth of July*

I

Is this fair? You leave your home in Salthill-on-Hudson on the muggy afternoon of July Fourth for a cookout (an invitation you didn't really want to accept, but somehow accepted) and return days later as ashes in a cheesy-looking funeral urn: bone chunks and chips and coarse gritty powder to be dumped out, scattered, and raked in the crumbly soil of your own garden.

Fertilizer for weeds.

You leave home, with the highest intentions. No suicidal urges! Anything but. Securing your faithful German shepherd to a lengthy sliding leash in the back lawn, leaving him a big bowl of water spiked with ice cubes and his favorite dry food with a promise you'll be back by midnight at least, by which time fireworks will have been bursting into the sky above the Hudson River for hours, by which time you will have been dead for hours, declared dead of a burst heart, your body temperature rapidly cooling in the Jones Point Medical Center morgue. You (or the body you've become) present the usual problem for professionals. Whom to notify? Who's this man's next of kin? "Adam Berendt" is the name affixed to the body, if the ID in his water-soaked wallet is correct.

What to do with "Adam Berendt," the man of mystery.

I WAS "Adam Berendt." For so long a period of time, I came to believe he was my life.

YOU LEAVE HOME, you drive up the river to Jones Point, New York. You find yourself among people you don't know, and will not know. Invited to join your host and several others on a dazzling-white twenty-five-foot sailboat, *The Albatross.*

On the river you hear children's cries. You're panicked, thinking you hear children's cries. Then in fact you hear: children's cries. For help?

2

NOT WHERE I was born, which I've long forgotten. Or where I would die, which I would not know. But where I lived, *where I was known.* The Village of Salthill-on-Hudson, New York. Where by a sustained act of will through twenty-one years I created ADAM BERENDT as you might fumble a human, or humanoid, figure out of such materials as clay, earth, dung. Rotted wood and driftwood salvaged from the river. Bits of glass, plastic. Crude materials to be shaped by crude fingers.

ADAM BERENDT: if you glanced at this guy once, you'd possibly glance twice. One of those ugly burly fellows you can't imagine other than middle-aged. A big jaw, Cro-Magnon head, thinning steel-colored hair he's shaved close to the skull so the baldness will seem intentional. Even aesthetic! He has a flushed oniony skin, a peeling-flaking skin, of varying textures, but generally coarse, scarred-looking. A single functioning eye, the left, often bloodshot from strain; the right eye, amid scar tissue, glazed over like marble and glaring white, blind. (This eye, I'd explain, had been injured in a childhood accident. Which was, more or less, the truth.)

ADAM BERENDT, the body. Not a work of beauty. Not monumental. Not heroic! Nor even (in my own opinion) especially brave. Only just impulsive. Stubborn. Maybe reckless. *What I do, I do on principle. The hell with the rest.*

Because I was a sculptor. Or tried to be. And even mediocre sculptors are not easily discouraged or dissuaded.

3

Help! Help us! Save us! The cries tore at his heart, he turned to see a small sailboat capsizing, children sliding overboard, screaming and thrashing. And no life jackets.

This was about thirty feet from *The Albatross,* itself about thirty feet offshore. The drunken careening speedboat, a luxury Chris Craft item, continued on its way.

No time to think, only to act. *The hell with the rest!*

One of the children was a little blond girl and it was this child he swam for, this child he was determined to save.

4

ADAM BERENDT, whose official age would be a matter of speculation among his Salthill friends. For no birth certificate would be found among his papers. His closest friends, one of whom was his attorney, had no absolute knowledge of ADAM BERENDT except what he'd told them, carefully. It was generally conceded he was in his early or mid-fifties. It was generally conceded he'd been born somewhere in the Midwest. Or the West.

Blinded in one eye in a childhood accident, he said. And scar tissue, burn-scar tissue, lightly tattooing his body, on his burly hairy chest, and elsewhere. (More private. A few women have seen.) It was a shame, it was tragic, ADAM BERENDT wasn't in better condition when he dived into the river to swim to the capsized children's sailboat, maybe he was being reckless, maybe it was poor judgment, he didn't pause to think, only just to act; maybe this qualifies as heroic, maybe just reckless, a man who acts before he thinks; a man who, having acted, will have abrogated forever the possibility of thinking.

But won't give in. God damn, will not. The terrified blond child is only a few feet away, *Adam Berendt will save her*.

5

EIGHTEEN OF MY TWENTY-ONE YEARS in the floating paradise of Salthill-on-Hudson I lived what people thought was *beyond his means*. Because I was an impoverished-looking and -behaving sculptor with no reputation beyond the local. Because I threw together my junk-art with a disdain for how it might better be done, more professionally, more permanently. ADAM BERENDT living for the moment. And never quite completing anything, never achieving perfection. Like my fellow-eccentric Albert Pinkham Ryder, who so poorly prepared his canvases, painting and repainting untreated surfaces, that his beautiful dreamscapes are flaking and peeling away into Eternity.

Beyond his means because somehow I'd gotten together enough money to purchase one of the township's picturesque ruins. An old stone house on the river north of the village. In the 1750s the building had been a mill owned by a Dutchman. After the Revolution, it saw service as a tavern, and later as a brothel. In the mid-1800s it was purchased, with fifteen acres of land, and rebuilt by a well-to-do farmer named Elias Deppe, and the Salthill Trust lists the property as *Elias Deppe House*. Not a distinguished house by local standards but there's an air of nostalgia and romance about it. Two storeys, steep shingled roofs, pewter-colored stone that exudes damp in all weather. Built on a promontory above the river where the sun rising in the east floods its interior as if with flame.

Living *beyond his means,* no one exactly knew how. He'd die *beyond his means,* too.

6

YOU LEAVE HOME one afternoon, you never return as yourself.

Leaving home, you don't anticipate not returning as yourself.

The home you've left ceases to be a home once you've left. If you fail to return. It reverts to being a house, a property. An estate to fall into the hands of others who survive you.

7

ADAM BERENDT, the recluse. ADAM BERENDT who was sociable, gregarious. ADAM BERENDT, who was living alone at the time of his death but for Apollo (whose formal name was Apollodoros), the mongrel husky-shepherd with beautiful melancholy eyes and coarse silver-tipped hair. ADAM BERENDT, who was frequently seen hiking into the village along the River Road. Or riding his bicycle (English racing style, purchased secondhand). Or driving his Ford station wagon or his 1979 Mercedes-Benz. ADAM BERENDT, who occasionally taught sculpting and figure drawing in the Salthill Adult Program. ADAM BERENDT, who gave blood in the annual Salthill Blood Drive. ADAM BERENDT, the volunteer fireman. ADAM BERENDT, who canvassed through Rockland County on behalf of education, environmental, and gun control bond issues. ADAM BERENDT, who'd been invited to run for local office himself on the Democratic slate. (And politely declined.) ADAM BERENDT, who confessed to friends in an unguarded moment that he had never traveled outside the United States but had a hope of doing so before he died: to Athens, Greece, where Socrates had lived more than two thousand years ago; and to the Far East, that region of Buddhist mystery.

Socrates was his hero. He'd first discovered the philosopher when he was a boy of sixteen, a lifetime ago. Already blinded in his right eye and yearning for a higher knowledge, a knowledge not of the body but of the spirit; craving not religious faith but faith in reason. *Know thyself!* Socrates taught. And through *knowing* the self, *knowing* the world. Socrates had been an ordinary-seeming ugly-burly man. A common man, a stone mason. By a vote of the Athenian court he was sentenced to death at age seventy. (Why? For asking penetrating questions and for inspiring young people to ask questions of their elders.) Yet it was a death of Socrates' own choice, for he refused to flee into exile. It was a death of his own choice for he chose the exact means of dying. (Drinking hemlock.) *The philosopher is one who practices dying, practices death, continuously, but no one sees it.*

8

Adam, please don't go! You don't know these people.

Of course I know these people. In essence, I know them.

Stay with us in Salthill. We're having a barbecue, just a few close friends. We'll watch the fireworks over the river as night comes on. Say yes!

I gave my word, I'd go to Jones Point.

It will be a big event, won't it? A fund-raiser? A hundred guests, at least? No one will miss you.

I can't, I gave my word.

WHAT MORE TRIVIAL MATTER than a Fourth of July cookout to raise money for a liberal cause. What more trivial decision to make, which Fourth of July event to attend. *It is trifles that constitute our lives. It is trifles that kill us.*

9

NOT DROWNING, as it would be generally believed, but *cardiac arrest*. Not in the river but in the ambulance en route to the emergency room.

Though his lungs would be filled with river water. And his skull that looked concrete-hard would be severely fractured from striking the side of the rescue boat.

10

The Albatross: a witty name!

You were inclined to be witty, ironic, self-conscious when you had money, when in fact you were rich, and involved in underdog idealistic causes like the National Project to Free the Innocent. (These "innocent" were mostly black indigent death-row prisoners abandoned by the American criminal justice system to die for crimes they had not, in fact, committed.) Adam Berendt wasn't known as rich, far from it, but he'd been taken up by rich people, liberal-minded rich people like those who'd organized the July Fourth cookout in Jones Point. *No, I hadn't much wanted to attend. But it was in a good cause, certainly. And I gave, for whatever it was worth, my word.*

The injustice of the world depressed him, he must do his part to help. Driving the traffic-slowed highway 9W north along the wide glittering Hudson River to Jones Point thirty miles above Salthill-on-Hudson. A town Adam didn't know, had never before visited. A riverfront home, quite splendid, contemporary glass-and-redwood split-level overlooking the river, with a dock, at which *The Albatross* was moored.

ADAM BERENDT, who lacked all capacity for the supernatural. Who could believe only in man. Not God.

ADAM BERENDT, without wife or children. (Yet there would be speculation: surely he'd been married at one time? Surely he, the most masculine-paternal of men, had sired children? Somewhere?)

ADAM BERENDT, who was known to be a "partner" of some ambiguous kind with a woman named Troy, Marina Troy of the Salthill Bookshop on Pedlar's Lane. (What was the relationship between Adam Berendt and Marina Troy? Were they lovers, or only just friends? Or only just partners in the bookshop? And how much could Adam have invested in the doomed little store? For Adam had no income, no holdings except his house and land—did he? The subject of money, finances, business of any kind made him restless, uneasy; if he couldn't escape, he became irritable; roused to repugnance.)

ADAM BERENDT, who'd unconsciously taken for granted he would live forever.

II

THE HUDSON RIVER at Jones Point was wide, rough, slate blue in reflected light, its surface like something metallic, shaken. The wind was ideal, steady at about fifteen miles an hour. There were clouds high overhead but these were not storm clouds. There appeared to be, late in the afternoon, no threat of lightning or rain. The men intended to sail to West Point and back, and this was a reasonable goal—wasn't it?

No, Adam Berendt hadn't been drinking. Amid many others who were. His quick stoic smiling response when drinks were offered: *Thanks, but no! Not for me. Club soda?*

Possibly his host, the owner of the sailboat, had been drinking. The other men on the sailboat had been drinking. Everybody on the river! It was that kind of festive American holiday.

Firecrackers detonating like maniacal laughter.

Adam Berendt gave his companions on *The Albatross* the impression, as they would afterward recount, of being a capable, calm sailor. He'd told them he lived on the river, at Salthill. He was a thick-bodied muscular man, very self-possessed, with powerful shoulders, arms, legs; of only moderate height, but he'd seemed taller. He wore a white visored cap, a navy-blue pullover sport shirt that fitted him tightly at the midriff, rumpled khaki shorts, and rubber-soled canvas shoes. These shoes, and the bulky shorts, would immediately become water-soaked when he dived into the river, the weight pulling him down. Pulling at his heart.

The medical examiner at Jones Point Medical Center would confirm that Adam Berendt had no alcohol or drugs in his blood at the time of his death.

After a delay, the four men set sail at about five-thirty. The sun still high in the sky. Just enough wind, edged with a taste of something cool. Of course, a sailboat on the Hudson River, there's always some measure of danger. What pleasure would there be in sailing, otherwise?

What pleasure in life, otherwise?

12

THE COOKOUT WAS HELD at the home of L—, a lawyer attached to the New York branch of the American Civil Liberties Union. L— was also a successful litigator in private practice. Adam Berendt had met L— once or twice previously, the men had shaken hands but no more, they'd scarcely spoken before that day.

S—, another ACLU lawyer, a woman in her mid-forties who wore, that day, a youthful red halter-top sundress, told of how she'd been talking with Adam Berendt, whom she'd only just met, and he drew her aside and "on the spot" made out two checks for the cause, each for $2,500. One to the ACLU, and the other to the National Project to Free the Innocent. S— stared at the man in startled gratitude, and impulsively hugged him, kissed his coarse-skinned cheek; felt a sharp frisson of sexual attraction between them; and drew back blushing fiercely. "Adam, thank you! This is much appreciated."

S— determined she would be seeing Adam Berendt again, soon.

S— determined she would be seeing a good deal of Adam Berendt, and intimately, soon. Or so she hoped.

The checks to be cashed on the day of Adam Berendt's cremation.

13

IN PRINCIPLE Adam distrusts lawyers, why's he with lawyers?

Speedboats rushing noisily past. Treacherous as giant wasps.

Rap music from a passing yacht. Dazzling white like *The Albatross*. Adam has strapped on a life jacket like the other men. His left eye is leaking tears from the wind.

On the river, seen from a distance, boats appear graceful and swift as paper cutouts in the wind; but when you're in one of the boats, on the water, there is little grace involved, there are clumsy maneuvers, shouted commands, trying to get along amicably with bossy strangers. The river, beautiful at a distance, is without color; composed of ropy strands of water; frothy, smelly. A mild taste of panic, imagining the underwater world. What it is, beneath the surface, in that dense, dark place. What it is to drown.

Not now. Not today. Don't think of it.

He isn't thinking of it. Nor does he allow himself to think as *The Albatross* lurches north along the river amid a discordant flotilla of other craft. *Why the hell am I here, why am I doing this?*

Hoping he won't throw out his back.

He'd been such a tough kid. A young man in his twenties, built like a steer. Now he's grown a gut, he's short of breath. Worried about his back. God damn: a man should have more dignity, ideals. Helping his host good-naturedly with the sails. And damned heavy sails they are.

"Some life, eh?" one of Adam's cheery new friends shouts at him, except Adam hears, "Some strife, eh?"

Thinking of Marina. Suddenly, guiltily. He should have called her that morning. She's been waiting to hear from Adam for several days, she has a question to put to him. *Yes. I love you. But no, I can't.*

Don't make more of me than I am. Forgive me!

It's then that Adam begins to hear screams. Not certain at first what he's hearing, the noise of waves and wind. For a moment his brain fails. He sees the terrible fire leap. The first flames, and the soft explosion. Liquid flame flowing from his outstretched fingers rising to the low ceiling of the trailer, like lightning in reverse. And the screams. The screams! His mother, his six-year-old sister Tanya. Trapped by fire you scream, scream until you have no more breath to scream. Strangulated cries of pure agony, animal agony. *Help! Help us! Save us! Don't let us die like this!* Adam is dazed, his consciousness gone, obliterated. He's telling himself he can't be hearing screams, not here, it's firecrackers, chains of firecrackers like gunfire.

But no. These are human screams. Children's screams, on the river.

About thirty feet from *The Albatross,* which is rocking in the wake of a careening speedboat, there's a small orange Day-Glo sailboat rocking more dangerously, violently, the boat is swamped and capsizing. A boy of about twelve, skinny, in bathing trunks, and two younger children, helpless, screaming, suddenly in the river.

Adam, squinting, sees, or thinks he sees, that the children are not wearing life jackets.

Within seconds, Adam Berendt is in the water.

Swiftly, without taking time to think, to register wariness, or caution, or fear, Adam dives into the water and begins swimming. His dive is a slap-dive, clumsy, awkward; he's an overweight out-of-condition middle-aged man; in the adrenaline-rush of the moment recalling his young self, a vanished self, a boy lithe and wiry-strong and as expert in the water as a water rat, and as reckless. Now, he has time to register only *Something's wrong.* The water is damned unyielding, thick and sinewy as snakes, resistant, surprisingly cold, Adam senses he's in trouble, he has overestimated his strength. Lifting his head, tries to keep the children's sailboat in sight. Glaring fluorescent orange, the mainsail floundering in the water. He tries to shout, "Hang on! I'm coming—" but swallows water, sputters and chokes. The other men on *The Albatross* watch in alarm, but only watch.

14

As a boy what a damned good swimmer. In the swift-flowing creek behind the trailer camp, after heavy rains. Rising to the girders of the bridge. The cattle and lumber trucks rattling past into Helena, over that plank bridge. The raw smell of water and sewage mixed. But you didn't mind the sewage, didn't give it a thought. Just breathe through your nose. Don't swallow.

Though Adam weighs now possibly one hundred pounds more than he weighed then. Aged eleven, twelve. The angry animal-happiness of that time. Before the other, the time to come. As a boy he'd been afraid of nothing. His name was Frankie: he was admired, he was feared, even older kids respected him. Certainly he hadn't been afraid of the water, of swimming. Of diving from the bridge. A boy had drowned in the rushing water but not Frankie, who dodged and swam like a water rat, his limbs suffused with a powerful radiant strength, his sleek glistening combative soul shining like reflected light on the mucky, mud-colored water.

Always you believe you will live forever. Though others may fall away from you, and sink into death, oblivion.

15

Adam is swimming in the direction of the capsized sailboat, arm over arm as always he'd swum, a pulse beating in his good eye, his blind eye useless. No reason for his sudden fear—is there? He can't drown, that's impossible. He's wearing a life jacket, he can't drown. But it's difficult to swim with the life jacket on, it's difficult to swim *(he knows now: this is a mistake)* with his shorts, his shoes, soaking wet, heavy. Sodden. Like concrete weighing him down. Like trying to swim uphill. (How, pedaling up the steep hill before entering the village of Salthill, passing the old Salthill Community cemetery, where weatherworn, mossy stone markers tilt in the mossy soil like tossed-away playing cards, etched with the faint fading numerals of the 1700s. So long ago, Death couldn't have been very real. Adam, pedaling his bicycle, begins to feel his breath shorten, just perceptibly, a quick strange tightness in his chest he doesn't acknowledge. Though remembering, since the previous April, how sweat breaks out on his forehead when he ascends this hill, when he hikes too briskly uphill, and Apollo trotting eagerly before him. What is it but weakness, God damn he will not give in to weakness.)

"Hang on—I'm almost there—"

Only a few feet away there's a small blond girl in the water, her hair streaking down her face, face very pale, contorted in terror, she's buffeted by waves, sinking, rising, clawing at the edge of the boat. The older boy, who'd been the sailor, has disappeared. Maybe he's on the far side of the boat, maybe he's under the boat, maybe he's drowning, or swimming to shore to save himself. Adam sees only the little girl. He swims to her, he's got hold of her. At last! He's got hold of her. Grips her small shoulder, meaning now to wrest both himself and the child away from the sailboat, so that he can swim freely to shore, or to a dock, must be a dock nearby, except—Adam's vision is blurred, he has only the one eye, streaming water. And he's breathing hard, panting. And the child is kicking and struggling, panicked as a terrorized animal. Adam shouts at her, he's got her, he will save her, Christ! he's exhausted suddenly, an old man suddenly, the terrible leaden weight in his muscular legs, his arms, he has always depended upon his strength, now his strength is ebbing from him. Hours have passed, in less than three frantic minutes. Splotched sunlight moves like fireballs in the waves. He's confused about directions. Which way—? There's another boat, a rescue boat, approaching. A swelling fiery ball in his chest. He's wanted to hide it, this shameful fact, but it will no longer be hidden. His mouth opens, gasping for breath like a dying fish's. His left eye, like his right eye, now blind. Except for the life jacket keeping him afloat he would sink, he's useless now. The hysterical little girl is being lifted out of his arms into a boat. Into the arms of strangers? But where has this boat come from?

Adam doesn't see. The fiery ball in his chest will not be placated. Pain, paralyzing pain of a kind he's never felt before in his life, except the pain of that original fire, perhaps it's the identical pain, and something strikes the crown of his head with such violence he's beyond pain. Not thinking *At least—the girl is safe*. Not capable of thinking *I succeeded in this, at least*. He has no breath. No strength. His left eye has gone out like a burst lightbulb. Adam Berendt, dying. The life jacket keeps the moribund body afloat like sodden laundry.

He will not know the name of the blond child for whom he has given his life.

PART I

If You Catch Me . . .

SURVIVED BY . . .

1

HOW DEATH ENTERS your life. A telephone ringing.

And maybe you're still waiting for Adam Berendt to call. And maybe you're confused, your heart already pumping absurdly, when a stranger's voice utters the name *Adam Berendt* and you answer eagerly, hopefully.

"Yes? I'm Marina Troy. What—what is it?"

That instant before fear strikes. Fear like a sliver of ice entering the heart.

2

Thwaite was the bearer of Adam Berendt's death. She would learn.

An ugly name, isn't it? Though the child's name, Samantha, is beautiful.

It was *Thwaite* that would stick in Marina's brain like a burr. *Thwaite* that became her obsession, she who would have defined herself as a woman free of obsession. A reasonable intelligent unemotional woman yet how *Thwaite* lodged in her brain as suffocation, choking, tar-tasting death. *Thwaite Thwaite* in her miserable sleep those nights following Adam's death. Sobbing aloud, furious: "If I'd been there with him on the boat, I wouldn't have let Adam die."

In the derangement of grief Marina Troy quickly came to believe this.

3

LOCAL TV NEWS! How Adam would have been embarrassed, if, just maybe, secretly proud.

Good Samaritan. Adam Berendt. Resident of Salthill-on-Hudson. July Fourth accident. Hudson River. Rescue of eight-year-old. Adam's face on the glassy screen: squinting his blind eye, smiling. That big head like something sculpted of coarse clay. A mere moment on the TV screen. Swift cut to the much younger Thwaites, parents of the rescued child. *Thwaite. Harold and Janice. Jones Point residents. Devastated by. Tragic episode. So very sorry. So very grateful. Courageous man sacrificing his life for our daughter. Our Samantha. Our prayers will be with Adam Berendt. We are hoping to make contact with his family, his survivors. Oh, we hope . . .* Marina switched off the TV in disgust.

How could she bear it, the banality of Adam as a "Good Samaritan." The banality of the Thwaites' emotion, how disappointingly ordinary they were, and young, stammering into microphones thrust into their dazed faces.

"Well. I must learn to bear it. And more."

She was an adult woman, she knew of loss, death. She was not a naive, self-pitying person.

Her mother was chronically ill, and her father had died three years ago at the age of seventy-nine, so Marina knew, Marina knew what to expect from life, every cliché becomes painfully true in time, yet you survive until it's your turn: you don't become middle-aged without learning such primitive wisdom. Yet, when Marina's father had died, Marina had not been taken by surprise. That death had been not only expected, but "merciful." After cancer operations, and months of chemotherapy, the fading of Marina's father's life had been a slow fading of light into dusk and finally into dark. And there you are: death.

Not like Adam's death.

"Adam, God damn you. *Why*."

She was desperate to recall the last time they'd spoken. She shut her eyes, rubbing her eyes with the palms of her hands: Adam's face!

A doctor at the Jones Point Medical Center had prescribed a sedative for Marina Troy. (Did that mean she'd become hysterical? She'd lost all dignity, and collapsed?) Next morning staggering from her bed that was like a grave, at the top of her house on North Pearl Street. Her storybook house, as Adam had called it fondly. As Marina Troy was a storybook creature to be rescued. (By him?) In sweat-smelling nightclothes, a strap slipping off her shoulder, tugging at a window to raise it higher *must breathe! must breathe!* There was some fact that plagued her with its cruelty, its injustice: what? *The last time we spoke, I didn't know. If I had known.* The ceiling careened over her head with an air of drunken levity. Lilac fleur-de-lis wallpaper of subtly mocking prettiness. *Thwaite* mixed with the church bells. *Thwaite Thwaite* clamoring jeering in her head.

Marina's bedroom was a small charming room with small charming windows of aged glass, dating to the mid-1800s, windowpanes badly in need of caulking, overlooking St. Agnes Roman Catholic Church with its heraldic spire floating in the night sky, and its ancient bumpy churchyard. (In which Adam Berendt would certainly not be buried. Adam had been pagan, not Catholic; and Adam had wanted to be "burnt to a crisp" when he died.) North Pearl Street was one of Salthill's oldest streets, hilly and very narrow, and it dead-ended with three charming woodframe houses, one of which was Marina Troy's.

Somehow it had happened (when, exactly?) she'd become thirty-eight years old.

Young enough to be his daughter, Adam Berendt used to joke.

Don't be ridiculous! You're, what?—fifty? Fifty-two?

Marina, to be perfectly frank, I've lost count.

She removed her sweat-soaked nylon nightgown and wadded it into a ball to toss onto the floor. She'd have liked to peel off her sticky itchy skin and do the same. In the silence following the church bells came the echo *Thwaite! Thwaite*. The sound of death, those hateful people, negligent parents, youngish, scared, reading off prepared statements to TV reporters, uncertain whether they should smile, or not smile, but one should always smile on TV, yes?—if only fleetingly, sadly? In truth, Marina didn't detest these people. It was *Thwaite* that had insinuated itself into her head. *Thwaite* snarled like her long crimped dark-red hair, which by day she wore plaited and twined about her head ("like Elizabeth I") but by night it snagged and snarled, snaky tendrils trailing across her mouth. *Thwaite* a mass of such snarls no hairbrush could be dragged through. *Thwaite* that was the fairy-tale riddle: what is my name, my name is a secret, my name is your death, can you guess my name? *Thwaite* the helpless tenderness she'd long felt for Adam Berendt, who had been neither her husband nor her lover. *Thwaite* powerful as no other emotion Marina had ever felt for another person.

And the anger. *God damn how could you. Without saying good-bye. Did you know, did you wish to know, why didn't you let me tell you, how I felt about you. And now!*

A boating accident. So many, each Fourth of July. Across the United States. Boating and traffic accidents. And accidents with fireworks and firecrackers, especially illegally purchased firecrackers, Marina found herself listening in a trance to—what? —a stranger's voice, a radio voice this time, before switching it off and pounding at the little plastic radio (on her kitchen windowsill) with her fist. Oh, what did she care for the accidents of strangers? Even their "senseless" deaths.

Now Adam was gone, it was going to be difficult for her to care about much.

The official diagnosis was that Adam Berendt had died of *cardiac arrest*. His skull had been badly fractured, as well. He'd died, evidently, within minutes of being lifted out of the river; in the speeding ambulance. At approximately 6:20 P.M. of July Fourth. Marina hoped that he'd died unconscious, unknowing. But she hadn't dared ask. *Thwaite, death*. Nothing to be done. A tragedy. If an accident can be a tragedy. You heard yourself utter that word *tragedy* as others did. It was a way of speaking, a way of attempting to assuage pain. You would not say of a good man's death that he'd died accidentally, and therefore stupidly. *Tragedy* was the word for there was no other. *Never kissed me. As I'd wanted him to*. Never her breasts, her belly, between her thighs. That not-touching and not-kissing was her secret. She would ponder it in the night for a long time. She would ponder it in the bookstore, knowing that Adam Berendt would never drop by, not again. If the telephone rang it would not be him, and if someone knocked at her door it would not be him. Through the barbiturate haze that slowed her heartbeat almost to stopping she would ponder these simple facts.

The Thwaite family had expressed a public wish to meet with Adam Berendt's family. His "survivors." To thank them for Adam's sacrifice. Anyone other than Adam's immediate family, a wife or a blood relative, wouldn't qualify.

Hypocrite sons of bitches. I was as close to Adam as anyone who knew him.

But she wouldn't hate them. She wouldn't become obsessed with an illusory enemy. Mr. and Mrs. Harold Thwaite of Jones Point, New York. Within twenty-four hours they'd received their share of public media attention and censure: newscasters hadn't accused them of being "negligent parents" but there'd been that implication, and police were going to "investigate" the accident in which the Thwaites' eight-year-old daughter, Samantha, and ten-year-old son had gone out onto the Hudson River in a neighbor's sailboat manned not by an adult but by a thirteen-year-old boy. The boat had been equipped with child-sized life jackets but none of the children was wearing one. Yes, it was stupid. It was negligence. Possibly criminal negligence. But how much more merciful, simply to forgive.

She would hear her voice on the telephone, commiserating

with friends, "Being bitter won't bring Adam back. And Adam was the most logical of men."

And again, "Wasn't it just like Adam! If—he had to go—without warning, suddenly—he would have wished for—something like this."

But was this true? There came *Thwaite Thwaite* to taunt her, when she was being most rational, responsible. *Thwaite* the tarry black phlegm of death.

4

MARINA HAD BEEN CALLED to Jones Point because, in Adam Berendt's wallet, there was no information regarding next of kin. *In case of emergency* had been left blank.

Had the man no family? *No one?*

What was found in the badly worn wallet was a water-soaked little white card:

> THE SALTHILL BOOKSTORE, EST. 1911
> 7 Pedlar's Lane
> Salthill-on-Hudson, NY
>
> *proprietor Marina Troy*

On the reverse of the little card was Marina's home telephone number, scrawled in pencil, and it was this number authorities called.

So Marina was summoned. By a voice of authority. Like a sleepwalker she obeyed. Too stunned even to think, *It can't be, can it? Not like this.*

In a calm sort of panic she was driving. She would not recall afterward getting into the car. Starting the motor. That suspension of time before she would see the irrefutable body. Yet she'd had a sense, for Marina Troy was a woman with an appreciation of bittersweet ironies, that this was a cruel time to be driving to

Jones Point on such a mission. For dusk was the luminous time, the romantic time. At dusk, she'd often thought of Adam Berendt. At dusk, she'd often been with Adam Berendt. Now across the wide gleaming river was a scattering of lights like startled thoughts. On the river, there were ghostly sailboats and speedboats' winking lights. Marina wondered: Was it safe to be boating on the river, as night came on? There were occasional freighters, enormous commercial barges beside which the pleasure craft seemed of no more substance than moths. Why had Adam been on the river, in a sailboat? Whose sailboat, where? Why at Jones Point? *If I'd been with him. Why wasn't I with him.* Marina and Adam were planning to see each other, with Salthill friends, the following evening. That had been their plan.

Why didn't you call us, Marina. Let us go with you. What a shock for you. Are you sure you're all right?

She was sure. Oh, yes! Only just she was so furious, and so heartsick. Wanting to drive up to see him, alone. Not wanting any talk. Not even commiseration. Shared tears. *Maybe he isn't dead, it's someone else? Another man?* Marina had been told only the stark fact that Adam, or a man purported to be "Adam Berendt," had died a short time before of complications resulting from a "boating accident" on the river.

The river! Marina recalled how from Adam's studio, at the rear of his house, you could stand staring across the river, those long mesmerized moments as light faded on the agitated waves, and dusk deepened at the edges of things; dusk, a quality of earth; while an eerie oily-glistening light remained on the water. In the west, the sun was chemical red and gorgeous, bleeding at the horizon like a burst egg yolk.

On both sides of the river fireworks erupted. Fourth of July: the American holiday celebrating gunfire, rockets, aggression, death to the enemy. Across the river on the east bank of the Hudson, in the vicinity of Tarrytown, gaudy pinwheels of crimson, gold, blinding-white light were rising, soaring and falling soundlessly into the river. And a moment later replaced by more explosions, gaudy glittering colors rising, sinking soundlessly to extinction. "Stop. Stop. *Stop.*" This idiotic celebration, at a time of death. As if in mockery of a man's death. Even in Jones Point, where death awaited her. Lurid bright carnival colors pitching up into the now-darkening sky over the river. Exploding yellow calyxes, crimson eyeballs, streamers of rainbow guts. Hideous, hellish. Marina recalled that fireworks are jokey symbols of sexual orgasm, and the thought repelled her. *Never us. And now never.*

In her state of suspended shock she located the Jones Point Medical Center. Not a large facility. Parked her car, and ran to the rear entrance. She was breathless, breathing through her mouth. As, on their hikes in Eagle Mountain Preserve, Adam had cautioned her never to do. Inside, in a brightly lit lobby, Marina was met by strangers who'd clearly been awaiting her. She heard her name—"Marina Troy?" She who was the friend of Adam Berendt. These people not known to Marina, a half dozen of them, yet a crowd, introduced themselves as "friends"—"new friends"—of Adam's, organizers of that day's fund-raising cookout. (Fund-raising *cookout?*) Marina stared at these individuals, wordless. A weepy woman in her forties, raw-eyed, in a very young halter-top sundress with a shawl draped over her shoulders, dared to call Marina "Marina" and to embrace Marina's stiffened shoulders as if they were two women linked by mutual loss; as if Marina Troy's shock and mounting horror were to be so easily shared. "Marina, we are so very very *very sorry.*" Marina, breathing through her mouth, pushed away, managing not to scream.

The Thwaites were not present. Marina was spared knowing of *Thwaite* until a later hour.

The next several hours would pass like a delirium dream of distortions and quick dazzling cuts.

"Marina Troy? You're here for Adam Berendt? Please come with us."

Escape! Marina was being led away from the guilty-faced "friends" in sports clothes, one of whom managed, as she'd discover afterward, to slip into her hand the keys to Adam's car. What had Adam to do with these people, why hadn't he told her about them, a Fourth of July cookout in Jones Point? Had that awful woman been one who'd adored and pursued him? Marina was trembling with fury, at them and at Adam for his poor judgment. Wasn't it like him! Impulsive, impetuous! A young man in hospital whites and an older Asian-American woman who'd looked upon Marina sympathetically were leading her to the morgue for the viewing and identification, and they spoke softly to Marina, preparing her for the ordeal (was this a fixed script? though Marina had never heard it before, she seemed somehow to recognize it) but Marina was having difficulty comprehending, nor was she in this breathless blinking-eyed state aware of the shiny corridors through which she was being taken; an elevator entered, and exited on a lower floor. Underground? "Adam? *Adam!*" She had only a vague awareness of someone speaking aloud. Possibly it was her. Wiping her nose on the edge of her hand. Rummaged in her purse but couldn't find a clean tissue, God damn. And God damn why was it so cold here? While outside the air was warm and heavy as an expelled breath.

Couldn't stop shivering. Adam had commented, sometimes on their hikes, Marina's fingernails turned blue, she must have low blood pressure, was she anemic? and Marina laughingly protested, no, certainly not. She wasn't a woman comfortable with being *looked at, considered*. She hadn't a normal store of vanity, and that was indeed a handicap. She'd run to her car after the summons came to her, drove twenty-three miles in whatever clothes she'd been wearing, denim shorts, a T-shirt that fitted her slender torso loosely, bare pale legs and well-worn sandals. Tendrils of damp hair stuck to her forehead and neck like seaweed. She hadn't glanced at herself in any mirror in hours and she wondered how desperate she would seem, to Adam's critical eye. *Marina for Christ's sake get hold of yourself.*

Or would he say, sobered by his near-escape, *Marina, thank you! For coming to me on such short notice.*

Marina was being warned. Of what? The young man and the Asian-American woman in their crisp hospital uniforms. Warning her she should prepare herself? How, her*self?* Car keys clutched in her hand. Her sweaty palm. She'd been entrusted with these keys, and told that Adam's Mercedes was parked behind Emergency. (How anxious they'd been, the cookout couple, to transfer the car keys to Marina, and to be rid of the nuisance of Adam's car.) She was being led into a large refrigerated room. The morgue. Stark lighting here. A powerful chemical odor. "Yes. That's—him. You have the right man." Idiot, why had she said such a thing? Yet her voice was even and calm, and reliable. Marina Troy was one of those whose concern is to behave in a civilized manner; in a way helpful, not hurtful, to others. She was not a woman of raw emotion. She was not a woman to break down in tears. She was not a woman to break down at all. In public. Yet her vision had narrowed strangely (good, for she was in a medical facility, if she were having a hemorrhage or a stroke it could not be happening at a more convenient time) so that she was able to see little in the fluorescent-lit space except the man who lay motionless on a gurney beneath the strongest of the lights. "Adam?" How bulky this body was, how graceless. Yet profound. Had Marina ever seen any person, living or dead, looking so profound? Adam might have been a sculpture of subtly colored lead. It would weigh, what would it weigh!—a literal ton. This thing both was and was not Adam Berendt, her friend. The indignity of being near naked, in strangers' eyes! Marina had seen Adam in swim trunks, she'd been struck by his barrel-like torso covered in swaths and swirls of silver-glinting hair thick as an animal's pelt, but at such times he'd been in motion; always in her memory, Adam had been a man in motion; and that made all the difference. Here, lying exposed on his back, no pillow for his head so that his head too rested flat on the aluminum surface, Adam was clearly "dead"; "deadness" lifted like a vapor from his ashen, slack skin, the sightless eyes, the mouth partly agape. Which of the eyes was the blind eye, now you could not have told. Both were nearly shut, sickly-white crescents. "Adam? It's Marina." She was whispering. Though she knew that Adam was dead, yet she was close beside him whispering. As if some secret might pass between them, unknown to observers. Marina fumbled to take hold of Adam's hand. So heavy!—she could lift it only with difficulty. Adam's muscles were rigid in the death-lock of rigor mortis, was that the explanation? This man who'd been so special in life, unique, subjected now to the most common of death symptoms. And decay to follow. "Cremation. His wish was for cremation." Marina spoke distractedly. She was but half conscious of being questioned. "He must have next of kin, in the Midwest I think, or the West, but—I don't know who they would be. I—I'm not the one to know." If her questioners had believed her the lover of Adam Berendt, now they must be reassessing her. But she'd taken Adam's hand firmly in hers, as if to assure him. Knowing his instinct would be to draw away from her in manly embarrassment. How mortified Adam would be, laid out naked like this beneath a flimsy sheet, and he'd not have liked to see Marina here, nor any of his Salthill friends. Any of his women friends. Marina's voice echoed faintly in the room that seemed so vast, her vision severely diminished, focused upon Adam. "Yes. I can give you his lawyer's name. But just not now. Can I be alone with him, please. Now." Her voice rose sharply on *now*. This hand gripped in both her shaky hands: clearly it was a "dead" hand. Yet it was her dear friend's hand. The big, bruised knuckles, thick fingers and thumbs twice the size of her own, and the nails discolored and ridged with dirt. Adam was a gardener, a handyman, a stonemason, an occasional sculptor; a man who loved to work with his hands, and put them to hard use. You could see, in Adam's use of himself, how a man wishes to pay little heed to how he wears himself out physically. Adam's fingernails had begun to crack recently, Adam had casually complained, and this made getting the dirt out virtually impossible even with a knife blade; Marina had said it must be a mineral or vitamin deficiency, concerned for him, but Adam had been indifferent and changed the subject. "Adam. Oh, my God." Her head was ringing. Her heart was beating strangely. (Maybe it *was* a cerebral hemorrhage? A gathering of pressure as of water building up outside this lighted space; as if, and for a fleeting moment, as in dream logic, she thought this might be so, she'd descended into a vessel like a submarine, deep under water.) The strangers in white had left her alone with Adam. She had the idea that they were observing her through one-way glass brick. She touched

Adam's face as perhaps she wouldn't have done, quite like this, in life. His cheeks had gone slack. Crepey flesh beneath his jaws. Strange, he looked ashen, who in life had always seemed flushed, overheated. Now his blood was draining out of his face. Draining downward. Blood thickening in its own rigidity, as if congealing from a massive wound. There was a gash in Adam's skull and forehead where he'd been struck by a boat (a rescue boat?) and the gash had bled, but had ceased bleeding; it would not bleed now; if cut elsewhere, Adam wouldn't bleed; his flesh was "dead." Marina hated it that Adam was looking so *old*. She wanted to protest to the hospital staff, *Adam Berendt didn't look like this*. So old, and so ugly. Deep shadowed creases beneath his eyes, his bumpy skull visible through his thinning, short-trimmed hair, that slack mouth. In the corner of the mouth, something white and crusty. If Marina could coax a smile from him, for Adam was the sort of man you could tease, he'd be himself again, and good-looking, with that bold funny sexy swagger, but she was beginning to feel desperate, she could not make him respond. *Here I am. Marina. Adam, you know me*. Of course she knew that he was dead. Yet she couldn't help thinking that, in Adam's sly way, he was kidding; had to be kidding; breathing very faintly, but breathing. "Could this man be in a *coma?*" Marina spoke sharply, accusingly. She was shivering, her teeth chattering. Her skin puckered and pimpled in goose bumps, hairs stirring at the nape of her neck. Whispering, "Can you hear me, Adam?" Yes, this was ridiculous, but she had to ask, didn't she? "They think I'm your lover. But who is your lover? I don't envy her." Often, Marina was angry with Adam without informing him. She was angry with him now for behaving recklessly. Stupidly. Diving into the Hudson River? "Saving" a child from drowning? Where were the child's parents? Who will *pay?* Adam Berendt had died of *cardiac arrest* in a "boating accident"? Wasn't it like him: offering aid to total strangers. Bad enough, helping his needy friends. Straining his back, after a New Year's Eve party at the Hoffmanns', helping a drunken friend dislodge his enormous luxury Lexus from a snowy ditch on Old Mill Way.

When Adam remarked to Marina that he wanted to be cremated, not buried, in a simple, private ceremony, and his ashes scattered on his property, mixed in the soil of his garden, he'd continued to ask Marina if she would be his "personal executor"; and Marina, deeply moved, but agitated, not at all wanting to pursue the subject of her friend's mortality, had quickly said yes, yes of course—whatever "personal executor" might mean. (Seeing to his household effects, maybe. Assuming care of his dog. Oh, poor Apollo! Marina had tried, but she'd never been able to feel affection for Adam's part husky, part shepherd mongrel who eagerly licked any part of Marina's body he wasn't prevented from licking.) Nor had she taken the opportunity to ask Adam about his family, relatives, who should be notified in a time of emergency, where did these mysterious folks live; would Adam be leaving a list of instructions with his lawyer? None of these practical questions had Marina asked. Instead, she'd laughed nervously and allowed Adam to change the subject. She hadn't wanted to think that Adam would die before her. (As if, considering that Adam was in his early fifties and Marina in her late thirties, this wasn't likely.)

If you catch me and I don't escape you. These mysterious words were from Plato's *Phaedo,* which Adam sometimes quoted, the lyric, long death of Socrates who, having drunk poison, awaiting death, in the company of his friends, had turned playful. But the dead are easily caught, Marina was thinking. The dead escape no one. "Oh, poor Adam. You weren't ready, I know. Darling, I'm so sorry." She was greedily kissing Adam's hands, both his hurt, stiffened hands. She was pressing against him, absorbing cold from him, the terrible bulk of him, a fallen colossus, heavy as lead; she kissed his forehead, his half-shut eyes. She cradled his head. She stroked his quill-hair. Kissed his lips. Dared to kiss a dead man's lips. She'd been going to ask him frankly *Do you know how I love you, Adam?* Though risking the end of their friendship. *Adam, why don't you know?* She pressed herself against him. She was shameless, desperate. She passed out of consciousness, in a swoon. A smothering wave rose in her, again came the sensation of being deep under water, and doomed.

Her strength drained from her, she was weak, falling. She was wracked with spasms of vomiting. She would strike the side of her head against something metallic and sharp and when they lifted her, to wake her, speaking her name urgently, she would discover that the front of her shirt was covered in a foul-smelling glutinous liquid, she'd coughed up the rank river water that had drowned Adam Berendt but of what help was this, Adam was still dead.

5

"SO, MARINA! Tell me: what's the purpose of life?"

They were hiking together, Marina and her friend Adam Berendt, in the Eagle Mountain Preserve, north of Hastings-on-Hudson. They were not a couple, though often together. "Just friends. But very close friends." Marina understood that Adam had many friends, and he was a man who enjoyed plying them with sudden sharp questions. It was known that Adam's interests were impassioned but curiously impersonal. You would never get to know the man intimately. But you might get to know yourself.

It was May of the year preceding Adam's death. Marina was the only woman friend of Adam's who enjoyed the out-of-doors and who was hardy enough to accompany him on hikes. He teased and baited her, he embarrassed her, but she didn't mind. She said, "Do you mean what's the purpose of 'life,' or what's the purpose of 'my life'? There's a crucial distinction." Adam said, "Answer one, and you'll answer the other." Marina laughed, though feeling a bit rebuffed. "The purpose of life, Adam"—she drew a deep breath as they were ascending a steep hill—"is to get to the top of this hill." Adam said, "And beyond this hill?" Marina said, "I can't see beyond this hill, yet. It's just theory."

Was it a form of sex, she wondered. Adam Berendt prodding, probing, querying his friends. His women friends.

Adam said expansively, "Beyond all hills, Marina."

"Beyond all physical hills?"

"What other sorts of hills are there, Marina?"

Marina knew. Marina knew where this was going. She was a

young headstrong dog, untrained. Her master directed her, with only his voice that was kindly, hypnotic, and tireless.

"Inner hills. Spiritual hills."

"Do you feel that there are spiritual hills in your life, Marina, that you have yet to climb?"

"Yes. I suppose so."

"And how would you describe them, Marina?"

Don't do this to me! Don't expose me.

I don't need to answer you. Who are you, to me?

Adam Berendt had come into Marina's life unexpected. With the authority of a protector, one who'd known her from childhood.

Knowing that the Salthill Bookstore was in a financial crisis, Adam had invested as a silent partner; often he dropped by the store to help her openly, greeting customers, shelving books and doing inventory, talking her out of becoming discouraged. (Oh, Adam sensed she was suicidal! In that way of American women, whether unmarried or married, young or not-young, brooding at twilight through windows that, as twilight deepens, become ghostly smirking mirrors of the soul.) *To be discouraged, depressed, over business, mere money, when the world is a place of rapture, Marina! No.* He did touch her, with his big, rather battered-looking hands. He was one to touch while speaking, smiling. Marina's forearms, Marina's shoulders. He might cup his hand on the top of your head, patting in approval as (for instance) he might pat his dog Apollo's head in a similar gesture of approval, or easy affection. He might kiss Marina's cheek, he might hug Marina in greeting, or in farewell. In Salthill, such kisses and hugs, and some of them quite extravagant, were social displays: women hugging men, and the men needing to mime passivity; women hugging women, with emotion, affection. Or the ritual display of it. Marina Troy was likely to be a stiff partner in such displays, for she felt herself insufficiently female, or feminine; and, being unmarried, she had not quite the freedom to embrace men, especially a man like Adam for whom she felt strong emotion, as her married women friends did. *Oh, Adam! If I dared touch you.*

Here was a mystery. How Adam Berendt, a part-time teacher and not-successful sculptor, mostly unemployed, had enough money to help Marina repay her bank loan and to invest in the Salthill Bookstore. (And he'd invested quite a bit, Marina was surprised.) And he wanted no one to know: "This is our secret, Marina." Adam might drop by the store several days in succession, fluttering Marina's heart, and then stay away for a week, or more; he disliked telephones, and rarely called; if you called Adam, as Marina sometimes did, in a weak mood, his telephone might ring, ring, ring forlornly; he had no answering machine. He was one to chafe at the expectations of others. He might come to a party, but he might not. Impulse seemed to guide him. Unless it was strategy. You couldn't predict Adam Berendt, he was a master who didn't need his subjects. Yet, in his presence, it was impossible not to think *This man! He loves me, alone.*

". . . my spiritual self? The hills I haven't yet climbed."

Marina felt embarrassed, saying such things. She felt like a child, anxious yet trusting; as, in her own childhood, she'd never been, for there'd been no Adam Berendt in her family or among her acquaintances. Saying, goading, in his expansive, kindly voice, "Marina, what are these hills exactly? That you haven't climbed?"

It was the pure Socratic method. The impersonal quest for Truth. Marina felt the unease, and the excitement, of the hunt. Not she was the hunted, but the elusive Truth. For there was nothing personal here. Was there?

Adam, you. You are the hills! Loving you.

Loving a man. Fully, sexually.

Instead, Marina said, in a lowered voice as if ashamed, stumbling on the path and blinking away tears, "I—I'd wanted to be an artist. As long ago as I could remember. There was no one else in my family who had such notions. We were a practical family. My father was a high school teacher, it was a job. My mother, before she got married, a nurse. They worked, they earned salaries. Me, I had 'visions.' I was an excitable, nervous girl. In college, at the University of Maine, I understood that, to be an artist, you must filter your vision through technique. I became interested in sculpting and pottery. But not conventional pottery—experimental, odd work. Pottery that doesn't sell! It was calming, I seemed to fly out of myself in a kind of trance. After graduation, this was in the eighties, I lived with some friends in Provincetown, very cheaply, and I was happy there, a local gallery sold some of my things, then I got restless and moved to San Francisco, and for a while I was living in a wonderful ramshackle old ranch house in Mendocino, you'd have loved that place, Adam!—instead of the river outside your house, you'd see mountains. A mountain is a kind of vertical river, isn't it? And the light cascading down. I was happy there, and doing some decent work; for a long time I'd been out of contact with my family, they hated my life, they didn't want to understand it, then my father got sick and I came back east, and something happened there, between me and what I was doing, between my hands and what they touched, and that's fatal for an artist, isn't it? It was as if I'd lost my nerve. A young artist has courage, maybe the courage of ignorance. Then you lose that courage. I didn't know it at first. I kept going for a while, mechanically. I loved my work but it became too important to me. It was my life, my breath. It was obsessive. I did sculpting, I suppose you could call it, on a smaller scale than your work, and in natural forms, not metal, but it exhausted me, I couldn't sleep, my head was filled with 'visions.' I wanted to create astonishing things that hadn't been imagined before. I wanted so badly—" Marina felt the old, sick excitement; she'd been speaking rapidly, heedlessly. *Why am I doing this. Exposing myself. As if it could make this man love me!*

They'd ascended the hill, and were in an open, grassy area; wild rose was blooming in white clusters; to the east, miles away, the Hudson River was of the hue of weathered stone, flattened by distance, without motion as a design in wallpaper. Adam, who'd climbed the hill without betraying exertion, he whose legs were hard-knotted with muscle, twice the size of Marina's slender legs, waited a respectful moment before asking, "How long was this phase of your life?" "About a year. A year and a half. I ran away to live again in New York, with a friend. He was an artist, too. And he had a commercial job in graphic design. I believed I loved him, it was part of my desperation." Adam asked, "And then what happened, Marina?" Marina said, "I don't know. I've tried not to think about it. I don't 'dwell' upon the past. I had a collapse, I guess. I suppose I was sick, physically. I seemed always to have a fever. I was terrified to sleep, I was anxious and angry all the time. Everything I touched, I seemed to destroy. My hands had turned against me. My lover couldn't live with me, he said. I drove him away, and begged him to come back; I drove him away again; I hated what I was doing, my work, I destroyed most of it, I lost all faith in myself; I even threw out most of my clothes. I returned to Bangor, I got a job. It was my duty, I believed, to visit my mother, even if she didn't know who I was, or care. When there's someone very sick, you can measure yourself against that person, and take comfort that you're not so bad. That's *sanity*—that thrill of relief. Even with the sorrow, relief. But this confirmed my resolve not to risk mental breakdown. 'Art' isn't worth it. And there was another side of me: I'd worked in bookstores, and I love books. I love the look and smell of books, the culture of books. There's a romance, too, in sanity, isn't there? I like the kind of people who come into bookstores. Thank God, I thought, I'd given up on the other—that craziness. I came into a little money and I borrowed money and I took over the mortgage on Salthill's 'quaint' little bookstore and I've been happy here." Marina laughed. She was stubborn, and just slightly angry. "I am happy."

But was Adam impressed? In his droll, blunt way evidently not.

He said, "Maybe you've embraced failure too quickly."

Marina was stung. Failure!

"I'll give you another chance, Marina. A choice. A way back into the life you abandoned."

IT WAS THEN that Adam proposed to Marina Troy that he make a gift to her. *Make a gift* was the expression he used. He would sign over to her the ownership of a forty-acre property in the Pocono Mountains, in Pennsylvania, approximately one hundred miles west of the hill upon which they were standing. An old lodge, but in good condition; of fieldstone and half-timbering; seven miles from a small town called Damascus Crossing, and about thirty miles from the city of East Stroudsburg, on the Delaware River. Marina listened to this, without fully comprehending. Adam was pointing westward, and Marina turned to see a sequence of hazing receding hills, a horizon of trees that must have been only a few miles away but seemed distant. "Don't look so alarmed, Marina," Adam said, bemused, as if this were the crux of Marina's alarm, "—the place has been winterized, insulated. It's furnished, more or less. There's a deep spring well, the purest water I've ever tasted. You could live alone there, Marina, undisturbed, and undistracted by any of us in Salthill. You could do the work for which you were born." Adam spoke excitedly, sincerely; Marina had never heard him, or any of her adult acquaintances, speak in such a way. *This man does love me. But on a spiritual plane. Not human.* Tears sprang into her eyes, she was so deeply moved; yet of course it was impossible, an absurd proposition. "But Adam, what of the bookstore? I couldn't—" "What of the bookstore? It will be there when you return, if you want it. If you return. Say you're gone a year: we'll hire a full-time manager. There's your current assistant who seems very capable. And of course I'd be in town to oversee things." Adam let his hand fall, and clamp, upon Marina's shoulder; the weight of this hand, and its heat, nearly made her stagger. Marina continued to protest, and Adam continued to make plans. "Your Pearl Street house, you can rent it for a high price. I happen to know about Salthill real estate, and it's as inflated as properties in Westchester County. Your droll little place, the size of a dollhouse, would be snapped up within twenty-four hours, and with your rental money you'd have more than enough to support yourself." Marina stared at her friend's face that seemed now to be glowing, glaring more fiercely. And his hand on her shoulder, so warm. *I can't. Can't breathe.* Long Marina had yearned to be touched by Adam Berendt, yet this touch was strange to her, disconcerting. They were standing so close together they might have been mistaken for a couple. Marina had to resist a sudden impulse to step into Adam's arms, to embrace him around his burly chest, lay her head against him, and be comforted in her distress, even as Adam was the agent of her distress. She disengaged herself from the weight and heat of his hand. "Adam, of course I couldn't accept such a gift. How have you come into this property, that you can throw it away? What are you thinking of?" Adam said, surprised, "What am I thinking of? I'm thinking of *you*." "I'm not a young woman any longer, Adam. And even if I— " "Bullshit."

Abruptly then, Adam turned away, and continued on the hiking trail. He was offended, thwarted. He would speak no more on the subject that day. Like a woman who has crawled out of a wreck, Marina glanced down at herself to see if she was still there. She wiped her damp, clammy face carefully with a tissue, tightened the laces of her hiking shoes, and followed after Adam who was nearly out of sight.

Marina hoped the preposterous offer he'd made to her would be discreetly forgotten, but a few days later, Adam stopped by her narrow lavender house at the top of North Pearl Street, beside the Catholic churchyard, to present to her several fully executed legal documents deeding a property in Damascus County, Pennsylvania, to her; and, in a manila envelope, a hand-drawn map in colored inks, labeled keys, and a page-long list of instructions regarding the operation of the house. With maddening aplomb he said, "Anytime you wish, Marina. It's yours now, it will be waiting." Marina was frightened, furious. She wanted to strike Adam with her fists. "Adam, are you crazy? I can't accept such a gift from you." Adam said, winking, "From whom, then, Marina, would you accept it?" "Adam, God damn it, I *can't*." But Adam merely placed the items on a table in Marina's front room, and strode back into her kitchen to brew himself coffee. (It was Adam's custom to drop by houses in Salthill where he was known and, in his words, tolerated. How vast were his friends, acquaintances, neighbors, Marina had no idea. Sometimes he bicycled about, sometimes he walked. Sometimes he was accompanied by his dog, Apollo, "Apollodoros." If you invited Adam, he was sure not to come; if you did not, he might.) Marina begged Adam to take back the gift, and Adam said pleasantly, "Marina, a gift from the gods can't be rejected without invoking a curse. In time, you'll come round." Adam took his coffee mug back into the sunroom, and Marina joined him, with a mug of her own, and for a half hour or so they talked of other things; when Adam left, declining her offer of dinner, he squeezed her hand hard, wetly kissed her cheek, and laughed at her. Marina thought, *Is he mad?* She could hear him laughing to himself halfway down the block.

The gift as she would come to think of it. She couldn't bring herself to touch the items he'd left for several days. This was to be Marina's fate, was it? "No."

It was as she'd known: she wasn't strong enough. She couldn't have borne freedom in the Pocono Mountains, or anywhere. She'd lost the courage of her youth. The audacity of her youth. Never again, to her relief, did Adam bring up the subject of the farmhouse in Damascus County, Pennsylvania, and Marina never brought it up. Of course, there was the knowledge of it between them, unspoken; as, Marina supposed, the knowledge of an unborn child, a creature aborted in the womb, must hover between a woman and a man, forever in consciousness yet never spoken of.

Marina put *the gift* away for safekeeping. She dared not try to return it to Adam. After this, though she continued to love him, she feared him, too, and rather resented him. No man should be so powerful, meddling with another's soul.

And a year and six weeks later, Adam was dead. Marina was herself the personal executor of his estate. With a pang of dread she supposed *the gift* was still hers?

6

How death enters your life. Following Adam's death, and that stranger's body in the morgue, things began to loosen and unravel. Marina was a passenger in a careening vehicle that at high speed begins to shudder. Your instinct is, hide your eyes.

But in fact she was a responsible woman. The owner of the last independent bookstore in the village, widely admired as a still-youngish woman of independent means. Adam Berendt's friend, and the "personal executor" of Adam's estate.

Marina would make arrangements for Adam's body to be cremated, by way of a funeral home in Nyack. She must try to notify his relatives. (But who were Adam's relatives?) Somehow, his car would have to be driven back to Salthill. And there was the emergency matter of Adam's dog: what had happened to Apollo? When Marina returned to Salthill in the evening of July Fourth, groggy and exhausted from her ordeal at the medical center, she drove directly to Adam's house on the river thinking, *I alone am responsible for that dog*. But at Adam's house, where was Apollo? When Adam was away for brief periods he usually left the dog outside, on a long leash, but Marina couldn't find Apollo in his usual place, had he slipped his leash, knowing somehow that his master was in distress, and run away? The silver-tipped husky was nowhere on Adam's property, Marina called and called for him until her throat was hoarse, tramping through the tall grass, through a wooded area, at last along the River Road wild-eyed and disheveled, crying, "Apollo? *Apollo!*" How furious she was, at both the dog and his dead master! Her drawn white face was illuminated in oncoming headlights that flared up, blinded her, and mercifully disappeared. Salthill was such a small community, Marina dreaded one of these drivers recognizing her, but no one did, nor did any residents of the River Road at whose houses she stopped to report having seen the lost dog. No one had heard "unusual barking." Marina thought *Apollo knows that Adam has died*. Marina reported the missing dog to the Salthill Animal Watch, and went home, staggering with exhaustion.

Envy Apollo! Adam once said. *Of all of us, Apollo alone doesn't know he must die.*

AT THE TIME of Adam's death, Marina had been living for seven years, contentedly enough, in the magical Village of Salthill-on-Hudson, where everyone was middle-aged.

She'd noticed immediately: Salthill residents who appeared to her young—"youthful"—in some cases strikingly attractive, in their late twenties or early thirties—were in fact middle-aged. Well into their forties, fifties, sometimes sixties. Salthill residents who looked frankly "middle-aged" were elderly. The only really young couples who could afford to live in Salthill were sons and daughters of the rich, and these had about them a vigorous, health-minded, resolutely "upbeat" American-middle-aged aura. Adolescents and even children in Salthill, staggering beneath the weight of their parents' ambitions for them like overburdened camels, were middle-aged in spirit. The most commendable thing you might say of such offspring was that they were *wonderfully mature for their ages* even as the most commendable thing you might say about the elderly, if you could identify them, was that they were *wonderfully young for their ages.* No matter the demographics of Salthill and its environs, the median age had to be fifty.

It was possible, Adam Berendt refuted these observations. He was believed to be in his early fifties, and he looked exactly that age. But of course, he *was* middle-aged—"The very essence of that state of the soul."

Marina Troy, who on her last, startling birthday was thirty-eight, could console herself at least, if consolation was what she wanted, that she looked "much younger" than her age. If one didn't look too closely, in too unsparing a light.

Long she'd imagined herself as a girl, not quite a woman, with a curse blighting her maturity. Though in fact she wasn't a virgin, she'd long led a virginal life. She'd become, in Salthill, a "character" in others' imaginations. Like Adam Berendt, though Marina wasn't so strong, nor so popular, a "character" as Adam had been. *A minor character. An eccentric.* All communities are myth-making, and none more so than communities of the privileged and the sequestered, like Salthill. *Where some of us have turned to salt, like Lot's wife?*

The Village of Salthill-on-Hudson, population 2,300, was less than an hour's drive north of the George Washington Bridge; by train, you arrived at Grand Central Station in twenty-eight minutes, at least ideally. It was both a "historic" region—an old

Dutch community founded in 1694 on the west bank of the Hudson River, rebuilt and enlarged in 1845 by devout members of the utopian Salthill Community under the messianic leadership of Captain Moses Salthill, who would in time, overwhelmed by angelic and demonic voices in "fiercesome contention," take his own life—and zealously, vibrantly contemporary. Here was *community spirit* in an almost literal sense. Even Salthill Republicans, it was fondly (if not altogether accurately) claimed, voted liberal. There was a palpable community *self,* a *soul.* You couldn't avoid it. Owner of the landmark Salthill Bookstore on Pedlar's Lane, in the heart of the "charming" historic district, Marina Troy could not avoid it.

Adam had said, of Salthill, that it was a place that, lacking legends, except for the long-dead early settlers, had to invent its own. And maybe this had become true, since World War II, of America itself. There were no true "heroes"—for there could be no "heroics." Yet the instinct for "heroes"—"heroines"—"legends" remained undiminished. At any time, a number of individuals must be designated as "legendary" by the media; a number of individuals must be designated as "local characters" in their communities. The wish to believe that Adam Berendt had been a recluse, for instance, a man of mystery, could not be borne out by any actual behavior on Adam's part over the years; though Marina sensed it would be intensified after his death. And there was Marina Troy, a "character" on a smaller scale.

The unmarried, never-married, virginal-appearing and "fiercely independent" Marina Troy. A figure of romance, to others at least, in this green suburban world in which everyone was married, or had been married. "They speculate about us," Marina's friend Abigail Des Pres told her, "—I'm the lonely, sexually rapacious neurotic divorcée, forever in quest of a man; you're the mysterious maiden, with the long glamorous hair like what's-her-name in the fairy tale. Not Rumpelstiltskin—" "Rapunzel?" "—a sort of unconscious temptress. Men are drawn, intrigued, but frightened away." "Are they? How?" "The collective sense is there must be some secret in your life, Marina. So they think." Marina laughed, though this disclosure alarmed and annoyed her. Her true secret, her repudiated hope of being an artist, she intended not to share with anyone (except Adam, who would never betray a secret).

"But, Abigail, who is this 'they'?"

"'They.' Who surround us."

So tales were told of Marina Troy. Those beautiful somber stony-gray eyes! Her face in repose, so melancholy! Marina could be made to laugh, but silently. Though she was the daughter of a high school science teacher in unromantic Pike River, Maine, north of Bangor, and a woman who'd been briefly a registered nurse, yet her Salthill legend was of a "patrician New England" family who'd lost their fortune (shipbuilding? banking?) in the Depression. Though Marina frequently traveled back to Maine to visit her mother in a Bangor nursing home, and an older, married sister, it was widely believed that Marina's "patrician" family had disowned her. (Surely the estrangement had to do with sex? And maybe politics? Marina Troy was "very left, very liberal.")

Marina protested none of these tales, for they were never told to her directly. But she was aware of them as we're uneasily aware of reflections of ourselves in mirrors or shiny surfaces at which, in the company of others, we don't want to glance. Except with Adam, Marina knew better than to speak of her private life to Salthill friends. She knew how the most reluctantly uttered confidence was soon taken up by the Salthill circle, tossed into the air and batted about, as a pack of dogs might take up a hapless creature, tossing its body into the air, yipping and barking excitedly until nothing remained but a patch of bloody skin or a few beautiful, bloody feathers.

She understood, though, that Salthill most admired Marina Troy for her "devotion" to the Salthill Bookstore. This cramped little store was situated in a block of rowhouses that veered uphill from Salthill's Main Street like steps, each of the woodframe buildings painted a different color, maroon, yellow, pale green, brick red, chalk white, like an illustration in a nineteenth-century children's book. Of course, Pedlar's Lane was cobbled, and one way, and so narrow that trucks moved along it slowly, like hunks of coarse thread pushing through the eye of a needle. Of course, no parking was allowed on or even near Pedlar's Lane, which cut down on customers considerably. A gigantic Barnes & Noble store at the gigantic White Hills Mall twenty minutes away in Nyack, and Internet book sales, were gradually drawing off even long faithful customers of the store, yet there was romance in such doomed idealism—wasn't there? Especially to the affluent who had no firsthand knowledge of it, as Marina did.

Salthill was intrigued, too, that in a gallant or quixotic gesture a few years before, Adam Berendt had invested in the Salthill Bookstore. Or he'd at least lent his friend Marina money. (How much, no one knew. No one supposed that Adam had much money. A sculptor who gave most of his work away, and seemed never to be working? Who drove a 1979 Mercedes through the decades, and lived in an eighteenth-century stone house badly in need of renovating?)

Marina lived at 388 North Pearl Street, a brisk ten-minute walk from 7 Pedlar's Lane, or a five-minute bicycle ride, in a Victorian shingleboard painted lavender, beginning just perceptibly to peel, with purple grapevine trim; seen from the street, Marina's house had a quaint storybook quality, like her store; its façade was so narrow, a man might almost encompass it by stretching wide both his arms as, in a playful gesture, a male visitor had once done. "Marina, you live in a dollhouse!" Marina felt obliged to plant purple pansies and petunias in the windowboxes of her house. Her small front yard was bounded by a three-foot wrought-iron fence; on her front step, there was a braided welcome mat. Inside the house were three rooms downstairs, and three rooms upstairs; the stairs were unnervingly steep, and warped; the floorboards of each room were warped; the old glass of the windowpanes was wavy as if afflicted with astigmatism. You could love such a house, and be terribly tired of living in it. As you could love books, and be terribly tired of the commerce of books.

Adam had visited Marina many times in the house at 388 North Pearl, but not once had he lain in her brass bed at the top of the house. The Salthill circle was curious about this possibility, and neither Marina nor Adam felt obliged to enlighten them. In fact, Adam had climbed the steep stairs, making their aged wood creak, and he'd entered the bedroom with its slanting ceiling, but only to help Marina paper the walls. He'd fixed drips in her bathrooms, upstairs and down. He'd offered to caulk the windows and would surely have done so before the first frost of that year, except he'd been killed in midsummer.

What is the romance of a Marina Troy, for her married female friends? She supposed it must be her *aloneness*. Women who couldn't bear a few minutes' solitude in their lavish homes, who frantically telephoned friends through the day and filled up their calendars with dinners, cocktail parties, luncheons, tennis dates, excursions into the city, charitable organizations; women who collapsed when their children departed for college, or for summers abroad, or even for summer camp; women who panicked at the possibility of divorce, yet also at the possibility of spending a quiet weekend alone with their husbands; women who kept lengthy, annotated lists of individuals who "owed" them and whom they "owed," and to what degree, nonetheless spoke of admiring Marina, and of envying her. Yet they were keen to contaminate her *aloneness*. They invited her to their continuous stream of parties, not minding that, though she owed everyone in town, she rarely reciprocated; they took care to seat her beside such eligible bachelors as Adam Berendt, who, it seemed, had never been married; and Roger Cavanagh, whose marriage had dissolved, leaving him witty and ironic, handicapped as with a wizened or missing limb. These women, most of them beautiful well into middle-age, spoke kindly of Marina's "unique" beauty; her "patrician" profile; for a woman prized by their circle could hardly be plain.

Marina wore striking clothes, quite unlike her Salthill women friends who shopped exclusively at designer stores; but these were "striking" perhaps by accident. Long hobbling skirts, often with alarming slits in the sides; velvet jackets wearing out at the elbows, and too tight in the shoulders; expensive but water-stained leather boots to the knee; curious carved-looking shoes with or without heels, or black running shoes with floppy black shoelaces. She was known to be one of Salthill's "runners"; it was a matter of common knowledge that she and her friend Adam Berendt went hiking together, on ambitious treks. She wore shorts, trousers, slacks, jeans; often these were a size or two too large; and cable-knit sweaters that looked as if they were hand knit, but were not. In fact, Marina was not very domestic. When at last she couldn't avoid it, and invited friends to dinner, the meal tended to be hastily prepared; often, she hauled it home from Chez Hélène, Salthill's premiere food shop. (If Marina's friends sighted Chez Hélène containers in her kitchen, they passed along the good news to one another: "We're in luck tonight.")

Marina's dread of domesticity had a darker side. She feared opening that vein, for what if she bled to death?

It was seven years before Adam's death she'd been introduced to him by an older Salthill couple, the Hoffmanns. Fondly it would be recounted how at that meeting Adam Berendt had shaken the young red-haired woman's hand and fixed her with his critical left eye and loudly, lavishly declared she was a contemporary Elizabeth I—"You know, the Hilliard portraits." Impulsively Adam lifted Marina's hand to kiss the knuckles, even as Marina, the abashed Rapunzel, stared at him in astonishment. *Who on earth is this man?*

She'd avoided Adam for the remainder of the evening. The mere sight of him provoked a blush like a hemorrhage into her face.

But she'd been touched with pleasure, too. For she was a vain woman, at heart. *Marina Troy, Virgin Queen.*

In fact, the celebrated Hilliard portraits of Elizabeth I, which Marina sought out the next morning in her bookstore, depict a very pale, unsmiling, eyebrowless red-haired woman of indeterminate age, neither young nor old; her nose long and narrow, her eyes wary, vigilant. Except for the Queen's excessively ornate attire, which exuded an air almost of madness, you couldn't have guessed that this individual was a *woman, female.*

* * *

MARINA THOUGHT of these things, as a way of not thinking of Adam's death. Upstairs in her crooked little woodframe house at the top of North Pearl Street beside the churchyard. She couldn't hope to sleep just yet. It was only midnight. July fifth, and the maddening fireworks silenced at last. She'd been making telephone calls, and speaking quietly over the phone, and finally she'd asked other friends to make the rest of her calls for her; and now the phone receiver lay off the hook, utterly silent as if the cord had been cut.

She'd embraced him, or tried to. Stroked his grimacing face. Kissed his discolored eyelids. *The body he'd become. Not Adam.*

A vigil for Adam. She'd rummaged through her bureau drawers, retrieved *the gift,* placing it quickly on a table; not examining the documents. She'd found snapshots of Adam and herself, and several charcoal sketches she'd made of him a few years before. *Evidence. He did exist. In my life.* For some reason, one day she'd had an urge to sketch Adam, though she hadn't picked up a charcoal stick in years. "My ugly mug?" Adam asked. "Hell, why?" He hadn't really wanted to pose for Marina, sitting still in such a way was too passive for him, made him restless, but he'd given in, for Marina had prevailed upon him and he was a good-natured guy, a good sport. And maybe he'd been curious to see just how talented Marina was.

So Adam had posed for Marina, in the solarium at the rear of her house, and she'd tried, God how she'd tried to capture his likeness, his spirit; finally giving up, and putting the sketches away, though she hadn't showed them to Adam, knowing he'd have laughed at them, and wanted to rip them up. She'd saved the sketches for they were a sign of their intimacy, hers and Adam's; and of the highly intense, concentrated hour they'd spent on that January afternoon that would otherwise have dissolved into oblivion. (Except: Marina recalled how that evening she and Adam were officially involved in a public occasion at the Salthill Arts Council hall. An anonymous, presumably wealthy local donor had given the organization, in which Marina was an officer that year, a tall columnar sculpture in travertine marble and cherry wood, by the distinguished Argentine sculptor Raul

Farco, and the Arts Council had talked Adam into publicly presenting the sculpture, to an audience largely unfamiliar with Farco's work. Adam professed to dislike events of this nature, yet, once on his feet, assured of his audience's interest, he spoke with zest and enthusiasm, and was warmly applauded. He'd worn a bulky tweed green-heather sport coat, gray trousers that didn't match, a midnight-blue shirt and a necktie of style and beauty, Marina suspected it must be a gift from a woman. But she wasn't jealous.) Examining the sketches now, Marina was sharply disappointed. She had been half hoping, after the horror of Jones Point . . . But she'd failed to capture the man's mysterious essence. You could identify this brute-looking character as Adam Berendt, but it wasn't Adam Berendt; it was a dummy, a mannequin; a simulacrum of a middle-aged, stocky man with a creased face, balding head, and unnatural eyes, from which all youth, vigor, mystery had departed. *As in the morgue he'd lain inert. Both eyes now blind. Mouth partly open as if he had one more thing to say—but what?*

Marina picked up a charcoal stick and tried to correct Adam's likeness. Willing herself to remember Adam as he'd been in life. Not in death but *in life*. Standing before her, here in this room as he'd done in life. Smiling. Reaching out to her. Was he teasing her? About what? *The hills are still there, Marina!* But he'd laughed at her, too. He'd laughed at all of Salthill, yet without meanness. Marina began to tremble, seeing the man so clearly. Hearing his voice. Yet, fumbling with the charcoal stick, as unable to express what she saw as a young child. "Oh, Adam." It was true: by any criteria, he'd had an ugly mug. His skin had looked singed, and his nose had been broken, and there was a startlingly white barbed-wire scar through his right eyebrow. Yet, why wasn't he ugly? On the contrary, Adam seemed to Marina beautiful . . .

In Plato's *Phaedo* Socrates assures us *Our soul is imperishable and immortal and existed before we were born.*

"Oh, Adam. Is this true? I don't think this is true."

It was 1:08 A.M. Marina's hand faltered. The charcoal stick that had been so inept fell to the floor. The drawings were crude, hopeless. The man had gone. Adam had departed. How to endure this night? Marina should have torn up the drawings, these testaments to her loss, but even this act of defiance was beyond her.

7

How death enters life. And life is altered. She knew that Roger Cavanagh, who was Adam's lawyer, and had been his friend, would call her soon, and within minutes of her replacing the phone on the hook, cautiously, with dread, the phone rang, and it was Roger. Instructing her to please come to his office in town, if she was free. He had private, urgent business with her. "Is it—Adam's will?" Marina asked, and Roger said, "Yes. Adam's will."

Marina had wakened in a state of suspended emotion. She'd slept poorly the previous night. Struggling not to drown as *Thwaite Thwaite* entered her dreams with nightmare logic. *Thwaite* that was a foul licorice substance pushing down her throat. In an overly bright daylight she moved like a sleepwalker. Or like a woman suffering a classic hangover. Thinking how, under normal circumstances, she'd have been irritated with Roger Cavanagh, so absorbed in his lawyer-mode that he hadn't even commiserated with Marina about Adam's death.

Roger Cavanagh, whose wife had divorced him, and won custody of their daughter. How often Marina had been seated beside this man, at Salthill dinner parties, as if, somehow, in their friends' eyes, Marina and Roger must be "fated"; yet neither seemed to feel much for the other except wariness, a vague sexual unease. Roger rarely came into the Salthill Bookstore. He was a man who acknowledged almost boastfully that he "hadn't time" for serious reading; newspapers, TV, and professional journals were all he "had time" for. How Adam had tolerated him, Marina couldn't imagine. Roger put her in mind of sharp, dark things: shark fins, spikes of wrought-iron fences, painful jolts in the darkness as you stumbled from bed. Years ago, he'd called her several times to ask her—what, Marina couldn't recall.

The essence of an unmarried man telephoning an unmarried woman in such circumstances must mean, to be blunt about it, *Will you have sex with me?* Marina laughed aloud, blindly coiling a braid around her head, not caring to observe herself very closely in the mirror. Yes, a hangover! Why not think of grief that way.

A dog was barking somewhere close by. In the churchyard?

Apollo?

Adam had brought the dog to visit with Marina numerous times, could Apollo have found his way to *her?*

But when Marina hurried from the house calling, "Apollo? Apollo?" the barking had ceased.

She drove to Roger Cavanagh's office on Shaker Square. And there was Roger waiting for her, on the front steps, smoking a cigarette. That air of barely restrained impatience. It was late morning, Sunday: Fourth of July weekend. The Square was empty. Roger's firm, Abercrombie, Cavanagh, Kruller & Hook owned one of the eighteenth-century brownstones, prime real estate at the heart of the "historic" village. Roger was known to be a reputable Salthill lawyer, capable, trustworthy, conservative. Marina had never stepped inside one of the Shaker Square brownstones, which mostly housed lawyers; expensive lawyers; when she couldn't avoid hiring a lawyer, she chose one with an office in an outlying district, or in a mall. As Marina approached, Roger frowned in greeting, glancing up and down the street as if in worry they might be observed, and urging her inside. "Please. Come in." As soon as Marina did, Roger shut the door and locked it.

The suite of offices was deserted, of course. Marina felt uneasy, alone here with Roger. And how unlike himself he looked: he'd shaved carelessly, leaving stubble, and a thinly bleeding scratch on his jaw; his dark hair that was usually impeccably styled and combed was disheveled, as if he'd been running his fingers through it. And his eyes were shadowed, more recessed than Marina recalled. "Terrible news," Roger murmured. "Unbelievable." Yet he spoke curtly as if not wanting to waste breath. Or emotion. Where usually this man exuded an astringent-masculine scent of cologne, he smelled now frankly of his body. And he wore sports clothes, rumpled clothes. He, too, has had a bad night, Marina thought; feeling, for a moment, for this calculating man, a stab of tenderness.

"Adam, of all people. Who'd been so—" But Roger was only just talking, in that obligatory social way of people with something else, something far more crucial, on their minds, and scarcely knew what he said. "—filled with life. Of all of us. Terrible news!" He was leading Marina briskly, with no ceremony, through the lavish suite, to his own large office at the rear; though it was a sunny midsummer morning, the plate glass windows' thin-slatted blinds were tightly shut. On Roger's desk, amid piles of documents, a plastic cup, very likely hot coffee; an ashtray and cigarette butts. Out of deference to Marina, who'd drawn back from his cigarette, Roger stubbed it out in the ashtray. He sniffed, made a snorting sound as if clearing his sinuses; shifted his shoulders inside his sports shirt; and asked Marina please to take a seat. Marina wondered what was so crucial, why she'd been called. Her eye moved restlessly about the office, which was furnished in expensive teak, black leather, chrome. There was a decorative paneling of glass brick setting off what Marina supposed was a private lavatory at the rear of the office; and this paneling reminded her of the Jones Point Medical Center morgue and what she'd seen there . . . Marina murmured, "Yes. Terrible."

Roger Cavanagh's stylishly decorated office was a showcase to be admired, but damned if Marina would say the expected thing, the Salthill-social thing, nor would she embarrass Roger with an outburst of sorrow, grief, tears. She saw, on a teakwood cabinet, a sculpted brass figure about the size of a violin, with a smooth raised oval surface that suggested a human face in which dim protoplasmic features were only just crystallizing. This was an old work of Adam Berendt's from a series Marina thought beautiful though Adam had long since repudiated it, and had no pieces from that era in his studio or house. *Too arty and self-conscious—too Brancusi*, Adam had dismissed the brass pieces. Roger said, "He gave me that. He wouldn't let me pay him for it even in trade." There was an air of shame and frustration in this admission, though Marina didn't know why. Roger was leafing through documents on his desk, breathing harshly. Marina pretended to be interested in, and then became genuinely interested in, several framed photographs displayed on Roger's big glass-topped desk. As if Roger Cavanagh meant to say, *You see? I'm a normal man. This is what truly matters to me.* One of the photos was of a child of about eleven, evidently Roger's daughter, an unsmiling little girl squinting in sunshine, oddly posed so that Marina surmised that another person, the ex-wife probably, had been scissored out of the scene; in another photograph, the girl was older, square-jawed and plain, with Roger's small squinting eyes and thick coarse dark hair, now smiling tentatively; in the third and largest, the one that exuded the most hope, Roger and the girl, both in tennis whites, gripping racquets, were posed side by side squinting and smiling in front of a tennis net; the girl now looked to be about fourteen, almost as tall as her father. Marina said, "Your daughter?" and Roger said, without glancing at the photographs, "Yes." He spread a bulky document of about twenty pages in front of Marina. *Last Will and Testament of Adam Berendt.* The date was April of that year. Roger said, "Possibly you know, Adam has left most of his estate to charitable organizations. His house and land to the Rockland Historic Trust, and enough of an endowment to establish and maintain it as an arts center. Other endowments to environmental organizations, the ACLU and related liberal causes, the Rockland County Homeless Animal Shelter, and so forth, exactly what you'd expect of Adam. Apart from the property on the river, which might be worth a couple of million dollars, I doubt that Adam has much of an estate, but I could be surprised. Lawyers, like priests, are often surprised. Death brings out not usually the worst in us, nor even the best, but the muted, the secret; you get used to surprises, which aren't invariably unpleasant. But you'll be relieved to learn, Marina," Roger said, glancing sidelong at her, with such a look of strain that Marina couldn't comprehend how this could be relief, "that Adam didn't leave sums of money or significant gifts to any individuals, including his closest friends, or any of his possessions except 'random works of art' as he calls them, to be disposed of as his 'personal executor'—you—sees fit. I'm Adam's estate executor, as you know." Marina said, uneasily, "He didn't designate any heirs?—relatives?" "He did not." "But we have a moral obligation to locate them, don't we? I mean, Adam's relatives? To notify them of the—funeral." "We can try to locate them. We'll drive over to his house this morning, and see what we can find, if you're comfortable with going through his papers so soon after, well, what happened yesterday, but Adam himself never supplied me with the names of any relatives, and you can be assured that I asked him, I asked him more than once, so I doubt very much that we'll find what we're looking for." Marina objected, not liking Roger's preemptory, lawyerly tone, "But we have to make the attempt. It's our moral obligation. Even if Adam wanted to cut himself off from his past, his relatives have a right to be informed of his death, don't they? He was only in his early fifties, at least one of his parents might be still living. From remarks Adam would sometimes make, without knowing what he said, when we were hiking especially, I have the idea he spent his childhood in a western state like Montana or Wyoming." Marina considered, but decided against, telling Roger about *the gift;* she felt uneasy, guilty over it, and the secrecy of the transaction; the moral thing might be to return the property to Adam's estate, somehow—but was it possible to give something to a dead man?

Roger was saying, "This is more important, Marina. Adam's will." Roger had opened the document to its final pages where Adam's characteristic scrawl *Adam Berendt* had been signed above *testator*. But other spaces, above *witness* and *notary public*, were blank. Marina said, "Adam has signed the will, but no one else? Why?" Roger said, "There were circumstances." Marina said, "Why didn't you get witnesses to his signature, at the time?" "Because, as I said, Marina, there were circumstances." Marina blinked, not understanding. The night before had been such a misery, she'd returned home from her futile search for Apollo to fall onto her bed exhausted, too demoralized to remove most of her clothing and her brain racing on the edge of madness; no wonder now she was having difficulty understanding simple things. There were Roger's evasive eyes, and Roger's small bruised-looking mouth, a curious mouth for a predator, what was he saying? Something about the will being "not quite complete"—"not quite fully executed."

"Marina? Look here."

Roger was sounding annoyed. He explained to Marina that though this was the will Adam had wanted, in every detail, yet Adam had postponed having Roger draw it up for years; after Roger prepared it in April, Adam had postponed coming in to sign for weeks, and then months, until it was too late. "But isn't this Adam's signature?" Marina asked naively. A moment later realizing *He has forged this signature. That's it!* Roger was saying, with the air of a man arguing a case, "It was the damndest thing. Adam would make an appointment, then fail to come in. We'd have used, of course, witnesses from this office. For an intelligent man he could behave very stupidly. Stubbornly. Well, you know Adam."

MARINA STUDIED the final pages of the will, seeing how the scrawl Adam Berendt on page twenty-one closely resembled, but wasn't identical with, the scrawl Adam Berendt on page twenty-two. The signature was skillfully executed but hadn't been traced. For some time she contemplated the signatures, and the blanks above witness, not knowing, yet certainly knowing, what was expected of her. Why Roger Cavanagh had so urgently called her in. Roger said, "Legally speaking, Adam has died intestate. This will isn't binding. It would be sent to probate court to languish for years. Much of the estate would go to death taxes, and since Adam's next of kin may never be located, the bulk of it would go to the State of New York. Adam's special wishes would be completely thwarted, do you see? Marina? For Adam's sake, not for our own, we have to help him."

"Isn't this—illegal? Criminal?"

The question hovered in the air unanswered. Roger sighed, and smiled his quick mirthless smile.

"But you've done it, the signature, for him. For Adam."

"Someone has done it."

"Am I to be a witness, then? And who will be the notary public?"

Roger said, "I'm a notary public."

"And the date today is—?"

"June twenty-second, a Wednesday. The date of Adam's most recent appointment, which is in the firm's computer."

"Roger, this is—a criminal act?"

"We have no choice, Marina. You know that Adam would be desperate for us to do it."

"What would happen if you, a lawyer, were—"

Roger said sharply, "Marina? Will you sign?"

"Yes."

Marina took up the pen Roger was offering her, and signed.

How Death enters your life. And all is altered hereafter. In separate cars they drove to Adam Berendt's house on the river, a mile and a half from Shaker Square. Marina's new mood was elation, hope; floating upon the older mood of despair and desolation. For now she was a criminal, for her dead lover's sake.

Impossible not to imagine the dead observing us. Our love for them a soft shimmering gossamer trailing behind us.

When Marina turned up the long rutted gravel driveway between stands of slatternly trees, she felt her old quickening of excitement, coming to Adam's house, though telling herself *No! not now.* Yet she watched anxiously for the silver-haired dog to come bounding out to greet her, as Adam's dog would have done under normal circumstances if Adam were home, but no dog appeared, and she swallowed hard, and when she came into view of the house above the river, screened by evergreens Adam hadn't gotten around to trimming after last January's ice storm, the house that had always seemed so romantic to her, the weathered old burgundy-gray stone, the steep slate roofs and tall chimneys, looked to her now melancholy and abandoned. Beside the house was a field of overgrown grasses and wildflowers, predominantly chicory, not a tended lawn; Adam had laughed at, scorned, such suburban lawns; he never troubled to clear away fallen leaves, year after year. His garden grew among weeds, a lush hive of green. Moss grew on the roof of the old garage, formerly a carriage house. Parked at the rear of the house was Roger Cavanagh's new-model American car, the wrong car. Marina would have to arrange to bring Adam's car back from that place of death. She saw for the second time that morning Roger Cavanagh awaiting her in an opened doorway, except he was now looking at her in a way that quickened her pulse, and her unease.

My co-conspirator. For Adam's sake.

Her new mood! Marina smiled to assure Roger that she wasn't upset, she was fine. That grimace of the mouth in smiling so closely akin to the grimace of the mouth in anguish. In sexual yearning.

When Marina stumbled on the front steps, Roger took her arm, and the sensation of his touch, his quick firm grip, stabbed through her.

"This is a strange thing we're doing. But it has to be done."

In silence they entered the stone house which was cool on even a warm midsummer morning. Marina was beginning to tremble. Wanting desperately to call out *Adam? Adam!* Still she was waiting for the noisy, excitable Apollo to appear, barking at them, and thumping his tail. But there was only silence. They stood in the vestibule in splotched sunshine and shadow. A fiercer sunshine spilled into the large, cluttered living room, where you'd expect Adam Berendt to be greeting his visitors, since he hadn't been at the front door to greet them; but the sunshine was blank and soulless. Marina moved slowly, staring at familiar sights with altered eyes. Adam's battered leather sofa with mismatched cushions; the Shaker-style chairs he'd built carefully by hand, which matched the six chairs he'd built for Marina's dining room; tables piled with books, magazines, newspapers, CDs; on the lofty fireplace mantel, the pair of antique pewter candlestick holders Marina had given Adam for one of his mysterious birthdays. (Mysterious because Adam never provided an exact date, only an approximate; and never specified his age.) Against the farther wall was a six-foot metallic and ceramic grandfather clock Adam had fashioned out of various idiosyncratic materials. Everyone who visited Adam admired this object, which had a working pendulum but no chimes, and no hands on the shiny ceramic clock face; Adam shrugged off the piece as "too likable, in the Rauschenberg mode"; he didn't want to sell it. Marina saw with childlike relief that the pendulum was still moving. Its tinny heartbeat filled the room.

Marina said uneasily, "It's wrong of us to be here. Adam wasn't expecting visitors."

Roger said, "There's no Adam now. Adam is beyond all expectations."

They moved through the house. Like phantoms, Marina thought.

As if they, not Adam Berendt, were dead.

They passed by the kitchen without entering, only glancing inside. Tears started in Marina's eyes: Adam's kitchen! Except for his studio, this was his favorite room. When he invited guests for dinner, which he did rarely, everyone would gather in the kitchen and help Adam prepare the food; if Marina visited Adam, by day, it was usually the kitchen in which they sat. His windows looking out upon the river. A vista that shifted constantly. He'd spoken to Marina of a strange absence of all desire, a profound peacefulness, in winter especially, as he leaned on his elbows on the counter, gazing out. "Not that I'm a happy man, nor even an unhappy man," he'd told her. "But happiness, unhappiness, are too trivial to matter. In such a place you become your own imagining. You feel nothing, or everything. You melt out into the sky."

Marina said, trying for a brisk practical tone, "The refrigerator. I'll come empty it, and the cupboards, some other time. Not now."

Roger was walking swiftly ahead. But Marina, seeing a stack of books on the floor, beside a closet, its door partly ajar, paused to inspect them, and this was the first of her shocks: these books in their bright, glossy covers, newly purchased, were from the

Salthill Bookstore. Marina swung open the closet door to see more books, a hundred books perhaps, stacked sideways on the shelves. Poetry, fiction, art, history. She stared at first without comprehension. Then the realization came to her, like a blow to the chest: Adam had purchased these books himself.

Since Adam's investment in the bookstore and his frequent visits, especially when he took over in Marina's absence, she'd noticed an increase in sales and profits. Some months, the increase was modest; at other times it was—well, heartening, exciting. "Adam, there's good news: we're *making money.*" Marina had attributed this business upsurge to her new partner's simple presence in the store: Adam was a popular Salthill figure whom other men liked to talk with and to whom women were attracted. Individuals who'd never entered the Salthill Bookstore dropped by when Adam was around. It was his idea to buy some rattan chairs, get a coffee machine, encourage customers to sit down in frank imitation of the big chain bookstores; he'd envisioned expanding into the adjacent store, where a picture framing business was on the wane; unlike Marina, he never worried about the future. *Because he was subsidizing the business. Our best customer.*

Marina recalled with a pang of embarrassment packing a box of unsold books back in January, mostly poetry books from distinguished small presses, and asking her assistant to return them to the distributor, and returning next day to the store to discover that the box was gone. Marina's assistant reported that Adam had "sold" the entire box—to a "collector from New Jersey." Janice hadn't been in the store at the time of the purchase, and hadn't seen this serendipitous customer, who was described as a retired English professor from a women's Catholic college with a special interest in contemporary American poetry, but the sale was in the computer, an astounding $618.95. How naive Marina had been, how desperately she must have wanted to believe! Seeing some of the titles now on Adam's closet shelves, stuck away unread, Marina recalled how adroitly Adam had deceived her. Though she'd been mildly suspicious, in a teasing sort of way, about Adam's special customers ("Women, obviously") who only appeared when Marina was nowhere near.

When will I meet this customer, Adam?

Marina dear, she's so much older than you are, have pity on her. We all must have our romantic fantasies.

"Marina, is something wrong?"

Roger, who'd gone on ahead, had returned to see why she wasn't following him. Marina lifted angry tear-brimming eyes to his face. "Adam was humoring me. Buying books from the store, all *these*." Roger frowned and seemed embarrassed. In a clumsy gesture of sympathy he picked up one of the poetry books and leafed through it as if seeking evidence to refute Marina's suspicions. She said, "I wanted so badly to believe that . . . business was improving." *And a good man, a gallant man, had entered her life, to change it forever.* "I suppose—everyone in Salthill knew?" Roger said, in his lawyerly, argumentative voice, "Knew what, exactly? There's no proof that these books are from your store." Marina wasn't going to argue. This man was humoring her, too. She shut the closet door hard and turned away.

In Adam's office at the rear of the house, with its dusty latticed windows and stained flagstone floor that opened into Adam's studio, Marina felt his presence keenly. And the tension between Roger Cavanagh and herself, tense as the electrical charge before a storm. She couldn't bear it that this man might pity her as Adam Berendt had done.

"Where did Adam get his money, Roger, do you know?" Marina meant to sound indifferent, detached; as if money were the crucial issue, and not a man's deception. As if Adam Berendt's worldly identity had nothing to do with *her*. But the question sounded anxious, pleading. Roger had approached Adam's desk, a massive old rolltop with numerous crammed pigeonholes and heavy drawers; with a grim expression he was pulling out manila envelopes and files, leafing through them. Going through a dead friend's papers! There was something jackal-like about this, distasteful. "Real estate, I think. Investments. He was mysterious about his background, of course. I never asked him personal questions, I wouldn't have seen that as practical. Some men live by boasting of their successes, but Adam seemed embarrassed by them; you had to infer that he'd had some success in business. At least, he had money. But he seems to have felt he was a man of such purity he shouldn't have had money. He paid my fees in cash." Roger's small wounded mouth contracted further. *Cash!* In a prestigious Shaker Square law firm. Marina wanted to laugh at the vision. *Like handling shit, is it? Cash. But you took it.*

Marina, silent, carried away a vase of limp, browning zinnias from a windowsill. Zinnias from Adam's garden. In which, shortly, his ashes would be scattered, and raked. Such a horror could not be, yet it was. She, Marina Troy, would see that the ceremony was done properly. Everywhere she went in Adam's deathly silent house she expected to see him. His look of astonishment, his slow baffled smile. *Marina? What are you doing here?* He would come forward quickly and take her hands, which were trembling. *Marina? Why are you crying?*

Marina noted that Adam's windowsills were grimy; the windowpanes rain-splotched and stained; yet sunshine blazed through the glass, idiotic and unmournful.

Why then should I mourn? Adam wouldn't want it.

Within the hour, Roger discovered another of Adam's secrets: he had credit and savings accounts under several names in New York, New Jersey, and Pennsylvania banks. He owned $180,000 in municipal bonds issued by the City of Philadelphia, $240,500 in municipal bonds issued by the City of New York, $325,000 in bonds issued by the Long Island Power Authority, hundreds of thousands of dollars in miscellaneous securities. The names were *Adam Berendt, Ezra Krane, T. W. Bailey, Samuel Myers*. Perhaps there were others, in other files. Marina tried to study the documents Roger passed to her, but the names and figures blurred in her vision; she felt light-headed, and frightened. She said, "I don't understand, Roger. Why?" Roger said quickly, "There's nothing illegal about having accounts under other names. We mustn't judge Adam without knowing more." Marina said, "But—why? Why would he have used these names? And where did so much money come from?" Roger said, with maddening evasiveness, "At a point, money begins to yield money." Marina protested, "But Adam was poor! He wasn't rich. He made fun of the rich.

He was—you know how Adam was. You were his friend, too." Roger said, shifting his shoulders uncomfortably, "Yes, I was Adam's friend. But no, I don't believe I knew him."

Apart from financial and legal documents, Roger hadn't located any personal papers of Adam's, any letters or documents suggesting that "Adam Berendt" had relatives, a background, a history. In one of the pigeonholes he found a half-dozen vouchers from Las Vegas casinos; in another, a crumpled document he passed over to Marina without comment, a bill of sale from a Manhattan art gallery? a receipt for $45,600 for the purchase of a work of art by Raul Farco? This must have been the sculpture donated to the Salthill Arts Council by an "anonymous" donor. Adam Berendt! Marina was stunned. She remembered how Adam had been persuaded to formally present the graceful columnar marble piece in the Arts Council hall; how, once Adam overcame his initial awkwardness, speaking in front of a gathering that contained so many friends, he'd seemed to soar, not eloquent exactly but warm and enthusiastic, explaining why the marble sculpture was an important work, speaking of the community's gratitude to the "unknown" donor. For once, Adam said, artist and donor need not be conjoined, only the artist and his work would be celebrated. Everyone had clapped enthusiastically. It had seemed to them that Adam's insight was profound. *But he was speaking of himself.*

Beneath scattered newspaper pages on a table, Marina found Adam's filthy, much thumbed address book. Quickly she looked under "B"—but there were no Berendts listed. Many names in the little book were messily crossed out and entire pages were missing. There were numerous insertions, business cards and slips of paper, falling out of the dog-eared pages. Marina couldn't resist turning to "T"—and there was *Marina Troy* listed. Her hand began to shake. How sordid it was, this business of recording the names of human beings, addresses, and telephone numbers as they intersect with our lives; when they no longer intersect, we cross them out, or tear out their page. Adam had marked occasional names with ↓; she seemed to know that ↓ indicated an individual no longer living. For some reason her heart was pounding quickly. What did it mean that *Marina Troy, 388 North Pearl Street,* was included in Adam Berendt's address book, with so many others? It meant nothing, of course. Marina said with sudden bitterness, "What do we want from one another, really? All this frantic 'collecting' of one another. Friends, social life. After death, it must all seem so futile." Roger, seated at Adam's swivel chair, made a snorting sound. "Maybe before death, too." Marina tossed the address book down onto the desk in front of him, with sudden vehemence.

Quickly Roger leafed through the little book, as if its secrets might spill out at once. She knew he was seeking "C"—*Roger Cavanagh*. Marina felt a stab of dislike for the man. Why couldn't he be Adam, why couldn't he have died in Adam's place? His forehead was oily and furrowed with fine cracks; his small, hurt, sullen mouth was offensive to her, as if she'd kissed it once, and tasted rot. Roger must have been fatigued by the morning's effort but he sat drumming his fingers on the desk top and Marina had an impulse to lay a hand on his. But she'd never touch the man! *We're co-conspirators. Criminals together. But neither of us understands the extent of the crime*. She felt shame, to have invaded her dead lover's home; to have learned facts about him he had not wanted known, at least not by her; and the shame was compounded by Roger Cavanagh's presence, as if both were looking upon Adam naked, each having to know that the other knew. Marina tried for the right tone, saying, in an undertone, "The strangest thing is, Roger, that Adam was alive twenty-four hours ago, and now he is not. The rest of this, his private life, his secrecy—is not so strange."

But was this true? Marina meant to be brave.

She understood that Roger both wanted to look at her, and did not want to look at her. Here was the true strangeness! Roger was acutely conscious, as a man, of being alone with Marina, a woman; his friend, and Adam's friend, yet a woman; he was aware of Marina's distraught state; her flushed, hurt face and angry eyes; unless her eyes were filled with sorrow, and threatened to infect his own with their emotion. He wasn't a man who trusted emotion. Not his own, and certainly no one else's. He was a lawyer not just by trade but by nature. That was why Marina instinctively disliked him: unlike Adam, he was a man who required control. A man with a short temper, with a reputation for taking offense. His divorce had badly shaken him and he disliked and distrusted all women on principle; even as he felt an aggressive, impersonal sexual desire for all women, a wish to seize, to maul, to pummel, to penetrate; yet, more powerfully, a wish not to touch, nor even come near. No, not near! His revulsion for women, Marina guessed, was both physical and moral. Shrewdly she saw that, if he could hurt you without touching, he would hurt you; but not at the price of touching. And there stood Marina Troy uncomfortably close, only a few feet away in this sunlit but deathly silent house above the river, Adam Berendt's house where they'd never before been alone together, and perhaps had never been together at all, even in Adam's company. And now Adam was gone. Marina was saying, faltering, not knowing what she said, wanting to dispel the tension between them, "I—don't feel that I'm equal to Adam's death. To death. I'm not worthy of—whatever it is. I resent it, I think, that he died the way he did, among strangers. For strangers. This hideous name 'Thwaite' is choking me."

This rush of words caused Roger to regard Marina yet more keenly. He lifted his eyes, that seemed to Marina eerie, reptilian eyes, heavy-lidded and yet quick-darting, curiously beautiful eyes, with a burnished-gold sheen, taking in Marina's carelessly plaited red hair that was falling loose, in damp strands and tendrils; and her slender, angular girl's body beneath her clothes, her skin that gave off the heat of despair. She was thinking that Roger Cavanagh had never seen Marina Troy so exposed; unprotected by the bright, brittle armor of her personality.

Roger stood, and made a movement toward Marina as if to comfort her, but Marina instinctively stepped back.

He asked, "What did Adam look like, last night?"

Marina stared at him, offended.

"Please, Marina. You were the only witness. I need to know."

"You can't know!"

"Tell me."

Those reptilian eyes: Marina shuddered.

Yet saying, calmly, "Adam was—noble in death. Like a statue. A Rodin." She touched her fingertips to her eyes. Seeing again the actual man, the body her lover had become. Stiffening of rigor mortis yet the jaw and mouth slack, losing their shape. Marina had a dread of this man, a rival of Adam's, seeing Adam through her eyes, naked and exposed. Roger asked, "Was death—instantaneous? He didn't suffer, did he?" and Marina said, "No. He didn't suffer. The emergency room doctor told me." Why was she saying this, why when this was a lie, simply to placate Roger Cavanagh who was behaving so strangely, wholly unlike himself; why, when she detested him. With a bizarre half-smile Roger said, "That's good then, Marina, isn't it?—that Adam didn't suffer." Marina was going to say yes, yes that's good, but instead she laughed harshly, "No! There's nothing 'good' about this. Don't be ridiculous."

She ran from him. Had he been going to touch her with his repulsive fingers? Comfort *her?* Blindly she ran into the long rectangular room that was Adam's studio. The air was cooler here, the ceiling higher. Always in this room that smelled of clay, paint, turpentine there was a faint chill of the ancient cellar beneath, its earthen floor. Adam had joked (but was this funny?) that in the old days before Salthill had become civilized, in the time of the notorious tavern-brothel, that earthen cellar had surely been used for quick burials. (They asked Adam if he'd been digging down there, and Adam said certainly not, he hadn't the slightest curiosity about finding, or not finding, two-hundred-year-old bones.) Of all the rooms in the stone house this was the one most associated with Adam. If you couldn't find Adam anywhere else, you would find him here; and Apollo close by. "Adam. Adam! *For God's sake!*" It was possible to think that the man was hiding from her, willfully. A rivulet of perspiration ran down her face hot as a tear. What did Cavanagh want from her! She felt his sexual interest, an impersonal interest, and his revulsion against it; perhaps she felt an identical sensation, she who would have described herself as stunned, unsexed, by grief. She hadn't spoken harshly, or spoken her heart, to anyone in the past ten years or more, as she'd just spoken to Roger Cavanagh; she'd never raised her voice. *Adam's death opening in me. A black wound.*

Was Roger following? She wished the man would go home and leave her. *She* was Adam Berendt's personal executor. She would oversee the house, arrange to have it cleaned, begin putting Adam's mysterious life in order. Moving now through the studio touching Adam's things that had taken on a new significance now, having outlived him. Artworks, furniture, massive stone fireplace; on a bench, a discarded shirt of his, an ordinary T-shirt, shamelessly she snatched it up and pressed it against her face, breathing in Adam's briny, clayey odor. She wasn't going to cry. Not here. She'd cried enough. She stumbled against a crude, uncompleted clay figure on the floor. It was a wood floor covered in places by rug remnants and outspread newspapers, splattered with dried paint. In her haze of grief she imagined she saw—what?—Apollo?—a ghostly-gray shape dozing in his usual place by Adam's work table, but no: don't be ridiculous: it was a patch of sunshine maggoty with dust motes.

Why was she here, she couldn't remember. If Adam wasn't here to greet her, and he wasn't. But if she was in Adam's house it must be for a purpose, and Adam must be that purpose. She was searching for—what? She knew she must not scream "Adam!" because someone, a man, a man she scarcely knew, was in the house with her, observing her, and would report back to others, *Marina Troy is deranged with grief.*

Here was Adam's long, cluttered work table shoved against a window. On the windowsill, desiccated husks of dead flies, wasps. And the window—all the windows—needed washing. And she would wash them. There was Adam's broken-backed easy chair, covered with a stained bedspread; and there was Adam's garage-sale sofa with its worn, pumpkin-colored corduroy upholstery where sometimes he slept, working late in his studio and too lazy to undress and go properly to bed, even to remove his shoes. *How could such a man marry, obviously he could not. Nor live with any woman.* Everywhere in Adam's studio there were uncompleted works, clay figures Marina had been seeing for years, collage-sculptures made of scrap metal, driftwood, storm debris, pieces of lumber, mirror fragments, bits of crockery and ceramics. There were hulking humanoid forms made of wood and awaiting the magic of life, and now that Adam was gone they would never receive it. Dozens of canvases of various sizes leaned against the walls, festooned with cobwebs. Most of these were uncompleted, Adam hadn't glanced at them in years yet he claimed to remember them all and intended to return to each of them, someday.

Had the man thought he'd live forever?

For months Adam had been working on a convoluted sculpture, his personal vision, he said, of the ancient nightmare Laocoön: the sea serpent that crushed a father and his sons in its coils, exacting a god's terrible vengeance. Except in Adam's American vision the human figures resembled slender elongated fish, poised as if swimming in a striated amber substance. This strange sculpture stood about six feet tall and measured about four feet in circumference at its base. How beautiful it was to Mariana, you could circle it and see undulating patterns of light through its partially transparent material; Adam had fashioned it from layers of plastic melted together and stained the hues of wood, straw, rushes. Standing before it now, Marina had the idea that the Laocoön was alive. She reached out to touch it and found it unexpectedly warm.

Why had Adam encouraged Marina to return to her long-abandoned art, and remained so indifferent to his own? Marina had known many talented artists in her earlier life, but no one less driven, less ambitious, than Adam. He was so without "ego," you'd worry he might forget to breathe. His "male ego" was of no more significance to him than a trailing shoelace. Yet he'd thought himself vain. He'd thought himself ugly. He'd sketched himself as a Cro-Magnon male with a low, bony forehead. If a woman dared to suggest that she found him attractive, Adam laughingly dismissed the very possibility. You could not make him think what his inner logic refused to allow him to think. Once when Marina and some others, at a dinner party, chided Adam for not taking his talent more seriously, he'd told them that, in middle age, he took nothing seriously except Truth; he'd become far more interested in the moral life than in the aesthetic life.

But isn't art a form of Truth?

No. Art is a cruel falsehood erected upon the corpse of Truth.

This was a bit dictatorial for Adam Berendt, who usually spoke without emphasis. He'd laughed at his pretensions, attributing the remark to Spinoza; or, better yet, Walter Benjamin.

Marina was opening drawers and cupboards in Adam's studio looking for—what? Behind her in the doorway stood Roger Cavanagh, sucking at his wounded mouth and watching her, uncertain what to do. Had Marina Troy actually screamed at him, or only just spoken harshly? As women in Salthill never spoke. At least, to men not their husbands or lovers.

This man would make her pay, Marina knew. If he could. She'd seen those reptile eyes beneath the puffy lids, fixed upon her.

Then, this happened.

Like a fevered scene in a film.

Until this moment of the headlong plunge of the past eighteen hours Marina would have described the film as somber, tragic; painful as if something were inside her guts twisting and churning. She would not have described the film as comic-grotesque. Yet somehow it happened that Marina opened the door to a cabinet near Adam's work table, which she'd always assumed Adam had used for art supplies, and there she discovered a cache of personal items: hand-knit sweaters neatly folded, in stacks; cashmere mufflers; elegant silk neckties still in their boxes. There was a small black box from Cartier containing platinum gold cuff links engraved *A. B.*—a card enclosed, *Love to Adam on his mystery-birthday, Gussie*. (Augusta Cutler? Owen Cutler's wife?) There was, attached to a bulky Aran wool sweater, a floppy black satin rose of the size of a woman's fist, with a card inscribed in crimson ink ♥ *Leila*. (But who was Leila? Marina knew no Leila in Salthill.) Marina's face flushed with blood. These were Adam's gifts-from-women-who-adored-him. And most of them looked as if they'd never been worn.

On a high shelf of the cabinet was a cardboard box, and this box, like her predecessor Pandora, Marina could not leave alone; though knowing (for how could she not know, her heart beating in fury and mortification, face burning as if she'd been soundly slapped on both cheeks) that it would be in her best interest to close the cabinet door with dignity, and retreat. But Marina tugged at the box, ignoring Roger Cavanagh who offered to take it down for her, and ingloriously the box toppled over, and its contents spilled on the floor: a cache now of cards, perfumed letters, and glossy photographs.

Even now, Marina might have retreated with a modicum of dignity. Yet there she was kneeling amid these lurid scattered things, hair falling into her face. From a distance, she might have resembled a greedy penitent.

Adam's women. So many? It should not have surprised Marina, yet it surprised Marina, for (she would understand this later, in a calmer time) she'd long refused to think of Adam's life as it failed to touch upon her; she'd long refused to consider that, if he had not been her lover, he must have sought other women sexually, and even romantically; not for Adam Berendt the role of celibate, yet she'd wished to imagine him that way. Now, here was evidence to refute her delusion. A packet of handwritten letters from—was it Camille Hoffmann, Lionel's wife? These were dated over the past seven years and were signed *Love, Camille*. On pale blue stationery, wispy as lingerie, a lengthy handwritten letter dated May of that year signed *Love, Abigail*. Marina's friend Abigail Des Pres! Marina quickly looked away, not wanting to see even a fragment of what Abigail had written to Adam. There were many birthday cards, holiday cards, *Thank you* and *Thinking of you!* cards which Marina didn't wish to examine. There were numerous postcards, and many of these were reproductions of works of art, for Adam's women would have wished to indicate their good taste. In dread Marina turned over a card that looked familiar, a surreal landscape painting by the German Caspar David Frederich, to discover her own handwriting on the back, and *Love, Marina*. The card was dated two summers ago when she'd traveled in Europe. Wincing, Marina thrust the card away, not wanting Roger to see. But probably he'd seen. Those eyes missed nothing! Marina would have ripped the card into pieces except it belonged to Adam's estate.

Thinking *Of all utterances of the past none are so painful as those written in the hope of winning another's love.*

Snapshots of Adam with Salthill friends, and with strangers. So many smiling people! So much happiness! Marina snatched up to examine closely a luridly colored picture that resembled a publicity photo, a ruddy-faced Adam Berendt in sports clothes, with an unfamiliar moustache, in what might have been a casino; Adam was looking just slightly embarrassed, in that one-eye-squinting way of his, while a heavily made-up blonde in a red sequined dress leaned familiarly against him, resting her upper arm and part of her ample bosom against his shoulder. Adam looked like a winner. He might have been in his early forties, with still thick graying hair and a relatively unlined face. The glamorous blonde might have been a high-priced hooker. On the back of the photo was stamped *The Dunes, Vegas. Nov. 23, 1989.*

And what was *this?* Several soft-filtered photographs of a naked, fleshy woman reclining on a sofa in the pose of Manet's Olympia; with alarmingly full roseate-nippled breasts and a swath of dark pubic hair; extravagant pearls around her neck, and an insolent-looking flat-faced white Persian cat at her feet. The woman wasn't young, though still very attractive; like the Vegas hooker she was heavily made up, and rings glittered on her fingers; her smile was studied and lascivious. One of her plump hands rested on her round little belly. Marina felt a tinge of disgust, and dismay, for her sex; the female sex; how pathetic we are, offering ourselves like meat. Marina saw suddenly that this woman was—Augusta Cutler? She recognized the Persian cat.

"This is hateful."

Adam Berendt, striding like a Cyclops among these ridiculous women. Stooping to pick them up at will, devouring female flesh. Oh, and Marina Troy was among them! She began to slap and tear at the photos, cards, letters, gifts, as Roger, squatting beside her, tried to calm her. "Marina, no. Don't. You can't know what any of this actually means."

"I know! I'm not a fool."

"Women liked Adam: you knew that. He was friends with both women and men, but women are inclined to write, and to be effusive. This will all remain confidential, of course."

"Augusta Cutler! That woman has *grown children.*"

This was the true horror, worse than Adam's suspicious finances: a low sexual comedy, where Marina in her grief had hoped to find pathos, pure cleansing emotion.

Roger may have thought this was funny, a comedy, or he may have been upset like Marina, startled and disoriented; it was difficult for Marina to interpret his behavior, except that it oppressed her, and her nostrils pinched at the cloying odor that wafted from his skin of cologne and male underarm sweat. She hated this man! This man who was a witness to her humiliation! He wouldn't even let her claw at the evidence, he kept seizing her hands, restraining her gently, yet firmly too, as if she were a child, and he the child's father, the male, supremely in control. Marina had begun to cry now, angrily. There was nothing of grief in these tears. She was flammable material, and Roger was a lighted match leaning dangerously close. Marina said, "Leave me alone, God damn you! Don't touch me. I hate you," and Roger said, "You don't hate me. That's bullshit." She felt his breath against her face. He was gripping her hands more tightly. Without transition they were struggling, in a grunting sort of silence. There was an air of the improbable and the fantastic about what was happening. A blazing light seemed to illuminate them, as on a stage, before an invisible audience. They were in Adam's house, and where was Adam? Why were they in Adam's studio, alone together? Why on their knees, on the floor? There could be no explanation. The previous morning at this exact time, Marina could not have comprehended such an event. *I don't even like Roger Cavanagh. He dislikes me.* Yet Roger was kissing Marina, pressing his bared teeth against her mouth and neck; as if he wanted to hurt her, and Marina was in a mood to be hurt; overcome with longing for him, or for whoever he was; a man, a sexual being, in Adam's place; in the exigency of the moment, stricken with desire like a violent thirst, she could not have recalled Roger's name. Yet her hands groped over him. Her hands clutched at him. There was the surprise of his hard-muscled back, his superior size and weight. She heard herself moan, in misery. In sexual longing. Was this, so suddenly, a love scene? Had the pathos yielded to frenetic comedy, and that in turn to a frenetic love scene? *It has been so long. I've forgotten how*. What was happening was clumsy, harried, blind; she and the man blundered together like swimmers in a rough surf. Roger pulled at Marina's clothing, nearly tearing it, and Marina's dazed grasping fingers pulled at his shirt, and at his trousers, where he was guiding her hand. Marina had not remembered how quickly excited a man becomes, sexually aroused with a woman for the first time; the hot, accelerated breath like a dog's panting; the strength of the arms, and the urgent thrusting body; between his legs, the wondrous thing-come-alive which Roger brought her hand to touch, to caress; even as he unzipped his trousers. They were kissing, groaning. They would have made love then on the floor, the hard hurting stained floor, the floor that smelled of clay, paint, turpentine and the ancient cellar beneath, except as Roger pushed apart Marina's thighs, hoisting himself upon her like a flag, he must have had a glimpse of something in her face that alarmed him, her eyes squinting shut and lips drawn back in a grimace of anticipated pain, and the discomfort of her plaited hair crushed against the back of her head and against the floor, or maybe each heard their friend's footfall approaching, Adam's raised, amused voice *What the hell are you doing, Marina? Roger? I haven't been dead twenty-four hours yet, and you're fucking in my house?* Almost at once, Roger's erection faded; he muttered what sounded like "I can't. I'm sorry." Marina struck the man with both fists. She was wild, uncontrollable; she kicked at him, and raised her knee into his groin; afterward she would recall her frenzied behavior with deep shame; at the moment, she took a savage joy in it, clawing at the man, drawing blood on his face and beneath his ear. His face, contorted with alarm! She had to laugh. He grabbed at her wrists and held her still; he bit at her shoulder where her shirt had been torn away, and he bit at her breasts; he was panting, furious; his penis had gone limp as a deflated balloon, mashed against Marina's crinkly red swath of pubic hair.

Abruptly then it was over. The madness had passed through them, and from them. A summer squall, blown into the air. They lay together on the floor of Adam Berendt's studio, spared the need to look at each other, for a long time, exhausted and defeated.

Old Mill Way: The Cave

I

Through the walls of the stately old Colonial house, through hardwood floors and layers of thick carpet, distended as if by Time, came the sound of a woman sobbing.

Her heart was broken, and not for him.

Once there lived together on Old Mill Way north of the Village of Salthill-on-Hudson, in a meticulously restored eighteenth-century Colonial house on a hillside, a man and a woman of youthful middle age who'd been married so long ("Half our lifetimes at least") they no longer saw each other, like moles in a burrow.

There was a distinct comfort in this, and the satisfactions of custom. For this man and this woman were the offspring of families of Custom. (Meaning good breeding and good money, though not a showy excess of money, on both sides of the marriage.)

Strange!—that the burrow, the house, was spacious and much admired and very expensive on four acres of prime Rockland County real estate, and yet remained a burrow. Strange that it was so confining and airless, though the present owners as well as previous owners had expanded it, and refurbished it, and spent a good deal of money on making it a showcase. ("It's like a dream, living here. Sometimes I worry I'll wake up suddenly—and all this happiness will have *gone*.")

The oldest part of the house, made of wood, was kept freshly painted, oyster-white shingles that glowed like radium in early dusk. And there was fieldstone, and there was faded red brick so aged it looked as if it might crumple at the touch, and there was practical white stucco like exposed bone. So many windows upstairs and down, but the windows were small and narrow, Colonial-style; the glass was so old it looked wavy. In the festive holiday season, which in Salthill-on-Hudson was taken up with Christian exuberance, each window visible from Old Mill Way was lighted with an electric candle, and strings of chastely white, glittering lights twined across the façade of the house and wrapped like cobwebs in adjacent trees. The shutters were dark green, a familiar patriot hue, and the sturdy front door was old oak, adorned with a brass American eagle knocker forged in colonial times. Through the summer, clay pots of bright red geraniums were placed on the front steps, and through the autumn, clay pots of chrysanthemums were placed on the front steps; the pots were carefully roughened with sandpaper, for a "countrified" look.

"It's hard to believe, such happiness. Not that we haven't worked for it, of course! Lionel is embarrassed to speak of such things, you know how a man like Lionel *is*. So we never speak of it."

The original house had been built in 1763 by a prominent Manhattan tradesman named Elias Macomb. Little was known of Macomb except that he'd been a Tory converted in 1774 to Federalism and to a generous financial support of the Revolution against Great Britain by the expedient threat of being tarred, feathered, and publicly lynched from a "liberty pole"; in 1781, the house would come into the possession of General Cleveland Wade, intimate friend and aide of President George Washington, and numerous rooms would be added, and the roof raised, and a barn and outbuildings constructed. With equal authority you could refer to the property as the "Macomb House" or the "Wade House," as subsequent owners felt obliged to explain in that earnest, animated way of homeowners who take their guests' polite questions about their property seriously, and have memorized passages of local history to be recited like sacred script. Beyond the house was the barn, of weathered wood, with a high stone foundation; at the peak of its roof, a brass rooster preened in unchanging profile. In front of the picturesque barn was a pond bordered by cattails, the rich sickly green of pea soup, and exuding a powerful odor; in April, dozens, hundreds! of vivid yellow daffodils bloomed and "danced" in the hilly lawn and at the roadside. Beneath this picture, *Happiness dwells here.*

This was the showcase home of the Hoffmanns, Camille and Lionel. Their children were grown and gone. Their marriage persisted like a brave boat caught in an eddy. It was a classic vehicle so pridefully crafted and maintained, it would never break into pieces. Camille, the wife of the house, was naturally the more sensitive to the burden of History, the privilege of living in such a house; she'd furnished it with antiques, whenever possible, and had long been one of the local amateur experts in Revolutionary-era New York State history. Lionel was an enormously busy man, a senior vice president of Hoffmann Publishing, Inc., his family-owned firm, and one of the most successful of American publishers of medical textbooks and manuals, headquartered in Manhattan. Still, the Hoffmanns were intensely social like most Salthill residents. Now that their children had departed, in middle age they required another family, a more expansive and in a way more reliable family, close at hand, sociable as they, intimate without being familiar; they were rich, but not wealthy; they knew enough of wealth to understand that a true fortune involves the potential for tragedy, and tragedy was not a concept with which they felt comfortable. *We love Salthill because it's a true American melting pot.* Few in their large circle of friends had much interest in what had been known in an earlier, more primitive era as "social climbing"; for where, after all, was there to climb *to,* when you lived in Salthill-on-Hudson? Serious golfers belonged to the Salthill Golf Club, and boaters belonged to the Hudson Valley Yacht and Sailing Club, and there was the Lost Creek Tennis Club, but most members of the resplendent Salthill Country Club were the suburban *nouveaux riches*. (True, there were a dismaying number of these in Rockland County, and each year brought more as high-rise condominiums and $2-million tract homes were being constructed along the scenic river or gouged out of rolling farmland.) The Hoffmanns and their circle were sensitive about being characterized as "suburban"; they thought of themselves as very different, another type of American entirely, Village-dwelling, or country-dwelling.

The Hoffmanns and their circle were as likely to be friendly with odd, independent, quirky types like Adam Berendt the sculptor and Marina Troy of the Salthill Bookstore as with neighbors on Old Mill Way, Old Dutch Road, Sylvan Pass, Wheatsheaf Drive, Deer Link, Derrydown Lane, Pheasant Run, Sparkhill Pike. They were as likely to be friendly with the founder of the Salthill Pro Musica, and the elderly Frenchwoman who taught ballet to children, and the minister of the Unitarian Church and his poet-wife, and with the bearded editor of the *Salthill Weekly Gazette,* and the retired merchant marine officer who raised orchids in his tiny Village rowhouse, as they were with people who owned National Historic Register houses like the Hoffmanns', and in whose sloping pastures thoroughbred horses, pedigree cattle, and black-faced sheep peacefully grazed as in a dream of Old Europe. Just possibly there was a sharp class distinction between Salthill residents whose property was bordered by old stone walls and those whose property was bordered by mere fences—redwood, chain-link, picket, post and rail—but this was not a distinction that seemed to matter much, in terms of friendship. *We need our friends. Constantly. Why, we don't know.*

In their spacious burrow furnished, for the most part, with period antiques or precise reproductions, the Hoffmanns were known for their hospitality. The quaint old barn had long ago been converted into a wholly modernized guest house, and the Hoffmanns often had guests. Even their guests had guests. They gave numerous parties, reciprocating parties to which they'd been invited. By custom in their circle, the Hoffmanns hosted a New Year's Eve dinner-dance party to which about forty of their closest friends were invited. Black tie for the men, long dresses for the women. The locally famous house would be lighted with candles. The fifteen-foot Christmas tree in the two-storey front foyer would be ornately decorated. Banks of poinsettias, fires burning companionably in each of the several downstairs fireplaces. The first time Adam Berendt was a guest at this annual party he'd lingered outside on the flagstone steps in a lightly falling snow as other guests streamed past. He'd joked, "I'm afraid to cross that threshold. It looks like perfection inside." This was seventeen years, six months, and one week before his death. In the prime of young middle age, Adam was stocky, but not heavy; twenty pounds lighter than he would be in his fifties; with hard-muscled broad shoulders that made him look like a manual laborer, a homely-handsome face less battered and creased than it would become, and hair that was thick and spiky and only just laced with gray. For the formal occasion he wore not black tie (as the invitation had suggested) but a salmon-colored satin coat, and a black-and-white-checked silk shirt, and black dress trousers with satin trim. His bow tie was so white it appeared luminescent and just slightly oversized. Adam Berendt hadn't been so well known in Salthill at this time, not yet a "character"; he'd surprised only a few residents by buying the old Deppe House on the river, moving there from a rented carriage house on an estate in the hills. No one who saw him at the Hoffmanns' that night knew with certainty if the man was being ironic, or playful; if he was mocking the Hoffmanns' New Year's Eve party, or all New Year's Eve parties; or if, in his bluff social innocence, rough-hewn as a frontier type, Adam imagined that this costume was appropriate attire.

Soon, perspiring in the clamorous crowd, dancing with one beautiful woman after another, Adam removed the salmon-satin coat, and rolled up his shirtsleeves.

Adam Berendt the local artist, sculptor. That was his identity in Salthill. He'd been Camille Hoffmann's instructor in a night school art class; like other women in the class, Camille had fallen under Adam's spell. (There were few men in the night classes, and of these all were quite elderly.) *What was different about Adam, oh, how to say!* Certainly he was unlike other night school instructors of art, yoga, dance, pottery, creative writing, tennis, golf, and so forth, who shamelessly flattered their rich married-women students with the fervor of a freezing man tossing sticks of wood into a fire; nor did he charm, or seduce. He was friendly—but impersonally—to all. He was "inspiring"—cautiously. He spoke of genuine artistic talent as rare, and needful of cultivation; to be a professional was a commitment, and so to be an "amateur" might be preferable. Where he couldn't praise a woman's effort he stood silent and musing before it; there were evenings when he said very little, but communicated much with his facial expressions, the movement of his body. At other times he joked, teased. If a woman (never Camille Hoffmann, who was shy and uncertain of herself, especially in Adam's presence) smashed her clay figure out of disgust with it, Adam laughed and said, "My dear, it takes guts to take yourself so seriously." He seemed sometimes to speak in riddles. He paced about the room in clear enjoyment of his physical being, as one woman observed, like a steer on his hind legs, reciting poetry in a swinging cadence, to inspire and to disturb—Lucretius' *On the Nature of Things*. Blake's *Marriage of Heaven and Hell,* Whitman's *Leaves of Grass*. For the remainder of their lives these Salthill women would recall the shuddering sensation in their loins engendered by Adam Berendt's passionate baritone—

> You will hardly know who I am or what I mean,
> But I shall be good health to you nevertheless,
> And filter and fibre your blood.
> Failing to fetch me at first keep encouraged,
> Missing me one place search another,
> I stop somewhere waiting for you.

He hired a mini-bus to take them into Manhattan, to the Metropolitan Museum of Art where, like a brooding centaur, he led them, his herd of mortal women, through the echoing halls of the Greco-Roman world; forbidding them to speak to one another, or to him, even to think—"Only just *see*." They saw so much! They were filled to bursting, like balloons being blown up beyond their capacity.

Adam Berendt gave off an odor, some evenings, of negligently washed male flesh. His clothes were often rumpled, and not very clean. He had only one "good" eye—the left—and this eye often gazed through them, and through their efforts at art, as if they didn't exist. Or, merely existing, in finite space and time, could not compete in Adam's imagination with another, more lofty and imperishable world. "The world of Forms. The world of Ideas. The world of the Soul. We know it's there, even if we can't always experience it." (But did they know this? The Salthill women were hopeful but confused.) If they dared to ask Adam personal questions he gently rebuffed them, and there was something thrilling in being so rebuffed, as they rarely were in Salthill among their set. Never would they learn where Adam Berendt had been born, and where he'd been raised; if he had a family; if he'd ever been married; and—what had happened to his right eye?

In their imaginations grown fevered and romantic from disuse, Adam Berendt exuded a mysterious authority. But it was an authority he did not exploit. *Or so we believed.*

"AM I JEALOUS? Certainly not."

For he was Lionel Hoffmann and not by nature a jealous man. Tall, loose-jointed, taciturn, "very intelligent, and very rich" (as he'd once overheard a woman describe him, to his embarrassment); with a finely chiseled face that was handsome, or rather bland, depending upon the mood and taste of the observer; and dark hair that began to turn a distinguished gray at his temples when he was in his early thirties. On the commuter train, Lionel often glanced up from his newspaper to perceive numerous other men like himself; out of shyness, or chagrin, these others quickly glanced away as Lionel did, concentrating on the earnest, data-surfeited columns of print that constituted the *New York Times* as if he were reading a breviary. As older men in the Hoffmann family were young-old men, active in the family-owned business well into their nineties, so younger men like Lionel, Jr., were old-young men, and even in boyhood Lionel had been a model of maturity, a reproach to his younger and more imaginative brother. *A boy you can depend upon.*

He'd fallen in love and married, young. He could remember Camille as a bride, but not himself as a bridegroom. Sometimes he had difficulty remembering Camille precisely, for she'd looked like so many young women in those years, and he was inclined to confuse her with—who was it?—one of his Colgate roommate's girlfriends? Kitzie, or had it been Mimi? The one who'd wept in his arms, and surreptitiously wiped her nose on the shoulder of her dress.

No man in the Hoffmann family was likely to be jealous for no man in the Hoffmann family was sexually insecure. You were a man, and thoroughly a man, and good-looking, and intelligent, and you worked for Hoffmann Publishing, Inc., the most successful American publisher of medical texts and reference books, and there was no ambiguity in this. Life was not a riddle for the Sphinx to answer (unless it was the Sphinx that asked the riddle), but something like a printout. Numerals, equations. Once married, the Hoffmanns remained married, and had no further romantic inclinations. (But was this entirely so? True, Lionel Hoffmann in his poised, remote and whimsical way was drawn to the wives of certain of his friends, but never would he have approached them; nothing was more repugnant to him than the mere thought of an intimate relationship, a messy sexual relationship, with a social acquaintance. *Never foul your own nest* was Lionel, Sr.'s, most eloquent advice to his sons.)

"Jealous of—who? *Him?* Never."

Adam Berendt, a local oddball artist. Sculptor. With one missing eye. Or maybe blind eye. Built like a fireplug. Before the New Year's Eve party, Lionel hadn't been introduced to Berendt though he'd been hearing of him, in Salthill, for several years.

If Camille was romantically attracted to Adam Berendt, Lionel was obliged to feel a husbandly possessiveness, like a dull toothache. She was his wife, and vulnerable; and under his protection. *If she makes a fool of herself, O God.* Salthill was insular as an island.

(Most Salthill men commuted to work in Manhattan, and were often away five full days a week; many, like Lionel, maintained apartments in the city, and were frequently away overnight; you could imagine that the work life of a Lionel Hoffmann occupied most of his waking hours, not out of greed for more money but out of a genuine perplexity about what, other than work, a responsible adult man was meant to do? In the absence of their devoted husbands, which might one day be tabulated as an absence of years, Salthill wives were inevitably "drawn" to men not their husbands. Rarely were these catastrophic love affairs that resulted in divorce and remarriage, but rather romances of an indefinite nature: there were discernible cyclical patterns in which a woman might imagine herself in love with the husband of a friend, and when that infatuation dissolved she might imagine herself in love with the husband of another friend, and, in time, with another; and yet another; over a period of years in a social circle as constricted as the one to which the Hoffmanns belonged, a woman would eventually come round to imagining herself in love with a man, or men, with whom she'd imagined herself in love at an earlier time. So long as a woman didn't become involved with a man outside her social circle, such behavior was perceived by husbands to be harmless. This was Salthill-on-Hudson, where marriages, families, property were sacrosanct, and it was not the seventies.)

At the New Year's Eve party, Lionel covertly observed this "Adam Berendt" whom his wife had invited, and of whom he'd been hearing rumors. Lionel was discreet as Lionel was always discreet. (Where another host would have winced at the salmon-satin coat, Lionel maintained a deadpan expression.) But over the course of the long, gay, champagne-enlivened evening, Lionel concluded that Adam Berendt was nothing more than warmly courteous to Camille; he didn't appear to be in love with her, nor did he encourage her to be in love with him. You could see, through Camille's pained eyes, how much more enlivened Adam was dancing, disco-style, energetically if not very skillfully, with Owen Cutler's opulently fleshy wife, Augusta, than with sweet-faced Camille Hoffmann.

Lionel concluded, *He's crude. But a gentleman.*

And later that night, at about two A.M., when most of the Hoffmanns' guests had departed, and after a reckless kiss for both her husband and Adam Berendt, the hostess herself had disappeared upstairs to bed, the two men sat before a smoldering fireplace, and quietly talked. That is, Lionel talked. Pleasantly drunk on champagne, and stimulated by the occasion. Both men had removed their coats, and their ties were loosened. Lionel wasn't a man to speak easily, especially at one of his own parties. His sense of being a host was something like a conscience. But now that the party was more or less over, he was speaking with animation, almost warmly. He liked Adam Berendt! A man so different from himself as to belong to another species. The subject was politics, morals, "human values." Lionel had been a boy in the sixties and disgusted by much of what he saw. Outside his family and relatives, that was. The "deterioration" of America as a serious moral nation. Then he'd gone to college—at Colgate, where his father had gone—and his life had been changed. His inner life. Though possibly Lionel hadn't so much as glanced into a book of philosophy or poetry since graduation, it was his fervent belief that in certain of his humanities classes, his soul had been "forged." Of course, he'd gone on to the Wharton School as planned, and he'd made his way steadily enough in the world of business—"But what I remember best is 'Know thyself.' That's Socrates, isn't it? And the Greek tragedies, I remember. A man makes a mistake, he owns up to it: puts out his eyes, or hangs himself. There was no self-pity and pleading for justice or mercy. It was all a weird kind of justice. If you were guilty, you paid. Even if you weren't guilty. Because sometimes it wasn't clear what the crime was. And that's how life *is*. What a world! I'm a Christian, but—you know. 'The meek will inherit the earth'—I wonder! It's more like winners and losers. Isn't it? People turning into birds, or trees, or rivers; a woman who's turned into a swan and she's raped by a—bull? Or is it the other way around? But really a god. The bull, I mean. And sometimes the gods were invisible. It was all a kind of parable, I guess? It sure wasn't Christian. This hunter who's torn apart by his own hunting dogs because he'd seen a goddess bathing naked in the woods. Just by accident he saw her, what's the blame? But he's punished anyway. He's turned into—what? I forget."

"A stag."

"A *stag*." Lionel pondered this fact. His voice was slightly slurred but steady. "What he'd been hunting. He's turned into it, and he's killed, and there's a weird justice there, yes?"

So he and Adam Berendt talked. Lionel talked. In the early hours of the New Year he was seized by nostalgia he hadn't known he'd felt; it was nostalgia for a lost youth, that in fact he'd never had. These things he would confess, almost!—to Adam Berendt. *My friend. Adam is my friend.* Afterward he would recall with a vague glowing happiness the conversation he'd had with Adam Berendt that night. He would tell Camille that he liked her art instructor "very much." He would thank Camille for introducing them. He would tell friends how "sensible, solid" Adam Berendt was; "down-to-earth," "no bullshit." It was certainly Lionel's intention to see Adam again soon, and to cultivate a friendship with him, for the truth was that Lionel hadn't many friends, in Salthill or in Manhattan; it might even be said that since college, and his early bachelor days, he hadn't any close male friend. He had numerous "friends" in Salthill but no actual friend. (For in Salthill as everywhere, women kept the wheels of social life moving. Continuously these wheels move, up and down the familiar rutted ways.) Yet months passed after that New Year's Eve, and years. And Lionel Hoffmann who was so immersed in work never sought out Adam Berendt in quite the way he'd hoped to. And Adam, tactfully, didn't approach him. Their handshakes were brisk and matter-of-fact. And their greetings, standard Salthill-style, uttered with smiling good cheer: "How are you, Adam?" and "Lionel, how are *you*?"

2

Adam, how's a man to live when he knows he must die?

IN THAT LONG-AGO TIME, the sixties. When Lionel was ten years old and a dependable boy. An A-student in the fifth grade at Broom Hills Country Day School, Westchester County. When Lionel saw his first dead body, in fact two. *And never never told!*

The sixties. Drugs! Long unkempt hair and slovenly clothes! Even such old, settled villages as Broom Hills, Bedford Hills, Katonah were not immune. Even revered families like the Thayers, the Briscolls, the Listers (neighbors of the Hoffmanns in Broom Hills Heights on spacious wooded lots overlooking the man-made Broom Lake) were not immune. The men commuted faithfully to New York City on early trains, and in fall and winter never returned before night; the women dealt with domestic servants, sent out handwritten invitations to parties and personally addressed and signed upward of five hundred Christmas cards each, each year. The Vietnam War waged on the far side of the moon. Why it mattered so much, so suddenly, wasn't clear. If you didn't switch on the TV except for New York and local news, and again after eight P.M., and just rapidly skimmed certain newspapers, you could mostly avoid it. Children who attended Broom Hills Country Day were protected from it. In Broom Hills, as not everywhere else, life remained serene and more or less controlled. Moral control, and aesthetic control. Up-zoning was the voters' most passionate issue. Boundaries had to be drawn, Custom had to be maintained. For if Broom Hills was not the ideal, there could be no ideal; and the human spirit cries out for the ideal, not in a faraway place and time but here and now. Yet, in Broom Hills as in less scrupulously zoned parts of the country, there were sometimes problems. Some of these were "drug problems." The legacy of the "hippie culture." For had not a hippie guru threatened America's parents with the terrible prophecy *We'll get you through your children!* And when children grew up but remained children, there was danger. When children left the protection of Broom Hills to attend college (in urban areas especially) there was danger. So it happened in the heat of August 1966 that the twenty-year-old Yale dropout son of the Listers, the Hoffmanns' neighbors in the prestigious area known as Broom Hills Heights, injected his girlfriend and himself with a powerful amphetamine, and somewhere in the night they wandered barefoot in the woods behind the Listers' sprawling contemporary house, and they'd lain down to make love by moonlight, unless it was simply to die, and their bodies wouldn't be found for three days. Three days! The Listers would claim to believe that their "troubled" son had returned to New Haven where he lived with friends, they'd had no idea that he and the girl, who was sixteen, from Katonah, were anywhere nearby. In the heat of August, bodies decompose rapidly. These would be discovered in the woods about twenty feet from the mirror-smooth man-made lake, by several young boys who ran shouting for help.

Lionel Hoffman, aged ten, was not one of these boys. But Lionel's secret was, he'd discovered the bodies himself the previous day, drawn by the terrible smell, and had run away in terror, and an obscure sort of shame, and said nothing. And would say nothing. That stench! And the horror of what he'd seen: what his eyes had fastened upon. He'd gagged and nearly vomited, and forced to eat at mealtimes he'd gagged and vomited, right in the dining room, and it was attributed to the "flu"—this was an era, and it continues to the present time, in which much that's unspeakable within families can be attributed to "flu."

To Lionel, this was the sixties. This was what threatened, and awaited, when you brought into the scrupulously zoned villages of Broom Hills, or Salthill, foreign toxic agents.

Of Lionel it would be said by the women in his life, he was "sensitive" about food, mealtimes, odors. He had a "sensitive stomach" which surely indicated a sensitive soul.

SENSITIVE, TOO, to dog hair. And cat "dander." His sinuses clogged up as if with wet, wadded tissue. His brain ached and eyes watered. Through the seemingly interminable years of their growing-up in the eighteenth-century restored burrow on Old Mill Way, Lionel's children, a boy and a girl, would pine loudly for a pet. For it was a fact that all their friends had pets, a dog or at least a cat, everybody's mom had cats, why couldn't they? why were they different? why was Daddy so selfish? Camille intervened in snatches of dialogue overheard by Lionel, approving when she was reasonably stern, hating her when she was apologetic, or plaintive as the children themselves. "Your father is *allergic*. You know that. He's so sorry. I'm so sorry, but there's nothing to be done about it."

Eleven-year-old Graeme protested, "Couldn't Daddy live in the barn? It's all fixed up."

In the barn forever afterward he imagined himself. And smiled. While in the beautifully restored eighteenth-century Colonial on Old Mill Way with his wife and children, he was really *in the barn*. Or maybe *in the woods*.

He'd never told his parents or anyone in Broom Hills about discovering the hippie couple (*hippie couple* was the formula phrase he'd settled for, derived from a news item about the drug deaths in a Westchester newspaper), nor would he tell his wife, Camille, whom he never told anything that might disturb; or might provoke in that alarmingly maternal way of even the least erotic women, to embrace a man passionately and comfort him. *Oh, Lionel. How terrible for you. Ten years old. Oh!—I can imagine the smell.*

He didn't want his wife, or any woman, touching him in such sympathy. Sympathy was too damned close to pity.

In the barn was his place of refuge at home. In the city, in the two-bedroom apartment on East 61st, where Lionel stayed two and sometimes three nights a week, in the grip of long hours at the office and an unexpected liking for the anonymity of city life, he required no place of refuge. But he felt a tinge of guilt in Manhattan, for his burrow, his home, was in Salthill after all.

When Lionel's younger brother, Scott, died unexpectedly, of an aneurysm, at the age of thirty-six—*thirty-six!*—Lionel had been stunned beyond grief by the news. For days after the funeral, in Broom Hills, he'd been unable to speak. He was forty-one at the time and obsessed with the thought *Is it beginning so soon?* He saw Death as the glistening mirror-lake of dark water near where the hippie couple had died, and rotted, their young exposed flesh swarming with maggots. *So soon! Our ending.* Camille was sick with anxiety, fearing that her husband, too, had had a stroke of some kind, impairing his speech and hearing, and leaving his face frozen into a kind of pained grimace, like a handsome death's-head. She cautioned the children to be quiet in their father's company, for he'd had a shock, and was feeling sad. It was a fact that Lionel had sometimes resented Scott, but he'd loved him, too.

Loved him! Never. You're damned glad he's dead.

That isn't true! That is not true.

Now Scott can't have a better time than Lionel. Now people can't like him better than they like Lionel.

That is not true!

So grief paralyzed Lionel. His hair that had only been touched with gray at the temples was now riddled with silver. His manner was sombre, preoccupied. Weeks passed, he moved like a sleepwalker. The children avoided him. He carried with him the very spores of mortality, decay. Camille went to parties and gatherings by herself, a brave, shaken woman, nervously smiling as she assured friends that Lionel was fine and would be seeing them again soon. ("Fine" had long been the most popular of Salthill adjectives, used in a great variety of contexts.) But inevitably there came the sun-spangled April morning when driving to the Village to catch the 7:08 train to Manhattan, in a procession of new-model gleaming luxury cars (his own was a cream-colored Lexus with four-wheel drive, sunroof, CD, and tape deck), passing along daffodil-lined Old Mill Way, and Old Dutch Road, and crossing the scenic woodplank bridge at Lost Brook and cruising south along Wheatsheaf Drive to Pheasant Run, and so to Fox Pass, through Battle Park to Linden Lane, West Axe and

Depot, Lionel felt his gargoyle mask relax at last, and heard wild hyena laughter filling the interior of his car.

Laugh, laugh! It burst from his pursed lips, out of his tight constricted throat. He hadn't felt so good in twenty years.

Requiescat in pace. The Latin was a consolation, grave and sonorous. You knew, but half-didn't-know, what it meant.

But the Hoffmanns were Lutheran, not Catholic. They'd been Lutheran for centuries. Camille, who'd been Presbyterian, had joined the Lutheran church when she'd married Lionel, and they'd exchanged vows in the First Lutheran Church of Broom Hills, New York. In Salthill, Camille attended Sunday services more frequently than Lionel, and while the children were young and tractable she'd brought them; Lionel tried always to observe Christmas and Easter though he had difficulty during services keeping his mind on what the minister was saying so earnestly, and when the congregation sang hymns or joined together in prayer he had to clench his jaws tight to keep from uttering—what, he didn't know. Or maybe it was wild hyena laughter threatening to spill out.

Those Sunday mornings waking early with that sense of sick dread to be expiated by driving his family to the First Lutheran Church of Salthill. A community of churchgoing folk, Sunday-morning Christians. The good news of the Gospels is that Jesus is your savior if you let Him into your heart, won't you let Him into your heart? Lionel had done so, numerous times.

But did Lionel truly *believe?*

He imagined himself speaking with Adam Berendt. Lionel at his most rational, sincere. "There is—must be—something greater than just *us*. Something beyond—*us*."

But there was no Adam with him, Lionel was alone. He paused. He listened. Distant as thunder at the horizon, or earth-gouging machines in the new tract development off Wheatsheaf Drive, that laughter.

* * *

So ashamed! she'd wept. He'd said, *Hey, don't be, please*. How many times he and the girl in the pink chiffon repeated these words, Lionel wouldn't recall. Quite a few times.

Not Kitzie or Mimi, in fact it had been Camille. The girl with the runny nose, mascara-tears streaking her face. She'd tried to wipe her nose on the shoulder of her dress as Lionel held her awkwardly, to comfort her.

Poor Camille: he hadn't known her last name. She'd stammered out "Camille" as a child might, as if he must know her, she was the younger sister of a guy in Lionel's freshman-year dorm. Now it was Lionel's junior year and he lived at the handsome Deke house on the hill and homecoming weekend one of his drunken Deke brothers had ditched this poor shivering girl and it was ten P.M. and the house so blaring, you couldn't hear yourself think. Couldn't hear yourself speak. This girl, hiding in the cloakroom. A flushed flower-petal face that made Lionel blink hard, and swallow hard. The palms of his hands sweaty. By accident he'd discovered her crying. Pink chiffon, and breasts, and curly fair-brown hair like a doll's hair cascading to her shoulders. Camille's young figure in the pink chiffon was shapely yet her effect upon Lionel wasn't sexual, he felt instead a brotherly compassion for her, a need to protect her from his crude fraternity brothers, and from further humiliation. Yet when she turned her damp, smeared face, her quivering lips, to him, wholly without disguise, without subterfuge, lurching into his arms, he wasn't prepared. She'd come to Colgate from Ithaca College for the weekend, staying at a hotel in town, oh, it was only Friday night and what was she going to do, what was she going to do she wanted to die, so absolutely ashamed she wanted to die, she'd been insulted by that horrible person, treated like dirt and laughed at, yes and she'd been made to drink more than she'd wanted, and she was sure there was something in her drink, LSD maybe, her head was swirling, heart beating so fast, she was staying at a hotel in town but hadn't any way of getting there, didn't even know where the hotel was, how far from the Deke house, oh she was so ashamed! so ashamed! wanted to die! how could anybody be so cruel, crude, treating her like this, he'd seemed so nice on the phone, and she'd been looking forward to this weekend, this was a new dress she'd bought for the weekend, her brother had arranged for the date, would he have something to answer for! would he, ever! she'd be telling their father about this insult, tomorrow morning! she'd come to the campus in a car with three other girls from Ithaca College, they wouldn't be driving back till Sunday afternoon, how would she get home, oh, she was so ashamed! everybody at her college would know, everybody would be talking about her, pitying her, oh, she couldn't bear pity, she'd never been treated like this by any date before, she wanted to *die!* absolutely to *die!* And Lionel told her please don't be ashamed, for God's sake it was his asshole fraternity brother who should be ashamed, Lionel was comforting this weeping shivering girl awkwardly, trying to remember her brother's last name, homecoming weekend at Colgate was frat parties like this, wild earsplitting drunken and not for sensitive girls like Camille, even her name was sensitive, delicate, *Camille* was to Lionel the most beautiful name he'd ever spoken, like music, he was helping her find her coat, would she like him to drive her to the hotel, he had a car, he'd like to drive her to the hotel, it was the least he could do, to try to make amends for how badly she'd been treated. And in Lionel's car driving to the hotel as Camille's tears subsided, as she dabbed at her heated face with a tissue (she'd found in her coat pocket), and blew her nose, Lionel felt that he was behaving well; he was behaving like a gentleman; his father would be proud of him; for once, he'd be proud of himself. *And it was so easy. It all just happened.* Later he would learn that Camille's family was rich: they owned extensive investment properties in Rhode Island, where Camille had grown up. She was two years younger than Lionel and three inches shorter, which seemed just right. A good Christian girl as unquestioning of biblical authority as of hair and clothing fashions; not an honors student, but a "dedicated" education major at Ithaca College. Her desire was to teach elementary grades, maybe join the Peace Corps first, oh, but she wanted to be married someday, of course, and she wanted to be a mother, of course!

In this way (though not immediately: Lionel went out with

other girls after graduating from Colgate, moving to New York to work in Hoffmann Publishing, Inc., and sweet vulnerable Camille had "disappointments") they were destined to marry, and to have two children, and to move to Old Mill Way in Salthill-on-Hudson where, as year followed year, they would be so happy.

3

Adam was the only one of them I could talk to. Even if I couldn't talk to him.

One of the profound shocks of Lionel's life in Salthill, that Adam Berendt was so suddenly and unexpectedly dead. And Lionel would never see him again!

"Adam? Dead? For Christ's sake *how?*"—so it would be exclaimed through Salthill, by Salthill men.

The women reacted very differently. But then, women always reacted very differently. They stared, and burst helplessly into tears. The response was instantaneous, there was no defense, resistance, incredulity. Though they cried, "No! Oh, *no! Adam!*" there was immediate acceptance. Like Camille, the women were likely to instinctively cover their stricken eyes, their faces that were cracking like cheap crockery.

For the men the crucial death-question was *how,* for Adam had been in their aggrieved words *so much alive*. He'd been *filled with life,* and had seemed *indestructible.* And the next crucial question was *how old.*

Not even Roger Cavanagh seemed to know, exactly. Somewhere beyond fifty, presumably, but not too far beyond. Lionel thought of his own age, fifty-two (fifty-*two!*) with a tinge of anxiety. As a boy he'd been unable to imagine being even twenty-one. In his early twenties, he'd been unable to imagine being thirty. In his thirties, forty had seemed the absolute terminal point; and, in his forties, fifty had seemed the absolute terminal point. And now. Strange how Adam's death shook Lionel more forcibly than even Scott's death had shaken him. Though Scott had been so young, and Lionel's own brother.

In the late evening of July Fourth and through the following day the terrible news of Adam Berendt's death (by drowning? heart attack?) was relayed through Salthill. Lionel had learned when he'd walked into a room and seen his wife standing with a telephone receiver pressed against her ear, her face stricken, eyes welling with tears and shoulders hunched as if to ward off a blow, no more aware of Lionel than if he were himself a ghost, bodiless. Camille cried out, wounded in her heart. Bursting immediately into tears of grief, and so Lionel knew.

By quick degrees a narrative unfolded. An air of childlike reproach underlay it, as in a fairy tale in which even the innocent—especially the innocent!—are punished for behaving incautiously. For if Adam hadn't left his Salthill friends to attend a fund-raising event in Jones Point, among strangers, having told not even Marina Troy where he was going, he'd be alive now; if he'd gone to the Archers' annual barbecue, he'd be alive now. If he'd had an urge to go sailing (but Adam hadn't been much interested in boating, and he lived right on the river), why hadn't he gone with Owen Cutler and others, that afternoon? It was understood, Adam had had a standing invitation from Owen, so how could you explain his behavior? He'd accepted an invitation from strangers. He'd gone sailing with strangers. He'd died among strangers. Drowned in the Hudson River rescuing a woman when their sailboat collapsed, or drowned rescuing a child, or, no, a heart attack after he'd made the dramatic rescue, having dived into the river from a "dangerous" height. So the narrative was relayed through Salthill. By telephone, and in person. Not Roger or Marina but others had become bearers of the terrible news, and its amplification. Always the refrain was *Why did he—! Why, so reckless—!* It was said, it had become a tragic secondary theme, that Marina had driven to Jones Point, "desperate" to see Adam in the hospital, but she'd arrived too late. It was said that Marina had "collapsed," and was "under medication." The refrain was *Poor Marina! What a loss to Marina!* Though not everyone believed that Adam and Marina had been lovers, there were dissenters on this point, and the dissenters were likely to be women. Lionel was repelled by such speculation. His strained nerves couldn't bear it. He retreated, fled the house. He would drive in his Saab into the hills. Couldn't bear Camille on the phone commiserating with one or another of their friends, weeping as if her tears were inexhaustible. And that hurt, shocked, plaintive-child voice, he'd first heard more than thirty years before in the Deke cloakroom. *That girl. Her runny nose. Oh God, my life—why?*

The earth opened at Lionel's feet, as it must have opened for Adam.

"WHY SHOULD I console *her?* Adam was my friend, too."

Prowling the darkened house. Like a nocturnal animal in its burrow. Hearing, at a close distance, yet muffled, a woman sobbing. Through floorboards and layers of expensive Oriental carpets. As if in the history of the Macomb House, or the Wade House, numerous unknown women had hidden away to weep in secret for men not their husbands, and their accumulated grief was a harsh, heartrending music.

Lionel, downstairs in the room called the pantry, adjacent to the kitchen, unscrewed the top of a bottle of Kentucky bourbon and drank from the bottle, just a sip, to wet his parched mouth; and the taste and slow burn of the bourbon in his mouth, in his throat and beyond was deeply pleasurable. Lionel was not a drinker; Hoffmann men were not drinkers; or, if they were, they drank in moderation and in dignified secrecy; they did not call attention to themselves, ever. Lionel would take another small sip, and possibly another. But no more. "I'll miss you, Adam. God *damn.*" But he wanted Adam's death to be private, for himself alone. He hated the public ceremonial nature of Death. So much in Salthill was public, as if one's soul had to be turned inside out, bared to the world. In his solitary moods on the commuter train, in his Manhattan apartment, on airplanes when he felt the plane shudder as if at the apex of a death dive, Lionel turned his thoughts eagerly inward, to discover that *inward* was perilous, too; his soul was a sort of curved reflective surface that distorts, as in a funhouse mirror, the face of one peering into it.

You might be anyone, any face. The face is mere skin. Accident. He seemed at such times to be approaching a profound yet unspeakable truth: that our identities are accidents. He recalled, not very precisely, Plato's Allegory of the Cave, from that forbidding book *The Republic:* mankind is imprisoned inside a cave of flickering shadows, mesmerized by illusion. But to be free of the cave is to risk blindness because the light of true day is dazzling. And to be free of the cave is to risk ostracism from those who remain blind.

Through the floorboards, the weeping continued. Lionel hardened his heart against the sound. His face froze in a half grimace of sorrow or of contempt for such sorrow. *Whatever you do, don't laugh. At the cremation service, don't laugh.* He would not weep for Adam, he hadn't wept for Scott. The Hoffmann men, on the whole, were not the sort for easy grief. Wouldn't seek out Camille hiding away in her bathroom, the hell with consoling a wife who'd committed adultery in her heart, with her husband's closest and most trusted friend. Let the woman console *him.*

"Adam was my friend, too."

He took another small sip of bourbon, replaced the top and hid the bottle away in the cupboard.

Ashes to ashes, and dust to dust.

There would be no funeral for Adam Berendt, and no church service. Only the stark ceremony of "cremation" miles away in Nyack. Nyack! No one ever went to Nyack willingly. Lionel panicked at the thought of the cremation of Adam Berendt, but told Camille he didn't want to attend for moral reasons, the very thought of cremation offended his Christian temperament, and Camille stared at him in distress, asking would he let his wife go alone? was he so heartless? had he cared so little for their friend Adam? and as her voice quavered on the brink of hysteria Lionel quickly acquiesced, for Camille was right, of course. *If she makes a fool of herself in public.*

He loved his wife, he'd forgive her. But no man can bear public exposure.

Like a dream this was. On a weekday morning in July when Lionel should have been in his executive office at Hoffmann Publishing, Inc., on the fiftieth floor of one of the newer Park Avenue buildings, grateful to return from the overwrought four-day holiday weekend, instead he and Camille were turning into a large asphalt parking lot off ugly Route 9W. Nyack Burial-Cremation Services, Inc. A number of cars—Lionel recognized friends' cars—were already parked in the lot. "What a nightmare!" Lionel shuddered. Except for the tall, ominously stained chimneys the crematorium resembled a suburban public library, low, flat-rooted, of cheap buff-colored brick. Inside, before they could get their bearings, the Hoffmanns were forcibly greeted by the crematorium director, Mr. Shad, a tall, dark-suited gentleman with a gravely twinkling eye and a skin that looked as if it had been lifted and stretched; Mr. Shad welcomed them on this mournful occasion in their lives, shaking hands vigorously with them both, gravely smiling, urging them to ask questions about the procedure if they had any, after the service perhaps, and the Hoffmanns said yes, yes, they would, eager to move on, for the gleam in Mr. Shad's eye was fearful. A youngish usher with dark sideburns and oily pompadour urged them into a fiercely air-conditioned lounge designated The Chapel, where there were rows of seats and, on a raised platform at the front, a plain pine coffin. Adam's coffin! Lionel smiled in confusion, looking for his friends. The Chapel was windowless and shadowy as the inside of a lung. Numerous persons stood awkwardly, not wanting to sit down so soon; if this was a social gathering, it was one in which things had gone wrong. "There!—our friends." Like wraiths with the impediments of bodies they stumbled in the direction of Salthill faces. Their well-dressed friends and acquaintances were so out of place here as to seem like imposters. And there were strangers, persons at whom they would not glance. Camille was taken up in female embraces, blinking back tears. Lionel's hand was vehemently shaken. "What a nightmare, eh?" "Christ. Isn't it." This was a gathering of individuals in which you'd naturally glance about for Adam's good-natured battered face. His absence was conspicuous. And the time of day was wrong. Not yet noon, and Lionel had been awake for hours. He'd poured himself a half glass of bourbon to steady his nerves but it seemed not to have had any effect upon him, none; hadn't even burned going down. And he'd gargled, and regargled with Listerine, that mouthwash he detested. Camille, he seemed to know, though certainly he hadn't been spying on her, had medicated herself with one or two of her "calming" pills. (What these prescribed pills were exactly, Lionel didn't know. Hadn't wanted to inquire. Antidepressants, probably. Antidepressants were all the rage now, said to be enormously popular in Salthill among the wives of Lionel's friends as, several decades before, tranquilizers had been popular among the wives and mothers of Broom Hills.) How disoriented they were, these friends of Adam's. His survivors. Mourners. Trying not to stare at the aggressively plain pine coffin on a raised platform at the front of the chapel. Trying not to think the obvious thought *Adam is inside? A body?* What was the smell in this place, despite the frenetic frigid-air currents. Lionel's sensitive nostrils pinched. He prayed not to become nauseated.

Mozart's *Requiem Mass* was being piped into the chapel. The tape seemed to be just slightly defective, playing at an accelerated speed.

Lionel had never attended a cremation service before. He supposed it was a good, necessary procedure: burning, not storing the dead body; if you didn't believe in the resurrection of the body at the Second Coming of Christ, what point in hoarding the dead? The earth was rapidly filling up, for sure. You read about cemetery-plot scarcity all the time. Worse than housing shortages. The Asian nations with their great surplus of humanity weren't sentimental, knew what to do, funeral pyres, burning beside "holy" rivers, of course, those people were heathens. Cremation offended Lionel's sense of protocol. That behind those somber burgundy-velvet drapes there was a roaring furnace, or an oven, prepared to reduce a human body to ash. *Ashes to ashes, and dust to dust.* The chapel walls seemed to press inward. Covered in innocuous nature-murals of a nineteenth-century type, like the faux-primitive landscapes of that French painter Rousseau. Their overdone leafy veined green was muted, faded; the deep vibrancy of life's green, of Adam's actual garden, would be out of place here. "Please. Take seats." Camille had been whispering with women friends, and now turned to Lionel, her face dazed and melting. She stumbled in her impractical high heels and Lionel instinctively took her arm, to steady her. They sat in a middle row of seats, shivering. A woman directly behind Lionel startled him by leaning forward to growl into his ear, "It's so perverse, Lionel, my God! Adam in that *box*. And us stumbling around like brain-damaged sheep." The woman's voice was husky, sexy; her breath smelled of something rich and ripe, like port wine. She'd been a lover of Adam Berendt, too, it was generally believed, though Lionel hadn't ever quite believed it: Owen Cutler's wife, Augusta, the smoked-ham heiress. It was flamboyant Augusta's habit to murmur such intimate remarks into Lionel Hoffmann's ear in the presence of his wife and others, for of their circle Lionel was the most stiff, the most reserved, the most easily embarrassed and offended; and such was Augusta's way of flirtation. Her eyes were slanted and sly as figs and she outlined them elaborately in blue-black ink that quickly smudged, so that her eyes looked blackened, as by a cruel lover. Her mouth was a perfect crimson heart, oozing blood. To kiss that mouth, Lionel often thought, was to invite hemorrhage. *Had Adam loved this woman, had he rooted in her soft ample body?* There was something both arousing and repugnant in the thought. Augusta Cutler was of an ambiguous age, the mother of grown children, the wife of gentlemanly Owen whom everyone liked, to a degree; Adam had certainly liked him, and would not (would Adam?) have drawn his wife into adultery. *She's too old for it. Too fat!* In fact, Augusta was a sumptuous female in the Rubens mode, big-boned, sensuous; with cascades of highlighted blond hair; though Lionel avoided looking at her when she was aware of him, he often gazed at her during long, slow dinner parties when she was involved with other men. Her necklines were tight and dipping and as hours passed, and Augusta drank and ate, her breasts became ever more engorged and tiny beads of perspiration glittered on her rosy skin. Once, at the Hoffmanns' New Year's

Eve party, Augusta had pressed herself boldly against Lionel as they danced a fox-trot, peering at him sidelong, the tip of her pink tongue protruding between her moist lips. Her crimson nails dug into his arms like plastic claws. "Lionel. Someday. Yes?" Lionel, embarrassed, pretended not to hear. The amplified dance music was very loud.

Lionel shuddered, passing his hands over his eyes. "What a nightmare!"

"Will you please *stop saying that.*" Camille nudged him, pleading.

Lionel hadn't realized he'd spoken aloud. Someone was addressing the gathering of mourners: Mr. Shad. Explaining the service which would be brief. Shad's black-dyed hair fitted his head like a shiny shoe. As he spoke, his lips lifted from his gums in a way that fascinated and repelled; his teeth, or dentures, gleamed very white, and gave a sort of dignified echo to his words. Lionel frowned in a pretense of concentration. *Adam? In that—box?* The perversity of death swept over Lionel. It was a sickening sensation he'd had at his brother Scott's funeral though his brother's funeral had been beautiful, in the family church in Broom Hills; banks of flowers, and an excellent organist playing Bach with a light touch, and two hundred in attendance at least. It was a sensation he'd had most powerfully at the age of ten, on the grassy bank of Broom Lake, seeing the dead young couple entwined and softly rotting together in each other's arms. *But I didn't see! I saw nothing. I wasn't the one.* Mr. Shad wanted the gathering of friends of Adam Berendt to know that, if they had any questions about the procedure, he would be very happy to answer them, after the service. And there was "educational" literature available. Lionel's nostrils pinched. He could smell the hot oven. Just behind that wall of velvet drapes. Adam's coffin, the most frugal Lionel had ever seen outside a film of the Old West, was cleverly hooked to a mechanism that would tug it forward, through the velvet drapes and an opening in the wall and into the fired-up oven and eternity. Lionel swallowed hard, and reasoned that this was what Adam wanted, wasn't it? That gruff no-bullshit guy, who'd have said take my dead body and trundle it off with the trash, what the hell. Lionel was trying to listen to the second speaker: Roger Cavanagh. One of Lionel's old Salthill friends with whom he exchanged perhaps a dozen words a year, and with whom he sometimes played squash, and tennis, both men killers on the court, seeking the jugular; but Roger had a reputation for shady behavior, cheating maybe, while Lionel was the quintessential good sport, gracious in defeat. This morning Roger's eyes were ringed with fatigue as if he hadn't slept in nights. His skin was coarse and pasty like something applied with a trowel. But he was wearing a handsome dark summer suit, his thinning hair brushed back neatly from his keen raptor's face. Lionel hadn't quite understood why his friend's marriage had disintegrated years ago, and why Roger had been left behind in Salthill bereft, hurt, enraged, and of course he'd never inquired. The sexual lives of friends are best left unimagined, and unimaginable. Roger was speaking hesitantly of the suddenness and the shock of Adam's death; there would be a memorial service in the fall; this ceremony had been delayed two full days as he and Marina had tried without success to locate relatives of Adam's. In his flat, cryptic lawyer's voice Roger said, "There seem to be no 'Berendts' who have heard of our Adam." The remark was blown about in the churning air currents, like a stricken moth.

Meaning—what? Lionel was annoyed as hell.

Next, Marina Troy came forward to speak. Always, there was something enigmatic and unpredictable about this woman; she was one of the younger women in the Hoffmanns' circle, but you'd have characterized her as an older-young woman, a girl who'd grown up missing her youth. Or so it had always seemed to Lionel, who dropped by the Salthill Bookstore sometimes to purchase books he'd seen reviewed enthusiastically, mainly history, biographies of financiers, statesmen, and other men of the world, rarely did Lionel read these books through, but he meant to, someday; in the meantime, he was accumulating an impressive library; and he liked, as he said, to support poor Marina in that store. What was striking about Marina was that you never quite knew what she might say or do, as she seemed not to know herself. "Th-thank you for coming, on this sad occasion. Adam would be—would be—oh, you know how Adam would *be*—so happy to see you, and only just s-sorry that, that—" Marina was breathless, radiant-faced and strange to her friends, who stared at her as if they'd never seen her before, in dread of what she might say next. The shock of her friend's (lover's?) death seemed to have devastated her; to have rendered her young, as if the layers of her brittle personality, carefully constructed in adulthood, had been peeled violently away. She was deathly pale, with the redhead's translucent skin; faint bluish veins quivered beneath that skin, like wires. Her eyes were enormous, damp and blinking. Her pale mouth resembled an animated wound. Like a sleepwalker she seemed but dimly aware of her surroundings. She wore black, but a curious iridescent-purple black, loose and indefinable, crinkled, possibly a tunic over a long skirt, a black knit shawl wrapped around her shoulders; she was visibly shivering from the cold air, and from excitement; as she spoke, she glanced repeatedly at the plain pine coffin a few yards away, that seemed to glow in the indirect lighting, as if she expected—what? Some sort of response from it, or from the man inside? Lionel saw to his disgust that Marina was bare-legged; on her naked feet were old, water-stained sandals. What poor taste! Obviously, the woman had no husband to oversee her public apparel, or her grooming. The red-glinting hair that Lionel in his remote way admired, and often found himself gazing at, had been plaited so tightly that the corners of Marina's eyes looked slanted; its crownlike bulk was covered in a black lace mantilla, and affixed to this was, improbably, a black satin rose with floppy petals. It was the sort of cloth rose you'd find on a woman's hat. It had a cheap theatrical look, of showy excess; pinned to Marina's head, it bobbed distractingly, disfiguring as a growth. Lionel frowned in disapproval as, years ago, he'd often frowned in disapproval of his children when they embarrassed and displeased him. Marina was speaking in a deceptively calm voice of Adam Berendt, their "beloved mutual friend"; of the "terrible loss" of such a good, generous man, in their community; of his "heroic"—"sacrificial"—death. She paused, as if she'd lost her way. She smiled in confusion. She regarded the coffin almost coquettishly. "What we all want to know, Adam, is, why?—why did you throw your life away, if that's what you did, and what does it mean for *us?*" In the startled silence, no one moved; Lionel had a sense of everyone in the chapel, some fifty or sixty people, including Mr. Shad and several ushers at the rear, remaining very still. But Marina, staring and blinking and smiling, like a sleepwalker managing to wake, if only for a few seconds, to get her bearings, went on to speak in a more normal manner, telling her listeners that the cremation service was what Adam had requested; he'd told her, once when they were out hiking, and they'd come upon the carcass of a dead creature, that what he wanted, when he died, was to be "burnt to a crisp." At this, there was an eruption of nervous laughter in the chapel. Marina's lips twitched, too. She glanced at the coffin as if in approval of Adam's wit. "And so, Adam," she said, almost merrily, "we will honor your request." Marina ended by taking out of the folds and layers of her curious costume a battered paperback book, *Great Dialogues of Plato* Lionel was able to read, for he was far-sighted in middle age, and with schoolgirl earnestness Marina read a short passage from the *Phaedo* which, as she explained, recounts the death of Socrates by state-mandated suicide, in the company of a few followers who were his disciples, and loved him. Asked on his deathbed how he would wish to be buried, Socrates said, "How you like, if you catch me and I don't escape you . . . I shall not be here then with you; I shall have gone away . . . Be confident; and bury my body as you please and as you think would be most according to custom." Having read these words, Marina ceased abruptly as if someone had jabbed a knife against her spine. "Oh! Oh, God." The smooth taut girlish face shattered, Marina began to cry, anguished. In that instant, to the horror of all who were watching, Marina Troy aged thirty years.

In this way, the formal ceremony ended.

Mozart's *Requiem Mass* was immediately resumed, in the midst of a phrase of music, pitched rather too high, and demented-sounding. Adam's type of music? You wouldn't have thought so: Adam was in the habit of whistling brisk tuneless tunes. He'd had few classical CDs in his possession, so far as Lionel knew. "What a nightmare!" At this point the plain pine coffin had begun to move. There was a cinematic quality to its departure. It was being tugged jerkily forward, then more smoothly, on its partly hidden rubbery hook; pulled out of sight through an opening in the velvet draperies as everyone, aghast, stared. What was happening? *Was* this happening? The tacky velvet drapes promised a theatrical experience but there would be no further revelation: Adam's coffin disappeared, and the drapes fell back into place.

Gone! So quickly.

To be burnt to a crisp.

LIONEL EXCUSED HIMSELF to flee to the men's room. Where, locked in a stall, in dread that someone among his friends might come in, and hear him, and recognize his shoes, he vomited into a toilet bowl.

Not that he'd eaten much that morning. But there was the acid-bourbon, more fiery in its upward trajectory than in its downward.

TIME TO LEAVE, to escape. Yet no one could leave just yet. With no religious ritual to make an ending, how to make an ending? They were in the parking lot, amid their glittering cars. How many hundreds of thousands of dollars worth of cars. They were dazed by the action of sunshine on black asphalt. The sun glared and glowered from all directions. Lionel felt better for having vomited, he'd vomited up not only the hot little knot of bourbon in his guts but the nauseating smell of the chapel. Poor Marina!—her tears had provoked many of the women into fresh bouts of weeping, so that their meticulously prepared faces were beginning to resemble melting wedding cakes. Even a few of the more sensitive, or weaker, men. But not Lionel Hoffmann, who was stoic; determined not to betray emotion, in public; or in private. Hysteria disgusted him as it disgusted all Hoffmann men. And what was this in his hand: a stiff little ivory card, pressed upon him by Mr. Shad as he'd left the building, a business card Lionel tore into pieces, and tossed away. Had everyone been given these despicable little cards? "It's no worse, is it, than a coffin lowered into the earth, I mean witnessing it," Owen Cutler was saying, reasoning, "and clumps of dirt shoveled onto it, and we actually didn't—see. We saw nothing." Augusta Cutler who'd hurriedly put on dark glasses, pointed above their heads, "Oh, but look." Puffs of pearly-white smoke lifted from a chimney, trailing upward. "And what is that *smell.*" In a tragic voice Camille said, "This is the end of an era." And burst into fresh tears. Lionel looked at his wife for the first time in recent memory. That woman, his wife? *His?* The runny-nosed girl in the cloakroom at the Deke house, thirty years later. And she was thirty years older. The round childish softly pretty face was plumper, flaccid at the jawline; the pink-flushed skin was rubbery as a doll's. Grief, and the anger of grief, had deepened lines in her forehead usually disguised by makeup, and bracketing her mouth. A pike's mouth it seemed to Lionel, contorted by suffering. Lionel felt both tenderness and repugnance, seeing Camille like this. Exposed to the world. He knew it was unfair to believe that only the young and attractive should display such emotion publicly, yet he wanted to hurry to Camille, literally with his arms, or his coat, to hide her from the laughter and pity of the world. But as he turned, blinking in the dazzling light, to take in the others, his friends, he realized his mistake. The change had come upon them all, all were middle-aged, and ravaged. *Camille Hoffmann was the world, the world was Camille Hoffmann.*

4

THAT NIGHT, in the house on Old Mill Way, the Hoffmanns slept. In their burrow-marriage, the Hoffmanns slept. In the antique four-poster bed at the top of the old Colonial Macomb House, or was it the Wade House, a landmark of local history, the Hoffmanns, exhausted, slept. Always they slept in a single bed by custom; for their marriage was sanctified by Custom. (Except when Lionel was forced to be away overnight in Manhattan, or was out of town on business, which was frequently the case in recent years. Then they slept in separate beds.) Their intense, separate, far-flung bouts of sleep.

For sleep is not one, but many. These regions of the soul inaccessible to all others save the sleeper; and even the sleeper is helpless to determine the course of dreaming, the spillage of emotion. No matter how others press against us, or grasp us in their arms. *Take me with you. Where are you going? Don't you love me?*

In their expensive burrow-marriage from which oxygen had leaked, leaving the air humid and stale as soiled bedclothes. Though the bedclothes on the four-poster bed were expensive linen, and scarcely soiled. And the enormous pillows were stuffed with goose feathers, expensive and luxuriant. And the bedroom, the "master" bedroom as real estate agents call such rooms, was beautifully furnished in Revolutionary-era things; and the walls papered in a net of silken dove-gray fleur-de-lis and serpentine tendrils, an exact reproduction of the wallpaper in the bedroom of General Cleveland Wade and his wife. In such surroundings the Hoffmanns slept. In their burrow of thirty years the Hoffmanns slept. In the aftermath of grief the Hoffmanns slept. On opposite sides of the double bed they slept. They were spent, exhausted; like swimmers who have only barely made it back to shore, through a treacherous surf; swimmers who've survived a common wreck, and dread the knowledge of what happened, and what almost happened, in the other's eyes. *No! I can't look. Don't make me look. I don't know you.*

In the history of the Colonial house on Old Mill Way, how many wives and husbands had slept beneath the high ceiling of the master bedroom, such spent, exhausted sleep.

Camille, who lived now, understood that Lionel, her husband, was deeply disappointed in her. Her weakness, her tears. Her public breakdown. In the car returning from Nyack, he'd said virtually nothing to her except "Blow your nose, Camille.

Please." And in fear of him, his severe eyes, Camille had crept upstairs to bed while Lionel was in his downstairs study with the door shut against her; as years before he'd shut the door against the children whispering and giggling outside it. Their daring soft pummelings against it with the palms of their hands. *Daddy? Dad-dy? Why are you hiding?* Camille had sometimes pressed the palms of her hands against that door and listened intently, and hearing nothing inside had not dared to speak; tonight, she hadn't dared to approach the door. The house was so large, you could be lost to another person for days. But Lionel was required to come upstairs to bed, in the "master" bedroom as Custom dictated. He was faithful to Custom, Camille knew. In gratitude she knew. She'd bathed luxuriantly, and put on a floral-checked flannel nightgown (though the night was hot, Lionel kept the house air-conditioned and their sleeping quarters were wintry), and lay on her side of the four-poster bed to wait for him; she'd left a dim light burning on the table by Lionel's side of the bed. Her lips moved in a silent prayer for Adam Berendt, and for herself and her husband. *O God let us endure. Let us be happy again!* She had not committed adultery except in her heart. She was not guiltless, neither was she guilty. Should she confess? That she'd loved another man? While continuing to love her husband, she'd been desperate with love for another man? Lionel in his remoteness could not know; he'd have had no idea. What an insult to his manhood! Must Lionel know the full truth, in order to forgive her, if he would forgive her? *O God, instruct me. Adam?* Camille had always been a religious person but her relations with God were formal and not very comforting. There were long periods when she no more thought of Him than she thought of the elderly white-bearded man who'd been her Grand-da-daddy, her mother's own grandfather, who'd given her so many nice presents including a Shetland pony, who'd disappeared from her life forever before she was ten. (When she'd asked where Grand-da-daddy was, her mother always said, with a quirky little smile, "Grand-da-daddy's gone back to the Highlands, where he came from.") Camille squinted into the darkness. She was in a wild place, approaching the mouth of a cave. She was alone, and in her nightgown, and frightened; but someone, perhaps Adam, was close by, protecting her. She couldn't see him but knew he was there. As in life, he'd protected her. She was drifting downward to sleep, which was inside the cave. Yet at the same time she was fully awake, conscious of that sequence of creaks on the stairs. In fact, her mind was racing, like a rabbit chased by hounds! She was exhausted from these racing thoughts! Since that terrible telephone call of the other evening. *Camille, I have such sad news for you. For us. It's Adam. Adam has—in an accident, Adam has—died.* (The caller hadn't been Marina Troy but Abigail Des Pres, who'd been one of the women in Adam's art class at the high school.) The caller broke down into sobs, and Camille, stricken to the heart, sobbed with her. Not that she'd been able to quite believe that Adam was dead, so quickly. Since that hour, Camille's mind had had no peace. Her thoughts were sharp as razors. They spun, they glittered. In the midst of the glittering a door opened stealthily, and it was her husband coming finally to bed. The house was deathly quiet, it was the middle of the night. Lionel Hoffmann barefoot, carrying his shoes; out of gallantry, not wanting to wake his exhausted wife. (Not wanting, Camille knew, to have to speak to her, touch her.) A rapist he was, creeping into her shadowy room. Camille smiled at the thought, for Lionel was not a man with rape on his mind. "Lionel, darling?" Camille whispered, and Lionel, startled, had no choice but to reply, "Yes? What?" Camille stirred, sitting up, the enormous goose-feather pillow sighing behind her. "What—what time is it?" and Lionel said quickly, "What difference does it make? It's late. I'm sorry I woke you." "I haven't been asleep." "I think you were, Camille, and I woke you. I'm sorry." "But I wasn't asleep, Lionel. I was waiting for you." "You were asleep, I think. I could hear you breathing. I'm sorry I woke you." Camille smiled into the darkness at the elusive man hovering just beyond the arc of light. She wanted to scream, *Stop being sorry! I hate you* but instead she said plaintively, "Lionel, do you l-love me?" But Lionel had already slipped away into his bathroom, which opened off the far side of the spacious bedroom; already the fan inside was clicking and whirring. "What will I do if you don't love me? And Adam gone."

It was Lionel's strategy to take a very long time in his bathroom before coming to bed. Camille understood that he was waiting for her to drift back to sleep. Since the news of Adam's death he hadn't wished to comfort her, nor even to touch her. Nor even to look at her. "Adam was my friend, too"—so strange a remark to make, as he'd turned away from her in a kind of reproach. Yet Lionel's remoteness was hardly new. How many months, years. Since about the time the children departed? Now she wasn't Mother, but again Wife. She'd served him and the children well, as Mother. As Wife, possibly she was deficient? Often she overheard Lionel complaining of his office staff, the "girls" he was forced to hire, none of them capable, and she understood that, if Lionel were to interview her for Wife, he wouldn't hire her. Somehow, her personality had begun to fade in her early forties. As her fair, wavy brown hair had faded. When they'd first met, Camille had been a vivacious eighteen-year-old college freshman; very pretty, and very popular with boys; at Ithaca College, she'd been frenetically busy with activities like Glowworms, HiSky, PIPS, Slipper & Pen, Lancettes, Icicles, and the women's intramural volleyball team; she'd nearly been elected class public relations officer, a position of responsibility. She'd met Lionel Hoffmann at a Deke party at Colgate one evening when Lionel's date had gotten shamelessly drunk, and was dancing with a succession of Dekes, and Lionel had stalked out of the fraternity house, furious; and Camille's date who was a friend of Lionel's had asked Lionel to join him and Camille for the remainder of the weekend; and somehow it happened that Lionel, in his fury and heartbreak, had focused on *her*. And so he'd loved Camille for several years before finally Camille agreed to marry him, giving up her hope of a career in education, and a stint in the Peace Corps. (Camille had begged Lionel to join the Peace Corps with her, they might have spent their honeymoon in exotic Africa, but of course, Lionel vetoed the idea.) Almost immediately after the marriage their relationship altered. By degrees, Camille lost her "sparkle"—her "dancing" eyes—as her Grand-da-daddy had called them. But she'd been very capable as Mother, with nannies, housemaids, and cooks to assist her, and this had pleased not only her demanding husband but her husband's yet more demanding parents; and in the pleasure of such knowledge, Camille had basked innocently for years. Then the children were grown and gone, overnight it seemed. And Camille began to lose her looks. In mirrors, often she saw an unrecognizable face. It was known by Camille to be hers, as in dreams we "know" people who don't at all resemble their real selves; yet parts might be missing—an eye, a nostril, the right side of the jaw melted away. In family snapshots, Camille was a blur. Her figure was ectoplasmic, shapeless. Her hair lost its color, its lustre, its texture; what beauticians call "body." Her eyes faded: where once they'd been a deep blue, now they were a pale gray, like wetted newsprint. A number of times Camille answered the phone only to hear the caller say, "Hello? Hel*lo?*" though Camille had distinctly said hello; when Camille protested she was there, she was Camille Hoffmann, the caller seemed not to hear, and hung up. It was so frustrating! It was heartbreaking. To be a wraith while still alive, and still relatively young. Only Adam Berendt in his kindness had seen *her*.

Time had passed, the bathroom fan still whirred. Camille was determined to remain awake though it was 2:06 A.M. by her bedside clock. Thinking how their lovemaking, hers and Lionel's, had become so rare in recent years as to have acquired, for each, a new and alarming awkwardness; as if they were inexperienced newlyweds, or strangers by some mysterious chance (a lottery?) forced to sleep in a single bed. This bed! Camille stifled a sob. She adjusted the enormous pillow beneath her head. Oh, why had Adam Berendt never climbed the stairs to this room, to this bed? *Why didn't you love me as I loved you, if you'd made love to me in this bed the bed would be sanctified now and I could sleep*. She'd bathed, and powdered her soft slipping-down body with talcum that smelled of lilac, to erase the gritty-acrid odor of the crematorium, but it was difficult to find a comfortable position in this bed. If Camille lay on her back, her right breast sagged to the right, and her left breast sagged to the left, to a degree that disconcerted; if she lay on her side, her heart seemed to beat faster, and her left breast was mashed against the mattress while her right breast was mashed against her upper arm. (For she could only face the left side of the bed, since Lionel lay to her right; that was his territory.) And her breasts had become fearful to her. Even as their maternal function rapidly retreated in time, they seemed to be growing larger. (In fact, Camille hadn't nursed either of her babies. Her obstetrician, male, hadn't recommended it. And Lionel had wondered aloud in his remote, whimsical way if nursing wasn't a bit aboriginal for their time and place.) How unnatural it had seemed that day in the crematorium "chapel," that Camille felt herself both a ghost and a mammalian physical being, burdened with the impediments of female flesh. *And there is no one to whom I can speak of such things, now that Adam is gone.* If she dared to bring up such a topic to Lionel, he would have been dismayed and embarrassed; he disliked what he called Camille's "metaphysical" tendencies, fearing his emotional wife might come to believe in spiritualism, séances, New Age notions like reincarnation and "channeling" and communing with animals. *Because I am not my body. I am so much more!* Not long ago at a fund-raising luncheon for Planned Parenthood, the unpredictable Augusta Cutler shocked women friends by declaring she was God damned bored with her female body; she'd outgrown the thing, even as, ripening and spreading, it seemed to be outgrowing *her*. Lifting her breasts in both beringed hands, and they were sizable breasts in taupe jersey decorated with myriad tiny pearls, Gussie said in her husky growl, "Sometimes I feel like a rubber sex doll some guy blew up, and discarded." Abigail Des Pres, the only divorcée in their circle, who'd lost so much weight since her divorce that she'd become ethereal, like a fading watercolor, glanced down at her narrow torso saying, "Me! I'm a rubber sex doll that's been deflated, and discarded." Camille snorted with sudden laughter.

Oh, but was it funny, any of it? Camille knew that Lionel was furious with her, and that his fury had something to do with the size of her breasts, and her hips and thighs, and their ectoplasmic nature; he was furious with her *femaleness;* even as he honored her as his wife, and would never dream (Camille knew!) of being unfaithful to her, still less leaving her. But he was upset with her grieving for Adam before witnesses, their Salthill friends. Camille lay listening to faucets being turned on, and off. The toilet flushing. Reproach vibrated in these sounds. A medicine cabinet door being opened, and shut. And opened again? *It's a test of wills. If he can outwait me. If I fall asleep before he comes to bed.* Camille smiled, thinking this might be a TV show. *Marriage at Bedtime: The Test of Wills.* How popular it would be!

At last, the fan ceased. A door opened quietly. A man's shadowy figure, barefoot, in pajama bottoms and white T-shirt top, came stealthily to the bed. Switched off the bedside lamp. Slipped beneath the covers, stiff and on his back and breathing as inconspicuously as possible. Camille was awake (wasn't Camille awake?) yet she seemed incapable of moving her head, or speaking in even a murmur *Lionel? I'm so afraid.* Her sprawling soft body felt as if it had been shot with novocaine. No, it was the coarse white pill she'd taken before coming to bed. *Lethesse* was the brand name. She'd had three, possibly four of these today? The powdery, slightly bitter taste of the pills was confused with the powdery, gritty, acrid-bitter taste of the air in the chapel, and in the parking lot outside Nyack Burial-Cremation Services, Inc. Oh, the shock of it: looking up to the tall stained chimney where big puffs of smoke drifted skyward with balloon-like ease. *My card, ma'am. I will be happy to answer any questions you may have, ma'am. At any time.* The gravely smiling Shad had pressed his card into Camille's hand, murmuring in her ear as if making an assignation. (And Lionel only a few yards away, oblivious.) Camille shuddered, remembering. She'd torn the card into tiny pieces. She was a Christian woman. Lionel would never permit her to be otherwise. He, too, was thinking rapidly; Camille could feel his brain, a finer mechanism than her own, working; his thoughts humming and vibrating, like the bathroom fan. Lionel still lay on his back, though facing the outside of the bed, having shoved his pillow aside (for Lionel had a decades-old, irrational fear of being "smothered" in the goose-feather pillows) and of course, he would begin to snore as soon as he drifted into sleep;

and Camille wouldn't dare nudge him awake. When she did, he responded with irritation and hurt pride. ("Camille, I wasn't asleep. How could I be snoring? I'm as wide awake as you.") Lionel's snoring was surprisingly loud for a man with a lean, lanky frame and fastidious manners. It had the power to penetrate her sleep as a bore penetrates a plasterboard wall. For thirty years Camille's dreams had reshaped themselves into narratives to absorb the man's snoring. Often Camille found herself in airports, or on airplanes roaring through the sky. She was on a train, rocked by rhythmic deafening wheels. She was involved with sewing machines, lawn mowers, lathes. Sometimes there was a wet, gurgling sound to Lionel's snores and Camille found herself in her nightclothes, barefoot in a turbulent surf. How eternal is a single night, and of what eternities are our long marriages composed! Yet the most upsetting of sounds was silence; the abrupt absence of sound. If Lionel ceased snoring, Camille would wake in alarm. "Lionel? Is something wrong? Darling?" She would shake him gently, not into wakefulness but into the comforting rhythm of his snoring. Only then could Camille resume her own sleep. As now she was making her way through an unfamiliar yet teasingly familiar landscape: Battle Park? She was stumbling in rocky soil, snagged by a snoring-thorn bush. Lionel's deep resonant snores were mixed with wild rose brambles. Sharp little thorns catching at Camille's clothing, and her bare, exposed skin. In a cave in the hillside Adam Berendt was awaiting her. She was desperate to get to him. She understood that something terrible had happened to him, yet if neither of them acknowledged it, this terrible thing had not yet happened. It was no longer summer but the wintry afternoon years ago when, boldly, she'd come to Adam's stone house on the river. Adam's studio was somehow in the cave, yet simultaneously in the stone house. And the cave wasn't dark but warmly lit; it was the outdoors, the winter sky, that was shadowy, the color of heartbreak. Camille, entering, kicking snow off her boots, stepped into an illuminated space like no other she'd seen. *An artist dwells in light,* Adam had told his students. And there was Adam Berendt in stained work clothes, jaws glinting with stubble, square-built, startled to see her. She'd interrupted him in the midst of deliberating on an unwieldy collage-sculpture. "Don't send me away, Adam! I need to speak with you." Camille was wearing a raffish fox fur jacket from the twenties, inherited from a grandmother, and hounds-tooth woolen slacks and knee-high boots; her cheeks blazed; her honey brown hair, just beginning to be streaked with silver, was wind-blown. She was in her mid-forties, still in the unconscious prime of her Renoir-female beauty. But she had no vision of herself, for her vision had been taken from her, and she had no confidence. In the quizzical stare of Adam Berendt's single sighted eye she began to tremble. If he sent her away! "I'm so deeply unhappy, Adam," she whispered. Gently Adam took her hands in his. Smiled at her, but in silence. Nudging against Camille's legs were two dogs, the older a yellow Labrador called Butterscotch, the younger a mongrel husky-shepherd called Apollo who quivered and barked excitedly, forbidden by his master to leap up and lick Camille's face. This dog, new to Adam's life, was less than a year old yet nearly full grown; his fur sleek and healthy, a mixture of black, dark brown, and silver, with black ears and muzzle. Adam had found Apollo abandoned as a puppy on a state highway, and brought him home. Camille stared at the handsome dog so quickened with life he seemed about to spring at her, not viciously, not with bared teeth, but with an unnamable animal affection. Adam dragged him away, laughing in apology. "The power of Eros," he said. "No matter your 'species' isn't his."

"Oh, Adam. What a beautiful dog. 'Apollo'?"

"His full name is Apollodoros. You remember—Socrates' youthful loyal friend."

Camille, who had no idea what Adam was talking about, nodded in smiling agreement. Oh, yes!

There followed then this haphazard scene, which Camille would recall in flashes and fragments for the remainder of her life. *In this lighted space, waiting for me like a stage.*

Adam banished the dogs to another part of the studio, and returned to Camille, whose eyes gleamed with tears of yearning, and of love. How many months, in secret she'd adored this man!

Now she seized Adam's hands, and would have lifted them to her lips to kiss except Adam, surprised and embarrassed, drew away. "Adam, I l-love you," Camille said pleadingly. "You must know it." "Camille, my hands are dirty. They smell of mortality." Camille said, "I don't expect you to reciprocate my feeling, Adam. I know this is terribly intrusive. It's in terrible taste. I can't believe that I'm here—like this. But please accept my love, Adam. Will you?" Across the room, the husky-shepherd Apollo whined as if in a parody of sexual yearning, shimmying his lean rear quarters and lowering his muzzle to the floor, barely restraining himself from leaping forward. Adam, rarely at a loss for words, seemed confused now, and chagrined; a deep mottled flush rose into his face. "Camille, dear! You know you love your husband. You love your family, not *me*." Camille protested, "Yes, I love them, but—not as I love you." "But what is it you 'love' in me, Camille? Seeing that you hardly know me." "I—love everything about you, Adam. I think I did from the first—when we first met. Your face—" "My face?" Adam smiled incredulously. "Yes. I do love your face." "Not my blind eye, surely?" Adam's right eye did make Camille uneasy, as it made others, even Lionel, uneasy; for it seemed neither a truly blind eye, nor was it a normal eye. The eyeball appeared larger than the other, protruding beneath a grizzled, scarred eyebrow; it had the resiliency of glass, the iris unmoving. Sometimes there was a tawny-golden light reflected in it, uncanny. Adam's other eye, the left, was alert, alive, human; often bloodshot as if with strain. This eye winked, this eye communicated. It was gazing at Camille now with a look of bemused patience. "I don't think about your eye, Adam!" Camille said. "I love *you*." It was a time when, in this compulsively rehearsed romantic scene, Adam would have come to Camille, to touch her; to hold her, perhaps to kiss her, to comfort her at least. To make her feel less ridiculous, exposed. Instead, he crossed his burly arms and said, in the manner of a stonemason, or a carpenter, hired to work for the Hoffmanns, and wanting to be certain he knew what their expectations were, if only to respectfully challenge them, "But what exactly do you think you love? In me? A man you scarcely know? That's what we're trying to determine."

Camille drew breath to speak, but stood confused, blushing. Adam had slipped into his Socratic mode of speech; almost, there was a sexual swagger in his manner at such times. "My face you 'love'—? But not its components, surely? My psoriatic skin? My bumpy forehead, my Cro-Magnon skull? My crooked teeth?" Camille said, hurt, "Adam, when I say I love you I mean I love *you*. Why are you being so cruel?" "I'm not being cruel, Camille. I'm only just trying to understand you." "When a woman loves a man, she loves—all that a man *is*. The physical part is—just a part." "But a part of—what?" "All that you are." "'All that I am'—how is that possible?" Adam's forehead was creased with genuine perplexity. "You hardly know me, Camille. You don't know my background, my history, my private self; you've seen me with others, as you might see a performer on a lighted stage. That isn't knowing *me*." Camille said stubbornly, "I know—someone. Who tells the truth. As so few people seem to." "But Camille, how *would* you know? You'd have to know the full truth about me, and about yourself, which surely you don't?" Camille said, "But I—I know you're the person you *are*. Your presence in the world, Adam, makes me feel less—" she paused, searching for the word, "—futile."

Futile! Yes, that was it. Adam Berendt's presence in the world made others feel less *futile*.

Camille's uncharacteristic eloquence seemed to take her by surprise. But square-built Adam stood his ground, shaking his head, frowning. If only the man would let her touch him! wrap him in her arms! hide her heated face against his neck. "Camille, you're a lovely woman, and I feel very tenderly toward you. But I don't think you understand what the consequences could be, of your coming to me like this; coming to any man, like this. Your marriage which has been your life might be destroyed, and your life devastated. It isn't worth it, dear. Not with me, not with anyone."

Camille said, her voice rising, "I don't want 'anyone,' Adam, for God's sake! I want you. I love *you*."

"But what exactly does this 'love' attach to, Camille? *What do you love?*"

Camille stared incredulously as Adam began tugging at his clothing, baring parts of his anatomy as both dogs barked in excitement, leaping about. "My chest?"—Adam opened his shirt to reveal a broad, muscular torso, fatty at the waist; beneath an untidy pelt of graying hair, his skin was mottled, flaking and peeling, and looked scarred as if with burn tissue; his breast-nipples were tough little pink-rubbery knobs. "My belly?"—it was a flaccid, sagging belly, both unnaturally pale and red-mottled, blemished like his chest, and scarred with old burn tissue. "My cock?"—a thick, stubby growth, like a thalidomide arm, purplish-red, moist at the tip, partly erect. Adam's pubic hair was copious, bristling, sprouting even on the insides of his thighs. Camille, blushing fiercely, turned away, hiding her eyes. Adam laughed. "I don't blame you, dear, it *is* ugly, isn't it? I've never been one of those men who imagines his cock is impressive."

Both dogs were nuzzling at Camille's ankles with their damp inquisitive noses. Camille didn't know whether to cry, or to laugh; didn't know whether she'd been deeply insulted, or treated with an original sort of consideration. The intense romantic scene she'd been fantasizing for many months had swerved out of her control like a careening car, and had become comedy. Adam was matter-of-factly shoving his penis back into his pants, zipping himself back up, adjusting his clothing as if nothing extraordinary had occurred, even as Camille retreated stiff-backed, with what dignity she yet retained. Adam called after her, "Camille? You aren't offended, I hope? But possibly enlightened?" He sounded like a mildly repentant, mostly amused host. Both Adam's dogs, the aging yellow Labrador Butterscotch and the lean young husky-shepherd Apollo, trotted protectively beside Camille as if charged by their master with escorting her through the drafty, cluttered house, and back to her car in the driveway.

Had she left the keys in the ignition? And the headlights on, in a thickening wintry dusk.

The river's surface was opaque, the hue of stainless steel.

Still, I love him.

Camille drove home, cautiously, like an impaired person. She was deeply mortified, stricken to the heart, and yet: the absurdity of the scene swept over her, and she began unexpectedly to laugh. She was still laughing, tears streaking her face, when she returned to the house on Old Mill Way, and entered the warmly lit country kitchen where the Jamaican woman who came twice a week to clean house was sitting in the breakfast nook drinking coffee. When she saw Camille, she said with a gap-toothed grin, "Mrs. Hoffmann! That sure must be some joke you been told, the way you laughin." Camille agreed, wiping at her eyes. "Felicia, it *is*."

Immediately she was elsewhere. The kitchen vanished, Camille was staggering into a monstrous vibrating machine like an upright lawn mower. Or was it a helicopter. Near to waking—to be rudely awakened, by Lionel's snoring—but clutching at the protection of the dream. Where was Adam? She knew now that something terrible and irrevocable had happened to him; but that he would not leave her, he was with her still. *I must tell Lionel! I must confess. Bare my soul. My love for you, Adam. It isn't too late.*

Camille. Of course it's too late.

No. I love you!

But now I'm gone. Even my ugly battered body, gone.

My love isn't gone.

You can't love a dead man, Camille. Love the living.

But, Adam—

Love the living.

With a shudder Camille awoke. The green luminous numerals of her bedside clock read 3:02 A.M. Beside her, turned from her, Lionel was not only snoring fitfully but grinding his back teeth as if arguing. Heat lifted from his long lanky back and his mussed hair. Camille, shaken from her dreams, slipped from bed and into her bathroom, to wash her feverish face and to drink a glass of water. (She deliberated, but decided against, taking another of her coarse white pills.) Oh, what had she been dreaming? What visions had Adam brought her, from the Land of the Dead? She contemplated in a mirror above her sink a puffy girl's face, and dilated eyes. She was thrilled, trembling. A decision had been made for her in her sleep: she would not tell Lionel of her love for Adam, as she'd intended. Her hopeless (yet somehow still radiant) love for Adam Berendt.

Love the living, Camille, he'd instructed her. And so she would.

AND THERE LIONEL SLEPT his own secret agitated sleep. Tangled in sleep as in the bedclothes of the handsome four-poster bed, and in the enormous goose-feather pillows which (no matter how he shoved the damned things aside) were always pressing against his face, tickling his nose. Before coming to bed he'd had a small glass, or two, of bourbon. Rinsed his mouth, gargled. Hadn't kissed Camille good night. (By the time he came to bed, Camille was peacefully sleeping.) In bed, in his usual posture, he turned from her, gazing out into the dark. What a nightmare of a day! What sorrow. *My best friend. Dead of a heart attack. Cremated.* And how perverse it was that, drifting into sleep, Lionel was becoming sexually aroused: moaning softly to himself, grinding his back teeth. He seemed to be crouched at the mouth of a cave. Or maybe it was a cellar: one of those old, earthen cellars built into a hillside he'd seen on farms in upstate New York, in the Adirondacks when he'd been a boy. He was crouched awkwardly on his haunches, his groin throbbing with blood. Inside the mysterious hole in the earth, which was approximately the width of an ordinary doorway, but not so high, what appeared to be a naked female figure lay curled. Her hair was long, matted, and greasy. Her body was naked, and smeared with dirt. Lionel squinted, seeing that the soles of her feet were filthy. She repelled him yet was sexually arousing, inviting. A sexual creature, purely female, still in the womb. *He* must give birth to her, if he dared. *The earth is the womb. Daylight is birth.* Adam Berendt was explaining. Lionel inched squatting closer to the mouth of the hole. God, how his penis bobbed taut with blood, painfully erect as a fist! He dared to lean inside the hole inhaling in a swoon the rich, rank smell of the female. Her flesh-smell, the smell of her hair, the smell between her legs, the musky blood-smell that so powerfully repelled, and invited.

The girl was awake, pretending to sleep? Moving her body provocatively in the dirt. Her belly and thighs were a lurid milky-white, but smeared with dirt. Girl's breasts, tight and hard, with eye-like nipples; tufts of armpit hair (what a shock to a man of Lionel's sensitivity, when first he'd glimpsed such tufts of wiry hair in female armpits, for Camille, of course, fastidiously shaved all unsightly hairs from her body, Camille would have been ashamed to acknowledge that such hairs grew on her body); toes that curled lasciviously in the dirt, like a monkey's. *Bring her into the light, you must bring her into the light. You must give birth to her.* Lionel understood that the purpose of the dream was to instruct him. He was a hypocrite, he'd been a hypocrite for a long time. Adam Berendt, who was his true brother, had brought him to the mouth of the cave, now it was Lionel's task alone to fulfill the command. He must crawl inside the cave, into that place of fetid darkness, and he must rouse the sleeping female, and bring her into the light. *No shame. Never again. The broken halves of your life.* Lionel woke with a shudder, on the precarious brink of orgasm. For a long time, his heart pounding, skin oozing sweat, he dared not move.

By slow degrees the blood drained out of his groin.

He felt his brain quicken, his thoughts rushing clear. Beside him in blissful ignorance, turned on her side, breathing wetly and sleeping that sleep that seemed to Lionel placid, bovine, dreamless, Camille lay inert as one of the goose-feather pillows. Now and then she sighed. Poor Camille! Lionel did love her. Always he would love her. Though knowing she'd been in love with their friend Adam, and Adam hadn't loved her in return. *My wife's sad, meager secret. I must grant her that secret.* Lionel felt his heart swell with magnanimity for the first time in memory.

Though when he'd come to bed he'd been exhausted and depressed, now he felt exhilarated, inspired. *The broken halves of my life. I must make one!* Determining that Camille was safely asleep, Lionel slipped from bed.

Barefoot in pajama bottoms and T-shirt, both damp with perspiration, he made his way quietly out of the bedroom, along the darkened corridor to the rear stairs. Like the eye of a benign god, faint moonlight guided his way. In his study, he shut the door behind him. Smiled. Sighed! By the digital clock on his desk, it was 3:58 A.M. *Call anytime, darling. By magic I will know it is you.* Lionel held his breath as he punched out the memorized number, his fingers moving swiftly and unerringly. Miles away in the third-floor walk-up loft on West 20th Street a telephone rang, and rang; and at last the receiver was lifted. Her soft shy tentative lightly accented voice—"Yes? Who is it?" Lionel cupped his hand over the receiver and said in a rush of words, "Siri, darling, it's me. Something terrible, and wonderful, has happened."

FORTY MINUTES LATER, exhilarated, swaying like a drunken man, Lionel was leaving his darkened study to return to bed when to his surprise the stairway light was switched on, and there stood Camille frightened, staring, a dressing gown hastily pulled over her nightclothes, at the top of the stairs. "Lionel, what's wrong? Why are you *here?*" When Lionel stood stunned, unmoving, Camille quickly descended the stairs, her plump breasts quivering, her anxious face crosshatched with shadowlike spiderwebs. She came to Lionel, a short, soft-bodied, anxious woman, laying her hand on his arm. "Lionel? Darling, what is it? You look—stricken." Lionel stammered he was too restless to sleep, couldn't get that ghastly visit to Nyack out of his head, he was sorry he'd disturbed her. Camille hugged him, pushing into his arms and laying her head against his chest. He stood unmoving, trapped. He could not resist. Camille was shivering, and smelled of sweet, stale talcum. "Oh, Lionel! I know. I'm so afraid. Hold me!" Lionel dutifully closed his arms around his wife. Thank God, she couldn't see his guilty, flushed face! "You do love me, Lionel, don't you?" Camille asked wistfully. Lionel stroked her soft, boneless shoulders, her fine disheveled hair, murmuring, "Of course I love you, darling. You know that. Always." Lionel had regained much of his composure and took strength in comforting the trembling woman. Next morning he would tell her. Next evening. He would tell her about Siri. He would bring the broken halves of his life together.

Camille stiffened suddenly. "What's that?"

"What?"

"That—sound."

They listened, huddled together at the foot of the stairs. A noise as of desperate scratching? sticks being rubbed together, raked against wood? "It must be an animal," Lionel whispered. The hairs at the nape of his neck stirred. Hand in hand the Hoffmanns made their fearful way through the shadowy house to the kitchen, where Lionel boldly switched on an outside light. Camille crept to a window to look out. Camille cried, "Oh, Lionel! Come see."

There, in the sudden ellipsis of light on the walk, dragging a wounded hind leg and his eyes brimming with sorrow, was Adam's lost Apollo.

The Madonna of the Rocks

I

In the binoculars' lenses the face of an adolescent boy leaps at her. *So beautiful!*

Eleven days after Adam Berendt's death.

She tells herself she is not violating the terms of the agreement. She is not in *personal contact* with her son Jared.

Jared Tierney. Abigail Des Pres's fifteen-year-old son who bears his father's name, not hers. *Her* son, named for her enemy.

Through the binoculars' magnified, slightly distorted lenses she stares. She isn't accustomed to the heavy, clumsy instrument, her hands with their guilty tremor grip it tight, pressing it against the bridge of her nose. Already the sensitive bridge of her nose has begun to chafe. *Is* Abigail Des Pres so sensitive? A pervert posing as a concerned mother. No, a mother in strenuous denial she's a pervert.

In actual life, Abigail could not stare at her son so avidly. So without shame. He'd be deeply uncomfortable, even disgusted; he'd slam out of the room. But this isn't actual life, this is something else. *Since Adam's death, all is unreal. A thin covering like sparkly cellophane wrap over oblivion.* Abigail bites her lower lip, hard. Contemplating the boy's cheekbones, the curve of his jaw, a dimple in his right chin like a tiny incision; the thick eyebrows darker than the chestnut-brown hair. The eyes she knows are steely-blue though she can't see their color, at this distance. Steely-blue, seeing too much.

But Jared can't see her now. Walking with his friends beneath tall trees, through spangled sunshine, talking and laughing and oblivious of his mother's transfixed eyes upon him. A man once pressed his thick stumpy thumb against an artery beating in her throat and that artery is beating now, hot and urgent. *Jared! Jared. I want you.*

It's nearly noon of a bright summer day. In a northerly place: Vermont? Why has Jared gone so far away from home, to summer school? But it was necessary, Abigail concedes. She understands. Jared had a difficult year at the Preston Academy, emotional pressure exerted by both his parents, he'd received a D in English, an outright F in math, he'd been resentful at the prospect of going away for six weeks to summer school yet now he looks very happy, even relaxed, and Abigail his mother concedes yes, that's a good thing—isn't it? You do want your only child to be happy even if, clearly, you are not the agent of his happiness.

For a fleeting moment Abigail thinks that Jared might see her. The way he's lifting his head, frowning. His desperate mother-in-disguise at a distance of about forty feet, hidden inside a parked car. If he sights her, if he discovers her, she'll drop the incriminating binoculars and throw herself on the boy's mercy. *Jared, forgive me! I didn't realize what I was doing. I didn't realize the lenses would actually magnify. I didn't realize that boy was—you.*

Maybe he'd laugh? Shake his head in adolescent dismay at her, and laugh?

Maybe not.

Yet the painful fact is, Abigail Des Pres, forty-two-year-old divorcée, former debutante, former beauty, a reasonably intelligent and educated woman, not an intellectual, but endowed with common sense, a moral woman, a decent woman, a woman-with-a-sense-of-humor, a moderately active participant in such civic-minded organizations as Planned Parenthood, Literacy Volunteers of America, Friends of the Salthill Trust, is stalking her own son.

The painful fact is, Abigail Des Pres is doing exactly what she's been forbidden.

It's different now, Adam is gone. I have no one now.

And Jared will never know.

She doesn't plan to stay another night in Middlebury. She will be leaving that afternoon. Returning to Salthill. *She vows.*

And Jared isn't aware of her, in any case. Not Jared nor the boys he's walking with. Abigail Des Pres, the former Mrs. Harrison Tierney, crouched behind an olive-tinted window of a rented luxury Lexus; frowning and squinting through a pair of binoculars; the Lexus was chosen for its discreetly darkened windows, it's a rental because Abigail doesn't want her own car to be recognized by her son. She has thought this through, hasn't she? Not impulse but premeditation. Shameless, unconscionable. She knows. She has parked the Lexus inconspicuously with other vehicles on a residential street in a metered place for which she has paid, a quarter for a precious hour. Abigail has a pocketful of quarters, clinking like pirate's gold! She's been willing to wait all morning here at the edge of the Middlebury campus, to sight her son whom she has not seen, has not touched, has not kissed in nearly two weeks.

She'd telephoned Jared when the terrible news came. Jared had always liked Adam, he'd been close to Adam for some months during the worst of the divorce siege, but Jared didn't return Abigail's calls for a day and a half, and then on the phone he sounded remote, detached, sullen. *Oh, honey, isn't this terrible tragic news,* Abigail wept. *I can't believe he's gone, honey, can you? Oh, my God.* Far away in Vermont the boy said quietly, *Yeah, it's real sad, Mr. Berendt was O.K. You better get hold of yourself, Mom, y'know? I'm not coming home.*

Abigail was shocked, she'd had no idea of taking Jared out of summer school.

It's fascinating, it's dangerous, to watch Jared like this, without his knowing. And be invisible herself. When Abigail stares at him through the powerful lenses, he's unnervingly close; when she lowers the lenses, his figure leaps back, his face becomes a miniature, she might not recognize him. He's safely distant. *She's* safely distant.

So far as Jared knows (and Abigail doesn't flatter herself he's actually thinking of her) his mother is at their Salthill home, the spacious lonely Cape Cod on the more rural stretch of Wheatsheaf Drive, 312 miles to the south; while Jared is in leafy Middlebury, Vermont, where the Preston Academy, for a hefty fee, holds its six-week summer session. So far as Jared knows, there is nothing to know, nor to suspect. *Of course you're not coming home,* Abigail told him, hurt. *I just thought you'd want to know about Adam.*

Maybe, after they hung up, Jared broke down in tears? Is that possible?

Jared might be in mourning, he's wearing the baggy black T-shirt Abigail especially dislikes, though in fact he may own several of these T-shirts bearing a cryptic codified message no adult can decipher (the word SUCKS in lurid red prominence on his chest) and oversized khaki shorts falling down his hips; the filthy Nike running shoes that must have some mysterious sentimental value to him, he refuses to give them up, and unlaced laces, and of course, no socks. No socks! Which is why (Abigail's nostrils pinch at the memory) her son's feet smell like damp-rot fungus. But the other boys are sockless, too. Maybe their smells compose a singular smell, the statement of an American generation born in the mid-1980s? Commingled with boy-hormones?

Desperate-mother humor. The shameful fact is, Abigail Des Pres adores her son exactly as she'd adored him when he was a baby, when he was a toddler, fitting not only uncomplainingly but very happily into her arms. Maybe more, now her marriage is over, and her emotional life a wreck. Gladly would she live among the smells of Jared's size-ten feet in those running shoes, greasy-hair smells, armpit- and crotch-smells, if only Jared would adore his mother half as much as she adores him. A kernel, a crumb, a nanosecond of adoration!

If Jared would meet her gaze unflinchingly. And say he loves her, and his love *is not pity*. He loves her *and respects her*. In her ceaseless and exhausting struggle with the ex-husband who happens to be Jared's father, Jared sympathizes with *her*, his mother. *Hey, Mom, it's O.K. I'm on your side.*

Abigail, if caught, can't claim this is an impulsive act. Spying on her son. After all she'd driven deliberately to Middlebury, Vermont. She'd gone to the gigantic nightmare Nyack Mall to purchase the binoculars, also known as spy-glasses, in a sporting goods store. Coolly she'd identified herself as a novice bird-watcher with myopia, she'd needed a high-powered instrument and price was no object.

"Adam, don't judge me harshly! I tried. But Jared is gone for six weeks, and now you. Gone forever."

Since the ghastly morning of Adam's cremation, Abigail has lapsed into the habit of murmuring aloud. Since that morning when, sedated, swaying on her feet and her eyes seared from continuous crying, she'd glanced innocently skyward . . . As smoke lifted in bland powdery puffs and tendrils bearing away the spirit of the only man she'd ever truly, purely loved; the only man, in her long embattled life after childhood, who'd seemed to her worthy of an intelligent woman's adoration. "Now turned to ashes, smoke? A jar of *waste?*"

And then, the scattering of ashes. Abigail had refused to attend. She'd been called, by both Marina Troy and Roger Cavanagh, but she'd declined. They planned to rake Adam's ashes into Adam's garden above the river, as Adam had requested. On the phone Abigail was suddenly rude, abrupt. "I can't! No more! I want to remember Adam as a man, for God's sake. Not fertilizer."

Abigail sits crouched behind the wheel of the rented Lexus, pressing the heavy clumsy binoculars against the delicate bridge of her nose, where they'll leave a mark. Since the death, Abigail's skin is sensitive, hurtful. Her moist mouth falls open. In contemplation of the remarkable boy who is *her son*. (She's hoping her breasts won't leak sweet warm milk inside the black silk Shanghai Tang tunic top.) Spying on him like this, yes, it's contemptible, yes, she's ashamed, but Jared wouldn't allow her to look at him like this, ever. He hates her looking at him at all, with her dark somber heavy-lidded erotic gaze. He's too normal, he's fiercely normal. *He wants to be average*. The American boy not as Michelangelo's blandly perfect *David* but as Bernini's *David*, with a furrowed brow and mutinous stance.

Jared is the hot, beating core of Abigail's life. As if her very heart stands outside her, raw and vulnerable, suffused with its own mysterious unknowable life.

At an intersection of paths Jared and his friends pause to talk with other boys. Boys smoking cigarettes! All wear baseball caps reversed on their heads, all wear backpacks. Baggy T-shirts bearing inscrutable codes and logos of rock bands, slipping-down shorts, bare brawny down-covered legs, bare feet inside unlaced running shoes. A herd of them. Patiently Abigail waits as tall loutish strangers obscure her vision of Jared. Hulking boys who are the precious sons of other mothers; mere blurs here beside the upright flame of her son. The Preston summer session is composed mostly of students like Jared who have failed or done poorly during the academic year and whose parents are becoming anxious they won't be admitted into first-rate universities, and Abigail wonders if Jared is one of these, an average low-achieving teenaged boy amid the herd, or whether he's in disguise as such a boy.

Abigail watches in dismay as Jared takes a cigarette offered him, and lights up. "Oh, honey. No." Though she isn't truly surprised. (She'd several times smelled smoke in his room, in his hair and clothes this past year. No matter Jared denied it. Rolling his eyes and informing her she was being paranoid. Later claiming he possibly smoked now and then for his nerves. *No big deal, Mom.*)

Jared and his friends move on. Jared exhales smoke as he shakes his head to flick hair out of his eyes. What ease in his most ordinary motions: so long as he doesn't know he's being observed. Someone tosses a Frisbee in his direction and Jared leaps to catch it, leaps like a dolphin, his cigarette clamped between his teeth, and with a twist of his wrist sends the Day-Glo orange object skimming back. So quick, so graceful, Abigail is dazed. It's as if the boy has shaken out a bolt of silk in the sun, a banner of shimmering light, silk that is his own soul, and a second later lets it drop.

Through splotched sunshine the boys move. They pass girls in tank tops and shorts, slightly older girls, Middlebury College students probably, no exchange between the groups of young people, and as they walk on Jared and his friends mutter slyly to one another and erupt into laughter. Abigail can't hear the laughter at this distance, the car windows rolled up tight, but she flinches, knowing it's crude. And what crude words spring effortlessly from Jared's beautiful mouth?

Abigail Des Pres who has many times (inadvertently!) overheard her son with his prep school friends, visiting their home in Salthill, feels a blush rise into her face.

Oh, Jared, honey, must you and your friends use such—language?

Fuck, Mom, you spying on me again?

Jared! I am not spying, this is my house. I'm asking you why—such words?

Don't listen, Mom. Then it won't upset you, O.K.?

This exchange they'd had earlier in the summer. Jared hadn't been angry or defensive, really. There's a peculiar sweet reasonableness about him at such times. As years before he'd wanted to know why *nigger* was a nasty word, but if you said the *n-word* like on TV, it was all right?

A good question. All children's questions are good. But how to answer? Abigail can't any longer kiss her little boy's frowning forehead with the serenity of a Botticelli madonna and murmur *Why? 'Cause Mommy says so.*

Jared and his friends have been approaching the street where the Lexus is parked, not head-on but slantwise. They appear to be heading not for a dormitory or dining hall but in the direction of a small commercial area, a block of stores and restaurants. Abigail stares greedily, she has only these few snatched minutes before she loses Jared. (She isn't going to telephone him from her hotel, she'll be leaving in a few hours. *She is not going to contact him.*) Her eyes feel bloodshot. Her heart is beating like a gong. Jared is beginning to loom in the binocular lenses like a cinematic image in close-up. His smooth taut tanned skin is slightly blemished, there's a scattering of pimples at his hairline it looks as if he's been scratching. His hair sticks out in taffy-like tufts beneath the soiled Yankees cap, it has grown long on his neck and looks stiff with grease. Almost certainly, Jared isn't clean. Two-minute showers, a few rough swipes with a bar of soap, soiled mangled towels tossed to the floor. What can you do? During the long months of separation and divorce, when Harrison moved out to live in New York City with a new woman said to resemble a younger Abigail, one of the forms Jared's deep unhappiness took was a refusal to wash thoroughly; a reaction that mostly amused her ex-husband Harry, but upset Abigail. Yet—what can a parent do? It was a custody compromise that, instead of living part time with each parent, Jared would board at the Preston Academy, near Springfield, Massachusetts; during the summer, he would mostly live with Abigail, but spend some time with Harry; they would alternate, or somehow share, school breaks and holidays. The Preston Academy was a respected, and very expensive private school for students not quite good enough for Andover, Exeter, St. Paul's, Lawrenceville; it was reputed to be less drug-infested than most, and no student had ever killed him- or herself on its premises. (Though as Jared pointed out, this pristine record didn't include Preston students who'd "offed themselves off-campus.") At Preston, Jared has shared a suite with boys no more disposed to keeping themselves clean than he, *what can you do?*

Abigail isn't one of those mothers obsessed with dirt, dirtiness. A nag of a mom. A TV mom. No, she wishes only that she could monitor her son without his knowing. By remote control, for instance, like an expensive electronic toy.

A faint moustache on Jared's upper lip! Or maybe just a shadow. Jared has begun to shave, Abigail believes. How many times a week, she has no idea. This she knows not from Jared (who would die before telling his mother such an intimate fact about himself) but from the ex-husband Harrison, who can't resist telling Abigail about things he believes might roil her, unsettle her; any stray fact to suggest how the stability she so yearns for is going to be denied her. In one of their few recent phone conversations Harry allowed Abigail to know that he'd lent Jared a razor one weekend when Jared was visiting, and so Jared's lifetime of shaving has begun. It was like Harry, sly and cruel and charming when he wished, to worm his way back into their son's emotional life after years of indifference. *A growing boy needs a father. Not just a mother. Even you, Abigail, must know this.* Abigail responded with dignity, thank God it was a phone conversation and her ex-husband couldn't see the sick, beaten look in her face. Yes, she did concede the point, yes, she knew. *A boy needs a father. Not you.*

Since the divorce there have been men romantically interested in Abigail, but Abigail can force herself to feel no interest for them. No more! She has become sexually anesthetized—neutralized—and intends to remain in that state. So it isn't likely she will be remarrying soon, it isn't likely that Jared the growing boy will be living with a stepfather soon.

Had Adam Berendt loved Abigail? Yes. But not in *that way*.

(Abigail's tender ears still ring with the cruelty of Harrison's *just a mother*, as one might say *just a minor head cold*, or *just a side order of coleslaw, please*. And the insulting *even you, Abigail*.)

By this time Jared and the other boys are striding away, in the direction of a McDonald's. As if hypnotized, Abigail continues to stare at the back of Jared's head, the reversed cap, the narrow shoulders in the baggy black T-shirt, the downy glint of his swinging arms and legs. It cheers her to see, or to imagine she sees, Jared tossing his cigarette into a gutter. "Honey, take care. I love you." Now what? She's both relieved he didn't see her, and acutely disappointed. Now nothing remains for her except the long drive back to Salthill, to that lonely house. Before leaving for Middlebury, Jared suggested that she spend a month on Nantucket, she had old, very rich friends with an enormous house on the ocean, but no, Abigail hadn't wanted to leave Salthill, for there was Adam, her dear friend Adam . . . The other morning, very early, she'd been wakened from her sedated sleep by a frantic scratching below her window, and a high keening sound, and looked out to discover Adam's silver-haired Apollo, heartbroken Apollo, at the back door, an old gardening glove of Adam's in his jaws.

She fed Apollo, petted and stroked his coarse hair, and wept over him. Two of a kind, they were. Lost souls of Hades.

Though Jared has nearly disappeared from view, Abigail continues to hold the binoculars to her eyes, hurting the delicate bones above her nose. Now she's leaning forward, her elbows over the steering wheel. There's a sudden rapping on the windshield. Abigail lowers the binoculars, and sees to her horror that a uniformed man is peering into the car at her. "Ma'am? Will you open this door, please?"

A nightmare!

Abigail, blushing, fumbles to open the door, which is heavy as lead. The Middlebury cop, in dark-tinted aviator sunglasses, a crisply ironed short-sleeved blue shirt with a tin-looking badge, leather holster and smart polished pistol riding his hip, doesn't help her with the door, but stares at her, frowning and bemused.

"Ma'am, what are you doing?"

"Officer! I—can explain."

Abigail's wrists are too weak to support the heavy binoculars, she lowers them to her lap. Her eyes that feel bursting with capillaries lift in soft female supplication. Her eyelids tremble. Her lips tremble. At such times Abigail Des Pres's social poise can help. To a degree. Women in the Des Pres family have been bred through the generations to exude this softness, this pleading-for-understanding, in the face of masculine suspicion and hostility. In youthful middle-age Abigail is still a beautiful woman, if very thin; out of fearfulness she always dresses expensively, in good taste, and her hair, face, and nails are impeccably groomed. For this shameful expedition she's wearing the elegant black silk Shanghai Tang tunic, matching trousers, open-toed Gucci sandals. The rings on her long thin fingers, the jewel-studded gold watch on her slender wrist; the rented Lexus with olive-tinted windows; Abigail's French perfume—all these, the Middlebury cop, a flat-bellied man of about thirty-five, is taking in. Abigail says in a hoarse whisper, "Officer, I've been—watching over my son. That's all. At a distance. I don't want him to know I'm here. He thinks I'm back home. His father and I are divorced. He's only fifteen, he's here for the Preston Academy summer session, I promised him I wouldn't try to see him, but I—I couldn't stay away. I was so lonely without him. Officer, I'm so embarrassed. Please don't arrest me!" Abigail smiles plaintively, wiping at her eyes. She knows she isn't going to be arrested.

And so she isn't. The cop checks her driver's license and the car registration. He notes she still has four minutes of meter time remaining. He says, with a half-smile that might be pitying, or flirtatious, or mildly contemptuous, "O.K., ma'am. Good luck."

DRIVING TO THE Mountain View Inn, giddy as a soaring balloon.

"I'm free! Not arrested."

Abigail laughs, she isn't remorseful in the slightest. Still less repentant. She's eager to get to her hotel room and move into the next phase of her strategy.

A beautiful, not inexpensive suite overlooking the fabled Green Mountains. Will Jared be impressed? It takes a lot to impress a spoiled fifteen-year-old kid, but Abigail will try.

She calls the front desk to inform the management that she'll be staying another night. She calls Jared's number in the residence hall, which she has apparently memorized. No surprise—Jared isn't in. In a warm, but not heated voice Abigail leaves a message: "Jared? It's your mother. I'm in Vermont. I'm staying in an inn about two miles from the college. Don't be alarmed, honey"—(here, Abigail's voice is beginning to waver, she can envision Jared's scowl)—"it isn't an emergency. I just—became a little lonely, suddenly. Missing you. And—Adam. And the house is so empty . . . Don't be angry with me, please? This visit will be just between you and me, your father doesn't have to know." Abigail pauses, breathing quickly. It's a scene in a foreign film of another era, a murky tale of sexual obsession and impending doom. She sees her face, a pale floating petal, in a mirror across the room. Why are beautiful women so shallow, like cutouts? Presented at the 1976 International Debutante Ball, Waldorf-Astoria, New York City. Trying not to beg: "Call me when you can, Jared. I'll be here waiting. We'll have dinner tonight, that's all. I promise! Just one night. My number is—"

Abigail gives the number and quickly hangs up. Too late, her fatal incriminating words can't be revoked!

Exhausted suddenly. She removes the black silk tunic that has become unpleasantly damp beneath the arms and the silk trousers wrinkled and damp at the crotch, kicks off the elegant Gucci sandals and collapses in her underwear, ribs and collarbone pushing against her pale-pasty skin, onto the high, hard bed with the ruffled bolster to drift into a sleep of delicious delirium-oblivion. In that region where Adam Berendt is not yet dead, and her baby is not yet born but tight and warm and snug inside her where he's safe.

2

Like a sparrow's heartbeat.

The artery in Abigail's throat, he suddenly pressed his big thumb against where it throbbed. Alarming her who had not been prepared for the sudden intimate gesture.

She didn't recoil from him, she gripped his hand and pressed it tighter against her throat. *Oh! Adam.*

Why so intense, Abigail? You'll burn yourself out.

To this reasonable question, which Adam Berendt would ask her, in varying ways, many times, Abigail has no answer even now.

That evening. After the divorce. Jared was gone, at boarding school. She invited Adam for dinner, nervously she prepared dinner for just the two of them, the telephone off the hook. They were not—yet—lovers. They were very good friends. Though sometimes reckless Abigail would press herself against the man as a hostess has the privilege of doing, greeting a guest who's a dear friend, saying goodnight to a departing friend who has been a guest, smiling dreamily, yes perhaps seductively; yet playfully, too; for Abigail Des Pres is a playful seductive unaggressive female, willowy, hot-skinned despite her pallor, the kind of divorcée who mocks her loneliness even as she presents it, as one might present a heart, torn bleeding from its breast, on the palms of one's trembling hands. *See? Mine. But, hey—you can ignore it!*

Adam was rummaging through the deep frayed pockets of his sand-colored camel's hair coat (purchased at the Trinity Church secondhand fair for forty-five bucks, as Adam boasted) looking for his gloves, and pulled out a handful of vouchers from Caesars Palace, Las Vegas; which Abigail flirtatiously snatched from his fingers, saying she hadn't known he was a gambler, he patronized casinos, was this his secret life?—and Adam hesitated a moment before saying yes, he gambled sometimes, he had a weakness for craps in particular: "To see, not if you will win, but if you have luck; and if you don't have luck, how far the absence of 'luck' will take you, and do to you." Adam spoke so strangely, with such an air of vulnerability, Abigail could only ignore his enigmatic words; she played almost exclusively to the man's exuberant side, not the other, the brooding and philosophical, saying, "Take me with you, Adam? Next time? Vegas? I've never been. But I love to gamble—I think!" (Was this true? Half of what sprang from Abigail's lips surprised her utterly.) But Adam merely laughed, his face warm, his single sighted eye narrowed in a wink.

He snatched the vouchers back from Abigail and slowly, thoughtfully tore them into pieces.

Like a sparrow's heartbeat beat beat.

Such yearning.

A growing boy needs a . . .

. . . a second penis, a giant Daddy-penis, in the household.

Shaving? A fifteen-year-old boy shaves, how often who knows, it's a small enough secret, a touching small secret; but a secret from Mother.

Among other secrets. For instance how much Harrison allows Jared each month on his credit card. (Under the custody arrangement, Harry is in charge of their son's allowance but, of course, Abigail, who has money of her own and has, with dignity, refused to ask her ex-husband for money, can't resist contributing, too. And buying the boy things directly.) Like how much Harry spends on the skiing trips, backpacking trips, mountain-hiking trips calculated to win back their son's love. Excursions to Costa Rica, Ecuador, Alaska (Mount McKinley). One memorable Christmas break, to the Seychelles Islands in the Indian Ocean, a world away. (When Abigail was weak with grief, and flu, mourning her mother's death.) And how much Harry has paid for his condominium in New York City, on Beekman Place; and for his new country house in Cornwall, Connecticut; and what Harry and the new wife, the glamorous twenty-nine-year-old stepmother, say of Abigail Des Pres that isn't meant to be repeated to her.

Abigail persists in querying Jared—"What do they say of me, Jared? Is it cruel? It it accurate? Do they laugh? Do you all laugh?" Provoking Jared to laugh, and blush, and shrug his neck in that way of his when Mom asks such uncool questions. As if he's got a crick in his neck. "Oh, jeez, Mom."

"'Oh, jeez, Mom'—what?"

"They never say a thing about you. We never do."

Secrets. Abigail told Adam, her chief adviser through the crisis of the divorce, and the depressive aftermath, that the *fatal split* between her and her son began when Jared was about eighteen months old. Baby's first attempt at obfuscation. Baby's first untruth! Trying to make Mommy believe he has eaten his pureed beets when in fact he has cleverly sloughed the mess off his plate and onto the floor. In that futile but somehow noble little gesture Baby set himself in opposition to Mommy, like a mutinous cherub against an omnipotent God. Following this, Abigail makes an entertaining anecdote of it, a Mother's Fable, a flood of untruths followed; in time, once Baby could actually speak, these became outright lies.

Abigail and Harrison, who were still in love at the time, young parents, laughed at Baby's awkward deceptions, not alarmed but delighted. Jared was normal. Telling transparent baby-lies is funny—isn't it? Abigail mused, "Gosh! I wonder if all our lies are so obvious, even as adults?" Harry said in his evasive mumble, "Yes. I wonder." Now in weak moments, which seem to be ever more frequent, soaking in a hot bath, sipping whiskey, sleeping this drugged delirium-sleep in an air-conditioned hotel room, Abigail recalls with a stab of pleasure that once-upon-a-time when there were no secrets, absolutely none, between mother and son. When Baby was still in the womb, for instance. (She'd expected to be sick through the pregnancy, all Des Pres women are, her neurasthenic mother warned her, but in fact Abigail had been surprisingly healthy, and in good spirits, happy and thriving and taking for granted that her boy-baby would be perfect.) Nor were there secrets during Jared's infancy. Tenderly she'd presided over nursing, which she quite liked, and which seemed to her (almost!) better than sex, and tenderly she'd presided over the diaper-ritual, which Jared's fastidious father couldn't bear (Abigail was required to virtually scrub herself down after a diaper-changing session, before she could again approach Harry); tenderly she'd presided over bathing the baby, an exuberant kicking baby, at times a fretful willful baby, shampooing his thin fawn-colored hair, rinsing his head, his skull delicate as an eggshell it seemed to her, and gently washing his penis, that tiny appendage, smooth as a snail, hardly snail-sized, silken-smooth and so much nicer, Abigail couldn't help thinking, than anything adult-male. In awe Abigail held the tiny sac in her fingers, in the warm bathwater.

How to foresee the rage that would one day quiver through her beautiful son's body. His contorted face. His boy-maleness. During the worst insomniac months of the divorce siege when Jared was thirteen, likely to break into furious tears shouting—"I hate you, see? Hate both of you! He's a bastard fucker and you're a, a—what you *are!* Why don't you both die!" And

Abigail, struggling to remain calm, stoic, conceded yes Jared was right, he was right to be so angry, none of this was his fault— "Only mine, and your father's."

(But mostly the father's fault. Yes?)

Secrets. Bound up with that tiny penis-snail, silken-smooth and perfect, that would grow inevitably into an adolescent boy's penis, hidden inside his clothes; of which Abigail, *who is not an incestuous mother,* refuses to think. Of course there must be secrets in a fifteen-year-old boy's personal life. There will be ever more secrets, a rush of secrets, mostly sex-secrets, to be kept from Mother. *For my own good. He wouldn't want to shock or disgust me. His seed welling up in him frantic to spill. Oh God I know.*

At least Abigail Des Pres has never behaved like the obsessive mothers of prized adolescent boys in certain Mediterranean and Middle Eastern countries who check their sons' bedsheets every morning to determine if . . .

"Never!"

Abigail, sleeping fitfully amid damp twisted bedsheets, wakes suddenly, in revulsion.

3

HOURS LATER. The bedside phone has failed to ring. She is a woman floating on the surface of a now disheveled bed like a cluster of rotting water lilies on the surface of a stagnant pond. Yet swallows down defeat, that sour but familiar taste. Swings her slender sword-legs off the bed, sits up smiling and hopeful and dials his number another time.

The telephone rings in Jared's room in the residence hall on the Middlebury campus two miles away. Abigail has seen this dormitory beneath tall oaks, built of solid-looking brick, from a discreet distance earlier today; she now sees a boy's hand hovering over the receiver, hesitating—and lifting it. But no one speaks. Abigail says softly, "Hello? Jared?" In the background, there are voices, rap music. After a pause, a boy says guardedly,

"H'lo?" It isn't Jared. One of his suitemates. Abigail identifies herself and asks to speak to Jared and the boy says vaguely, in that appealing, adenoidal way of a lying boy, "Jared isn't here right now, Mrs. Tierney. He's—" But there's another pause, and an exchange of voices. Abigail can envision the receiver snatched from the boy, in fury and dismay.

"Yeah? Hello?" It's Jared, sounding as if he's been running.

"Jared! It's me, did you get my message?"

"Sure." Jared speaks in his flat voice. Abigail can see his deadpan expression. "I got your message."

"I'll—pick you up at the residence hall? Is seven-thirty good?"

"Six-thirty is better, I have work to do tomorrow."

"Six-thirty! I'll be there."

"O.K., Mom. Sure."

"And, Jared—"

The line is dead. Jared has departed.

IN THE SHOWER, Abigail turns her smiling face into the warm spray and tries not to think of *whatever it is: a death, a departure*. She understands that Jared is angry with her for violating the terms of the agreement with his father (not a legal agreement, nothing truly binding), and for putting him in the difficult position, which Jared is frequently in, of needing to protect one parent from knowledge of the other. *He won't inform on me, I can trust him.* At the same time, Abigail would be devastated if Jared protected his father from her; if, for instance, Harry had violated the terms of the agreement himself and driven up to see Jared. *But Jared would tell me! I can trust him.*

Abigail's too-thin body, streaming water. Her knobby vertebrae, ribs and collarbone and wrists; the smooth, creamy pallor of her skin, which gives her the look, as Adam once remarked, of an Italian Renaissance madonna.

Abigail's face, at least.

Her body is no longer a maternal body. She's been sexually neutralized. Her breasts have shrunken. The incision in the left breast (she touches it gingerly with her fingers, never looks) has mostly healed, the scimitar-shaped scar faded.

"Proof of my good luck! So far."

Six years ago, Abigail was made to realize that Harrison no longer cared for her, still less loved her sexually, when he'd become upset and angry after a routine mammogram showed up a pea-sized cyst in her left breast. Abigail's Salthill gynecologist scheduled her for surgery at Columbia-Presbyterian Hospital, a biopsy that might, if necessary, be followed by a mastectomy if the cyst was malignant, and Harrison warned her not to tell anyone. "I don't want this getting out. I don't want other men pitying me." Abigail wasn't sure she'd heard correctly. "Pitying *you?*" "That's right." "Because you have a wife with—cancer?" "No. With a missing breast." A moment later Harry added, as if only just hearing what he'd said, "I mean, honey, I'm not ashamed of cancer. Anyone's cancer. It happens. I just don't want people around here feeling sorry for us. Discussing us. You know Salthill, Abigail." Quietly Abigail said, "Yes. I know Salthill." *And I know you.* The fact was, Harry hadn't hugged her. Hadn't even touched her. *Already I am flawed to you. Yes?*

In fact, Abigail had already told several women friends about the cyst. Of course! They'd been immediately sympathetic, supportive. They'd told her of similar scares, and biopsy experiences; each woman offered, independent of the others, to accompany Abigail into the city if Harrison was out of town.

Later, Abigail would realize that her friends knew, or guessed, what she hadn't: Harrison was unfaithful to her, and Harrison would likely be "out of town" when she needed him.

The pea-sized cyst turned out to be benign. The healthy breast was not removed. Subsequent mammograms turned out negative. Harry chided her for taking a "morbid attitude." Still, Abigail is in the habit of crying. In the shower, where no one can hear her. As she is crying now, shyly stroking the subtly scarred breast.

Always buy designer clothes, Abigail. Understated, never showy. That way, you will be unassailable. This was Abigail's mother's most profound advice, but it has turned out to be worthless.

Still, Abigail dresses with care. It's become a ritual with her, like saying the rosary for Catholics, by rote, without thinking; a talisman for good luck. Though she knows that in Salthill, among even the protective friends of her circle, Abigail Des Pres has a reputation for vanity; her diffidence and insecurity misinterpreted as a kind of arrogance. *Look, I can't help it. If I'm not beautiful—what am I?* For this illicit visit to Middlebury, Abigail has brought with her several changes of clothing, and is wearing, for this evening with her son, an Italian import, a cream-colored silk shift with spaghetti straps, a fitted jacket and a skirt that just skims her slender knees; and a pair of cream-colored kidskin pumps with medium heels. Jared, at five feet eleven, will loom over her. Abigail wears the shift with no bra beneath, and the jacket loosely buttoned. She brushes her smoke-colored, wavy, very fine hair until it rises and floats about her head, and she makes up her face with care, porcelain-pale, black-edged eyes, long lashes, a pale opalescent mouth. Gold hoop earrings, platinum wristwatch and rings. But no wedding ring. Though knowing that Jared will be wearing his usual baggy clothes, filthy Nikes, and baseball cap and that he will react to her with a sneer or, worse, a chill stony stare; but it's true, Abigail can't help it. Every quiver of her eyelids is a plea. *Only love me!* Eager and anxious as a young bride she drives to the idyllic college, parks the rented black Lexus and crosses a quadrangle in the direction of Jared's residence hall, it isn't yet dusk, still a balmy summer day, Abigail has put on dark-tinted designer glasses and a floppy-brimmed straw hat; the campus is populated with young people, in shorts, jeans, tank-tops, and many of them barefoot playing Frisbee on the lawn. Abigail seems to move in her own element. Gliding, glimmering. Among the noisy Frisbee players is her son, Jared, who sights his mother by way of others who are staring at her as if trying to place her. A model? A TV personality? Maybe there's filming on the Middlebury campus? Jared, his face darkening with blood, tosses the Frisbee back to his friends and mumbles, "Got to go now. It's my mom." He comes quickly to meet her, to head her off, no need to introduce her to his companions, and there's a painful moment when it looks as if Jared's anxious mom is going to grab him, kiss him wetly, burst into happy tears, as sometimes she has done, as if they were survivors of a cataclysm, only just finding each other; but, thank God, Abigail is restrained, though clearly anxious, trembling, squeezing Jared's hand and lightly kissing his cheek. Her greeting is a breathless sigh—"Hello, honey! You washed your hair?"

Together, but not touching, they cross the quadrangle to the rental car. Jared hates it, though he's excited too, that his mother is so conspicuous; imagining herself shy, in fact she's fantastically vain; strangers' eyes tracking her don't seem to upset her, like a performer blinded by stage lights, earnestly playing to a fellow actor. "Jared! It's so—such a relief—to see you! You seem well?"

"Sure, Mom."

"And this is all right—isn't it? Coming up to see you?" Her voice is wistful, and willful. "It was just so damned lonely back home."

When Abigail wants to link herself with Jared, a co-conspirator, a fellow adolescent, she will slip in a mild profanity. Jared is unmoved. "Sure, Mom."

Abigail looks around, smiling blindly. "It's—lovely here. It seems so—" She pauses, unable to think of the appropriate word. "Do you—like it? Are you happy here?"

"It's O.K."

"Only 'O.K.'?"

Jared shrugs. "It's summer school, Mom. It's just what I'm doing."

"And this," Abigail says gaily, squeezing her son's surprisingly brawny forearm, "is what I'm doing."

If Jared is surprised at the unfamiliar car, he tries not to show it. He has become accustomed to his mother's impulsive, irrational surges. Throwing out "old" china, potted plants, furniture—redesigning rooms of the house, even the gardens and lawn—with such fervor, you'd think it meant something, had some purpose. Possibly Jared's mother has totaled the white Acura, and has no car of her own to drive; he isn't going to inquire. The wrong question, she'll burst into tears. Almost, Jared wouldn't be surprised if she has been driven up to Middlebury by someone, a man, whom he won't meet: but it can't be Mr. Berendt, her friend who *has died*.

Jared understands that his mother, though middle-aged, terribly old in his eyes, embarrassingly old, somewhere beyond forty (he doesn't want to know how far beyond, but he knows that his dad is even older) is a seductive woman, a woman to whom adult men are attracted, and this is infuriating to him, unspeakable. He hates it, he refuses to think about it. He's made anxious by the fact, and resentful, though possibly excited, too. Guys saying to him *Jeez, Jared, that's your mom?* The looks in his male teachers' faces. *Jared! Say hello to your mother for me, will you? Next time you speak to her.* And the Preston headmaster casually inquiring *Will your mother be visiting us anytime soon?*

No! No time soon.

Jared has told himself he's profoundly relieved that his mother and father have finally worked out a custody agreement, removing him from Salthill for most of the year, and allowing him to board at the Preston Academy, on neutral territory. There are other kids at Preston in exactly the same situation. Divorce and custody suits, embittered former spouses who now hate each other's guts. Mostly, the mothers are the left-behind, pathetic ones. Losers. The fathers have new, young wives, why not? It's a free country. Times have changed. God is dead. One of Jared's Preston suitemates asked him didn't he get lonely, and Jared replied contemptuously—"Lonely? I wish I knew how."

Maybe he is lonely, sometimes. Sure. But he prefers *lonely* to the other.

It's ironic that men are attracted to Abigail Des Pres, with one notable exception: Jared's dad. In a memorable phrase that man once confided in Jared he'd "had it" with Jared's mother.

Had it. This might sum up both a man's desire for Abigail, and a man's desire for Woman. Jared is contemplating both.

Inside the car, Abigail can't resist hugging Jared. "C'mon, a real hug. A hug-hug!" And a wet kiss on his cheek, narrowly missing his twisty mouth. She tugs off the ridiculous baseball cap, runs her fingers through his springy fawn-colored hair, comments that it needs trimming—"Just a little. By your ears. Maybe tomorrow morning?"—and smiles happily, joyously, at him. The baggy black T-shirt with SUCKS prominent on the front, hip-hugging jeans, smelly Nikes worn without socks. *My Jared. My love.* Jared submits to this with a reluctant smile. It isn't actually so awful, once nobody's watching. He likes his mom O.K. And he's hungry.

Driving out of town Abigail says in her throaty, co-conspirator voice, "I did miss you, honey. Gosh! And this is just for tonight, I promise."

"It's O.K., Mom. I won't tell him."

What do you want from your son, Abigail?

Adam, what a question!

Well. Answer it.

I want—him to be happy.

And—?

I want—well, I want to be happy, too. With him. Forever.

4

AT THE HISTORIC Mountain View Inn, Abigail has arranged for them to have dinner alone together in her suite. In a bay window overlooking the sloping lawn of the Inn and, miles away, a dreamy postcard-view of the sun melting behind shadowy mountains. "You're certain this is all right, Jared? We could go somewhere else if—" "This is O.K." "I thought, just the two of us—" Abigail sees Jared hesitating. Possibly he is going to say yes he'd rather go out to eat, anywhere, a real restaurant, with other people, not here, not in such intimate quarters, but since the collapse of his childhood a few years ago he's become a tactful, even stoic boy. He curls his lip at the ornate tassled menu but orders a T-bone steak. With french fries. And a double Coke.

He is dreading something. What?

With a flourish a waiter wheels a cart into the room. White linen tablecloth and napkins, a single red rose quivering in a vase, steaming hot dinners, steak for Jared and fillet of sole for Abigail, beneath silver covers; and a bottle of burgundy wine for Abigail. "Isn't this—festive? Like something in a movie. In the south of France?" Why is Abigail saying such inane things: what does Jared know, or care, about the south of France? The most profound adventure of his young life has been a treacherous white-water rafting trip his father took him on the previous summer in the Grand Canyon region, no matter if Jared sprained his ankle in an upset, and another rafter was nearly killed. Abigail sips wine, and asks Jared careful questions. Unlike his father she will not inquire closely into his summer session courses; she would never bluntly ask what his grades have been so far; *she is not spying on him,* she isn't the one who obsesses that Jared will be "sloughed off" from his generation when his generation advances to the next hurdle of the American meritocracy, college. (Not Abigail Des Pres: who studied "arts" at Bennington in the late seventies and graduated with honors knowing less math, science, and history than she'd known when she graduated from high school, with a further handicap of not knowing how to think or write except "creatively"—"spontaneously.") So she takes care to ask Jared questions he can answer without shifting his shoulders edgily inside the black T-shirt and avoiding her gaze.

"Sloughed off"—a cruel term. Abigail has heard her ex-husband use it numerous times. There's a Darwinian-evolutionary sense to it, a ring of fatality.

As they talk, Abigail tries not to stare too avidly at Jared. Tries not to touch him too often. She's well aware of the social decorum: a woman may lightly touch a man's wrist while they speak, in harmless flirtation; a man, touching a woman in a similar way, is perhaps being aggressive. *But Jared will never touch me. What choice do I have?*

Abigail says, "When the session is over, I'll drive up again to bring you home. You're with me, you know, till school starts."

There's a breathless pause here. Abigail tries not to watch Jared's face. His eyes that seem suddenly heavy-lidded, his fleshy sullen mouth. He's chewing steak, forehead creased in concentration. "I thought we might go to—Nantucket? Sailing. You've always liked—sailing."

Jared doesn't reply, chewing and swallowing. He gulps down a large mouthful of his Coke. "O.K., Mom. Cool."

"—the full month of August, through Labor Day. The Sorensons have offered us their guest house on the ocean—"

Abigail has abandoned her food but continues to drink, slowly. She isn't one to drink alone, alcohol goes to her head, red wine especially gives her a heavy sodden headache. She hears her bright scintillate voice echoing in the handsomely furnished sitting room. She hears Jared's monosyllabic replies and occasional forced laughter. *My mom has a sense of humor!* There is something unspoken between her and Jared. Always there is something unspoken between her and Jared. The constant weight of it pulls at her heart, though her heart is young she is becoming exhausted. *Look, I didn't even want to marry. Not that man. Not any man. I was just a girl. God damn, I wanted to be a dancer! No, I was not pregnant at the time. I married for—love.* Suddenly she can't remember who the man was whose love she'd accepted so passively, like one succumbing to the plague. The face—Harrison Tierney's?—is a smear like the uneaten mashed potatoes on her plate.

Adam's death. That must be it. Unspoken between them. But, Christ! She's afraid.

That rambling incoherent message she'd left on Jared's answering machine, the night of Adam's death. When Abigail was paralyzed with shock, grief. When Abigail got frankly drunk. (Roger Cavanagh had come over. To console her. *No, they had not slept together* though possibly that was Cavanagh's intention.) Well, she shouldn't have called Jared. He's fifteen, just a boy. He must have been shocked, overwhelmed: he hadn't answered Abigail's call, or calls. And when she finally spoke with him he'd been taciturn, sullen-sounding. *I'm not coming home.* Abigail feels ashamed, and wonders how to bring up the subject of Adam's death, now. She's worried she might become emotional. The strain of this visit, and the glasses of burgundy. And the memory of Jared striding across the campus, talking and laughing with his friends, lighting up a forbidden cigarette, oblivious of her. For those minutes, magnified in the binocular's lenses, Jared had seemed no one Abigail knew, or could claim. The memory frightens her. But Jared must be feeling grief for Adam's loss. Knowing he will never see Adam Berendt again. Yes. He must! During the worst times Adam had behaved "like a father" to Jared. He'd talked with Jared in private, and would never tell Abigail what they spoke of. He took Jared out walking, bicycling, to quick meals at McDonald's and Burger King. Trying to explain to him, Abigail surmised, what divorce is, how common it has become, what his mother was going through, why she was so—"emotional"—"unpredictable." And what Jared's own natural feelings might be. Abigail knows that Jared liked Adam very much for he always asked after him, as he never asks after Abigail's other friends. But since Adam's death, Jared has been virtually silent on the subject. Abigail sent him clippings from local newspapers—SALTHILL MAN, 50, DIES IN EFFORT TO SAVE CHILD. And SALTHILL RESIDENT A. BERENDT, 54, DIES IN BOATING ACCIDENT ON RIVER. But Jared never responded to the clippings.

In the boy's hooded eyes she can see that he fears her. Perhaps he believes that Adam was her lover. That she has lost, another time, her love. He's deeply embarrassed by her. He pities her. He knew of the biopsy, after the fact; Abigail had wanted to spare him as long as possible. *Your damaged mom. Don't remember this breast, do you? I don't use it anymore, anyway.* She feels her face tightening. A danger of laughing. And laughter is a hairsbreadth from hysteria.

The Madonna of the Rocks. Suddenly, Abigail remembers.

On one of their Manhattan excursions Adam took her to the Frick Museum, that beautiful setting, a setting for romantic love, where Beauty and the Beast (both were Adam's wry terms) might wander in their gilded fairy tale, untouched by Real Time; for Adam loved her, or seemed to love her, while keeping a certain distance from her, unworthy of love he'd claimed, he was unworthy of love, and of happiness, it was wrong of him to tangle himself in another's soul he said, but there Adam was pulling Abigail by the hand to position her before *The Madonna of the Rocks*, by an unknown Florentine artist, circa 1540; forcing her to gaze at the ethereal, waxy-skinned, somewhat fretful and peevish-looking Virgin Mary clutching a squirmy Holy Infant in her rather large hands; against a curious Magritte-landscape of rocks, boulders, sea cliffs, and a dramatically darkened sky; the Holy Infant's head was disproportionately large for his small shoulders, and his halo was alarmingly metallic, as luminous as the Virgin's. Abigail stood astonished and staring, before the centuries-old oil painting as before a mirror only just slightly distorted. Adam nudged her in his chummy way. "So, who's she remind you of, dear?" Abigail's first instinct was to laugh. "But I'm not—am I—like that? Her?" Abigail stammered, "—clutching at her baby with those *hands?* And that desperate—fanatic—look in their faces."

Virgin Mary and Holy Infant, gigantic figures in a rock-landscape.

Virgin Mary and Holy Infant, bathed in holy—or was it unholy?—light.

Beneath the Virgin's bare foot, a writhing, defeated, wicked-eyed serpent.

Adam said, "See? The snake? The Madonna of the Rocks has the power to subdue Satan. And so do *you,* Abigail."

The caressing-melting sound of *Abigail* in Adam Berendt's roughened voice. In memory, as at the time, Abigail feels a shiver of something like dissolution; her eyelids quiver shut.

But what does it mean, she wonders: the power to subdue Satan?

She drains her glass of wine. It's another time. This unexpected place. And Jared glaring at her as if he can read her dazed erotic mind. "Hey, Mom? How's about dessert?"

Jared dials room service to order for himself. Abigail is impressed, as she is at such times, by her son's capable manner. He can talk to desk clerks, airline personnel, taxi drivers, in mimicry of adult authority. More relaxed now, actually smiling at his mom. *Hey. We get along O.K., it's weird!*

But how long can Abigail hold on to her son, here? It's not even eight P.M. He will want to get back to the campus by nine. As usual Jared devoured his meal swiftly. Abigail hardly touched hers.

Day before yesterday, pondering this trip, Abigail went to the Salthill Bookstore under the pretext of buying some paperback novels to take along (she hasn't read Jane Austen in years, feels it's time to reimmerse herself in that sentimental-astringent seriocomic world of triumphant female will), but really she wanted to speak with Marina Troy; Marina, Abigail's most elusive Salthill acquaintance, whom she hadn't seen since the morning of Adam's cremation. Abigail hoped to commiserate with Marina, yes, she'd heard that Marina had been ill, was going to invite her to lunch to ask her, with some embarrassment, if as Adam's personal executor Marina had yet come upon any of Abigail's personal letters to Adam. *Yes, I'm ashamed! Love letters written to a man who didn't respond. But—I couldn't help it.* But this was a surprise, something of a shock, as soon as Marina Troy saw Abigail step into the store, the little bell tinkling over the door, she turned away, rigid and white in the face, distracted, nearly rude, fleeing from both Abigail and another customer—"I'm sorry, I can't help you now. I'm too busy." Marina Troy in one of her ratty jumpers, bare-legged, unshaven legs, rust-red hair straggling down her back. Amid stacks of unsold books, some of them piled on their sides, on the warped-tile floor. Those eyes! Brimming with tears of alarm and fury. In that instant Abigail saw the eccentric woman as a sister-mourner, a sister-widow. And a rival. *Is Marina jealous of me? And I, of her?* Adam would have shaken his head at their folly, laughing.

Abigail says suddenly, as if this were the solution to a riddle she and Jared have been puzzling over, "'Thwaite' was the name." Jared is eating pecan pie and vanilla ice cream, skimming TV channels. Mostly local Vermont news, which interests him not at all. He won't like it that the Mountain View Inn doesn't have cable, Abigail steels herself for his scorn. "—the child in the river. The eight-year-old girl whom Adam tried to save."

Jared says, not looking at her, clicking fiercely through the small cycle of channels, "'Tried to'—? He *did*."

"Well, he did. But—"

"What you sent me, in the papers, they're saying he *did*."

"Well, yes. He did."

"Mr. Berendt was, like, a hero. And those asshole kids, fooling around in a fiberglass sailboat, on the Hudson River!" Jared is almost speechless with disgust.

"It was," Abigail says slowly, conscious of the pitiful inadequacy of her words, "—an accident. Oh, God."

Jared says, "Some people think there aren't any accidents."

"Well, when you get older, you see, honey, there *are*. In this case the conjunction of—unsupervised children in a sailboat, and Adam, and Adam's personality, and his—cardiac condition."

Jared doesn't want to hear about Adam Berendt's cardiac condition. Any discussion of the physical conditions of his elders, including even their ages, makes him squirm in adolescent mortification. To acknowledge that such old people have bodies—! Jared says disdainfully, "There's a 'Thwaite' at Preston, a guy. I don't know him." Almost inaudibly he mutters, "*He's* an asshole, too."

Abigail, who despises the Thwaite parents, the ignorant selfish strangers whose parental neglect precipitated a tragedy, feels she should defend them, as one erring parent might defend another, to lighten the charge against herself. "The parents are very—stricken. They've said so, publicly. The little girl, Samantha is her name—you wonder what she'll be told. That a man died for her."

Jared says, sharply, "Mr. Berendt didn't die for *her,* jeez, Mom! You exaggerate all the time. He didn't know who the hell she was, or any of them. He just did it. You know what he's—he was—like."

Was. Abigail shivers at that word, in Jared's mouth.

Abigail has had dreams of *Thwaite,* not that pretty little blond-haired girl whose picture was briefly in the local media, but

Thwaite as an impersonal force like electricity, mud; a substance into which you fall, and sink, even as you struggle to escape; the muck into which Adam fell, and sank. *Unworthy of love, why? Unworthy of happiness, why?* For a long moment, staring blindly at her angry-looking son surfing TV channels, punching at the remote control with childish violence, Abigail can't speak. She feels how close she is to that dissolution, herself. A sudden turn of the car's wheel as she'd sped north along the interstate, oblivion in flaming wreckage against a concrete overpass upon which fading red graffiti proclaims LOVE FUCK SUCK BELLINGTON H.S. '00.

Well, Abigail Des Pres did not succumb. And will not.

Pouring herself another half-glass of this quite good, tart, thrilling burgundy.

For the fifth or sixth time Jared clicks onto a baseball game being played in some luridly bright-green space. "Fucking Mets. Those shits." Clicks onto an overloud overbright advertisement for razor blades. Clicks onto an overloud overbright advertisement for—

Abigail cries, exasperated, "Jared, God *damn*. Turn that damned thing off."

Jared clicks the set off and tosses the remote control down onto the carpeted floor with enough violence to break it.

Abigail laughs.

"Apollo! You should see that poor dog."

"What about Apollo?" Jared asks, immediately concerned.

Jared who has never had a dog of his own, loved Apollo. Walking with Adam above the river and in Battle Park, and Apollo trotting ahead. The husky-shepherd invariably barked excitedly at Jared's approach. Jared hugged the dog, buried his face in the dog's silvery coat. Once, appalled, Abigail witnessed her son who shrank from her kisses as from a bad taste, turn his face to Apollo's lavish tongue-stroking kisses, letting the dog lick even his eyes, his grinning mouth.

Abigail says quickly, "Apollo is—all right. He's heartbroken, of course. He keeps turning up. People's houses. Early in the morning. Before we're awake. He brings us things of Adam's, an old glove, a shirt." Abigail has saved the old gnawed gardening glove, a talisman from the other world. She recalls the mysterious scratching beneath her bedroom window: how could the dog know precisely where Abigail's bedroom is, in the sprawling house with six bedrooms upstairs, and a guest wing? *Not Apollo, it's Adam.*

But did Adam know the location of Abigail's bedroom?

Abigail sighs dreamily. Thinking of how a few days before his death she'd seized both Adam's hands in hers and kissed them and when he tried to escape she laughed and pressed his hands against her breasts saying, teasing *Oh, what an old prude you are, you're ridiculous* and she'd kissed Adam Berendt full on the lips, laughing even as she kissed him, feeling his sexual arousal, and Adam grunted, his face flaming red, and grabbed Abigail's elbows, and—

Jared is asking, incensed, "But where is he? Where does he *live?*"

"Who?"

"Apollo!" Jared glares at her.

Abigail shakes her head to clear it. It's as if her head is a glass paperweight, filled with snowflakes and a mysterious transparent liquid. "Oh, yes—Apollo. I think he stays with Camille Hoffmann most of the time. Sometimes Marina Troy. I've tried to keep him, I feed him in the kitchen. And he sleeps, sort of fitfully. Then he whines and sniffs around looking for—Adam, I guess. He has actually growled at me. When he can't find Adam, he scratches to be let outside, and I let him out, and he trots off sniffing. Poor thing." Abigail doesn't want to tell Jared that Apollo now limps, his left rear leg was injured.

Jared says with childish hurt, "I hope you guys aren't gonna let Apollo be put down by, like, the Humane Society. Or shot by some cop."

"Camille Hoffmann wants to keep him. She's quite emotional about him. And she's gotten into this strange state where you can't talk to her about Adam being *dead;* you can only talk about Adam being *gone.* 'I think of him as traveling,' poor Camille says, 'and he's out of touch right now. But he'll be back.' Unfortunately Lionel Hoffmann has, I guess, allergies. Dog hairs give him asthma."

A telling little gossipy detail, Salthill adults would want to know more, but the adolescent Jared twitches with indifference.

"Look, *I* can take Apollo. He can live with *me*."

"Oh, honey. You're away at school most of the year."

"Fuck it, if he's *lonely!* He'll get hit by a car, on the road. He's looking for—something he can't find." Suddenly Jared sounds frightened.

Surreptitiously, with one of the linen napkins, Abigail wipes at her eyes. A smudge of mascara. Oh, she's tired of tears! It's laughter she wants.

"If you took in Apollo, he would be living with *me,*" Abigail points out with a mother's tedious logic. "And he doesn't seem to want to live with *me*. He stays overnight, and drifts on." Suddenly this seems a mistake, such an admission. Why doesn't Apollo want to live with Abigail Des Pres? She has rushed out to buy hefty cans of dog meat, dog biscuit. To no avail.

Jared says with sudden wistfulness, "Where is Mr. Berendt buried?"

How many times Adam had asked Jared to call him "Adam." But it's "Mr. Berendt." Like Jared's friends at Preston, who call her "Mrs. Tierney." Or nothing at all.

"Honey. I told you, he isn't."

"He isn't?" Jared looks alarmed. "But where is—"

"His remains, I told you— He requested— He wanted to be cremated."

"Oh. Yeah." Jared swallows hard, shifting his shoulders inside the baggy black T-shirt. Abigail has been able to decode, she thinks, the words on the front: SUCKS floats inside the black cloud DEATH. Meaning, what?—DEATH SUCKS? That sounds right.

Abigail says, trying to smile, "You know Adam, honey! The most practical of men. And funny. Not that he expected to die anytime soon, he was in perfectly good health, but he told Marina

Troy that when he did, die I mean, he wanted—'to be burnt to a crisp.' Isn't that just like Adam?" Abigail tries feebly to laugh.

Between mother and son, what heaviness of emotion. The Madonna of the Rocks clutching with claw hands at her squirmy big-headed baby who knows, God damn, he's the son of God, not just his mother's son. This weight between Abigail and Jared that's so much more palpable here in the Mountain View Inn outside Middlebury, Vermont, than it is back in Salthill where Jared can creep away to his room, to his computer and TV and the telephone, and escape. This weight that has begun to seep and spread, like something leaking from a paper bag. Jared says, hesitantly, "So he's—it's just, like, ashes?—in a vase or something?" and Abigail says, "He requested his ashes be spread, honey. In his garden." Abigail doesn't want Jared to know that she hadn't attended the small private ceremony. Just a few friends, people who'd loved Adam. But not Abigail Des Pres who out of terror, cowardice, smallness of soul stayed away. "His garden, you know how much he loved it. Always a lot of weeds, tall thistles, but so lush and beautiful, pole-beans, and tomatoes, and peppers, sunflowers, goldenrod, that exquisite little orange wildflower that grows like a vine, in the fence—touch-me-not? Adam never worried about weeds, so long as they're green, he said. He—"

Jared interrupts. "That's pretty crappy, Mom, that Mr. Berendt doesn't have a *grave*. You guys should've paid for one, if he couldn't."

You guys. Abigail is both touched and nettled by this remark. Is Jared now going to blame her for Adam's death? She says, "Honey, Adam did have money. He wasn't poor as people thought. In fact, I gather he had quite a bit of money, in bonds, stocks, real estate, and of course his property, he has left to the township—"

Jared persists, an adolescent tracking down adult hypocrisy, trickery, "You guys could've set up some kind of—memorial, monument. Like with some of his ashes?—in a vase?—in an actual cemetery, buried, in a plot? Like normal people? So, if somebody wanted to visit the grave, he could."

"Why do you say 'you guys'?" Abigail protests, hurt. "We were—we are—Adam's closest friends. He seems to have had no living relatives. He was just—Adam Berendt, of whom very little seems to be known. We did what he requested. You can visit the garden. When you come back from summer school, honey, we'll go together! And maybe Apollo will be there, and—"

"Yeah. Cool."

Jared is breathing hard, clearly unhappy. Abigail wonders what he's thinking? And does he blame her, somehow? *For what? I am guiltless!* He has no idea she was spying on him that morning—does he? *Yes. He senses it. Senses something. They all do.* When men desire Abigail Des Pres, she's bored, even angry, with them; when men elude her, she's fascinated, filled with yearning that isn't—she is certain, after all she's been neutralized—sexual, but spiritual.

Adam often dropped by the house, and he and Jared went hiking together in the fields above Wheatsheaf Drive. Apollo trotting ahead. Abigail caught a glimpse of them from the road, the stocky middle-aged man and the lanky adolescent boy talking earnestly together, but when she asked Jared what they'd talked about he told her with an embarrassed shrug *Nothing*. "Jared, it can't be 'nothing,' I saw you," Abigail objected. Jared said, "Mr. Berendt mostly lets me talk." Abigail said, deeply wounded, "Lets you talk! You never talk to *me*."

When Abigail asked Adam what he and Jared talked about, Adam refused to tell her. In that maddeningly reasonable way of his he said he'd never violate Jared's confidence.

Jared's confidence. Abigail thought, what about *hers*?

Adam was damned brave. A true friend. During the worst of the divorce wrangling, when Abigail was sick with despair and anxiety as with a flu, hid in bed twelve hours a day and spoke to virtually no one except Jared, Adam, and her attorney she'd come to despise, Adam went to New York to attempt to reason with Harrison. The men knew each other slightly from Salthill, and had seemed to like each other well enough, in that cautious way of men who meet in social circumstances who would never otherwise meet, and who have little fundamentally to say to one another. Adam had believed he might reason with Harrison Tierney, who was suing for complete custody of Jared on the grounds that Abigail was an unfit mother; a "disturbed, congenitally neurotic woman with no aptitude for motherhood, or life"; the custody suit was futile, for no responsible judge would have ruled in Harrison's favor, yet Harrison in his malevolent, blind way persisted, as if he must now defeat, demolish utterly, this woman for whom he'd once had a fatal weakness, and had loved, and married. Adam, the voice of reason, argued, "The only people to profit from this will be lawyers, you must know that." Harrison said coarsely, "Fuck what I know and don't know, Berendt. I have to set my son an example. What's worth fighting for is worth fighting for all the way." Adam said, astonished, "But, Harry, you aren't going to win full custody, your son doesn't want it, the judge won't rule that way, what's the point? You're punishing Abigail and yourself both." Harrison said hotly, "Bullshit! The point is, Berendt, you and that neurotic bitch are screwing, you want her ass and you want her money, you can have her skinny ass, and all her money, but you're not getting my ass, friend, you're not getting a dime of my money, and my kid, my son, he comes with *me*." There was a curious gloating crudeness in Harrison Tierney's speech, as if, liberated from Salthill-on-Hudson, he was liberated from civility. The two men had met in a midtown bar. Adam, deeply offended, and possibly injured in his pride, that his role as intermediary was so rebuffed, stared at Harrison in silence, then excused himself, paid for his drink, and walked away. ("Wanting to punch the bastard in the face, but then hell, I'd only be arrested, and sued.") Harrison called loudly after him, "Good luck, friend. You're going to need it."

The identical error his hero Socrates made, in his dealings with mankind. That all men are, and wish to be, rational! Abigail Des Pres knows better.

Saying now to her glaring son, with the air of one confessing a crime, "You know, honey—Adam and I were not lovers. We were very close friends. I loved Adam, and I—I think he loved me; but not in *that way*. I'm sorry, honey."

Jared's cheeks flame. His crazy mom!

"Whatever some people have thought. Whatever your father has said." Abigail persists, humbly.

Jared mumbles what sounds like *O.K., Mom.*

"Now he's dead, and—well, he's *dead*. It's the end of that story."

Jared says, a wild edge to his voice, "Death sucks! And it's bor-ing."

"Oh, honey. Don't be upset. I'm sorry."

"The thing about death is," Jared says, stammering, "—I don't give a fuck about it. As far as I'm concerned we're just, like, algae on a pond. Our fucking scummy pond out back of the house! That Dad was always pissed at, it looked stagnant! Well, it was stagnant. Fucking green scum. Like the algae thinks it's a big deal, we think we're a big deal, but we're *not*. Death is just a big nothing—like cyberspace if the last computer went down, and the last memory went out. No big deal. Adam—Mr. Berendt—knew this, for sure, but he wouldn't say so 'cause he was too, too—" Jared searches for the right word, his forehead creasing like an adult man's, can't find the word, fuck it, "—he wanted just to accept things, like in the universe, and get along with people. He'd say, 'Don't wound anybody, but don't get wounded, either.' He'd say, 'Hang in there, kid.' But the fact is, Mom, it—it's all *bullshit*."

"'Bullshit'—what? I thought it was pond algae."

Jared laughs, a harsh barking noise. "Same thing."

Abigail laughs. "Long as you're not smoking, sweetie. Remember, you gave your word. To both Adam, and me."

(Did he? Jared stares, guilty-eyed.)

Saying with childlike sincerity, "I'm sure *not,* Mom. I see those billboards about cancer . . ."

Abigail drains the last of the wine, immediately she's drunk. She'll pay for it in the morning but what a good cozy snug feeling now. "*I* believe in life-before-death," she says, wriggling her bare toes in the plush carpet. "And any kind of bullshit that's attractive and, I don't know, tender." She is still wearing the Italian import cream-colored silk shift, hiking up her thighs. The little jacket has long since been tossed aside. The thin straps keep falling over her naked shoulders. Inside the bodice, the tops of her loose, very pale breasts are just visible. Her smoke-colored hair is disheveled and her dark dreamy eyes are dilated. *What do I want, Adam?—I want my son to be happy. I want to be happy, too. With him. Forever.* Feeling giddy, Abigail alarms Jared by lurching to her feet and pirouetting in his direction, "Honey, it's so damn good to *see you.* So damn lonely *back home.*" Wetly kissing Jared's burning forehead, his burning earlobe, just missing his abashed mouth as he turns, ducks his head, deeply embarrassed. "Jesus, Mom!" Close up, the boy's beautiful smooth contorted face is magnified as in binocular lenses.

Breasts loose and unencumbered inside the silk shift, Abigail smells of her favorite scent *l'Heure bleu* and this is in fact the blue hour, that hour of imminent night and of unquenchable thirst.

Even as Jared squirms away from her without precisely wrenching away, and without shoving her, as he'd like, Abigail thinks calmly that there is a rational, pure, impersonal self inside her; inside even Abigail Des Pres. Beyond her despairing love for Jared there is a place in her that is no one's mother, and loves no one. As Adam has said we are all asleep in the outer self. The self that is perishable, passing. And the boy, her son Jared—in him, there is this identical impersonal self, a being she doesn't know, who loves no one. Swaying, almost losing her balance—"Jeez, Mom!" Jared mutters, keeping her from falling—she feels a thrill of certainty, almost defiance. From now on, she will love both Jared and Adam less.

Time to drive Jared back to the dormitory? Or will he be staying the night?

There's the king-sized bed in the bedroom, and, in the sitting room, this cushiony sofa. In the morning, a room service breakfast?

"Mom, I better go. O.K.?"

Jared backs off, goes to use the bathroom. Abigail, pressing a glass of melted ice water against her heated cheeks, manages to breathe calmly. *Yes yes yes yes.* Or is it *No no no no.* Abigail briskly dials room service to please have the sullied things taken away, there's a food-smell permeating the room. She frowns at herself in a mirror, adjusts the straps that keep slipping over her shoulders, smooths her wild-looking hair, yes she's a beautiful woman, if deranged, and neurotic; hot-skinned, though frigid. *Apollo scratching at my door?* What's it mean? Adam never stayed the night, either.

She's drunk. Or this must be funnier than it is? Or, maybe—she isn't drunk, and it isn't funny? "Oh, hell, it *is*."

Jared emerges from the bathroom, his young face freshly washed, hair flattened, and his steely-blue eyes brave, defiant, fixed upon her. His mom. Abigail sees his mouth moving before she hears his terrible words. *What what what what?* A breathless little speech he has obviously rehearsed. His dad wants to take him to Kenya in August, to visit a wild animal sanctuary "on safari"; and to Tanzania, to hike as far up Mount Kilimanjaro as they can. Jared says, licking his lips, "I'd really like to go, Mom! If it's O.K. with you? Dad says it has to be next month, because—"

No no no no no.

But Abigail hears herself say calmly, "Oh, of course, Jared. If that's—what you want, that's what I want, too. Of course."

"It's O.K., Mom? You're not, like, mad?"

"Oh, Jared. Of course not."

"Jeez, Mom! *Cool.*"

Breaking into a wild radiant smile. The first Abigail has seen from Jared on this visit.

I know, I love him too much. But I am his mother, Adam!

Abigail, the boy knows you love him. But he'll tear himself apart, and you, if he can't love you as much in return.

THE BINOCULARS ARE safely locked in the trunk of the Lexus, Jared will never know.

Driving Jared back to Middlebury. To his dorm.

As Jared chatters excitedly about Kenya, Mount Kilimanjaro, the new camcorder Harrison has bought for their mutual use, Abigail finds herself thinking of the last time she saw Adam. Of course, not knowing *This is the last time;* just as, when Jared leaves her, to travel to Africa with his father and glamorous stepmother ("Kim is crazy about backpacking, too") it may be the last time she will see her son. The words *The last time* echo in her head that feels empty in the way that old public lavatories with filthy cracked tile floors and peeling walls can be empty, and prone to dull echoes.

The last time. Like this?

The last time with Adam, she hadn't known. But she'd known the first time. Years ago. How much younger, less wounded Abigail was then. Abigail Tierney. Mrs. Harrison Tierney. A rich man's rich wife. Attractive couple, in the striking Cape Cod on Wheatsheaf Drive. It was before Abigail heard of this man Adam Berendt, before she saw his witty junk-sculptures around town, or signed up for his course in figure drawing and sculpting, in the Salthill night school. Before she'd fallen in love with him, or imagined it was love. *But how can you love me, Abigail, if you don't know me? C'mon! We've never even slept together. Maybe I'd disgust you, naked. God knows, sometimes I sure disgust myself.*

He'd never given her a chance, God damn it. To be disgusted by him.

She'd felt his aroused penis through his trousers, more than once. It had felt fine, in good operating condition. "God damn *you.*"

Jared, chattering happily, doesn't hear Abigail muttering to herself. The Yankees cap is now visor-forward, at a cocky angle on his head. If he turned to look at her, his eyes would be hidden.

That first time, a man not-Adam. For she had not known him.

By the side of the road, the River Road, a man trudged in the rain. Two dogs trotting beside him. One of the dogs was a bedraggled yellow Labrador, the other resembled a young wolf. Abigail felt a shiver of dislike, repugnance. She knew what Harry would have said, seeing such a sight, on the River Road, Salthill-on-Hudson. Could a homeless man be living here? Somewhere near here? Abigail, slowing her car, regarded the stranger with sharp, critical eyes. He was graceless, primitive-looking. His head, the set of his shoulders, the relative shortness of his legs in proportion to his stocky body, reminded her of—what were they?—Cro-Magnon man, or Neanderthal?—ugly brutes! The stranger wore mismatched clothes, a plaid wool shirt, workpants splotched with what looked like paint, or mud, flapping rubber boots. A dented felt hat, beneath which quills of iron-gray hair escaped, and the collar of his shirt turned up, as if that would make any difference in this chill soaking April rain.

A vagrant, by the look of him. An intruder. A threat.

Vehicles were passing him, on the River Road. As Abigail drove past she felt a sudden pang of—was it guilt, embarrassment, pity?—a nursery rhyme running through her head *If wishes were horses, beggars might ride*. For a fleeting moment she thought she might stop for the man, trudging in the rain, offer him a ride; but, no, what of the dripping dogs, impossible.

So Abigail drove past Adam Berendt, pressing down on the gas pedal so she wasn't tempted to glance over at him, and meet his eye.

As now, driving along a curving road, back into Middlebury. The road is black asphalt, reflectors loom like animals' eyes in the dusk, Abigail is driving at forty miles an hour, maybe forty-five, not fast, her eyelids strangely heavy, hooded, her lips strangely slack, even as Jared continues chattering, excited as a four-year-old about whatever it is, a trip with his dad, he's so excited about, and there's a rising winking moon, a moon like a man's battered face, and Abigail can't for the life of her remember where the hell she is, the car handles differently tonight, the dashboard strangely lighted, and the windshield curving in a way unfamiliar to her, and the windows dark-tinted, so visibility isn't good, and still her foot on the gas pedal wants to press down, a little more pressure, she's in a hurry to get somewhere for the night, must be a town ahead, a motel reservation waiting, oh, but her head is empty! yet aching! and by the side of the road she sees him, a sudden hulking figure, he lifts an arm to beckon to her, can't see his face, she squints, she leans forward anxious, breathless, her headlights illuminate a sign that warns DANGEROUS CURVE 20 MPH and it's at that moment, just as the unfamiliar car flies into the curve, that the demon hand seizes the wheel and wrenches it hard to the right, almost she sees this hand, she will recall seeing it, she will swear she has seen it, not the boy's hand but a demon hand, the rushing asphalt road rapidly narrows, falls away, hardly more than a footpath, she hears screams she could not have identified, a crashing as of a forest of dry sticks being broken, and then—

Nothing.

The Game

I

THERE WAS a man, forty-seven years old. Once he'd believed himself lucky, now he understood that his luck had drained from him. Like his life's blood, or his sperm. These precious liquids you imagine in the prime of young manhood are infinite, and in middle age you understand are finite, and will one day fail you.

What is mortal wishes to be immortal.

"Oh, Adam. Hell. I'd settle for being just mortal, if it meant at least I was alive."

ROGER CAVANAGH. A very good lawyer and among his friends and business acquaintances in Salthill-on-Hudson, New York, a model of integrity.

But God damn: here he was three hours late leaving for his daughter's school near Baltimore. When he'd promised Robin he'd be arriving early in the afternoon so that they could "relax" before the game.

Sure, Dad, I know what your promises are worth.

But his promises did mean something! At least, his professional promises. His word and his handshake were as binding to him as fully executed contracts to others. Roger Cavanagh was a very good lawyer and a model of integrity and since the breakup of his marriage he lived for his work, and for his reputation as *Roger Cavanagh a very good lawyer and a model of integrity.*

"What else is there, really?"

Not women. He'd had enough of women, he was sick of women. His soul, if he had a soul, if that hungry angry emptiness at the core of him was his soul, recoiled in loathing.

IT WAS mid-October. The carefully forged signatures on Adam Berendt's will had not been detected. Roger Cavanagh's integrity remained inviolate.

In his law office that Sunday morning the red-haired woman stunned in grief had asked him naively, not in reproach but with her blunt childlike innocence (that so aroused Roger, even as it annoyed and maddened him, as a man) *Isn't this illegal? Criminal?* and fixing her bruised-looking eyes upon him asked *What would happen if you, a lawyer, were—*

He'd cut her off. Roger Cavanagh would not engage in any conversation with Marina Troy on the ambiguous matter of Adam Berendt's last will and testament, as with other ambiguous matters regarding their deceased friend's estate, that might be considered conspiratorial.

As grounds for disbarment.

"I won't be disbarred. I won't be caught. Who could prove the signatures aren't Adam's? Who would wish to?"

"Marina would never tell. Marina is in love with him."

"Marina would never tell. Marina is implicated, too."

"I had no choice! I had to protect Adam's interests after his death. Since the man didn't do a very good job of protecting them before his death."

Not that these remarks were made to Marina Troy, or to anyone. They were not. They were tersely uttered, as so many of

Roger Cavanagh's most heartfelt remarks were uttered, in the privacy of his BMW.

ROGER CAVANAGH THE MAN of integrity was thinking these things on the harried drive south from Salthill, New York, to the Ryecroft School in Nicodemus, Maryland. He was deeply unhappy. He was anxious about this visit with his daughter, in dread of things going wrong. No, he wasn't unhappy, or anxious: he was angry. His guts like writhing snakes. Strapped into the powerful car like a pilot strapped into a bomber. Shifting from one lane of I-83 to another, impatient to get to his destination yet resentful of having to get there, being obliged to be Dad, yes, but *he was Dad, he loved his daughter*. Muttering aloud, "Fuck. Fuck. *Fuck*."

Late leaving the office, and now he was beginning to be caught up in Friday afternoon traffic. The field hockey game in which Robin was playing began at four P.M. He'd promised Robin he wouldn't be late for the game.

Sure, Dad, I know what your promises are worth.

Adam Berendt had died more than three months before. Yet the wound was still raw. Roger scratched compulsively at it with his nails. Must've liked the raw oozing blood, the dull throb in his veins.

"Your death is an infection in us, survivors. Fuck you!"

No. Bitterly Roger mourned Adam Berendt, he missed his friend enormously. He had a quarrel with Adam that smoldered like an underground fire.

Roger Cavanagh was Adam's attorney, the executor of his estate, he would keep those secrets of Adam's he could. Surprise, shock, incredulity, a kind of baffled hurt—so Adam's Salthill friends had reacted when they learned of the estate Adam was leaving behind. How was it possible! Adam Berendt who'd lived so frugally in the midst of affluent Salthill. Adam Berendt who'd seemed always to subtly disapprove of their lives, in his dry, witty way. Adam Berendt who'd been a local "character" of whom they'd liked to speak warmly, admiringly, and always with that air of condescension. Adam who'd bought secondhand overcoats, suits, even a tuxedo to wear to Salthill parties. He would play their clothing-game, and even seem to enjoy it, basking in their attention; at the same time he was slyly mocking them. He drove an elegantly rust-stippled secondhand Mercedes, even rode a secondhand English racing bike. His dogs were handsome, noble dogs, dogs to break your heart, yet they were strays, cast off by their original masters. *Was it some sort of game? A masquerade?* Adam had postponed, for years, having the rotting, leaking roof of his "historic" house repaired; some of his friends conferred, should they offer to pay for the repairs? Or would Adam be offended? (They'd never summoned up quite the courage to make the offer.) Adam was passionate and idealistic about art, he seemed truly to believe in the high worth of art, but scavenged his own art materials from town dumps; to the frustration of friends like Roger, he gave away his curious, odd-sized sculptures to nearly anyone who expressed an interest, rather than trying to sell them. ("Adam, what kind of compulsion is this?" Roger once asked, "—are you afraid to be a 'professional,' afraid of defining yourself as an artist, and of competing with other artists? But why?" and Adam said, with an embarrassed shrug, and a wincing smile, "Roger! I guess you got my number.") And all along, Adam had been investing in Internet and biotech stocks, and real estate, in utter secrecy from his friends. His brokers were scattered over four states, his savings accounts were under a half-dozen names. Apart from giving away isolated sums of money, often anonymously, to organizations like the National Project to Free the Innocent, the Rockland County Homeless Animal Shelter, the Salthill Arts Council, and the Salthill Environmental Watch, he seemed to have no use for his money. *As if ashamed. Was he ashamed? Something is not right here. Something is very wrong here. Adam Berendt leaving—how much behind?* Ridiculous rumors made their way back to Roger. That Adam was leaving fifteen million dollars, twenty million dollars, to charities; that he owned numerous properties on the river, worth additional millions; that he was a professional who gambled in Vegas under aliases; that he had grown children from whom he'd long been estranged, to whom he was leaving millions of dollars . . . Roger refuted these rumors as he heard them. He was reticent about the actual worth of Adam's estate, but allowed himself to be quoted that it would probably add up to no more than six or seven million dollars once fees and taxes were settled, and this included the "historic" Deppe House.

Ashamed. Sure. Having so much money. More than some of his friends in fact. Saying he didn't deserve happiness. Who the fuck deserves happiness? Not wanting us to know him. That's the reason. That he had money, and didn't spend it on himself. Gave it away. He'd have been ashamed to reveal himself as better, more generous, than the rest of us.

"Except he didn't factor in dying so soon. And 'Adam Berendt' exposed."

2

Uncle Adam. When Robin was a little girl, and very sweet with soft honey-brown curls, and big honey-brown eyes, and very smart with a love of reading and writing though she was such a little girl, and her daddy was still married to her mommy, and Uncle Adam was a family friend, in that long-ago lost time, for Robin's fourth birthday Uncle Adam brought her a big funny book he'd constructed out of papier-mâché covers painted robin's-egg blue, and cream-colored pages of stiff construction paper decorated with friendly cartoon farm animals. The title of the book, in gold leaf script, was ROBIN CAVANAGH: MY STORY SO FAR. Each of the pages had a headline—

PEOPLE I LOVE BEST
PEOPLE I LOVE NEXT
WHEN I WAS *REALLY* LITTLE
WHEN I GROW UP
ON MY NEXT BIRTHDAY
MY SECRET WISHES

What a nice birthday surprise! Childhood is made of such nice birthday surprises, though of course we forget.

Robin loved the robin's-egg-blue book, she'd loved her funny Uncle Adam with the queer staring eye that never exactly looked at you, Uncle Adam who was always making her and her mommy and daddy laugh. While the adults sat at dinner, talking and laughing for hours, how strange we have the passion, the energy, the mutual fluent love that allows us to spend so much time with one another, Robin lay stretched out on her stomach on the fuzzy wool rug in front of the fireplace, and excitedly filled in the entire book. When it was brought to show him, Adam was astonished. "Robin! What a special little girl you are."

Did Robin remember, now? Maybe. Sort of vaguely. ROBIN CAVANAGH: MY STORY SO FAR has long been lost.

That night, eleven years ago, saying good-bye to his hosts, Adam Berendt was deeply moved. He was sober, but shamelessly sentimental. Made you embarrassed, though you loved the guy. Never knew what he'd come out with! Taking Lee Ann's and Roger's hands in his, squeezing, didn't know his own strength, saying, earnestly, "I guess you know how God-damned lucky you are, don't you? Yes?"

"Oh, Adam. Yes." Lee Ann smiled beautifully.

"Yes. We certainly do." Roger smiled, standing tall.

He was a man of hardly five feet ten inches. Always, he made a conscious effort to *stand tall*.

Sure, they'd laughed at Adam afterward, undressing for bed. Adam Berendt was easy to laugh at. Their heated skins pressed together, wine-sweetened mouths kissing, nuzzling. *How God-damned lucky you are*. They knew!

After the divorce, furious with Adam for having been sympathetic with Roger as well as with her, Lee Ann refused to speak with Adam, ever again. She left Salthill to remarry, took Robin with her, and lived now with her investment banker husband in Rye, New York. Much of the summer they spent in Aspen, Colorado, and it was the Aspen number Roger called to inform Lee Ann and Robin of Adam's death. It was Robin who picked up the phone. "Oh, hi—Dad? *You?*" Robin pretended at first not to recognize her father's voice. Her manner with her father (whom she saw not very frequently) had become archly flirtatious in the past two years. Roger never knew how to respond to her, and usually played it straight. He was somber now, trying not to sound agitated. He asked Robin if her mother could come to the phone and Robin said quickly, with an air of satisfaction, that her mother and George (Robin's stepfather) were out, and she didn't know when they'd be back. Roger said, "I'm afraid I have upsetting news, Robin." Always quick at repartee with her father, Robin said, "Upsetting for who, Dad? You, or us?" Roger said severely, "All of us." With a sharp, girlish laugh Robin said, "Then don't tell me, Dad. Tell Mom. *She* can deal with it. You know old armor-plated *Lee Ann.*" Roger winced at the girl's juvenile sarcasm. He tried to envision her plain-pretty face, her hazel eyes so like his own, but could not. *Look, honey. I didn't want the divorce, I didn't want to leave you. Your mother wanted me gone.* He told Robin to tell her mother that he'd call back that evening; he knew that Lee Ann would never call him; if Roger Cavanagh lay on his deathbed, Lee Ann would never call him. But when he called back that evening, Lee Ann picked up the receiver, and said in her cool, languid former-wife's voice, "Yes? What do you want, Roger?"—as she might speak to a telemarketer. Roger told her about Adam's sudden death, and Lee Ann murmured, "Oh! Oh, God." For a long moment she was silent though in the background (was Lee Ann out-of-doors? speaking on a cellular phone?) there were raised excited voices, it sounded like a tennis game, Roger had a blurred image of the flashing of a white ball, tanned legs and swinging arms, his daughter's face screwed up in concentration, but who was Robin playing?—the stepfather?—and Lee Ann said, sadly, sighing, "Adam! But he was always overweight, and didn't take care of himself. It doesn't surprise me. Heart failure! What can you expect, at his age, if you don't take care of yourself? Remember," Lee Ann said, in that impassioned breathy way of hers, building a case against the victim, "how Adam postponed seeing a dentist?—for so long? He was superstitious about his health, so many men are, even intelligent men, and he absolutely hated to spend money, and when finally he went he had to have all that root canal work, poor Adam, remember . . ." Roger listened to this, and to the tennis players in the background, and at first Roger was shocked, and then Roger was disgusted. "That's all you have to say, Lee Ann? I call to tell you that Adam Berendt is dead, in his early fifties, and you're blaming him for his *teeth?*" Lee Ann said sharply, "Adam was your friend, Roger, not mine. He chose you." "Fuck that shit, Lee Ann. Just fuck it!" "And don't use your obscene language with me, I'm not one of your hookers." Before Roger could protest, Lee Ann hung up.

Hookers! It was a tale Lee Ann had wanted to believe, she'd told it so many times she had come at last to believe it.

3

No one else has the power. No one! The lethal power of the ex-spouse.

Roger stopped at a Big Boy on I-83 for black coffee. To bring the fist-banging sensation in his chest under control. The mere thought of Lee Ann and that disgraceful three-minute call left him shaken. Flooded with adrenaline! He sipped steaming-hot bitter-black coffee from a plastic cup. Fuck it, if he burnt his mouth. A red-haired woman seated in a nearby booth distracted him, that freckled pallor, skimpy eyebrows and lashes, but a bloodred juicy mouth, this one was nothing like the Troy woman, the woman he guessed he was in love with, if *in love with* wasn't a lurid joke at this point in his life; this one had two small fretting children and a good-looking linebacker husband, woman of about twenty-eight, normal-seeming, at ease in her female body, not-crazy, with that translucent redhead skin that drew Roger's rapt attention, a virtual kick in the groin . . . "Not her. Don't think of *her*." He was pondering the time: he had about ninety miles to the Ryecroft School, most of it on I-83, which was fairly clear, but then he had to exit on 695 West and from 695 he'd have to drive north to Nicodemus on a busy state highway, and on Friday afternoon . . . Before leaving his law office he'd called Robin, left a message on her answering machine, wincing at the girl's flat dismissive voice. *Hi. I'm not here, I guess! Leave a message at the sound of the beep if you think it's worth it.* A mirthless giggle. *Your message, I mean.* He left a message explaining he was a little late starting out, Dad was going to be a little late but Dad was definitely coming to see her play field hockey, wouldn't miss it for the world, don't wait for him in her residence but go get ready for the game, he'd be there for the game, absolutely. Now, since it was past two P.M., and the game began at four P.M., it looked as if he wouldn't make the start of the game, but—"God damn, *I will be there.*"

Lee Ann had told Roger, via e-mail, their preferred means of correspondence now, that she was "concerned" about Robin. She was concerned that Robin "obsessed" about field hockey, and was neglecting her studies, and seemed to have few friends, and never, "repeat: never" spoke of him to her and George, which, Lee Ann said, "I'm sure you'll agree is not a healthy thing. For after all, you are the girl's father."

Doubtful about the wisdom of calling the baby girl *Robin.* So close to *Roger.* "Robin"—"Roger." *He* hadn't made the decision, Lee Ann had.

He hadn't remarried within eighteen months, Lee Ann had.

He was the wounded one, not Lee Ann.

"Never." Meaning, he'd never remarry. Never again.

He wasn't in love with Marina Troy, the thought was absurd. Their single bungled attempt at lovemaking . . . on the gritty floor of Adam's studio. (In Roger's furious imagination, someone or something was watching them. The damned dog?)

Half-consciously Roger was watching the red-haired woman in the booth. If her beefy husband was aware of him, Roger didn't notice. Lost in a dream. But it was a caffeine-dream, the beat of a heavy pulse. The woman half-carried a fussing round-faced toddler into the women's lavatory, kissing and scolding, and Roger, turning to stare after them, felt a faint, sick sensation. The truth was: he'd loved Robin so much, as a baby; he'd loved Lee Ann so much, as his young, high-spirited wife; he'd even loved, to a degree, the young man he'd been. *Yes, we were happy. And not deluded.* Was disillusion inevitable with middle age? Or was it just a fact that, with the passage of time, things fracture, break, split into pieces? From the age of thirty-one to the age of forty-three he'd been married, and his daughter Robin, his only child, had been born in the second year of that marriage. That long-ago time. Twelve years married! Now, it felt like an amputated limb.

He would marry again, sometime. He was a man of fierce passions and appetites and he would love a woman again, he had to believe this would happen.

Pathetic asshole. Even as a lawyer you're mediocre.

Roger bought a second steaming cup of coffee to take with him in the car. Since his friend's death he'd become acutely conscious of his heart: if it was going to beat oddly, he wanted to know the cause was caffeine. Yet still he lingered in the restaurant. Gazing toward the door of the women's rest room, which was continually being pushed open, swinging shut, pushed open and swinging shut and at last the red-haired young woman emerged with the toddler, and Roger saw to his disappointment that she wasn't so attractive as he'd believed, she really looked nothing like Marina Troy. The young woman glanced up quizzically at him as if wondering should she know this man, this sharky-looking guy in his mid- or late forties with a narrow dark calculating face and graying dark hair receding from his forehead, and in the same instant Roger sighted a tall figure approaching in the corner of his eye, the woman's linebacker husband, no thanks! Clamping the lid tight on the cup, Roger fled the Big Boy.

Not wanting to hear the exchange.

That guy, he's somebody you know?

Him? No.

The way he was looking at you.

So? Let him look.

Ashes. Quietly she'd murmured, in that low-throaty voice that seemed deliberately to provoke him, and the corners of her mouth twitching, "It isn't a dead man's ashes you spread, is it?

It's the dead man himself." This bizarre statement was made as Roger, with a strained smile, conscious of eyes upon him, carried the urn into the garden. Thinking *Jesus Christ! Let us not fuck this up, too.* At least it was a still, windless day. An opaque pale sky through which sunlight penetrated like the beginning of a migraine. Adam's ashes dumped from the urn, mostly bone chunks and powdery grit would at least not be blown back into their faces.

They'd invited only Adam Berendt's closest friends to the ceremony. Ten days after his death. Marina, who'd been keeping the urn in her house, said she couldn't bear it any longer, they had to put Adam's ashes *to rest.*

Roger agreed. No point in keeping Adam's ashes in an urn on a mantel, if you knew Adam wanted to be raked into the soil of his garden. (Except in fact would Adam now give a damn? That is, would Adam, if he could know, have seriously cared where he, or his ashes, ended up? Not likely.)

"Ceremonies! They mean nothing really, yet without them we sink into grief."

Since the morning of their bungled lovemaking in Adam's studio, of which neither Roger Cavanagh nor, he assumed, Marina Troy wished to think, the two were stricken with shyness, and a deep disgust and rage beneath, in each other's presence. Roger was a man for whom impotence of any kind, especially sexual, was humiliating; if he'd been impotent once, very likely he'd be impotent again; it was the start of a curse, and Marina Troy was to blame. No, Adam Berendt was to blame. Marina Troy was the witness, the innocent victim. Incredibly, Marina Troy had *struck Roger with her fists.* But it was Roger's fault, he knew. He loathed himself, knowing. The woman scarcely looked at him now. There was still the powerful sexual attraction between them but it had turned spiteful, mocking. Roger was conscious of the woman's heavy-lidded eyes, her gaze that brushed past him as if he were no more than a cloud of gnats, even as she spoke with him, and was obliged to speak with him, for they were connected through the dead man, and could not so easily avoid each other. Roger called Marina, and Marina never picked up the phone, even when Roger knew she was home; if he called the bookstore, Marina's assistant claimed that Marina wasn't in; even when Roger called from his car parked on Pedlar's Lane, and knew absolutely that Marina was in the store; he thought, *This is how a man becomes a stalker, a criminal: he is driven to it by a woman.* But no. This was absurd. Roger was not a man to force himself upon any woman, even in the interests of a third party. He would win over Marina Troy as he won the majority of his law cases, by the force of his seriousness, his integrity, his lawyerly cunning. He understood that Marina was afraid of him and that she resented him for being alive, while their friend was dead, and with this sentiment Roger sympathized. *But I am alive, and Adam is dead.* He could not believe that Adam and Marina had been lovers, no matter what others believed. He seemed to know that Adam had resisted the Salthill women who adored him, perhaps he'd always resisted women who adored him, not for a moment had Roger supposed that the cache of letters and gifts Marina had discovered in Adam's studio meant that Adam had been the lover of any of these women. He wanted to assure Marina of this, to console her, but of course, he could not speak to her of such things, she'd been too deeply wounded, made ashamed. *And I am her witness. No wonder she hates me!* Roger called Marina, and left messages on her answering service; she never failed to call back, for she was a courteous, scrupulous person, but invariably she called when she knew that Roger wouldn't be home, and her messages on his answering machine, which made him shiver, were almost inaudible, but precise; she sounded like someone speaking from a coffin buried in the earth. Always when she returned Roger's calls she identified herself as *Marina Troy*. As if Roger might confuse her with another *Marina* of his acquaintance.

Both Roger and Marina had keys to Adam's house on the River Road but if one saw the other's car in the driveway, of course, that one drove quickly away.

Except, that morning. Spreading Adam's ashes in his garden. It was to be a joint effort, this ceremony. Roger and Marina, and the others looking on.

(Abigail Des Pres had stayed away, she'd told Roger she was sick with grief, and anyway she hated ceremonies—"Any kind of ritual that's impersonal, and phony." And Camille Hoffmann had stayed away, her husband Lionel reported, with mild embarrassment, because it was too painful for Camille to acknowledge that Adam was dead—"She prefers to think that he's alive, only just traveling and out of touch. Temporarily." But there was Augusta Cutler, glamorous as a fashion mannequin in dark glasses, wide-brimmed straw hat, and a low-cut summer dress the color of poppies, staring avidly at Adam's garden, at plants and wildflowers and weeds, as if all were sacred, and she meant to memorize it. A nymph ripened to middle age, yet unbelieving she was middle-aged and not rather young, younger even than her grown children; Roger could sympathize with Augusta, though she made him uneasy. Her sweet rich perfume wafted through the garden, overwhelming even the hearty, musky smell of the tomato plants. She leaned on her husband Owen's arm only because her stylish high-heeled shoes sank into the soil. Augusta was the only person smiling in Adam Berendt's garden and her smile was porcelain-perfect, adamant. Even as she swiped at her brilliant smudged eyes she continued to smile as if for Adam's sake, at this ceremony in honor of Adam. Her fingers curled into Roger's hand and squeezed, hard. She leaned close, perfumey and bosomy, to murmur in Roger's ear, "Roger! Thank you *so much* for arranging this. Only *you* have really taken charge, in this disaster. How happy Adam would be, wouldn't he, if he could see us! Adam loved his Salthill friends, *we were all he had.*" This pronouncement, which seemed dismaying to Roger, was clearly a joyous pronouncement to Augusta. Roger was reminded of the nude photos of the voluptuous Mrs. Cutler inscribed to Adam, the lush mammalian body on the sofa, dreamy but masklike face offering itself to be kissed. Unless Marina had taken them away, or destroyed them, which seemed unlikely, these photos were probably still in Adam's studio amid the cache of adoring women, and it seemed to Roger that Augusta knew this, and knew that he knew, she looked at him so pointedly, with that mysterious smile.

Whispering, "It isn't really over, is it?—with Adam, I mean. Our love.")

Adam's weedy garden! It was beyond the old stone house, marked off by a five-foot wire fence Adam had himself erected; in his practical mode, Adam was one to get things done, and capably. But he'd never been a fastidious gardener, and now his garden was overgrown with weeds. In a promiscuous tumult it seemed to be celebrating his absence. The very air was thicker here, more moist. Clouds of gnats drifted against your mouth, caught in your eyelashes. There were monarch butterflies with wide pulsing wings, and other varieties of flying insects glittering like tiny gems in the air. And bees making their way from one ripe blossom to another, especially thick amid the pale yellow tomato blossoms, bent upon the task of spreading pollen. There came mosquitoes out of the tall grasses above the river, drawn by the scent of living blood, and gently these frail creatures, hardly more than line drawings by, say, Saul Steinberg, alighted upon their victims' bare skin; Roger absentmindedly crushed a mosquito against his forehead, his fingers came away stippled with blood. He saw a mosquito hovering near Marina Troy's neck and daringly brushed it away and Marina, white-lipped, frowning, took no notice. *I love you. Can't you forgive.* For an occasion of such gravity, Marina wasn't very well groomed. She wore a shapeless black sheath that drooped to mid-calf, shimmering fabric that clung to her slender hips and thighs with static electricity; you could see, if you chose to look, the impress of her pelvic bones; her legs were very pale, and bare. Tangled dull-red hair falling down her back. The sight of this hair, its imagined rich rank scent aroused Roger's senses, even as he carried the urn into the garden, he saw himself as Marina's lover shutting his fist in that hair, pressing his mouth against the white neck beneath the hair, licking the clammy skin, except the thought was repugnant, Roger Cavanagh who was fastidiously groomed, clean-shaven and his hair recently trimmed, like his friend Lionel Hoffmann, like his friend Owen Cutler, like his friend Avery Archer—*Roger Cavanagh was one of these men.*

Spreading human ashes, raking them into the soil: not so easy a task as Adam had imagined. (But Adam hadn't imagined any of this, really. Roger was pissed at Adam, setting these wheels in motion.) Before you can rake ashes into the soil you have to dig up the soil, you have to tear out weeds, and plenty of weeds there were in Adam's garden, among the tomato plants, among the sweet-corn stalks, among the pole beans, the bush beans, the zucchini and squash vines; dominating over the remains of the lettuce, now bolted and gone luridly to seed like exposed genitals. Everywhere in the garden were dandelions, thistles grown knee-high, a stringy-nasty bastard of a vine with tiny golden flowers that, when you tugged at it, as Roger had done, cut into your hands like wire. Marina had tried to help but wasn't very effectual, swinging a hoe, so vacant-eyed, clumsy. Roger, who had absolutely no patience for outdoor work, was the one who'd cleared a patch of soil near the tomato plants, before the others arrived, but now that they were here, naturally they had opinions, Beatrice Avery was saying how, last time she'd visited this garden, in Adam's company, in June, Adam had been particularly proud of the sunflowers, look how tall the sunflowers were growing, taller than any man, ruddy-faced, blazing-yellow, let's spread Adam's ashes beneath the sunflowers at the back of the garden, but Roger cut off the woman's proposal, before someone else could chime in, God damn it was too weedy there. He wasn't doing any more weeding, hoeing, and raking in this God-damned garden, now or ever.

This quieted Beatrice Avery, and anyone else who'd had a new idea. Roger thought *Fuck you all, if you don't like my attitude.* He was sweating, conscious of a sick churning sensation in his gut as awkwardly he held the urn, turning it sideways, and Marina pressed near, breathing quickly, as if Adam's very spirit were present, and his dignity at risk, Marina murmured, "Let me do it, please *let me do it.*" Roger would recall afterward that she had not called him *Roger,* she had called him nothing at all as if he'd had no identity to her. Almost forcibly Marina took the heavy urn from Roger, and with misgivings, Roger relinquished it, and suddenly it slipped from Marina's fingers and fell heavily to the ground, and on all sides there were indrawn breaths—

"Oh!" Roger cursed under his breath, or maybe not under his breath, "Fuck it," and, face burning, squatted above the urn and dumped the ashes out of the God-damned thing, not very ceremoniously, simply lifting the bottom of the urn and shaking the ashes, bone chunks and powdery grit, out onto the soil. *How'd I deal with this absolutely freaky thing,* Roger would afterward recall, *I pretended it wasn't me doing it and what came out, wasn't anything human.*

Solemnly they hoed and raked this residue of a human being into the soil. It took some time, for it was more than simply an idea, it involved actual hoeing, raking, patience, concentration. Overhead an enormous airliner passed with excruciating slowness, both the air and the ground vibrated, it was maddening, yet had to be endured. Some twenty of their Salthill friends were witnesses, mostly silent and solemn and only just Augusta Cutler broke into unexpected tears, but just possibly these were tears of ecstasy, the moment was for her a moment of sacred consummation with Adam Berendt, who could tell? Roger's concentration was on not sneezing but he began sneezing anyway—"Excuse me! God *damn.*"

Following the ceremony everyone quickly departed. Except Marina Troy lingered, kneeling amid the fresh-tilled soil. "Marina, you'd better come with me," Roger said in his severe-lawyer manner, but Marina scarcely acknowledged him. He knew, if he touched her, the force of that touch would strike him in the groin, sharp as a knife blade, halfway he wanted this sensation, but no, he was a man of reason and wanted nothing to do with it, or with the woman. She wasn't even attractive! If he wanted to be involved with a woman, he much preferred a beautiful woman, a woman like Abigail Des Pres. He hurried to his car, eager to escape. Spreading Adam's ashes had been strangely exhausting. And being in Marina Troy's company was strangely exhausting. His sexual being had been nullified by that woman, she seemed utterly unaware how she'd insulted him in his masculinity, why was he drawn to her again?

"I'm not. Adam, you had the right idea: *don't get involved.*"

The last glimpse he'd had of Marina Troy she was kneeling in the garden, a small figure nearly obscured by vegetation, bright-winged butterflies fluttering above her head.

Since that time he'd seen Marina only infrequently in Salthill, at a distance; out of tact and resignation he stayed away from Salthill Bookstore, and never called her. He would never! Except, one evening in early September, returning from an engagement with a woman he knew in Manhattan, with whom sometimes, as if to keep up a fading acquaintance, he slept, there he was dialing Marina Troy's home number, intending to leave a short, neutral message, "Marina? It's Roger. I'd like to see you, O.K.?"—but the phone rang and rang in the shingleboard colonial on North Pearl Street, unanswered. Next day Roger entered the Salthill Bookstore to learn, from a woman he'd never seen before, who introduced herself as manager of the store, that Miss Troy was "away." Astonished, Roger asked, away where?—but the woman shook her head gravely and only just repeated, "Away."

"But for how long?"

"For"—the woman hesitated— "a year."

"A *year?* Did you say—*a year?*"

Roger was more than astonished, he was beginning to be enraged.

"That seems to be the plan. That's all I know."

"But—where is Marina? She's a friend of mine."

The woman was young, but prim-faced and disapproving. She frowned like one entrusted with a secret that weighed upon her like a giant key on a chain around her neck. "If you're a friend, Mr. Cavanagh, Miss Troy would have told you where she's gone, I think."

Roger said angrily, "Marina is more than a friend, she's involved in Adam Berendt's estate, she has responsibilities, she can't just disappear for a *year.*"

But the young woman shook her head, adamant. No she would not tell Roger Cavanagh where Marina Troy was. And there was some ambiguity in her remark, some slight, subtle evasiveness in her face, that led Roger, trained to decipher the most subtle nuances of speech in any adversary, to conclude that possibly she didn't know where Marina was, herself. "But you must be in contact with her, if you're managing the store while she's away?"

"Miss Troy contacts *me*. When she wants to."

In a fury of disgust Roger left the Salthill Bookstore, the little bell trembling above the door.

Not one of their mutual friends knew where Marina had gone. Several women expressed surprise and hurt that Marina had left without saying good-bye. All shared Roger's sense of having been betrayed. Camille Hoffmann admitted knowing that Marina was planning to be away for a year, that she'd leased her house to a tenant, but Marina had refused to tell her where she was going, or to provide a telephone number or a P.O. box. "It's as if everything is falling apart now, into chaos," Camille said, with a forcefulness that surprised Roger, who'd never taken Lionel's wife very seriously; the woman's warm brown eyes brimmed with hurt, yet with the courage to withstand hurt, "but we won't despair, will we? None of us. *I* certainly will not."

There came into the room suddenly a large wolflike dog—Adam's Apollo. He seemed not to know Roger, he was growling menacingly, toenails clicking on the floor and hackles raised, his tawny eyes widened. Roger hadn't seen his friend's dog for months and was surprised that Apollo was so healthy-looking, though lean, with something feral about his jaws. His silver-tipped fur was coarse and gnarly, yet he was a handsome dog. "Apollo! You know me." In that instant Apollo recognized Roger, his master's friend, and began to bark excitedly as a puppy. You could see him transformed into a puppy. Sniffing about Roger's legs and crotch, licking his hands, an old eager friend.

Quietly Camille said, "He's boarding with me. Until Adam returns from wherever he is—the Grecian islands, I think."

4

THERE WAS ROBIN on the hockey field!—his heart leapt with pride, Roger sighted his daughter immediately. Her fair-brown hair swinging in a ponytail, that was new. Swiftly and determinedly she was charging at the edge of the pack of girls, hockey stick at the ready. The ball, not at the moment near Robin, was struck by an opposing player, the ball flew, skidded on the field, a Ryecroft center in a green uniform snatched it away, a tall platinum-blond wide-shouldered girl, there were cheers at the sidelines, shouts of encouragement. How beautiful the girls were at this distance, most of them taller than Robin, strong-limbed, bearing their wicked hockey sticks like Amazon warriors. Roger stared, transfixed. It was hard for him to keep Robin in sight amid the confusing action, he'd arrived too late for a seat in the small three-tiered bleachers and stood at the sidelines far from the center of play. There came Robin again swinging her stick, and this time snatching the ball from a rival, her hard-muscled legs pounding as she guided the ball zigzag fashion down the field in the other direction, passed it to a teammate who seemed literally to fly with it, the ball leapt, skidded, slammed into the rivals' net, as the desperate goalie lunged and fell. More cheers! Roger joined in, shouting. "Great play! Great!" He was hoping that Robin had caught sight of him. She'd know now that her dad was here, hadn't let her down.

As in the past, not often but once or twice, unavoidably, for very good reasons he'd been at pains to explain, he had.

He hadn't been very late after all, he'd missed only the first quarter of the game. The other team was ahead by only two points. He stood with cheering Ryecroft supporters, a scattering of adults and adolescents, mostly girls. Though the Ryecroft School was now co-ed, it had been a girls' school for a century, and had a reputation in the east as a girls' school of the hardy second rank, attracting fewer boys, and not very good students among these; as Robin said scornfully, the girls were what boys are supposed to be, and the boys were mostly losers.

At halftime Roger made his way to the Ryecroft side to wave to Robin, say hello, and saw to his shock that the tall adroit pony-tailed girl wasn't his daughter! There was Robin in fact, shorter, with a thicker frame, her hair a darker brown, frizzed and damp from perspiration; Roger waved at her, caught her eye, and Robin smiled a restrained smile, lifted her fist in a gesture of victory, which Roger mimicked in return. He cupped his hands to his mouth. "Love ya, honey!" Robin didn't appear especially elated to see her dad, playing it cool perhaps, of course she'd been disappointed to get his phone message, he hadn't been able to make it before the game as they'd planned, or maybe she was simply distracted by the game, the pressure and excitement. Team sports: Roger knew the intoxication, the almost unspeakable animal-joy that runs through a pack of young people united in a single, finite effort. He knew, and halfway envied Robin.

The referee's whistle, and play resumed. Roger had found an empty seat in the third tier of bleachers. He was drawn into the game, began to care about the game, wanting the green-clad team to beat the blue-clad team, willing his girl Robin to excel. (The fact was, Robin had never been a graceful loser even as a little girl. Even playing kiddie games with her dad she'd needed to *win*. He dreaded her sulking through another dinner, this time at the three-star Hanover Inn in Baltimore he'd reserved for them that evening. And beyond that was Washington, D.C., a father-daughter weekend together.) Roger was often on his feet, squinting to see Robin, trying to follow the action. Shouting with other supporters until his throat was hoarse.

A game, any game is any game, a game like any other game, indistinguishable. Except if you're on the playing field, then each game is unique. It's your life.

In high school, Roger had been on the track team for a while, and on the swimming team for a while. He'd been quick and clever and fairly well-coordinated but, shorter than most of the guys on teams, he hadn't the stamina required for competitive sports, maybe he hadn't had the necessary will, the drive to win at mere games. In college, he hadn't gone out for sports at all. Sports seemed to him an idiotic squandering of time, energy, talent. Student athletes revered by others seemed to him frankly deluded about the world. Victory isn't to the swiftest of body but to the swiftest of mind. Roger Cavanagh would cultivate not his body, though he liked his body well enough, but his mind. *And this too, a game. You have no choice but to play.*

Ryecroft scored a goal, the game was tied. Then the other team scored two goals. In the final quarter, the teams were tied again. Tension! Suspense! Roger stood and shouted with the others, trying to keep his girl in sight. But kept losing her. And kept losing the thread of why he was here. *Look, Robin: you know I love you, don't you?* But he kept thinking of Marina Troy. Wondering where she'd gone, and without telling him. For they were co-conspirators. They'd committed a misdemeanor together. Especially, such a violation of law could have serious consequences for Roger Cavanagh, attorney-at-law. Yes, but he was concentrating on Robin's game. Yes, he understood that his yearning for Marina Troy was absurd, and beyond that it was futile. He did care about the ferocious Ryecroft girls, these Amazon warriors thundering up and down the field, up and down the field, brandishing their scythe-like hockey sticks. The ball might have been a human head. No, too small. Male genitals? Maybe sometime in history, anthropologists would know, morbid research, what it unearths about mankind's playful customs, decorum, civilization itself. Adam Berendt had seemed to view their suburban-Salthill world as if he'd drifted into it from another planet, a place of cooler, drier air, clear-sightedness, that single staring eye, yet he'd seemed to forgive them, too; he'd seemed to like them as, mysteriously, they had not always been able to like or even tolerate themselves.

Cave-dwellers. Dwellers among shadows. How to escape? But—escape to what?

Good athletes become better athletes under duress, less-good athletes begin to falter. Roger felt pain seeing that his daughter was being outplayed by the blue-clad wing as the game continued, she'd become flush-faced and surly and clumsy. (In all fairness to Robin, she wasn't the only girl whose playing had visibly deteriorated, as that of two or three star athletes was becoming spectacular.) But there, determined, dogged, Robin galloped on her powerful legs, swung her stick, colliding with other equally determined and dogged girls. Roger recalled his daughter in a bathing suit, the previous summer, those thick fatty-muscled thighs, amazing, sturdier than his own, far larger than Lee Ann's;

not that Robin was heavyset exactly, but big-boned, a girl who could never be slender. And she was easily flummoxed. In the midst of a protracted play, as the ball flew by her, she turned desperately, lunged with her stick, swung and missed and at a clumsy angle, the ball was taken from the Ryecroft girls and went flying down the field for an easy goal, and—where was Robin? Fallen to the ground.

But immediately on her feet. Before anyone could help her.

Still, she was limping. Time was called, the coach removed her from the game. *God damn, just our luck. Oh, honey.* She was his little girl again, in need of her dad.

BUT ROBIN INSISTED, with a bright plucky smile, that she was all right, she'd only just made a mistake and slipped—"Or maybe she elbowed me. But it was my mistake."

She was trying not to cry. A big-boned flush-faced girl who smelled of exertion, hair plastered to her forehead and her breath still quickened. After the game, which in the last few minutes of playing the Ryecroft team narrowly won, she gave her anxious dad a quick, hot kiss, twisting away from him even as she pressed against him even as he meant to hug her. Since the divorce there was a physical awkwardness between them. Roger said, "Honey, you were great. You all played wonderfully. I was watching every—"

Robin cut him off, embarrassed. "Sure, Dad."

Somewhat flippantly, though possibly with pride, since Roger was still a reasonably youthful, attractive man, Robin introduced him to several of her elated teammates who smiled shyly and called him "Mr. Cavanagh." Then she went off, trying not to limp, with the team to shower and change, and would meet Roger at her residence hall in about an hour. Roger watched the girls walk away. Their mood was rowdy and jubilant, they'd won by a single goal, and that had been a fluke—the most delicious kind of victory. The kind you don't really deserve.

He was grateful for the free hour. He went for a drink at the town's single hotel, a Hyatt Regency with a cocktail lounge behind a waterfall. God, how shaken he was! He hadn't realized. The excitement of the game, the shock he'd felt seeing Robin down. The strain to the heart in being somebody's dad. Did you ever get used to it?

A double Scotch, with water.

Madonna of the Rocks. She'd told him about the painting in the Frick. She couldn't recall the artist's name. *Mother love gone wrong*.

She called Roger often when they were both in Salthill, to invite him for dinner. Sometimes with friends, and he'd accept; sometimes alone, and he'd decline. He knew what might happen if he and Abigail Des Pres were alone together in her house. That beautiful lonely-echoing Cape Cod on Wheatsheaf Drive in which the tragic divorcée continued to live, out of inertia perhaps. Like a princess under a spell. Sleeping Beauty. *But I'm not the prince to wake her with a kiss*. Abigail Des Pres was a lovely appealing woman, and not in need of money, but she was one of those women who adored Adam Berendt even after his death, and Roger wasn't going to compete with a dead man. Adam had been formidable enough when alive.

Still, he saw Abigail occasionally. They were romantic friends. They shared certain secrets. Abigail had been a friend of Lee Ann's for much of the Cavanaghs' marriage and believed, with Roger, that he'd been unfairly treated by Lee Ann. "If a man isn't absolutely 'faithful' to his wife it should be discounted, to a degree. But when a woman . . ." Abigail's voice trailed off in disapproving silence. Roger said, annoyed, "I was not unfaithful to Lee Ann. That's one of her stories." Abigail listened gravely. "Yes. I suppose."

He and Abigail were like brother and sister. Their relationship had become, since their mutual divorces, subtly incestuous. They even resembled each other, dark-haired, intense, inclined to suspicion and paranoia. Where Abigail's laughter was high-pitched like glass shattering, Roger's laughter was low-pitched, like gravel being shaken. Abigail was a woman who eroticized her friendships with men, even the husbands of her women friends, out of a nervous desire to please, not out of actual desire; Roger believed that, like many beautiful women of her class, Abigail had been raised to feel no physical desire for anything, not sex, not food or drink. Like one of those exquisitely overbred greyhounds so taut with nerves you can see them trembling. Where Marina was all will, steely and remote, Abigail was without will, soft, yielding, unresisting as water to the touch. Roger knew he could be Abigail's lover if he wished. Sink and sink in the woman, finding no bottom.

In July, shortly after Roger had helped spread Adam's ashes in his garden, Abigail telephoned Roger in distress. She called him at his law office and insisted to his secretary that he speak with her at once, though he was in a meeting—"This is an emergency. It can't wait." When Roger came on the line, Abigail burst into tears. He had difficulty understanding her. "Roger! I need your help. Something terrible has happened."

Roger would recall: something *has happened*. Not *I am to blame. I nearly killed my son and myself*.

Roger drove at once to Middlebury, Vermont, to bring Abigail home. The rental car had been wrecked, Abigail and her fifteen-year-old son Jared had been treated for minor injuries in a local hospital. Abigail's face was bruised and lacerated, one of her eyes blackened. When Roger came into the room she seized his hands and wept with gratitude—"Roger! I will never forget this." Later she would say, "I should have died. It was meant to be." Roger told her not to be ridiculous, she'd only just had an accident. But when he spoke with Jared, separately, the boy was furious, hostile. He too had a battered face, a swollen jaw, cracked ribs and a badly sprained forearm. "Keep her away from me, Mr. Cavanagh! I hate her. I never want to see her again." The boy's father, Harrison Tierney, whom Roger had never much liked, was en route to Middlebury to deal with the crisis.

Roger identified himself to Middlebury authorities as Abigail Des Pres's attorney. Charges against Abigail were serious. It seemed Abigail had been drinking, the alcohol level in her blood was beyond Vermont's legal limit. She'd been speeding along a narrow country road, lost control of her vehicle going into a turn, crashed through a low guardrail, through a ditch, and into a stand of trees. The front of the Lexus had collapsed like an accordion. There were no skid marks on the road. It was purely luck that neither Abigail nor Jared had been seriously injured or killed. Jared hadn't buckled his safety belt, he might have been thrown headfirst through the windshield.

No skid marks. No attempt to brake the car?

Roger told authorities that his client was by nature a gentle, loving mother who since a difficult divorce had been under "severe mental strain." He told authorities that the boy was emotional, and what he might be telling police (that his mother was crazy, had tried to kill them) should not be taken altogether seriously.

Roger would not intervene between Abigail and Jared. The boy refused to see Abigail no matter how she pleaded. He was rude to Roger, whom he called, with obvious contempt, "Mr. Cavanagh." He wanted to quit summer school, he wanted to go home with his father for the rest of the month, then to Africa —on a safari?—mountain-climbing?—if he was sufficiently recovered?—and never see his mother again. Nor did Roger want to meet with Harrison Tierney. In Salthill he'd played doubles tennis with Harry a few times, the man was vicious. Alone among the Salthill men, Harry was known to cheat at tennis. And at golf, and squash. Other Salthill men were gentlemen and would not contest Tierney's claims. Roger had disapproved of Harry, found him personally abrasive but had to admire the man's air of bravado. He seemed always to be having a good time. "Harry doesn't care what we think of him," Lee Ann said, "that's why we think of him." "Don't tell me you find him attractive?" Roger asked incredulously, and Lee Ann said with her thin infuriating smile, "Of course. Women are masochists, haven't you noticed? It's the unspoken cornerstone of marriage." Roger recalled an evening at the Tierneys' house some years ago, one of those large dinner parties that mean so passionately much to women, and which are mostly tolerated and endured by men. Harry joined Roger where he was leaning in a doorway after dinner, smoking a cigarette, for it was a time before cigarette smoking had been completely banished from such occasions. Harry was the evening's host and might have been expected to behave like a host, except he nudged Roger in the ribs, said laughingly, "What's it all about, eh? Some riddle, is it? Chr-ist." Roger smiled, confused. His lawyer-training kept him vigilant at all times. The men were watching a ring of Salthill wives, Harry's wife Abigail, Roger's wife Lee Ann, Beatrice Archer, and one or two other women talking together excitedly, their faces shining like fresh-opened flowers. Candlelight made these women, in their late thirties, strangely beautiful. There was an uncanny innocence and simplicity to their beauty, as if it had never been tested; as if none of these women had ever screamed in the agony of childbirth, writhed and groaned in orgasm, sweated, defecated. As if beneath their expensive clothes their bodies were sleek in perfection as expensive dolls. They floated in that state of party-euphoria when they needed to touch one another, their praise of one another's hair, skin, clothing, beauty was extravagant. Of course, these women were all friends, they'd known one another for years. They were sisters, hatched from the same great egg. It was as if—Roger saw, with Harry's hand on his shoulder in mock-brotherhood—the women sought in one another, as in magical reflecting surfaces, some measure of their immortality. They were bright shimmering petals floating upon the lightless, depthless chaos beneath Salthill which reached to the very molten center of Earth. Roger shuddered, and eased away from Harry Tierney's hand. Harry said, "It means so much to them, doesn't it?" Roger said, "What? Friendship?" "*Is* it 'friendship'?" Harry seemed to consider this for a moment, then dismissed it. "I don't know what 'friendship' is. Call it 'social life.' Like pond algae. Tiny organisms locked together in the most intense intimacy, symbiotic and 'synergistic' and yet—it's only just, in the end, pond algae." Roger, who valued friendship, or wanted to think that he did, as well as love for Lee Ann and his daughter, said, "Harry, come on. You're hosting this terrific party tonight. You come to all our parties." Harry laughed. He had the ease of a killer for hire, he couldn't be touched, himself.

"It wouldn't matter in the slightest if I never saw anyone in Salthill again. And you feel the same way, Cavanagh." Roger said stiffly, "I do? Thanks for the insight." "No need to thank," Harry said, punching at Roger's shoulder as if they were high school kids, "it's gratis."

Through Vermont and New York State countryside of surpassing beauty, Roger drove Abigail Des Pres back home to Salthill. He'd dealt with the car rental agency. He'd arranged for his client to pay a stiff fine for charges of DWI and reckless driving. Abigail's driver's license would be suspended for six months. He did not ask her pointedly about the absence of skid marks on the road, but after some time, roused from her lethargy, examining her bruised and lacerated face in a compact mirror, Abigail began to speak of having been "under a spell" and unable to act at the time of the accident. She was always such a careful, cautious driver; such a timid driver; but something had forced her to drive fast that evening, though she wasn't familiar with the Lexus, and didn't know the road. She had not been actually intoxicated, she insisted. She'd experienced everything with a terrible clarity. "It was as if a hand turned the wheel. Turned the wheel to the right. To take us off the road. A demon-hand." Roger said casually, "A 'demon-hand'?" Abigail said, "Yes. It had the power to turn the wheel to kill us but it wasn't, I don't think, *actual*. I mean, *physical*." She hadn't told the Middlebury authorities about this demon-hand because it would have seemed like an accusation of Jared, that Jared had reached over to twist the wheel, and Jared had not, Jared too was innocent; she hadn't dared tell them for fear of being considered mad. She would not tell anyone except Roger, and begged him not to tell any of their friends for word would spread everywhere in Salthill—"I'd be so ashamed!" Roger questioned her about the "demon-hand" and Abigail conceded, possibly it had been a force rather than an actual hand. But it took the shape of a hand. She'd seen it! Certainly, she'd felt it. "As soon as the hand took hold of the steering wheel, I became paralyzed, I couldn't react. I could no more have brought the car out of the skid, turned the wheel the other way, put on the brakes, than"—she paused, breathing quickly, her anxious bruised eyes on Roger—"I could perform these actions now, in this car. With you in opposition." Roger laughed uneasily. Abigail was joking? Or—Abigail wasn't joking? "Jared refuses to speak with me now. He says I tried to kill us both. *And I did not, Roger.* You believe me, don't you?" Roger said, "Abigail, of course. I'm your attorney." He laughed, it was a joke. "Hey, no. I'm your friend."

As they crossed the Tappan Zee Bridge high above the Hudson River, Abigail began to speak resignedly of having lost Jared, so soon after having lost Adam. "It was fated, I guess." Roger objected, "'Fated'? Hardly." But Abigail, picking at the bandages on her face, squinting into her compact mirror, said, sighing, "I feel it, you know. My age." "Your age?" Roger laughed. "You're the youngest of us all." "No. Marina Troy is the youngest." Roger went quiet, wondering what Abigail knew of him and Marina. In Salthill, that pond of teeming algae, everyone seemed to know everyone else's affairs despite the greatest efforts to maintain secrecy. As if she could read Roger's thoughts, delicately Abigail brought up the subject of the letters and cards she'd sent to Adam, had Roger come across them amid Adam's papers?

"No. Don't worry."

"Oh, I'm not worried. It's nothing to be ashamed of. Loving." Abigail peeled off one of the smaller bandages, lifting her chin. Her face resembled an exquisite vase that has been mysteriously smudged, cracked. "Even when you're not loved in return."

"Adam loved you, Abigail."

"Did he?"

"In his way."

"Did he ever—talk about me with you?"

"You know Adam had too much tact for that."

"Yes, but—did he ever talk about women with you?"

"Not really."

"Do you know if he was married, ever?"

Abigail spoke anxiously. Roger was annoyed, this should mean so much to her even now! "No. I doubt it."

"You do?" Abigail considered this. "But Adam was a man you would swear must be a father. He should have been a father. He loved children, and he loved—well, life. But—he hadn't had children? This rumor about grown children of his coming forward to make claims on his estate—"

"There's no truth to that," Roger said, irritably. "We can't locate any heirs."

"It's still early, isn't it? Heirs may show up."

"Yes. But somehow, I doubt it."

"Why would a man like Adam, such a good man, not have children; and a man like Harry Tierney, who isn't at all a good man, and frankly hates life, have a child?—a son? And want so badly to hang on to him?" Abigail shook her head, sighing. "It seems wrong."

"It is illogical," Roger said. "Adam would have agreed."

After a while Abigail said, as if unable to resist, "Adam was a gambler, you know. I mean sometimes. In Vegas."

"Was he?"

"One year, 1997 I think, he 'earned' eleven thousand dollars. He had to report it to the IRS!"

In fact, Roger knew this. And he knew more. But he said only, admiringly, "That's a lot of money, he must've been serious. I suppose—poker?"

"I guess. He wouldn't talk about it much. He did seem ashamed. Or maybe he pretended to be ashamed, to keep it to himself. Gambling was some kind of experimenting with him, he said; with, like, the universe, and its 'intersection' with his own mind. He didn't seem to be serious about anything," Abigail said, thoughtfully, "that was only just, you know, an action." What a strange, unexpected thing for this woman to say! Roger was impressed that, since the accident, so very recently, Abigail Des Pres was becoming a more thoughtful person; unless it was since Adam's death. "To be serious about any action, if it's only just an 'action,' is to commit yourself to some principle it represents, assuming some kind of future, and this, I think, Adam never did. No, he wasn't serious about gambling because it was just making money, business, in another guise. He despised all that. He was only serious about life, and that's something you can't talk about."

"He sought the truth. Like Socrates."

"Socrates!" Abigail sounded uncertain. "He's a character invented by—is it Plato? Or are they two separate people?"

Roger had to think. "It's believed they were two people. But, who knows—it was a long time ago."

"How long? A thousand years?"

"More like two thousand."

"Two thousand! And we live so briefly." Abigail sighed, and touched her tender skin with her fingertips. In the corner of his eye Roger saw her glittering rings, which somehow assured him. No woman can be profound whose fingers glitter with expensive rings. "Strange that Adam would care so much, isn't it? About those long-ago people. He didn't believe in time, maybe? That human beings change much? That we 'progress.'"

"No. But he didn't believe in the reverse, either. What about you?"

"*Me?*" Abigail laughed, showing her perfect white teeth like another accessory. "What does it matter what I think? A cast-off wife, and now a cast-off mother. I'm"—she wiped at her eyes with a carefully folded tissue—"pond scum."

Roger laughed, in that instant disliking the woman. Abigail Des Pres was still Harry Tierney's wife. "Well. So are we all, I suppose."

"But we try to be more, don't we?" Abigail pleaded. She touched Roger's wrist, sensing she was losing his sympathy. And she was a woman whose nourishment was sympathy. "Some of us try so very hard."

"Yes. I suppose."

Roger drove the rest of the way to Salthill in silence.

In Abigail's darkened house, Roger set her suitcase down in the vestibule and would have quickly departed except Abigail seized both his hands in hers. "Roger! I'm afraid, I can't be alone. Not just yet." If he'd been vigilant enough, and forceful enough, he might have escaped; but a perverse inertia gripped him, like quicksand. Soft and yielding as water, yet possessed of a childlike will, Abigail stepped into his arms and held him; her own arms were thin, trembling, but strong. "We have so much in common, Roger. I've been watching you for years. We've both been wounded. And we have children the same age. Like brother and sister they are. That does link us, doesn't it?" She spoke wistfully, raising her face to his. Roger felt a thrill of panic, and a razor-sharp stab of sexual longing. *I am so physically lonely. God help me.* The woman's luminous bruised face, her luridly blackened eye excited him; as if he were the cause of her hurt, himself. "I'll never see Adam again. I'll never see Jared again, I know it." She spoke almost calmly, she was resigned. As if in fact she'd killed her own son, and there was a bitter satisfaction in this, as there would be in Roger if Robin ceased to love him, and joined with her mother in despising him, there would be a bitter satisfaction. "Love me? Just a little? Please." She was kissing him avidly, and Roger found himself kissing her, in the shadowy cathedral-ceilinged living room of the house, the scene of so many parties. As if those years of parties were a prelude solely to this, an exquisite consummation. Roger and Abigail staggered to a silk-upholstered sofa and fell clumsily together. They were excited, breathless, fumbling as adolescents. Abigail's breath was fierce as licorice. "I love you, oh, I love you, love you." Roger supposed she no longer had any idea who he was, she'd lost his name. And he was forgetting her name, and where they were. In haste, pushing aside, knocking to the floor, what were they?—small but bulky silk-covered pillows. God damn! They began to make love, how quickly and easily it was happening, the woman's slender thighs, the woman's suddenly bared, very warm belly, a soft-curly swath of pubic hair like down, as if their eager ferretlike bodies had taken control, their personalities were nulled, obliterated. A woman's fleshy, ravenous mouth against Roger's mouth, it might be any woman's mouth, or any mouth, Roger was immensely happy suddenly, knowing that the pressure in his groin would soon be relieved, would explode in a delirium of brainless pleasure. "Do you love me? A little?" the woman was pleading, "—say you do. You can lie to me. Oh, please!" Boldly she was pulling open his shirt, her fingers worked at his trousers, Roger pushed them away to open his trousers himself, his penis lifting hard, hot as a boy's, and the woman was guiding him into her, shimmering as a pool of water, except suddenly an agitated sound interrupted them. "What? What was that?" Tense as drawn bows they lay together, listening. A strand of the woman's hair was caught in Roger's mouth. Her narrow rib cage, beneath his, rose and fell anxiously. At first, the sound seemed to be in the room with them, in a darkened corner—or in the fireplace perhaps? Then, it was evident that the sound came from outside, a frenzied scratching at the front door.

Apollo?

5

THERE CAME ROBIN limping and thudding down the stairs.

Seeing him staring at her, she said, teasing, an angry flush rising into her face, "Guess I've grown some, huh, Dad, since you saw me last year?"

His first surprise, no, it was frank shock and disappointment, and it must have shown in his face: Robin had dressed for dinner in baggy unclean pants, a parrot-green Ryecroft hockey T-shirt with a flannel shirt partway buttoned over it, straining against her big, broad breasts, and filthy running shoes. Her hair, damp from the shower, hung lank and limp about her round childish face; her skin shone coarsely, as if she'd rubbed it with a washcloth. Amid the prettier, more girllike, more attractively dressed Ryecroft girls Roger had been observing in the residence hall, Robin stood out as defiant, conspicuous. Seeing her dad trying to smile at her she laughed outright at him. A quick cruel smile tightened her jaws.

Roger's face burned, he would let the remark pass. The implication that Roger hadn't seen her since the previous year when in fact he'd seen her more recently, and she knew it. The implication that he might be discomfited—disturbed—by her maturing body, her sizable breasts and hips. Roger said, trying to sound neither severe nor pleading, "This inn we're going to, it's a nice place, honey. I was expecting you to dress a little more—"

Robin laughed. "'Nice'? You're dressed 'nice' enough for us both."

Her duffel bag was slung over her back, Robin refused to carry her things in a suitcase. When Roger offered to take the bag from her, she resisted. "It's how I build my muscle, Dad." Roger recalled Lee Ann saying that their daughter had become, in the past year, obsessed with hockey, and with other sports at her school. He felt dismay: was this antagonistic young person *his daughter,* a plain homely chunky girl with dangerously bright eyes, watching him defiantly, daring him to criticize her? For a half hour Roger had been waiting for her in the visitors' lounge of the residence hall, having to observe other girls, not wanting to compare his daughter with these girls yet unable not to think, with a sinking heart, *What a crapshoot, fatherhood. I played, and fucked it.*

For all her insouciance, Robin's eyes brimmed with emotion Roger wasn't about to provoke. Not him! It was the first phase of the father-daughter weekend. Lee Ann had told him that Robin never ("repeat: never") spoke of him any longer, obviously Robin was furious with him, he meant to regain her love for him, her trust. He said, sympathetically, "Well. You look fine, honey. We could always have dinner somewhere else. The crucial thing is, you didn't get hurt out there."

Robin had been smiling, mugging, for the benefit of others, a group of girls dressed like herself, and turned her attention back to Roger, saying hotly, "It *does* hurt, not just my ankle but all over. I'm banged up like hell. But I'm not, you know, *hurt.* Like needing an X ray or the infirmary or whatever."

They left the residence hall, something must have been decided. Robin was jocosely complaining of the aches, bruises, sprains you had to endure playing hockey. All the girls were banged up, even the stars. It was, like, a "badge of courage." One of the centers, the girl with the platinum-blond hair, the very best player on the Ryecroft team, ached so much sometimes she could "hardly lift her head" from the pillow, waking next morning after a game. As they crossed the quad, Robin waved and exchanged loud greetings with a number of students, both boys and girls, Roger was given to understand that she was a popular kid, a school personality. She was called "Robin," "Robbie," "Rob." Her eyes gleamed with a sort of frantic pleasure. She walked fast and hard, on the heels of her feet, Roger had to hurry to keep pace. "You seem to like it here, honey? That's good."

Robin shrugged, Dad's remark was too banal to warrant a reply.

In the car headed for the Hanover Inn, Roger tried to talk to Robin about the game, wanting to praise her, he understood that she was seething, still excited, though physically tired, and resentful, no doubt there were turbulent emotions connected with the team and the coach who'd pulled her out of the game, but Robin answered only in grunts. Roger asked her how she liked her teammates, they seemed like "nice girls," and Robin snorted with laughter. "Oh, Dad. 'Nice.' You're like Mom. Your vocabulary is so *limited*." Roger laughed, for this was true, not that Roger Cavanagh was *nice*, in fact Roger Cavanagh was *not-nice*, but there were words you said, like *fine*, even *great*, and these were code words whose meaning had long since dissipated. Roger said, "Well. They did seem—'nice.' Just in the few minutes I met them. You all get along so well . . ."

Robin said with a shrug, in a suddenly somber tone, "Why ask me how I like *them*? It's if they like me that matters."

To this, Roger had no reply.

Wondering: does she matter so little to herself, her own feelings don't count?

"Let's face it, Dad: if they liked me better, I'd like them."

"I thought you did like them. I thought—"

"Oh, sure. I'm crazy about them." Robin laughed, wiping at her nose with the edge of her hand. She sat with one muscled leg crossed over the other, at the knee; her calf bulged against the khaki pant-leg. From time to time she rubbed her ankle, the flesh of her lower leg. She wore white cotton socks very like his own. Roger caught a glimpse of raw, reddened skin.

He said, "I hope to hell that isn't a sprain. Why didn't you let somebody check it?" Robin shrugged. Roger said, "If it doesn't get better, we can take you to a doctor in the morning."

Robin made a gagging noise.

"Oh, sure, Dad. Real cool. Instead of going to the Air and Space Museum."

"If you're injured—"

"I am *not injured*. I'm tougher than you think. I'm not pretty-pretty like Mom, she melts in the rain practically. Or pretends to. So Georgie can come mop her up." Robin laughed harshly.

Roger wasn't going to follow her in that direction, no thanks!

Tenderly he said, "You girls certainly played well. Both sides. Everybody I was near, watching, was impressed. *I* was impressed. I hope you weren't disappointed, honey, being taken out. Your coach had to do that. You certainly were playing well—"

Robin interrupted, impatient, "I played lousy. It was my worst game this year. Even practice."

"But when I first arrived—"

"That's just it!" Robin said, excited. "Before you came, I was *hot*. I almost made a score. I got the ball away from their hotshot player. Then, when I see you there, and could feel you *watching*—and, like, *willing* me not to fuck up—for sure, I *did*."

Roger was so stunned by this outburst, he drove in silence. His daughter had uttered the word *fuck* to him! The first time. And in that rude way. And she was blaming him for her poor performance. He said, hurt, "Robin, I don't think that's fair or even logical. You wanted me to come see you play, and so I did. And you didn't play badly—"

"I did. I played 'badly.' I turned my ankle on purpose and fell, because I knew I was going to be benched." Robin spoke indignantly, as if her dad was such a fool he required these simple, demeaning explanations from her. "And it was because of you, your presence. You always ruin everything."

"Always? What—?"

"One of our teachers says, there is such a mental phenomenon as 'telepathy.' Some people send signals, other people receive. You, Dad, are a sender. And the signals you send, they're bad news to the receivers."

Roger said, "That is pure bullshit."

"*You* should know."

"What's that mean?"

Robin shrugged. She turned on the radio, punched through a half-dozen stations. They drove on. Blurred suburban landscape. Growing Friday-evening traffic. He should have had two drinks, he'd have had enough time. Abigail Des Pres was right: she and Roger had this in common. Adolescent children. It was a true bond, like hemophilia or hemorrhoids.

In her e-mail messages to Roger, Robin sometimes addressed him as DEARDEADDAD. Was that funny? It was not funny. He'd never responded, he ignored it. Frequently Robin signed off her brief, cryptic messages with LOVEYLOVE FROM NIBOR. "Robin" spelled backward. Was that funny?

Roger said, "Robin, honey, it hurts me to see you like this. I'd been looking forward to this weekend. Is something wrong?"

"Our teacher says life is 'essentially' wrong. Because Nature is a continuous struggle, species pitted against one another and, within the species, individuals pitted against individuals. 'Red in tooth and claw.' Who'd have designed that, for Christ's sake?"

Roger glanced at his daughter in alarm. Such emotion in this child, you'd think Darwinian evolutionary theory was a new, radical idea. Maybe, if you're fifteen and just starting to seriously think, it is?

Roger protested, "But your teacher must have told you that human life has evolved beyond that level. We have civilization, we have morality, law—"

"'Law'! Tell that to the Jews. That the Nazis gassed in the ovens."

"—we have things we believe in, things we would die for, beyond just eating, and territory—"

"These 'beliefs,' they're just flimsy little canoes, O.K. to paddle around in, in good weather, but if there's a storm—it's every man for himself."

How to drive in snarled suburban traffic at Friday rush hour, and simultaneously defend humankind, and civilization, against the charges of a furious fifteen-year-old? Roger heard himself say, in the tone he'd used when Robin had been a little girl gazing up at her daddy with beautiful liquidy-brown eyes,

"You're forgetting, Robin: love makes a difference. Human beings are a species capable of love. Especially within families. People sacrifice for one another, sometimes give up their lives for one another, it's an instinct. A parent for a child . . ." Roger's voice trailed off hopefully. He steeled himself for Robin's snorting derisory laughter that cut him to the quick, he felt he couldn't bear it.

But Robin surprised him by saying, in a quieter voice, "I was sorry to hear about—you know. Uncle Adam." She mumbled the name as if embarrassed to speak it.

"Oh. Yes."

"Mom told me. After you two talked. Some of it, anyway." She glanced at Roger, intent upon his driving. Something was being exposed in her, a tremulous little flame, she dreaded its exposure. She was roughly kneading her ankle and the surrounding bruised flesh.

"Well. It was sudden. We were all very shocked, and saddened. He died of heart failure, your mother probably told you, showed you the clippings?—trying to rescue a little girl in the river."

"Yeah. I saw. That was shitty."

Shitty! Roger stiffened, he hated such words in his daughter's mouth yet knew better than to protest.

"I mean," Robin said, relenting, "—it was, like, tragic. I got so mad at those assholes, the parents of 'Samantha,' I wanted to, God I don't know! Drown 'em." She paused, breathing hard. "Did he ever ask, much, about me? After Mom moved us away."

"Of course, honey. All the time. You know, Adam was so fond of you."

"Was he!"

She knew, but had to be reassured. Roger reassured her.

So they talked, about Adam mostly. Roger was relieved to see the Hanover Inn ahead. He was feeling much better about Robin, and she appeared to be feeling better about him. If there was a single adult whom Robin had liked, from her years in Salthill, it had been Adam Berendt.

She said, hesitantly, "Mom was telling me, she'd heard from

some friends there, Mr. Berendt had—some things?—people were surprised to find?—in his house?"

"What things?"

"Oh, I don't know."

"What kind of things?"

"It's just gossip, you know Mom. She'll say anything people tell her."

"Honey, what kind of things? I'm Adam's estate executor, and I know."

"Mom was saying, she'd heard Mr. Berendt had, like, lots of money hidden away? In boxes? Like, buried in the cellar of his house? Millions of dollars?" Robin was watching him closely. Seeing his grimace, she said, "*I* never believed it, why'd Uncle Adam hide money like that, if he had it? If, like, anybody had it? You'd put it in a bank, right? I told Mom that. She's so credulous, it's pitiful."

Roger said carefully, "Of course, Adam didn't have money hidden in his house. That's an utterly unsubstantiated rumor."

"I told Mom it sounded ridiculous. Uncle Adam scorned money, he had no wish for material things."

"That's right, mostly."

"I was in Uncle Adam's cellar, a few times. When we were there visiting. I must've been, like, ten. A long time ago."

"Were you."

"The cellar was *old*. It was sort of creepy. Uncle Adam said maybe there'd been dead people buried there, a really long time ago? Like, if they'd been murdered in the tavern, that the house used to be, they were buried in the cellar. Was that so?"

Roger disliked the drift of this conversation, not knowing quite why. "I doubt it, Robin. Adam liked to tease, you know."

"He was so *funny*. He could make me *laugh*." Robin wiped at her nose, fiercely. "Even when there wasn't anything funny, Uncle Adam could make people *laugh*."

"He had that gift. Yes."

Roger was parking the BMW at the rear of the inn, when Robin unexpectedly burst into tears. He hugged her, she pressed her face against his shoulder. "It's like, it came over me, I won't be seeing Uncle Adam again. Wow."

They checked into the inn, where Roger had reserved a suite on the top, fourth, floor. The Hanover Inn was an "historic" inn on the Baltimore Pike, many of the furnishings were Colonial antiques. Scrutinizing the high-ceilinged, rather chilly rooms, Robin said, "It wouldn't surprise me, lots of people have died *here*."

In her baggy khakis, in her parrot-green T-shirt and flannel shirt buttoned tightly over her mature-woman's breasts, Robin stood with her hands on her hips, rocking from side to side as if taking the measure of the place. Elegant surroundings intimidated her, yet also provoked her to childish behavior. Roger, hanging clothes in a closet, saw her twisting her head, winking and smirking at herself in a mirror. The outburst of tears in the parking lot had embarrassed her but excited her as well. Her eyes still shone, she tilted her head to catch the light in the mirror; smoothed the ratty flannel shirt over her breasts, smirked again, and smiled. In the mirror, at a short distance, Robin's round Eskimo-face, her coarse soapstone skin, looked almost attractive. Casually she asked, with the air of a bright student, "Dad! You have a logician's mind, you're a lawyer, and all? What if I told you—this is just a hypothesis, Dad, see?—that a man who looked just like Uncle Adam 'touched' me, kind of, sometimes? When I was—"

Roger turned to stare at her. "Robin, what?"

Robin stared back, deadpan. She'd ceased her rocking but stood with arms akimbo. "*What if?* Just a hypothesis."

"You—don't mean it, do you?"

"I told you, Dad. It's a hypothesis. Like, an experiment? In logic? I'm just asking *what if*."

"Robin, I don't think this is—funny." Roger swallowed hard. He held something in his hand, a wire hanger, and had no idea what he was doing.

Robin said, impatiently, "It *isn't* funny. It's, like, experimenting with what's real. Like, if you introduced an alien element, sort of, when people are serious? Like in church? At a funeral?

Where people just say the same old things? There are counter-worlds to this world, you know. Antiuniverses? Our math teacher says so."

"'Antiuniverses'? What are we talking about?"

"We're not talking about Mr. Berendt per se, Dad. You don't need to look so sick, or—guiltylike, whatever. We're talking about *what if*. Like in logic. The antiuniverse."

"What kind of nonsense is that?"

"You can't prove that an antiuniverse doesn't exist, and as rightfully as our own." Robin spoke in triumph; Roger could hear the echo of a preening adult here, impressing and confusing his young students. He wanted to bang some heads together.

But he said, reasonably, "What can't be disproved isn't scientifically valid as a proposition. It's bad logic, too. Like fairy tales."

"Our math teacher says— "

"Tell him," Roger said, hanging the wire hanger in the closet with such force that the handle bent, "he's full of shit."

"*Her*. It's a *her*." Robin was elated that Dad should fall into such a trap. She said mockingly, "O.K., I'll tell her: 'Miss Ringler, my dad, a hot-shit lawyer, says to tell you you're full of shit. Too.'" She laughed uproariously. Roger backed off, not trusting himself to respond. He disappeared into the bathroom. He would shower, shave for the second time that day. He would cleanse himself of the filth this angry child had dumped onto him as, a naughty little girl, she'd taken fiendish delight in overturning her food onto the kitchen floor for a red-faced nanny to clean up.

ONE OF THE cryptic e-mail exchanges between DEARDEAD-DAD and NIBOR of the previous summer, which Roger had more or less forgotten until now, was:

> Why did you & mom get married, it seems like it was such a mistake.
>
> N.

* * *

We married for the obvious reason: we fell in love. We were very happy together for many years. It WAS NOT a mistake. There's—YOU.

D.

* * *

EXACTLY!!!

N.

6

A truce. At dinner in the Inn, soothed by tiny flickering candles like votive lights, Roger and his daughter behaved cordially with each other. They were polite, they were smiling. They were patient with each other; Dad merely laughed at Daughter who kept changing her mind about her entree. Daughter had even washed her flamey face, made a gesture toward combing her disheveled hair, removed the offensive flannel shirt and replaced it, over the T-shirt, with a handsome cable-knit black sweater. She'd dabbed lipstick on her mouth, Roger hoped not in mockery, and was looking, in the flattering light, rather striking, exotic. Smiling at her, Roger wondered if there might be Native American blood in his or Lee Ann's family? Eskimo, or Inuit?

They would not speak again of Uncle Adam. No more hypotheses.

Roger had been shaken by the exchange upstairs but consoled himself thinking, *She's angry. Not at Adam but at you. Yes?* He would have to accept it, though he believed her anger was unjust. He understood that, this evening, having pushed a little too far up in the room, Robin was now relenting, respectful and wary of Dad. Maybe her own coarse, cruel words had shocked her.

When her food came, Robin ate hungrily. Such a big, growing girl: appetite raged inside her, a fire that had to be fed. A porterhouse steak, french fries, hard rolls with butter. She ate Roger's french fries, drenched in catsup. Roger laughed and joked with her. She was a funny, quick-witted girl, mimicking her teachers, yes, even the revered Miss Ringler was slyly mocked, all adults seemed to her subjects for laughter, so self-regarding, pretentious. Roger couldn't disagree. He was charmed by her. He wanted to be charmed by her. He ordered a second carafe of red wine. He was feeling mildly depressed. No: he was feeling optimistic. *This is going well. You saw her play hockey. She doesn't hate you.* Because they were laughing, and running out of things to laugh about, Roger told Robin about Abigail's misadventure in Middlebury, Vermont. Robin had known Jared Tierney in the Salthill Middle School. "Jared's lucky to be alive, huh?" Robin laughed. "*You* wouldn't try to kill me, Dad, would you?"

"Robin," Roger said, wincing, though he knew she was joking, "that isn't funny."

"No. I was just kidding, Dad."

"Well. I know, honey."

Eating dessert, pecan pie with a double scoop of vanilla ice cream, Robin said, "You're a pretty close friend of Mrs. Tierney's, I guess, to drive up to Vermont to help her?" She squinted across the booth at Roger, as if she'd only just thought of this.

"Yes. I suppose I am."

"She wasn't one of the women Mom was saying—what she said?"

Roger's jaws tightened. "No, Robin."

"Are you in love with her, now?" The question was playful, almost mocking. But Roger understood the ferocity beneath.

"No. I am not."

"With Abigail Tierney, you *are not?*"

Roger loathed having to answer. When Lee Ann had interrogated him like this, in their bedroom, often as he was undressing for bed and therefore vulnerable, exposed, resenting his wife and yet not wanting to antagonize her, for he knew how she longed to lacerate both his flesh and her own, how she longed to be hurt, devastated, humiliated—he'd behaved stoically, calmly. He'd thought, *I can't let it begin.* Now he told Robin what was simply the truth: "No, honey. If it's any of your business. I'm not in love with Abigail." He paused. "She's Des Pres, now. Since the divorce."

Dogged as on the hockey field, trailing after faster players, Robin said, "But. You were in Vermont with her."

"Robin, I wasn't 'with' her. I drove up to help her and Jared. It was a pretty desperate situation. I'm Abigail's attorney."

"Since when?"

"Since a while."

"Is that what you are!—her *attorney*." Robin pronounced the word as you might pronounce the name of a rare disease.

Roger smiled. A sudden dark fury rose in him. He was watching his daughter spoon ice cream into her mouth, twisting the spoon in a way repulsive to him. "Look, Robin. My work, my profession, my life—you have no right to scorn. My income—"

Robin continued to lick the spoon. Calmly she said, "Sure, Dad. I know."

"The law is an honorable profession. The law is certainly not an easy profession. But my income has—"

"Dad, cool! I know."

Roger's lips were numbed as by novocaine. He could not believe he was uttering, to this sardonic, beetle-browed daughter of his, such empty banal self-condemning words.

They sat for a while in silence. Roger's eardrums throbbed. He'd have liked to give his daughter a hard shaking. She was so maddening, as a small child is maddening, without skill or finesse; without seeming to know what she wanted. *Like her mother. Wanting to hurt.* Lee Ann's taunting of Roger had sometimes ended in lovemaking; a hard swift unsentimental lovemaking; the kind of lovemaking that, in marriage, signals the onset of the end of marriage; for marriage isn't passion but tenderness, pure sentiment. But with Robin, Roger felt a physical animosity, repugnance. He wanted simply to knock the smirk off her childish face.

Still Robin persisted. "Basically, Dad, you defend white-collar criminals. What's to be proud of?"

"Criminals? That's ridiculous."

"Aren't they?"

Roger wondered if his daughter was truly so uninformed about his work. His life. Or whether this was part of her tormenting of

Dad. He said, "Most of my work is contracts, wills. Legal agreements. More and more our firm works with corporations, not individuals. We rarely go near a courtroom. What gave you the idea your father is a defense trial lawyer?"

"I thought you were. Sometimes?"

"Rarely."

"You don't actually help people, do you? Poor people—"

"'Poor people' are not the only people who require the help of the law." Roger spoke calmly, though the pulse was hammering in his head. "I think you must have a very narrow concept of the law."

"Nothing you do is a matter of *life and death,*" Robin said, with an air of exasperation, "—it doesn't *matter!* Not really."

Roger tried to smile, an affable dad, though steeped in corruption. He said, "Most actions in our lives don't 'matter'—ultimately. Yet—they matter to us. My clients wouldn't agree with you, honey."

Calling this beetle-browed disdainful young person, hair hanging in her face, jaws chewing pecan pie with mechanical precision, *honey!* Dad was trying, trying pitifully hard. It would be noted that Dad was trying pitifully hard. But Robin dismissed this ploy with a wave of her fist. "What's the law *for,* Dad? Basically to make money for lawyers, isn't it? I mean, basically."

"Law is—" Roger faltered, a man on the edge of an abyss, "—the cornerstone of civilization. Without law—"

"What's civilization," Robin interrupted vehemently, "just a power structure, isn't it? A *hegemony,* it's called. To keep the masses, and women, in subjugation? Sure, people like you love 'law,' the 'law' is always on your side."

"Without law," Roger said, gritting his teeth, "we'd be savages."

"We're not savages, now?"

"If we were, honey, you would know it."

Robin regarded her father across the white linen table top. Across the soiled remains of plates, cutlery. Something was exposed in her for an instant, a dark raging knowledge between them, of how far Daughter might push, and how far Dad might consent to be pushed, before there was a catastrophe. But, how delicious the possibility of catastrophe! Roger saw in his daughter's widened blinking eyes a look of spiteful innocence that must have preceded the deliberate twisting of her ankle on the playing field. *I hate myself, why shouldn't you hate me, too?*

Quickly she looked down. Her heavy face darkened with blood. She pushed her dessert plate away, with just her fingertips, in a sudden fastidious gesture of repugnance. As if finally she had disgusted herself, and was frightened.

7

ROGER SLEPT POORLY that night. In the bedroom that was his, adjoining the bedroom that was his daughter's. (Quietly she'd locked the door between the rooms. He'd heard her.) His eyes kept opening, he was disoriented, confused. His guts were writhing snakes. He could not envision what the weekend would be. The whole of Saturday and much of Sunday in Washington, in the company of his daughter.

Yes, but Roger was the girl's father, he loved her.

Certainly, yes, he loved her.

He had not wanted the divorce, only his pride kept him from begging.

Why are you unfaithful?

Why? Out of loneliness.

Loneliness for who, for what?

Out of the fear of loneliness, maybe. Adam, I don't know!

But to jeopardize your marriage, your family, for a reason you can't explain?

If I could explain it, Adam, fuck it I wouldn't have to do it, would I?

When he woke, his eyes stinging, tears of rage, disappointment, loss, he couldn't remember where the hell he was. But he was alone, Adam had departed. He'd lost his best friend and what had he, instead?

He got up to use the bathroom. Quietly. Not wanting to wake Robin on the other side of the door.

He would have liked to talk with Adam. To talk and laugh together. He had yet to tell Adam about the misadventure in Middlebury. Adam was the one to appreciate the pathos, and the grotesquerie.

This helpless yearning to come together with a woman: with the lost half of one's soul. Lost half of something.

How he and Abigail Des Pres had scrambled from each other's embrace like guilty children. Abigail went to open the door, why Abigail was compelled to open the door to that furious scratching Roger would have no idea, and in bounded Apollo, wolflike, tawny-eyed, burrs in his coarse silver-tipped coat. He was limping and panting. Though the dog must have been crouched outside the door it seemed, now the door was opening, that he'd been running, the force of crazed momentum carried him inside. He was ravenously hungry, Abigail fed him in the kitchen. Abigail and Roger watched the husky-shepherd eat. Politely then Abigail asked Roger, who'd adjusted his clothing, and more or less managed to regain his composure, if he would like to stay for dinner; but Roger coolly declined. Was Roger Cavanagh no more—or maybe less!—than a dog, to be fed by this woman out of pity?

He went away, he wanted never to see her again. The very thought of her, the lurid soft mouth, the discolored eye and bruised face, the thin tremulous yearning body, was repugnant to him. It was an insult to his manhood, to be so treated! And the other woman, the red-haired woman, he would not think of, at all.

Still, Roger Cavanagh felt responsible for Abigail Des Pres, he worried about her, and found himself calling her; he wanted not to call her, and felt relief when she didn't answer her phone, and no answering machine clicked on to take his message. Finally, a week or so after the Apollo episode, Roger drove out Wheatsheaf to Abigail's house. In the circular driveway there was a lawn service truck, and Roger parked behind it. If Abigail was home, if Abigail would see him. *If this was meant to be, then it was meant to be.* He would obliterate utterly his love for the red-haired woman, he would sink and sink in this woman, and make an end of it. If he made love to her just once, she would adore him, she would become his wife, he seemed to know. He did want to marry again, he was in horror of remaining alone much longer. But when he went to ring the front doorbell, the foreman of the lawn service crew told him, above the roar of motors so powerful that Roger's skull vibrated, that Mrs. Tierney was gone for the rest of the summer—"To Nantucket."

IN THE MORNING they drove in the direction of Washington, D.C., in pelting rain. Wind rocked the car, Roger seemed to know they would never get to their destination.

The previous day had been autumnal, beautiful. This day was a raw churning cloud-mass, spewing rain like gunfire. Breakfast at the Colonial Hanover Inn had not been a pleasant experience. At first Robin refused to order anything, screwing up her pug-face in a juvenile mimicry of nausea. "I never eat breakfast." Reprovingly Roger said, as any parent must, "You should, breakfast is the most important meal of the day." Deardeaddad's lips moved numbly. He had no idea what he was saying. Deardeaddadspeak. As if simply needing to be courted, Robin was easily won. "O.K. If you insist. I'll eat!" With grim satisfaction then ordering an enormous breakfast of eggs, sausage, waffles which she ate greedily, at times lowering her head toward her plate. Roger, skimming *USA Today,* which was provided free for hotel guests, tried not to observe. He had no appetite himself except for black coffee, fresh-brewed, as many cups as he dared. In the BMW, lurching through rain, Roger's heart leapt and thudded in his chest. Robin complained of the "gross" meal she'd had, rubbing her belly, blaming Deardeaddad, which was only logical. She began to fiddle with the car radio. No CD in the glove compartment was to her liking. They were bound for the nation's capital to see, mostly, museums. Such great museums! On the phone planning their weekend, their first father-daughter weekend in more months than Roger cared to recall, Robin had been excited as a young child. Especially, she was enthusiastic about the Air and Space Museum. A few years before, in eighth grade, she'd announced that she intended to study space; the "universe"; she would be an astronomer, or an astrophysicist; possibly, she'd even travel in space. Earnestly she told her parents, "Space travel will be common, in the twenty-first century. We can all go!" Roger had smiled, hearing his daughter, thirteen at the time, make such a proclamation. Maybe the young are gifted, to see into the future?

While the middle-aged are captives of the past.

Midway to Washington, at about ten A.M., Robin was suddenly stricken with what seemed to be stomach cramps. Diarrhea? "Dad, exit *please*. I need a rest room *fast*." She moaned softly, rocking in her seat beside him; sweat beads were forming on her forehead. Roger exited immediately, at an interstate fast-food restaurant and gas station, and Robin climbed out, groaning, and stumbled through the rain to the entrance, bent over with stomach cramps. Anxious, dazed, Roger followed Robin into the building. Now what? What now? He didn't want to think that his daughter had made herself purposefully sick, gorging at breakfast. Or, was it the case, once she'd begun eating, her hunger was such she hadn't been able to keep from gorging . . . Roger waited, guiltily. *Whatever this is, it's your fault. And you know it.*

After some minutes, Robin emerged from the women's room. Her face was the color of paste and her lips chalk white. Tears shone in her eyes with an odd sort of elation. She approached Roger shakily, smiling. As he was about to touch her gently, to ask how she was, Robin murmured with pitiless candor, "Morning sickness, Dad."

Teenaged rock music was being piped into the lobby, loud. Roger cupped a hand to his ear. "I—didn't hear you, honey?"

"You heard me, Dad. You heard me exactly."

Robin pushed away from her stumbling Deardeaddad, baring her teeth in a grin, and stalked out of the restaurant. Numbly, a man in a dream, yet not a dream he recognized, Roger followed.

Morning sickness.

Morning sickness?

He had not heard. Yes, but he'd heard.

He felt as if his head was trapped inside a giant clanging bell.

"Robin! Honey, wait—"

He was sure it was a misunderstanding. A joke. Robin was a clever mimic, a gifted satirist. She was not the kind of girl who . . .

Roger tried to help Robin, who was swaying as if faint, walk to the car, but she shrugged away. In the car she hunched far over, arms crossed over her stomach. A sharp odor of vomit lifted from her like a befouled breath. Roger slid into the seat beside her, trying to remain calm. "Honey, you said—morning sickness? Does that mean—?"

Robin said flatly, "You know exactly what that means, Dad."

"Does—your mother know?"

"No."

"Does—*he* know?"

"Who's *he?*"

"The, the—" Roger couldn't bring himself to speak the word, it seemed in that instant an obscene word: *father*.

They sat in a tense silence for what seemed a long time but was no more than two or three minutes, rain streaming down the windows of the new-model metallic-gray BMW. Roger's mind was working rapidly. Trying to recall if Lee Ann had ever mentioned that Robin had a boyfriend; that she saw boys. Trying to recall if at the school Robin had breezily introduced him to a boy whose face should have lodged in his memory. Trying to think how much a fifteen-year-old at a progressive private school would know about pregnancy, the option of abortion.

Panting, trying not to sob, Robin said, "You know who the father is, Dad. Don't you?"

"I—do?"

"Think!"

"I c-can't, honey. Who?"

Robin turned on him, pushing out her lower lip in a monkey-like gesture of disdain. "'Honey.' How many females have you called *that?*"

Roger was stymied. He sat in a paralysis of indecision. He

would have to telephone Lee Ann, immediately. They would have to confer. A decision would have to be made. It didn't occur to Roger to ask his daughter how long she'd been pregnant; when *the baby* was due. He would recall afterward that the very concept *the baby* was no more real to him than the concept of eternity, or space travel.

Robin blew her nose extravagantly. Clearly she was enjoying her own misery as well as his. Again that morning she'd put on the ratty flannel shirt, buttoned halfway over her big breasts, the green T-shirt beneath. Her thighs were bulky in the khaki pants, her feet like wedges in the filthy running shoes. What boy would have been drawn sexually to Robin Cavanagh! Almost, Roger sensed an air of pride in her. *You see, Daddy? Somebody desires me even if you don't.*

Then she turned to him, and spoke. Such words, Roger couldn't comprehend. "*You,* Dad. You're the one."

Seeing the sick stunned look in Roger's face, Robin laughed. Opened the car door again and climbed out, into the rain, leaving Roger staring after her. What was this? What was happening here? What had Robin said? Obscene, unspeakable! He would never forget, through his life. *You, Dad. You're the one.*

He'd begun to shake, his teeth chattered with cold. His daughter was accusing him of—what? Incest? Rape?

It wasn't possible. Yes, but it was possible.

His daughter's accusation, her hysteria. A fifteen-year-old's revenge.

Even if no one believed her! Lee Ann, for one, would never believe her.

Sick with dread, his knees nearly buckling under him, Roger climbed out of the car and followed Robin behind the building, through chill pelting rain around a corner, beneath an overhang, close by a dumpster overflowing with trash. He could not have said, if he'd been questioned, where they were; what place this was. Robin was huddled against the stucco building, arms folded tightly across her breasts, her round childish face curdled with spite, yet with a kind of dark ecstatic glee. Rain had darkened her clothing, droplets ran down her cheeks like cartoon tears. When

Roger moved to touch her, gently to cup his hand on the nape of her neck, she jerked from him like a nervous young horse. She laughed again, daringly. Slyly she said, "Hey, Dad: I'm *not*. I was just kidding."

Roger required a long moment to absorb this new fact.

"You're not—pregnant?"

"Whoever said that I was? God, Daddy: gross!"

"You mean—you've been joking?"

Robin made her pug-face. "You'd believe anything, Dad, I guess! Any low, nasty, disgusting thing about your own Robin." Another time she giggled and ran from him, slipping by him as a skilled hockey player might slip by a clumsy player; she ran back to the car, where the door had swung open in the rain, and climbed inside. It was a game! This running in the rain, making Daddy follow. In a daze, another time, Daddy followed.

Robin announced, blowing her nose, "I guess I want to go back to school, Dad. This wasn't such a great idea. I've got a lot of work to do, O.K.?"

"You don't want to go to Washington after all? The museums—?"

"I guess not."

"But, Robin, why not?—we'd planned."

"I *said*. I have work to do, I'm failing two courses. And my roommate's got some friends visiting today and tomorrow, these kind of weird, wild characters from Exeter."

Blindly Roger jammed the key into the ignition. His daughter wasn't pregnant. She was not accusing him of incest, rape. It had all been a joke, a prank. One day, possibly, they would laugh at it.

Roger returned to the interstate highway, to take an exit that would allow him to reverse his course, to return north to Nicodemus, Maryland. The rain had lightened, though it still ran in rivulets down the BMW's windows. Overhead the sky was dense with clouds like mucus. Robin, shivering with delight, daring, barely suppressing a childish attack of the giggles, glanced sidelong at Roger. "Your face, Dad. You should see your face." She pushed the rearview mirror in his direction, so he had no choice but to see the face reflected there.

FAREWELL!

I

M*adness*. There came the morning, at last she drove up river to Jones Point. She located the Thwaite house. It was a redwood and brick ranch overlooking the river. This was a chill neutral day in October. He'd died in the heat of summer. It seemed a foreign country by now, the circumstances of his death. For a half hour she sat in her car, parked just up the road from the house, smoking a cigarette. Not a deranged neurotic woman, truly she didn't blame the Thwaites for Adam's death.

Yes but someone is to blame. A man is gone.

She'd had no clear intention, setting out. She was a woman of lush emotions, of impulse and instinct; through her life as a vital, seductive woman, she'd "followed her heart"; this was the quality in Augusta Cutler that most characterized her. She feared that, without this quality, she'd have had no personality at all.

It was a Saturday, the child wouldn't be in school.

Quaking with excitement, like walking onto a brightly lighted stage. For weeks, for months she'd rehearsed this moment. Yet only in fantasy for she'd never truly believed she would do such a thing. Adam, for one, would not have approved.

Gussie! For God's sake. Let me go.

Quaking with excitement, which wasn't like Augusta Cutler. A woman of calculated effects. A woman usually thrilled to be perceiving herself, admiring the beauty of her face, her body, her clothes, her style, through others' eyes. Unless it was fear? Fear of what she might say, or do. As the door was opened at last, a harried-looking young woman stood in the doorway, staring at Augusta. She said:

"Yes? What do you want?"

This was the wife of Harold Thwaite. Augusta wasn't certain of the name. Janet, Janice? Mrs. Thwaite seemed to the elder woman impudently young. There was a further insult here. Young Mrs. Thwaite wore a sweatshirt, jeans. She was slender, twenty pounds lighter than Augusta Cutler; her breasts were hidden inside the sweatshirt that bore the legend JONES POINT COMMUNITY COLLEGE. It was a Saturday morning, children's voices were raised in the house behind her. A telephone rang. Mrs. Thwaite's expression was tight with suspicion.

Quickly Augusta said, "Mrs. Thwaite? You don't know me. I'm Augusta Cutler, I live in Salthill, I was a, a—" not knowing how to describe her relationship with Adam, disliking to claim intimacy, not wanting to sound sentimental, "—a close friend of Adam Berendt's. I—wondered if we might speak? For just a minute."

The young woman stared at the middle-aged woman with alarm and a growing revulsion. Yet something constrained her, a need to be courteous; she dared not shut the door in Augusta Cutler's face.

Behind her a child's voice lifted. *Mom-my?*

Augusta said, a little stiffly, "Mrs. Thwaite? I think you know—who Adam Berendt was?"

Mrs. Thwaite said, "No. Not actually." She was surprisingly prim, nervous. A nerve twitched in her left eyelid. "We didn't know . . . that man."

Augusta's heart was beating rapidly. There were times, even

before Adam's death, when she'd felt faint; ascending even a brief flight of stairs, she might feel light-headed; her moistly radiant skin, her still-youthful beauty, maintained by moisturizers, creams, oils, facials, and collagen injections, was deceiving to her as to others, for she was fifty-two years old, and not a woman devoted to exercising.

"I understand. I realize. You didn't know . . . him. And so I was hoping," Augusta said, half-pleading, "you might want to? You, and Samantha? I've brought along a few things." In her handbag, a packet of snapshots. Adam Berendt, with his Salthill friends. Adam Berendt, with some of his sculptures. Adam Berendt, alone. "May I come inside?" Something was being exposed in Augusta, like the white flash of bone piercing skin. The raw white pain that accompanies it. Behind the woman, in a farther room, the child appeared. A little fluff-haired blond girl carrying a small object.

"Samantha? Is that—Samantha?" Augusta called. She would have stepped into the house except the harried-looking woman in sweatshirt and jeans, quick as a girl athlete, blocked her way.

"I'm sorry. Whoever you are. You'd better leave."

"Let me talk to your daughter, please? For just a minute."

"I said I'm sorry. No."

"It would mean so much to her, I think," Augusta said, "not now so much as in the future? When she's older, and thinks back? You will allow her to—think back, won't you? You will keep Adam's memory alive—won't you?"

In an angry shaking voice the younger woman said, "I said go away! You're not welcome here! Upsetting us! I'm going to call the police if you don't go away. This is a private home, you're not welcome here, we've been through all this, *no more!*"

Augusta drew breath to protest, but the door was shut in her face.

"How can you! He died for—for your family! Your well-being, your selfish happiness!"

It was an absurd melodramatic scene. Afterward, Augusta would but dimly remember except to think *Was that me? That desperate woman.*

Of course she retreated, she returned to Salthill and the refuge of her home. She'd had a final impression of the little blond girl staring in her direction, listening. *It will matter to her. Someday.* There was that solace, of which she was certain.

No one in Salthill would ever know. She'd had no close confidante except Adam. But now the madness had touched her, ah! she was *alive*.

Departing. There was a woman of Junoesque beauty, fifty-two years old. She announced to her husband, "I'm quitting." Their children were grown and departed, they lived alone together in a six-bedroom French Normandy house on Pheasant Run, in a semirural neighborhood of similarly large, expensive homes a few miles west of Salthill-on-Hudson, New York. "Whatever this is, this mausoleum, I'm quitting." Since early childhood she'd had magical dreams of flying along the surface of the earth, leaping into the sky, breaking into a strange beautiful singing speech all would hear and admire, and none would comprehend. Sometimes in her dreams she was splendidly naked, defiant and unafraid. "Because I can't breathe. And I must breathe, to live." It was true, the air in the Cutlers' house was sometimes unnourishing. You could breathe deeply, yet not get enough oxygen. Ascending even a brief flight of stairs, you might feel light-headed, dazed as a time-traveler. *What is this place, why am I here?* The house was surrounded by tall elegant trees, Scots pine and blue cedar, their fragrant piercing needles entered her sleep and caused her to cry aloud. "Yes, dear? What?" Her husband smiled his vague distracted smile. He was reading the *New York Times* business section. He had heard his wife's voice, but not her words. Often in the night, when they shared the same bed, when Augusta poked him awake because he was snoring loudly, or turning restlessly, Owen would say, "Just a minute, dear," and he said this now, frowning at something in the paper, "Just a minute, dear. Yes?" It was an epoch of magical transformations, the onset of the twenty-first century. It was an epoch of abrupt stops and starts. Of acquisitions, mergers, blunt and irremediable disappearances.

You might have your old frayed face peeled away, and a new, tender face sculpted in its place. You might have your very vision redesigned by laser. The husband frowned, glancing over his reading glasses. In the eyes of some, Owen Cutler was still a handsome man; in the eyes of others, he appeared unnervingly puffy, parboiled. Another Salthill man of integrity. Yet romance dwelt in his heart, often in public he was observed gazing at his wife with a sort of appalled admiration. "Gussie? What did you say just now?" How fierce, how invigorated Augusta felt, having made her decision! The one-eyed man had entered her soul, he had forced her to see her life without illusion. And the Thwaite woman, shutting a door in her face. Yes, it was time. "How long have we been married, Owen?" Though she already knew the answer yet she counted on the fingers of both hands, twice, three times. Before coming downstairs on this breezy Sunday morning in late October she'd washed her face in very cold water. Her eyes were dilated, blazing like Christmas lights. Fifty-two years old, which is not young, yet not old. This man did not know her, knew but the shell, the husk of her, the feminine mannerisms, the makeup and clothes, the inexhaustible spring of emotion. Her grown children did not know her, certainly her friends did not know her. Only the one-eyed man had known her soul. For what was Augusta but a swath of brilliant sunshine breaking through thunderhead clouds, ah! she was *alive*. "Thirty-one years. By the end of this week, thirty-two. That's enough." The husband's face was of a porous, florid hue. The mouth was strangely small, pointed like a beak. Over the tops of his half-moon glasses he regarded his wife, an emotional woman, a woman dear to him in her very excesses, with something like astonishment. He was fifty-five years old, he took a powerful medication to control high blood pressure. His genitals drooped like skinned organs, somewhat shrunken, inconsequent, in his boxer shorts, hidden by his clothes; always, he was aware of them, without knowing why. So strange to think that his once-hot seed had engendered children: *his*. These were long since grown and departed but sometimes in the quiet house you could hear their jarring footfalls, their quarrels, the echoes of raised child-voices. "Gussie, what? What is *enough?*" For thirty-one years she'd been held hostage by her children, no one could have guessed how bitterly she resented it, as she resented her wifehood, her motherhood, her very comfort as the wife of Owen Cutler, her diminished soul beating against its confinement like a bird trapped in a chimney. "Gussie, you're feverish. Your hair in your face, no shoes on your feet, you're *unwell.*" The husband had no idea how she'd loved Adam Berendt, he had no idea of her passionate inner life. He would not know. With his partners he owned medical facilities in Rockland County and upstate. His investments were narrow but carefully chosen. He, too, was a dreamer since childhood, he had magical dreams! dreams of intense happiness! that dissolved tragically when he opened his eyes. In Salthill he was a prominent citizen, everywhere he went his hand was warmly shaken. It astonished him, that no one had yet guessed that Owen Cutler was a froth of bubbles floating upon a void. It filled him with wonder, both guilt and gratitude, that others should shake his hand, that women should teeter on the toes of their expensive shoes, to graze their lips against his cheek, as if he were as real as they. "Gussie? What?" He saw his wife's mouth moving but could not comprehend her words. Suddenly, she seemed to be speaking foreign words, distasteful gibberish-words. And her mouth that was always made up lusciously red-gleaming as a work of art was raw and pale, thin-lipped. At the age of nineteen Augusta Fitzgerald had been the most gorgeous and the most "vivacious" of that season's crop of debutantes in Atlanta, Georgia, she'd quickly fled north to escape her fate. Yet here was her fate, a man rising to his feet, approaching her to claim her. "Don't! Don't touch me. I've told you *all this is over.*" A thin cold autumn wind had been blowing through the night, the sky had been washed clean. Like isolated thoughts through the night evergreen needles fell on the slate roofs. The husband saw the dangerous feral-flash of his wife's eyes yet dared to touch her. He wanted merely to calm her, he dreaded a hysterical woman. "No! Never again." Wildly she slapped at him. He could not believe the strength in her soft fleshy body. "Gussie, please! You *are* feverish. You *are* unwell." It was an epoch of diminished souls and yet an epoch of thrilling public romance. The President and the Girl Intern. These were Jove and Io, inflamed by passion. Both were blundering, clumsy, bovine yet handsome creatures. No mortals could presume to judge them. The childlike exultation in the face of the Girl Intern in the fetching beret as she leans forward to be publicly hugged, kissed, raised to stardom by the boyishly grinning President. And there was the tragic romance of the Black Athlete and the Blond Beauty, his former wife and the mother of his children. All of America had thrilled to their story. The Black Athlete was a handsome hot-blooded man in the prime of life who'd loved the Blond Beauty so much he'd had to murder her. His passion was such, he'd nearly severed her head from her body with a butcher knife. This was a manly passion lesser individuals might thrill to, and envy. Owen Cutler accepted it that he was no longer moved by passion, yet still in his heart there remained romance, or the memory of romance. His own beautiful girl-bride in her lacy dazzling-white bridal gown. The love of his youth. Now, this middle-aged woman who denounced him. "Owen, we've lost all mystery for each other. We're corpses embalmed together, this is our mausoleum. I can't bear it any longer." She began at last to weep. But when he tried sensibly to restrain her, she raked her nails down the side of his face, slapped and kicked at him like a maddened cat. "Augusta! God damn you." He was a man who rarely cursed, and now the woman had goaded him into cursing her. She ran from him. She fled upstairs. He was quaking with shock and fury, he would not pursue her. How he dreaded, despised, loathed hysterical women! These Salthill women. They were keening harpies mourning the death of the one-eyed man. A rogue, that Berendt. A suspicious character. In death, yet more suspicious. He, Owen Cutler, scarcely gave death a thought. If queried, he would have boasted that he was indifferent, stoic. He'd been baptized in the Episcopal church and he believed in the immortality of the soul, to a degree. Not all souls, not mass-souls, the teeming populations of the under-earth, but the souls of civilized Western populations. He'd long ago made out his will. Signed, sealed, fully executed. Just another legal document among a lifetime of such documents. He would not indulge his hysterical wife, that was no good. The Salthill women fantasized about Adam Berendt because Berendt had been an old battered rogue elephant living at the edge of the clearing. He'd avoided marriage, domestic life. There was something infuriating about Berendt. Always, the one-eyed man was *right;* even in acknowledging he might be mistaken, he came across as *right;* the kind of man to put the rest of us in the *wrong;* when Owen heard of Berendt's death, the first word that crossed his lips was "Good!" If he seriously believed that Augusta had been the one-eyed man's lover . . . Her warm sensuous female body opened to that brute . . . If she'd been unfaithful to Owen . . . "No. Impossible." Women fantasized, invented. To save their lives. Men had to understand, forgive. These women, still physically beautiful, desirable, retaining as if by magic their youth well into their fifties, and beyond, past childbirth, well into menopause—their penchant for romance and exaggeration had to be forgiven. Though of course it was a sickness. He refused to trot after Augusta like a trained dog. "Let her come to *me.*" He dabbed at his face with a tissue and was surprised to see how lightly it had bled. Thirty years ago, his and Augusta's quarrels had risen swift as wildfire, Augusta had sometimes struck at Owen and he'd grappled with her and they'd ended making love, panting and ecstatic. Now, no longer. All that was finished. Owen was glad that Berendt had died, and was gone from Salthill. Through one of the house's exquisite leaded windows, Owen saw sunlight winking and jeering at him, that he took his bubble-life so seriously.

Upstairs, Augusta threw on clothes. She had money: in fact, she had wads of money, in large denominations: in secret she'd been making preparations for just such a flight. She would buy her ticket at the airport. "But where? Where can I *go?* Adam, give me a sign." Her eyes gleamed like the eyes of one deranged by a vision. She would not be deterred from her vision. The damned children had held her hostage, well into their twenties. The man downstairs had held her hostage. And yes, her "femininity" had held her hostage. *But no more.*

"Adam, this is the right thing to do, isn't it? I must *breathe.*"

If only he'd allowed her to love him. As only Augusta knew how.

Gussie darling, no. We can't.

She'd said, laughing, *Bullshit!*

Laughing at Adam who'd seemed just slightly shocked by her. Though they joked a good deal, and exchanged bawdy witticisms, he was a man you didn't touch carelessly, or provocatively. Yet that side of Adam that was brooding and preoccupied with his sculptures and the pursuit of old dull things like philosophy and truth, Augusta ignored. Why didn't he pay more attention to *her*, why didn't he adore *her?* Augusta's luscious female mouth that, in private, with uninhibited men not her husband, loved to utter profanities. And obscenities. Teasing *Why not fuck me just once, Adam, give it a try? C'mon!* He'd laughed, turned away from her yes but Augusta could see he was flattered, and aroused.

You know it wouldn't be just once, Gussie. And it wouldn't be just a fuck.

She knew! She shouldn't be endangering their friendship. For this friendship with Adam Berendt had become the most valuable thing in Augusta's life. Not even motherhood had meant so much to her.

It was in June, several weeks before Adam was to die, that he came to swim in the Cutlers' pool, as often he came at Augusta's invitation, and that afternoon only Augusta was present, and she saw another time the shiny burn scars on Adam's chest beneath the grizzled hairs, and more fine, feathery scars on his back, and for the first time she dared speak of these scars, because she and Adam were alone together and it was a moment of possible intimacy, and in the pool she dared touch him, and felt him shiver at her touch. *Was this a childhood accident, Adam?*

Augusta knew, she shouldn't pursue the subject. But she couldn't resist. *Were others injured in the fire, Adam?* It was a sudden terrible hunger in her, almost a mother's hunger, to know! But Adam drew away, and seemed not to hear, swimming to the far end of the pool. *Swimming away from me. Swimming to his death.*

The quaking bright water through which Adam Berendt swam

with short choppy splashing strokes, wet head lifted and alert like an otter's, seemed to float in a distant reflected sky. Only a single time, mildly medicated, had Augusta returned to Adam's property on the River Road. To contemplate in horror-awe the soil in which her lover's ashes had been raked. It was late July, the garden was overgrown with weeds, tall thistles and blossoming vines, life was teeming here, sun-baked and except for the sounds of insects and birds utterly silent. Adam's tomatoes were stunted, black-blistered from heat and no rain; the pole beans were withered, stricken by some sort of disease. Everywhere were aphids, Japanese beetles. Sunflowers drooped along the back fence, not nearly so tall as they'd grown under Adam's care in the past. *Life devours life,* Adam had said, *but man breaks the cycle, man has memory.* But was that so? How trustworthy was memory? How ephemeral, how doomed to oblivion? Augusta, wandering in the garden, a full-bodied woman one might have mistaken for a much younger woman, a still-questing, still-yearning woman, slapped at flies and gnats with increasing exasperation, and began suddenly to cry. Then she laughed. Oh, it was ridiculous! Why was she here! Staring at the crumbly earth beneath her expensive sandals, looking for—what? Grains of powder, Adam Berendt's lost being? Adam himself would be laughing at her. *Gussie! Christ's sake, go home.* He was a God-damned prude, Adam Berendt; always advising Salthill women to go home to their husbands, families; easy for him, the bastard, who had no wife, no family. She might have defied Adam, for Augusta, years before, had had lovers; not many, but a few; carefully chosen lovers who were not Salthill residents, but were men of her social class; men who knew, if only distantly, her husband; men who respected her husband, and by extension beautiful Augusta Cutler; yes, the penises of numerous men had been taken into her soft sensuous desirable body, yes and given her pleasure, though an intermittent and erratic pleasure, and Owen had never known. (*Had* Owen guessed? Suspected? Sometimes seeing his gaze drift onto her in social gatherings, that strange impersonal look of possession, and pride in possession, she'd felt a thrill of fear, and she'd wondered.)

Not long after the visit to the garden, there came in the mail, addressed to MRS. AUGUSTA CUTLER, a plain manila envelope marked PERSONAL, no return address, postmarked Salthill, and inside the envelope were the six or seven nude photos Augusta had taken of herself with a timed, tripod camera, lying nude on a sofa in the pose of Manet's Olympia, opulent-bodied Augusta wearing only pearls, a flower in her hair, with her pug-nosed snowy-white Persian cat at her bare feet—the photos she'd given to Adam, as a joke. (Well, not entirely as a joke. The poses were glamorous, sleazy, lurid, lascivious, and inviting.) How they'd roared with laughter. Adam had loved the photos of his pal Gussie, he'd put them away for safekeeping. But he'd died. You never quite think: my lover might die. And then? Another woman was executor of his personal estate. The photos had been found. No note accompanied them but Augusta surmised they'd been sent by Marina Troy. Such a tactful gesture was typical of the quiet red-haired youngish woman. Augusta was deeply grateful to Marina, for the photos might have been used to blackmail Augusta; she'd left herself open for such a predicament, such a scandal; at the same time, Augusta was deeply embarrassed, even mortified. God damn: what business was it of Marina Troy's, that Augusta Cutler had been in love with Adam Berendt? (Even more she dreaded the younger woman knowing that Adam hadn't quite returned Augusta's love. *That* was the true insult.) Yet Augusta, a generous woman, a good-sport sort of woman, visited the Salthill Bookstore on Pedlar's Lane, and in a typical flurry of buying purchased more than three hundred dollars' worth of books in a short period of time. Augusta was an avid reader of romances so long as these were disguised as "serious"—"literary"—novels; otherwise, prose failed to grip her imagination, she fell into a romantic-erotic reverie that no fiction could penetrate. But, that day in Marina's bookstore, Augusta was disapppointed that Marina hid in her back office while a young college-girl assistant waited on her. *Please tell Marina hello from her friend Gussie. I'll be calling her soon for a dinner party.* Yet somehow, Augusta never called Marina; she'd planned to return to the quaint little store on Pedlar's Lane soon again, and buy more books, yet somehow she had not; the summer slipped away; she began to avoid Marina Troy, whenever they chanced to meet; the very sight of the lanky melancholy red-haired youngish woman became an annoyance to her; and in the fall she heard from mutual friends that Marina had abruptly left Salthill, leasing her house, hiring a manager to supervise the store; rumor was, Marina had gone to live in the Catskills, unless it was the Adirondacks, or the Poconos, on property Adam Berendt had left her in his will. This news was devastating to Augusta, for Adam had left her nothing. She instructed herself *Don't be jealous, you don't know the circumstances. Adam felt sorry for her. You are the one he loved.*

Now she was packing her things, she would fly away, her heart lifted in exaltation. Since childhood she'd had such magical dreams! Even the eye of God looked upon her in loving approval. *Oh, Adam. My love. I will come to you. I swear.*

2

The Search. There came the husband seeking the wife, repentant, or seeming so, for perhaps in his heart he was still very angry with the hysterical woman, and he looked for her in the bedroom, but she wasn't there; he looked for her in adjacent rooms, including her steamy-fragrant bathroom, but she wasn't there; he looked for her in the guest wing of the house, but she wasn't there; he looked for her downstairs in the formal living room, and in the informal family room, in the dining room and in the kitchen and in the solarium, but she was in none of these places; he looked for her in his own study, and he looked for her in the basement, and he looked for her on the rear stairs, and in closets, but she wasn't there. "Augusta?" he cried, "Augusta darling?" the alarmed husband cried, but there was no answer, there would be no answer, his wife of almost thirty-two years had vanished, no sound in the house except the familiar ghost-echoes, mere vibrations of sound that, even as you strain to listen, fade.

PART II

. . . And I Don't Escape You

The Fell of Dark

I

Damascus County, Pennsylvania. Where I have come as a pilgrim to discover—whatever awaits me, to be discovered.

And here was the first surprise of her new life: in a rear room of the house Adam Berendt had deeded to her in the Pocono Mountains, she discovered a number of unfinished sculpted pieces, obviously Adam's work. Pushing open a door to what she assumed would be another barely furnished bedroom and seeing, in this shadowy cave with tattered sheets of newspaper strewn on bare floorboards, in air that looked congealed with time, objects of about the size of stunted human beings, crude constructions of scrap metal and Plexiglas, plastic and aluminum foil, soft-rotted wood, dried bullrushes, pieces of clay and glittering glass. Marina's first reaction was fright—were these things *alive*? But her second reaction was gratitude.

"Adam! You've left these for me."

* * *

ALREADY IN THE first hour of her new life. Already, taking possession of the stone house on this fine blazing autumn day. Already in the first flush of ownership, walking through rooms she scarcely saw. Already she was talking to herself. As she would never have done in Salthill. Even alone in her house at the top of North Pearl Street. For here in the foothills of the Poconos, in northeastern Pennsylvania, on forty acres of uncultivated fields and pine woods, in the handsome old stone house Adam Berendt had deeded to her, there was no one to hear. Silence like a glass to be shattered.

"All this? Mine? It's beautiful."

It was beautiful. Views of hills, pines, mountains from nearly every window. In a haze of first possession walking through the rooms of the old stone house. A roaring-in-the-ears like a distant waterfall. For this was so new, so utterly strange to her. *My house*. The gift her lover had bequeathed her, for no other reason than that: he'd loved her.

He'd loved the Marina Troy who was yet to be. The artist Marina Troy who'd abandoned her art a decade ago, out of cowardice. Out of terror. Out of a very practical fear of failure. That Marina Troy, Adam Berendt had loved.

"Not the 'anesthetized' Marina. Of course!"

Now she had the documents of ownership to this property at 1183 Mink Pond Road, Damascus County, Pennsylvania. She had the keys. She had the sketchy map Adam had left with her, and a list of names, telephone numbers. But these were years old, and probably outdated; Marina would make her own queries in town.

The stone house, built in 1923 by well-to-do Philadelphians, was at least a mile from its nearest neighbor on the unpaved, curving mountain road that dead-ended a mile beyond Marina's mailbox. From the road you could see few dwellings, all were hidden behind thick stands of birches, pines, scrub oaks, and enormous clay-colored boulders. The nearest town—if you could call Damascus Crossing, population four hundred, a town—was seven miles to the west. Thirty miles to the nearest city, gaunt and bravely ugly East Stroudsburg, on the Delaware River.

Marina was alone in this remote beautiful place breathing in air that tasted chill and stony as the air of a well sunk deep in the earth and she wanted to believe she'd made the right decision, not out of grief and despair needing to escape Adam's death, the nightly morbidity of obsession thoughts, mourning like chewing the inside of her lips or, as in the later stages of starvation when the body begins to feed upon the protein of the very brain, self-devouring, lethal. *Marina. Go away. Save your life. One of us, drowned, is quite enough.*

To save her life, then. That was why she was here.

"Oh, God, Adam! Don't let me fail."

With a clearer eye she began to see: the house was old, much work would have to be done to make a few rooms habitable through the winter. Badly the house needed airing, and cleaning. Everywhere there were cobwebs, the floors were covered in stained sheets of newspaper, venetian blinds were broken and emitted a jocose sort of autumn sunshine. How entirely different from Marina's tidy constricted Salthill house. Here, dust motes writhed in the air. Grimy sheets had been draped over the few pieces of furniture. Two floors to the house, a narrow stairway connecting. Cramped bathrooms, plumbing that worked, but only barely. The kitchen was an ample room, modernized in an outmoded seventies style, pieces of loose linoleum on the floor, covered in grime. Marina tried to imagine Adam in this room, sitting at the plain wooden table that faced a window, stocky shoulders hunched forward as he peered out the window at a distant mountain but the vision eluded her, just yet. The truth was, Adam hadn't lived here often. He hadn't visited his "stone house in the mountains" for years. A local caretaker was hired to tend to it, and a local real estate agent rented it out to summer tenants.

Was there nothing of Adam here, would she discover nothing of him, how could she bear such solitude.

Marina was too restless to sit down. Nerved-up from her drive across northern New Jersey on I-80. This plunge-into-the-unknown. Walking another time through the house, counting rooms upstairs and down, but each time she counted a different number, like a fairy-tale heroine under a spell, for were there three bedrooms upstairs? or four? and downstairs, what?—the large open living-dining room, an aged fieldstone fireplace measuring perhaps twelve feet across to accommodate cross-sawed tree trunks, fireplace and stacked kindling festooned in cobweb like gossamer confetti. In the next room, overlooking a steep hill strewn with boulders, there were tottering bookshelves crammed with paperback romances, mysteries, crossword puzzles, and knitting patterns; the walls covered in a blinding poppy-red print Marina couldn't imagine Adam tolerating, let alone having chosen. For here was a stranger's house, an unexpected house. And everywhere underfoot, tiny skeletons of birds and rodents; everywhere the desiccated husks of insects; a large number of silver-gray moths with wings beautifully marked in black, as with hieroglyphics.

What strange moths! Large as hummingbirds. Marina picked one up to examine closely. Its wings were covered in a fine luminous powder, its tiny black eyes shone like mica.

"Adam, see here? A true work of art!"

Marina came to herself, and with a shiver let the thing fall.

Wiping her powder-smeared fingers unconsciously on her clothing Marina continued through her new house. *Her* house! *Her* possession, and her responsibility. She did not want to think that beneath her excitement was an undercurrent of something very like dread, panic. For this was an adventure out of her lost girlhood—wasn't it? Each room was a surprise, floorboards creaked beneath her feet as if in warning. Strange: the view from one window seemed subtly different from the same view from another. Where was Mount Rue? She'd found it before: at just under three thousand feet, the highest peak in the Poconos. There was High Knob, a smaller peak. Or was she confusing them? Her view was obscured by vines growing over windows, grimy panes. She heard something overhead, a scuttling sound along the roof: squirrels? hawks? (Red-tailed hawks were plentiful in the Poconos, Marina had noticed them drifting in the sky above Mink Pond Road as if leading her onward. This way! This way!) She listened carefully, telling herself it was nothing, of course.

It was then she pushed open the door to the back room. The door stuck just perceptibly as if it were latched shut, but the latch was loose, and did not hold. She couldn't recall if she'd already seen this room on her quick excursion through the house. So many doors in the old stone house: one that led downstairs to the cellar, opening off the kitchen, others to closets, a storage room. But this was a door to a room Marina hadn't noticed previously, apparently built as an addition to the rear of the house; boldly Marina pushed the door open, stepped inside, and her breath caught in her throat, for—what were these strange things?

Crude works of art, unfinished sculptures of Adam's. This must have been his workroom, much smaller and darker than his Salthill studio. It was cavelike and shadowy and smelled of dust, damp, and disuse. A melancholy odor. Gnarly vines grew across the windows like exposed veins. Though it was a whitish-glaring autumn day, little light came into the room. Marina switched on an overhead light, but nothing happened, of course, she hadn't yet made arrangements for electricity to be turned on. *I am the new owner of the property at 1183 Mink Pond Road, Damascus Crossing. Will you please supply me with power?*

Marina entered Adam's former workroom shyly, wondering at her good fortune. Here was something of Adam Berendt, left behind! Forgotten even by him, it seemed. (Or had Adam deeded the house to Marina years ago, knowing she'd one day discover these?) She was fascinated to see that several of the sculptures were constructed like sculptures of Adam's she knew, including the ambitious Laocoön, but these were hardly more than skeletal, rather like sketches. Even when completed, they would have been small-scale, coming barely to Marina's shoulder; Adam's completed work was often sizable, monumental. Unable to resist touching—for Marina was a sculptor, sculptors must *touch*—Marina ran her fingers over the twisted scrap metal, the sheets of brittle plastic, aluminum foil, cellophane, and shards of glass embedded in clay. How many years had it been since Adam had touched these? Dust in layers, everywhere cobwebs like powdery lace. Adam had been negligent about securing his materials, binding them together with wire, twine, or clothesline, and some materials had broken away from the construct and fallen to the floor. "Oh, Adam. Look what you've done." She could hear his voice in protest: he'd wanted, he said, the haphazard ephemeral fluidity of life; of things called *art* happening by accident, even clumsy or ironic accident, and but once. Most sculptors want permanence. Adam had thought permanence "overrated." And so he'd been careless, sloppy. Sometimes. For look at the condition of these pieces.

His Salthill friends had had to rescue some of Adam's best work from him and now, ironically, these works would outlive the man.

The constructions left behind in the old stone house in the Poconos were crude and sketchy and would certainly look to an unsympathetic eye not very promising, but Marina Troy knew better! She knew how such sketches might evolve by slow, groping degrees into something very different, if the artist persevered. Sometimes, you were simply struck by lightning. Inside each construction was a vision, the artist's vision, and this vision might even now, years later, be realized. Marina could imagine filling in certain of the pieces, determining the trajectories of curves and completing them. These abandoned sculptures of Adam Berendt's, what were they but riddles?—precious gems obscured in sludge?

It had become late afternoon. This warm whitish day in early September. Nine weeks after Adam's death. A day that had begun in some anxiety, in an obscure dark, but already so long ago, in so distant a place, Marina scarcely recalled. Calmly her heart was beating now. A great happiness suffused her like a light coming slowly up.

"Adam! I can finish these for you. That's why I'm here."

OUTSIDE IN THE waning light Marina tramped through tall grasses gone to seed. Like frozen waves they were. Yet buzzing with gnats, tiny flies. She was wearing trousers, a long-sleeved shirt. Prickly vines caught at her like importunate strangers. Wild rose, hidden amid the grass. It would have to be cleared away lest it take over everything. At the front of the house was a screened-in porch made of wood painted magenta-gray, though peeling now, and the screen was rusted and pocked, and would have to be replaced. A sinewy vine resembling wisteria was pushing through the screen and would soon cover the porch and the windows. It, too, would have to be cleared away lest it take over everything. *Hello! My name is Marina Troy and I'm the new owner of the property at 1183 Mink Pond Road, will you please help me?*

Yet how beautiful the grasses like stilled, frozen waves, and the wild rose and vines. Soon it would be autumn, deciduous leaves turning color against the unchanging pines. And overhead a sky pale as a watercolor wash of no distinct color, a faint sepia-gold shading into blue.

A phone?

She would not have a phone.

But shouldn't she have a phone?

No.

In case of—

No.

Wasn't it irresponsible as well as dangerous, a woman alone in this remote place, without a—

No.

She feared Roger Cavanagh telephoning her. Between them was a shared memory like a shared flap of skin. No, no! The thought revulsed her. In weak moments she felt a dull sullen ache between her legs, waking in the night from dreams of sexual yearning in which she opened herself to the man, moaning with desire, unless he'd become any man, the beautiful supple warm body of the male to be touched, caressed, kissed, enjoined *Come to me! Oh, please.* And waking agitated, ashamed. What did a woman lacking a lover do, that was not ignoble, piteous, self-disgusting, when sexual yearning came so strong? She half believed that Roger Cavanagh must sense her feeling. Did he dream of Marina, too? Almost, they'd become lovers. It had nearly happened. But then it had not happened. A slapstick scene! Marina had a vague absurd memory—of course it was absurd!—of Adam watching the two of them as they'd grappled like drowning swimmers on the gritty floor of Adam's studio, laughing uproariously. She knew that Roger would never forgive her for that episode, and she did not want to forgive him. How awkward they'd been, spreading and raking Adam's ashes into his garden. When by accident he'd touched her arm, Marina had recoiled in distaste. No, no! She was not an irrational person (was this what irrational persons told themselves?) and yet she could not bear Roger Cavanagh's touch. Yet he'd called her through the summer. She knew from mutual friends that he'd asked about her, often. Roger Cavanagh was a man, a lawyer, for whom the telephone is an automatic extension of his will; and his will, a lawyer's will, must be consummated. She knew, and she dreaded knowing. But she'd escaped him, and would escape him. She had fled to Damascus County, Pennsylvania, to escape him. *I don't want you, it's Adam I want. Adam I love.*

In time, she supposed he would acquire her address. She would not think about it. Her responsibilities in Salthill she'd delegated to others. A young woman named Molly Ivers was managing the bookstore in her absence and when Marina wanted to speak with Molly she would telephone her from Damascus Crossing, and she'd given Molly the number of a real estate agent in the vicinity if there was an urgent reason for them to speak. And Molly had Marina's post office box number in town, which she had sworn not to give out to others. And Marina had left information with relatives in Maine, in case of an emergency involving her mother. Enough, enough!

Circling the house in a distended loop, walking with difficulty through the wavy grass, Marina stumbled upon the remains of a stone well. She had a childhood dread of such deep, depthless things, like elevator shafts descending into—what? Don't look. The drinking water for the house came from an underground spring that must have flowed into this well, but the well itself was covered with heavy planks, no longer in use. There were several outbuildings on the property: a small asphalt-sided garage, a guest cabin made of authentic-looking logs, a storage barn and a dilapidated shed. The garage was crammed with useless old things, rusted hand mower, cracked earthware pots, a bicycle with a flat tire. Nothing of Adam's. The guest cabin was a single unadorned room with a braided rug faded to no-color, a pot-bellied stove covered in cobwebs, bunk beds and bare, stained mattresses. On the floor lay a boy's laceless sneaker. And the mummified remains of a small gray bird, a junco. In the storage barn were a tractor with flat tires, gardening equipment, boxes, and items of furniture, everything covered in cobwebs and not a thing that would seem to have belonged to Adam. The detritus of strangers' lives that might have been fascinating to Marina if converted into art but otherwise held no interest. As Marina stood in the doorway, something behind the tractor scuttled violently away, Marina had a glimpse of a dark-furred creature blurred with speed, rather large for a raccoon but she wanted to think it must be a raccoon, nothing more dangerous. Her heart was beating with adrenaline as if she'd been running. She knew there was no reason to be afraid, she was alone here. Yet she stood in the grass, trembling.

Forty acres. Hers.

The vehicle in the driveway, parked near the house, a steely-gray Jeep with a military look, startled her—it was new, Marina's new purchase, she'd decided she wanted a larger, heavier vehicle for Damascus County and had traded in her compact car for a Jeep and driving westward to Pennsylvania amid a thunderous roar of trucks and trailers she'd been grateful for the vehicle's heft, and had come to appreciate its height. But she wasn't yet accustomed to owning it. She wasn't accustomed to seeing it.

"All mine?"

This property, this gift, in Damascus County! She'd told few Salthill friends about it. Roger Cavanagh had to know, but she'd never discussed it with him. Years ago when Adam had first spoken of it to Marina she'd been annoyed with him, upset, hadn't wanted to listen because the gift, though well intentioned, was hurtful to her. She'd wanted to protest, "But Adam, I love you! Won't you miss me? How can you send me away for a year?" The very word *Damascus* was painful to her. Now as waning sunshine in this beautiful remote place in the mountains swiped across her face and upper body like a scythe's blade she began to wonder: Maybe Adam had intended to visit her, during that year away? Maybe he'd intended to stay with her in the old stone house? Away from Salthill-on-Hudson. The scrutiny of their friends.

Maybe she'd misunderstood.

She wished now she'd asked Adam more forcibly about the property. Why he'd purchased it, and when he'd actually lived here. Why he'd never sold it. (But he'd owned numerous remote scattered properties. Some of these under different names.) Marina recalled Adam mentioning in passing that he'd spent weekends here—"In retreat"—when he'd been living in Nassau County, Long Island, but when Marina pressed him to inquire what he'd been doing at that time in his life, why had he been living on Long Island, Adam had shrugged and said evasively, "Nothing of monumental interest, Marina." It was like a door shut gently but firmly in her face. He'd come to remind her of a man afflicted with amnesia who has grown contented with his condition, you dared wake such a man at your own peril.

Yet Marina bitterly regretted she hadn't wakened Adam Berendt.

Possibly another woman had. But not Marina Troy.

All this while, distracted by her thoughts, Marina was skirting the edge of the clearing, down beyond the storage barn where the land was flatter, marshy. Beyond this, the pinewoods began again. You could see how the woods were pushing inward, always inward into the clearing, saplings, tall bushes, wild rose and briars. Always nature was pushing, and man resisting. You felt a thrill of horror, and yet of satisfaction: when man gave up this resistance, nature rushed in triumphant. If Marina didn't prevent it, within a few years the property would be inundated by the forest, obliterated. The very driveway leading back from Mink Pond Road would be obscured. "It's my responsibility, is it? Yes." She felt heartened. She was confident. Adam Berendt had given her this gift for a reason, she would be equal to it.

A strong, sickening odor wafted to her. The ground was spongy underfoot. Here was scattered trash: pieces of rotted lumber, a bucket of hard-congealed tar, children's toys, a naked and hairless rubber doll with widened glass-green eyes. Marina was disgusted, that Adam's former tenants had littered his property like this. Half-consciously she picked up the doll. A bland blank face, but the eyes glittered like jewels. Marina pried out the eyes, dropped the doll and studied the glass eyes in the palm of her hand. A strange thing for her to have done. Already she was beginning to think like an artist, one for whom any stray object might be an inspiration: "What does it mean, I've found these?" But the odor was distracting. Her nostrils pinched, she felt a tinge of nausea. Her instinct was to depart quickly but instead she pushed forward through wild rose and rushes, drawn by curiosity, staring in horror at—what? The naked body of a woman with matted brown hair, sprawled lifeless, partly hidden in the grass.

No. It was an animal.

Was it? An animal, it must be a dead animal.

Marina's eyes filled with tears of shock. Scarcely could she see. Now her heart was truly hammering in her chest.

Cautiously she crept forward, she had to determine this. Seeing to her relief of course it wasn't a human being, but the carcass of a white-tailed deer.

A doe. Partly decomposed. Much of the belly and torso was missing, cruelly torn away by predators, but the head remained, the slender neck craned far to one side and the mouth frozen open in the anguished pose of the dying horse in Picasso's *Guernica*.

2

IT HAPPENED IN Marina Troy's thirty-ninth year, unexpectedly and more or less contentedly she lived alone in an isolated stone house in primitive surroundings in the Pocono Mountains, in northeastern Pennsylvania; in Damascus County near the crossroads town of Damascus Crossing of which, only a short time before, she'd never heard.

It was madness! It was to be the great adventure of her life.

From her arrival in September through the remainder of the year Marina immersed herself in completing Adam Berendt's fragmentary constructions. You could not really call these "sculptures"—they were embryos she would bring to life. By turns she was exhilarated and despairing. It was a risky thing she did. She'd set aside plans for her own work, indefinitely. This was far more urgent work. Some mornings she woke inspired, suffused with energy and a need to begin work immediately, still barefoot, in her flannel nightgown with a sweater twined around her shoulders, and her mouth still tasting of sleep; other mornings, when autumn rain pounded against the windows of the drafty stone house, she woke groggily to a sense of oppression, as if a weight lay upon her chest, a heavy dark-furred creature the front of whose bullet-head she could not see. *Yet it has a snout. It sucks at my breath. It has small beady yellow-glass eyes.* She had to push the furry creature from her in order to fully wake. She would lie then breathing hard, panting, in the unfamiliar bed, blinking and staring at the unfamiliar ceiling, for some minutes until she recovered her senses, and remembered where she was, and why.

Damascus County, Pennsylvania. In an old summer house built of stone, on forty acres of hilly, wooded land, this lonely beautiful impractical place deeded to her by Adam Berendt. Yet she was coming to think it a legacy. Left to Marina in Adam's will.

Bequeathed to my friend Marina Troy. Beloved friend Marina Troy who has survived me.

She knew what they were saying of her in Salthill-on-Hudson. Where has Marina gone, why has Marina behaved so recklessly, is Marina in a state of shock, is Marina in a state of mourning, how can Marina break away from her own life, her responsibilities, is it true she's going away for a year to live alone, and—why? Marina's heart beat in indignation, imagining. She would not explain or defend herself. She was determined. She'd made her decision. She would break with her anesthetized Salthill life. So Adam had described it—"anesthetized." No more! Her house on North Pearl Street was leased to tenants, she'd hired a capable young woman manager for the bookstore, she'd resigned as personal executor of Adam Berendt's estate, not wanting to learn more of Adam's private, secret life. *I will remember the man as I knew him. I will never surrender that.*

Once Marina was fully wakened and out of that deep seductive clinging sleep and once she'd begun working in the studio at the rear of the house, the narrow windows now cleared of vines on the outside, and cobwebs on the inside, and sunlight, if there was sunlight, entering from the east, she felt much stronger. It was a fact, she was happy. Now she'd so radically simplified her life, she was happy. She'd come to Damascus County with the original intention of working on her own art, which she'd abandoned years ago in her twenties, and she fully intended to take up her "own" art again sometime in the future, only just not yet. "This is more important. This is crucial." She felt that she was arguing with Adam himself, and she would convince him. Entering into a trancelike state, working tirelessly. She was not inventing. This was "restoration"—"divination." No objects she added to Adam's uncompleted pieces, no scrap metal, or plastic, or broken glass, or tree limbs, were merely her idea. On the studio walls she'd taped photos of Adam's finished sculptures back in Salthill (as it happened, among the few things she'd packed to bring to the Poconos were these photos, for Marina hadn't wanted to go away without mementos of Adam's work) and often she stood staring at these for long periods of time, almost unseeing, under the spell of their mystery. *Come to me. Enter me. Give life to me!*

Strange it seemed to her, unfair and unjust, that Adam Berendt hadn't been recognized during his lifetime as a sculptor of genuine talent. His work should have been represented by major galleries. It should have been purchased by major museums. If only he hadn't lacked ambition! Surely Adam had been as gifted and original a sculptor as Raul Farco, whose work he'd purchased anonymously for the arts council. Surely he was as American-idiosyncratic as Rauschenberg, and in his more austere pieces as powerful as Henry Moore . . . "But it's no good to think in that way. It's demeaning to Adam."

As time passed two pieces of Adam's, reproduced in the photographs, exerted a strong influence on Marina. The "natural crucifix" made of a grotesquely twisted oak limb, with oddly shaped rocks and stones at its base, and the six-foot "American Laocoön" of translucent plastic, which seemed, even in the photograph, to be constantly changing hues as if living, breathing. Yet while Marina recalled this large unsettling construction in Adam's studio as heroic, in this space, which was smaller and less brightly lit, it seemed to have acquired a taunting, malicious air. *Catch me if you can. But you will never catch me.*

But Marina was not directly copying any of Adam's existing work. She was not!

When she completed these sculptures, if they seemed to her of merit commensurate with Adam's previous work, and not an insult to his memory, she intended to find for them a New York gallery of distinction. It was a bold, risky thing she was doing, unprecedented. The Poconos work of Adam Berendt, as these pieces would likely be called, would be recognized immediately as by Adam Berendt, yet it would be entirely new, unique. *Works of Berendt the man had not lived to create. A miracle.* Marina would have to acknowledge her role in their creation, for to fail to do so would be to commit a forgery, but in fact as she worked she emptied her mind, conscientious as a Zen monk in meditation, of her personal ideas, memories, reflexes, impulses, that she might be guided by Adam's vision. She'd brought a number of his books with her, and at mealtimes and in the evening she read avidly; and reread; committing to memory certain of the passages Adam had underlined in Plato, Ovid, Blake, Walt Whitman, Gerard Manley Hopkins. Were these clues to her lover's deepest, most elusive soul, he'd never revealed to Marina Troy—

> I wake and feel the fell of dark, not day.
> What hours, O what black hours we have spent
> This night! what sights you, heart, saw; ways you went!
> And more must, in yet longer light's day.

When she worked with Adam's sculptures, she felt his power directed through her nerves and fingertips. For long hours she worked entranced. She was only part-conscious, all her life was in her fingers. If she happened to glance up at a sudden movement outside the window, at the edge of the clearing, or in the forest, or in the sky beyond Mount Rue, she scarcely registered what she saw. For she saw *inwardly*. As her fingers worked, she might hear, or seem to hear, a vehicle approaching her house, along the rutted drive; she might hear a voice, rising in the wind yet immediately fading; she might catch a glimpse of a fleeting figure (human? animal?) at the edge of the woods. Yet she was protected from alarm, she could not be distracted.

Through the autumn and into early winter Marina worked in this way, and was happy. Slowly, very slowly she was making progress! It was her strategy to focus upon an individual piece of Adam's at a time, conceiving of it as a riddle, as a heroine in a fairy tale is confronted with a riddle she must solve, or suffer what fate, she didn't wish to know. This work she built up slowly, expanding it, deepening it, then when she hit a snag moving to another, and to another, for she hoped to bring the eleven pieces to completion more or less simultaneously. Adam had worked this way, on numerous pieces in sequence, in varying styles and modes.

Until her head spun so she wanted to laugh. Her senses were dazzled. Until at last (by mid-afternoon) she was emptied of the vision of the other who inhabited her, for the time being.

AND IN THE NIGHT, the furry weight on her chest. Pressing its snout against her mouth, to suck away her breath. Flattening her breasts against her rib cage. She would suffocate! Yet the creature was warm, strangely comforting. She tried to lift her arms, to embrace it. Its fur was long, rather coarse, the hue of wood smoke, thickening for the upcoming winter.

SOMETIMES FROM the doorway Marina contemplated her handiwork. The fragmentary stunted things she'd found in the old stone house were beginning to take shape, to be of interest to the eye. Maybe.

Marina, what about your own work?
This is my work, Adam!
Your own work, I said. Marina.
Adam, this is my work. Have faith in me.

ON A PLANK TABLE in the kitchen, a scarred but handsome old piece of furniture pushed against a window, she was accumulating odd objects, as she'd done years ago as a girl. A giant gray moth with hieroglyphic wings. Hawk feathers, tiny bird skeletons, buttons, a wooden baby's rattle she'd found in the barn. The green-glass eyes she'd prized out of the rubber doll in the marsh. Sometimes eating her first meal of the day in the afternoon, ravenous with hunger, Marina contemplated these objects, too.

3

THE CALLS MARINA MADE to Salthill were on business. Once a month she spoke with the real estate agent who oversaw the rental of her North Pearl Street house, and each Monday promptly at six P.M. she spoke with the capable young woman who oversaw the bookstore in Marina's absence. Marina hadn't yet had a phone installed in the old stone house, stubbornly and superstitiously she resisted. For even an unlisted number would make her vulnerable to unwanted calls. *And in lonely weak moments, calls I don't want to make.*

Vaguely she'd promised her women friends she would call them, but that didn't seem possible, now. They would have wished to give her advice. (For what are women friends, except givers-of-advice both wanted and unwanted.) She would have found herself impersonating "Marina Troy," and doing a poor job of it.

The young bookstore manager, Molly Ivers, was resolutely cheerful, upbeat. Business in the quaint little woodframe store on Pedlar's Lane was "good"—"not bad, considering the lousy weather"—"*really good*"—"*fantastic.*" A popular Salthill mystery novelist, with a *New York Times* bestseller, had dropped by the store at Molly's request and signed a stack of books, thirty-two had been sold in a few days. Marina in her remote outpost in the Pocono Mountains, speaking from a pay phone, agreed. "*Fantastic.*" She meant to be upbeat as her employee who was ten years her junior. She meant to be upbeat as a way of not arousing Molly Ivers's concern. Yet it did all seem—fantastic. To sell thirty-two copies of a book, or two; thirty-two hundred, or -thousand. To sell, to peddle; on Pedlar's Lane, you were obliged to peddle; what did this mean? *What begins to elude, Adam, is meaning. My former life.* Marina recalled her love of books since girlhood, so much more innocent than her passion for art, but she could not now comprehend how this love had been mixed with trying, or wishing, to sell them. For when you sell, quantity matters. Quantity is the point of selling. If it isn't, why are you in business? And what exactly is *business?* Like Socrates, Adam had asked such questions involving the obvious. But questions involving the obvious are the hardest to answer.

"Marina? Are you still there?"

"Molly, yes. Such good news!"

"Next week Sallie Bick is coming in. The food writer? To sign books and meet people. I'm opening the store, Sunday from two to six. I'll be serving some refreshments." Hastily Molly added, "It won't cost much at all, Marina. The author is going to provide the food."

"Molly, that sounds wonderful. I wish I could be there."

An awkward pause. Even Molly Ivers who doubted nothing doubted this.

Molly said, lowering her voice as if someone might overhear, "There's a man named Roger Cavanagh, who drops by? The lawyer? I guess you know him? He always asks about you."

"Does he!"

"He's a good customer. He always buys a hardcover book. But he seems concerned about you."

"I've told you, Molly. Just tell him I'm away."

"Marina, he knows you're away. But he wants to know where."

"'Away' is enough explanation." Marina felt her face flush with annoyance, chagrin. "I must hang up, Molly. Someone is waiting to use this phone."

He will track me down someday. He will make me fall in love with him. But it won't happen! It will not.

IN DAMASCUS CROSSING, Marina sometimes made calls from a public phone booth outside Pryde Gas & Auto Repair, where since September she'd become a regular customer; when the stone house on Mink Pond Road grew too lonely, and too confining, after hours of work in Adam's studio, Marina had to escape by driving to the Delaware River and back, or up into the mountains, or to a discount shopping center outside East Stroudsburg, and such drives, which she tried to see as part of her meditation as an artist, required a considerable amount of gas. She understood that she was becoming, in Damascus Crossing, population four hundred, a figure of speculation. "Miss Troy"—"the woman who lives on Mink Pond Road, alone." She tried not to notice the garage attendants observing her when she parked to use the phone booth, furtive as a woman slipping into a port-o-john under the scrutiny of male witnesses.

At other times, not wanting to brave the men's stares, Marina made her calls from County Line Realty, also in Damascus Crossing. This was the agency that for years had overseen Adam Berendt's property as a rental, provided services and a caretaker in the owner's perennial absence. An aggressively friendly middle-aged woman named Beverly Hogan seemed to be the sole agent, running the business out of a small simulated-redwood ranch house festooned with banners that flapped in the wind, like frantic applause. Marina worried that County Line had no business, in these off-season months; except for Beverly's compact Toyota, the graveled lot was nearly always empty. Beverly Hogan was the first person Marina had become acquainted with in Damascus

Crossing and had provided Marina with invaluable information. (Including the names of "highly recommended" rodent and insect exterminators, for instance.) She'd insisted that Marina use one of the agency phones "gratis" for local calls; long-distance calls, Marina was invited to make on her card. That Marina hadn't a telephone was a matter of aroused concern to Beverly as if Marina were a headstrong young girl in need of an older woman's good sense. Except for her overeager social manner, her excessive makeup and perfume and inexpertly dyed ash-blond hair, Beverly Hogan reminded Marina of certain Salthill matrons: rich women ravaged by loneliness as by sexual desire, afflicted with a compulsion to talk as physical as a tic, with mysteriously remote husbands and grown children who'd proven disappointing. What good-hearted women these were, how generous, how kind and solicitous; and how one fled them, with stammered apologies and averted eyes. Several times since Marina moved into the stone house, Beverly had driven out uninvited, alarming Marina by knocking on her front door, and when Marina at the rear of the house failed to hear, tramping cheerfully through the tall grass to knock at the back door. "Just to see how you're getting along, Marina. If you need anything." Marina had not encouraged these visits, and felt guilty afterward. She would rather have made her telephone calls in the outdoor booth smelling of urine, but she understood that Beverly kept close tabs on Marina Troy's movements in Damascus Crossing, and would be hurt and resentful if Marina didn't drop by her office from time to time, to confirm a gratitude she didn't feel. Beverly Hogan was the kind of woman you might not wish for a close friend, but you would certainly not wish for an enemy.

Always Beverly gripped and shook Marina's hand, as she was doing now, on a blustery November afternoon. Always she asked, "How are you, Marina?" intently raking Marina's face with her sympathetic eyes, behind red plastic glasses. Her attentiveness was oppressive, Marina knew she was being memorized. Her innocuous calls to Salthill were perhaps being overheard and memorized, too.

While Beverly typed away rapidly on a computer, Marina

made a swift call to Molly Ivers. A surprising good week for book sales, Molly reported, considering the lousy weather; and things were sure to pick up as Christmas approached . . . When Marina hung up the phone, there was Beverly with two cups of instant coffee and peanut-butter cookies, homemade. She said, with the air of one not liking to interfere, "I'd miss you, Marina, if you didn't drop by to use the phone, but like I've said, *I* couldn't live without a phone on the premises. And out in the woods like that. I'd have one connected before winter sets in, if I was you."

Marina murmured, "Yes. I probably will."

"The first real snowfall, you could be isolated."

"Yes."

"It's a friendly community here. We look out for each other. Lots of families go back generations." Beverly told tales of widows—living alone—on remote roads like Mink Pond—an elderly aunt of hers, who'd had a stroke—and a neighbor checked in on her, and saved her life. "Dialed nine-one-one from Aunt Louise's kitchen. But she had to have a phone, you know. To make that call."

"Oh, I know. Beverly, you're right."

"There's not somebody you don't want to be calling you, is there, Marina?" Beverly's eyes opened wide in disclaiming a wish to intrude. "Or maybe you moved here, to—get away? From?"

Marina laughed ambiguously, blushed and shook her head. The hot coffee burnt her mouth. She picked up a cookie and crumbled it in her fingers.

"People wonder, you know. *I* tell them, an adult woman has a right to her own life. Her privacy."

"I suppose so."

"An ex-husband, maybe? My sister, what she went through with her ex! 'Court injunction'—the least of it."

"I'm sorry."

"*I'm* sorry. Guess who has to hear about it." Beverly smiled grimly, adjusting her glasses. Inside the bifocal lenses her eyes hovered like small fish. "Gory details. There's two kinds of men: the ones who all they can 'get up' is the remote control, and the ones who go crazy and want to kill you, they 'love' you so much." Beverly laughed loudly. Marina heard herself laughing in Beverly's wake, like a smaller vehicle pulled in the wake of a speeding larger vehicle, out of control. Shrewdly Beverly said, "You have the TV connected, do you? I know there was a set in the house. Nice one."

"Yes."

But was this true? Marina couldn't remember.

"The reception won't be what you're used to in the New York area. Out here, in the mountains, you need a dish satellite. Like we have."

Marina nodded sagely. At a point in this oddly intense conversation enough wisdom would have been communicated, and the older woman would release the younger. Marina's eyelids fluttered. How tired she was! She'd begun work early that morning, in a soupy slate-gray dawn, had despaired of all she'd managed to do through the day, beginning to be frightened that she was deluding herself, and bitterly disappointing Adam. How had she imagined she was capable of "restoration"—"divination"—what madness!

Beverly, seeing that Marina's thoughts were drifting away from her, yanked them back in her cheery-commandeering way. "Marina! You bought that wonderful old house from Mr. Berendt directly, I guess? No agent?"

Marina hesitated. "Yes."

"Or did Mr. Berendt list it with an agent in New Jersey? I never heard."

"No. I don't think so."

Beverly nodded mysteriously. "A true gentleman, he was. But not what you'd call easy to read." When Marina said nothing, Beverly continued, pursing her lips, "We were all real shocked to hear—he'd passed away like he did. Only in his fifties."

"Yes. It was—unexpected."

"Of course, we didn't see much of Mr. Berendt, the past few years. He had a busy life lots of other places, I guess! When he'd come to Damascus Crossing it was for weekends mostly. He never hunted or fished and he never came in the winter to ski.

He'd be alone, mostly. One summer he stayed for a month, he was a sculptor? That's what he was?"

"A sculptor, yes."

"But not statues. He didn't make statues of people. It was more what you'd call modern. 'Abstract.' Hard to figure out." Beverly sighed. She'd been eating cookies in delicate bites, as a way of not devouring them with Marina looking on, and crumbs clung to her ample bosom. "You'd wonder what it is, makes a man care about things like that? Of course a great artist, like Picasso, makes *money*."

Marina smiled. What was this leading to? She felt both uneasy and hopeful. Beverly had known Adam Berendt at a time when Marina had not known him; a younger Adam, remote now in time. She said, lowering her voice as if someone might overhear, "There was something sad about that man, wasn't there! In his face. His eye that was blind, and his other eye that was so sharp-seeming, like he saw inside you. I came out once and asked him, point-blank, that's the way I am sometimes, I asked him about his family, did he have kids, and—know what he said?"

"What?"

"He said, 'No and yes.'"

"'No and yes.' What does that mean?"

Beverly laughed sadly. "Damned if I know, Marina."

How clearly Marina could hear Adam Berendt telling this woman *No and yes*. Meaning *no* he had no children of his own, *yes* he had children in another sense.

Beverly said shrewdly, "He liked dogs."

"Did he!"

"There was a handsome dog, he had. A shepherd. One of those older Seeing Eyes." When Marina looked blank, Beverly explained, "You know: dogs for the blind. They only use them for a few years, then they're 'retired.' They only want young dogs. So you can get older Seeing Eyes, they make excellent pets. At a place in Stroudsburg you can get them. Mr. Berendt had one when he came out here, sometimes. But they die, you know. Sort of young. A shepherd is a large dog and large dogs don't live as long as small dogs, that's a fact. Why, I wonder?"

Marina shook her head slowly. She was feeling slightly dazed by all this, like one trapped in a speeding car, forced to listen to the rapid chatter of its driver.

"It's a tragedy if you get to love the dog. You get attached."

"Yes. I know."

Marina half shut her eyes: seeing Adam, in shorts, his muscled legs tanned and hairy, squatting to hug Apollo, and the dog lavishly licking Adam's face. She'd felt an absurd pang of jealousy, knowing that Adam dared show his affection, his really boundless, boyish physical affection, with one of his dogs. To have touched Marina Troy in such a way would have been impossible for him.

Marina's eyes stung with tears, surreptitiously she brushed them away.

Sharp-eyed Beverly Hogan saw, of course. Possibly she'd been nudging Marina toward this moment. *Now I know: you loved him. And you knew him no better than I did, you stuck-up bitch.*

Marina glanced at her watch. She hoped she was freed now, she could leave. The sky above the mountains was an alarming mass of bruises, there was a taste of snow in the air. Beverly walked her to the door with an invitation to drop by for coffee, for a drink, for a meal anytime, at Beverly's home which was close by; and to think about getting a phone, seriously. Marina murmured a vague assent. She was seeing those stunted unfinished pieces of Adam's awaiting her at the back of the stone house, like aborted embryos they were, reproaching her for failing to give them life.

Beverly was saying, in a warmly reminiscent voice, "I took Adam Berendt to a farm auction once. Beautiful big old ruin of a brick house on the Delaware. He bought some things. He had money, just in his wallet. One of the things he bought was this ring." And she thrust it into Marina's face, a glassy dark amethyst in an intricate silver setting; she wore it on the third finger of her right hand, amid other, less distinctive rings.

Said Marina quietly, "It's beautiful."

"It is." Beverly continued to hold out her fleshy hand,

frowning at the ring, smiling a hard little gratified smile. "Everybody says so, that's ever seen it."

Why is it when I'm inside this stone house I have come to love I can't remember what it looks like from the outside. And when I'm outside I can't remember what it looks like on the inside.

Why is it I keep losing my way. The things in the back room, taunting me.

The views from the windows don't seem to mesh somehow.

Mount Rue has been lost in mist for days.

My breath catches in my throat. The heavy furred warm thing on my chest in the night. Damp muzzle against my mouth. Sucking.

4

STILL, THERE WERE good days. Very good days!

It was not madness, what she was attempting. She could distinctly see, yes, she'd made progress. These past twelve weeks.

She woke early and was filled with energy, inspiration, hope. She sloughed off the doubts of the night, splashed her face with cold water and smiled at herself. *Marina, dear!* Adam's encouraging voice. In the studio she worked through the morning, into early afternoon, she refused to be discouraged, she refused to be despairing, it was true she was groping and uncertain as a blind woman, yet by degrees the blind woman was finding her way.

There came a thin scratching at one of the windows behind her, on the far side of the room. Like fingernails, or claws, against glass. Not a loud sound but rather more tentative, questioning.

Marina? Whose house?

And sometimes, trying to concentrate on her reading, she was distracted by sounds directly overhead. Floorboards creaking, almost imperceptibly. She'd shut off those rooms for the winter, of course no one was there.

One night she heard voices in the near distance, coming from the direction of the barn. Mixed with the wind. The wind! Always lately there was wind. Marina shook her head to clear it, confused. She'd been reading Adam's copy of Pascal's *Pensées,* and was feeling Adam Berendt's nearness as she hadn't felt it in some time, his voice that was quiet, bemused, teasing, yet kindly. *A mere trifle consoles us, for a mere trifle distresses us* he'd underlined in red ink and in the margin of the page marked *Yes!* And, which made Marina smile, *All the unhappiness of men arises from the single fact, that they cannot stay quietly in their own chambers.* But there came muffled laughter from somewhere outside, a man's coughing. And silence.

Marina's eyelids were so suddenly heavy, the book slipped from her fingers, falling hard, striking her ankle, waking her rudely.

AND THEN ONE MORNING she saw it: the dark-furred creature of the night.

The thing that settled on her chest in the night. So warm, so seductive. Comforting and smothering.

It was utterly still. Silhouetted against one of the large clay-colored boulders, in the wan, whitish sunshine of November. An intricately marked large cat, far too large to be an ordinary domestic cat, a wild cat or a lynx, with upright tufted ears, a flattish owl-like face, clearly discernible whiskers, and alert tawny eyes. Marina was in her kitchen, and crouched low to watch the creature through a window. Her heart caught at its beauty. The way wind rippled its fur. A dark-mahogany fur, that would be smooth to the touch. And the plumelike smoke-colored tail. *Looking for a way in. It knows what it wants.* After a moment the cat made its way through fallen leaves close beside the house, Marina could hear it, this, too, was a sound she heard frequently in the night. How lithe the great cat was, how stealthy; it did not trot as a dog or wolf would, but glided with an uncanny grace; its head and body remaining level while its supple legs moved. Almost, there was something cartoon-like and comical in this movement of the legs while the body remained level as if motionless. *The way it moves in the night. No one to see.* Marina followed the cat around a corner, and at a dining room window, too, quickly lifted her head, the cat must have seen her for its eyes seemed to glare, in an instant it had turned away and ran, and vanished into the woods.

"Damn."

The beautiful dark-furred creature had come to Marina's door, and like a fool she'd frightened it away.

She set chicken scraps out for it near her back steps, in an aluminum plate. Within a few hours the scraps were gone.

"NIGHT" SHE WOULD call it. For its fur was so dark, even in sunshine it was clearly a creature of night. "What we see of it, in the day, isn't fully it."

She seemed to be explaining this to Adam. He was frowning, noncommittal. You couldn't predict, with Adam. There was that side of him so rational, so sane; argumentative in the service of truth, like his master Socrates; yet there was the other side of Adam, of which Marina hadn't known until after his death, the left-hand side of secrecy, of darkness and outright lies, unexpected wealth and Vegas casino coupons and lurid sexy photos and false names, how many false names had the man used, and of exactly what use, when you come to think of it, is a false name . . .

"Night" she would call it.

5

IN M. TROY'S tubular box at the Damascus Crossing post office, mail accumulated, most of it forwarded. One of these forwarded items was an envelope with the return address ABERCROMBIE, CAVANAGH, KRULLER & HOOK, ATTORNEYS AT LAW, 1 SHAKER SQUARE, SALTHILL-ON-HUDSON, NEW YORK. Marina had time to wonder, as so many of us wonder, why lawyers' names in the aggregate sound like the punch line of a joke.

"Oh, *why!*"

Hurriedly she stuffed the envelope with other items of mail into her shoulder bag, or maybe into a pocket of her khaki jacket; her cheeks burned as if she'd been slapped. For why did the man persist in trying to contact her! She'd resigned her position as Adam Berendt's personal executor, an assistant of Roger Cavanagh's had been hired in her place, surely there was no official reason for Roger to write to her.

Marina drove home, annoyed. She supposed, if Roger Cavanagh was pursuing her, it was to revenge himself upon her. One day. *He will make me love him, he will seduce me into making love with him, and then in triumph he will repudiate me. I know.* Yet this happened, so strangely: when Marina returned home, and unpacked her things, and emptied her pockets onto the plank table in the kitchen, though other pieces of mail were there, the envelope from Abercrombie, Cavanagh, Kruller & Hook was missing.

Marina searched for it in the Jeep, on the driveway, amid fallen leaves by her front door, that damned envelope from Salthill she didn't want, and in so not-wanting had somehow willed out of existence, and of course now she felt guilty, and remorseful, for perhaps she was being irrational in her dislike of Roger Cavanagh, or was it fear of Roger Cavanagh, his eyes hungry upon her, the hurt in his face when she'd struck him, in her fury she'd struck at him, oh, never would she forget, what shame, what an exposure of Marina's crude animal appetite, and her clawing at the man, in sexual misery, never would she forget, never could she forgive herself.

And never would Marina find the envelope.

THERE CAME a sudden frost. An encrustration of fine feathery white in the tall bent grasses, and in the piles of dead leaves. A new sharpness in the air, an urgency.

Dragged to the back door, the partly devoured remains of a

young rabbit. The head was missing, the torso clawed open. When Marina first saw it, and the trail of blood through the frost, she'd imagined it must be a wounded animal that had crawled to the house in the clearing, seeking help. When she looked more closely, she saw *Of course, it's prey. The remains of prey.*

She was stricken with pity. She may have felt a touch of panic. In newspaper she wrapped the poor mutilated flesh, and carried it away to hide behind the barn.

(YET KEEPING BEHIND a memento. Part of a newspaper page smeared with the rabbit's blood. What does it mean, such a design. Imprinted upon print. As print is imprinted speech.)

Night, the predator.

Night, that brought her such bloody prey.

Night, that could not be predicted! Neither summoned, nor kept away.

Night with tawny-lemony eyes. *Night* with sharp razor teeth. *Night* the carnivore, muzzle smelling of blood. *Night* leaping onto her chest. *Night* the heavy furry weight pressing her soft breasts against her rib cage. *Night* she could not lift her arms to push away. *Night* that made her moan softly, a sob catching in her throat. *Night* whose snout she dreaded, wet, whiskery, pressing into her partly opened mouth, her parched lips, in the paralysis of sleep the horror of *Night* sucking away her oxygen.

6

"JUST TO BREATHE. To see the sky."

Restless! Driving aimlessly along mountain roads. Roads with unfamiliar names. Avoiding busy highways, avoiding commercialized strips: BUCK HILL SKI AREA, POCONOS VACATION SITES BARGAINS, TIMBER HILL RESORT MOTEL. In spirals descending toward the river. Those small scattered towns on its banks whose names intrigued her: Dingmans Ferry, Bushkill, Welshtown, Shoemaker, Echo Lake. "The names of romance, Adam."

Though these little crossroads towns were never so romantic as their names.

She stopped to take Polaroid shots. Mountains, sky, Delaware River. That sullen leaden light on the river. And the river choppy, sinuous. As if a living organism. Deadly to enter. She was fascinated by the limestone outcroppings rising above her, vertical, steep, raw and wet, looking sharp as gigantic claws. "Silver Thread Falls. There's a lovely name, Adam, yes?" There was also Kane's Mills and Foxboro. Marina took photos of long-abandoned glove, textile, canning factories on the river. "These are beautiful. Not the kind of beauty that hits you in the eye, but . . ."

Give me up, Marina, dear. I'm a dead man, you know.

But I'm not dead, Adam. Have faith in me.

"Am I jealous? I am not."

The ring probably wasn't an amethyst.

Crafty Beverly Hogan hadn't claimed it was.

It *was* beautiful, obviously an old ring. But no older than the century. Probably what Marina had mistaken for an amethyst was just attractive purple glass cut to resemble a precious stone. Buying the ring for Beverly Hogan at a farm auction, how typical of Adam Berendt, one of the man's impulsive acts of generosity.

Still, Marina couldn't bring herself to return to County Line Realty. Not just yet.

"Miss Troy, ma'am! How ya doin, huh?"

How ya doin. Marina had no idea but always she smiled and indicated with her mouth *Fine!*

The greeting was exuberant, with an undercurrent of something aggressive, insolent. A cross between a yodel and a sexual assault with a blunt weapon. Each time Marina pulled the Jeep into Pryde's Gas & Auto Repair to get gas, and lowered her window, she steeled herself for it. For there came the old-young RICK (name stitched onto the bib of his grease-stained coverall) with hot resentful eyes, dragging his bad leg and calling out his loud greeting. "Fill 'er up, Miss Troy, ma'am?"

"Yes. Thanks, Rick."

Unless Marina bought gas elsewhere, which was inconvenient, she had to endure Rick Pryde. She'd come to be fascinated by Rick Pryde. And of course she was intimidated by Rick Pryde. Beverly Hogan had warned Marina that the Prydes knew by extrasensory perception if you bought gas or had your car serviced elsewhere, and they'd let you know they knew, it was the way of Damascus Crossing that everybody knew everybody else's business for better or worse.

Rick seemed always to be lurking behind the steamy windows of the service station, when Marina pulled up to the gas pumps. (She seemed to know, too, that Rick observed her making her few, furtive telephone calls in the phone booth beside the garage.) Rick was mysteriously crippled, with a pronounced limp and alarming scalded-scarred skin. *Like Adam's. But so much more disfiguring.* He had a jocose jack-o'-lantern grin, big crooked nicotine-stained teeth, and a full droopy dark moustache and wiry whiskers hiding a weak chin. Rick never hurried to service any vehicle yet managed to give an impression of alert and earnest and determined courtesy. Rick grinned and grunted to indicate the effort he was putting in to clean Marina's broad front windshield and her outside mirror with a rag that left greasy smears on the glass. Always he was chewing a big lump of something very juicy that required him to frequently pause and spit, with a look of concentration, a jet of brown liquid that might have been acid; then he swiped at his mouth with the back of his big-knuckled grimy hand, smiling at Marina who wanted to avert her eyes yet somehow could not. Marina wondered if the hot-eyed old-young man was the son or younger brother of the gruff, taciturn elder Pryde who owned the service station.

One afternoon while Rick was pumping gas into Marina's Jeep he said unexpectedly, "I see you looking at my freaky face sometimes, Miss Troy? And my leg? I should explain how I got in this condition, I guess!" He laughed good-naturedly at Marina's look of distress. Clearly he was enjoying his power over her. He told her he was the only Damascus County casualty of the Persian Gulf War. He'd been a Marine sniper. Marine snipers were the best of the best. But you had to pay for being the best of the best and he'd paid, and was paying. He'd had skin-graft surgery on his face and six operations on his leg and if Marina was thinking, hell, those operations didn't work worth shit, she'd be wrong, 'cause he'd been in a helluva worse condition before the operations, his own dog wouldn't of recognized him.

Rick asked Marina offhanded and sly if she could recall the dates of the Persian Gulf War.

Marina's face heated with blood. Her mind was swept blank.

A decade ago? Or more? In the nineties.

Rick said, baring his chunky discolored teeth in a semblance of a smile, "Ma'am, don't be embarrassed, *nobody knows*. Except poor bastards like me an' their folks. And the Iraqis. They'd remember, I guess." A mischievous boy, Rick laughed. He chewed at the lump in his mouth, leaned over to spit carefully between his boots, swiped at his stained moustache, and continued to smile at Marina. "January 1991 to March. The dates."

"That long ago!" Marina sighed.

"Bet you can't guess how old I am."

It was a challenge. Marina squirmed uncomfortably. Rick was both a boy and a ravaged middle-aged man. If you glanced at him, on the street, in passing, taking note of his scabby skin and pronounced limp, you might have thought him forty-five years old.

"Thirty?"

Rick's mouth twitched. He smiled, a little. "Pret-ty close, ma'am. You got sharp eyes. But you can figure, 1991, how old I'd of been then."

"No! You look young."

"Well, I'm *not*."

Rick laughed. The numerals on the gas pump whirled. Marina wondered uneasily how long this interrogation would last.

"I'm sorry, Rick. You must have undergone terrible pain . . ."

"Pain's the least of it, Miss Troy, ma'am. But hell, I ain't complaining, see I'm alive, and I'm here. That can't be said for some of my close buddies." His mouth twisted as if he were getting ready to spit, but he didn't, not at the moment.

"I'm sorry." It wasn't adequate, but it was all Marina could find to say. The words like soiled cotton batting in her mouth.

Rick shrugged, "Us guys were kind of cocky, I guess. Our motto was 'Put us anywhere, and we can put it in the head at eight hundred yards.'" He paused to see the effect of this remark on Marina, who winced as you'd expect a sensitive woman to wince. "But hell. It's ancient history now."

Rick removed his grimy cap and brushed his black hair back in a swift savage gesture. In that instant, Marina felt a stab of something like sexual attraction; a sensation she had not felt in months. Until this moment she hadn't seemed to realize that Rick in his grease-stained coveralls, with singed eyes and skin, was a sexual being; not much younger than Marina; and he took pride in the fact, displaying himself before a woman.

At last the numerals on the gas pump were slowing. Rick said, bemused, as if the subject were altogether natural, "This bad habit I picked up in the Gulf, trying to keep awake for long hours, y'know what guys would do?—rub tobacco on our eyeballs." He made a gesture as if licking his forefinger, and brought the finger near his eye. Marina winced another time, and Rick laughed, pleased. "Naw, ma'am. I ain't desperate, I don't do it *now*."

At last Marina's gas tank was full. The amount of purchase was disconcertingly high. Marina paid in bills, and Rick briskly counted out her change, all business now.

Casually he said, "You're living on Mink Pond, ma'am? The stone house? Used to belong to Mr. Benedict? Pryde hires out to plow driveways, y'know." Rick explained it was forty dollars each time if arrangements were made beforehand; but if customers waited until they were snowed in, and called, it was fifty dollars. Pryde only plowed out customers if there was a sufficient accumulation, Rick said emphatically, as if there were snow removal services of which this wasn't true. "We're careful about that, ma'am. But in an average winter say we plow you out ten times, you'd pay five hundred dollars altogether if you hadn't made arrangements beforehand, but if you do it's only four hundred. Plus you won't find yourself in any emergency situation out in the woods, if you sign up now."

A pickup truck was pulling in behind Marina at the gas pump. Quickly she said, "That's a good idea, Rick. I was going to ask about your snowplow service, my driveway is a half-mile long and difficult to—"

"No, ma'am. It ain't more than a quarter-mile. But you could get really stuck back there. I've seen it happen." Rick spoke ominously.

So Marina hired Pryde's snowplowing service to keep her driveway cleared through the winter. She would think of this, in retrospect, as one of her wise, practical decisions, amid others that were neither.

Several nights later, on December 2, there came the first serious snowfall of the season. Through the overcast blustery day Marina uneasily observed particles of snow swirling past her windows, pinging like bits of sand against the glass, blown against the northern sides of trees; she prayed her power wouldn't go out; and in the evening lit a fire in the fireplace, and huddled beside it, a book in her hand, waiting.

But snow ceased falling by midnight, less than three inches accumulated. Pryde's snowplowing service did not show up.

7

The fell of dark. Not day. There was the dark-furred cat silhouetted against the snow. Marina stared from her window, as if the creature had called her name.

How brief days were. A patch of lighted cloud surrounded by gigantic storm clouds. Virtually no sun.

"Could mankind imagine a sun, if there'd never been a sun?"

But there was night, so reliable. There was *Night*.

The snow-creature outside her window. Its coat was thicker now with winter, and lustrous. Tufted ears, flattish owl-face, eyes glaring like reflectors. *Marina. Marina!*

"I must be terribly lonely. These delusions . . ."

Hair in her face as she crouched at the window. Crept like a clumsy animal from the darkened bedroom and into the next room, to another window, crouched at the sill, hoping to follow the big cat as it circled the house. If she made a careless gesture *Night* vanished.

Except: she was wakened from sleep by something making its stealthy way through dead leaves, where they'd been blown up against the house.

Marina left meat scraps for the cat. Though probably raccoons got there first. Behind a curtain she waited to see what creature approached, but none did, not so long as she was watching; yet in the morning the scraps were gone, the aluminum plates tossed rudely aside like trash. And in place of the food was the part-devoured carcass of a rabbit or squirrel. Mangled bloody flesh-remains the size of a man's fist; how curious, the heart and inner organs had been removed as if with surgical precision, and left conspicuously in the snow beside the carcass. Sometimes Marina gagged, but always Marina looked. *Night* was leaving these for her.

WHILE ON THE WINDOWSILLS of the drafty old stone house Marina's things were accumulating.

The moth with wide ragged beautifully marked wings. Skeletons of birds delicate as lacework. Buttons prized from the cracks between floorboards. A baby's wooden rattle, green-glass doll's eyes. Newsprint smeared in rust-colored patterns like distant constellations. And more, small random *things* of no value that struck Marina's eye, touched at her heart.

She was a bird making a nest, of materials found close by. She was a pack rat, greedy and ingenious.

In the frigid air of early morning, her breath steaming, Marina took Polaroid shots of the *things* left for her in the snow behind the house. Bloody mangled fetuses they seemed to her. A mockery of her childlessness. Ugly, obscene, piteous the suffering of such defenseless creatures, Marina half-shut her eyes yet she was determined to take the photos, for this felt like fate.

The wild cat's footprints in the snow, amid the blood-trail, these too Marina photographed, in fascination.

Such *things* Marina Troy accumulated through her winter in the old stone house, stark square Polaroid prints on her window-sills, for what purpose?

Night, Marina was never to photograph.

AND IN THE BARN one day while searching for materials for Adam's sculptures, she discovered a box of mildewed papers.

It was a small cardboard box hidden amid tattered lawn furniture, filthy with cobwebs and mouse droppings. Most of the papers appeared to be badly faded computer printouts of columns of figures. Bank statements? If these belonged to Adam Berendt, there was no identification. Eventually Marina came upon a name on another document: *Ezra Krane*. Teasingly familiar, but Marina couldn't remember why. At the top of a printout from *Revenue Canada—Statement of amounts paid or credited to non-residents of Canada*—there was another vaguely familiar name, *Samuel Myers*.

Marina continued to rummage through the printed documents, few of them of much interest, until by chance she saw a torn sheet of paper with familiar handwriting on it.

Adam's handwriting! Marina would recognize it anywhere.

But the name, the signature, was unknown to Marina—

Francis Xavier Brady
Francis Xavier Brady
Francis Xavier Brady
Francis Xavier Brady
Francis Xavier Brady
Francis Xavier Brady

—repeated in a column covering the page.

Why? Why would Adam sign another's name?

"Adam? Was 'Francis Xavier Brady'—*you?*"

If so, keep the secret.

Who Brady was, where Brady came from, Adam hadn't wanted us to know.

If you love him keep his secret.

Yes?

Marina tore the paper into shreds. Though she would remember Francis Xavier Brady as keenly as if Adam himself had revealed it to her.

8

ONE MISERABLY COLD MORNING Marina plaited her hair carelessly, wound it around her head headache-tight and secured it with pins and pulled a wool cap low on her forehead. Pale and plain and capable-looking she was, in her trousers, boots, fleece-lined khaki jacket. She liked the relief of being sexless; at first glance she looked like any youngish guy in Damascus County, driving a Jeep. She drove through town and out onto the highway past the Timber Hill Ski Resort where in good weather skiers were visible from the road, flying down the dazzling white slopes fearless of accidents, injury. Marina envied these strangers their courage and their playfulness for it seemed to Marina that life required almost too much courage, and there was no time for play. She was in an anxious mood. She wasn't making much progress with Adam's sculptures, and why? How badly she wanted to complete them! She'd taped photos of his best work to her walls but these images weren't inspiring her. She was feeling constrained, intimidated, for under the spell of Adam's work she could only imitate him, yet of course she couldn't openly imitate him, that wasn't at all what she intended.

Adam Berendt's most successful sculpted pieces were blunt, clumsy-seeming yet to Marina's eye magical combinations of wildly disparate elements. Scrap metal, wood, plastic, earth tones or transparencies, with abrupt, sometimes jarring touches. These might be whimsical sculptures or they might be starkly beautiful, they might be purposely ugly, disturbing. It had been Adam's intention to make them appear haphazard, but Marina knew there was nothing haphazard in their creation.

At the Shawnee Scrap Yard, Marina asked the bull-necked owner if she could look around. "My husband is a sculptor and he sends me out for materials," she said, and the proprietor regarded her with curiosity, saying, "We don't have 'sculpture' supplies here," and Marina said, "He doesn't want supplies, just things. 'Found' things. Anything." The proprietor shrugged and told Marina sure, look around all she wanted. Marina would see the man watching her from his trailer office as she drifted about the yard. She was trying to "see" with Adam's eyes. She'd had a week of frustrating days but was feeling optimistic now, in the open air.

It was Christmas week. A week of unbridled American optimism. Though Marina wasn't celebrating Christmas, and had come to dislike the tyrannical holiday, she felt the Christmas buoyancy in the air. Even the Shawnee Scrap Yard was decorated with ugly flapping tinsel and a shiny red plastic Santa Claus perched on the trailer roof.

"Adam, what looks good? What do you like?"

She selected twisted, discolored pieces of metal from wrecked vehicles. A cracked headlight, a stained floor mat, a broken stick shift. Badly rusted license plates. Kewpie dolls lewdly dangling from rearview mirrors, stiff with grime. Knobs, handles, mirror fragments. So much broken glass in this world, and much of it mirror fragments. The owner of the yard, who called himself Steve, came outside, to ask Marina if she needed help lugging these things to her Jeep and quickly she told the man thanks, but no, she was fine. And she was fine: she'd become strong, in her new arduous life. When she asked the man what she owed him he waved her away. "Hell, ma'am, it's just junk. You're welcome to it." "But five dollars, at least? Please?" The man frowned, backing off; as if Marina had inadvertently offended him; but she too had been offended by the "ma'am"—it so distanced her from the life of this community, set her off as a stranger, worse yet a tourist. She heard herself telling Steve that she and her husband lived close by, on Mink Pond Road north of Damascus Crossing, in an old stone house built in the 1920s; she heard herself asking (but why, why was she doing this!) if he'd ever met her husband Adam Berendt, and the man shook his head, no he didn't think so. Steve was younger than Adam but had Adam's stocky build and peely-flaky-burnt-looking skin. "I bet you've met him, a few years ago," Marina said, "he'd have come here, looking for things. 'Adam Berendt,' the sculptor."

"'Berendt'?" Steve frowned as if trying seriously to remember but finally, no, he shook his head. "Guess not, ma'am. Sorry."

DRIVING HOME then Marina wondered: why would it have mattered so much to her, that the scrap yard owner remember Adam?

"What is happening to me?"

PRE-CHRISTMAS SALES at the Salthill Bookstore were "pretty good"—"some days bustling, almost"—"not too bad, considering." (Considering what, Marina wondered.) Molly Ivers cheerfully reported having to keep the store open until seven P.M., sometimes eight P.M. But even her cheery voice sounded frayed, like sound piped into the telephone receiver. Marina who'd wished to take the young woman's enthusiasm for granted felt a stab of dismay. *Are we losing money? Going bankrupt?* The bookstore, like the village of Salthill and its suburban environs, had become remote to Marina, as an anesthetized part of one's body becomes remote; yet Marina knew, whether she felt pain or not, there might be pain to feel. The damned—"quaint"—bookstore was her livelihood, unless she quickly found another.

"That rude, pushy man who used to come in here asking about you, that lawyer, Cavanagh, I think his name is—he's stopped coming in. *That's* good news, Marina, at least!"

9

POST-CHRISTMAS SALES at Home Depot, Kmart, Wal-Mart, Sears, JCPenney, Discount King . . . Marina drifted through the giant warehouse stores like a ghost among solid fleshy Brueghel figures. Why were these Americans so much more real than Marina Troy? And so many of them: pushing shopping carts heaped with merchandise, returning presents, making exciting new purchases at "slashed" prices. Christmas carols were still being piped loudly into stores, the holiday spirit prevailed. In January would come the slack, dead season, but not just yet.

Marina, a home owner, was alert too to bargains. She could not afford to scorn sales. Kitchen appliances slashed by 40 percent, terrycloth towels in untidy heaps, women's waterproofed boots slashed by 50 percent, snow shovels, mousetraps, shower curtains, underwear, television sets, carpet remnants slashed by 60 percent . . .

There must be something I want? Something I need?

Sometimes in the warehouse stores Marina thought she saw individuals she knew. At the far end of a crowded fluorescent-bright aisle there was Beverly Hogan with rouged cheeks and ash-blond hair shiny as a wig. In Wal-Mart, a shock to see Beatrice Avery—but of course it couldn't have been Beatrice, the woman would never have set foot into a Wal-Mart anywhere. Yet Marina saw men who resembled Salthill acquaintances, she saw women who resembled glamorous Augusta Cutler, always at a distance. Crowds of shoppers blocked her view, loose-running children collided rudely with her, the piped-in Christmas music made her head ache. Yes, she saw Adam Berendt, sometimes. She stared, and her vision wavered. Adam Berendt, heavier, shopping in Sears with his stout middle-aged wife, pausing to consider linoleum tile "drastically reduced" . . . Marina turned blindly away. "Am I lonely? *I am not lonely.*" In the parking lot between Sears and the garishly lighted Mexican Villa, Marina saw a couple seriously quarreling, the angry youngish man was Rick Pryde, with long straggly dark hair, drooping moustache and beard, in a crimson satin jacket with a black logo (wolf, wolverine) on the back; but this Rick Pryde didn't limp, and his voice was higher-pitched. The girl was young, no more than nineteen, with a full petulant-pretty face, very like the girl-cashier at the 7-Eleven in Damascus Crossing with whom Marina had brief, friendly exchanges. The quarrel appeared to be escalating by quick degrees. Marina, who never quarreled, Marina Troy, who was of a class, and in Salthill-on-Hudson an entire society, in which voices were never raised in public, listened in fascinated alarm. No man had ever, no man would ever, speak to her, Marina Troy, in such a way. "You bitch—" "God damn you, you can't—" "Listen, you—" "*You* listen—" "Fuck you, *you listen—*" Marina was standing beside the Jeep and unlocking the driver's door slowly, distractedly. She seemed to have misplaced her gloves, her fingers were bare, chilled. It was very cold, gritty soiled snow underfoot, above the garish Christmas lights of the mall was an achingly clear night sky. Marina had driven to the Delaware River in daytime and had lingered, taking photographs in a trance, and on the way home she'd stopped impulsively at the East Stroudsburg mall, in no hurry to return to the drafty deserted house on Mink Pond Road. Now, so unexpectedly, she stood listening to strangers quarreling. The sexual fury of young people unknown to her. *Don't get involved*, Marina warned herself even as she positioned herself where the young man could see her, staring in his direction, for now he'd backed the girl against a car, and appeared to be twisting her arm; the girl was sobbing and slapping at him in a way that looked, to Marina, dangerously provoking. It was a movie or TV scene of a kind Marina Troy rarely saw and yet she spoke boldly—"Excuse me? Is something wrong?" Her voice sounded stronger than she felt. "What's happening there?" The face turned toward her was a variant of Rick Pryde's raw, male, aggrieved face, furious at being challenged. "This ain't none of your business, ma'am. Best mind your own fucking business, ma'am." His voice was heavy with sarcasm.

Marina's heart was beating violently. Never had she behaved in such a way. Yet she couldn't turn away as if nothing were happening. She asked the girl, "Is he hurting you? Do you need help?" The girl burst into louder sobs, broke suddenly away from the man in the crimson jacket, and ran clumsily to Marina. The young man cursed them both, but advanced only a few feet before he halted, for there were security guards at the mall, he wouldn't have wanted to draw their attention.

The girl begged, "Could you give me a ride, ma'am? I just want to get the hell out of here." Her young face was damp, swollen, flushed, with small close-set eyes luridly smudged with mascara. She was panting, hair in her face. It occurred to Marina to wonder if she and the angry young man were married.

What am I doing, this is a mistake!

But Adam too behaved recklessly. He, too, was brave.

Marina unlocked the Jeep, the girl clambered inside. There was Marina, hand trembling so badly she could barely insert the key into the ignition, starting the engine, and driving out of the lot as the young man shouted after them. *Bitches! Cunts!* It was a TV-movie scene. And how would it end, Marina had no idea. She would recall afterward that she'd been both excited and calm. Inappropriately calm perhaps. But how does one know how to act, how to behave, in such circumstances, what is appropriate behavior! She saw the crimson jacket, the furiously gesticulating man with the full moustache and beard, following briefly after the Jeep, his face contorted with rage, and his fists clenching and unclenching. Then Marina left him behind, driving the Jeep bumpily along the shoulder of an access road. Traffic lights swirled and spun toward her. Not knowing what she did she ran a red light. Now she was driving on a county highway, a sobbing girl, a stranger, beside her. The girl was muttering, "I hate him. Hate hate hate him." Striking her thighs with her fists. Marina offered to drive the girl home but the girl seemed not to hear. "All he wants, ma'am, the bastard wants to hurt me, *he* don't show up and *I'm* the one to blame. *I wish we were both dead*."

Marina drove blindly, not knowing what to do, or to say. In the face of such emotion. She appeared to be headed south toward the city of Stroudsburg, in the opposite direction of Damascus Crossing; it was past seven o'clock. The sobbing girl took up so much space! As if a giant baby had climbed into the Jeep, bursting out of her tight showy-sexy clothes. Big-hipped, with a large glistening face like a glaring moon, and hair that looked electrified. The girl wore designer jeans with metallic studs, a smart fawn-colored suede jacket opened over a cheap yellow sweater that fitted her young, jutting breasts snugly; there were numerous glittering studs in both her ears, and what looked like a tiny pearl pierced into her left eyebrow. She smelled of cigarette smoke and hair spray, spilled beer and hot female anguish. Quarreling with her lover had aroused her, clearly; her eyes were dilated and her nostrils widened. Marina could hear her harsh breathing.

Another time Marina asked where she should drive the girl, yet still, stubbornly, the girl seemed not to hear. She was incensed, indignant. "He hurt me, the fucker. You saw it, ma'am! I've got witnesses! He's got no right."

Marina asked, "How did he hurt you?"

"Different ways! All kinds of ways."

"Should we go to the police, then? Should I stop, and call the police, and report him?"

Now the girl turned to look frankly at Marina. Her expression was one of mild shock. "Jesus God, no! No ma'am, no cops." With an air of disgust she said, "*He's* a cop, Christ sake. And so's his brothers."

Afterward Marina would think calmly *He could trace my license plate number. If he's a police officer. He could find me, if he wanted to*. But at the moment, she had no thought for anyone except the sobbing girl beside her.

They stopped finally at a diner. The girl wanted to get cleaned up, and make a telephone call.

It was a large place, noisy with mostly young customers and blaring rock music, brightly lit as a stage set. They were given a rear, corner booth. Never would Marina learn where the girl lived. Her first name was Lorene, she refused to disclose more. "You're not, like, a social worker, are you, ma'am?" Biting her thumbnail, crinkling her forehead so that her soft doughy skin puckered alarmingly. "Like—for the county?"

Marina laughed. "No, I am not. I'm a private citizen."

"Not from around here, though?"

"Yes. I live near Damascus Crossing."

The girl shook her head doubtfully. As if she'd never heard of Damascus Crossing. "You don't sound like from around here. Or look like from around here."

"I'm originally from Maine."

"Maine! Jesus." The girl laughed uneasily. Was Maine a foreign country to her? Maybe a province of Canada. She said, "Well, it's sure nice of you, ma'am, to do this."

"Please call me Marina."

Lorene frowned, not wanting to call her benefactress by her first name. As you wouldn't want to call a high school teacher by her first name. It wasn't proper, it was maybe distasteful.

Almost shyly she said, "Marina—that's a pretty name."

"Lorene is a pretty name, too."

Lorene shrugged, grimacing. "Oh, hell." As if to say *you don't need to flatter me, ma'am, you don't need to be nice to me, come on!*

Lorene went to use the rest room and was gone for some time. Marina ordered two cups of coffee. She leaned shakily forward, elbows on the table, pressing her chilled hands against her warm cheeks. From a short distance there was Adam Berendt observing her. If she looked directly at him, she wouldn't see him; yet in the corner of her eye she almost saw him. Was he surprised, baffled? Wondering why Marina was here? In this noisy place, just outside Stroudsburg, Pennsylvania? Had it to do with *him?* But how had it to do with *him?* Still, Adam was pleased with her. She knew that. He liked Marina acting impulsively for once.

When Lorene returned, sliding heavily into the booth, Marina saw that she'd washed her face; she'd wiped away the runny mascara, but her small bright eyes were reddened. Her face seemed boneless, her lips were thin, a glossy crimson. She might have been a mature seventeen, she might have been an immature twenty-seven. Strangely attractive she seemed to Marina, with her savagely glittering ear studs, the little pearl in her left eyebrow. Her hair was bleached in uneven streaks and fell past her shoulders, constantly she pushed it back, always she was brushing it out of her face in a luxuriant sweeping gesture. Her eyes were somewhat glassy, the pupils dilated, Marina wondered was she on drugs? or only just excited, anxious? Marina felt a stab of arousal as if she were in the presence of danger, and drawn to it.

A waitress brought their coffee. Lorene emptied two sugar packets into hers. She was sniffing, rummaging through her jacket pockets for a tissue, Marina gave her a small opened packet of Kleenex and she blew her nose, obedient as a little girl, and laughed and said, "Y'know? Ma'am? This could be, like, a change in my life. This, tonight. It's what I'm thinking."

"That's good, Lorene. Isn't it?"

"It's got me thinking! I need to think."

Lorene spoke in a rushed rambling elated way of making new plans, it was time to make new plans, there were people she'd "kind of let down" and she was feeling guilty, and "you, tonight, ma'am" had caused her to think in a different way, and she was grateful. Marina had the idea that Lorene had been married, was now divorced or living apart from her husband; possibly, there was a small child, somewhere; this child was living with relatives

. . . Marina was about to ask more specifically when Lorene said suddenly, "What I need to do, I need to make a phone call, ma'am. That's what I need to do." She was excited, nervous. "I need to make that call. Somebody could come get me, then." But she hesitated, as if awaiting Marina's permission.

Marina said, "Yes, why don't you, Lorene? That sounds like a good idea."

Lorene swiped at her nose, embarrassed. "I don't have any change, I guess."

Marina gave her several quarters and dimes.

Lorene said, "Thanks, Marina!" with a flashing smile. It took so little to transform her sullen face, Marina could see why men would be drawn to her.

Lorene went away again, and was gone for perhaps ten minutes, and when she returned, she shook her head, disappointed, evasive; the people she'd tried to call hadn't answered, she said. "I'd need to take a bus. To get where I'd like to go. Tomorrow, I could go. But I need to call them first."

"Where would you like to go? Maybe I could drive you."

Lorene shook her head again, not meeting Marina's eye. *She doesn't trust me. But why?* "I'm O.K. I'll get a bus."

"Where would you get the bus, Lorene? In Stroudsburg?"

"Oh, anywhere." Lorene's voice was vague, annoyed. "I just need to make another phone call, I guess."

Things were becoming confused. Marina knew she was being rebuffed but she smiled, and gave Lorene several dollar bills since Lorene had run out of change; and Lorene mumbled thanks, and slid out of the booth again, a big-boned, pretty girl with a tiny pearl glinting above her eye and flyaway streaked hair, and she was gone again for perhaps ten minutes while Marina drank her coffee, heedless that the caffeine would thrum along her nerves through the night. She glanced around, and her heart stopped: there was Rick Pryde entering the diner, no, it was the young man who'd cursed her, no, it was a stranger, with a scruffy black beard and straggling black hair but no crimson jacket, a tall narrow-shouldered man Marina had never seen before.

When Lorene returned to the booth she was holding an

unlighted cigarette in her shaky fingers. "I just bummed this from a guy up front," she said, laughing. "Christ! I'm so fucked up. It's no smoking in here, I guess?" She slid into the booth heavily. Her young face was flushed as if she'd been running. She laughed again, and wiped at her nose with a crumpled napkin. "I could take a bus from, like, Stroudsburg. Tomorrow morning."

"A bus to—where?"

Lorene murmured what sounded like "Pittsburgh." Her lips barely moved.

"Pittsburgh? Do you have a—relative there?"

"I got some family there." Lorene raised her eyes frankly to Marina. *See? I'm not lying.*

Marina asked if Lorene needed money for the bus and Lorene shrugged, embarrassed, and murmured what sounded like "no"—or possibly "I don't know"—shifting self-consciously in her seat. She said, "See, if I can get through with this call I'm trying to make? Then maybe not."

This was ambiguous. Marina didn't understand. But Marina was reluctant to press the issue. "Well. I'll be happy to lend you what you need, Lorene. Please."

Lorene stared at her hands, a dull flush rising into her face. Her fingernails were polished, but the maroon polish had begun to chip. On both hands she wore a number of rings. She shook her head as if trying to clear it. "I don't accept, like, charity."

"It wouldn't be charity, Lorene. It would be a loan."

"Ma'am, you're real nice. You're kind. But I guess not, O.K.?"

"My name is Marina," Marina said, smiling.

"Well. Marina." Lorene tried to smile, too.

All this time Lorene was brushing her hair out of her face, and glancing behind Marina's head, her close-set dilated eyes perpetually moving. She was restless as a trapped wild creature. Marina tried to draw her out but she was distracted, and seemed only partly aware of their conversation. The effort of talking to this girl was like pushing a large unwieldy boulder up a hill, but Marina was determined not to give up easily.

"That man, the one who was threatening you—what sort of police officer is he?"

Lorene stared at Marina, frightened. "Who said that?"

"You did."

"I did! Hell."

What this meant Marina couldn't interpret. In an instant Lorene's childlike face was closed like a fist.

Marina said, "You aren't married to him, are you?" and Lorene laughed scornfully, saying, "Married to *him*? That'd be the day," and Marina said, "If he's threatened you, you could get a court injunction to be protected against him." Marina spoke adamantly though in fact she wasn't so sure of this.

Lorene snorted in contempt. "'Court injunction'! Against guys like him! Know what them things are, ma'am—*bullshit*."

Marina recoiled from the girl's fierce scorn. She asked if Lorene would like more coffee and Lorene said irritably, "No, thanks!" and then, "O.K., maybe." The waitress came by. Marina gave their orders. She had the distinct impression that Lorene was waiting sulkily for her to do something; or for something to happen; she was both restless and passive, licking her lips, brushing her frizzed hair out of her face. Through a wall mirror Marina glimpsed a man of about forty in an unzipped windbreaker, wearing a baseball cap, staring distractedly at Lorene as he passed their booth. He seemed not to know her, only just to be attracted by her. His gaze passed through Marina Troy as if she were invisible.

Marina was saying, "It's such beautiful countryside in the Poconos. Except it's becoming so developed . . ."

Lorene stared at Marina, as if unhearing. Marina's oddly ebullient words seemed to come to her slow as balloons. "'Developed'—yes, I guess. I don't notice too much." The waitress brought them more coffee, and Lorene quickly emptied another two sugar packets into her cup. "It's hard to remember, like, how anything *was*."

"Have you lived here all your life?"

Lorene lifted the coffee cup to her thin-lipped mouth. The coffee was steaming but she was impatient to drink. Distracted, she seemed about to ask *lived where?* but managed to murmur, "Yes. I guess." But a moment later, with an annoyed laugh, she said, "No. Just a few years." She seemed about to add more, but hesitated.

Marina said, "Where I live, in Damascus County, it's very hilly. It's beautiful but remote. My road is an unpaved road."

Lorene said, with just perceptible disdain, "Why anybody'd move here if they could live somewhere else, I mean like year-round, *I* can't figure. It's O.K. in the summer, sure. And if you like to ski. But just to live here, Christ!" She laughed breathily to signal to Marina she didn't mean to be insulting or confrontational, only just matter-of-fact.

Marina said, a little stiffly, "A friend left me the property. It's a beautiful property."

Lorene said, rousing herself to take an interest, "Oh, yes? Who?"

"A man. He was very special to me."

Lorene's eyes widened in sympathy. "Uh-uh! 'Was.' He's—passed away, I guess?"

Marina nodded. That quaint tactful phrase. *Passed away*. She was grateful for it.

Lorene said, sniffing, but with an air of reproach, "My dad, too. Two years ago, around now. Christmas. Why I'm so fucked up, I guess. Lung cancer, and it met-as-tized to the brain. That's ugly. Daddy didn't leave us much to want to remember, y'know? Poor guy couldn't kick the habit." Lorene lifted the cigarette she'd been half-consciously shredding.

Marina said, "I'm sorry to hear that, Lorene. Please accept my condolences."

Lorene said, embarrassed, "Well. It was, like, two years ago."

"Still. You must miss your father."

"*Your* friend? You were, like, in love?"

"Yes."

How suddenly blunt Lorene was, as a child might be blunt, and not rude. Marina was grateful for this, too. She smiled, not wanting to cry. Her face burned pleasantly. *No one has spoken to me like this. No one in years.*

Lorene asked with genuine curiosity, leaning forward, hair swinging in her face, "What happened to him, Marina?"

Marina said quietly, "He died. In an accident on the Hudson River last summer."

How strange it seemed to her, in a way wonderful: she could speak of Adam's death in such a way, to a stranger. As if it had been an event, fixed in time. Not a condition but a single event, Adam Berendt's death.

"Like, swimming? Or in a boat?"

"A beautiful white sailboat," Marina said, with sudden emotion. Her eyes brimmed dangerously with tears but she felt her heart swell. "He dived overboard to save a drowning child. It was reckless, under the circumstances. The girl was going to be rescued by others. But Adam, he had to be the one! And it killed him."

"God. You were there? You *saw?*"

Marina hid her face, for the moment overcome.

As if she were skilled in loss and in speaking of loss Lorene said quickly, "That's real sad, Marina. It must've been real awful, like a nightmare. How old was he?"

Marina hesitated. "My age."

She knew that Lorene was rapidly assessing her age. A woman in her thirties who maybe looked younger than she was. Or maybe older.

Marina hadn't wanted this impatient young woman to dismiss her lost Adam as an old man.

Thinking afterward, *Of course I'd be old to her too. Anyone of another generation.*

Marina dried her eyes, and turned the conversation to more practical matters. What should Lorene do? She, Marina, felt the burden of a not-unpleasant responsibility. Like an older sister. For once. She brought up the subject of the bus ride to Pittsburgh, the return to Lorene's family, and offered to "lend" Lorene fifty dollars; and Lorene declined the offer; and Marina persisted; and finally, deeply embarrassed, Lorene gave in. "Well. O.K. I guess. But I will pay you back, Marina, I promise. You give me your address, O.K.?" She smiled a quick, pained smile. Her eyes shone with gratitude and resentment in about equal measure. Marina counted two twenty-dollar bills and three five-dollar bills out of her wallet, and added a ten-dollar bill, excited by her own generosity; on a fresh napkin she carefully printed her name and address—

Marina Troy
R.R. #3, Box 139
Damascus Crossing, PA 18361

Self-consciously as if she feared she was being watched, Lorene accepted the bills from Marina, without counting them; the napkin she folded neatly, as if it were precious, placing it with the bills in a pocket of her suede jacket. Almost inaudibly she murmured, "Thanks!"

Marina said, "But where will you spend the night, Lorene? If the bus doesn't leave until morning?"

There was that to consider. Lorene's gaze went blank.

"I need to try that number again," Lorene said with sudden animation. "Like I said."

You could stay with me, Lorene.

I know you won't. But you could stay with me.

Their eyes met. Lorene looked away, fiercely blushing. Again things became confused. Lorene was eager to get to the phone, but slid out of the booth as if reluctantly, her small eyes very dark, glassily dark as marbles, and an odor of perfumy perspiration lifting from her skin. On her feet, hovering over Marina, impulsively she leaned down, murmured, "Thanks, Marina!" and kissed Marina wetly on the corner of the mouth. Then she was gone.

Marina sat unmoving, as if she'd been struck.

Her mind was a flurry of wings. Moths' wings. The kiss burned at the corner of her mouth.

IN RETROSPECT, recalling that disjointed, confusing evening in her life Marina would think calmly *Of course. Why was I surprised?* But at the time, to her chagrin, she had no thought of the girl who'd called herself Lorene walking out of the East Hills Diner and leaving her forever. In fact she was keenly alert waiting for Lorene to return; watching in the mirror for the big-boned streaked-blond girl in the suede jacket to loom up behind her.

Ten minutes passed. Fifteen. Marina began to suspect that something might be wrong. On the table top, across from Marina, were spilled sugar and a shredded cigarette and a crumpled napkin smeared with maroon lipstick.

Marina went to look for Lorene by the public phone at the front of the diner, but Lorene wasn't there. No one was using the phone. Nor was Lorene in the women's rest room. In a haze of alarm and mounting worry, Marina walked quickly through the crowded restaurant, looking for Lorene. She saw several girls who resembled Lorene, or the girl who'd identified herself to Marina as "Lorene," but she did not find the girl she sought.

Anxiously Marina asked their waitress if she'd seen Lorene leave the diner and the waitress said, "Your friend? I guess so. She left with some guy. Maybe ten minutes ago."

Marina swallowed hard. *Some guy!*

In dread she asked what this guy looked like.

The waitress shrugged. "Just a guy."

"Did he have a moustache? A beard? A crimson jacket?"

The noise level in this part of the diner was so high, the waitress had to cup her hand to her ear. "A what-color jacket?"

"Crimson. Red."

"Yeah, ma'am. He sure did."

The folly. The shame! And worse to come.

The adventure didn't end in the East Hills Diner but in the parking lot. Where I discovered that all four tires on the Jeep had been expertly slashed. And the windshield cracked like a crazed star where he'd slammed a baseball bat, probably, against it. Bitch! Cunt! Dyke! *Almost, I could hear him. Fortunately the windshield wasn't shattered so I could drive back to Damascus Crossing that night, late that night, after the tires were replaced. (For almost six hundred dollars.) Just laugh at me, don't pity me!*

Let's just say Marina Troy got what she deserved.

10

It was at the end of December, at the turn of the year, that the warm furred creature came in stealth to settle upon her chest. That smothering weight. Heavy, and heavier. *Can't breathe. Help me!* In the night the dark-furred thing with a snout that smelled of blood, pushing wetly against Marina's mouth. Nudging, kissing. The heavy warm dark-furred smothering thing with teeth, claws. *Thwaite, Thwaite!* came the muffled guttural cry. In desperation Marina recoiled in her sleep, threw the thing off herself, woke nauseated and repelled. "What is happening to me! I can't bear this." She was going mad. *Thwaite* was madness, and *Night* was madness. She climbed out of her messy bed as you might climb out of a shallow messy grave.

Barefoot and shivering she went to the studio at the rear of the drafty house. The things, Adam's things, were waiting for her. She switched on the light, exposing them in crude glaring light lacking the mitigating filmy shadows of romance. She saw them for what they were: ugly aborted "sculptures" she'd been laboring at, with such hope, for months. The vanity of her effort swept over her like a wave of dirty water. The futility. The delusion. Almost she wanted to laugh, she'd failed utterly. The fragmentary artworks Adam Berendt had left behind in this house haven't been completed by Marina Troy, but sabotaged. Clearly Marina Troy knew nothing of Adam Berendt, the man was finally a stranger; Marina had no access to his vision, as she'd had no access to his heart. She was only herself.

Old Mill Way: The Transformation

I

Everything in the universe is a coincidence! Adam Berendt once said. *Or nothing is.*

Yet it couldn't be merely coincidence that the day Lionel Hoffmann at last confessed his secret to his wife, Camille, was the eve of the day Shadow entered Camille's life.

"Camille, I have something to tell you."

I have something to tell you. These words. Dread-words. Chill-words. Words no middle-aged wife wishes to hear uttered numbly, yet with a ghastly hopeful smile, by her middle-aged husband.

I have something to tell you. Lionel Hoffmann spoke awkwardly, guiltily. He was not a man to speak falteringly yet he spoke falteringly now. How absurd that his eyes should water, and his sinuses ache, as if he were having an allergy reaction . . . Though he'd prepared this scene for weeks. Since the terrible night of Adam Berendt's cremation he'd prepared this scene.

He'd murmured these words to himself countless times, like stones in his mouth they were, clumsy, distasteful. Yet they must be uttered, at last.

"Camille? You are listening—aren't you?"

He did not say *Camille darling, Camille dear*. Not even to soften the blow he did not say *Camille darling, Camille dear*. Never again *Camille darling, Camille dear*. The horror of that realization swept upon her like the taste of impending death.

Yes, Camille was listening. No! Loudly Camille was humming to herself, squatting in a corner of the kitchen as Lionel stood in the doorway behind her. This, too, was a TV scene, a movie scene, yet raw, original, painful as a dentist's drill without novocaine for the participants. *I had no idea. Not a hint. No! We were so happy in that house*. With dampened paper towels Camille was vigorously cleaning the tile floor. It was an expensive tile meant to suggest the hard wood of an eighteenth-century kitchen floor with knot-holes, blemishes, and cracks. Camille Hoffmann had long been the wife of the beautifully restored Colonial on Old Mill Way; and Lionel Hoffmann had long been the husband of the house. Joint owners the Hoffmanns were of a property estimated at $2.5 million. *We will never sell! Never*. It was rare for the husband and wife to see each other so vividly, let alone embark upon a dramatic scene; since their children were grown and gone, drama had largely departed from their lives. *No, I never guessed. How could I, when we were so happy!* Yet now the household air quivered like the air before an electric storm.

Camille was wiping the floor clean in wide, guilty swipes. For Apollo had made a mess, eating. And Lionel wasn't supposed to know that, in his absence, the dog was often fed indoors and not outdoors as Camille had eagerly promised he'd be fed; Lionel wasn't supposed to know (of course, Lionel knew: his allergies could hardly fail to alert him) that during the week, when he was in Manhattan, Apollo had become Camille's constant companion, and was given his meals in a corner of the kitchen where Camille laid down newspaper to set his dishes on; but so ravenous was the lean husky-shepherd, so anxious and edgy since his master's disappearance from his life, that Apollo ate nervously, messily, scattering food beyond the margins of the *New York Times*.

(Oh, Camille scolded Apollo. Camille tried to discipline him as Adam had gently but firmly disciplined him. "Mind your manners, Apollo, please!" Camille begged. "Be a *good dog,* please!" So Lionel overheard when Camille didn't realize he was within earshot. And how offended he was, hearing his wife begging a dog to behave . . . Those interminable weekends in Salthill, Lionel had to endure shut up in the house with Camille, living their blind cave-existence, while his mistress, Siri, long milky-pale limbs and dark eyes brimming with both hurt and passion, was miles away in her flat in the East Village, leading her mysterious life as distant to him as if she were in Tangier . . . *Siri, darling! Think of me, as I think of you.* Lionel would not have wished to acknowledge that he, too, was begging. While in the house on Old Mill Way Camille tried gamely to eradicate all signs of Apollo, as an adulterous wife might try to eradicate all signs of her lover, naively hoping to deceive her husband. Camille didn't even trust Lina, their cleaning woman, to rid the house of dog hairs, dog dander, that unmistakable doggy odor that so offended Lionel's sensitive nostrils, there she was vacuuming, mopping, opening windows herself, and gently scolding Apollo, who was a lonely creature, and rather demanding. Lionel, overhearing Camille with Apollo, gritted his teeth. Camille's manner with the dog was pleading and reproachful, frantic and seductive. "Apollo, *please.* You must learn to *obey.* For Adam's sake if not for mine." Lionel might have banished the damned dog permanently except he didn't want to cause a scene; he didn't want to be cruel to either the dog or his emotional wife; he didn't want to be crueller than he would have to be; he wasn't a cruel person, but a gentleman. Lionel wanted to be known among the Salthill circle as a gentleman. *I love it that you so respect your wife,* Siri murmured, in his arms, *but have you no respect for me?*

"Camille? Can you look up here?"

Lionel's grave guilty voice. God damn, what was wrong with

Camille? "The floor is clean, Camille. I don't mind—much—that you've been feeding the dog in the house. But I"—and here Lionel hesitated, like a man easing out onto cracking ice—"have something to tell you."

"Oh, Lionel! I didn't realize you were here."

Camille smiled. Blinking as if a bright light were shining in her face. And her softly flaccid girl's face shone like the floor she'd been wiping. For here was a woman who clearly suspected nothing; a woman of childlike innocence. She was dressed somewhat oddly in a gardener's denim coverall, over a salmon-colored turtleneck; squatting, she bulged alarmingly at the thighs. Her graying brown hair was brushed back and fastened with a clip. She wore no makeup, she seemed to have no eyelashes. Surely, Lionel thought, annoyed, Camille had had eyelashes at one time? Her smiling mouth had a rubbery resilience that made her husband think of a doll's mouth which a man would never, never wish to kiss.

He could not recall when he'd kissed that mouth last. The thought filled him with guilty revulsion. *Oh, Siri!*

"Camille? Why don't you stand up, please. It's difficult to talk to you like this."

Camille laughed lightly, and straightened; she swayed as if the sight of Lionel made her dizzy, and this, too, made her laugh, nervously. Lionel had to resist the impulse to steady her as one might an elderly or infirm person.

"Lionel! You're home early. This is—Thursday? Or no: Friday."

It was Friday. The end of the week. On Friday evenings, Lionel sometimes returned on the 7:08 P.M. Amtrak to Salthill, and sometimes he returned on the 7:45 P.M. Amtrak. He was a man of routine like all the Hoffmann men. But tonight, with Siri's encouragement, he'd returned early, on the 6:48 P.M.

You must tell her. You have promised me!

"Camille, I'm sorry to startle you. I thought you'd heard me drive in."

(Of course she'd heard. Why otherwise had she been desperately cleaning the kitchen floor? Why otherwise had Apollo been hastily sent out of the house, barking and whining forlornly in the backyard?)

"I'm afraid—I have something to tell you."

Those words. Such weak, hollow, unoriginal words! Lionel felt a thrill of disgust. He was a six-foot puppet through whose hole of a mouth someone, or something, spoke words of such clumsy banality he could not believe they might be mistaken as his.

Yet Camille, that good woman, managed to smile as if to encourage him. Her lashless eyes were damp with terror.

"Lionel, dear? *What?*"

SHE WAS DRIVING the new car, the white Acura. Beside her in the passenger's seat was Apollo, panting and eager. This was no dream for it was morning, and a new day. She turned off Salthill Road, north onto West Axe Boulevard. She had not slept the previous night and was grateful for dawn and now she was driving, as if nothing were wrong, as if her life had not been rent in two as with the terrible stroke of an axe, to the farmer's market in West Nyack. Her swollen eyes stared. On the grassy median a dog cringed in terror as traffic streamed past on both sides. Had the poor creature been abandoned? So cruelly abandoned? Was it lost? Camille slowed her car to watch in horror as, hesitating, the dog ventured off the median, leapt back up onto it, then ventured off again, gathering its courage to run blindly across the right-hand lane. It was instantaneously struck by a speeding minivan, the small dark-furred body lifted and flung twenty feet along the edge of the road like a bundle of rags. "Oh, God! Oh, God!" At once Camille braked her car, heedless of horns behind her and of her own safety as she left her car to run to the stricken dog, which dragged itself off the pavement and into weeds, a trail of bright-glistening blood in its wake. The dog, a small-bodied mongrel with Labrador retriever blood and no tags, was whimpering in pain and terror. Beside Camille, Apollo barked excitedly.

This was no dream. Traffic sped past on the notoriously busy boulevard. The minivan had vanished. No one else would stop. It was a Saturday morning in October, the first morning of Lionel Hoffmann's departure from the house on Old Mill Way, the first morning of Camille Hoffmann's left-behind life. She pressed the heel of her hand against her broken heart and wept for the injured dog. "You, too! You, too!" She knelt in blood-splattered weeds daring to put out her trembling hand to the writhing dog whose mouth frothed with saliva. Sunlight glittered on her beautiful useless rings.

Words once uttered, that can never be revoked.
How could you, when we were so happy!

Guilt darkened Lionel's face like blood seeping into a translucent sac. His hoarse voice was unrecognizable, his throat felt as if he'd swallowed thorns.

He stammered, "Camille, I'm—sorry."

"*I'm* sorry!"

Gamely Camille was trying to keep the mood light. Though the floor tilted drunkenly beneath her. Though her mouth ached with smiling.

"Camille, I had to tell you. It was—time."

"Yes?"

"We couldn't continue, obviously—as we were."

"We couldn't?"

Was Camille in shock? Stunned? Smiling in that bright-blind way of hers. Lionel wasn't smiling for this was hardly a smiling matter. This was hardly an occasion for levity. His sinuses were impacted as if with cement. That damned dog! Almost, Lionel was furious with his friend Adam Berendt for dying so carelessly and leaving the animal in their care. For after all that was what Apollo was: an animal. When the children were young it was explained that Daddy had allergies, Daddy couldn't live with animals, not dogs, not cats, not even parrots, and perhaps that was true; or true to some degree. And now it was certainly true. Lionel's eyes were watering with pain, misery, excitement. He said, urgently, as if to involve Camille in his drama, "You know that, Camille, don't you? I think—all along you must have known."

"'Must have known'—?"

Camille smiled, leaning against the kitchen table to keep her balance. She saw in her husband's face an expression of commingled pity, guilt, sympathy, and annoyance. For this was a scene for which she had no preparation. It was a familiar scene from TV and films, yet Camille had no more idea of how to play it than she would have known how to play her own death scene. *So sudden! So raw! Cruel as a blow in the face.*

"These months," Lionel was saying ecstatically, as if his words made perfect sense, "—this past year. Since last November, to be exact."

"—November?"

Camille was having difficulty not only with her balance but with her hearing. This was all so strange! The refrigerator's motor throbbed in both her ears. Or was it blood drumming in her ears. On the kitchen counter were several dampened, dirtied paper towels. But the floor shone. Spotless.

"—I've known her. The woman I—with whom I—have become involved."

Involved? The curious neutral term hovered between them like a swarm of dust motes.

"Camille, I never intended it to happen. It began with pain—in my upper spine, my neck? D'you remember? 'Cervical spine strain' the doctor called it. And, after that—" A dreamy confused look came over Lionel's face, like butter melting on warm meat. He lifted his hands in a gesture of helpless acquiescence to fate.

Camille was trying to comprehend her husband's bizarre words. Had he been drinking on the Amtrak? It wasn't like Lionel; but then, none of this was "like" Lionel. Vaguely she recalled his complaint of neck pain months ago, but—what had neck pain to do with *this?* The throbbing in her ears had become a roar. Her husband's mouth moved, and she saw his excited anxious eyes, and felt his words like chunks of mud flung at her. Hesitantly Lionel approached Camille as if to touch her, but finally he did not touch her. She stood dazed as one who has been mortally wounded but has not fallen. Lionel stood rigid, staring in dismay at the woman he'd injured, and did not move toward her.

Already he won't touch me. Already my marriage is over. My life.

At this awkward moment the telephone began to ring.

The telephone! Like a sleepwalker Camille moved forward to answer the phone. Still she smiled. A phone call was a happy event, usually. Lionel couldn't bear his wife's bright warm brave voice. "Hello? Oh Marcy, hel*lo*." Like a criminal in retreat from the scene of his crime, Lionel quickly fled.

Marcy, their daughter. Twenty-seven years old.

Lionel dreaded her, and their twenty-five-year-old son Kevin, learning his news.

Oh, Daddy, how could you! Breaking Mother's heart.

Lionel's plan was to pack a few things and drive back into the city, in his car; Lionel's was a Lexus, the older of the Hoffmanns' two cars, but the one he preferred. Siri had promised to be waiting for him in the apartment on East 61st Street. (Maybe she would have prepared for him one of her exquisite vegetarian-Indian meals.) For months Lionel had been smuggling items of clothing, documents and papers, into the city in his briefcase; unobtrusively, trusting Camille not to notice. Camille had not noticed. In Manhattan in Siri's company he'd been buying new clothing and furnishings for the apartment, which Siri believed was a beautiful apartment but rather somber and unimaginative. *Not at all like you, Lionel! Your special nature.*

At a distance Lionel heard Camille speaking with their daughter as if nothing were wrong. What a good, gracious woman Camille was! He hid his burning face in his hands. What the hell had he done? Was it irremediable? When he lowered his hands, his mouth was twisted in a grimace like laughter. It was a gargoyle-mouth, wracked in pain.

A WILD RIDE! Through Saturday-morning traffic on Route 9W Camille drove a mile and a half to the emergency clinic of the

Rockland County Homeless Animal Shelter north of Salthill-on-Hudson, the bleeding, writhing, whimpering dog beside her on the passenger's seat of the Acura. At the clinic, where she'd taken Apollo for treatment some months before, there was a youngish veterinarian on duty, a Dr. Lott, who seemed to remember her, and stared in amazement as Camille carried the injured dog into the examining room heedless of the fact that her clothing was blood- and urine-stained and that the dog in her arms, in agony, was alternately licking her hands, and snarling and snapping at her, and wagging his stump of a tail. Fiercely Camille whispered, "You will *not die*. You *will not die*. I swear!"

But the veterinarian, after a quick examination, recommended putting the dog down. It was a male, badly injured; hind legs, spine, spleen; the external bleeding could be stanched, but there was internal bleeding, which would require emergency surgery. "It could be very expensive, Mrs. Hoffmann. And it isn't very practical." Camille was prepared for this. She drew herself up to her full height, and fixed both Dr. Lott and his young woman assistant with a look of absolute determination. "No. This dog will not be 'put down.' Do what you can to save him." Dr. Lott said, frowning, "But whose dog is this? Where did you find him? He has no tags, no collar." It seemed to Camille that the dog, strapped onto the aluminum examining table, understood these words, and lay panting and shivering in apprehension, looking at her. Quickly she said, "It was meant to be, that I rescue him. He was struck by a minivan on West Axe Boulevard and left to die and at that precise moment I happened to be there, I was a witness, it must have been for a purpose, Dr. Lott! There are no coincidences in the universe—unless everything is a coincidence—which can't be so! You must save this dog." Camille was breathless, her voice rising. Still the veterinarian was shaking his head, and looking grim. Again he told Camille that the surgery would be very costly, and he couldn't guarantee that the dog would survive; and Camille said loudly, "Dr. Lott, I will pay you. Whatever it costs. I will not give him up, *this was meant to be*." The veterinarian was staring at Camille as if, until that moment, he'd never fully looked at her before. He was a vigorous youngish man in his early forties, accustomed to telling others what to do, especially women; Camille's presence made an impression upon him. How visible Camille felt, suddenly. And how good the feeling. *Now I am no longer a man's wife, I don't need to be a woman, either.*

WHAT HAD HE DONE, what had he done!

Fled the house on Old Mill Way.

Free! He was free. His heart swelling with happiness like a balloon close to bursting.

At last, he would join the two halves of his life. No more hypocrisy. No more subterfuge. *Bring her into the light, you must bring her into the light. You must give birth to her.* By degrees Lionel had come to believe that his friend Adam Berendt had advised him. The dream-vision of the cave. Adam's voice. *No shame. Never again. Bring together the broken halves of your life.* His family and friends would understand, when they met Siri. When they saw how transformed Lionel was, in love. "In love for the first time in my life." For years, for decades!—he'd been a living mummy. Speaking mummy-words, enacting mummy-desires. Until at last his body had rebelled, bringing him pain, stabbing pain, dull aching brooding pain in his neck and upper spine, until he'd been nearly paralyzed. Unconsciously he'd come to despise himself. But now, he was a new man. Since Siri entered his life he'd become a new man. They would understand, his family and friends; and they would forgive him. In time, the more generous would rejoice with him.

In the steel-green Lexus that held the road like a tank Lionel drove south on 9W to the soaring George Washington Bridge. In a transport of joy he drove. In bliss. He took the upper level of the bridge, crossing the wide river that glittered below like shaken foil. Adam Berendt had not died in that river for nothing!

Through the girders of the great bridge a luminous full moon shone, a staring eye.

"Siri, darling! I've left Salthill."

* * *

"IT IS NOT a coincidence. Adam has brought me here."

The badly injured dog was in surgery. Hopeless, it was hopeless! Yet Camille had hope. She tried to sit in the waiting room, but soon stood, and paced about. Apollo, that good dog, was nervous, too, but sat obediently on his haunches, his anxious intelligent dog-eyes fixed upon Camille, as if the fate of the strange dog, and his own fate, rested with her. "Yes, I will save you! I will save you all." In the lavatory Camille had washed as best she could, ridding her hands and forearms of the dog's blood, but her clothes, which were expensive sporty Ann Taylor clothes, cotton-knit beige trousers and matching jacket, were irrevocably stained. Ruined. Camille saw how other customers in the partly filled room looked at her. In other circumstances Camille would have been mortified, but now she scarcely cared. Most of these individuals had dogs on leashes, or cats in carrying cases, and were anxious themselves. A woman whom Camille knew slightly, who'd brought in her bulldog to be examined, asked why Camille was at the clinic, and Camille told her about the abandoned, injured dog—"His name is Shadow. Out of nowhere he came, and he came to *me*."

The woman, stroking the wheezy bulldog's head, told Camille she knew exactly what Camille meant.

So nervous! In her stained and smelly clothes, her hair disheveled, Camille paced about the waiting room. She did not much resemble a Salthill millionaire's wife. At the rear of the room she could hear the barking of dogs in an adjacent kennel. A disjointed chorus of barking, never-ending barking, as in mirrors reflecting mirrors to infinity. "So much animal sorrow," Camille sighed, "and who is responsible?" She spoke to no one in particular. The barking dogs tore at her heart. Animal sorrow, animal suffering. Had she made an impulsive, selfish decision, to try to keep the dog alive? Alive for *her?*

Adam, too, had taken in homeless animals. Apollo had been one of these, abandoned by the roadside. Adam had left the Rockland County Shelter thousands of dollars in his will.

It is not a coincidence, you've brought me here. Oh, Adam!

Shadow would survive the surgery, which lasted for seventy

minutes. Never would he fully recover the use of his hind legs, Dr. Lott explained, but at least he was alive—"For now, Mrs. Hoffmann." After six days in the clinic, Shadow was released into Camille's care; she was presented with a bill for over two thousand dollars, and without hesitation she made out a check for this amount and a second check, for four thousand dollars, to the Rockland County Homeless Animal Shelter. The receptionist rose immediately to summon Dr. Lott, who came to shake Camille's hand, and to stare at her in wonderment. "Mrs. Hoffmann! Thank you."

Said Camille firmly, "No, Dr. Lott. Thank *you*."

2

HE'D FALLEN IN LOVE innocently, with the girl's *touch*.

Scarcely had he seen her, falling in love. His head wracked in pain as in a demonic halo. She was no one to him: "Siri": a young woman therapist assigned to Lionel Hoffmann, purely by chance, at the Park Avenue Neck and Back Clinic. She was an angel of mercy in white nylon. Chaste as a bandage, and of as much interest to him, initially. (Though Lionel's sensitive nostrils quickly detected her subtle nutmeg scent, which seemed to arise from her skin, and from her remarkably thick dark hair fastened in a coil at the nape of her neck.) "Siri" was primarily her hands: deft, gentle, skilled, patient. During their session she said little except to murmur when Lionel stiffened or winced in pain—"Mr. Hoffmann. Please try to relax."

Not in reproach but gently. As one might admonish a small child, for his own good.

For weeks, unless it had been months, years, Lionel had been aware of quick stabbing pains in his neck. Since the previous summer the pain had gradually increased until it resembled icicles radiating downward from his neck into his upper spine; and, with alarming frequency, upward into the base of the skull. Lionel would wake dry-mouthed to the terror he had a tumor there. Of course, a tumor! Like a tiny seed it would take root in his flesh, it would grow, and grow, and suck his life from him. In one of the medical texts published by Hoffmann Publishing, Inc., he read about the *cerebellum:* that part of the brain that regulates equilibrium and the coordination of muscular movements. *Injury or organic disease in the cerebellum may produce such symptoms as a staggering walk, palsy, slurred speech, chronic malaise.* There were days when Lionel could barely hoist himself from bed. He was only fifty-three years old!

With guilty anxiety Lionel thought of his younger brother, Scott. Dead at thirty-six. Moldering in the grave for how many years. To Scott, fifty-three would have seemed old. Fifty-three would have been old. "But I'm not ready to die. I haven't yet *lived.*"

Telling himself the pain couldn't possibly be a tumor, more likely just a pulled tendon, neck strain caused by playing tennis, racquetball, golf. (Not that Lionel had much time for these activities.) If you're a middle-aged man who imagines himself "active"—"energetic"—you would wish to decode pain in reference to some form of masculine behavior. You would not wish to decode pain in terms of a sedentary life, a defeatist posture, the inevitable process of *aging.* You would not wish to decode drastically waning sexual desire, indifference to sexual stimuli (a beloved wife's familiar body, for instance), inability to sustain a serious erection, to the inevitable process of *aging.*

It was Harry Tierney, whom Lionel saw occasionally at the Century Club, who directed Lionel to the Park Avenue Neck and Back Clinic. Lionel would not have brought up the subject, which was far too personal for him to discuss with Harry Tierney, except during their exchange of greetings Lionel winced with pain, and held his head at an odd angle. Harry asked what was wrong, and Lionel told him he'd strained his neck playing golf, he thought; it was a pain that came and went; not severe, but it forced him to think about his health more than he was accustomed to thinking, and he resented it. Harry saw at once through Lionel's pose of detachment and told him he'd better take the pain seriously. He gave Lionel the name of a "first-rate" orthopedist and suggested he make an appointment immediately.

"Spinal trouble is nothing to ignore, my friend. He'll send you to a clinic for therapy, and they'll save your life."

How unexpected, how strange, that Harry Tierney should be speaking to Lionel with such apparent sincerity. As if indeed they were friends, or had been at one time. Tierney was known for his irony and cynical wit. In their Salthill circle, Lionel had avoided him, disapproving of the man's jocose manner and his mock-cavalier tone with women, including Camille. (And Harry's own wife, Abigail. That wanly beautiful woman whom all the Salthill husbands contemplated, with a sort of lustful dread, from a discreet distance.) But Tierney behaved as if he respected Lionel, CEO of Hoffmann Publishing, Inc., which was flattering. Since leaving Salthill, divorcing poor Abigail and marrying a younger woman, Tierney looked like a younger version of himself, with darker (dyed?) hair and even a moustache, evenly tanned if somewhat lined skin, and oddly light, luminescent eyes that put Lionel in mind of a deep-sea fish's eyes. There was something predatory yet crudely innocent about Harry Tierney, of whom Adam Berendt had once said *The man's a bastard, like a scorpion's a scorpion. Can't help himself.* Adam's sympathies had been entirely with Abigail, the left-behind wounded wife.

Harry was saying, tenderly rubbing his own neck, "If you're in pain, Lionel, life shrinks to the size of a cocktail napkin. No matter how many millions of dollars you have. Save yourself!" Lionel smiled, uncertain of what they were actually speaking. Pain? Money? He didn't trust Harry Tierney. Still, Harry seemed to be utterly sincere, and wasn't drunk.

At the time of this conversation Adam Berendt was still living. Though Harry Tierney and Lionel spoke of mutual Salthill acquaintances neither mentioned Adam, with whom it was generally believed Abigail had had a passionate affair of long standing. In parting, Harry laid an uncomfortably warm, heavy hand on Lionel's shoulder, that made Lionel wince, for it smelled moist and urinous as a kidney, saying, "Remember me to Salthill, my friend! 'That hell of a paradise.'" Harry laughed uproariously as if he'd coined a brilliant aphorism, and Lionel was enjoined into laughing with him though he was offended.

That hell of a paradise: what did Harry Tierney mean?

Lionel took Tierney's advice, however, and made an appointment with the Park Avenue orthopedist Tierney recommended. He entered the doctor's lavishly appointed office listing to one side, in a haze of throbbing pain that felt like neon tubing in his spine. The examination was brusque and brutal and within a few minutes tears streaked Lionel's smooth-shaven cheeks. The orthopedist informed Lionel that his problem appeared to be "cervical spine strain" caused by the "overstretching" of neck muscles, the probable result of decades of "postural stresses"; the underlying tissues in his neck muscles, capsules, and ligaments, had been "severely strained," and "scar tissue" had been formed. Lionel listened in fascinated dread. In these minutes he'd become vulnerable as an infant. *So long as it isn't malignant. So long as I will live.* "Is the damage—reversible?" Lionel asked anxiously. The orthopedist, a pink-skinned, pudgy man in his mid-forties, slightly mishearing as he scribbled a prescription for Lionel, said, "Yes, if you begin therapy immediately, Lionel. No drugs! We don't believe in pain-*killing* but in pain *control.* I'm recommending therapy three times a week. This, plus exercises you can do on your own, will help you control your pain, and eventually banish it."

As Lionel dressed, with shaking fingers buttoning his shirt, the orthopedist smiled at him in a brotherly way, and said, "You're fortunate, Lionel. Your pain is not organic, but merely 'mechanical.' To a large extent, a human being is a mechanical assemblage of bones, muscles, organs, tissue, nerves. We inhabit these robots but we need feel no sentiment, for they are not *us;* we are not *them.* Always remember: the management of your spine is your personal responsibility. If you have developed spinal problems, then you must learn how to deal with them, and how to prevent future symptoms. I will see you again in three weeks, Lionel, and by then, I predict, you will be walking upright. You will be feeling much, much better." The man's handshake was warm and reassuring and just perceptibly bullying. Again, Lionel had the discomforting sensation that their topic was more profound than simply physical pain.

At the lavishly appointed Park Avenue Neck and Back Clinic, Park at 52nd Street, Lionel was assigned a young female therapist named Siri. In his haze of pain he scarcely noticed her. In his haze of pain, resentful and wincing with each step, embarrassed to be gripping his neon-throbbing neck in both hands, Lionel followed the therapist through the atriumlike clinic, where pain-wracked individuals, most of them middle-aged men like himself, were exercising on machines. There was a steaming whirlpool. There was a larger pool of gemlike aqua water where individuals swam laps with cautious strokes. There were discreetly veiled mirrors, there were tropical-looking potted plants and sleek chrome works of art in the Henry Moore mode of aesthetic physicality, featureless and smoothed to perfection. Impressionistic music, Debussy or Ravel, was being piped in, quietly. No soft-rock music here as in a Midtown yuppie health club. No beautifully proportioned young people working out on the floor, gazing with narcissistic ardor at their own reflections. No healthy clients! All this, Lionel understood, would be very expensive, and no doubt the orthopedist was a part-owner in the clinic, shrewdly profiting from others' pain.

Lionel staggered into the therapist's windowless, white-walled cubicle, which opened off the atrium. He removed most of his clothing as directed by the therapist and lay down gingerly, with the young woman's assistance—"Mr. Hoffmann! Slow-ly"—on a firmly cushioned table. He was terribly ashamed to have whimpered aloud. A stab of panic gripped him, that he might not be able to sit up again, except with assistance. He lay very still, his eyes shut. Willing himself to be strong. Yet thinking *I, Lionel Hoffmann, have become one of the walking wounded. No one must know.* Not his staff at Hoffmann Publishing, Inc., and certainly not his wife and friends in Salthill. He dreaded being the object of others' scrutiny and pity; it infuriated him to imagine Camille's women friends inquiring after his health, in that eagerly solicitous Salthill way. (In Salthill it was primarily women, of course, who were afflicted in myriad mysterious ways. Nerves, "migraines," loss of appetite, depression. There was a free-ranging malaise commonly if vaguely referred to as "flu," and there was a near-ubiquitous condition known as "chronic fatigue"—"Epstein-Barr syndrome"—which particularly afflicted women without work or responsibilities, like Abigail Des Pres. Where in another era such women might have passed around recipes to one another, dress patterns and outgrown baby clothes, in present-day Salthill-on-Hudson they passed around their symptoms, which constituted a strong bond among them. Camille's physical complaints were so clearly psychosomatic, rooted not in her body but in her fantasies, out of embarrassment for her Lionel never inquired after them, nor did he question Camille's choice of doctors and her reliance upon prescription drugs.) Lionel could not bear it, that he might be confused with such weak-willed individuals!

"Mr. Hoffmann. Please try to relax. The pain is greater, if you do not relax."

The therapist spoke quietly yet with authority. Lionel shut his eyes tighter. He was resolved not to cry out, nor even to shudder with pain if he could avoid it. The first session was strenuous and intense, lasting fifty minutes. By slow degrees Lionel managed to relax as the therapist's remarkably strong, deft fingers sought out what she called "pain sites"—"stressed muscles"—and massaged them into compliance. Lionel was made to retract his neck like a turtle and to extend his neck like a snake. He was made to "sidebend" and "rotate" his neck. His vertebrae were loosened and shaken like dice. His eyeballs rolled white in their sockets with intermittent flashes of blinding pain, beads of sweat broke out on his body and trickled down his sides. From time to time there came the warning murmur *Don't stiffen, please. Mr. Hoffmann.* Some of the exercises were performed while Lionel was lying on his back or stomach, and some while he was sitting up. He began by disliking the lying-down exercises which put him, as a man accustomed to authority, at a disadvantage; in time he would come to prefer these, for he was a man accustomed to authority, and weary of exerting it. The therapist leaned over him, clad in crisp white nylon, intimate as Lionel's mother of decades ago; yet, unlike Lionel's mother, the therapist rarely spoke, to Lionel's immense relief. How accustomed he was to female chattering! Where he hadn't the obligation to speak, or to deal with being spoken to, which constituted the major portion of his adult life, he could feel himself free, and anonymous. Tears streaked Lionel's face, for the exercises were in fact painful; but these were tears of gratitude as well.

So quiet was the therapist, Lionel began to wonder if perhaps she didn't know English well. What was her name—"Shura"—"Siri"? Possibly she was Middle Eastern? Indian? Yet she seemed to speak without any evident accent; her throaty voice was purely musical. Through half-shut eyes Lionel had a dim vision of the girl's olive-pale face, pursed lips, and large exotic deep-set black eyes fixed intently upon him. *Yet she doesn't see* me. *I am free of her knowledge of me.* That musky-nutmeg smell, that rose from her thick dark plaited hair, neatly fastened at the nape of her neck.

He wondered how long her hair was, when unplaited. He had a vision of velvety hair falling in glistening strands.

At the end of the session the therapist placed around Lionel's neck a collar heavy and clumsy as a horsecollar, surging with hot water. For ten astonishing minutes Lionel drifted pain-free and entranced. How happy he was! Like a disembodied spirit he contemplated his life from an elevated distance and was forgiving of others, and of himself. He resolved to be kinder and more attentive to Camille; to be less impatient with his children, who seemed to him insufficiently mature for their ages. That weekend he would arrange to see Adam Berendt, his most worthy friend. *Adam, what an insight I had! The secret of life is—*

But when Lionel pressed several bills into the therapist's hand, as he prepared to leave, the young woman stepped gracefully back, and murmured, with an air of apology and regret, "Mr. Hoffmann, thank you but *no*." Suddenly Lionel was looking at her—they were nearly the same height—and his heart thudded absurdly in his chest.

"Forgive me," he said, staring. "This was my first time."

* * *

When did I fall in love with you, I fell in love at once. Your hands. Your touch. Oh, Siri!

Very quickly it would come to seem to Lionel Hoffmann that the remainder of his life, all that was not Siri, was of little more substance than those hypnagogic images that flash against our eyelids when, in a state of exhaustion, we begin to sink into sleep.

YET LIONEL WAITED, and didn't inquire of Siri until the end of his third week of therapy, when things were going very well for him, whether he might "see" her sometime; and Siri declined at once, though with downcast, embarrassed eyes; and that air of apology and regret that suggested (unless Lionel imagined it?) how much she regretted being in a position obliging her to decline Lionel's offer, and to disappoint him. Lionel saw in the mysteriously silent, darkly beautiful girl a sensitivity to another's feelings that could only have been foreign, for it was certainly not American. "If I weren't your patient, Siri? Would that make a difference?" Lionel asked, and Siri turned away, stricken with a deeper embarrassment, forced to murmur, "Mr. Hoffmann, how can I say!"

Which left the issue, Lionel thought, ambiguous and open to interpretation.

BY THIS TIME he knew her name: Siri Joio. Frequently he spoke it aloud when there was no one to overhear. He knew from the few remarks he'd been able to draw out of her that she lived in Manhattan, in the East Village; it seemed likely that she lived alone; she had few relatives; always she'd wanted to be a physical therapist, and to devote herself to helping "alleviate pain" in others. Lionel was deeply touched by the girl's idealism, which reminded him of his own idealism, years ago; before he'd gone into the Hoffmann family business. Lionel assured Siri that she was certainly helping him, and he was very grateful. Except—

"When I'm well, will that mean we'll never see each other? That doesn't seem fair."

Siri's only response was to laugh nervously.

OVERNIGHT HIS DREAMS were engorged with her. His neck, shoulders, upper back, and spine were erogenous zones. The blood of lost youth pumped into his groin, waking him on the brink of orgasm. During the day, at Hoffmann Publishing, Inc., in meetings and at luncheons and on the phone, Lionel was seized with irrational surges of happiness, and hope. *You won't abandon me, Siri! I know it.* At other times, when the pain returned to his neck and spine, a dull sullen throbbing, he was overcome with a sense of desolation, self-disgust, hopelessness. *Of course I'm too old for you. And you've seen my weaknesses, exposed.* It had been years since Lionel had felt so irresolute. His emotions so mercurial. Years since he'd understood that love brings fear: our worry that we won't be loved in return, that our emotion will be flung back into our faces.

He could not recall having loved Camille like this.

He could not recall having loved anyone like this.

He'd told Camille only that he was having minor neck and back problems, and seeing an orthopedist in the city. Preoccupied with her own problems, and the intensity of Salthill social life which resembled a high-speed roller coaster from which one might never alight during one's lifetime, Camille was sympathetic, but not very involved. "So long as you've had X rays, darling? And there was nothing—serious?"

Lionel reassured Camille, there was nothing "serious."

Liking it that he felt so little unease, in her presence. And when he was away from her he scarcely thought of her at all. *Siri, you have taken over my life. Siri, have mercy!*

ONE DAY, in their fifth week of therapy, when Lionel lay grimacing and panting in pain after an arduous exercise in neck "flexion," Siri gently continued to massage his neck; and paused, and stroked his forehead, which was damp with perspiration. Lionel's eyelids opened at once. He saw Siri's dark, tender gaze fixed upon his. He gripped her hand and held it for a long, tense moment.

Walking wounded. He saw them everywhere, now. He pitied them, and felt contempt for them, and looked quickly away when their eyes that shimmered with pain sought his.

Head retraction in sitting. Neck extension in sitting. Head retraction in lying. Neck extension in lying. Sidebending of the neck. Neck rotation. Neck flexion in sitting. Each of these exercises was to be repeated ten times. Each complete set to be performed twice daily in Lionel's bedroom, or more often, as Siri said, depending upon need.

"But I need my pain, too! My pain is my bond with you."

Not in Salthill but in the apartment on East 61st Street, Lionel slept, or tried to sleep, with a rather hard tubular cushion called a "cervical roll" between his pillow and pillowcase. He'd purchased it at the clinic, as Siri recommended. Sometimes he dreamt that Siri of the smoldering-dark eyes and warm nutmeg scent was pushing a bar against the tender nape of his neck. Her throaty almost inaudible voice. *Mr. Hoffmann! Relax, please.* Sometimes he dreamt he was naked, in a public place, awkwardly kneeling, his neck throbbing with pain outstretched above a bucket as, above his head, a guillotine blade was being raised, preparatory to slicing his head from his body.

HE KNEW, he knew! One day soon she would consent to see him.

(But would she? *This is ridiculous, I'm too old. Adam would laugh at me.*)

Yes but Siri was so kind. He'd overheard her speaking with other patients, before and after Lionel Hoffmann entered her cubicle. He'd overheard her speaking on the telephone. And her strong deft capable fingers were so kind. It was her task to alleviate pain. She was an angel of mercy clad in crisp white nylon. A smock, trousers. The smock was loose-fitting so one could not make out the shape of her breasts except to know that they were not small, though obviously not large, crudely mammalian. Siri was of an entirely different physical type from Camille: slender, boyishly lean, with perfectly proportioned thighs, hips, torso, shoulders, and arms, subtly muscled, not an ounce of fat. Poor Camille: with her fleshy hips and breasts, her pink-skinned round face so eager to please, she was one whom evolution had bypassed; young women no longer died in childbirth because their pelvises were too narrow, they no longer required hefty milk-bags for breasts. The thought of Siri's flat smooth belly made Lionel sweat. *This is ridiculous! Help me.*

Still, he seemed to know she would consent to see him. One day soon.

SIRI'S SHIFT AT the Park Avenue Neck and Back Clinic ended at six P.M. Lionel arranged to be awaiting her at the curb, on Park, in a hired town car. She was startled to see him, she was disapproving, yes, but surely she was flattered, "Siri, I must talk with you. In private." "Mr. Hoffmann! This isn't allowed." "'Talk' isn't allowed? That can't be!" Lionel laughed. An unexpectedly lighthearted lover he was, like Fred Astaire or Gene Kelly of yesteryear. Except for his problematic spine he might have broken into dance right there on the sidewalk. How boyishly eager he was, how seductive his smile. Gaily improvising as he'd never have done in mummy-Salthill—"Under the U.S. Constitution, Siri, we're guaranteed freedom of speech. You are a U.S. citizen, dear, aren't you?" This was teasing but pointed. Jocular but urgent. Siri laughed uneasily. Cutting her softly dark exotic eyes at him. Shaking her head in a way he couldn't interpret. Maybe yes, maybe no. Today Siri wore her lustrous dark hair parted neatly in the center of her head and brushed back in a way that put Lionel in mind of ancient Egyptian female figures, in profile. How beautiful she was! "We can talk in the car. On your way home. You won't have to take the subway." "Mr. Hoffmann. If my supervisor should see . . ." "We can have dinner. Drinks and dinner. Then I'll take you home. We must talk, Siri. You know that." "But Mr. Hoffmann . . ." The girl appeared genuinely concerned. But who was watching them? Lionel saw no one. He dared to take Siri's arm, and led her to the waiting car, and she didn't resist, though seeming not to acquiesce, either; and then they were together, alone together, in the back of the car, and the driver was easing into traffic, and dark-tinted glass protected them from prying eyes. Now they were free of the scrutiny of the clinic, and they were free of the protocol of the clinic. What relief! In the town car in intimate quarters, both rather breathless, but Lionel was in authority. Lionel was the one to assert authority by touching: closing his fingers around Siri's fingers. Laughing at his own boldness. Siri tried to smile, looking frightened, demurring, "Mr. Hoffmann—" and Lionel simply tightened his grip.

They were moving in a procession of glittering vehicles. Midtown traffic. Lionel Hoffmann was a Salthill citizen and he owned property in Manhattan and he was worth many millions of dollars and Siri Joio, who was no fool, nor perhaps so naive as she appeared, could not help but know.

"Please call me Lionel, Siri. You must know by now that's my name."

Now it begins. Now, nothing will stop me! In the town car he kissed her lightly, in an East Side restaurant they sat at a corner table by candlelight, Lionel's handsome graying head inclined toward Siri's as he talked. Siri was very quiet through the meal, and Lionel talked. He hadn't known he was so aggrieved, and so eloquent. A sexually aroused male yet a gentleman. He would see to it that Siri knew: he was a gentleman. Telling her of his life. Never had he considered his life a story until, that evening, he began to tell it to a beautiful young woman who gazed at him avidly, now and then, always rather shyly, stroking his hand. If

Siri had heard the life stories of numerous men of affluent middle age, her clients at the clinic, she certainly gave no sign. If Siri's mind wandered during Lionel's quietly impassioned monologues, she certainly gave no sign. She appeared fascinated by Lionel Hoffmann's life which had been, as he expressed it, a life of deprivation and stoicism and duty—"The Protestant ethic. The theology of quiet desperation. *You* have been spared, Siri, I hope!" It began to seem to Lionel as he told his story that every action of his dating back to his boyhood had been in compliance with others' wishes; his only private, secret act had happened by accident, the terrifying discovery of the dead hippie couple by the lake in Broom Hills, when he'd been a child. "It was like finding treasure. An appalling treasure. Except I had no idea what it meant." What could Siri possibly make of this amazing statement? Yet she listened attentively. Her eyes were fixed on his. That glisten to her eyes. Her hypnotic eyes. The scent of nutmeg, of heated skin. Heavy hair at the nape of her neck Lionel was mad to unplait, he was mad to press his face against her neck, to bury himself in her. Waiter, another bottle of wine! (Though Siri was drinking only mineral water.) He was compelled to tell her of his life. His life until he'd met her. "Thank God for the pain. The pain that brought me to you. I see now, the purpose. There are no coincidences in the universe, Siri." As he spoke she murmured *Yes* and *Oh yes?* and showed by the warm intensity of her gaze and a frequent baring of her teeth in a smile how impressed she was with him, and how erotically attracted; how she admired him, yet was rather intimidated by him; for he was telling her in some detail of Hoffmann Publishing, Inc., the preeminent publisher of medical texts in the United States; he was telling her of his family's pride in his accomplishments, and of his own resentment that he'd bartered so much of his life in exchange for "success." And he'd married too young; he'd married primarily to please his parents; he'd married a sweet girl whom he hadn't truly loved, but one of whom his parents had approved. "My wife. My children. My life until meeting you. These belong to the past, Siri. I feel as if I'm drowning in happiness. Yet—what a riddle it is!"

After the restaurant. In the apartment on East 61st. Entering, gripping Siri's hand, Lionel felt a thrill of panic: what if to surprise him in her blundering way, as once she'd surprised her reticent and easily embarrassed husband with a fortieth birthday party, Camille had come into the city that day, and was waiting for Lionel . . . Thank God, the apartment was empty. Lionel laughed aloud at the look of childlike awe on Siri's face. "Yes. I live here. Four nights a week. It is attractive, isn't it?" The apartment, which the Hoffmanns had owned since 1975, was elegantly if unimaginatively furnished; there were six rooms, with high ceilings, antiquated light fixtures, silk brocade curtains, and thick-piled Oriental rugs. Lionel, who'd scarcely glanced at the apartment in years, took pleasure in seeing it now through this girl's widened eyes. How he adored her, and desired her! There was something powerfully erotic about a girl-therapist who, removed from the setting of her own authority, must submit to the authority of another. In a hesitant voice she was saying, "Mr. Hoffmann. I shouldn't be here. I should leave," and Lionel made no response except to kiss her. She said, breathless, trying to pull away from him, "Mr. Hoffmann! You're married, this is wrong. You know this is wrong. Oh!" She broke away from him, and ran into another room. He followed, trapping her. Lionel felt tall, looming, threatening, potent. For Siri wasn't wearing her trademark white nylon, Siri wasn't his therapist now, Siri was wholly in his power as his children had been, years ago. "Don't be afraid, dear. I won't hurt you," Lionel said. "Mr. Hoffmann. Please, *no*," Siri whispered. They were in Lionel's study. On his gleaming mahogany desk were framed photographs of the Hoffmann family. As in a Hollywood film, light seemed to play about these photographs, even to emanate from their miniature smiling faces. Lionel and his pretty young wife, Camille, Marcy and Kevin as smiling youngsters, what an attractive family, what an American family, these figures at whom Lionel hadn't so much as glanced in memory, that would have been obscured by dust if a cleaning woman didn't come in to the apartment, and into this room, once a week. "Mr. Hoffmann! This is your—wife? These are your—children?" How sorrowful

Siri seemed, in that instant. How vulnerable. Lionel loved her all the more, and desired her. He closed his arms around her, pressed his warm face against the nape of her neck and inhaled the spicy scent, that aroused him almost beyond endurance. "Mr. Hoffmann. This is wrong. I must leave. Oh, please!" She pushed away from him, but Lionel held her; he kissed her, moving his mouth hard against hers, and parting her lips that resisted him initially, then gave in. They staggered together. In a swoon together. Lionel could feel her heart beating against his chest. He could feel her pulses, her panicked rushing thoughts. He'd unloosed her hair, that fell in a cascade of glossy rippling strands. They stumbled against a satin-covered love seat. Lionel began to pull impatiently at Siri's clothing. As, for weeks, he'd longed to pull at her white nylon smock and trousers. He'd been mad to pull at her white nylon smock and trousers and only his extreme self-restraint had prevented him. Now Siri laughed, startled. Her laughter was rather wild. Lionel, grunting, was pressing his body against hers. Letting her feel his massive erection. In this place Camille had furnished and decorated, at the bidding of an overpriced interior decorator, that Lionel had never much liked. *Where I've been so physically lonely, and so bored.* "Mr. Hoffmann. This is wrong! Oh—you know this is wrong—" Siri murmured; and Lionel grunted in reply, unable for the moment to speak. It had been years since he'd so much as fantasized holding a woman as he was holding Siri. You didn't seize your wife in such an embrace, the thought was absurd. Frenzied sexual passion was not an experience between husband and wife but an aberration. Angrily he demanded, "How is it 'wrong'? How is what we do 'wrong'? Anything we can possibly do, 'wrong'? I don't feel desire for my wife. I will never feel desire for my wife. Am I never to feel desire for the remainder of my life? Am I trapped, am I to die, a captive of my marriage? How can I endure such a fate? Why should I?" In his passion Lionel had grown grandiloquent, Siri shrank before him as if abashed. A strange knowledge of him, a dark glistening in her eyes, revealed itself to him. They were in the bedroom now. Tall narrow windows, filmy white curtains. Cream-colored silk wallpaper with delicate green stripes. Everything was so tasteful, here! Except Lionel's lurid dreams. Lionel's male body. Alone in that bed, too many nights. It was a ludicrous king-sized bed with a green satin cover and an ornate mahogany headboard. God knows where Camille and her decorator acquaintance had found such a piece of furniture. The "cervical roll" had been inserted into the pillow on the right, which was the side of the bed Lionel slept on; he felt a stab of masculine embarrassment that the girl he'd brought here should discover it, yet reasoned of course Siri knew of the therapeutic cushion, it was Siri herself who'd urged Lionel to buy it. "Mr. Hoffmann—Lionel—this is wrong—oh, please—" But she was resisting Lionel with only a fraction of the strength he knew she possessed. His will was dominating hers utterly. How strange it was, and how arousing to Lionel, that this young woman with the deft, trained hands, a therapist with the magical authority to dispel pain, should weaken before Lionel; her resistance to him was dissolving as if he'd blown out a flame. Yet Lionel's desire for her was whetted by this passivity. For women were hardly passive creatures, any longer. Even Camille, in the earlier, more experimental years of their marriage, inspired by soft-porn articles in women's magazines and sex manuals, had done her best to "initiate" lovemaking with her bemused and embarrassed husband . . . But here was Siri, gorgeous exotic Siri, so much younger than Camille, and far more sexual than Camille had ever been, who seemed truly frightened of Lionel, the maleness in him. Now that their situations were reversed. Now that he was master, and she was submissive to him. Where was the spinal pain that had held him in check for so long? Had Siri's ministrations banished it, had Lionel himself willed it away?—had sexual desire dispelled it? Lionel and Siri stumbled against the bed. Her clothes had been tugged open, Lionel's shirt and trousers were opened, Siri was murmuring his name in a swoon, no longer "Mr. Hoffmann" but "Lionel"—at last. Her face was very pale, flowerlike. Her eyes were downcast. Lionel might do with her what he wished. He understood that she would not reject him. Never in Lionel's life had his masculine will so exerted itself, a hot fountain within him. His groin, his penis, his very spine: his entire body was suffused with the triumph of desire. Now the woman was naked beneath his hands, a strand of her long dark loosened hair in his mouth, he knelt above her trembling—his erection was enormous as a club!—and pushed himself into her, he'd ceased thinking, what relief to cease thinking, his brain annihilated as by a searing white light. *I will not die, like Adam. I will not die!* Moaning softly the woman moved beneath his weight. Her will had been defeated by his, she lay in trancelike obedience to him. There was no female obstinacy here, no withheld acquiescence, that coyness that so infuriated the male. Lionel was pumping his life into this woman. Into that dark unspeakable place between her thighs. Pumping himself joyously into oblivion. He had but a vague awareness of the woman's slender, shapely, hard-muscled and milky-pale arms lifting to encircle his neck, and her final soft triumphant murmur—"Lion-el!" The long dark slightly sticky hair in tendrils on the pillow like a spider's velvety legs, spread out on the dazzling white linen. Her thin-lipped but rather wide, hungry mouth sucked at his. He felt her large, hard teeth. He felt her pelvis, rising to his, bucking and heaving in her own eager rhythm. They were drowning together. In the frenzy of their passion, the hard, tubular cushion inside one of the pillowcases was jarred loose, fell to the floor and rolled for several feet as if desperate to escape. Lionel's heart, so long unused, was pounding violently. An envelope of stinging briny sweat enveloped him. Never in his life had he felt such—power! Such energy coursing through his body! He panted, "My darling! My—"

In the cataclysm of orgasm he'd forgotten the woman's name.

3

THERE WAS A WOMAN who many times awoke in the morning to realize that her pillow was damp, her face was wet with tears, for she'd been weeping in her sleep.

How many times. Linen pillowcases embossed with satin floral ornamentation. Dampened, soiled by sorrow. In the late autumn of this year of sorrow. In the late autumn—or was it already early winter?—of Camille Hoffmann's life.

Yes. Already it was December, the darkest month. He'd moved away in October.

My shame. How to bear it. But I love him, I forgive him!

He must know, I forgive him. And I will always love him.

Yet: there was solace. For Apollo and Shadow slept each night on the floor at the foot of their mistress's bed. Apollo to the left, Shadow to the right. Like sculpted dogs of Egyptian antiquity guarding the funerary image of their entombed mummy-mistress.

During the night if Camille stirred in distress, moaned or sobbed in her sleep, both dogs awoke at once, rising onto their haunches, alert to danger.

They would never desert her.

AFTER HIS ABRUPT and astonishing departure from the house on Old Mill Way, and his removal to the apartment on East 61st Street in Manhattan, Lionel Hoffmann had made some attempt to "keep in contact" with Camille; he meant to behave "fairly, and justly"; through mid-November they spoke daily on the phone. Then, for some reason unknown to Camille, her husband began to be "unavailable" when she called his office; when she called the apartment, no one ever picked up the receiver, when she left a message Lionel often failed to return her calls. And when he did, he spoke in a vague distracted manner as if (but this couldn't be possible, could it!) he was having difficulty remembering who she was.

Once, during one of these awkward exchanges, Camille believed she could hear whispering at the other end of the line. And muffled giggling. And Lionel muttering, or groaning.

These distractions Camille courteously ignored.

Repeatedly in the weeks following their separation, like a soldier making a vow, Lionel had assured Camille, yes, he loved her, and respected her; he would always love her, as he loved Marcy and Kevin. But he was not, it seemed, at the present time, *in love* with her.

There was that crucial distinction. Those whom we *love,* we are rarely *in love with.*

Quickly Camille said, "Oh yes. I see, Lionel. I . . . understand."

"It isn't personal, Camille. You must understand."

"Oh, I can understand!"

"When lightning strikes, it is never personal."

"Not at all."

Do you know, darling, how I forgive you? Always, I will love you. And the house we've been so happy in, awaits you.

"Camille? I must hang up now."

"Oh, yes! Thank you for calling, Lionel."

"Camille, you called me."

"Well! Thank you for—"

"Good-bye!"

Though they had many things to discuss. Their jointly owned properties, investments, finances; the future of their marriage. (The ugly word "divorce" had not yet been uttered.) Their children's reactions to this wholly unexpected, jarring news. ("But surely Marcy and Kevin are not 'children' any longer, Camille, are they?" Lionel rather coolly said.) Never did they speak of the woman, no doubt a very beautiful younger woman, with whom, it seemed, Lionel had fallen *in love,* though Camille was eager and open and even, to a degree, sympathetic.

Once, at the conclusion of a brief, extremely disjointed telephone conversation, Lionel murmured, as if in pain, that he would never, never wish to hurt her, deliberately.

"How kind of you, Lionel! How thoughtful."

After she hung up, Camille laughed. With the palms of both hands rubbing her raw, reddened eyes. Her laughter was high-pitched, and brief. Apollo and Shadow came running.

HANDSOME HIGH-HEADED APOLLO, dwelling in the house on Old Mill Way in Adam's absence. Apollo, a noble mixture of German shepherd and husky, fiercely loyal, intelligent, whom Adam had entrusted to Camille, his closest woman friend. Apollo who was perhaps six years old, in his late-middle years, with soulful excitable eyes, silver-tipped fur grown thick and sleek with the vitamin-enriched dog food Camille bought, and her careful grooming, and unstinting love. And the smaller, less distinctive Shadow, a mongrel-Labrador, with melancholy rheumy eyes and a narrow fox face, battered ears, coarse dull-black wavy fur, discolored teeth; an oldish-young dog, in some ways still a puppy, immature and (fortunately, Lionel wasn't here to know!) insufficiently housetrained, in other ways aged, badly crippled with a twisted spine and a partly amputated left hind leg; poor Shadow who quivered at the slightest noise outside, or the telephone ringing; who had to be disciplined repeatedly not to bark inside the house; but who was insatiably loving, devoted to his new mistress. When Camille glimpsed in Shadow's watery eyes a veiled memory of terror, in the midst of whatever she was doing she immediately squatted to embrace and console him. "Shadow! Good dog! You're safe now, with me. Forever."

Shadow had a naughty habit of leaping at Camille, whimpering, barking, licking and kissing her, shimmying his twisted buttocks and his stump of a tail; sometimes, in his excitement, he nipped at her, even bit her, with surprisingly sharp teeth; broke her skin, and caused bleeding. "No, *no*. Shadow, that's *bad*." At such times Apollo came running, jealous, or eager to be included in the hugging; he rushed at Camille and Shadow, circled them, nudging and whining and covering Camille's face with lavish kisses. "Apollo! Mind your manners." Camille laughed excited as a girl, awkwardly balanced on her heels; sometimes she toppled over onto the floor; the dogs kissed and licked her face leaving swaths of acidic wet on her skin that, drying, felt like fleeting, fading sunshine.

"MOTHER, ARE YOU *serious?* Tell me you're *joking!*"

Camille winced. How little her daughter Marcy knew her, to imagine Camille could joke of such a thing.

"Daddy has moved *out?* Out of our *house?* To New *York?* What in God's name is *going on?* Mo*ther!*"

What to tell the children! What words, discreet yet matter-of-fact and unhysterical, to carefully compose, to tell Marcy and Kevin? The private hurt and social shame of being a *left-behind wife* were perhaps exceeded by a mother's sense of having failed to keep her family together. And the responsibility of explaining to Marcy and Kevin fell to Camille, of course.

It was cruel and inaccurate of Lionel to say that their daughter and son, though well into their twenties, were adults. As if "adults" were invulnerable to hurt and disappointment. Camille understood how attached both the children were to the house on Old Mill Way, how they'd revised, in memory, their somewhat disputatious adolescences, recalling idyllic years where in fact they'd professed to hate Salthill at the time, and to be utterly bored, like all of their friends, with "Caucasian-affluent suburbia." They'd come of age in the most competitive, materialist epoch in American history, excepting perhaps the last decade of the nineteenth century, and were of that generation of young Americans who were made to realize that they probably could not, by their own efforts, achieve the degree of success and prosperity their parents had had. Though Marcy had a liberal arts degree from New York University, she was working in Seattle for the online magazine *Slate* in a capacity so undefined, her parents understood it was hardly more than clerical. Kevin, with degrees from Harvard College and Harvard Business School, had yet failed to distinguish himself amid his brilliant rivals; he too had a vaguely defined job in cyberspace, logging in a frantic sixty-hour week in Boston for TechInvest.com; already he was beginning to lose his hair and suffered from spastic colon as a consequence of stress; as Lionel had done at his age, he was resisting joining the family business out of a hope, or a delusion, that he might make a career for himself independently. (Lionel's strategy was not to press his son. "When Kevin is ready to work with me, he will know it, and I will know it." Long familiar with her husband's tactics of gentlemanly evasion and duplicity, Camille took this to mean that Lionel secretly distrusted their son's business ability and didn't want him to join Hoffmann Publishing, Inc.)

Distraught and deeply ashamed, Camille had postponed calling Marcy and Kevin for weeks. Ten days before Thanksgiving she realized she must call, for Marcy and Kevin would naturally assume there would be a lavish family Thanksgiving as usual, prepared by Camille; a table of at least twenty-five guests, relatives from both sides of the family and a few local friends like Adam Berendt. (Camille couldn't bear to think that Adam would never again be a guest at her table, perhaps the wisest solution was simply to never again give a dinner party?) Neither Marcy nor Kevin ever expressed much enthusiasm about coming home for Thanksgiving, but usually they came, out of a sense of duty, or lacking other invitations; but when Camille apologetically informed them that there would be no Thanksgiving this year, both were shocked and distressed, and Marcy reacted with anger. Camille hadn't any choice but to stammer out the confession that she and Lionel seemed to be having "marital difficulties"—Lionel had "moved away to New York, temporarily." With Marcy, the conversation quickly took a downward turn. Marcy said cuttingly, "He's found another woman, hasn't he? I knew it. Mot*her!* You've drifted along in a dream, you've let yourself go for *years*. Daddy is a handsome man, and Daddy is not exactly an impoverished man, couldn't you *see?*" As her outraged daughter scolded her from across the continent, Camille began to feel faint. One of the dogs nudged her knees with his big head, and licked encouragingly at her hands: Apollo. The smaller, more wiry Shadow approached her from the side, whimpering almost inaudibly and pressing his warm furry weight against her, to comfort her. "Marcy, it isn't personal. Your father is anxious that we all understand that." "Not 'personal,' what does that mean? I can't believe this conversation!" "Lionel has said it—it's like lightning striking, it has nothing to do with—" "Daddy has done the striking, for God's sake, Mot*her*. Take your head out of the *sand*. Daddy is the *fucking lightning!*" "Marcy, please—" "I'm going to call him! I have a thing or two to say to good old *Dad*." "Oh, Marcy, I wish you wouldn't, dear, please. I'm sure this is just a temporary aberration and Lionel will be back home by Christmas. He has never done anything remotely like this before, and—" "In fact, I did call Dad last week, at the office, and was told 'Mr. Hoffmann isn't available right now.' And he never called me back," Marcy said. "He's afraid to speak with me!" "Marcy, I'm sure your father intends to call you very soon. You and—" "Don't tell me Daddy has a girlfriend, at his age. That's it, isn't it?" "Marcy, I—" "This is just the most shitty, shitty news I've had this week, and let me tell you, Mom, it has been a *shitty week*." Marcy was sobbing with indignation. Camille dreaded her daughter slamming down the receiver, as she'd done on more than one previous occasion, with less provocation; at the same time, Camille rather hoped Marcy would slam down the receiver. Marcy said furiously, "I'll get to the bottom of this! I might have to fly home, Thanksgiving or no Thanksgiving! Everybody's father is getting divorced and marrying girls my age and God damn it isn't going to happen in the Hoffmann family, not without a prenuptial contract Kevin and I see beforehand! Fuck, Mot*her*! You've put on twenty-five pounds at least, just since I left home." Camille shut her eyes against these blows. She knew they were deserved, but that didn't lessen the hurt. She was forced to recall how, when Marcy was in seventh grade at the Salthill Country Day School, Marcy had been the plumpest girl in her circle, and had become obsessed with dieting; she'd detested her "boneless" face which so resembled her mother's, and once, when Camille had gently chided her for trying to starve herself, Marcy turned in fury on her, saying these words Camille would never forget, "Leave me alone, Mother! I'd rather die than be fat like *you*." At the time, Camille had perhaps been eight pounds overweight.

She'd never told Lionel about that scene. She'd started to tell Adam Berendt but stopped, out of a sense that Adam, too, would pity her, and the last thing she wanted from Adam was pity.

As if sensing her mother's distress, Marcy began to relent a little. "Hey, Mom? You still there? Look, I'm sorry. I guess your heart is, like, broken?" When Camille, wiping at her eyes, didn't trust herself to reply, Marcy asked again if there was another woman, so far as Camille knew; and Camille said, with as much dignity as she could summon, "Marcy, you must ask your father. Only he knows."

Exhausted and demoralized by this exchange, Camille would have liked to lie down on the sofa, but she knew she had to call Kevin immediately, before Marcy in her fury contacted him. By a fluke, Kevin was in, and picking up his phone. He, too, was stunned to hear the news. "Dad has moved *out?* Of our *home?* Is he *crazy?* What's going on there, Mom?" Camille said carefully, "It's only just temporary, Kevin. I called your sister and explained, too. Lionel is—" "Wait. Let's get this straight, Mom. Dad has moved *out?* To New *York?* Since *when?* Why wasn't I told? When did you tell Marcy? Hey, is there—someone else involved? *Mom?*" Kevin's voice was that of an anguished adolescent, so very different from his usual bemused, mildly cynical drawl. Camille stammered, "I—truly don't know, Kevin. He may have said—he might have mentioned—it was all so confusing to me, I'm not sure I understood." In fact, Camille didn't quite remember. Had Lionel actually uttered the ominous words *woman—have become involved—since last November*—or had Camille imagined them, as in a cruel self-punishing dream? It seemed to her frankly unlikely that Lionel could have been involved with a woman, whatever exactly that meant, for a full year, and she, his wife, remained ignorant. Kevin who'd always been one to defend Camille, perceiving in his parents' marriage an unjust imbalance of power, and perhaps in Camille his only ally against his powerful father, said incredulously, "There *is!* God damn. You'd think, Dad's age, over fifty at least, he'd be *ashamed.*" Kevin began to laugh derisively as if the very idea of Lionel Hoffmann committing adultery, a renegade lover, was hilarious. Out of nervous sympathy Camille found herself laughing with him. Half-heartedly she pushed the dogs away, in their zeal to comfort their mistress they were licking her hands frantically, and pleading with anxious dog-eyes, she couldn't concentrate, oh! she was tired, since Shadow had come into her life (like grace, unbidden) she'd been so grateful to the Rockland County Homeless Animal Shelter she'd signed up as a volunteer, helping out two afternoons a week. Kevin too was incensed that there'd be "no Thanksgiving" this year and speculated in a young, sullen voice if maybe there'd be "no Christmas either."

Camille remained silent. Her head ached. She wondered why, if one might live with dogs, one would have wished to live with children, and a husband? *Dogs don't judge. Dogs love.* Kevin was saying petulantly he'd better come home to see "what in hell Dad's up to." He complained to Camille that he'd been sending Lionel e-mail ("on a private, professional subject") but that Lionel hadn't replied. *Was* he in New York? In the apartment? Camille murmured she assumed so. She too called Lionel, and he was slow to call back. Kevin said despairingly, "Just don't let Dad sell the house, Mom. It's jointly owned, I assume? All your property, investments, savings are jointly owned? Don't let Dad cheat you out of anything. Don't let him sell our *home.*" Camille, stroking the dogs' hard-boned heads, felt a stab of longing for her son; as a child Kevin had been prone to accidents, and tears; stymied by life rather than angered by it, like his sister; if they were together, Camille would have hugged him, and the two might have wept together. But Kevin was far away, and breathing harshly into the receiver. "Oh, no, Kevin! Your father would never be that cruel, to sell this house. In fact, I expect him to be home by—Christmas. When this madness has run its course."

WHAT A SURPRISE! Camille received a postcard from Lionel, from Barbados. He'd taken five days off, he said. He would be contacting her soon about *future plans*. He suggested she begin to think about *legal representation.* He apologized for being incommunicado with only the excuse that his life had become *mysterious and new again,* and *glorious beyond belief.*

IT WAS A SAD, cautionary tale of a left-behind Salthill wife.

Beatrice Archer, her eyes brimming with tears, would say: "I knew. As soon as I parked in the Hoffmanns' driveway and saw Camille's gorgeous mum plants blown over and some of the clay pots broken, that something was terribly wrong."

That day, in early December, Beatrice boldly came to visit Camille Hoffmann. She hadn't been invited. She'd several times called Camille, and Camille had never returned her calls. "But we can't just abandon Camille, as Lionel has done. The poor woman is in a state of shock." Beatrice Archer was a handsome woman of youthful middle age, the wife of a prominent Salthill internist, with fair gold-glinting hair that fell in sculpted wings about her perfect face and a forward-thrusting manner like the prow of a ship. She was a woman to care deeply about her friends especially now that her children were grown and gone. She was a woman of strong neo-Christian convictions. She'd urged her husband Avery to contact Lionel Hoffmann in New York and to arrange to see him if possible. "To talk some sense into that man. Lionel, of all people! He must know this is *demeaning*." (But Avery complained that Lionel never returned his calls. At Hoffmann Publishing, Inc., Lionel's secretary curtly informed him that Mr. Hoffmann was "unavailable at the present time.") Beatrice decided one morning simply to drive over to Old Mill Way, which intersected with Old Dutch Road where the Archers lived in a beautifully restored neo-Georgian house on three prime, wooded acres; it was Beatrice's reasoning that Camille would have no choice but to let her into the house. "How many times, after all, we'd visited in each other's homes . . ."

But there were the unsightly mum plants, disturbing to a fastidious home owner like Beatrice Archer. And blinds drawn on a number of the windows of the many-windowed Colonial house. And the dogs that unexpectedly rushed out of nowhere to circle Beatrice as she approached the front door, and rang the doorbell with a trembling forefinger. She recognized Apollo, Adam's much-loved dog she hadn't seen since Adam's death. Fortunately, Apollo seemed to recognize her. "Apollo? You know me: Adam's friend Beatrice. Apollo, good dog!" The mixed-breed German shepherd wagged his tail as he barked, though not so briskly as Beatrice would have wished. More worrisome was the smaller, more antic dog, a disfigured black mongrel-Labrador with three legs and watery eyes, that Beatrice had never seen before. Did these dogs both live with Camille? Or was the black dog a stray? Its bark was like fingernails drawn across a blackboard, and it was behaving belligerently. "I was terrified the creature would bite me, or tear my clothes, before Camille opened the door. Its hackles were raised, and it was growling. And so misshapen! An ugly little demon of a dog." By the time Camille came breathless to open the door, in a soiled coverall, her unkempt graying hair brushed back severely from her face, both dogs were poking their noses against Beatrice, and rudely sniffing. Camille called them off apologetically and explained that the dogs weren't used to visitors. "Not that they're dangerous, of course. Apollo and Shadow are both very gentle dogs."

Beatrice, mindful that she hadn't been invited, and that her friend Camille was clearly not herself, warmly embraced Camille and kissed her cheek. Tears of genuine compassion gathered in her meticulously made-up, large and luminous eyes. "Camille, it's such a relief to see you! We've all been terribly worried about you, not returning our calls, missing the Planned Parenthood fund-raiser, living out here alone. You've hurt your friends' feelings, Camille, and why?" It was like Beatrice Archer to express compassion in the form of reproach. Blushing fiercely, Camille could think of no reply and invited Beatrice inside, again apologizing, as the dogs trotted with them, continuing to nudge and sniff at Beatrice's legs. Beatrice would afterward recount how distressed she'd been, such an odor of dogs in that beautiful house; and stacks of unopened mail on a cherrywood table in the foyer. "As if the owners of the house had died and someone was doing the bare minimum, bringing the mail inside but not opening it."

The awkward visit lasted less than an hour. The women sat in Camille's spacious but badly cluttered country kitchen, which was flooded with winter light. On the windowsills were wilting African violets, on the floor in a corner were dogs' red and yellow plastic bowls, set on stained newspaper. Beatrice had the impression that much of the house had been shut off, to prevent dog-damage probably. She had the impression that an air of emergency prevailed, as if Camille were expecting something to happen; or something had already happened, and this was the aftermath. She would report that Camille hadn't been rude to her exactly, for poor Camille was incapable of rudeness. "She offered me coffee but never gave me any. She simply forgot, I guess!" Beatrice was disturbed and intrigued by her friend's altered appearance. It was less than two months since Lionel's departure but already Camille was letting her fine wavy fair-brown hair grow in gray. She wasn't wearing makeup and her skin looked ruddy and rather coarse as if she'd been outside in a cold wind. She was smiling nervously. Her lashless eyes blinked. She seemed to be staring at Beatrice as if trying to follow a conversation in another language, in which, in a strange halting way, she was participating. Beatrice noted the denim coverall that fitted Camille's wide soft hips snugly, dirtied at the thighs as if by dogs' muddy paws. She noted Camille's broken, dirt-edged fingernails. What a sign of female defeat, such fingernails! Almost, Beatrice would have liked to manicure Camille's nails for her. "But I didn't want to upset Camille, of course. I didn't want to seem to be intruding. I wanted her to realize that her Salthill friends care about her. I told her that Abigail Des Pres wanted badly to see her, to offer Camille 'spiritual commiseration' and 'good practical legal advice,' for Abigail of course had had something of the same problem a few years before, with Harry—but Camille interrupted me, and said, in this almost-angry stammering voice, 'That isn't necessary. I won't be needing a lawyer. You can thank Abigail, but our situations aren't at all similar. My husband will probably return by Christmas. We speak often on the phone. He loves me very much. He loves his children, and this house. We are both very attached to this house. We would never sell *this house*.' It was a sudden rush of words! Camille's cheeks were flaming. I thought we might cry together, it was such a—moment! I held her hands that were icy-cold and trembling and I told her of course that was so, that Avery had said, when he first heard the news, 'Lionel will be back.' And Camille said, brightening, 'Avery said that, Beatrice, really? Lionel will be *back?*' "

Following this, Camille began to speak more openly, if disjointedly. She interrupted herself frequently to laugh and to wipe at her eyes. With childlike trust she confided in Beatrice that it was Marcy and Kevin, not her, who'd been most upset by their father's strange behavior—"They so look up to Lionel, you know. He's a model of moral integrity to them. As he is to me!" She confided in Beatrice a remarkable story of emptying the liquor cabinet of every bottle, whiskey, Scotch, bourbon, gin, that had already been opened, a few days after Lionel had moved out; packing the bottles in boxes and taking them to the county dump so she wouldn't be tempted to drink—"The unopened bottles, and everything in Lionel's wine cellar, I wouldn't know how to open—so I'm safe." She and Beatrice laughed together at this revelation. How prudent of Camille, whom a single glass of white wine made light-headed; how wise. Beatrice, who was susceptible, too, to alcohol, and who avoided drinking except upon social occasions, and then sparingly, would have liked to think she might have equivalent sense if Avery ever left her. (But Beatrice could no more imagine her devoted husband leaving her than she could imagine her own death, except as an intellectual possibility.) Camille showed Beatrice a postcard from Barbados, which it seemed Lionel had recently sent her; the glossy picture was of a resort hotel and a wide white beach—"The Barbados Hilton where Lionel and I have stayed. So it must mean he's thinking of his marriage, yes? Of our happy memories? Otherwise Lionel wouldn't have sent such a card. It would be cruel, and Lionel is not a cruel man." Camille's voice trembled. Beatrice said quickly, "Certainly not! Lionel is very possibly the most gentlemanly, considerate man in Salthill. Much nicer than Avery." Camille didn't register the little joke, but was staring fixedly at the handwritten message on the postcard. Beatrice had to wonder if Lionel had slipped off to the Caribbean with his reported girlfriend, a gorgeous, exotic, very young physical therapist he'd met at a Manhattan clinic, but she would not have wished to ask.

Camille went on to apologize for having missed meetings of Planned Parenthood, Friends of the Salthill Free Public Library, Friends of the Salthill Pro Musica, Friends of the Salthill Arts Council . . . She was limiting her volunteer time to the Rockland County Homeless Animal Shelter where they badly needed help, and donations. She told Beatrice of how, driving on West Axe Boulevard the very morning after Lionel had left, she'd seen a dog hit and left to die at the side of the road; she'd stopped, and brought the dog to the Rockland clinic, where emergency surgery saved his life. Recounting this, Camille became quite moved. "Shadow is one of us who has not been destroyed. I call him Shadow because he came like a shadow out of the sunlight that was blinding, I looked up and suddenly he was *there*." The misshapen dog's ears pricked up at the sound of his name. His rheumy eyes lightened. Beatrice, who felt a fastidious dislike for deformed or disfigured creatures, had a sudden sense of the dog's inner life, if a dog might be said to have an inner life; she shuddered. "Camille, it's so generous of you to take a strange dog in. An abandoned dog. And now a crippled dog. At such a—difficult time in your life." Camille said reprovingly, "It's the right time. I knew. There are no coincidences." A thought came to Beatrice, suddenly. "Will you be taking in others? Dogs needing a home?" Camille said with an apologetic smile, "Oh, Beatrice, I'm afraid not! I wish I could, this house is absurdly large, but Apollo and Shadow are probably quite enough. Even if they spend most of their time outside, and sleep in the barn, Lionel is allergic to dog hairs, you know." Beatrice said helpfully, "How convenient for you, when the children were growing up. We had no such excuse, they nagged us constantly." Camille said, as if unhearing, "Of course, Apollo isn't with us permanently, you know." Beatrice murmured, "Isn't he!" Camille said, "Adam is traveling in Egypt now, I think." Her eyelids fluttered shut as if to spare her seeing Beatrice's embarrassment. "I'm not sure when he's returning. After the New Year, I suppose." Beatrice fumbled to open her purse to search for a tissue, suddenly preoccupied. Camille said, smiling, "I've been having such vivid dreams lately, Beatrice! I can recognize the Mediterranean, I think—Lionel and I took a Greek cruise there, ten years ago. But also desert, pyramids, and this strange luminous river that must be the Nile, it's so very old a river, its roots are in the beginning of Time. These sights Adam is seeing. I assume." She laughed girlishly. "Isn't it like Adam, not to send any of us postcards!"

Beatrice heard herself say haltingly, "Yes, it's—not like Adam, to forget his friends. I mean—well, yes, I guess it is."

At the name "Adam," Apollo stirred uneasily. Both dogs had been lying on the kitchen floor, close behind Camille, as if guarding her. Apollo's ears pricked forward, his silvery club of a tail thumped a few times. But, Beatrice could see, Adam's dog had not the faith in Adam's existence that poor Camille had. The melancholy moment passed.

Soon after this exchange Beatrice kissed her friend good-bye and left the house on Old Mill Way. What a relief! The doggy depressing smell, and the somehow too intense atmosphere, as if everything uttered had a double meaning; one in which the dogs somehow shared. On the whole, however, Beatrice was pleased with the visit, and she believed that Camille was grateful for it. She'd extracted from Camille a wan promise to come to dinner that weekend at the Archers', and to have lunch with her and Abigail Des Pres in the new Thai restaurant in Salthill the following week. The first principle of human sanity is to maintain the challenging external life that's called *social.* What the second principle is, Beatrice wasn't so certain.

Camille will take in Thor. Of course! This all makes sense.

Through the remainder of the day Beatrice would telephone a succession of women friends to recount for them the fascinating story of her visit to the Hoffmanns' house. Everyone agreed that Camille was in a state of shock and that they must all be very kind to her. Beatrice was viewed as an angel of mercy. One day perhaps Camille would tell the story of how Beatrice Archer had saved her life . . . That night Avery returned home late from a medical conference in New York. Or had it been Boston, or Chicago? As he undressed silently in the dimly lighted master bedroom Beatrice recounted for him the story of her visit to the house on Old Mill Way. "That poor woman is in a state of shock, Avery. She hadn't begun to recover from Adam's death, and now Lionel has left her, damn him. He never returned your calls? He snubbed *you?* He's ashamed, I suppose. He should be. Lionel Hoffmann, leaving Camille at such a time!"

Said Avery, "Maybe Lionel wants to save his own life, darling."

4

For this I would kill. There is nothing else.

Waking in a state of excited bliss, a woman's plaited hair flung across his mouth. Deeply he breathed in the musky female smell, mixed with the smell of his own body. They were naked. Swimmers who have drowned together and whose limbs have become entwined. His groin was suffused with blood, again he was a young man in the prime of his life. Desire slammed through him like a mallet crushing his bones. He had no resistance, he groaned in acquiescence.

Nothing! Nothing else.

"CAMILLE? Yes, I will be calling soon. I have time for only this quick message but I'm thinking of you. I know this has been difficult. It's a difficult time for me, too. But I want you to know that—"

Slyly her hands moved over him. From behind. Stroking, caressing, gently squeezing. Not-so-gently squeezing. She was his monkey-girl sometimes, smelling of musk. Whispering *Mr. Hoffmann. Be very quiet. No one must know!*

A groan broke from him, a strangled sob. The telephone receiver dangled at the end of its curly cord.

IN BARBADOS. How grateful like a greedy little girl she was, in the luxurious resort hotel, in a suite overlooking palm trees, the wide white beach, the dreamy aqua sea. *Maybe you do love me. Mr. Hoffmann.* Making love with him in bright sunshine Siri emitted cries like a child in pain. Never had Lionel been so stricken with desire. Slyly the woman abased herself before him, the male. Kissing his hands, his chest, his belly. Pressing her face against his groin. If his wife had ever done such a thing—! The very thought was preposterous, revolting. But Siri claimed him, Siri knew what he wanted even as he weakly protested. Even as he pushed her away she persisted, and his hands grasped her to clutch her tighter, to press her against him. In the night waking him with her mouth. His eyes shot open. Overhead the ceiling floated like gossamer. The balcony doors were open to the lapping sea.

Nothing! There is nothing else.

"SOMEDAY, SIRI WANTS to see where you live. Your true life."

Playfully she spoke of herself in the third person, as a child might. A willful sly-eyed child. Lionel supposed she'd been looking at the framed photos in the apartment. The Hoffmann family, of some years ago. The beautifully restored eighteenth-century house on Old Mill Way, Salthill. "Where your true life exists. And Siri isn't welcome." She was teasing, of course.

Playing monkeys with him, naked and scrambling in the bed, Siri panting, on top, straddling her patient with muscular thighs.

"Mr. Hoffmann. Be good. Try try try to re*lax*."

GRAVELY HIS SECRETARY informed him. His daughter, his son, yes and another time Mrs. Hoffmann, had all been trying to reach him. For days. "Thanks, Irene! I'll be calling them back soon." He was smiling, he was jaunty. He was in control here. "So if they call again, please tell them." Still Irene looked doubtful. "'Tell them,' Mr. Hoffmann?" "That I'll be calling them back soon."

MARIA, WHO CLEANED the apartment on Thursdays, was hesitant to inform him. Several bars of expensive French soap were missing from the cupboard in the guest bathroom. Mrs. Hoffmann's soaps, and Mrs. Hoffmann's Elizabeth Arden toiletries. Moisturizer, hand cream, bath salts. And maybe one of the washcloths. Thick white terrycloth with white satin trim. Shy-eyed Maria in her halting English, hopeful her employer will know that she, she was not the one to have taken these things.

IN BARBADOS, in November, they'd been happy. At least he'd been happy. She'd seemed so. And their long weekend in Santa Monica where he'd gone on business, and taken Siri, in early December. He'd swear. He was in love. Siri was so beautiful! If not beautiful Siri was—Siri. Lionel was crazy about her. He panted, trotting beside her in hard-packed sand beside the Pacific Ocean. How other men, and boys, stared at her. Siri in tank top, bikini bottom, and barefoot. And her wavy-kinky unplaited hair straggling down her back. Admit it: he loved the intensity of their eyes. Male-predator eyes. As a married man for decades he had not once glimpsed such eyes. He was thrilled! No, he was revulsed. It was low, lewd. Still it was exciting. The glisten of her skin. A smudged soiled skin it sometimes appeared. And her sly, insolent eyes. Her throaty laughter. *She doesn't love you, asshole. She doesn't give a shit about you. She's laughing at you with her young lovers.*

Disgusting! Such thoughts. Lionel was repelled by such thoughts yet even self-disgust excited him, where Siri was concerned. For so long his self-disgust had meant nothing except itself. "Bor-ing!"—as the kids would say. Bor-ing as the insipid feminine wallpaper Camille insisted upon. Bor-ing as the Pro Musica concerts Camille insisted upon where his handsome graying head nodded, brain swooning into the sweetest of oblivions even as Camille's elbow nudged him back to wakefulness. Now, his disgust was very different. His disgust had a sexual wallop. He carried it inside his shirt, against his slimy skin. Inside his shorts, against his swelling groin. It upset him—his upset, his agitation, were disgusting to him—if Siri wasn't available when he wanted her. If Siri had "other plans" for the evening, or the night. If Siri was "out of town" for the weekend. If another therapist was taking over Siri's shift at the clinic. He knew: Siri had a life of her own. He was a married man, and not once had he spoken of marriage to her. Not once had he spoken of divorcing his sad dull wife. Certainly Siri had a life of her own as she'd more than once informed him. Siri was not for hire. As a therapist she was for hire but otherwise, not. And even as a therapist at the clinic, she was not obliged to work with any patient she didn't wish to work with. This was a policy at the clinic, of course. For it sometimes happened that patients (male, predatory) began to be obsessed with their female therapists, tried to contact them outside the clinic, pursued and stalked them. "But Siri, Mr. Hoffmann, is not for hire. Yes?"

Yes. But no. Lionel loved to undress her roughly, yanking off her white nylon smock and trousers. By his request she wore her uniform to the apartment at East 61st. By his request she wore her hair plaited and knotted at the nape of her neck. It was his pleasure to unpin her hair, unplait the long crimped hair with its nutmeg-smell, its mildly rank unwashed monkey-smell he loved. While making love Lionel wrapped a strand of hair around her neck, in play. She taunted him *Mr. Hoffmann! Squeeze! Hurt me! I know how you like it.* Laughing at his face dissolving in orgasm like something softly rotted, dissolving in water. Laughing and biting his lower lip, drawing a bead of blood.

HE COULD NOT believe: he'd become such a man.

That painful episode. At Christmas. He and Siri were about to leave for Key West. Siri was late meeting him at the apartment. The phone rang. Eagerly and imprudently he'd lifted the receiver. And there was the shock of Marcy's voice. Whining accusing hurt-little-girl Marcy. "Daddy? Is that you? This is your daughter Marcy"—her voice heavy with sarcasm, he could imagine her glaring eyes—"I've been trying and *try*ing to reach you, Mother has told me, oh, Daddy what is *happening?*—we're not going to have Christmas this year—" And like a coward Lionel hung up.

"I can't believe this. I've become a man who hangs up on his own daughter."

He would not tell anyone this. Not even Siri to whom he told too many secrets. Instead, he poured Scotch into a glass and drank. Still, he laughed. It was funny.

IN JANUARY, in the New Year. Things began to change. Siri began to murmur in his arms lightly mocking *Yes you love me like this, but do you respect me?* He caught a glimpse of her sullen hurt-little-girl face in a mirror and was shocked at its coarseness. And the glaring-wet eyes, like Marcy's.

MARIA CAME PLEADING to him. Oh, Mr. Hoffmann! There was missing from his study one of the framed photographs. The frame was of fine leather, expensive. Maria was anxious to tell her employer, who stood grimly silent that she, she was not the one who took it, each week she dusted the photographs and always stopped to look at that one, Mr. Hoffmann so young and smiling, standing on the beach, and Mrs. Hoffmann so young and pretty, and the little girl so sweet, and the little boy, such a happy beautiful family, poor Maria was close to tears in the face of her employer's enigmatic silence begging him to understand that she, she was not the one who took away the photograph, like the other items, please did Mr. Hoffmann believe her?

Lionel passed his fingertips over his eyelids. "Maria. Of course."

HE SAID NOTHING to Siri. No accusations. Yet Siri seemed to take offense. Siri was silent, aloof. Siri refused to accompany Lionel to a cocktail party where, Lionel had planned this in his luxurious-erotic dreams, she was to wear a gorgeous lime-colored silk dress slit high up the thigh he'd bought for her at the trendy boutique Kyrie on Madison Avenue. *Yes, you love me. Mr. Hoff-mann. But respect? Like Mrs. Hoffmann, you respect?* Tearing at the silk fabric, the exquisite cloth buttons. Till he caught her, held her, her hard-muscled angry limbs, feeling the strength drain from her, Siri sobbing against him, or seeming to sob. *Because I am made to feel hurt by you, not respected by you. Only your wife, away in Salthill, in that house, you respect.*

CERTAINLY, Lionel respected his wife Camille. And loved her.

No matter what his children were saying.

No matter what all of Salthill was saying.

He would not be cruel to Camille. Would not treat his wife of thirty years as other men, for instance that bastard Harry Tierney, had treated their wives. *Oh Christ but I am suffocating. If only Camille would leave me. That damned house! Adam bores me, too. His death.*

Over drinks with Harry Tierney he vowed he would not be cruel to Camille. He would make a generous settlement with Camille. He'd give her the house. Camille loved that house, the kids loved that house, the decent thing to do would be to give it to her outright—"And good-bye." Harry Tierney looking very youthful, slick tufts of dark hair sprouting on his shiny head, grizzled dark eyebrows, his left eyelid drooping in a smirk, lifted his glass of Scotch, saying cheerfully, "I'll drink to that, friend." Was Harry, that notorious selfish bastard, laughing at Lionel? Laughing at Lionel Hoffmann, the man of conscience? Lionel began to speak quickly. *He* was a good decent man, yes, he was a Christian and proud of it. He'd been brought up to be a gentleman. Harry Tierney listened to this, chewing nuts. The men, who'd never been friends in Salthill, had become friends of a kind here in Manhattan where both now lived. They were in the Skytop Club, 200 Park Avenue, fifty-sixth floor overlooking nighttime sparkling Manhattan like jewels. At a distance, you can't discern between true jewels and fake jewels because both are sparkling, dazzling to the eye. And so Manhattan was sparkling, dazzling to the eye. After some minutes Harry Tierney interrupted Lionel to ask, "Who's your new love, Lionel? This sounds serious." Blushing, Lionel stammered, "I—I'm not sure." Harry laughed, "Not sure of the girl's name?" "Not sure if she's my—" Lionel hesitated as if his mouth were filled with something sticky, "— 'love.'" Harry asked how old she was, and Lionel, his judgment weakened by Scotch, answered, "She's about—thirty. I think." Harry nodded, as if this was a good answer. "And where'd you meet her, Lionel?" "At the clinic." "The clinic?" "The Neck and Back Clinic on Park. You know—you recommended it a few months ago when I had neck pain." Harry's eyebrows lifted. He was chewing brazil nuts noisily. "She's a therapist there? Which one?" Lionel swallowed. He was smiling in confusion. Did he dare—in this place, to this man—utter the name that meant so much to him! "S-Siri." "Siri!" Lionel felt a stab of apprehension at the tone of his friend's voice. Harry's gaze was veiled, his jaws grinding a little less forcibly. Clearly he was taken by surprise, and he was embarrassed.

For the first time in Lionel's experience, Harry Tierney was at a loss for words.

STILL LIONEL REMAINED a patient at the clinic. His neck pain had diminished, miraculously; but he was in terror of it returning. *Without Siri, there is only pain.* As Siri's patient, Lionel was required to partly undress and to lie quietly, passively, without resistance on Siri's table; sometimes they behaved as if they were strangers, addressing each other in formal voices as "Miss Siri" and "Mr. Hoffmann." The therapist's deft trained hands controlled Lionel. What a powerful erotic tension between them! Lionel's penis pulsed with blood, he groaned with desire Siri primly refused to appease.

"Mr. Hoff-mann! If anyone should *see.*"

DAYS WHEN SIRI disappeared. Where? With whom? Lionel dared not accuse her, she laughed in his face saying she hadn't disappeared to herself, had she, only to him.

"I am my own self, I hope. I don't belong to *you.*"

She wanted him to marry her, Lionel guessed. Just as, a lifetime ago, Camille had wanted him to marry her. An engagement ring, ritual celebrations culminating in a lavish wedding party, marriage and a house, a baby, and another baby. Vertigo overcame Lionel, he had already lived his life.

The babies, now grown, possessed of adult demands, bombarded him with telephone calls, the most embarrassing of which came to Hoffmann Publishing, Inc., and incessant e-mail messages. It was rare for Lionel to check his personal computer in the apartment on East 61st, he couldn't bear it. He prowled Siri's grungy neighborhood off St. Marks Square. Did it trouble him that he was the oldest individual in sight, excepting homeless persons dozing in doorways or babbling into their hands?

He called the clinic, he risked humiliating himself by dropping by the clinic. The receptionists knew him. Siri's sister-therapists knew him. Some of them smiled in sympathy, or in pity. Or were they laughing at him. "Mr. Hoffmann! Siri isn't in today." With as much dignity as the tremor in his voice allowed, Lionel inquired if anyone knew where Siri had gone, for instance had she gone out of the city? And when was she expected back? And who were her friends, her male friends, what were their names, surely names could be supplied, for a price?

"Mr. Hoffmann. No."

The pain in his neck returned. He listed to one side, clenching his neck in his hand. He was walking on a Midtown cross-street. He was headed for the Plaza Hotel where he'd made a reservation to have lunch with Kevin, finally he'd agreed to see Kevin who'd been pleading with him *Dad! We have to talk. We really have to talk. What all this craziness is doing to Mom, scares me!* But when Lionel arrived at the Plaza, Kevin wasn't there. When Lionel checked with the maître d', he discovered there was no reservation in his name. When the maître d' checked his reservation book, he discovered that Lionel's reservation had been for the previous day.

Siri returned. Siri telephoned Lionel. In a pocket of the sealskin coat Lionel had bought for her at I. Magnin he would discover a boarding pass for a Continental flight, San Diego to New York. Seat 3E which was first-class, window. Who'd paid for this, Lionel wondered. Him?

* * *

INTERMINABLE DAYS AT Hoffmann Publishing, Inc.! Siri had hinted that Lionel might sell the business, retire as a multimillionaire and travel the world, *why not, you are not getting any younger or any poorer, yes?* Siri had a friend, a divorce attorney. Siri's attorney-friend also dealt in prenuptial contracts. *That house in Salthill you have never taken me to, maybe it should be sold? Such a big expensive property for a sad old woman living there alone.* At Hoffmann Publishing, Inc., Lionel was CEO and very much respected and feared. Even the older Hoffmann shareholders approved of him. Of course, Lionel wasn't the man his father had been, but the company was doing exceptionally well. Riding the ongoing wave of American prosperity, they were selling more books, bringing in more revenue, year after year. There were interested buyers, of course, an immense American conglomerate. If Lionel sold, he'd make a fortune. But he'd have to confront his relatives. Oh, but he was bored with publishing eight-hundred-page illustrated books priced at two hundred dollars, on such subjects as endocrinology, gastroenterology, otolaryngological surgery, ophthalmological surgery, cardiovascular surgery! If once he'd been genuinely intrigued by medical science, as his father had been, he'd long since lost interest. Mankind was overwhelmed with specialized information, as the universe was composed of invisible wormholes in incalculable quantities, merely to contemplate the phenomenon of such quantities was to risk vertigo, nausea, spiritual exhaustion, and despair. *Money-making* was far easier. *Money-making* in a booming free market economy. *Money-making,* which he'd done, and might even take some pride in, if he wished. If Lionel Hoffmann still considered himself a man of pride.

He laughed aloud. Thinking how close to *monkey-making, money-making was.*

"NOBODY HAS the right to judge *me.*"

Thoughts like maddened wasps in Lionel's skull! He was

thinking he would not be bullied by self-styled moralists. Not by his intrusive children, not by his strangely uncomplaining wife, not by his Hoffmann relatives, not by Salthill friends. Former friends! Not by the pious dead.

Adam Berendt hadn't been any saint, far from it. Adam too had made money in real estate and junk bonds and there was something shadowy, possibly even illegal about his finances, but you'd never have guessed it from the man's pretense of living like Socrates, for Truth and Beauty. Lionel had heard plenty in the months since Adam's death. There were rumors that Adam had used false names in money-making schemes, that there was a cache of love letters from women, including certain Salthill wives, hidden beneath the floorboards of his studio; there were shocking photos of nude women, some of them depicting sex acts, taken by Adam himself.

Lionel smiled to think of it. No, it was disturbing. It was sickening. Yet perhaps liberating, too.

Maybe the rumors were exaggerated, and maybe not. Who knew.

(Lionel knew there were lurid rumors making the rounds in Salthill, for his daughter Marcy had e-mailed him the information, knowing it would upset him. Lionel Hoffmann involved with a woman "young enough to be his daughter." Lionel Hoffmann of all people involved with a "model," a "go-go dancer," a "soft-porn actress," a "high-class call girl.")

Still, if Camille had been involved with Adam, that would account for her readiness to forgive him. Sending him messages that clawed at his heart. *Lionel dear, I will always love you. I will always be your loving wife. Please know that! Your Camille.* If Siri discovered these, she was furious, and ripped them into bits. It was Siri's conviction that Camille wasn't forgiving at all, but manipulative.

"She'll do anything to keep you, but not for love. *I* am the one who loves you, my Mr. Hoffmann."

And Siri demonstrated how.

* * *

A FEW DAYS LATER, on a Midtown street, Lionel heard a familiar voice call his name, and turned to see an eagerly smiling Roger Cavanagh striding toward him. "Lionel! How the hell are you?" The men shook hands. Roger seemed to Lionel an apparition out of a dimly recalled and vaguely regretted past. But Lionel had always liked Roger, one of Salthill's battered souls.

"How am I? I'm—fine."

The men had drinks in a Sixth Avenue bar. Roger's eyes glittered with secrets. He was in the city on business: he was doing volunteer work for the National Project to Free the Innocent—"You know, one of Adam's causes. He left them fifty thousand dollars. I've gotten involved." Roger spoke with unnerving animation of the case he was appealing in federal court, the 1989 conviction for first-degree murder in Hunterdon, New Jersey, of a black man named Elroy Jackson, Jr. Lionel listened. Or tried to listen. How tedious, another's idealism. But no: he was feeling envy. To care about something other than oneself, one's ridiculous sexual needs . . .

Lionel was trying not to think of Siri. Their most recent disagreement. *His* disagreement, with her. He felt like a man who has devoured a rich gourmet meal, carrying it now like lead in his bowels.

Roger was saying, having shifted to another subject without Lionel's awareness, "Marriage! It's the great mystery, Lionel, isn't it? We can't live without it, and we can't live within it. Obviously men weren't intended to be domesticated, like animals. Men were intended by nature to be polygamous, promiscuous. This is common knowledge. Our glands know it. We were meant to impregnate as many females as possible before we collapse or get killed by some other zealous seed-bearer. That's 'nature'—and nature is irrefutable. At the same time, anything other than marriage with a woman you love is just shit. You know it, Lionel, and I know it." Roger drank, shaking ash carelessly across the table. The men were in a swanky lounge called The Cigar Bar where busty waitresses in black spandex tank tops and tights emerged out of the shadows like Nubian slaves bearing drinks, with luminous made-up faces like leering masks. Lionel laughed, resenting Roger's remark. "*Do* I know it? Know what?" Roger ignored Lionel's belligerent tone, saying, "There's no life in loneliness, even in being alone. How Adam did it, I can't comprehend. There was a man made for family life! I think he felt he wasn't 'worthy' of a complete life. He'd done something, or caused something to be done, I think. When he was a kid. I never asked him outright, of course. As his executor I've been making inquiries into his past but always come to a dead-end. He's from Minnesota, yet also from Montana. He was born in 1948, or in 1946. I'm pretty certain he changed his name, officially. And used other names, unofficially. If a man wants to erase his past it's for a useful reason, right? A friend should honor that." Lionel asked, intrigued, "Adam changed his name officially? From what?" It came to him that the folly of his life sprang from his remaining "Hoffmann" when he was no "Hoffmann." If he'd had the courage to change his name, and to choose another; to walk away from his family's money . . . Roger said, "A man needs a family as much as a woman does. I know, I've lost mine. I've lost my daughter, who hates my guts. I've been in love with a woman, and it hasn't gone well." Roger paused, and signaled for another drink. Lionel was embarrassed. He guessed that Roger was speaking of Marina Troy. At Adam's cremation ceremony he'd seen Roger with Marina, and at the ghastly spreading of Adam's ashes—that sick, stricken look in Roger's face when Marina pushed away from him. That, too, he'd envied. "She disappeared from Salthill. She left *me*. Though we weren't what you'd call lovers, I know she meant to leave *me*. The hell with it." Roger laughed harshly. The men drank in silence for a while. Lionel was resigned to a night alone, in anticipation of calling Siri in the morning. And he was becoming resigned to marrying her. For if he didn't marry her, he would lose her. And if he lost her, he couldn't bear it. And so he would have to divorce Camille, and that would destroy Camille. In a sensible, pragmatic, polygamous society, Lionel could simply have added on Siri as a second wife. A new, young, physically robust female. A fertile female. By now, in his prosperous early fifties, he'd have had several young wives. He wouldn't have become a mummy, pain throbbing in his neck.

He wondered what edgy, nerved-up Roger did for sex. For love.

Suddenly, with a guarded expression, Roger said, "My real news, Lionel is: I'm going to be a father." Lionel said, "A—*what?*" Roger said, grinning, "A father." Lionel said, "You already are a father . . ." and Roger said, "For the second time, I'll be a father. And this time I mean to do it right."

As Lionel listened now avidly, Roger told him that the woman was a young paralegal working for the National Project to Free the Innocent with whom he'd become "involved" since the previous fall but with whom he wasn't in love—"And Naomi certainly isn't in love with me." There had been the possibility of the young woman having an abortion but through a "mutual arrangement" she was going to have the baby, and . . . Roger spoke excitedly yet with an air of wonderment like one who has been struck over the head by a blunt weapon. Lionel listened in disbelief, and in dismay. A father! A second time! And by way of a woman Roger didn't love!

The thought of Siri pregnant with his child both excited and repelled Lionel. And yet: what a testament to a middle-aged male's virility.

Lionel had no option but to ask when the baby was due, and Roger said, proudly, July eleven. In a lowered voice he added, "When Robin learns she'll be disgusted." Lionel said, impulsively, "My children are disgusted with me, too." The men laughed suddenly.

They drank, and laughed. Lionel felt his sinuses aching. Elsewhere in the lounge men were smoking cigars. Luxuriantly, lasciviously. Busty waitresses in shiny black spandex moved through clouds of smoke with fierce, fixed smiles. Lionel was laughing but his jaws seemed to have locked. A searing pain lifted from the nape of his neck into his skull. Hot tears ran down his cheeks but in the smoky twilight of The Cigar Bar his companion could pretend, with impeccable Salthill tact, not to notice.

IT WAS THAT EVENING that Lionel returned alone to the apartment on East 61st to discover a faint stink of cigar smoke pervading the rooms. Innocently thinking, *It's in my clothing. My hair. Not here.* He tried to recall whether the president had smoked a cigar, and believed he had not.

In the bedroom Lionel discovered the green satin bedspread carelessly drawn up over wrinkled linen sheets; disbelieving, he stooped to examine coin-sized splotches of still-damp mucus on the bottom sheet. Another man's semen? Was it possible? There were smudges of lipstick on the pillows, the hue of dried blood, Siri's shade of lipstick. Amid the bedclothes, Siri's rich nutmeg smell and the smell of another, rank and animal, a sweaty male. In the dazzling white tile bathroom every towel appeared to have been roughly used and hung crooked from racks or lay damply wadded on the floor; the shower was dripping, and long dark snaky hairs were trapped in the drain. The air was still humid but steam had evaporated from the mirrors. In the zinc-framed mirror above the sink, a man's ashen, appalled face floated foolish as a child's balloon. His mouth was slack and his brain was struck blank as with a mallet.

5

"APOLLO! SHADOW! *Thor!*"

She had only to appear in the doorway, framed in sunlight, before she summoned them, and the dogs came running. She lifted her hands, clapping just three times. How they adored their mistress, and how beautiful they were to her!

First came Thor, panting and eager, the youngest, a two-year-old Doberman pinscher with a lean-muscled, burnished-dark body like liquid energy, urgent eyes and razor teeth. Next came the older Apollo, with the husky-shepherd's deep chest and solid hindquarters, yet puppylike in his eagerness to please. Finally, there was the smaller, spidery Shadow, coarsely black-furred, on three legs, shimmying his narrow hindquarters, panting so quickly his breath made a whistling sound. "Good dogs! Come." Where once Camille Hoffmann had taken pleasure in feeding her husband and children, and in feeding guests seated at her long dining room table, now she took a more ardent, less anxious pleasure in feeding her dogs in a corner of the kitchen, each in his separate bowl. "Here, Thor. Here, Apollo. Mind your manners, now! And here, Shadow. Don't spill. Good dogs." A yellow plastic bowl for Thor. A red plastic bowl for Apollo. A dark green plastic bowl for Shadow. And a large white plastic water bowl for all three dogs, neatly set upon sheets of newspaper.

These sheets of newspaper (usually the stock market pages of the *New York Times*) Camille changed every two or three days, depending upon how messily the dogs ate.

Now in the New Year the beautifully restored old Colonial house on Old Mill Way was no longer a burrow. It had become a space open to daylight. Camille laughed to think she'd once fussed so over her furniture, her curtains and carpets. She'd once allowed herself to be upset when the children tracked mud into the spotless downstairs rooms. She'd been physically ill when, the morning after one of the Hoffmanns' New Year's Eve festive dinner-dance parties, she'd discovered burn marks on the hardwood floor of a newly remodeled guest bathroom, where someone, presumably drunk, had stubbed out a cigarette. ("In our house, Lionel. One of our so-called friends. Can you imagine. Who could it be!" The probable suspect, both Camille and Lionel agreed, was Harry Tierney, who'd left Salthill soon afterward, thumbing his nose at them all.) What did such trivial things matter? On only his second day with Camille, the high-strung young Doberman, Thor, dashed past her into the dining room to throw himself with a savage snarl against a window (having seen what might have been a bird's shadow passing outside?), sank his teeth into the antique lace curtains, and tugged, and all came tumbling in a heap. Apollo and Shadow, not to be outdone in vigilance, and jealous of their mistress's new adoptee, barked excitedly. "Oh, you bad boys! You're destroying my beautiful house," Camille laughed.

In fact she was upset. She worried what Lionel would say when, one day soon, he returned home. "This is his house, too. He has allergies. He'll be appalled." And what would Camille's relatives say when they visited, both hers and Lionel's; and such

Salthill friends as Beatrice Archer and Abigail Des Pres, who telephoned often, concerned that Camille spent too much time alone. (Camille wanted to protest she wasn't alone: she had Apollo, Shadow, and Thor. And she had her volunteer work at the Rockland County Homeless Animal Shelter, which meant a good deal to her; she was making friends there, and would make more. *People like me. People who understand animals.* At Christmas, Camille had made a generous contribution to the New Jersey Friends of the American Associated Humane Societies and in the spring she would volunteer to help in their statewide campaign to influence citizens to vote yes in an upcoming election, for a proposal to make cruelty to animals and animal abuse felonies and not merely misdemeanors punishable by token fines.) In this new phase of her life Camille felt like an explorer who has blundered onto a strange, unexpected terrain, for which nothing in her previous life has prepared her.

But she would be prepared, in time. She believed this!

At least the dread holiday season was past. Somehow, Camille had managed to endure it. She'd never quite realized how onerous the burden was to be, or to pretend to be, *happy;* to keep up a brave, stubborn pretense of *happiness* because it's that season. Marcy and Kevin came to visit, glum and embittered, jealous of the dogs. "How can Daddy come home, if these dogs are here? You know he's allergic," Marcy said peevishly. Camille tried to explain, "But your father isn't home, dear. And in the meantime these poor animals deserve a home, too." Marcy said, in a voice heavy with sarcasm, "Mot*her!* Next thing we know, you'll be building a kennel out back."

But why a kennel, Camille thought, when there's the guest house? A useless luxury, under these changed circumstances.

THE HOLIDAY ORDEAL was worsened by the cloudy presence of Marcy and Kevin. Both complained to their mother that they'd had to cancel holiday plans in order to be with her at such a sensitive, painful time; both tried repeatedly to make telephone and e-mail contact with their elusive father, with no luck. She heard them declaring grimly over the phone to friends that "Poor Mom needs us, she's in a permanent state of shock" and "Daddy needs us, he's having a nervous breakdown." They went to Manhattan, to Hoffmann Publishing, Inc., and to the apartment on East 61st Street, in vain. At Lionel's office, his secretary swore that Mr. Hoffmann wasn't in, but had left the country for the holidays; and when Marcy strode past her to boldly open the door, there was no one at her father's desk. "It's like black magic. Dad's a magician, and he makes himself disappear," Marcy said, disgusted. At the apartment, they discovered to their chagrin that their keys no longer fit the lock. Their father so distrusted them, he'd had the locks changed! "It's like Kafka," Kevin said. "The shame of the father outlives the son."

Still, Marcy and Kevin were childishly adamant, as Christmas approached, that Lionel would, Lionel must, return to the house on Old Mill Way for Christmas Eve, at least! Camille, who'd pondered such a fantasy earlier in December, then gave it up, tried to warn them; most likely Lionel was out of the country; he and his new, young friend seemed to travel a lot, especially to lush tropical places. Marcy said derisively, "This 'new, young friend' of Dad's, know who she is? Know what she is? *I* know." Kevin said, "Yes? What do you know? Who told *you?*" "I know she's Third World," Marcy said smugly, "and she wouldn't be confused with a Caucasian. That's what I know." Irritated, Kevin said, "So who told you? This sounds like bullshit to me." "I know what I know," Marcy said, thrusting her bulldog face dangerously close to Kevin's, "I ran into a certain Salthill divorcée in the village, whose ex-husband 'double-dated' with Dad, both of them with Third World hookers, and—" Kevin began to shout at his sister, and Camille deftly intervened, daring to thrust herself between them. Exactly as she'd done nearly two decades ago. "Children, please," she said, resorting to the pitiful stage gesture of actually wringing her hands, "don't do this to me, not at Christmas. I beg you." Both children sneered.

Apollo was barking, and Shadow was close to baying, locked in another part of the house and fearful their mistress was being attacked.

Marcy, a big girl with a tendency to lurch, went about the house singing in a mock-sugary voice, "It's beginning to look a lot like Christmas—NOT." Kevin, obsessed with combing his wan, thinning hair in such a way as to minimize its thinness, or to maximize its rapidly diminishing thickness, took Camille aside and told her he was worried about his sister who was "clinically depressed" over their father's disgusting behavior and close to "burning out" with her "fiercely competitive job." Another time, Marcy took Camille aside to confide in her she was worried about her kid brother, who was "in a crisis of sexual identity" exacerbated by his dad's disgusting behavior and by his mother's "failure to deal decisively." Camille smiled weakly and promised to do what she could.

When it became embarrassingly clear that Lionel wasn't coming home for Christmas Eve dinner, had no presents to heap upon them, nor even a mumbled telephone apology to transmit, it fell to Camille to placate, or to attempt to placate, Marcy and Kevin. Marcy said tragically, "This is the first time in my entire life that my father I believed I loved, and I believed loved me, won't be spending Christmas with me." Kevin said vehemently, "This scene sucks. It isn't even Oedipal, where you could explore it as myth. It's just—shit." "The first fucking time! In my fucking life! Fucking Christmas! Sure it's materialist, our culture is sick with material things, but how the fuck else do you communicate your *love?* Name the ways." Just then the telephone rang, and Camille hurried breathless to answer it. In a stage play a ringing phone would signal a possibly happy ending, but in actual life, dogs barking and baying in the near distance, things weren't so logical. Yet her heart leapt like a girl's. Though soberly instructing herself *Just remain calm. Calm, Camille!* She had time for a quick pleasant recollection of meeting Lionel for the first time, how many years ago, in that rowdy smoky fraternity house upstate, and she'd been a calming influence upon him, upset as he was that his date had slipped away with one of his fraternity brothers; Camille, though very young, had been calm, sweet, steadying—and that had made all the difference. But, damn!—the telephone was only just Beatrice Archer, calling to wish

Camille a happy Christmas, and to mention casually that she knew of a "beautiful, sweet-tempered, loving dog," a young Doberman pinscher named Thor, in need of an immediate home. Had Camille any suggestions? "Thor is a purebred Doberman, too sensitive to be lodged anywhere impersonal like a kennel or a shelter. He needs a true home, Camille. I wish Avery and I could take him in, but—!" Camille tried to keep the disappointment, in fact the bleak despair, out of her voice. "Beatrice, thank you but I can't take in a third dog. I simply can't. I'm desperate to know what I'll do when Lionel comes home. Please understand!" Upset, Camille hung up on Beatrice's lilting soprano voice.

When she returned to the children, Marcy was loudly singing, "I'm dreaming of a white Christmas—NOT." Kevin said, "NOT Dad on the phone, I guess?" in a voice heavy with adolescent irony.

IN THIS WAY Christmas Eve was endured, and Christmas Day. And Camille Hoffmann and her two grown children exchanged presents, and no more mention was made of the absent husband-father. When, the morning after Boxing Day, Marcy and Kevin departed for their homes, Camille collapsed on a sofa and slept for six straight hours. She was awakened only by the dogs whining and scratching at the door. How happy!—her heart lifted. For a moment she couldn't remember why.

IN EARLY JANUARY, Beatrice Archer again called. "Camille! If you'd just consent to meet Thor. Just let me bring him over for five minutes."

"Beatrice, I can't. I've explained."

"Five minutes, Camille! I promise, no more."

"Beatrice, *no*."

"Camille, this isn't like you. There's a strange hardness in your voice. If only you'd consent to meet this poor sweet beautiful creature—"

How could Camille say no? How harden her ridiculous heart, that had already been cracked?

In this way, in the New Year, Thor came to live with Camille. "Three dogs! I'm becoming eccentric, I guess." Meeting Thor, seeing the dog's shining desperate eyes, Camille had known she couldn't turn him away. A purebred Doberman pinscher! He'd belonged to the Archers' eldest son Michael, who "wasn't able to keep him," as Beatrice evasively explained. Camille spoke quietly to Thor, and Thor seemed, shyly, to be responding. He was certainly a handsome specimen, though clearly high-strung and anxious; his fine dark-burnished hide rippled with nerves almost continuously, even when he slept. He was timid around the older dogs and frightened of sudden sounds and movements. The protracted noise of a neighboring executive's helicopter roused him to whining and snapping at the air. His teeth were young teeth, and sharp. (Camille knew! That first week, he'd growled and snapped at her several times, reacting out of fear.) While grooming Thor, Camille discovered to her horror that fur on the young dog's neck was rubbed away, and the skin beneath scarred, as if he'd been tightly tied. On other parts of Thor's body there were suspicious nicks and scars. He cowered in the way of a dog accustomed to being shouted at, or kicked. Camille was naively shocked. How could the Archers' son Michael, a classmate of Kevin's at Salthill Country Day, and now a Wall Street market analyst, have been cruel to his own dog? Camille stroked the dog's bony head gently, and murmured, "Thor, I promise: you will never, never be hurt again."

IN JANUARY, Thor. In March, Fancy.

"Fancy is my darling, and my orphan-to-be, I'm afraid. Let's speak frankly, dear."

Mrs. Florence Ferris of Lost Brook Farm, a twenty-acre estate bordering upon Old Mill Way, summoned Camille to her enormous Tudor home, and to her bedside. The old, ailing woman was somewhere beyond ninety, and badly incapacitated by strokes and other maladies of age. Along with her late husband the admiral, a golf-playing friend of Dwight D. Eisenhower, Mrs. Ferris was known for her charitable works and contributions to such organizations as the Salthill Pro Musica and the County Historical Society. Camille had met the renowned old woman only a few times, at fund-raising events. She was conscious of the honor of being invited to Lost Brook Farm, but uneasy; what did Mrs. Ferris want of her? A curly-haired French poodle, very white, was sprawled across the quilted bedspread beside Mrs. Ferris' shrunken doll-body. Camille thought *Not another dog! I will not.* Mrs. Ferris said, "My dear, I'm so sorry I never got to know you in life. And now—" Mrs. Ferris laughed sadly, yet forcibly. Camille was moved to protest but Mrs. Ferris continued, "Let me be blunt, dear. I have heard such good things of you. Will you adopt my darling Fancy? I love her so, I'm desperate for her to have a good, loving home not too many miles from here. She is eight years old, no longer young, possessed of a highly sensitive soul, and I don't want her uprooted and traumatized any more than she will be when I . . . depart." Camille smiled weakly, thinking *No! I swear, I will not.* The previous night she'd had a vivid dream of Lionel, not as the stiff, guilt-wracked man she'd last seen, but as he'd been fifteen or twenty years before, dark-haired, robust, often affectionate; in the lovely Technicolor dream they'd been ice skating hand in hand, beneath an incongruous Caribbean sky, and so innocently happy . . . Mrs. Ferris was saying briskly, "Poodles, you know, are the most intelligent of all the breeds. And Fancy is devilishly intelligent, I must warn you. And yet so sweet. And something of a mind-reader! She will snap, and I'm afraid she will bite, but only if provoked. Don't let fretful children anywhere near her, Camille!" Mrs. Ferris laughed fondly. "And Fancy is an heiress, too. Aren't you, Fancy?"

The curly poodle, with widened watery shrewd eyes, barked at Camille sharply, three times, like Morse code.

Camille said reluctantly, "Mrs. Ferris, I wish I could adopt your beautiful dog. But my husband is allergic to dogs and it's only a matter of time before—"

Mrs. Ferris commanded, "Fan-cy! Stop groveling and cringing and show some spunk. Here is your new, young mistress."

Fancy peeked at Camille over the quilted edge of Mrs. Ferris' bony hip. The Morse-code bark came again, and a growl deep in the throat.

"Mrs. Ferris, thank you so much for your trust. But I— "

"Fancy *is* an heiress, and it's never been said of the Ferrises that they are likely to *stint*." Mrs. Ferris winked lewdly. Camille blushed. She said, stammering:

"Oh, but I, I—I don't require money, Mrs. Ferris. I have more money than I can use, truly. Except to help out unfortunate animals, of course. In which case— "

"In which case, Fancy will be residing in just the right home, yes? And her mistress can 'retire' in peace."

Somehow it happened, Camille wasn't certain how, that Fancy was delivered over to her; and Mrs. Ferris thanked Camille profusely, squeezing her hands and weeping. Fancy, too, whined, and squirmed in Camille's arms. "Fancy, good-bye! You will leave me. You will live from now on with Camille, my dear friend and neighbor. You will be a good dog, and you will obey your new mistress. If you think of me, think of me kindly. Away!"

A uniformed nurse and a uniformed housekeeper helped Camille with the quivering, whimpering dog and its cushioned wicker bed, its wardrobe of little sweaters and coats and booties, and its cans and sacks of special diet food. In protest, and yet passively, Fancy leaked urine onto Camille's clothing, but did not bark hysterically as Camille feared she might on the way home, and did not bite. Not just yet.

AND IN APRIL, ten days before Easter, there came Belle to live in the house on Old Mill Way.

Of Camille's dog-family, as she would come to call them, Belle was by far the most pitiful. She'd been brought into the emergency clinic at the shelter one afternoon when Camille was on duty, a female mongrel, visibly pregnant, with bulldog blood, mud-colored and weighing about thirty pounds, profusely bleeding. According to witnesses who'd brought her to the clinic, the collarless dog had been dragged from the rear bumper of a pickup truck by sadistic boys and left to die by the side of a country highway north of Salthill. The pads of her paws were torn away, her right shoulder was dislocated, several ribs were broken, her stomach, hindquarters, and the contents of her womb a bloody mess.

Of the numerous volunteers at the Rockland shelter, only Camille was eager to work with the badly injured dog during her slow recuperation. Only Camille was patient enough to feed the traumatized dog, who had to lie on her side, her feet bandaged and her ribs in a cast. Camille fed her by hand, like a baby. Because there was the danger of the dog panicking and biting, Camille had to wear protective gloves to her elbows. She didn't at all mind. She came quickly to love this trembling, courageous dog who, the day following surgery, tried to wag her tail at Camille's approach. "'Belle.' That's your name. Because one day you will be *belle*. Don't be frightened. You're safe now." Camille rocked the bandaged dog. "Belle, Belle! You will never be hurt again, Belle! *You will be revenged.*"

THERE CAME the April morning, shortly after Camille brought Belle home to live with her and the other dogs, when the telephone rang, and Camille answered it expecting to hear the voice of one of her new friends, but it was a hoarse voice she scarcely recognized, with a quaver to it, like a nervous bullfrog at the bottom of a well. "Camille? It's Lionel." There was a pause. Camille's heart beat painfully. "May I come home?"

As in her dreams Camille tried to speak, and could not. She felt herself falling, fainting. The telephone receiver slipped from her fingers. The dogs rushed to her, to lick her face and hands, gathering in a tight, jealous ring about her.

The Girl in the Red Beret

There she is: that woman.

Through the fall and winter and into spring the whispering was relentless! pitiless! like dried, torn leaves blown by clouds with manic bulging cheeks! A rustling murmurous mocking sound. Never to Abigail's beautiful mask of a face but behind her back, of course.

There she is: the mother who lost her son. Whose son has repudiated her. She tried to kill herself and him in a speeding car, can you imagine! These were Abigail's friends. Her Salthill neighbors. They knew her soul that was in tatters. They wished her well, as one wishes a convalescent well. Yet they shook their heads in bemused disapproval. Smiled in astonishment that one of their own could so misbehave. Smiled, appalled. *And had she been drinking, poor Abigail?*

You know the answer to that one.

SINCE THAT NIGHT in Vermont when the *demon hand* reached out to yank the steering wheel, to bring Abigail and Jared to their deaths, Abigail hasn't had a single drink. She swears! Not even Salthill's alcohol of choice, dry white wine, and that's one of her problems: "Life, raw and sober, isn't 'life' as we know it. It's something else." What else? An autopsy report. Continuous traffic news over one of the breathless New York City radio stations. Or continuous MTV, if, middle-aged, not an American adolescent, you had to watch, trussed up like a turkey and your eyes taped open. Forever.

And so she planned her suicide for April 30. With characteristic modesty choosing the slack, anticlimactic Sunday following Easter Sunday, which seemed to Abigail, a lapsed Episcopalian, a fitting day, since Easter itself would be too pointedly symbolic, an elbow in the ribs—*Got it? No resurrection for this woman!* But inevitably something (a persistently ringing phone, her anxiety that the caller might be Jared who hasn't spoken to her in months) happened to deflect it. And the following morning is May 1, and maybe that means something? *The first morning of my new, posthumous life?*

And Abigail is driving into the Village of Salthill-on-Hudson, slowly (shakily!) along Pearl Street, a still young-looking woman in dark glasses wanly glamorous as a recovering-druggie rock star of another era, in her gleaming ghost-colored BMW sedan in a state of suspended animation waiting *to feel something! anything! since after all I'm alive, it's spring and I am NOT DEAD.* But her mind is blurred like the lipstick-smudged rim of a cocktail glass, since having failed to die the previous day she's obliged to carry on with her absurd and exhausting life, a life that would seem to be enviable to most of the world's billions, basically the life of a forty-three-year-old (yes, Abigail has acquired another birthday, during the winter malaise) suburban divorcée with a busy social calendar and no soul; a life of appointments, social events, and errands like beads on a rosary, and these beads looping continuously back upon themselves, now Adam is gone, now Jared is gone, now Abigail has failed to remarry, Abigail has failed even to stumble away from the wreckage of her marriage to find another man to love, and to love her; and for a weak moment on Pearl Street passing the Old

Salthill Cemetery where patriots of the American Revolution are buried, and the Salthill Free Public Library in its restored-historic Neo-Georgian building, and a corner of Shaker Square, her mind has drained so blank she can't recall if she has just driven into town to have lunch with the co-chair of the Friends of the Salthill Historic Society Annual Spring Festival of Flowers, or if she's on her way back to Wheatsheaf Drive, and home; that beautiful house empty of life as a mausoleum; she can't recall if, the day before, lining up her precious cache of barbiturates, painkillers, and Prozac on a kitchen counter, she'd decided to appeal to Jared one final time (just a single telephone call!) before washing everything down with vodka, or whether, with laudable magnanimity, she'd decided to spare the boy, who after all (she's his Mom, she should know!) is only sixteen and wounded by his parents' acrimonious divorce; when at the intersection of Pearl and Ferry, waiting for the traffic light to change, Abigail happens to see the girl in the red beret . . .

"She must be lonely. Always, she's alone."

The girl appears to be Chinese, about eleven years old. She's small-boned, with delicate features, a perfect petal of a face; dark gleaming-smooth straight hair to her shoulders, and straight-cut bangs across her forehead; carrying a cello case gripped tightly, and walking as if into a bracing wind. The girl wears a plain jacket, neatly pressed slacks, and the little red beret, a stab of bright color. By chance, Abigail has seen this child several times in Salthill, and her heart is touched . . . The girl is no one Abigail knows. And no one who knows Abigail. Sometimes she's carrying the cello case, and sometimes not. Salthill is a small enough community in which, without wishing to, you recognize individuals without knowing their names. The girl in the red beret is a student at the Salthill Middle School on North Chambers Street; Abigail has seen her walking from the school, alone. Abigail has seen her in the Salthill Public Library, alone. Surely there are other Chinese-American girls attending the middle school, but the girl in the red beret is always alone, or at any rate when Abigail has seen her, she's alone. The first time Abigail happened to notice her, the girl was trying shyly to make her way through a rude, noisy gaggle of middle-school classmates loitering on the sidewalk outside the library, the diminutive Chinese girl confronted by girls and boys of approximately her own age who ignored her as if she didn't exist, and jostled her as she tried to pass. The unconscious cruelty of young adolescents! Abigail was incensed and would have liked to come to the Chinese girl's rescue, taking her hand and pushing the others aside. Such louts! Caucasians! She felt her face burn with a pleasurable racial shame. Since Caucasians are the majority race, you can castigate yourself with racial shame, and not be held to account in any way. Abigail had lingered on the pavement a few yards away, pondering what she would do if, for instance, one of the show-offy boys snatched off the Chinese girl's beret; if anyone was actively rude, aggressive. Abigail was a Salthill mother, these kids would shrink before the authority of a mother. (Wouldn't they?) As Jared's mother, Abigail shouldn't have been surprised or shocked, overhearing the language of these bratty spoiled Salthill kids, the casually tossed-off *shit, fuck, suck,* and the sexual innuendo of their banter *blow, eat out, fuck you, man!* But she was shocked, and dismayed. These were hardly more than children, after all. Girls of twelve and thirteen sharing cigarettes on the street. Garishly applied lipstick and eye shadow and tight-fitting little skirts. The boys in baggy rap-style pants from Banana Republic and Gap, their expensive jogging shoes unlaced. Privileged Salthill children whose fathers were multi-millionaires, emulating what they believed to be the gangsta-street-style of the black ghetto where fathers were likely to be in prison, absent, or dead. At least, Jared had passed through this phase. Abigail hoped Jared had passed through this phase.

So sad! Abigail's son refuses to speak with her, let alone see her. She tries to be brave but there she is carrying the deformity of her shame about with her, in public, a giant goiter growing out of her neck.

That day last autumn Abigail tried not to be conspicuous watching as the child in the red beret managed to make her way through the rowdy group, too shy to speak, her face waxy-pale and masklike and her beautiful Asian eyes deep-set and solemn, downlooking, amid the giddy gaiety of her classmates. Abigail thought fiercely, *She is superior to them all. They must know it!* Though in fact the white Salthill kids took no evident notice of her at all. Now Abigail sits behind the wheel of her BMW, watching the same child passing within a foot of the car, carrying her cello case, and she feels again a stab of affection, a wish to protect. There's a melancholy precocity about this girl. An old soul, in a young body. Is that possible? And yes, the girl is beautiful, in Abigail's eyes, though harsher eyes might consider her plain. It's the pure young-girl innocence that quickens Abigail's scarred heart. *Why did I never have a daughter! What a blunder.* In fact, Harrison hadn't much wanted the first baby, who at least turned out to be a boy. A little DNA-carrier with a miniature penis, and Harry's moaning thrashing tantrum ways. The prospect of a second baby, meaning a bloat-bellied wheezing wife instead of a debutante beauty, and a season of stinking diapers and disinfectant and another "ethnic minority" nanny in the household—*No thanks!* Abigail sighs. Watching as the child in the red beret walks away, oblivious of the Caucasian woman in the designer dark glasses, behind the wheel of a ghost-colored BMW, gazing with such interest after her. Wondering who the child's mother is. What a lucky woman! Surely the girl is a model of the mother, those delicate features, the shining black hair, the self-effacing way in which she carries herself, but she'll become, by degrees, Americanized, and break the mother's heart. *Still, it's worth it. They give us a few years of happiness, it's selfish to ask for more.* The thought occurs to Abigail: maybe she should marry an Asian-American man? Are there any Asian-American bachelors over forty? She has a vague idea that Asian-Americans don't divorce frequently; they marry young, and remain faithful; if they have adulterous affairs, surely it's within their race and class; as her ex-husband Harry Tierney used to say, after business trips to Tokyo and Taiwan, Asians *are* inscrutable—"On purpose. To make us look like lumbering assholes." Abigail seems to think that, if she could inveigle an Asian-American man into loving her, and marrying her, this might be the solution to her problems? There's a small Asian-American population in Salthill and its affluent environs, but there are, strangely, no Asian-Americans in Abigail's immediate social circle, as, equally strangely, since Salthill is such a liberal-Democrat community, there are no blacks or Hispanics either. ("We try! We try constantly!" Salthill hostesses claim, quite sincerely. "We invite them, but they don't come to our parties. Or, if they do, they come only once, and we never hear from them again.") Abigail knows—her brain is awash with affable cultural clichés, like a washing machine churning laundry—that Asian-American children are "top performers" academically, and that Asian-Americans have "strong family ties." Each year there are more Asian-American faces in Salthill and Abigail thinks this is a good thing, on principle. She supposes that the child in the red beret is the beloved daughter of one of the new families, her father an investment banker, or a doctor, or a biotech executive, some of whom have bought million-dollar homes in new subdivisions with names like Lincoln Green, Pheasant Hollow, Liberty Vale.

Abigail is wakened from her trance by a horn lightly tapped behind her (this is Salthill, not New York City) and quickly she drives through the intersection. Where she's headed, she isn't certain, but knows it isn't important, since it's where Abigail Des Pres is headed; like her suicide, it can be deflected. Instead she takes a left onto Quaker Street, and another onto Front, with the intention of circling back to Pearl. (What is she doing?) (Her excuse might be, it's an overcast spring day, mean-looking storm clouds and gusts of wind spitting rain, if the child in the red beret gets caught in a downpour . . .) But, bad luck, Abigail is slowed down in Salthill's narrow streets, caught in slow, clogged traffic, waiting with mounting impatience as women shoppers (acquaintances of hers, Abigail can't honk rudely) struggle to insert their luxury vehicles into parking places, like hefty women inserting themselves into corsets. By the time she returns to Pearl and Ferry, and cruises along Pearl for several futile blocks, the child in the red beret is nowhere in sight.

Now what the fuck are you doing, Mom! Stalking somebody else's kid! You are one SICKO mom, Mom.

* * *

"NO, I'M AFRAID that Jared and I rarely speak these days. But I hear his voice often. He's always in my thoughts. I feel that I keep in contact with him, somehow."

ABIGAIL DES PRES IS *not stalking* anyone, let alone an innocent child of eleven! Observe how she proceeds dutifully to The Lemon Tree to have lunch with the co-chair of the Flower Festival. (Though it has crossed her mind that she could contact each of the music teachers in Salthill, there can't be very many, and inquire discreetly after a Chinese girl of about eleven who wears a red beret and studies cello . . . But what would she say next? That's tricky.) Abigail finds herself the brunette half of a pair of beautifully dressed, impeccably groomed Salthill women lunching at Salthill's most popular new restaurant, The Lemon Tree. Amid a bustle of white-uniformed young waiters and a clatter of gleaming cutlery and what sounds like an endlessly repeating Bach harpsichord tape and a buzz and murmur like the coursing of blood in one's ears. Before each woman is a plate profusely heaped with gourmet salad greens, vinaigrette on the side. "The Sunday following Easter, yesterday, seemed like a good idea. But I missed it."

"A good idea for what, Abigail?"

For killing myself. "For rethinking my life. Housecleaning, sorting through my wardrobe and throwing away clothes I haven't worn in the past year. Girl things."

"Excuse me? 'Gull things'? It's so noisy in here."

"Girl, gull." Abigail laughs almost too heartily. "I won't contest the point."

To her chagrin Abigail finds that she's drinking white wine after all. Since when? She'd promised herself *Never again!* And in fact she promised Roger Cavanagh, who'd gallantly saved her ass up in Middlebury, Vermont. *No more alcohol, ever!* Abigail's luncheon companion, Beatrice Archer, is a bronze-highlighted blond beauty of a mysterious age, somewhere between thirty-five and fifty, in a splendid wide-brimmed straw hat like a character in a Merchant-Ivory film, and she's sipping red wine, and talking enthusiastically of the upcoming Friends of the Salthill Medical Center Festival of Flowers, a massive annual fund-raiser scheduled for later in May, for which Abigail has volunteered, reasoning that she can't kill herself until the Festival is over, nor even succumb to the luxury of a nervous collapse. In fact it was Beatrice, a co-chair of the Festival, who telephoned Abigail the day before, interrupting her suicide plans to remind Abigail of their luncheon date, and of the crucial work they have yet to do, telephoning volunteers, coordinating public relations, finalizing arrangements with the Salthill Inn, where the lavish luncheon will be held, tickets one hundred fifty dollars apiece. Members of the Friends are donating flowers, local florists and nurseries are donating flowers, a Pulitzer Prize–winning poet (male, Irish-American, "romantic") has been engaged to read to the luncheon guests. Beatrice's wine-stained lips part in a glossy, happy smile.

Lean across the table and kiss Beatrice! Maybe you're a lesbian, that has been the secret of your sexual malaise.

". . . TWENTY-SIX, -SEVEN, -eight . . . thirty. Thirty-*one*."

On a spotless kitchen counter she'd lined up barbiturate tablets, miscellaneous painkillers, and nine remaining Prozac capsules. She'd located some of Harry's pills dating back to 1987. "You can assume you've lived too long in one house," Abigail sagely observed, to the invisible surveillance camera overhead, which was blurred in her mind with her lost friend Adam Berendt, "when your prescriptions date back to previous presidential administrations." Abigail took out the bottle of Absolut Vodka and set it before her as on an altar. She was starting to tremble, but maybe that was a good sign? *I am serious. I am determined.* If she wasn't going to go through with this, she'd be calm, wouldn't she? But maybe she could simply drink herself to death, ingest alcohol by slow steady increments until her flimsy heart fibrillated, and burst? In that way, "Salthill can say, 'Poor Abigail! She was drinking to chase away the blues, it was an accident.'" Thirty-one pills swallowed within the space of a few minutes, washed down with vodka, was a more incriminating tale.

"Adam! Here's my predicament. I'm miserable alive, as you can see, but I don't want to cause anyone misery, dead."

Abigail, stop! You know I can't hear you.

"But I must know: if I commit suicide, should I acknowledge it as a conscious, rational act, an existential act; or should I simply—do it? And leave no note behind?"

Abigail, you're being ridiculous. I told you I can't hear you, I've ceased to exist.

"But Adam! You know how insecure I am. You know how I want to do the right thing, but—what *is* the right thing? I haven't been very happy, you know. For a long time."

So, who has? You think it's a barrel of laughs, being dead?

"Well. I could join you, maybe."

Scattered in my garden? Raked? Who's going to do it?

"I miss you so, Adam."

Silence.

"Adam! Are you angry with me? Please don't be . . ."

Silence. Abigail could hear Adam sighing. There was a maddening way he had of rubbing his knuckles against his eyeballs, which made a muted, juicy sound, and this sound too she believed she could hear.

"Adam, don't do that! That's a terrible habit."

I'm blind in one eye already, so what?

Abigail laughs, without mirth. "Adam, please. I need your advice. If I kill myself successfully, shall I leave a note behind? For instance—

Dearest Jared,

This is my choice, the wisest course for me. My heart is broken. I guess I'm a coward. But don't feel guilty, darling, over *me*. Always know: YOU ARE NOT TO BLAME FOR YOUR MOTHER'S FUCKED-UP LIFE.

Anyway, I love you.

Love,
Mom

Even in death, see, Adam, I'm trying to impress Jared. A not-so-subtle form of flirtation. Using adolescent language like *fucked-up* which I'd never use in actual life. Adam, am I pathetic?"

A disapproving, sullen silence.

"Adam, please! Am I pathetic?"

Abigail, you're a woman who has been wounded. But you're a strong woman, and you'll heal.

"I'm a strong woman, and I'll heel. Is that what you said?"

Heal, Abigail. H-E-A-L.

Abigail began to laugh gaily. "Adam, I spend all my time heeling. Cringing and cowering. Tail between my legs. People stare at me and see an attractive woman, I guess. The worse I feel, the more 'exotic' I look. On the outside a purebred Afghan hound, on the inside a tremulous little mutt."

ABIGAIL'S SHINING BLOND COMPANION in The Lemon Tree is smiling at her, perplexed. "'Smut'? Abigail, what are you saying?"

Has Abigail spoken aloud? She stares at the heaping greens on her plate that take on, for an unnerving moment, the configurations of little green oleaginous snakes in a cluster. She shuts her eyes. The fork slips from her fingers. The buzz and murmur of The Lemon Tree continues without her participation, as the universe will continue after the extinction of our kind. *I'm not capable of living without love. God forgive me, I'm not strong enough.* Abigail makes an effort to dislodge Adam's battered-homely-handsome face from her mind. Beatrice leans forward in a conspiratorial gesture, a necklace of golden coins gleaming around her neck; she tells Abigail of Lionel Hoffmann's return, at last, to Camille—"Just in time! Poor Camille has been behaving so strangely. She's taken in every stray dog in Rockland County, and that beautiful house smells like a *kennel.*"

Abigail says stiffly, "Camille has been lonely, Beatrice. I wouldn't presume to judge her."

"*I'm* not judging Camille," Beatrice says quickly. "She's an extraordinary woman. No one of us could have guessed how extraordinary! Now she'll be nursing Lionel: he had to have emergency surgery for bleeding ulcers, and he'll be having spinal surgery soon. And he's had some kind of—Camille is very tactful in speaking of it—'emotional collapse.'" Beatrice speaks gravely, a small smile tugging at a corner of her mouth. "The girl he was involved with, in New York, is young as their daughter Marcy, I've heard, and quite treacherous."

Abigail, who has heard the same rumor, but also that Lionel had been introduced to the treacherous girl by Abigail's ex-husband Harry, who was sexually involved with the girl too, says nothing. Beatrice continues:

"Camille is terribly relieved, and grateful, that Lionel has returned, but has refused to give up her dogs. Lionel wants her to, of course. But Lionel has lost his moral authority in that household." Beatrice pauses, her smile now radiant. "He walks with a cane. He's become quite gray. It doesn't seem likely that he'll return to his CEO position, even after the spinal surgery. Avery has heard that Lionel's replacement is an aggressive younger man with plans to expand into the Internet and to start a line of popular medical and self-help manuals in foreign languages. Camille has more responsibilities than she's had in years, but she seems to be thriving. She's donating tons of flowers to the Festival, as always. 'I wouldn't surrender Lionel for my dogs, so why should I surrender my dogs for Lionel?' Camille said to me. 'They all need me equally.'"

Abigail is sensitive enough to recall her subtle, shameful hurt that Adam's dog Apollo preferred Camille Hoffmann to her. The few times Apollo came to her door, bringing an old shirt or sweater of his master's, Abigail had coaxed him inside, but he'd never stayed long. Restless as his master had been, in Abigail's house! She has never spoken of this hurt to anyone. Yet how unfair it is, that Camille, a plain, thick-waisted woman with no clothes sense, should not only have her husband returned to her, but be mistress of Adam Berendt's beloved dog; the more unfair, since Abigail had been a closer, more intimate friend of Adam Berendt's than Camille had ever been. *If he loved any woman, it was ME.* "And does Camille still speak of Adam as if he's alive?" Abigail half-shuts her eyes, asking.

Beatrice shivers. "Yes! It's the only subject I don't dare bring up with Camille. If you speak of Adam in the past tense, she becomes upset. She's quite emphatic on the subject."

"Where is Adam now?" Abigail asks casually. "I'm just curious."

"He's traveling to Benares, India. It's a Hindu sacred city, Camille says."

"India! I thought Adam was in the Mediterranean."

"Well. Camille now 'sees' him headed east."

"How does Camille know?" Abigail feels a moment's jealousy. Has Adam been sending Camille postcards?

Beatrice laughs, as if Abigail has said something witty. "I wouldn't have thought that Camille, of all people, who's so sort of peasant-earthy, like a hausfrau by Brueghel, would be such a fantasist, would you?"

Abigail, resenting Camille, feels the need to defend her. "We all deal with death in different ways, Beatrice. I'm sure we are all fantasists, while thinking ourselves 'realists.' I only wish I had Camille's faith—in Adam, in her dogs, in nursing her wreck of a husband who'd betrayed her." Abigail swallows dry white wine and half-shuts her eyes, seeing a wicked vision of sixteen-year-old Jared, limping from a mountain-climbing accident, or in a wheelchair, delivered over to his mother. Permanently.

"Oh, and sinusitis. A terrible bout of it!" Beatrice says suddenly, as if she's just thought of it.

"'Sinusitis'? What?"

"Lionel is also suffering from that. He's allergic to dogs, it seems."

The women begin to laugh. Tears sparkle in their carefully mascaraed eyes.

Their lunch would end on this jovial note, except, even as Beatrice calls for the check, insisting upon paying for both meals, their waiter approaches the table bringing them two tall glasses of—is it champagne? "Compliments of the gentleman at the corner table, ladies. With his warm regards, he says." The women glance around, startled, and see it's their friend Owen Cutler. Poor Owen, having lunch alone at The Lemon Tree, on a weekday! Owen has removed his glasses and smiles bravely at the women, but even at a distance they can sense his eagerness to be invited to join them. Beatrice murmurs, "Oh, my God. Owen is so *lonely,* and I don't feel quite up to hearing him lament over Gussie another time." Abigail shudders in agreement. Since his wife disappeared from Salthill, Owen has called Abigail intermittently, sometimes very late in the evening, wanting to talk; wanting to take her out to dinner; wanting (unless Abigail is imagining this?) to be comforted by her, if not sexually (it's difficult for Abigail to envision Owen Cutler as a sexual partner of hers) then romantically. A glass of champagne is exactly what Abigail would love, and would never order for herself, so quickly she protests, "Waiter, please take these glasses away. My friend and I are not *whores.*" Abigail speaks with such deadpan sincerity, both the waiter and Beatrice stare at her, appalled.

On their way out of The Lemon Tree, the women dutifully stop by Owen's table to thank him for his thoughtfulness, but don't accept his plea that they sit with him. "I've had such dreams lately," Owen says, clutching at their hands, "that Gussie has died. And I am to blame." The women slip from Owen's chilly grasp with assurances that Gussie is certainly alive, and will return to him, soon. On the sidewalk outside the restaurant Beatrice says, after a moment's hesitation, that she has been hearing an ugly rumor that possibly Augusta isn't any longer living— "And Owen *is* to blame." Abigail, who has heard the same ugly rumor, shivers visibly as she puts on her dark designer sunglasses. She says, in a playful rebuke to her friend, "Beatrice, that's ridiculous! No Salthill husband would murder his wife *literally.*"

What does it feel like, losing my son? Like an abortion performed without an anesthetic.

CRUISING PEARL STREET in the direction in which the girl in the red beret had been walking two hours before. "Adam, I know. It's ridiculous. But I'm not harming anyone, am I?"

Silence. This means disapproval.

"I wouldn't actually speak to her. I wouldn't alarm her. It's just that, if she should need a, an adult to . . . consult. If she should turn her ankle, let's say. And need a ride home."

Each time Abigail returns to the house on Wheatsheaf Drive it's with the forlorn hope that Jared would have called in her absence. His voice on the answering tape. Or he might have sent an e-mail message. *Hey Mom! How's it going?*

Jared used to send her such messages, not frequently of course—"But more frequently than fucking *never*."

Since the accident. Since the *demon hand*. Since the emergency room, and Jared's refusal to see his mother. His own mother! To Abigail's mortification he'd denounced her to Roger Cavanagh. To Abigail's shame he'd insisted that Harrison be called, to take him home. By the fall he'd recovered sufficiently to travel to Kenya "on safari" with his father and his father's new young beautiful wife, and to Tanzania on a guided hiking tour up Mount Kilimanjaro. And he hadn't said good-bye to his mother before leaving the North American continent; nor had he sent a postcard from Africa. "And he might have died there! What if he'd died." Useless to think of these things. Saying a rosary of pain. Abigail knows! Yet, entering the house from which all life has fled, even a ghost-echo of a memory of Jared's boyhood voice, Jared's boyhood laughter, Abigail can't stop herself.

Roger had consoled her, not very tactfully. "Jared will realize what a bastard Harry is, eventually, and make up with you."

Abigail laughed. "When Jared realizes what a bastard Harry is, his mother may appear minimally better to him? That's something to live for."

Roger, who disliked being challenged, even in a spirit of flirtation, said irritably, "Look, my daughter, Robin, won't have shit to do with me. And I didn't try to kill her."

Abigail said, hurt, "Roger, I didn't try to kill Jared. What are you suggesting?"

"This *demon hand* fantasy. Come on, honey."

Honey! Abigail stared at her friend. He'd been a marvelous lawyer on her behalf, he'd persuaded a Middlebury traffic court judge to feel sympathy for her. Clearly he was attracted to her. *The least I can do is make love with Roger. Maybe we should be married* . . . But Roger continued, crudely, "You aren't conscious of having tried to kill Jared, of course. Under the law, I'm sure you wouldn't have been guilty of anything more than involuntary manslaughter. And I could have gotten you off that. But your actions suggest an unconscious intention, as you must know."

Abigail's hand leapt out, slapping Roger's face. The act of a hysterical woman in a movie except Abigail wasn't hysterical, and this was no movie. Roger, shocked, lurched away from her, tears flooding his eyes. Abigail was no less shocked. She whispered, "Roger, forgive me." Roger seized Abigail's slender shoulders and kissed her, hard, as an adder might bite. There was no affection in the kiss, only anger and contempt. For hours afterward Abigail's shoulders and her tender mouth ached. She held ice cubes against her mouth, and melting water ran down her arms.

This sorry episode occurred in January, in Abigail's house. It was at least as embarrassing as the couple's thwarted attempt at lovemaking, in October, when Apollo interrupted them by scratching noisily at the back door. Now, lately, Abigail has been hearing from numerous sources the disquieting rumor that Roger is in love—not with Marina Troy?—but with a woman lawyer whom no one in Salthill knows, an allegedly "very young" woman, and that Roger is "fathering" a baby with her. Abigail has become sulky as a spurned adolescent girl.

"If we'd made love that day, that baby might be *mine*."

A MELANCHOLY SEASON for romance. But Abigail is yet hopeful.

And so this evening, in Pryce House (1771), a tediously restored faded-brick Colonial townhouse on Shaker Square, home of the Salthill Historic Society, Abigail Des Pres is listening, in a pose of softly feminine attentiveness, to a local architect of youthful middle-age speaking on a visionary subject—"Whither

Salthill? The Next Crucial Decade, and Beyond." How passionate the architect is, and how dull! The most striking thing about the man is his nostrils, enormous cavities in his beakish nose, that contract in shudders as he inhales, and expand as he exhales. Abigail listens intently, hands folded quietly in her lap and her torso pushed forward at about the angle of the Pisan tower, yet even as she hears each of the architect's words she forgets it, as if her consciousness is a TV screen surfed by a restless teenaged boy with a remote control. Like most of her social circle, Abigail has been a supporter of the Historic Society for years, but rarely has she attended meetings and evening programs; she's here this evening as an alternative to swallowing thirty-one pills with vodka, and with the hope of "meeting" an eligible man. And her conscience has been pricked by the revelation that Adam Berendt not only left $35,000 to the Society, to aid in its preservation of historic local buildings and environments, but had been actively involved in some of its plans. (Yet had Adam attended meetings? Abigail doubts this.)

It's a misty-rainy May evening. An evening for romance. Abigail is glad she isn't dead! Driving into the village from her house on Wheatsheaf Drive, she passed through a shimmering-green Monet landscape of fields, hillsides, flowering trees and shrubs; a landscape of large, single-family homes with lighted windows, their inhabitants hidden from view, yet tantalizingly present. It seems to her a lifetime ago that she was Mrs. Harrison Tierney and that, when she entered any room in which her young son, Jared, happened to be, the child would rush at her headlong and embrace her legs and cry, "Mom-my! I love you!"

How simple life was. Jared so young. A child knows that love is all.

Abigail is sitting in the second row of folding chairs in the rather dim, dusty-smelling parlor of the Pryce House. She's one of the younger women (that is, under fifty) in the gathering: and, though suicidal, she's looking radiant as usual, if rather too luminously made up. For the occasion, she's wearing a new spring Armani suit of a dove-gray-lilac linen, with subtly padded shoulders and a long narrow waist; her smoky hair has been "highlighted" only that afternoon, and floats beguilingly about her head. Her mouth is a rich ripe glossy plum any healthy man might wish to bite into, her eyes are vacantly shining. Her heart, the size of a toddler's fist, beats hard with hope! (And with caffeine. Abigail, trying not to drink alcohol, has become a caffeine junkie.) As the architect with the cavity-nostrils speaks earnestly of the "spiritual need" to preserve not only the region's precious historic sites but their "ecological environments" as well, Abigail glances surreptitiously about the room. Unconsciously she's looking (always, she's looking!) for Adam Berendt. Consciously she's looking for Eligible Men. Asian-American? In fact there are relatively few men here this evening, no more than fifteen in all, and most of these are what you'd call older gentlemen; the great majority of Historic Society members are older Caucasian females, some quite elderly and infirm. (What a gold mine Salthill is, for fund-raisers! Many of the citizens are not only rich, but elderly-rich, which is the very best kind of rich. The dowager Florence Ferris has recently died, aged ninety-three, leaving an estate of over $40 million to be divided among her favored local charities, including the Historic Society.)

On the far side of the parlor, beneath a faded oil painting of Vice-President Aaron Burr shooting down General Alexander Hamilton in their notorious duel of July 1804 in nearby Weehawken, New Jersey, there's a stranger with thick, dark hair who might be Asian-American; his profile suggests a rather flat face, and he sits without fidgeting, as if listening as intently as Abigail. (But why would an Asian-American care about Salthill history? How shallow all of "American history" must seem to individuals from civilizations ancient and vast as the Chinese and Japanese, in which millennia, not mere centuries, are the norm of measurement; and in which billions of human beings have lived, died, and been forgotten, of no more consequence than fireflies.) Abigail thinks naively *An Asian-American would bring perspective to my life. He wouldn't have to be a lover, only a friend. He could be a she! I am dying of a lack of perspective.*

Already Abigail is feeling a little better. To isolate a problem is to begin to solve it.

She's conscious of being in the midst of a powerful, if not youthful, gathering of citizens. For years, since the booming sixties, Salthill has been in a combative "patriotic" mood. Unlike other, less affluent American suburban communities, Salthill-on-Hudson has been able to afford costly litigation to preserve its heritage; to block developers' efforts to break zoning codes. There are local lawyers who have made fortunes successfully bringing suits against the federal and state and county governments, blocking interstate connections and the widening and improvement of state highways; blocking subsidized housing units; senior citizens' units; a mega-million-dollar biotech research park ("Germ warfare experiments in our midst"), new sewers, paved country roads, medical clinics, a branch of the state university; additional public schools; even new nature trails with facilities for the handicapped. The enemy is change, the enemy is "progress"—"profit." At least, within the township. Adam laughed at Salthill paranoia, yet left money to the Historic Society; he'd deeded Deppe House to the township. Abigail realizes it must have been guilt Adam was assuaging.

Guilt for what, she has no idea.

Guilt is always to be assumed, maybe? Once you're an adult.

The architect, whose name is something harsh and improbable, Gustave, Garrick, Gerhardt?—Oldt, or Ault—has been speaking for a half-hour, and shows no signs of slowing down. What a strange, ugly face: both boyish and vulpine, with a long beak-nose and prominent nostrils and gnarled eyebrows over deep-socketed melancholy eyes. His chin is long and narrow, yet receding. His teeth glimmer wetly as he speaks, smiling often, with a nervous excitement. He's in his late forties, perhaps. He wears a dark tweed winter jacket that fits him loosely in the shoulders, and may be missing a button, like an item of second-hand clothing Adam Berendt might have purchased. But he lacks Adam's poise, and he lacks Adam's confidence. He has not an ounce of Adam's playful sexual swagger. As he speaks he gestures excitedly. His hair has grown too long around his ears, his necktie is partly unknotted, and twisted. Still, Abigail feels a stirring of interest. Almost, she can convince herself it's sexual.

Oldt, or Ault, is a man of intelligence, and fiery principles. His eyes move restlessly about the room (where some of his listeners are attentive-seeming as Abigail, and others, mostly men, are nodding off to sleep) yet return repeatedly to her. He seems to be asking Abigail, pleading with Abigail. "Why do images of the future hold so little attraction for us? So little human appeal? Because we have not yet lived in the future. We have lived, through our ancestors, solely in the past. The past is a country we know, or believe we know. Our mission then is to preserve the past intelligently—and to preserve our own souls." But Oldt, or Ault, is so ugly. You simply could not kiss a man with such nostrils, even with tight-shut eyes.

The parlor lights are being dimmed, the architect is preparing to show slides. A relief, Abigail won't have to stare at his face.

Is it true?—the past is a country we know, a country worth preserving? Abigail wonders. In recent weeks, since brooding upon her death, she's been haunted by the careless words Jared had uttered in the Middlebury hotel room. *We're just, like, algae on a pond. Fucking green scum.* Jared's contemptuous eyes, the twist of his beautiful mouth. Abigail feels a sting of hurt, remembering. Why hadn't she gone to her son, to embrace him? Why had she been so—stupidly shy? Jared was needing her, the kid was brokenhearted, Abigail should have hugged him, wept with him. *No, no, no. We are not pond algae. We are HUMAN, we have SOULS.*

Abigail wipes at her eyes, distraught. She has failed as a mother. Not in trying to kill her son but in not knowing how to teach him to live.

Slides of regional landmarks. "Before" and "after" restoration. Abigail recognizes some of these. The architect Oldt, or Ault, is head of a firm that specializes in the preservation and restoration of historic sites; it seems that he's been very successful, and his work has won prestigious awards. In the semidark, the man exudes authority, even charisma. *If I could love him. Someone like him.* There's the old stone Griswold House (1683) in the nearby village Galilee-on-Hudson. There's the Old Post Office (1797) of Bethel-on-Hudson. The Union Cliff House

(1840), once a stagecoach stop on the River Road, not far from Adam's Deppe House. The Hudson Hotel (1883) of Hastings-on-Hudson, a Victorian extravaganza nearly razed by a rapacious developer but saved by the efforts of preservationists. Abigail sees these heraldic images through a shimmer of tears. Even ugly buildings are beautiful, redeemed by History. The Swan's Ferry Quaker Meeting House (1845), once a near-ruin and now a branch of the Rockland County Public Library; the Palisades Battle Memorial Bell Tower (1911); the classic-revival bank on Main Street, Salthill (1925), owned now by a real estate agent; the Rialto, the art-deco movie house (1934), also on Main Street, restored and reopened as a theater showing art films. Next, the architect shows slides of deteriorated regional buildings and sites badly in need of salvation. His conclusion is passionate: "The next decade, our first in this new century, will be the most crucial of all our decades. We hope you will give us your support. History is everyone's business."

Abigail thinks *Restore me! I'm in ruins.*

The lights come up. There's a reception. Abigail blinks, a little dazed. Her first impulse is to escape, and return home: to the safety of the mausoleum. Her second impulse is to remain. She's here for a purpose. (But what purpose?) She's being greeted by Salthill acquaintances and neighbors, her hand is being shaken, ritual kisses bestowed upon her cheeks. *We're just, like, algae on a pond. Fucking green scum.* These good decent dull people she's known for years. "Abigail Tierney! It's been ages." Abigail has a set response to such remarks, she's pert as a high school cheerleader—"I'm no longer Mrs. Tierney, I've reverted to 'Ms. Des Pres.' Harry and I have divorced." Abigail takes care to pronounce the absurd "Ms." like an ingenue in a situation comedy, signaling her listener not to wince on her account but to smile as Abigail is smiling. She hates it that the automatic response to her declaration is *Oh! I'm sorry to hear that* and has prepared another pert reply: "*I'm* not sorry, so you shouldn't be, either."

Now can we change the fucking subject, please!

Abigail Des Pres, Salthill's fabled neurotic divorcée, by far the most attractive woman in Pryce House tonight, as she's the youngest, finds herself the center of much masculine attention. Too much. Like a soccer ball shouted-after, and kicked. Men compete for her vacant startled smile. Her Old Mill neighbor, eighty-year-old B— in his motorized wheelchair. And there is S—, the distinguished federal judge she'd once dated, wearing beneath his dark pin-striped suit a colostomy bag; now nudging against Abigail in a way both intimate and intimidating. S— kisses her porcelain cheek and murmurs in reproach, "Abigail, where have you been keeping yourself? You seem never to be home when I call, and you never call me back." There are several men this evening who brandish the tokens of a lost, lamented manhood, two of them unwrapped cigars, the other an unlit pipe. One of the men, trying to engage Abigail in conversation, strokes the crinkly paper of his cigar as it nestles in his coat pocket; the other, smiling edgily, unable to push into Abigail's presence, is fondling his cigar, openly, clenching and clutching at it with subdued violence. And there is an old acquaintance, P—, whom Abigail might have loved a very long time ago, meditatively sucking as he often does on such occasions an unlit pipe. Smoking has been forbidden these men, you needn't ask why.

"Abigail! You're looking lovely as usual."

Abigail is stunned with disappointment. The dark-haired gentleman she'd fantasized might be Asian-American turns out to be just another Salthill acquaintance; a junk-bond millionaire and a former golfing partner of Harry's; G— swarms upon Abigail, outweighing her by one hundred pounds, kissing her cheek though she gives the man no encouragement. G— has had some sort of facial restoration and looks "young"; his hair is boldly black, raven's wing black, and suspiciously thick; beneath his expensive cologne there's a whiff of something very black, like shoe polish. G— peers at Abigail's mouth when she speaks. Their conversation is awkward, disjointed. At another time, Adam would have drifted by to rescue her. Oh, where is Adam! G— is telling Abigail with a smirk that he's been meaning to call her for a long time—years!—"to commiserate"—"to share memories of that world-class bastard H.T. who treated you, frankly, excuse my language, a lady like you, like *shit*." How'd Abigail like to slip away from Pryce House and get a drink at the Inn? And maybe they could have dinner together sometime soon? Abigail is desperate to escape G— but the man has backed her into a corner. Continuing to stare, avidly, at her mouth. (Is he going to kiss her? In this public place? Abigail is fluttered and panicky as a thirteen-year-old.) G— maneuvers Abigail beneath a light, explaining, in an undertone, that he's become a little deaf in both ears—"But I read lips." Unconsciously, G— smacks his lips. Abigail blushes and manages to slip away, somehow. A cocktail reception is very like a soccer game, you must keep in motion. "M-Miss Des Pres? Hel-*lo*." It's the architect with the vulpine-boyish face.

During the architect's presentation Abigail had become mildly uneasy, noticing how his eyes repeatedly drifted onto her, but she'd told herself maybe she was imagining it. Now the man is quite intent upon speaking to her. His name is "Gerhardt Ault"—it turns out that he was a friend of Adam Berendt. "Though not a close friend, as I know you were, Miss Des Pres. But I admired Adam enormously. He was a true American original." Abigail frowns. She isn't at all certain she likes Adam characterized as an *American original,* like a stunted folk figure in a painting by the primitive artist Edward Hicks. Reluctantly she shakes hands with Ault, whose grip is moist and overly eager. The man might be fifteen, not an adult of reputation and accomplishment. He wears no cologne. He exudes sweaty-clammy unease, a whitish odor like slightly rancid oysters. Close up, his nose is not only large but large-pored; the nostrils are cavernous. He has a faint stammer. Yet he's boyish, almost charming. Abigail smiles in her "feminine" way; Ault is a man after all, if an ugly man, and "feminine" behavior is a reflex with Abigail as with most women of her class, as a decapitated chicken is said to totter about comically while blood spurts from its throat, and just possibly the decapitated head flutters its eyelashes and attempts a coquettish smile with its beak preparatory to extinction. Gerhardt Ault has been talking of Adam Berendt's sculpted works, which he "much admires"; he seems to be under the misapprehension that Abigail is a "sculptress"; Abigail, who'd taken art classes with Adam a decade ago, and had no patience for the discipline of sculpting, is too annoyed to set Ault straight. *Is that what he sees in me: sculptress?* As he speaks, a strange animation suffuses Ault. He reminds her of—not Adam Berendt exactly; but Adam as he might have been, younger, not so stocky in build, with a narrow and not a broad face; less certain of himself, uneasy with women. Adam if he'd had two functioning eyes, and these eyes were deep-socketed, melancholy. Adam with a long beaky nose. What sense does this make? There are flecks of lint, or dandruff, on Ault's tweedy shoulders. The man is scarcely taller than Abigail in her high heels. And his necktie, a dull striped affair, is twisted about, its torn label exposed. Macy's! Absentmindedly, Abigail reaches out to straighten the tie. An instinctive wifely gesture. As she might have done, scarcely thinking, with Adam. The effect upon Gerhardt Ault is electric. A warm dazed flush envelops his cheeks. His nostrils widen alarmingly, like staring eyes. And his eyes flood with emotion. *As if I've touched his cock. Have I touched his cock? Oh, God.* Ault begins to speak, stammering, and Abigail says quickly, blushing, "I'm so sorry, Mr. Ault! I don't know what made me do—that." Ault says, "Miss Des Pres, thank you. Obviously I'm—disheveled."

He laughs shrilly. Clearly his teeth haven't been capped. He would say more, but Abigail excuses herself, and gracefully escapes.

Algae on a pond. Fucking green scum.

Abigail sits up, late. Thinking: Jared's generation is being educated to ecological interrelatedness and yet there is, for them, no higher, sacred vision. (How could Abigail fairly bring her son into the Episcopal church, in which she didn't believe? And Harrison Tierney liked to boast he'd been a "confirmed atheist" in the womb.) But "ecology" might be hardly more than cyberspace, to American kids. A video game. Fantasy. Nature consumes all, and defines all. Is there nothing beyond Nature?

No wonder Jared and his friends have no interest, not a scintilla of interest, in History. What's History but old, dead things done by old, dead people.

Life devours life, but man breaks the cycle, man has memory.

So Adam once said. Oh, why hadn't Abigail embraced Jared, to commiserate with him over Adam's death? Why had she been so reluctant to speak to him, frankly?

Because you were pandering to him. His adolescent angst. You were flirting with him. Your own son!

SUICIDE? It might be a mistake. (A terrible mistake!) Since Abigail's estate would go almost exclusively to Jared, her only child; Jared is a minor; so, Harry Tierney, that world-class bastard, would control it. *My mortal enemy. I've got to outlive him!*

NEXT MORNING at precisely ten o'clock the telephone rings and Abigail hesitantly answers it—"Yes?"—resisting the shameful hope this might be Jared (for of course it won't be Jared, never will it be Jared), and there's an adenoidal voice stammering in her ear, "M-Miss Des Pres? Abigail? Hello." Politely Abigail says, "Do I know you?" The caller says, "We met last night? At the Salthill Historic Society." A blurred vision of the architect's homely face rises before her, the melancholy eyes and enormous nostrils and that eager grimace of a smile. Oh God, why had she touched him. Why does Abigail do such things. How cruel she feels in her quilted Laura Ashley robe, barefoot, staring through a window at an edge of a sloping lawn that rises like a sharp green headache out of sight. "My name is Gerhardt Ault? We spoke briefly."

"Yes, of course. You were very—inspiring."

"I was? Thank you!"

Abigail shuts her eyes. Why say such things! As if her mouth, like the decapitated chicken head, must have its own way.

"I try, you know. I believe so—fervently. In what my associates and I are doing. Not just the buildings, you know, but—the environmental sites. Sometimes we look at the landscape first. Where, in the past, the landscape architect would be the last to be called in, and often there wasn't any money to properly—"

Abigail presses her face against a windowpane. She's in one of the many, too many, rooms of the Cape Cod mausoleum. She's exhausted by living alone. *Alone, you think too much. The brain never clicks off till bedtime.* God damn, when Roger Cavanagh kissed her, in this very room, she should have kissed him back, slid her arms around his neck and kissed, kissed. She might've brushed against his groin. That baby Roger is fathering might have been *hers*.

"Would you be free to have d-dinner with me? Tonight?"

"Tonight? Certainly not." Abigail has to think for a moment, to whom she's speaking.

"T-Tomorrow night?"

"I have another engagement. I'm sorry."

How cruel she's feeling. An Amazon, one of her breasts sawed off so that she can fire her arrows more expertly. She understands Camille Hoffmann's weakness for dogs. Doggy-eyes, yearning-panting, crawling to your feet.

"What about—Sunday?"

Abigail sighs. She wants to laugh incredulously. The caller, seemingly shy, tongue-tied Ault, is breathing down her neck! Abigail has to hold the receiver away from her ear.

"Sunday. I suppose so. Thank you. Good-bye!"

It's the only way to escape. Abigail hangs up the phone, and hurries from the room even as, almost immediately, it begins to ring again.

"Harry. Just tell me—how Jared is."

A pause. Harry is obviously shocked to hear her voice.

Or maybe he's trying to place the voice? So many women have passed through his life, sticky for a while, but ephemeral, like pond algae.

"We don't need to talk, otherwise. Just tell me how he *is*."

Harry swallows, hard. This, Abigail can hear.

"Abigail, it wasn't my idea, Jared living with me. But I had to accede to his wishes, you know."

Abigail says nothing. She grips the telephone receiver hard to keep it from trembling as her entire body is trembling.

"He did claim—you know. You tried to kill him."

Abigail shuts her eyes. *Not I! The demon hand.*

"Whether true or not"—Harry is being gracious, this is a surprise—"he seems to believe it. Or to wish to believe it."

"Harry, please. Will you please just simply tell me how Jared *is.*"

"He isn't e-mailing you? I thought he was."

Like hell, you thought.

"You mean he isn't? Like—never?"

Abigail makes a faint, fading sound of acquiescence. The last peep of a decapitated chicken.

"That kid! Well, he's a *kid.*"

"Harrison, don't make me beg. It always comes to this: I crawl, I beg. Just tell me how my son is, is he well?"

There's a long pause. Abigail is feeling anxious. At the other end of the line, background noises (the gorgeous young second-wife Kim, scolding a maid?) are suddenly silenced, as Harry has possibly (Abigail used to wince at such maneuvers) kicked a door shut.

"He's a kid. He's fucked-up like his friends. He's sixteen. You're asking is he 'well'?"

"How is he—'fucked-up'?" Abigail feels, despite her best maternal instinct, a surge of hope. Jared misses his mom! Jared is going through a phase, and will soon be reconciled with his mom.

Harry laughs irritably. "Let me count the ways. Academic, social, familial, psychological. His feet stink."

"It's the shoes. The running shoes. Without socks."

"Jared's feet stink without the benefit of running shoes," Harry says. Abigail sees him, her ex-husband, running his fingers through his thinning hair; screwing up his face like a gargoyle. That look that signaled intense disgust, or the very brink of orgasm. "Though, I grant you, they stink worse with the shoes around." Harry pauses, and now Abigail sees his nose twitch. Harry was always a fastidious man, nauseated by the faintest whiff of baby shit. And Abigail, a young besotted mother, grateful for the excuse to forgo designer clothes, tight-fitting Italian shoes and weekly trips to the hairdresser, had reveled in baby-mess. Even baby shit was fine since it indicated, didn't it, that the gastrointestinal machinery was working right?

"It's just that I get so lonely. I miss Jared."

Another pause. Sudden frank emotion embarrasses Harry Tierney, if he can't turn it into a joke. "Sure. But you two were always fighting, the kid says."

"We were not always fighting!"

"*I* know that, but Jared . . . What does a kid know."

"Has something happened between you and Jared, Harry?"

Harry sighs. Again Abigail feels an absurd little pinprick of hope. "He says you were always nagging him. About smoking. And he says he isn't smoking."

"Harry, I've seen him smoking."

"There're worse things."

"Is he—doing drugs? Is Jared—?"

"He's sixteen. He's at boarding school. When he's technically home, he's in Manhattan. What can I say?"

"Is that it? Drugs? What—kind of drugs?"

Abigail can see Harry screw up his face again, as with a bad smell. She recalls now that he'd come to be bored with her *maternalizing,* as he called it. She'd overheard Harry joke crudely with male friends. *When is a cunt not a cunt? When you call it Mom.* Abigail's face smarts, she wishes she were in her ex-husband's presence so she could claw at his smug-sour fattish face.

Abigail says, pleading, "I didn't nag Jared, truly. But I may have hugged him." *Nag, hug.* You could see how the two, so very different, actions might be confused by a teenaged boy.

"Well. There you are."

Abigail knows that this conversation will leave her exhausted and wounded, like one who has run naked through briars, but she seems incapable of breaking it off. She says, "I didn't try to kill Jared, Harry. You know that—don't you?"

A long pause. "I don't believe you deliberately wanted to kill Jared, or yourself. You aren't a deliberate woman."

Abigail laughs, annoyed. "What am I then, an instinctive woman? A primitive woman?" She has a flash of aboriginal females living in some desperate place like the outback of Australia, swollen with pregnancy, tubular breasts—"dugs"—drooping to their crotches.

"You're a very feminine woman."

"Meaning—?"

"Meaning you don't always anticipate the consequences of your actions. You act, then you reflect."

"And you never reflect at all."

Harry laughs. "Only in reflection do we feel regret. So why?"

Abigail thinks, you can never get the better of Harrison Tierney. He's one to agree with the most extreme interpretations of his motives, always he eludes you.

"'There are no accidents,' the kid says. Some crap he got from your buddy Berendt."

Abigail will let this pass. She reveres Adam Berendt too much to drag him into her old quarrel with Harry Tierney.

Harry laughs. "Except the kid nearly killed me, his dad. I'm limping from it."

"Harry, what happened?"

"We were skiing, in Aspen. Somehow, don't ask how, Jared loses control of his skis and sort of fishtails and slams into me, going down a pretty steep hill, and I'm down and skidding into Kim's skis on my stomach and next I know, I'm waking in an ambulance. Two bad breaks, I mean bad breaks, in my right femur. But at least I don't have a plate in my skull, eh?"

Abigail thinks quickly, he's going to blame her. This is what it will come to.

"Harry, I'm sorry to hear that. I'm—"

"You're smiling your dazzling-debutante smile. Every one of your beautiful teeth lit up." Harry laughs. "Don't bullshit *me*."

It's true, Abigail is smiling. Just her mouth, stretched and twisted.

"Was—Jared hurt?"

"Minor lacerations. You know the kid: unkillable."

"I'm sure it was an accident, Harry. Jared would never deliberately hurt *you*."

"Right."

Abigail knows she should hang up the phone. Talking with Harry is psychic Ping-Pong. But her pulse is quickened, it's impossible to resist. Harry says, "You've heard about Roger Cavanagh?"

"He's 'fathering' another child."

"Fantastic! At his age."

"Roger isn't *old*."

"None of us is old, Abigail. We just aren't young."

"Roger seems very happy. He— "

"He's in a state of shock. Poor bastard."

"Have you met the girl?"

"No, I have not," Harry grunts. Pregnant women have no attraction for him. "Frankly, I was surprised. Roger had a thing for you, I'd always thought."

Abigail lets this pass. She says, "You've heard that Lionel has come home? He and Camille are reconciled."

"Lionel is home, yes I know. The poor asshole is a wreck. But he isn't what you'd call 'reconciled.'"

"This exotic mistress of his, the rumor is"—(why is Abigail saying such things, like bringing a lighted match to something flammable, she knows she'll regret it)—"that you introduced her to Lionel. One of your 'therapists.'"

Harry laughs heartily. But doesn't deny it.

Another of Harry Tierney's stratagems. Don't apologize, don't explain. Don't deny. Abigail says slyly:

"A therapist who's also a part-time hooker. A light-skinned 'exotic' from Jamaica."

"Jamaica? Who the hell told you that?"

Abigail smiles. The look on Harry's face! She can imagine. Few of his friends know that Harry Tierney is a closet racist.

"People. You know Salthill."

"I know Salthill," Harry says furiously, "which is why I moved away."

"You didn't know that Lionel's girl was—is—a light-skinned black?"

There's a pause. Abigail can hear her ex-husband breathing. She wonders if Kim, the replacement wife, has quietly picked up the receiver to eavesdrop on her husband's conversation with his ex-wife; these intense, adrenaline-pumping sessions are a special sort of adultery, available only to the formerly married. Abigail wonders if Jared is anywhere near.

No, Jared would be away at school. On neutral territory, at a safe distance from both Dad and Mom.

Harry says, "Siri isn't. She is not. What you've said—Siri *is not.*" Harry makes a grunting noise to indicate the subject had better be dropped. Asking, in his own sly way, "And how the hell are *you,* Abby? I've heard things."

Abby! This translates into *you pathetic bitch.* "What sort of things?"

"Things."

This will be like poking a comatose body with a stick. Abigail's the body, Harry wields the stick. Not to torture, exactly. To see if the comatose can register pain.

Still, Abigail is alert, interested. Lacking an inner life, she requires knowing that others imagine a life for her.

"You 'date' a lot of men. Mostly cripples."

Abigail laughs, stung. "Actually, I'm thinking of quitting."

"Quitting what?"

"Dating a lot of men." Abigail laughs again, a sound as of a small creature being strangled. She adds, almost inaudibly, "No. Life. Quitting fucking *life.*"

Silence at Harry's end. Not a profound silence but an awkward fidgety silence. Here is a man who'd been embarrassed by a pea-sized growth in his wife's breast. He'd been embarrassed, and annoyed, by his father's death, which had been prolonged, and in the end, to Harry, needing to travel abroad for business purposes, impractical and tedious. Then Harry manages to laugh, nervously. Abigail can imagine his cheeks flaming crimson. Quickly Abigail amends, "Hey. I don't mean it, of course."

Flatly Harry says, "I know you don't," and hangs up.

"'LIVING.' What we take for granted other people have a knack for."

Abigail speaks aloud into the silence that surrounds her. She can't recall if Adam originally made this gnomic remark, or if it's her own discovery. "If Adam said it, it's profound. If I, 'Abby,' have said it, it's just another wistful little wounded-cunt remark."

Silence.

Abigail waits for Adam, or someone, to refute her.

She laughs. "Of course I date 'cripples.' Who else?"

Does Adam Berendt disapprove of Abigail's self-hating mood? Is the man being stubborn, or coy? Or is Adam simply—not there?

Abigail, cut the crap. You know I don't exist. I'm ashes. You said it yourself: fertilizer.

SHREWD! Abigail insists upon meeting Gerhardt Ault at the restaurant, the Swan's Ferry Inn on the river, so she has her own car, and the possibility of escape. Though she's hopeful. She is not cynical. "I like him. 'Gerhardt.'" She doesn't recall what he looks like very clearly. She wonders if Hitler's architect's name was Gerhardt. *You date a lot of men. Mostly cripples.* Abigail wants to protest, she doesn't date many men. She never has.

It's a mild spring evening. Daylight Saving Time has caused the sun to prevail through lengthy days. If you like lengthy days, this is an upbeat season. If you like manic fluorescent "splashes" of azaleas blooming everywhere, this is not a cynical season. Why not be hopeful. That very day, Abigail volunteered to introduce Donegal Croom, the Irish-American poet who will read from his work at the Festival of Flowers luncheon in mid-May; she has committed herself to remaining alive that long, at least.

"I would never let my women friends down. Never!"

Abigail arrives twenty minutes late at the Swan's Ferry. Gerhardt, seated at their table, squinting at a book he's brought along to read in flickering candlelight, has the look of a man who has arrived twenty minutes early. When Abigail approaches him, he glances up startled, as if he's forgotten who Abigail is, and why he's here. At once, Gerhardt struggles to his feet, and his napkin, unfolded in his lap, falls to the floor, somehow twisting in his ankles. "Abigail! This is so—it's—" Gerhardt stammers, blinking and smiling at Abigail, clumsily shaking her hand. "Yes! It *is*," Abigail says. Quickly she sits, smiling her most vacant smile. As always the koan *Why, why am I here, why here* begins in her head, but she beats it back like a housewife with a broom. The next swirl of words is *A drink, a quick drink!* but this, too, Abigail beats back. Gerhardt has already begun talking. His melancholy-dog eyes are fixed upon Abigail eagerly. He is telling her—what? She tries to listen. She tries. Gerhardt Ault is a very nice man. You see them everywhere in Salthill: very nice deadly-dull middle-aged men. Most of them are husbands. (Why isn't Gerhardt Ault a husband? Abigail has a sinking sensation, she'll soon be told why.)

In the romantically flickering candlelight Gerhardt looks alarmingly vulpine. Tonight he's wearing a very white boxy-looking shirt with a large collar, a checked bow tie (snap-on), and another loose-fitting tweed coat. His fair, colorless hair lies in odd collapsed tufts on his head like transparent Thai noodles. When he smiles, Abigail has an impulse to count his teeth: surely there are too many? Gerhardt is wearing bifocal reading glasses, which he hurriedly removes and stuffs into his coat pocket, with the vanity of a shy, homely man who hopes he isn't, somehow. *To be redeemed in another's myopic eyes. The aim of all romance*. Abigail asks what Gerhardt is reading, and Gerhardt tells her.

Drinks are ordered: Perrier water, with a twist of lime, for both.

Abigail would like to ask if Gerhardt, too, has a good reason for not drinking, but of course she doesn't. She's far too tactful. And it would only be depressing to learn that he's "always been" allergic to alcohol.

As Gerhardt talks, animatedly, his bright blurry gaze fixed upon her face, Abigail glances covertly about the restaurant to see if any of her friends are here tonight. Or maybe it's just Adam Berendt she seeks. The Swan's Ferry Inn (1791) is one of the "historic" sites on the river, a three-star restaurant, costly, dungeon-dark, with equestrian prints on the walls, riding crops and horse gear; on a nearby wall there's a large oil painting of President George Washington in ceremonial attire, stiff curled wig, royal-red coat, gold-braid epaulets, brass-handled sword, the jeweled insignia of the Society of Cincinnati on his lapel, and in the background, like a child's cartoon drawing, the president's gorgeous canary-yellow coach drawn by six white horses. Though Washington was relatively young at the time of the portrait, he looks dour and middle-aged as if his face has been baked. Washington had been a frequent patron of the Swan's Ferry Inn, it was claimed. As he'd been a patron of Deppe House a few miles away. (The tavern exclusively, or the brothel as well?) Adam used to joke darkly of bones buried in the dirt floor of his cellar . . . In the near-to-the-end days of Abigail Tierney's marriage she'd met Adam Berendt sometimes here; their favored spot wasn't the pretentious dining room but the pub, beside the fireplace. What a setting for romance! Abigail sighs. Abigail recalls with sudden clarity the winter evening her feet were freezing, in thin kidskin open-heeled sandals, and Adam lifted her stocking feet into his lap beneath their table to warm them with his hands. His strong sculptor's hands. The gesture was both intimate and nonsexual. As if Abigail were a child, and Adam her mildly chastising father. But Abigail couldn't resist wriggling her toes into Adam's groin. And Adam visibly blushed, and pushed her feet away. "Hey. I'm sorry," Abigail whispered. Not that she was. Abigail's rarely sorry. Adam shifted his shoulders uncomfortably, looking at her with his good eye, saying, "You're a married woman, still. You shouldn't play at adultery." Abigail said, "Play? Who's playing?" It was true, she and Harry were still officially living together, when Harry wasn't in their Manhattan apartment, but Abigail understood that her time as Mrs. Tierney was rapidly running out. Only a few weeks before, she'd had the biopsy; her husband had seemed repulsed by her, as if she were already disfigured. Abigail hadn't wanted to tell Adam about this (was she ashamed of herself, too?) but she did tell him, "When I was a girl, I thought 'adultery' was something you got to do, when you were an adult. Like playing bridge."

(Was this true? Were any of Abigail's disarming little tales of herself true?) Adam grunted a vague disapproving reply, and changed the subject.

Why had Abigail agreed to meet Gerhardt at the Swan's Ferry, of all places? Suddenly she's frightened, she'll begin crying.

Gerhardt is speaking of his "deceased wife, Gail." So soon! And at an awkward time, as the smiling waiter looms over them with enormous menus that look like engraved slabs of marble. As Abigail scans the blurry cursive script, appetizers, first courses, entrées, she tries to concentrate on her companion's words, a rush of words, a waterfall of words, as if the wounded man hasn't uttered such words to anyone, and has chosen Abigail, and this damned awkward moment, for a reason fathomable only to himself. Dividing her attention between appetizers and Gerhardt Ault's stammered grief! He confides in her that his wife died six years before, of pancreatic cancer—"The oncologist told us five months, at first. But it was less than three." The deceased Mrs. Ault had been an architect, too; her specialty was churches; Gerhardt has "yet to recover from the trauma." Abigail, nodding sympathetically, glances at the blurry column of entrées, no red meat for her, possibly coq au vin, possibly swordfish steak, scampi, no sweetbreads . . . Gerhardt is leaning both elbows on the table, leaning forward hunched, his melancholy eyes gleaming, big pit-nostrils contracting and expanding, pouring out his grief to Abigail Des Pres as one might blindly dump a gallon container of liquid into a teacup. She interprets Gerhardt's pronouncement perhaps unfairly: *Don't think you will ever wedge yourself into my life. I'm pure, I'm deep. I'm a mourner.* When Abigail says nothing, biting her lip, reluctant to offer the congealed remains of her own domestic sorrow, the Divorce and the Loss-of-Son, Gerhardt swerves on more severely, hunching farther forward with the crisis-look of a downhill skier on the brink of losing control. "And there's our daughter Tamar. She's eleven. She's adopted. She's still traumatized. She's mute sometimes—for days." Tears well in Gerhardt's eyes. Abigail swallows hard. "It must be hard to communicate with her," Abigail says, "—if she's, well, mute. It's hard enough to communicate with—"

(But what is Abigail saying? She can't possibly say *normal children.*) Her words trail off vaguely, apologetically. "Tamar is adopted," Gerhardt says. He has pushed aside his marble-slab menu, not having glanced into it. Abigail feels cruel, crude, greedy, for having glanced into hers, and shuts it. "Gail was so yearning for a baby—'Someone to live for, beyond just *us.*' I saw her point of course. A man might not be quite so r-ready for this next stage as a woman, but—I—I loved Gail—I would have done anything Gail wanted. To make her happy. There was this entire side of her I hadn't known about until after we were married, a sort of—maternal-spiritual side. I have to admit, I was surprised! I wasn't very mature perhaps. I've always focused on my work. I've been called a workaholic. Well, I w-wanted a baby, too. I mean—I didn't *not want a baby.*" Gerhardt looks as if he's drowning. Abigail murmurs, to console him, "Of course! It is different for a man." *A man shoots his seed into a small hole out of which, nine months later, a woman pushes a watermelon with arms and legs. That's the difference.* Gerhardt says, grateful for Abigail's understanding, "We tried! And we tried. We went to fertility specialists, clinics. We prayed! Finally we went to a Christian adoption agency—Gail's from a family of Presbyterian missionaries—and were put in contact with a 'birth mother' in, first it was Romania, but that didn't work out, and finally—" Gerhardt is speaking now with an air of mystification and aggrievement. Does this kindly, confused man regret his daughter? Does he wish the burden of her gone from his life? Abigail sees their waiter hovering a few yards away, with a frayed, stoic half-smile. Abigail begins to say something both conciliatory and practical, to nudge Gerhardt into acknowledging the very real, actual setting, the expectation that they will order meals and eat them and pay for them and leave, within a calibrated two hours at the outside, but suddenly tears flood her eyes, Abigail Des Pres is beginning to cry, Abigail Des Pres is crying, sabotaging her flawless cosmetic mask of a face; she's astonished at such weakness, such gauche social behavior; breaking down in a public place; she blames Adam, his damned puritanical behavior in their cozy pub corner. Abigail hides her flaming face in her white linen napkin. She rises from the table blindly. Murmuring an excuse, an apology—"I c-can't stay. Good night!"

Abigail flees the dining room of the Swan's Ferry Inn. In a haze of tears, mortification, grief, she hears a man calling after her—"Abigail!"—but it isn't a voice she recognizes, a voice to stop her dead in her tracks.

Cross what's-his-name off the list. One less cripple.

THROUGH HER LIFE, Abigail Des Pres has had "lost moments." As she calls them. When she understands what it will be like not to *be*. The atmosphere of the house on Wheatsheaf Drive, the tranquil emptiness of the rooms, from which the person she has been, or has thought she'd been, has finally departed.

SOMETIMES LAUGHING, surprising herself. What's so funny?

"The look on Harry's face. I could see it! When he told me about the skiing 'accident.' Jared plowing into him." Abigail wipes her eyes, it *is* funny, the spectacle of Harry, Jared, and the gorgeous second-wife what's-her-name Kim, sprawled on their assess in the snow.

"Adam? Hey c'mon, crack a smile."

Abigail. Why laugh at others' misfortune?

"Fuck you. 'Cause it's funny, that's why."

Do you want Harry to laugh at you?

"Sure. I'm funny as hell, let the prick laugh. We used to have great times together, Harry making me laugh. Like tickling with rough fingers. Harry doing his 'ethnic-minority' imitations. Of course they weren't funny in any human, moral way, but they were hilarious as hell in a sick, nasty way."

Are you still in love with Harry, Abigail?

"Asshole! I'm in love with you."

You're in love with the hurt he inflicted on you. It's become your ID tag.

"Like hell. Know what? I wish Harry was dead! Well, sort of dead. Not brain-dead. Paralyzed, maybe. Yes! If Jared had torn into him and sliced his spine in two, so he's just a head propped up in a wheelchair now, pushed around by Kim rolling her eyes behind his head, that's exactly what I wish."

Abigail, you should be ashamed of yourself. Such bitterness isn't worthy of you, have you been drinking?

"Fuck you, who wants to know? None of your business."

You promised Roger. He saved your ass up in Middlebury, remember?

"Fuck Roger. Roger has broken my heart."

You sent Roger away, Abigail. You don't love him.

"I did love Harry, at first. There's nobody like your first. I was a virgin, and there came Harry jamming his boot heel into my cunt. They say women aren't by nature masochistic, it's culture that makes us sick, but how can we know? There's no culture without nature. There's no—shit, what am I saying, Adam? Do I know what I'm talking about?"

You're making a subtle distinction, Abigail. But it's gotten away from you.

"Harry was our unconscious. Mine, and Salthill's. I don't love him but I do miss him. Almost as much as I miss you, Adam."

Now you've said a daring, profound thing. What an insight, for a Salthill resident!

"But, Adam, is it true?"

Silence.

"Adam, please tell me. *Is* it true?"

Silence. God damn Adam where is he, playing his *if you can catch me* game as always.

"Adam? Hey, c'mon." Abigail is on her feet managing to keep her balance. Once, she'd been a lithe, floating girl-dancer, now there are weights attached to her ankles. She's staggering—swaying—careening through empty rooms. A vertigo-sequence, as in an infinitely reflecting mirror, of empty empty empty beautifully furnished rooms.

* * *

A TELEPHONE MESSAGE from a man who mumbles his name, apologizing if he'd "upset" her, saying he would "very much" like to see her again or at least speak with her "sometime soon, I hope" and Abigail quickly punches "3" for erase. *No more cripples!*

IN THE SALTHILL PUBLIC LIBRARY on this fine May morning there's a sudden commotion near the entrance, just beyond the turnstiles. Abigail, drawn by curiosity, approaches to see a middle-aged woman with flushed cheeks and short-trimmed graying hair, in a denim coverall with sunflower pockets, confronted by one of the librarians—"Mrs. Hoffmann, please! You know that dogs are not allowed in the library."

It's Camille Hoffmann!

Abigail stares at her friend from a short distance. And keeps her distance.

How incensed Camille is! How firm she stands, legs like tree trunks. Camille's maternal-mammalian softness seems to have yielded to a tougher, more obdurate substance. Her voice is controlled, with an undercurrent of threat. "Excuse me. These are not *dogs*. These are not dogs *merely*." Camille is gripping, on leashes, two large, handsome dogs: Adam's Apollo, who has obeyed his mistress's order to sit; and a lean, sleek young Doberman pinscher, too skittish to stay in one place, tugging at the leash and growling deep in his throat. Abigail recognizes Apollo immediately, of course, but the Doberman is new to her.

A number of library patrons have gathered to observe the confrontation, discreetly. Such public-commotion scenes, in Salthill, are rare. Abigail feels a duty to intervene, but—what could she say? ("Frankly," Abigail would confide in Beatrice Archer afterward, "I was afraid of that Doberman pinscher.") The embarrassed, uneasy librarian insists that Camille must leave her dogs outside the library; Camille repeats that the dogs "are not dogs merely"; the librarian threatens to "call security"; at last Camille turns, with dignity, murmuring, "Apollo! Thor! We will not stay where we are not wanted. And we will cease all financial contributions, believe me, where we are not wanted. *Come.*"

In Camille's wake, a furtive outburst of applause, in which Abigail Des Pres, who is Camille's friend, does not join.

A sudden scratching at the door of her bedroom.

Boldly the door is pushed open before Abigail can rouse herself fully from sleep.

A furry animal! Apollo! Trotting into the darkened room, bearing in his strong jaws what appears to be an old red flannel shirt. Adam's gardening shirt, soiled with earth.

Abigail is out of bed, and tugging at the shirt. Apollo will not release it. Abigail persists. Apollo shakes his head, and growls in warning. Abigail persists, growing desperate.

Through the long panting night the struggle continues.

"I AM DEEPLY HONORED. I am thrilled. As an undergraduate at Bennington College . . ."

As an undergraduate at Bennington College in the late seventies, an idealistic "arts" major, Abigail Des Pres frequently fell in love with older, unattainable men; and one of these, when she was a nineteen-year-old sophomore, was the Irish-American poet Donegal Croom. At the time, Croom had just published his first collection of poems, *SeaChange,* and was being hailed in the United States as an heir of Dylan Thomas and "a more lyric" William Butler Yeats. Amid a pack of excitable, admiring young women in a white woodframe barn on the college campus, Abigail listened with a quickened heartbeat to the darkly handsome Croom read his passionate, incantatory poetry, which was less obscure than Thomas's and Yeats's poetry but lush, sensuous, "toughly eloquent" and "elemental, mesmerizing" (as reviewers on both sides of the Atlantic praised). Abigail wept with happiness. She'd never been so deeply moved by any public performance. Immediately after the reading she bought Croom's book, and waited in a long line of eager girls for the poet to sign it.

to Abrigail—

Donegal Croom

3 Nov. 1978

(He'd spelled her name wrong!—added an "r"!)

(Or was that a secret message?)

Abigail thanked the poet shyly and stumbled by. If Donegal Croom had given her so much as a second glance, a lithe, slender girl with gleaming dark hair to her waist, in black leotards and an oversized T-shirt, Abigail was too agitated to notice. She was of an age, still virginal, if only barely, and deeply romantic, to clutch the sea-green book to her heart. She, too, wrote poetry, in breathless fragments, and envisioned one day that she might set her poetry to music, and dance; she would be poet, composer, choreographer, and dancer in one. (Her Bennington teachers, former sixties radicals with predilections for the more esoteric, inspirational drugs, encouraged Abigail as they encouraged her classmates, talented and otherwise.) For days after Donegal Croom's reading, lines of poetry, musical, divorced from meaning, shimmered in Abigail's head; like butterflies with fluttering wings; almost, she could see them; almost, she could catch hold of them; but they eluded her. And yet—how beautiful. She knew!

Now, twenty-four years later, Abigail still has her copy of *SeaChange*, which has become in the interim a collector's item. Croom has written a number of books of poetry, he has won a number of prizes including the Pulitzer, his reputation in some quarters is still very high. (Out of curiosity, typing in "Donegal Croom" on the Web, Abigail discovers that a signed first edition of *SeaChange* in mint condition is worth as much as $3,000. "Of course, I would never sell it.") Rereading the slender book, Abigail feels a vestige of the old, visceral shock; not so strong as it had been, but palpable nonetheless. As the dust jacket claims, this is a poetry of magic and of Eros. "If only. When I held my book out to him, our eyes had met."

Abigail visits the Salthill Bookstore to purchase other books by Donegal Croom. In the window there's a display of a half-dozen books of his, as well as a publicity photo of the ruggedly handsome, long-haired poet in his prime. The face is older, but unmistakably Irish; the hair is coarsely threaded with gray, framing the weathered face. How old is Croom? In his mid-forties? Abigail has learned that Croom has been married three times but is unmarried, at least officially, at the present; this, she takes to be a good sign. *He's available. Maybe he's lonely.* The window display is in anticipation of Donegal Croom's appearance at the Festival of Flowers, which is being advertised everywhere in Salthill. What a good cause it is! Though for a moment Abigail can't remember what it is. She pushes open the door to the bookstore, the bell tinkles quaintly overhead. She feels a welcome sense of sanctuary in Marina Troy's old-fashioned quarters with its framed photographs of T. S. Eliot and Virginia Woolf, James Joyce, Willa Cather, William Faulkner, and other icons of the past century on the walls, as remote to the new electronic-Internet age as the gods of antiquity. These are noble figures Abigail admires and intends to "reread" sometime soon.

Entering the Salthill Bookstore, Abigail invariably glances about, with a tinge of guilt, looking for Marina Troy. (The guilt is because Abigail has tried, to a degree, to seduce Roger Cavanagh; and there's a prevailing sense in Salthill that Roger and Marina Troy are in some way, however undefined and perhaps unconsummated, a couple.) Abigail misses Marina! For years she's felt a one-sided attraction for Marina; as one might feel for an eccentric, difficult younger sister, or cousin; a solitary version of Abigail herself, bravely immune to the blandishments and temptations of men. *In her soul, she's a virgin. No one can conquer her.* But Abigail hasn't seen Marina for a long time.

"Mrs. Des Pres, hello!"

Abigail forces a smile as Marina's assistant Molly Ivers greets her, as always a little too loudly. Molly is a hale, hearty Girl Scout type, in a bulky purple caftan and black nylon trousers; her straw hair falls in a childish fringe around her broad puppet-face. Where Marina was shyly welcoming, Molly loves to greet customers! It's being said that, despite intense competition from mall stores and from the Internet, the little store on Pedlar's Lane has been doing surprisingly well in Marina's absence, the result of her intrepid manager's relentless campaigning: readings by local poets and writers, receptions featuring gourmet appetizers, the Salthill String Quartet, Sunday and late-night hours. How does she do it, Molly Ivers is asked, and in an interview in the *Salthill Weekly Gazette* Molly confessed, "I never sleep!"

In Salthill it's begun to be rumored that Marina Troy will never return. She'll lease or sell the store to Molly. *So devastated by Adam Berendt's death, poor woman.*

Abigail knows she shouldn't inquire, she'll only be rebuffed, but she can't resist asking how Marina is, and Molly says, circumspectly, "Oh, Marina is very well, thank you." Abigail wants to ask where Marina has been since last fall but already she has asked this question and been rebuffed, as others in her social circle have asked Molly, and been primly rebuffed; instead, Abigail asks when Marina is expected to return to Salthill, and Molly says, lowering her voice as if granting Abigail a special favor, "Oh, Mrs. Des Pres! Marina has been working on art, 'sculpted pieces,' and she's very happy, she says. She hopes to return in the fall, and to have an exhibit of her work then." Abigail is astonished by this revelation. She prefers to think of Marina Troy as a more neurotic, piteous version of herself. "*She's* happy? You mean she's—" Abigail pauses, not knowing what she's saying. *She's recovered from Adam's death? How can that be?*

Of course Abigail can't ask such a question. And if she did ask, Molly Ivers wouldn't have known how to reply.

Abigail buys several paperback books by Donegal Croom and drives to a park near the Salthill Middle School, to sit on a bench and read. She notes that cover photos of Croom depict the poet as virtually unchanging over the decades. His poetry, critics have marveled, is "elemental"—"fierce"—"lyrical and savage"—"potent as a force of nature." Abigail reads, enthralled, though not always with full comprehension, of the ancient Gaelic warrior-hero Cuchulain, and of the cruel god of the Mexican Aztecs, Quetzalcoatl, overseer of lavish sacrificial rites, flaying, and cannibalism. Croom's poems are populated with falcons, snakes, panthers, sharks, stallions, and bulls. Abigail feels a shuddery identification with the eviscerated horses of Croom's controversial poem, "The Bullfight"—

> As the screaming horses' entrails twist
> in dust & Time
> so my soul twists in mad resis-
> trance to Oblivion.

Abigail admires the clever slant-rhyme (if that's what it is) and the poet's "intransigent and stoic vision of nature 'before God was love,' to quote Croom's mentor D. H. Lawrence" (a quote from the book cover).

Abigail glances up, hearing voices and laughter. Young teenagers on their way home from school. She feels a pang of loss: Jared is gone from her, and shows no sign of wanting to return. She hasn't seen the Chinese girl in the red beret for—how long? Two weeks? For all Abigail knows the girl has vanished. Her family has moved away from Salthill. Or the girl had never been. Abigail feels a stabbing sensation in the region of her heart, the loss of a presence she never knew.

"I AM DEEPLY HONORED. I am thrilled. As an undergraduate at Bennington College . . ."

On the day of the Festival of Flowers, Abigail rises early. She anxiously rewrites, rehearses her introduction of Donegal Croom. What if the poet, notoriously "sensitive," is offended by her fawning praise! She has an appointment with her hairdresser at nine o'clock. She makes her face up with elaborate, talismanic care. *The eyes especially. His poetry is filled with eyes.* She changes her clothes several times, like a giddy young girl in another, more romantic era. At last, in a newly purchased Hermès suit of raw silk, champagne-colored, worn with a black silk scarf and a smart black straw hat and black Gucci pumps, Abigail arrives a half-hour early at the Salthill Inn, as Beatrice Archer has requested. So excited! *My destiny. My fate. Why not? I'm still young.* Abigail has spent so many hours reading and rereading Croom's poetry, writing and rewriting her five-minute introduction, the pupils of her eyes look as if she's been mainlining belladonna and her brain hasn't been so taxed since college, when she had to concoct twenty-page word-cocoons on such subjects as light and dark imagery in Joseph Conrad's *Heart of Darkness,* "original sin" in William Golding's *Lord of the Flies,* the theme of the "double" in Dostoyevsky's *Crime and Punishment.* She sees, in the lobby of the Inn, her friend Beatrice with an older, slack-faced man in a denim jacket. "Abigail, come here!" Beatrice is anxious, and clutches at Abigail's hand like a schoolgirl. The man in the denim jacket must be—Donegal Croom? Abigail stares, shocked. Of course she knows that the poet must be older than she recalls, but this is like meeting Donegal Croom's father . . . His hair is wanly leonine, falling in putty-colored wings that frame his red-cobweb face; his nose is frankly swollen; his eyes are bloodshot and appear not quite in focus. Yet he wears a youthful denim jacket and black T-shirt and jeans; his stomach pushes out above the buckle of his hemp belt. In his left earlobe he's wearing a single gold stud that winks like a perverse little eye. When Beatrice introduces Abigail, Croom peers at her rudely. His nostrils sniff like an aroused dog's. He's hardly more than Abigail's height: has he shrunken? He gives off a faintly sour odor, mixed with a fresher scent of toothpaste and cologne. He looks as if he hasn't shaved for a day or more, nor has he combed through his snarled hair. Abigail hears herself laughing giddily. "Mr. Croom, you called me 'Abrigail,' once. A long time ago." Croom says in a booming voice, "Good! That calls for a pre-luncheon drink, 'Abrigail'." He steers her away from Beatrice Archer and several other smiling women waiting to be introduced to the famous poet, and leads her into the dimly lit "tap room" off the lobby. It's only just twelve noon, there's no one behind the bar. "Bartender!" Donegal Croom bares his teeth in a grimace of a smile and pounds on the bar with his fist. "This is an emergency." Abigail, mortified, stands by his side; he's holding her wrist, as if keeping her hostage. Croom says, "Salt-hill. A suburb of New York City? Have I been here before, dear? You're very beautiful but you all look alike." Abigail tries to explain that Salthill-on-Hudson isn't a suburb really, it's a village dating back to the early 1700s, but Croom, distracted by his quest for a bartender, isn't listening. She wants to tell him how powerful his poetry is; how much it has meant to her, over the years; what a solace poetry is, as one experiences the turmoil of life . . . At last a moustached black man in a crisp white coat emerges, polite if unsmiling, and takes drink orders. "Two single malt whiskeys. Straight." Abigail isn't clear whether one of these is for her, or whether both are for the poet; she won't touch any drink that contains alcohol, she vows. Quickly Donegal Croom swallows down half his whiskey, with a sigh of satisfaction. He's sitting now on one of the bar stools, his head in his hands. At his feet is a battered canvas suitcase; he'd come to Salthill directly from La Guardia, and hasn't yet checked into his room at the Inn, where he's staying the night. He seems to have forgotten that Abigail is with him, raising the whiskey glass to his mouth, rocking a little on the bar stool, shoulders hunched. He's murmuring to himself—what? Abigail imagines Gaelic words, potent and mysterious. At such close quarters Abigail can see how thin Donegal's hair is at the back of his head; it looks as if his hair is sliding down, exposing his pale-pink scalp. Donegal finishes the second whiskey and calls for a third, but Abigail daringly intercedes: "No more for Mr. Croom, please! We have to leave now."

Croom turns to Abigail, scowling. He seems, for a moment, not to know who she is. Then, sighing, he says, "Good. You're quite right, dear. Always, you're right." He lays an unexpectedly gentle hand on Abigail's slender shoulder. His fingers crinkle the beautiful raw silk. "They've sent you to me, eh? My muse. Good." Swaying on his bar stool, Donegal leans in Abigail's direction as if he's about to kiss her; Abigail stands unmoving, as if hypnotized. What is happening? What does Croom mean by calling her his muse? In the doorway, Beatrice Archer and several other committee members are signaling anxiously. Abigail says softly, "Mr. Croom, excuse me? I think we must leave now. Will you come with me?"

"Anywhere, dear. With you. *La belle dame de merci.*"

Croom takes Abigail's hand and kisses the palm, in a gesture so sudden and so intimate, Abigail feels faint. *And my friends saw!* For the moment, Abigail Des Pres can't be happier.

LIKE A LARGE, ungainly fish on its tail Donegal Croom is led by Abigail into the noisy ballroom. Everywhere are banks of flowers, a giddy paradise of flowers, some fresh-cut and others in attractive pots. And there are pyramids of Donegal Croom's books, to be sold after the luncheon, and signed by the poet. What an elegant, festive occasion! Croom stares, like a man waking with difficulty from a dream. "Gaelic" music is being piped into the cavernous space, and Croom seems to be looking about for its source. "I *must* be dead. *Dead* would explain all." Abigail leads Croom through the maze of lavishly decorated tables, determined to get him to the speakers' platform. He's leaning rather heavily on her. He's breathing rather heavily. His hair is falling into his face, his skin is flushed. He stumbles on the steps to the platform, but Abigail steadies him, like an old, dependable wife. Abigail pulls out his chair for him, and sits beside him, smiling. Oh, smiling! Her friends gaze up at her, admiring the black straw hat, the gleaming helmet of hair beneath, the striking Hermès suit; possibly they're envious of Abigail Des Pres, for the first time in years. Abigail likes the feeling. Except she's very nervous. She has no more appetite than Donegal Croom for the luncheon, cream of asparagus soup dribbled with parsley and puff pastries stuffed with seafood, "baby salad greens" dribbled with low-caloric vinaigrette and fresh raspberries for dessert. And meager servings of a very dry, not terribly good chardonnay. (Seeing that Abigail isn't drinking, Donegal Croom unobtrusively appropriates her glass as his own.) Abigail gazes out into the enormous flower-festooned space through the poet's bloodshot eyes: she sees the tables of petal-faced, colorfully costumed women, so many tables, so many women, chattering like birds. What a din! And everywhere clusters of roses, lilies, irises, orchids, gardenias . . . Abigail sees the women of Salthill, her sisters: all of them beautiful. Strange, that all are beautiful. The plain have been transformed into beauties by the magic of affluence. And there are no longer "ugly" women, at all. Meringue hair, glaring cosmetic faces, piranha smiles, jewels that wink like semaphore signals. That commingled drunken smell of myriad perfumes. "Help me, dear. Oh, Chri-ist. I think I might be leaking." Donegal Croom mutters in Abigail's ear, she can't determine if he's serious or joking, his flushed cobweb-face drawn into a grimace of—what? Anticipation, dread? Acknowledgment of the Salthill women's girlish-thrilled applause? But Abigail Des Pres must precede him, and now Beatrice Archer introduces her. In her high-heeled Gucci pumps she's standing at the podium. Trembling visibly. Oh, so frightened! Her friends gaze up at her, willing her to do well. Yet not too well, so that they might envy her even more. "I am deeply honored. I am thrilled. As an undergraduate at Bennington College . . ." In a dream the introduction passes, and suddenly Abigail is returning to her seat, blushing fiercely, wanting to think that the girlish-thrilled applause is at least partly for her. Donegal Croom stands at the podium, nudging his protuberant belly against it. He has put on reading glasses that give him a mock-grandfatherly air, even as the gold stud glitters lewdly in his ear. In Salthill, no men of Croom's generation wear earrings: earrings are worn by gay waiters, and there are not many of these. Behind the podium Croom looms large, sighing improvidently into the microphone, with a sound as of distant thunder. He frowns as he leafs through much-thumbed paperback books with no air of great urgency. Hasn't he prepared his reading? Is he taking this occasion so lightly, that means so much to the Friends of the Salthill Medical Center? Eventually Croom begins speaking, his voice near-inaudible at first and then stronger, and more melodic, like a music box that has been cranked up. In an oracular tone he proclaims to the more than three hundred women in the ballroom, each staring avidly at him, that poetry is a "mystical revelation"—it is "anarchic"—it is "Dionysian"—it is "divination." He confides in them, that poetry has "saved my life." Poetry has "given my life its singular meaning." And that one must, to comprehend poetry as well as to create it, "succumb to the demon within. And have faith!" At this there's a flurry of applause. Croom's bloodshot eyes scan the room, the vertiginous flower-space before him, the rapt uplifted female faces, and begins at last to read, in a voice that rises to passion, or its convincing simulacrum. "The Gyrfalcon"—"The Dying Jaguar"—"The Old Man of the Bog"—"Young Lust"—"Festering Wounds"—"The Feathered Serpent"—"The Bullfight." There's a collective, delicious shudder through the ballroom. What will the genteel women of Salthill-on-Hudson tell their husbands that evening, of the Irish-American poet Donegal Croom's reading? How can they convey the frisson of illicit, brutal pleasure provoked by the man's sensuous words, the subtly erotic forward-thrusting of his pelvis as he drives his lines home? How to speak of the "anarchic-Dionysian" joy in pain; the "rough divination" that touches them at the core of their being, with an adulterous thrill? If the women's sharp eyes have observed that the Donegal Croom who stands before them is a battered-looking wreck in his fifties who bears only a fleeting resemblance to his handsome publicity photos, they are too tactful to acknowledge it; these are women accustomed to not-seeing imperfections in men, though anxiously aware of the smallest imperfections in themselves. Perhaps it gratifies some of the Salthill women to realize that Croom is no more manly or attractive than their own husbands, though assuredly he's a great poet. Hasn't he been awarded a Pulitzer Prize, and numerous other prizes besides? *What wonderful poetry. So inspiring. I bought all of his books! The Festival is such a worthy cause.*

As Donegal Croom reads his perversely sensuous, incantatory poems, Abigail half-shuts her eyes to summon back the Donegal Croom of her youth. A man with whom she'd fallen in love, if at a distance. A gyrfalcon of a man, exuding tenderness, strength, sexual confidence; hinting at mysterious wounds, failures, "losses of the race, and of the soul." In 1978, Croom had recited poems instead of merely reading them, with an air of excitement and discovery. Abigail tries too to summon back her nineteen-year-old self, the naively idealistic virgin with hippie-style hair, who believed she "wanted more than anything in the world" to be a dancer, in the style of the great Balanchine. Of course, by the age of nineteen Abigail Des Pres was already much too old. And she'd lacked, fatally, whatever it is that true dancers possess, that unnameable blend of talent, determination, and audacity. "No. I was a coward. I'm so ashamed!" It's to Adam Berendt she makes this confession, for she understands that, in her moments of most extreme folly, Adam watches over her.

With gusto Donegal Croom launches into what he describes as his most controversial, and most personal poem, "The Dark Muse: A Sestina." There's an apprehensive air in the ballroom as Croom recites in a hushed, incantatory voice what seems to be homage to, or repugnance for, the "female mouth lacking teeth only/ as Death lacks teeth." Abigail feels her face burn. Is she the only woman who knows what Croom is speaking of? The others are smiling vaguely, encouragingly. Abigail is grateful for a noisy clicking-on of the air-conditioning unit, which muffles Croom's words. Her attention is drawn to uniformed waiters moving with gigantic trays through the flower-festooned ballroom, expressionless and mechanical as robots. Mostly young males, of varying skin tones. Caucasian, Asian, black. There's a thin dark-haired boy who resembles Jared except his face is more mature and he carries himself with more manly dignity than Jared could in such circumstances. Abigail can sense the contempt these waiters feel, forced by economics to serve the Salthill women; she notes how pointedly they ignore the ranting poetry of Donegal Croom, as if it were of no more consequence than the vibrating hum of the air conditioner. *Don't judge us harshly! We were once your age.*

Croom cuts off his reading abruptly as if he's tired, or bored; or maybe his audience has annoyed him, listening in primly shocked silence to what was intended to be, Abigail guesses, a "savagely funny" poem. Croom has read less than a half-hour (though he'd contracted for forty minutes, for a $5,000 fee and all expenses) and now declines, with a dismissive wave of his hand, to "take questions" from the audience. Just as well, Abigail thinks. Abigail is on her feet, resplendent in her Hermès suit and black straw hat, leading the applause. Smiling her happiest smile. Her Salthill friends and neighbors applaud generously, for these are generous women, and the strained interlude comes to an end.

As the luncheon breaks up, there comes bronze-highlighted Beatrice Archer to hug Abigail and kiss her warmly on the cheek, smearing lipstick. Beatrice's eyes are damp, dilated. "You were wonderful, Abigail! We're all so proud of *you*."

A reason to live? Why not?

DESPITE DONEGAL CROOM'S ambiguous performance, a respectable number of his books are purchased, profits going to the Salthill Medical Center, and after a laconic book-signing session Croom insists that Abigail accompany him to his room. He's scheduled to spend the night in Salthill—"Recovering and recrudescing." He tells Abigail that he's "feeling shaky"—"on the brink of depressed"—which often happens when he reads his work before audiences "hostile to poetry." Abigail protests, "Oh, Mr. Croom! That audience wasn't hostile to poetry, they adored you." Croom laughs in a wistful-angry-adolescent way that reminds Abigail of Jared, and she feels a tug of sympathy for the man. Croom looks genuinely disappointed. Though he's signed a fair number of books, it isn't enough; no amount of books sold and signed in Croom's sweeping, florid hand will ever be enough. Abigail perceives that Croom is one of those men—invariably, such individuals have been men, in her experience—who take for granted the adulation of others, and are crestfallen when the adulation isn't so lavish as they expect. Her ex-husband Harrison Tierney was one of these men. Though despising others, he wanted their admiration; he'd been infuriated when it was withheld.

Only Adam Berendt was different. So different! Adam was always surprised when anyone liked him.

Abigail accompanies Donegal Croom to his hotel room, in a state of nervous exhilaration. She has been chosen by the famous poet to "be with" him and who knows what this intimacy might lead to? *He seems truly to be attracted to me. An almost mystical rapport.* Maybe Croom remembers Abigail from Bennington, in 1978; maybe she made an impression upon him, indelible through the years. Not very likely, but this is something to cling to! Abigail knows that Croom has had love affairs with several prominent women poets; he has lived with an acclaimed artist; he's been married three times, but has never had any children. ("By my own choice. One insatiable infantile ego in a family is quite enough." So Donegal Croom stated in an interview in the *New York Times,* posted on the Web.) Abigail knows this man is no one to be trusted, yes he'll break her heart, yet here she is helping him into his room, allowing him to lean heavily on her as he sidles toward the bed. He says, sighing, "Oh, God. Where are we. Salt-hill? Hill-of-*Salt?* Suburban-American paradise. The warm bath that leaves you waterlogged and dopey and uncertain—uncaring!—if alive, or dead." Even as he exaggerates his tiredness, Croom seems to be genuinely tired. His breath is short, labored. Possibly he's drunk: during the signing he'd somehow managed to get hold of several more glasses of chardonnay.

So romantic! We'd first met years ago, I was just a girl, an undergraduate at Bennington, then we met again in Salthill, and the old rapport was there, again it was instantaneous, who can explain such things? One must succumb to the demon within, and have faith!

Croom uses the bathroom noisily, leaving the door partly open, there's a long interlude of faucets and coughing-hacking and at last the poet reappears, hair dampened and slicked back, careening in Abigail's direction as she stands, innocently it seems, reading in a copy of Croom's most recent book of poems *The Flayed Heart.* He takes her hand, smiles at her enigmatically, and falls back onto the four-postered bed with a sound as of bones creaking. For a moment his flushed cobweb-face, male beauty in ruins, is contorted in pain. Though Croom seems to have freshened up in the bathroom, yet there's a residue of something sour and unwashed; Abigail's fastidious nostrils pinch against it. "Alone! You've saved my life." Abigail feels both a touch of pride and a touch of apprehension. Yet she obeys when Croom instructs her to untie and remove his shoes, and to loosen his belt, and to turn up the air-conditioning in the room. She obeys when he commands her to sit close beside him on the bed. "My Helen! You're the only one of those bitches who has an *ear*. They invited me to read to them purposely to insult me." Abigail quickly protests that no one has insulted him, on the contrary the audience adored him, the poem "The Bullfight" in particular, such a powerful controversial poem, yes and the audience was deeply engaged by the dark muse—"Of course, the sestina form isn't very familiar to them, Donegal. But they understood subliminally. Your poetry is deep-rooted in the sublime. It appeals to, it profoundly touches, even those unfamiliar with poetic 'form.'" This breathless proclamation, an inspired amalgam of reviewers' quotes, causes the poet, propped up on pillows, to open his broken-egg eyes and peer intently at Abigail. "Really? You think so? Those women understood?" "In their way, yes." Croom smiles slyly. "Poetry is fucking, dear. Subliminally. Did you know?" Abigail is startled by this revelation, but willing to concede Croom's point, for he's the poet after all. He says, "What the poet does, what I attempted, is fucking the audience, collectively; making them feel something, making them come, even against their will. All poets are male, all audiences female. Poetry is the triumph of the superior will, and I don't mean that I, Donegal Croom, am 'superior,' except in the service of poetry, the higher transcendental divination we call poetry, which is both mystical and erotic, Eros as the highest mystery." Croom speaks passionately, yet with an air of vexation. "Do you think this came through to the audience, today? The damned air-conditioning didn't interfere?" Abigail says, "Donegal, yes! Your reading was powerful, and profound, and erotic, and we will all remember it in Salthill for a long, long time."

Croom says, almost humbly, "I don't suppose many poets come to Salthill to read?"

"Not poets of your caliber, Mr. Croom."

Croom fumbles for Abigail's hand, and brings it to his lips. A soft fleshy kiss like a slug's caress. "My dear. My Helen. You *are* my muse. My lovely Hill-of-Salt muse in her ridiculous straw hat. We are strangers yet soul mates. In this hellish place. 'What hours, O what black hours we have spent!' You won't leave me, will you, dear? Until—" Abigail understands that Croom means *until I send you away* but she acquiesces with a smile, removing her ridiculous straw hat and setting it on the bedside table. Croom murmurs endearments, and kisses the soft inside of Abigail's wrist; with her free, slightly shaking hand she strokes his flushed face warm and soft as bread dough. She has become used to the sour-mashy odor of his clothing and feels a stab of tenderness, the poor man is so *tired*. A major poet, his work honored in all the anthologies of twentieth-century poetry, and so *tired*. And only fifty-four! Abigail says suddenly, shyly, fearing a rebuff from Croom, "I—I had a friend, the closest friend of my life, and he's gone from me now, and there's an emptiness in my heart that will never be filled, and—this friend so admired your poetry, Mr. Croom! He taught an art class here in Salthill and he read your poetry to us, to inspire us. Almost as beautifully as you yourself read your poetry, Adam read it." (Is Abigail lying? It's the poetry of Walt Whitman and Gerard Manley Hopkins of which she's thinking, not Donegal Croom's, yet Croom has clearly been influenced by both poets, so there's an unmistakable kinship.)

"Really? *My* poetry? Which poems?" Croom grips Abigail's hand more tightly, speaking with boyish eagerness.

Abigail says, "'SeaChange,' and 'The Feathered Serpent,' and 'The Bullfight' of course, and—'The Flayed Heart.' And many others." Abigail speaks softly, seductively, with widened sincere eyes. Like most women she discovers, in such impromptu, intimate moments, her true talent, and what ease in the talent: *tumescing* the male ego. As Abigail spins her tale, frothy and effortless as a spider spinning her web, Donegal Croom listens ardently, and inspires her, as if their situations are reversed, and Croom is Abigail's muse. "Who was this friend of yours?" Croom asks, and Abigail says, "A sculptor. I miss him." With surprising sympathy Croom studies Abigail, as if seeing her for the first time. "Someone you loved? Who meant a lot to you?" Abigail nods, yes. Her radiant-jonquil look. Almost, she can see herself. Croom asks, "He died, did he? How?" Abigail speaks carefully, not wanting to become emotional. "He drowned. In the Hudson River. Trying to save a child." Croom says, "Drowned! Like Shelley. But it was a hero's death, eh? Good for him, he had the guts. How old was he?" Abigail hesitates, assessing her options: to say that Adam was Donegal's age at the time of his death might arouse anxiety in the poet, and defeat the erotic urgency of this exchange; to say that Adam was older would be to suggest that Abigail herself is older; yet to pretend that Adam was younger than his age is somehow repellent. "Adam was—no age I knew. Ageless. We were lovers who touched each other rarely, yet so deeply, I don't think we ever knew, or cared in the slightest, about mere facts. The outsides of things." Croom is in agreement. He's been stroking Abigail's arm, her shoulder, her gleaming hair. He says, "It's strange, isn't it, profound and banal simultaneously, how we can 'love' only a few individuals of the thousands we meet in a lifetime. We try, sometimes—but it comes too late."

Defiantly Abigail says, "No. It can never come too late. Love can be—reborn."

Croom laughs sadly. He's been tugging at the crotch of his rumpled jeans. He says, in a lowered voice, "My dear Helen! In 'The Dying Jaguar' I touch upon a personal, private matter, I've told virtually no one, I suppose, yes, I am ashamed, I am deeply mortified, my male vanity has been wounded, but I must tell you: I've had prostate cancer, and my prostate has been 'removed,' as they so delicately say. The cancer was stopped in time, evidently. But I haven't much control over my bladder. I wear a diaper, dear. Continuously. I've grown accustomed to it, as I suppose women grow accustomed to menstruating, wearing sanitary pads, tampons, soaking up blood, and worrying that others might detect the odor. My predicament is worse, of course: my body is pissing all the time, like a leaking faucet."

Abigail stares at Donegal Croom, too astonished to react.

"Oh, yes: I'm impotent, too. That goes without saying, eh?"

Croom chuckles. Still he's stroking Abigail's hair, with an expression of tenderness. His breathing has steadied, he seems less distressed. Though very tired. His eyelids are beginning to droop. It would seem a very late hour, and not mid-afternoon of a sunny May day. It would seem a remote, secret place, a kind of cave, and not a handsome if rather overfurnished room in the "historic" Salthill Inn. Croom is rapidly sinking into sleep, and Abigail remains close beside him, reluctant to leave just yet; not certain if she has been dismissed. "I could love you anyway, Donegal. I love your poetry!" Abigail whispers. But Croom's bluish eyelids have shut as decisively as if invisible thumbs have shut them. His mouth droops slackly, his lips are moist, flaccid. Croom begins to snore wetly, and in his sleep he twitches, like a large dog trying without success to shake himself. And then he stumbles, as if tripping over a curb. Abigail strokes the man's face, his coarse hair, feeling a strange sort of contentment. *Is this it? It is!* She senses Adam Berendt watching. Adam has, Adam will, watch over her. She has no reason to live except Adam would wish her to live. And this encounter with Donegal Croom, she'll remember as poignant, spiritual. Shimmering lines of poetry come to her, soft and fleeting as petals, or butterflies' wings. A dancing flame, so lovely. Abigail's eyes flood with tears of gratitude. She reaches out to touch the flame—and it has vanished.

WHEN ABIGAIL RETURNS, exhausted, to the mausoleum-house on Wheatsheaf Drive, one of her phone messages is a faltering, stammering voice she vaguely recognizes, with a stab of guilt. And annoyance. "Abigail Des Pres? H-Hello! This is Gerhardt? Ault? You remember me, I hope—we met at—" Abigail Des Pres, *la belle dame sans merci,* fast-forwards the tape, "—was wondering if, one of these evenings, if you were free, and if"—(why are some phone messages so *long,* virtually *sagas,* by their conclusions you've forgotten their beginnings but aren't likely to replay them)—"and w-w-would you consider, I know this is abrupt, and unconventional, and it may offend you, Abigail, but w-would you consider, I mean *purely as an abstract proposition,* m-marrying? *Me?*"

Abigail is too exhausted to be shocked. Even incredulous. Nor is she certain she has heard this message correctly. She punches "3" to erase, without replaying.

A MELANCHOLY SEASON for romance!

Abigail would think no more of her shy stammering architect-suitor Gerhardt Ault (though she continues to hear encouraging things about him in Salthill: he's a "good" "kind" "decent" "very successful" widower) except, the following Monday, there she is driving into Salthill on another of her trivial but lifesaving suburban missions, and by chance she sees Gerhardt Ault and the petite Chinese girl in the red beret, hand in hand, crossing a wedge of lawn near the arts council. The two appear to be companionable, if not talking at the moment. Gerhardt is carrying the girl's cello case.

Abigail stares, astonished. "*His* daughter!"

Managing to drive past without being seen. Her heart beating in helpless, fainting love.

DEARDEADDAD

I

AT FIRST, on Roger Cavanagh's computer screen, the message from his daughter, Robin, glimmered like a small gem of a poem.

DEARDEADDAD

i doubt you are my
  true father
there is NOTHING of you
    in me
& I prefer it that way

  please NEVER contact
    me again
  to tell me the lie
   you "love" me

(r)

2

"Yes, it's disruptive to all our lives. But Robin is adamant, and maybe it's for the best."

. . . long fascinated minutes. Staring at the swiftly changing numerals of the digital clock, set in crystal, on his office desk. As a woman's voice penetrated his brain. As he pressed the telephone receiver against his numbed ear. How hypnotic, the flashing seconds! Heartbeats. The digital clock on Roger's desk was absurdly expensive, you could "tell" time as accurately with a drugstore clock, but such cheap practical merchandise wasn't for Roger Cavanagh of Abercrombie, Cavanagh, Kruller & Hook of 8 Shaker Square, Salthill-on-Hudson. ("Who the fuck am I?—'Cavanagh.'") There he sat at his desk, in his glossily furnished office, listening to a woman said to be his ex-wife speaking into his ear with maddening equanimity.

Once, he'd loved Lee Ann. He knew. As he knew random facts about his old, lost life, at a distance, with faint disbelief.

In this office, the previous July, he'd fallen in love with—who was it?—the red-haired woman, the difficult woman, the woman-who-owned-the-bookstore, the woman-who'd-left-him. Marina Troy. He'd fallen in love with Marina Troy when she signed her name as *witness* to Adam Berendt's forged signature. When he'd succeeded in inveigling her into committing an illegal act, compromising her integrity for Adam. And for *him*.

Now Marina was vanished from his life. Now Robin was vanished from his life.

The red-haired woman, he'd had to let go. He couldn't stalk her, for Christ's sake. *Yes, I could. But I will not.* The daughter, how could he let go? She was his daughter, his only child. Though she'd banished Deardeaddad. Though she was, as Lee Ann was saying with grim satisfaction, "dead serious."

After the unfortunate visit with Robin in Maryland, it seemed that Roger and Robin were as estranged as Roger and Lee Ann had been years before. The e-mail message was a shocker, yet not a surprise. Roger had tried to please the girl yet she hadn't been pleased. He had tried to demonstrate his love for her yet she hadn't wanted his love. Now she'd announced to her mother that she wouldn't be returning to the Ryecroft School for the second semester, the very school grounds were "tainted" for her since Daddy's visit. She was insisting upon transferring to a smaller school in Brunswick, Maine. *Maine!* "What's this, the fourth school in three years, or the fifth? And all to put distance between herself and her father." Roger tried to speak calmly, as if to a client. With clients, you were always calm. Lee Ann agreed yes, it was disruptive but "maybe for the best." Roger was baffled by his ex-wife's acquiescence. Lee Ann was a woman of good, stubborn sense: he'd expected her to refuse to give in to another of their daughter's whimsical demands. But Lee Ann was saying thoughtfully, "Better for Robin to make this break with you, Roger, than to love you too much." "Love me too much!" Roger laughed incredulously. "Robin hates my guts. She hates my profession. She hates my cock, and my soul." Lee Ann said primly, "Don't talk dirty, Roger. That's one of your less endearing traits. Robin has said you do it to 'assert masculine authority'—it's an act of 'sexual terrorism.'" "*Robin* says? That bullshit sounds like one of her teachers." "Roger, good-bye. I'm hanging up." But Roger slammed the receiver down first. He couldn't bear it, this was madness.

The personal life! He wanted no more of it. He would immerse himself in the impersonality of work, and it would be work that would save him.

Yet staring at the flashing numerals of a digital clock. *Is this all there is, finally? A mad rushing forward. Seconds, hours. Days. Years. Through a lighted tunnel for a while, and then—oblivion.*

Only the other day he'd had another birthday. He was forty-eight years old! No one loved him! Self-pity convulsed him like a belly of squirming eels. Didn't know if he was sick with despair, or with rage. Or shame.

He'd wanted to ask Lee Ann, almost he'd wanted to beg Lee Ann, what had he done to so offend their daughter?

Or was it something Roger Cavanagh *was?*

Nothing you do is a matter of life and death. You defend white-collar criminals, what's to be proud of?

3

ONE THING HE KNEW: not to allude to any personal weakness, and never to his predicament as a divorced, scorned father, in the company of anyone at Abercrombie, Cavanagh, Kruller & Hook. His reputation in the firm was: efficient, informed, methodical, and unsentimental as a guillotine. Roger was a skilled litigator who made money for his clients, and for himself.

What's a litigator but a money-making machine.

What's to be proud of? Robin had sneered, crinkling her nose against a bad odor.

Hell, Roger wasn't proud. Pride is a young man's prerogative. But Roger was functioning, and would function.

Above all he'd learned never to speak of personal matters to his Salthill friends. The men (with whom he played tennis, squash, sometimes golf) shrank from such revelations as one might shrink from a carrier of plague. The women were eager to invite him to dinner (especially during the week, when their husbands were in the city) and suck what remained of his life's blood from him in the name of delicious shuddering *empathy*.

And there was Abigail Des Pres. The woman infuriated him, he refused to think of her.

Yet, working with new associates whom he knew slightly (Roger had recently become involved with a local branch of the National Project to Free the Innocent), Roger sometimes spoke impulsively, unguardedly. "My fifteen-year-old daughter has cast me out of her life like an old shoe."

"And why not? Your daughter has the right."

This was a young woman named Naomi Volpe speaking. A paralegal assigned to assist Roger in the Elroy Jackson, Jr., case.

"She has the right? My *daughter?*" Roger was incensed.

Naomi Volpe said, "To herself she isn't 'your' daughter. Believe me. To herself, she's *herself.*"

Exactly, Roger thought. That was the trouble.

It was the first time that Roger Cavanagh and Naomi Volpe were alone together, outside the Project's offices in lower Manhattan. They were driving in Roger's car to Hunterdon County, New Jersey to meet with Elroy Jackson's public defender for his disastrous 1989 trial. It was an overcast day in late October not long after the shock of the *Deardeaddad* e-message. Roger, driving, was stung by the young female paralegal's tone. He wasn't accustomed to subordinates, especially females, confronting him so bluntly; but there was Naomi Volpe fixing her ferret-eyes upon him, as if Roger Cavanagh and his reputation as a litigator didn't much impress her. She said, "A man sees his daughter as a possession, an appendage, but the daughter has a totally different perspective. And remember: a fifteen-year-old today knows more than an eighteen-year-old did just ten years ago. American kids grow up fast." Naomi spoke with maddening certainty. No possibility she might be wrong. This was one of the woman's telephone voices that Roger had overheard since joining the staff as a volunteer and it made him itch to grab hold of the nape of Volpe's neck and give her a good hard shake. Instead he said:

"It isn't just Robin's only fifteen. She's a very immature fifteen."

"How so?" Volpe's response was immediate.

"She—has a cruel streak. She fantasizes, and—"

"You think only adolescents are cruel, Mr. C.?"

Mr. C.! Was this mockery, or an awkward form of deference? Or was it playful, even seductive? With Naomi Volpe—who'd asked Roger please to call her simply "Volpe"—you couldn't know.

"Of course not. But there's a particular sort of unthinking adolescent cruelty, that seems not to be connected with a sense of reality, and responsibility." Roger was thinking of Robin's teasing accusation that Adam Berendt had "touched" her. "Touched" her! The whimsicality of it. The treachery. *Just a hypothesis, Dad. See?* But Roger hadn't seen. In Robin's wish to harm him she'd have sacrificed Adam Berendt whom, Roger believed, she'd truly loved. He said, "It's painful to concede that maybe your own offspring isn't—fair-minded. Isn't 'nice.'"

"And you yourself *are?*"

A born lawyer, this Volpe. Except she wasn't. She was only a paralegal. Practically, Roger was thinking, a menial. Yet she had the lawyer's instinct for relentless confrontation, interrogation. A fired-up lawyer is like a buzz saw: get too close to the spinning blade, you'll be shredded. But Roger Cavanagh was accustomed to being the buzz saw, not its victim.

Roger said, deflecting the question, "Robin has demonized me, in her imagination, and I have no idea why."

Volpe was lighting a cigarette, exhaling smoke out her window. She laughed. "No, Mr. C. Probably you wouldn't."

Roger said, annoyed, "You've had experience with daughters?"

"Have I! I was a daughter myself for sixteen years."

"'Was'? Are your parents dead?"

"Dead to me."

Roger shivered.

This paralegal Volpe was a sledgehammer of a female, though hardly more than five feet tall and one of the newer staff members at the Project. She was claimed to be "very experienced" in assisting with death penalty cases; she'd worked in Texas, the heart of U.S. executions. She lived in Jersey City and commuted to East 15th Street, Manhattan. She wore mostly black clothes, sexy gay-boy attire: long-sleeved shirts tucked into trousers that outlined her round, hard little buttocks, black leather lace-up boots. A black leather coat. You could stare at her (as, half-consciously, Roger had done) and not know if Volpe was attractive or plain. Or if she believed herself attractive, or plain. Her mouth was so small as to appear invisible except when she smiled broadly, showing a flash of ferret-teeth. Her gravelly laughter was the obverse of infectious: a jeering sound to put you on the alert. *Is she laughing at me?* Roger half admired Volpe's wiry little-boy body with its unexpected, somehow perverse breasts like rocks shoved up inside her tight clothes. And her hair! It was a sleek dark brown, shaved up the back of her head yet spiky on the sides and top, moussed, or oiled, to give the feisty little woman a look, surely unintended, of a cartoon character who has stuck a toe into an electric outlet. Her skin looked smudged as if with a dirty eraser. Her eyes too looked smudged. Both ears glittered with studs and rings and there was a silver ring in her left nostril that gave her an aboriginal ferocity. She was much younger than Roger Cavanagh yet seemed to him not-young; there was nothing girlish about her, and certainly nothing charming. Even in repose her forehead was lined; her eyebrows were dark, heavy, quizzical. When Roger was first introduced to her she'd said, "Mr. Cavanagh of Salthill-on-Hudson. An honor." Roger hadn't wanted to think the paralegal was being ironic.

On this drive into New Jersey, they were becoming acquainted. Volpe confided in Roger that she'd been admitted to several top law schools and had started at NYU but dropped out, too much bullshit, torts, motions, briefs, judges' rulings and precedents, nobody gave a damn about justice, no attention paid to the ethical life. But now she wished she'd gotten her degree, you had to be a lawyer to have some effect upon this "shitty consumer society" where everything was for sale, especially justice. Roger guessed that Volpe hadn't done well in law school. She was smart, obviously, but had little patience. She was restless, and annoying. She'd lit up a cigarette without asking Roger's permission. (It was his car. This was his mission, primarily. And he was trying to cut back on his own smoking, which was becoming excessive.) Volpe's aggressive in-your-face style would rub law professors the wrong way, especially in a female. Among the congenial staff of Abercrombie, Cavanagh, Kruller & Hook there was no one remotely like Volpe. Even in Manhattan, among seasoned lawyers, individuals who'd been involved with various liberal organizations like the ACLU, Volpe stood out. She strode through the drafty high-ceilinged rooms of the Project's headquarters on the third, walk-up floor of an old brownstone tenement with the swagger of a jockey, her boy-buttocks cupped in snug trousers of some odd fabric that rustled and whispered *My ass. My ass. Hey, see? My ass.* Roger had heard rumors of Volpe's "intense, polymorphous sexuality" and even a rumor, he'd since discounted, that Volpe had had a baby, and given it up for adoption to a wealthy couple. He disliked her on principle. Though she was a very capable assistant so far. They were too much alike temperamentally, to get along for a protracted period. Roger knew! He knew the type. Volpe claimed to be from the Midwest but her accent sounded like Brooklyn to him. She spoke rapidly and impatiently and gave the impression of believing herself superior to anyone around her, which pissed Roger (*he* was the superior party, usually) but also intrigued him. Roger had had occasion to overhear Volpe speaking on a phone, in a voice heavy with sarcasm, to individuals (like Elroy Jackson's ex-attorney) who should have been treated with professional courtesy, if only in the interests of manipulating them. (A first-rate lawyer is a first-rate manipulator, or he's nothing.) Since joining the Project staff, coming into the office two or three times a week in the late afternoon and early evening, Roger had been fascinated to hear this spiky female chew out assistant district attorneys and defense lawyers and even clients, social workers, law professors. He'd overheard her speak in rapidfire Spanish. She'd been critical of one of the Project interns, a slow-moving cow-eyed Barnard girl whom other staff members treated with strained patience. On this drive Volpe managed to boast to Roger that she'd lived and worked in places as disparate as Arizona, Florida, Alaska, and Vancouver, British Columbia, as well as Texas, and Capetown, South Africa, where for a year she'd taught remedial English to black African adults—"The most exhausting and rewarding year of my life." (So why had she left Capetown, Roger inquired, and Volpe admitted she'd had to leave, she'd been mugged and "pretty badly beaten though at least not raped" by some drug-crazed black youths and couldn't take the pressure of continuing with her work.) She'd been a social worker's assistant in the Bronx. She'd been a paralegal in a Legal Aid office, also in the Bronx. She'd "repudiated" her Caucasian middle-class Indiana background by the age of sixteen. She was furious at what the "system" had done to Elroy Jackson, Jr., among others whom the National Project to Free the Innocent had taken up and she sincerely believed that there was in the United States an "unspoken but calculated apartheid" and that the emergence of selected African-Americans in sports, show business, the arts, and even the law was but a part of the conspiracy. "See, Elroy Jackson, Jr., is the basic unit. Not 'Justice' Clarence Thomas. The 'exceptions to the rule' are like brand names, logos, the ruling class can point proudly to. 'These minority folks have done O.K. in our capitalist-consumer culture, why not the rest of them?' Like female 'leaders' they can point to pretending this is an egalitarian society and not a sick-masochistic society in which women and girls are raped, battered, and murdered twenty-four hours a day." Roger, driving, staring at the rushing pavement before him, had a vision of a mammoth Wal-Mart store open twenty-four hours a day for such violent purposes.

Roger was certain he hadn't laughed, or indicated any sign of dissension, yet Volpe snapped, "If you'd been born with a cunt, Mr. C., you'd *know*."

"With a—what?"

"You heard me. *A cunt.*"

Roger winced. He resented it that, if he used a word like "cunt" he'd be vulnerable to a sex harassment suit, while fierce little Naomi Volpe with her ferret-eyes, spiked hair, and nose ring could shoot off her mouth as she wished.

Seeing Roger's expression Naomi said, with mock deference, "Hey, sorry, Mr. C. I should've said, if you'd been born female, and not white privileged male, you'd know."

"Know what, Volpe?"

Roger was losing the thread of their conversation. Talking with the paralegal was like playing Ping-Pong while driving a car: dangerous. Volpe said, "What it is to be mute and marginal. To be in sexual thrall."

"Somehow, Volpe, you don't strike me as 'mute.' And you don't strike me as a woman in sexual thrall to anyone or anything."

"Is that an accusation, Mr. C., or a threat? Or a come-on?"

But she was smiling.

4

ROGER KNEW BETTER than to become involved even casually with any woman with whom he worked. And yet.

In a rat's nest of a law office in Somerville, New Jersey, Roger and his assistant Volpe met Elroy Jackson's court-appointed attorney for his 1989 trial: Reginald "Boomer" Spires, an obese, doughy-oily, uneasily smiling individual of moderate height who must have weighed three hundred boneless pounds. "H'lo, come in. Wel-come. Not what you're accustomed to, I guess? Sor-ry." Roger, glancing about the cramped, cluttered office, was appalled. Even Volpe with her deadpan expression and jockey-swagger seemed taken by surprise. "Boomer" Spires thrust out his hand to be shaken, moist and clammy and the size of a catcher's mitt, and Roger had to resist the impulse to shrink away, for could a handshake be infectious? With the air of one making an elaborate joke Spires apologized to his visitors for the fact that there was practically nowhere to sit in his office, unless you shifted stacks of documents off chairs, which he hadn't gotten around to doing, and which he was reluctant to do since the floor was in use, too—"See, I share this space with another p.d. whose specialty is clients with psychiatric disturbances. *There's* a good time." Spires laughed wheezily. Neither Roger nor Naomi Volpe joined him. "Excuse me, folks, my knees are bad, have to sit down," Spires said, collapsing back into his swivel chair, "—hope I'm not being rude." Roger perceived that Spires didn't at all mind being rude but he, Roger, said civilly, "Of course not, Mr. Spires. 'Boomer.' We won't take up much of your valuable time."

Spires had promised to assemble for them material from his files on Elroy Jackson, Jr., but he had only a few court documents, material already in Roger's possession. It was impossible to gauge if Spires was genuinely concerned with Jackson's fate, or whether, for the purposes of this awkward meeting, he was pretending. As they talked of the case, Roger tried not to stare at Spires; but he'd never seen so repugnant a specimen of humanity, let alone a fellow lawyer, close up. Spires's body seemed to consist of layers of fat, oozing oily-fat. Slabs of fat at the back of his head, a puffy round ball of a face, sausage-fingers. Roger could not have said what offended him the more, that Spires was nominally male, as Roger was male, or that Spires was a lawyer, a member of the professional class to which Roger belonged, dubious in Naomi Volpe's scornful eyes as in Robin's. *What's to be proud of?* On a wall, just visible behind a stack of papers, was a diploma from Rutgers Law School. Roger would have liked to ask this character what the hell had gone wrong in his life, how did a man who'd earned a law degree from a good, solid, second-rank school like Rutgers wind up in this sinkhole of an office, wheezing and exuding the stink of failure, bloated as a drowned corpse? Roger shuddered. *It could happen to you, pal. Never too late.*

He'd committed an illegal act, after all. He'd forged a dead man's signature. He'd entered into a conspiracy with another party to perpetrate a fraud (no matter it was a beneficent fraud) upon the state. *Grounds for disbarment. You knew the risk.*

"Boomer" Spires was doing his best, which wasn't very inspired, to convince the skeptical visitors from the National Project to Free the Innocent that yes, he'd worked damned hard to defend Elroy Jackson, Jr., but no, truth was he hadn't much time to prepare, his client had been wounded by police fire, hadn't been "one hundred percent mentally" and had looked "pretty God-damned guilty" in the eyes of the mostly white jurors, see, it was one of those trials where you didn't have a chance. "Hello, folks, this is Hunterdon County? 'Guilty till proven innocent.' Things you folks in New York City pass off like misdemeanors, a little jail time and parole, over here in Jersey we go for the jugular. See, the death penalty here is popular as TV wrestling." Spires spoke with explosive mirth, shaking his fatty jowls. His eyes shifted furtively in their sockets, like melting Jell-O. The lawyer was crafty enough to know that Roger and his assistant weren't in Somerville for friendly chitchat and he was beginning to get defensive. Roger estimated that Spires was in his late forties—Roger's own age!—yet retained a puckish juvenile air, a fat boy hoping to be spared the ignominy of competing with adult men. His hair was scattered follicles in a white scalp. He smelled not only of nervous sweat but of those cardboard boxes in which pizza is delivered. Roger was particularly disgusted that Spires was wearing a faded Grateful Dead T-shirt and polyester trousers that ballooned around his hips. As if Elroy Jackson, Jr., incarcerated on death row at the Rahway State Maximum Facility for Men, scheduled to be executed by lethal injection in seven months, didn't merit at least a display of sobriety. Roger, examining the transcript of Jackson's trial, began to question Spires more aggressively. "Why didn't you insist that this 'co-defendant' take the stand? So you could cross-examine him? The man was lying, obviously. He'd cooked up a deal with the DA. Why didn't you object?"

Spires, shifting in his swivel chair, protested, "It was, what, a long time ago, in my lifetime, I'm a busy, busy man, and Jackson was one of an awful lot of 'disadvantaged' clients, you might call them. Like, blacks and Hispanics? Which there aren't that many of population-wise in this county, you'd think, but of the ones there are, mostly in Somerville, it's Boomer Spires who has the good luck to represent them, see? That's been more or less my career, Mr. Cavanagh. Just to explain our different perspectives, see?" Roger said coldly, "I've been going through this transcript and court records and frankly, 'Boomer,' I'm appalled. Back in 1989 you didn't put much effort into this case, did you? A capital case! You had plenty of cause for objections and you didn't object once. Here's this alleged co-defendant with a record of armed robbery, prison time, and your client Jackson with just petty stuff, and the original police report says there was no 'physical evidence' linking Jackson to the shooting, he'd gotten into trouble running from a crime scene when police called for him to halt, and he winds up shot, and charged with felony murder, and convicted and sentenced to death. What the hell were you thinking of?" Spires mumbled sullenly, "Ask me! How many hundreds of cases like this you think I've taken on, I don't mean death penalty but clients like this Leroy, Elroy, since the early eighties when I moved to Somerville? *You think I want to be in*

Somerville? See, folks, you have the advantage of hindsight. 'Hindsight ain't foresight.' See, you walk in here and think you can insult me—" Spires was working himself up, trying for moral indignation. The swivel chair creaked alarmingly beneath his bulk and his Jell-O eyes glared. "See, I'm not a partner at Abercrombie & Fucking Fitch. I don't make five hundred bucks an hour. What d'you think the hallowed State of New Jersey pays guys like me? I'm lucky if I get five hundred a *week*." Naomi Volpe, who'd been listening in silence, taking notes, suddenly turned fierce in Roger's defense. "Back off, you! Mr. Cavanagh is volunteering his time on this case you fucked up. His fee is zero bucks per hour."

By degrees Spires caved in. You could see he was a man who enjoyed caving in, at his own pace. A man throwing himself on the mercy of the court. O.K., he admitted he hadn't spent much time on the Jackson case because he hadn't had much time, the State of New Jersey Public Defender's office worked him and his colleagues like beasts of burden and if they didn't like it, they could always quit. "Plus I'd gotten into the mind-set, I'm reluctant to admit it, but why not be frank, maybe you can sympathize, see, when I'd more or less started to assume my clients were guilty? Because mostly they are? Somebody's got to be committing the crimes out there, holding up 7-Elevens and gas stations for chump change, dealing drugs on the streets, right?—so who's it likely to be except guys like Jackson? I don't mean one hundred percent, for sure the Jersey cops are racists to the extent, like all cops, they can get away with it, there's a willing populace supporting them, see, this 'racial profiling' is just the tip of the iceberg. Well, I know that. That I know. You're looking at me like you don't approve but you'd have to be blind and your head in the sand not to know that. So there's guilty clients, plenty of them, and psychotic. Did I say psychotic? Does a fish swim? Yes? A psychotic is a helpless individual but not an individual you much want to help, see. It's human nature. Not like the clients you deal with, Mr. Cavanagh. Over in Salthill, New York. Jackson might've been one of these, the cops shot him and possibly beat him and extracted a confession, you know how cops are, and this is Hunterdon County not Manhattan, see? His mental processes were interfered with. And now you're coming in, twelve years after the fact. 'Hindsight ain't foresight.' *I* had your hindsight, if it was foresight, I'd be a lottery winner. Sure as hell I wouldn't be here. O.K., Mr. Cavanagh, there's things I didn't see at the time, you want to hang me? O.K., Jackson got a lousy deal. Think he's the only one? Like getting hit by lightning, these guys on death row. Jackson's just one. *You* wouldn't know about that, would you, Mr. Cavanagh, getting hit by lightning?" Spires spoke in a childish whine. Roger could see that through his adult life "Boomer" had escaped punishment by pleading incompetence. He'd made a racket out of humility. His honesty was such, you wanted to punch him in the gut for not having the decency to fabricate. Roger was saying, "As a result of your incompetence, Mr. Spires, an innocent man has been locked away on death row for twelve years. He's had a stay of execution a half-dozen times. Sure, the prosecution withheld exculpatory evidence and the judge was prejudiced but that's them, and you're you, *you* were being paid to represent Elroy Jackson, Jr., in a capital case, an innocent man, and you did a fucking lousy job of it. You should be disbarred."

"Disbarred!" Spires was both scornful and alarmed. His lurid T-shirt had darkened with sweat beneath the armpits and across the swell of his belly. Behind his head, a grimy window overlooking Somerville's Main Street seemed to glower with derision. "Hey, look, friend, I do my best. Maybe it ain't great by your big-city standards but it's Boomer's best, see? They dump these shit cases on my lap, it's like paddling a canoe up the river with just bare hands, what can I do, easy for you to judge! If you—" Roger cut into this self-pitying bilge, saying, "One of the complaints the Project has filed says you 'nodded off' in court. This was Jackson's complaint and it was corroborated by others. I see in the transcript where the judge says, 'Wake up, Mr. Spires. You're not home watching TV.'" Spires protested, "I never fell asleep in court! I *do not*. Maybe I rest my eyes, I have headaches, I need to rest my eyes, that's a crime? That's moral turpitude? *You* try it. In my shoes. In that courtroom. You'd 'nod off,' too.

The both of you. Looking at me like I'm dog shit. I wasn't asleep *per se* and whoever says I was, judge or whoever, that's fucking *slander*."

"Your closing argument reads as if you were asleep when you gave it," Roger said. "It's rambling and repetitive. You never touch upon the central point: that Jackson was an innocent man, and his 'co-defendant' lied, implicating him and getting himself off with a lesser charge. You didn't examine prosecution witnesses. You didn't call any witnesses of your own. You let all these things slide by. What did you do to earn your fee?"

Spires said, "It's easy for you, sure, to criticize another lawyer, after the fact, O.K. where were you in 1989? When this guy needed a hot-shit defense? Why didn't you volunteer your precious time then, Mr. Cavanagh? And the appeals, what about the appeals, where were you then?"

Naomi Volpe cut in sharply, "You! You fat asshole. If I were you, I'd cut my throat. I'd give up practicing law and save clients like Elroy Jackson the death penalty."

It was then that Spires tried to heave himself up from his chair, or made a sudden defensive gesture as if imagining, or pretending to imagine, that Volpe was going to hit him; and Volpe mistook the gesture, or pretended to mistake it, as offensive, and struck out at him with astonishing quickness, using the edges of both hands simultaneously. This must have been a martial arts move, though one not known to Roger. He saw Spires catch Volpe's fast-flying blows on both sides of his fatty neck, saw the look of astonishment and pain on Spires's face and heard him whimper, like air rapidly escaping from a balloon. Spires spilled sideways out of his chair grabbing at the edge of a desk and pulling over with him to the floor a cascade of documents, plastic cups and containers. On the floor, Spires sat like an upright baby whale, red-faced and panting. "Go away. Just *go away*," he whispered.

Volpe would have replied, but Roger prudently touched the young woman's shoulder and drew her away. Without another word they left Spires's office. "No need to assault the poor bastard," Roger said, laughing. "Let him sue," Volpe said furiously, "I'm not ashamed of hitting him. *He's* the one who deserves lethal injection, not Jackson." Roger said, as you might placate a vicious dog, "Don't worry, Volpe. I'm the sole witness to the assault, and I'm yours."

After the meeting with "Boomer" Spires, Naomi Volpe was hot-skinned as if sunburnt. Too restless to sit quietly in Roger's car. Could they stop for a drink? "Sure," Roger said. "I could use a drink, too." The rat's nest, repugnant to enter, would become an adventure to recount. A shared adventure. Cavanagh and Volpe were now incensed comrades. Cruelly they laughed at the defeated enemy. "Fuck that asshole," Naomi Volpe said loudly, not caring that others might overhear, "can you believe that asshole! And the size of him. Call himself a man if that's what he calls himself, I wanted to laugh in his face. That size, a guy's got a prick this size." Volpe raised the smallest finger of her right hand. "Ask me, I *know*." The furrows in Volpe's forehead deepened. Her ferret-eyes glittered meanly. The smudged, triangular face seemed to Roger attractive, in the half-light of a barroom somewhere in Jersey. Roger liked it that the paralegal could get so worked up in a common cause. After a few beers and a cigarette or two he thought it touching, a sign of Volpe's loyalty, that she should be on his side, when no one was on his side, her fury directed at someone beside himself. He'd signed on as a volunteer for the Project to make his daughter respect him and if Robin didn't come to respect him at least he'd given her grounds for respect and maybe he could respect himself. The Project had been one of Adam Berendt's causes. It was a damned good cause. If Naomi Volpe was associated with the Project, she was a woman to respect. When they left the tavern it was dark, and dark felt good. You could get too much of daylight. You could get too much of sobriety. They'd lost track of time, but who cared. It was too late to return to East 15th Street for sure. As Roger drove, looking for a way back to the interstate, Naomi Volpe continued to speak hotly, passionately. She was leaning forward in her seat, the safety belt unbuckled. At a traffic light Roger noticed her picking at her face; in the bar, she'd been picking at her face; it was a nervous, angry gesture, a mannerism of Robin's, prodding blemishes in her skin and picking with her fingernails until sometimes she drew blood. Roger reached out to catch hold of Volpe's hand and pulled it away from her face. "Hey. Don't." It was the first time he'd touched her so intimately. Volpe stared at Roger, and smiled. She drew her hand out of his. They were both aroused, breathing quickly. Roger touched her face, and her spiky hair. Naomi leaned forward to kiss him, a hard quick kiss like a bite. Did Roger imagine it, or did the barbaric little nose ring brush against his skin? Desire flooded him like molten wax. He hadn't been with a woman sexually in memory. He fumbled to grip Volpe's narrow, hard-muscled shoulders like a man grabbing to save himself from drowning. He kissed her in return, with feeling. They laughed, breathless. "Why're you angry with me, Naomi? I'm on your side," Roger said. Volpe grabbed at Roger's hair with both fists. "Nobody's on my side, Mr. C."

Roger drove into a dead-end street of warehouses, a trainyard. He had no idea where he was. Already Naomi Volpe was tugging at his sport coat, at his white cotton shirt, crushing the material in her fingers as if wanting to tear it.

5

He was driving somewhere in snow.

A snowy mountain road? The air was heightened and clear as glass. Through a stand of evergreens a lighted window glowed. He had the power to see at a distance. Or maybe he had a telescope . . . There was the red-haired young woman in the window, passing by the window, her pale grave face and long tangled red hair illuminated. She was the woman he loved and yet she could not see him—could she?

He called, Marina!

He stared, and the woman was shutting the window against him. Shutting a louvered blind.

He wakened, in his bed in Salthill, sexually aroused and ashamed.

NEXT MORNING he telephoned Naomi Volpe at Project headquarters. She put him on hold.

6

CASUAL SEX! It seemed to Roger the behavior of another era, the 1970s. He'd never been "involved" with a woman the way he became involved with Naomi Volpe, though Lee Ann had accused him. Roger was more traditional, more romantic, possessive. He wanted sex to *mean something*. He couldn't have said exactly what it should mean but he knew it should *mean something*. It wasn't that he was in love with Naomi Volpe but he felt that she should be in love with him. At least, she should be susceptible to loving him. For his part, he wanted to feel protective toward her. He wanted to feel tenderness, affection. This was only normal, wasn't it? He'd entered her tight, frantic little body and he'd made love to her, unless it was only that he'd fucked her ("fuck" was a word Volpe uttered as casually as another might murmur "Well" or "Uh"), but he'd impressed her, he'd caused her to feel something, he was sure, and that was important—wasn't it?

In all, Roger and Naomi Volpe would make love less than a dozen times that fall, winter. Their relationship wasn't a love affair exactly, yet not a friendship. Volpe seemed bored by intimacy. Unlike any other woman with whom Roger had been romantically involved, she showed little interest in "intimate" exchange. She was physically restless, and in Roger's embrace, if they weren't actively making love, he could feel her thoughts churn. She talked a good deal, on her feet, but not in bed, and at no time did she encourage Roger to talk about himself, after their initial conversation about Robin; the next time Roger brought up the subject, to him fascinating and obsessive, of his "demonic" daughter, Naomi Volpe scarcely listened. Talking of Elroy Jackson, Jr., Volpe showed true animation. She was angry on behalf of the condemned man, she spoke bitterly of the "enemy"—the "white prosecutors." (Even when technically black-skinned, prosecutors were in thrall to the white élite.) Roger saw that Naomi Volpe was an impassioned hater, but an indifferent lover. Their sexual liaisons, scattered and unpredictable at least by Roger, seemed to begin with outbursts of bad temper on Volpe's part. (For a woman who aligned herself vociferously with the underclass, Volpe liked expensive restaurants. Her only requirement was that they were "downtown," which included Union Square.)

They made love a number of times in Volpe's rowhouse apartment in Jersey City, where it wasn't clear whether Roger was, or was not, invited to stay the night or didn't wish to, being eager to get away and back to Salthill for a morning in his office on Shaker Square. Sometimes, alone in the office on East 15th, and overcome by desire, they made love on a sofa there, as many times as Volpe could eke out of forty-eight-year-old Roger Cavanagh. The more pissed Volpe was with the injustice of the world, the more urgent her sexual need. She sank her fingers into Roger's hair, clutched and groaned and bucked beneath him, locking her ankles at the small of his back. He was made to worry, upon more than one occasion, about throwing out his back: this was sex a little too young for him, sex as aerobics, acrobatics. Not that he'd complain! Kisses were snaky-quick little bites. Sometimes lovemaking came too suddenly, for such safety precautions as condoms—"No. Never mind. I'm on the pill. Come *on*." Roger was sexually flattered, winded, and confounded. He was hurt, resentful. He would have been alarmed if the paralegal had begun telephoning him in Salthill, or left e-mail messages or notes for him at Project headquarters, but he was subtly insulted that she didn't do these things; if she told Roger she couldn't see him, she had an engagement with someone else, whether the "friend" was female or male Roger felt a stab of jealousy though knowing, of course he knew, that Volpe was a purely contemporary type, not promiscuous but amoral, indifferent to romantic conventions as she was indifferent to conventions of female makeup and attire. It couldn't be said that Naomi Volpe was "unfaithful" to Roger because the concept of "faithful" would have struck her as hilarious, or obscene. Roger told himself yes, he felt the same way.

Like hell you do. You want her to adore your prick. Above all others. Till death do you part.

True, Roger was pissed off when he called Naomi Volpe—a paralegal!—and she neglected to return his call. When, meeting up with her in the Project's offices, she scarcely glanced at him, smirked as she murmured, "H'lo, Mr. C.! Nice tie." *Is she laughing at me? But why?* He behaved cordially with her, coolly. He kept his distance. No one in the office could have guessed they were—sometimes—lovers. (*Was* that what they were?) Roger was incensed when Volpe put him off with a vague explanation that she had "other plans" for the evening. If Lee Ann should discover this! If Roger's Salthill friends should know! He felt the injustice of being so treated, by a woman of no special attractions with a smudged skin, a ring in her nose, a gravelly voice; a woman who merely assisted lawyers on the staff, and should have been grateful that one of them took an interest in her.

He had to wonder: was Volpe a lesbian?

He had to wonder: who were her other lovers?

He couldn't bring himself to discuss such things with her. He would not have wished her to know he was thinking of her in such a way; or that he was thinking of her much at all. From remarks she let fall he gathered she was bisexual—"At least in theory." (This was heartening: Volpe preferred men? The penis?) One evening over drinks she spoke of the "occult power" of fetishes. She said, "Everyone is a fetishist, except most don't know it. They haven't yet discovered their fetish. It's like your blood type, Mr. C! Before you're informed, you could be said to be 'innocent' of that knowledge, but that doesn't mean you don't have a blood type that's verifiable."

Roger was struck by this. He, a fetishist!

Bullshit. He was a thoroughly normal heterosexual male.

He said, "So what's your fetish, Naomi?"

"'Volpe,' please call me. I've asked you."

"*That's* your fetish, not being 'Naomi'? Why?"

Volpe looked startled. Her forehead creased in discomfort. Accustomed to asking questions, she wasn't good at answering questions. Nervously she said, "Mr. C, it's late. I think I'll take a train home tonight. Good night!"

In sexual thrall. But he wasn't, yet. Not to Naomi Volpe.

7

WHO'D LED ROGER CAVANAGH to this impasse? Who but his friend Adam.

As Adam's executor, Roger had discovered a file of documents and clippings relating to the National Project to Free the Innocent. He'd been impressed that Adam had left $50,000 to the organization, and he remembered a conversation he'd had with Adam a few months before Adam's death in which his friend had expressed the wish that he'd gone to law school, had a law degree, so he could "help fight injustice." Roger said dryly, "You think that's what lawyers do, Adam? Fight 'injustice'?"

"Yes. Some lawyers."

Roger, smiling hard, felt the sting of his friend's remark.

Fuck you, Berendt. Life isn't that simple.

It was nonlawyers who idealized the law, Roger thought. If anyone idealized it. To the lawyer, the law is pragmatic as a subway map. It's a function, a use. To get to X, you take a specific route. If you never wish to get to X (if you've made Y your life's work) you need never glance at the route to X. You may be aware that X exists, but it doesn't exist in relationship to you.

Adam had gone on to speak of "injustices" of which he'd become aware, the disproportionate number of black men on death row in the United States, the likelihood that innocent men were being executed by the state, possibly Adam had even spoken of Elroy Jackson, Jr., to his shame Roger wouldn't remember, afterward. He'd been feeling defensive. He'd been annoyed by Adam's naive indignation. You can't be confronted with another's idealism without wishing to refute it and if you can't refute it, you deny it; you do your best to forget it.

After Adam's death, when Roger began to discover surprising things about his friend (the size and variety of Adam's financial investments, for instance; the mysterious absence of family, relatives) he came to see that "Adam Berendt" had been an invention of a kind: the charmingly eccentric philosopher/sculptor whom everyone in Salthill had liked, and some had loved. Never a hint of the money he was amassing, and would give away to "deserving" charities. Adam had allowed his friends to interpret him in ways that were false. He'd allowed his friends to love a man who'd never existed.

It was while looking through Adam's file on the National Project to Free the Innocent that Roger became caught up in the Elroy Jackson, Jr., case, the most-documented of the cases in Adam's possession. Here were more than a hundred pages of photocopied material, court documents, letters, newspaper clippings, memos. In the margins of some of these Adam had made exclamatory notations. Here was a miscellany of pathos. To read through Jackson's case was to avidly wish not to be reading it; to push it impatiently aside, to shut one's eyes. Yet how familiar in outline the sordid story: a black man, running from a crime scene as police command him to halt; an unarmed black man, one not involved in the crime, the armed robbery of a 7-Eleven store in Somerville, New Jersey, and the shooting death of a young store clerk; a black man pursued on foot and seriously wounded by police who would later "confess" to being involved in the crime, under coercion; a black man with a record of minor convictions betrayed by another, more canny black man . . . Witnesses claimed to have seen Elroy Jackson "in the vicinity" of the 7-Eleven store and some would claim to have seen him run away before the shooting, and some would claim to have seen him run away "at the time" of the shooting. In the confusion of eyewitnesses, what was the jury to believe? Yet Jackson hadn't had a gun, and gunpowder residue wasn't found on his hands or clothing. It was his word against the actual shooter that he hadn't been involved. It was his word against a lighter-skinned, more intelligent and craftier black man who'd known how to make a quick deal with prosecutors, to blame an innocent man and plead guilty to reduced charges. Where there has been a shooting death, someone must pay severely, and luckless Elroy Jackson, Jr., turned out to be that man.

Roger read and reread the file on Jackson. Jesus! Here was a clear misapplication of justice. Much of the evidence that might have spared Jackson wasn't admitted into the trial, or Jackson's incompetent public defender hadn't brought it in; there were obvious inconsistencies in testimonies, yet the Hunterdon County prosecutor's office had managed to "prove" its case before a jury of mostly white, retired jurors. This jury would duly convict Jackson of a capital crime, a murder committed during a felony, and he would be sentenced to death by the new, humane method—lethal injection.

The execution had been several times postponed. No one had been executed in New Jersey for more than two decades. Pressure from right-wing politicians and their constituents was being brought upon the state to resume executions, and recent rulings by the U.S. Supreme Court were making it more difficult for the condemned to appeal. As Roger read further he became incensed, frustrated. No wonder Adam felt so strongly about this . . .

The file included photographs of Jackson: the man was dark-skinned, in his mid- or late thirties, with a wide nose, thick lips, deep-set anxious eyes; he hadn't any distinctive characteristics; it was his bad luck to look like a man whom jurors could readily imagine perpetrating the crimes he'd been charged with perpetrating. (It was worse luck that Jackson's supposed co-defendant had Caucasian features and a less generic, more "appealing" face. And a smarter attorney.) Roger could imagine the poor figure "Boomer" Spires must have cut in the courtroom. The trial must have moved along swift and pitiless as a bulldozer. There was the damning matter of Jackson's rambling, incoherent "confession" he'd made to police, which he later recanted but which remained a matter of record. And once a guilty verdict was entered into the record, the machinery of "justice" kicked into action like a meat grinder. Appeals in capital cases were automatic in New Jersey but Jackson's guilty verdict remained unshaken through nearly twelve years. Reading of such matters, the dark side of the law that was his life's profession, Roger felt sickened, ashamed. He understood his daughter's repugnance for his life's work and for him and could not have defended himself against her.

It was late. Roger was alone in Adam Berendt's office in the house on the River Road that would shortly become the property of the Salthill Arts Council. Discouraged, overcome by fatigue, Roger rested his head on his arms. Pulses pounded in his eyes. Strange to be alone in Adam's house without Adam present. He wasn't asleep yet there stood Robin a few feet away regarding him with—was it sympathy? *Poor Daddy. Daddy's tired. A matter of life and death. Something to be proud of, Daddy?*

Almost, Roger heard the girl's voice.

8

"THIS WILL BE an education for you, Mr. C."

In November, Roger and his paralegal assistant Naomi Volpe drove to Rahway, New Jersey, to interview Elroy Jackson, Jr., in the death row cell block in which Jackson had been incarcerated for twelve years. Twelve years! The intellectual knowledge of such a fact was hardly adequate to suggest the grim pitiless reality behind it. The visit was Roger's first to a prison, let alone a maximum security prison containing death row inmates, and the experience left him shaken, disoriented. He would dream of it, and the luckless Elroy Jackson, Jr., for months afterward. As they were being led by a taciturn guard into an interview room, after having been brought through a sequence of electronically monitored checkpoints, the prison air heavy with portent as an ether-soaked rag, Naomi Volpe squeezed Roger's arm in an unexpected gesture of—was it sympathy? Pity for the Salthill attorney's dead-white face? As if to say *It will be all right, I'm with you. I'm your friend.*

Roger would have squeezed the young woman's hand in return, but Naomi Volpe eased out of his reach.

Always, Naomi Volpe was easing out of Roger Cavanagh's reach.

Volpe had boasted to Roger she was no stranger to prisons, including maximum security prisons for men. She knew the protocol and took no apparent offense, as Roger was inclined to, at the brusque way in which they were treated by prison officials and guards. "They see you wearing a necktie, they register: lawyer. These guys hate lawyers. Even the lawyers on their side. But we're here to help our client, so just accept their shit. *We* get to walk out afterward, right?" Volpe spoke with a certain zest. She was wearing a black jumpsuit and black jogging shoes and her spiky dark hair was freshly razor-cut at the back and sides: at first glance you might mistake her for a Rahway inmate, boy-sized. She hadn't met Elroy Jackson, Jr., but she'd been corresponding with him and had spoken with him on the telephone so it was Volpe who introduced the prisoner and Roger to each other, explaining Roger's mission: to prepare a motion on Jackson's behalf, in tandem with a New Jersey ACLU lawyer, to be filed with a New Jersey federal court, requesting a retrial for Jackson, or an outright release. This information the prisoner absorbed with little emotion, a sardonic tic of a smile. He mumbled what sounded like, "Heard that before." Or maybe it was just a grunt, "Huh-uh." Roger found himself playing the role, a new and untested role for him, of the resolutely upbeat suburban-Caucasian-liberal attorney. *White man to the rescue!*

The interview, in a windowless cubicle glaringly lit by overhead lights, was brief and unsatisfying. Most of what Roger asked him, the prisoner had already answered in more detail, at greater length and more intelligently, in the past, according to documents in Roger's possession. After twelve years Jackson abbreviated his account of what had happened and seemed to Roger to be reciting, in a dispirited voice, words he'd many times recited. Roger had the impression that the slack-faced, middle-aged prisoner, who resembled the Elroy Jackson of 1989 as an aging, ailing father might resemble a son, recalled little of the actual incident that had sabotaged his life; he recalled what had been processed for him by others. His eyes were heavy-lidded and bloodshot, his dark, lustreless skin looked coarse as sandpaper. His body in the prison jumpsuit was shapeless as a sack of flour. He could make the effort only intermittently to relate to his earnest white visitors, grunting and mumbling in response, his breath audible as if he were suffering from a respiratory condition. Others had come to Rahway on his account over the years, his execution had been postponed, but the sentence of death had not been commuted and his life was wearing out, like a broken towel dispenser. When Roger assured him that prospects "looked very promising" for a retrial, even a reversal of the verdict, since Roger had discovered "unconscionable errors" in the trial, Jackson grunted in bemusement and smiled with half his mouth. He regarded Roger Cavanagh in his tailored gray pinstripe suit and crisp white cotton shirt as one might contemplate a mildly annoying fly buzzing nearby. "Are you following me, Mr. Jackson?" Roger asked politely, Jackson roused himself to consciousness like a large dog preparing to shake its coat, mumbling, "You tell 'em, Mr. Spires."

Spires! Roger flushed with wounded pride, and even Naomi Volpe shuddered, like one who has witnessed an obscenity. She said, in reproof, "Mr. Jackson, your new attorney is Mr. Cavanagh. And I'm Naomi Volpe, his assistant. We work with the National Project to Free the Innocent. You're a long way from 'Boomer Spires.'"

Jackson mumbled what sounded like an apology, except in its midst he began laughing; or was it a coughing fit; a violent discharging of greenish phlegm into a handkerchief Roger Cavanagh had no choice but to hastily provide, out of his coat pocket. This handkerchief was white cotton, monogrammed, freshly laundered and ironed. "Please. Keep it. It's yours," Roger said, with a shiver of repugnance as, in a gesture of utter sincerity that might have been a gesture of consummate irony, Elroy Jackson, Jr., offered the befouled handkerchief to its owner.

Quickly following this exchange the interview ended.

Outside, in the acrid air of New Jersey, which nonetheless tasted sweet to Roger after confinement in the prison, Naomi Volpe said with grim humor, "So, Mr. C.! How'd you like to live on death row? Not like Salthill-on-Hudson, is it?" Roger, aroused by his companion's careless nudge, as by the visceral frustration of the past hour, grabbed Volpe's shoulders so that she winced, and pulled her to him, and kissed her thin-lipped mouth, and told her in crude monosyllabics what he'd like to do to her, as quickly as they could find a private place. Volpe's ferret-eyes brightened. She'd pressed against Roger's groin when he embraced her, gripping him around the waist with as much urgency as he'd gripped her. "Right, Mr. C.! I was thinking the exact thing."

They spent the remainder of that dismal afternoon, and after a break for a meal another several hours, in a room in a Ramada Inn off the Jersey Turnpike, and afterward Roger wouldn't see Volpe except at a distance for weeks.

Which was fine with him, he thought. For all her sexual dexterity, the woman wasn't his type.

9

You're drifting away from Salthill. Where to?

Though he was spending increasingly more time in New York, and would shortly lease a one-bedroom flat on East 11th Street, Roger continued to live in the Village of Salthill. At the time of his divorce, when he and Lee Ann had hurriedly sold their house, he'd bought a red-brick town house originally built in 1901 and many times renovated since then, in another "historic" district of Salthill within walking distance of Shaker Square. It was a tall narrow austere-looking house of aged brick with black shutters and trim and a lawn bordered by a wrought-iron fence, a house that could only belong to someone with taste and money. Approaching it, Roger never failed to feel a thrill of ownership, and of deception. *Mine! I'm the man who lives here.*

He'd never brought Naomi Volpe to this house. He'd never brought Naomi Volpe to Salthill. He dreaded the spiky-haired young paralegal's response to his suburban life. "Mr. C.! None of this surprises me in the slightest."

He'd fucked the smirk off Volpe's face, more than once. He'd fucked her until the mouthy female was wordless, moaning and sweating and clutching at Roger without knowing who he was.

Mr. C.! He did resent it, Volpe's scorn.

This was unpredicted: by early winter Roger was spending as much time working on the Elroy Jackson case, or brooding about it, as he spent on his Salthill clients. His paying clients! He'd begun to resent these individuals, for whom he couldn't become impassioned. Their cases were solely about money and pride. Win, lose, settle high, low, in the middle—"Who gives a shit?" It was business, and Abercrombie, Cavanagh, Kruller & Hook were businessmen. They were multi-millionaires but not mega-millionaires and the distinction didn't trouble them, for in Salthill their reputation was excellent, they were men of comfortable middle-age, anticipating retirement and "golden" years. Their children were mostly grown, and gone.

Every morning, checking his personal e-mail, Roger steeled himself against discovering another cryptic little poem from Robin. But she'd ceased communicating with Deardeaddad. He'd have to accept it, her dismissal of him. *To herself she isn't your daughter. To herself she's herself.*

Almost, Roger was regretting his lost youth. Squandered in Salthill-on-Hudson. He should have gone into ACLU law, civil rights law, environmental protection, antipoverty. He should have married a woman who shared these commitments. He'd have another daughter now, possibly sons. These children would love and respect their idealist father. Instead he'd fallen in love with good-looking Lee Ann Stacey, a Pi Phi at Penn, whose canny mother had "registered" her at Tiffany's for wedding presents and whose insurance-executive father had insisted upon helping out the newlyweds with their first house . . . No wonder Volpe mocked him as "Mr. C." Roger was an initial, not an individual. *He didn't know who the fuck he was.*

Roger recalled the mingled admiration and scorn his law school classmates felt for the idealists who'd declined jobs with law firms to work for "worthy" causes. The deep-seated unspoken wish that they fail.

"Now I'm one of them? At my age? Jesus."

It was like bringing your hand dangerously close to a grinder: if you're not cautious, your hand will be sucked in, and if you can't get your hand out, you will be sucked in.

OWEN CUTLER CALLED, and dropped by Roger's townhouse at 11 Belle Meade Place, bringing a bottle of expensive French chardonnay from his wine cellar and an exquisitely prepared gourmet dinner from Salthill Seafood—"We never entertain any longer, you know. With Gussie away." If this seemed to him an eccentric remark, Roger gave no sign. All of Salthill knew that Owen Cutler had become increasingly eccentric since his wife's disappearance; he'd virtually retired from business, spending much of his time at home ("In case Gussie calls, or returns suddenly") where, Roger had heard, he'd begun to raise tropical flowers. Roger had known the Cutlers for many years but in the way of affluent-suburban friendships he hadn't known them well. He wasn't sure he'd ever had a serious, protracted conversation with Owen Cutler until now, when Owen's conversations were more serious than one wished, and far more protracted. "There's a terrible rumor, Roger, you've probably heard, people are saying that I have had a hand in Gussie's disappearance somehow," Owen murmured, in a faltering voice of hurt, chagrin, shame, not meeting Roger's eye, "but I have not. Roger, I swear *I have not*. Gussie had investments of her own she cashed in, she simply disappeared, she has *vanished from the face of the earth*. The private detectives I've hired come up with *not a clue*." Roger sympathized with Owen, but dreaded his friend staying much later, and so had few questions to ask; but Owen continued to speak, in a piteous monologue, rubbing his red-rimmed eyes and sighing; at last saying, in a rush of words, "Roger, I—I don't mean to offend you—I would never wish to offend *you*—

but were you and Gussie ever—close? Were you ever—lovers?"

Roger should have been prepared for this, he'd heard that Owen had asked this question of others, but in fact he was shocked. Not just the question was blunt and unexpected but the proposition was distasteful: Roger Cavanagh and Augusta Cutler!

The Salthill woman he'd loved, Roger wanted to tell Owen, was Marina Troy. Surely everyone knew?

Quickly Roger assured Owen no, he and Augusta were never lovers, only just friends.

"'Just' friends? But you were good friends, I think?"

"Of course, Owen. We were all good friends. I mean—we are all good friends."

"Gussie was drawn to you, you know. Your 'vigor' she called it. Your 'snaky' eyes." Seeing the look in Roger's face, Owen said quickly, "I'm not sure what Gussie meant by that, you know how fanciful Gussie could be, but—she meant attractive, obviously. She found you very attractive, Roger."

Roger sat wordless. What did you say, posed with such a revelation? *Thank you!* Or, *I'm sorry*.

"Gussie was even more intimate, I think, with Adam? Were you their confidant?"

"'Confidant'? How?"

"A friend to whom they confided. *You* know." Owen Cutler, his face abraded by worry, stress, time, smiled with ghastly intimacy at Roger, who stared at him uncomprehendingly. "Adam made Gussie very happy, I know. He was someone to whom she could talk, and unburden her heart. Our wives have much to say, Roger, much to confide in others, if not to us. I'm grateful to Adam for that. Truly, I'm *grateful*."

When at last after midnight Owen Cutler left, Roger impulsively telephoned Naomi Volpe in Jersey City. Her phone rang, rang, rang!—God damn, her answering tape switched on. "Naomi! It's 'Mr. C.' I'm missing you. Give me a call, huh?" Volpe was no more Roger Cavanagh's type than Gussie Cutler but in his loneliness, he'd have settled for either female.

* * *

ANOTHER DAY, Abigail Des Pres dropped by the Shaker Square office to take Roger to lunch (Roger politely declined) and to smile at him wistfully. "You're drifting away from Salthill, Roger. Like Marina Troy."

Roger said sharply, "No. Not like Marina Troy."

Was he rude to beautiful Abigail, Salthill's most eligible cocktease-divorcée? He hoped so.

10

AMERICAN LAW IS a paradigm of warfare "by other means." Maybe this was why Roger had liked it, as a younger man. Now he wished he could talk to his adversaries. Elroy Jackson's accusers. He believed he might reason with them, for surely they were reasonable men? (Everyone involved in the Jackson trial, prosecution and defense, and judge, happened to be male.) One of the names that leapt out at him from court documents was "Calvin Ransom": an acquaintance of Roger's from Columbia Law. Ransom had been an assistant district attorney in Hunterdon County in 1989, and had helped to prepare the state's case against Jackson and Jackson's "co-defendant." More recently, Ransom had the title of Hunterdon County comptroller; he'd become an elected official, a Republican. That figured, Roger thought. He recalled Ransom as an ambitious law student, not unlike Roger Cavanagh. They hadn't been friends but they'd been friendly acquaintances and had respected each other, or so Roger wanted to think.

"He'd talk to me frankly. No bullshit with *me*."

Trying to make an appointment to meet with Calvin Ransom wasn't easy, however. And when they did meet, in Ransom's executive office in a handsome new municipal building in Flemington, New Jersey, Roger was offended to learn, from Ransom's secretary, that Ransom had allotted only a half-hour for him.

A half-hour! The prick.

Since volunteering to work with the Project, Roger was

beginning to understand why Naomi Volpe, like a few other colleagues, was often so impatient, rude. Why a fury burnt in her like a gas jet that could suddenly flare up.

And here was Calvin Ransom, a two-bit success in New Jersey political circles, probably a multi-millionaire, what's a comptroller but a guy with deep pockets and developers throwing money at him in a county like Hunterdon, New Jersey, formerly farmland and up for grabs, the new American suburban-paradise. Ransom shook hands vigorously with Roger, plump-porcine, with glinting metal glasses and a guarded manner; immediately Roger distrusted him, detested him, and hoped to Christ Ransom wasn't feeling the same way about him. Like mirror-twins they were, except Roger still had his hair, was twenty pounds lighter, and in the abject position of asking for help. When he brought up the subject of Elroy Jackson, Jr., a glaze passed over Ransom's face. *Bored! A man is going to die and this fucker is bored.* Roger had an impulse to sink his fist in the other's soft-looking middle but retained his air of smiling, affable courtesy. Quickly he explained his involvement in the case and his hope of freeing Jackson and he saw that Calvin Ransom was listening with only a modicum of attention, though not daring to exhibit actual rudeness, yet. His strategy was to let Roger talk. And talk. Finally Roger said, "Cal, frankly I'm stunned by this. I'm new at investigating cases like this, criminal cases, death-penalty issues. I'm just a volunteer, I'm still with my law firm. What I'm discovering! Not just errors in Elroy Jackson's trial but what looks like deliberate decisions by the prosecution to withhold exculpatory evidence. The original police report, and witnesses favorable to the defendant not brought into the trial, and—" Calvin Ransom said coldly, "A jury found Jackson guilty. A jury sentenced him to death. Appeal is automatic. The man has been assured the protection of the law." Ransom spoke in a polite flat TV-politician voice of judiciously restrained contempt.

Roger said, "'Protection' of the law! The law has screwed this man. A black man—"

"They were all black. Both sides. The kid who was shot in the face was black. Wasn't he?"

"Hispanic, but what's that got to do with it? Elroy Jackson got a lousy break. Like getting hit by lightning. He wasn't smart enough to deal with what happened and his attorney was a moron—you know 'Boomer' Spires? He must be a local courthouse character, lots of laughs?"

Ransom shrugged. "Boomer" Spires was an embarrassment out of the Hunterdon County comptroller's past.

Roger heard himself arguing with law-student earnestness as Ransom, seated behind a massive desk, arms behind his solid-looking neck, pretended to listen. "You can see how this was rigged, Cal. A federal court will find for us. I'm not accusing you, Cal, but the prosecutor's office, you were just assisting. The shooter, the actual killer, who's serving a twenty-five-year sentence at Rahway, found out when he was arrested that another guy, Jackson, whom he knew, ran from the crime scene outside the store, and the cops shot him, so the shooter, who turns state's evidence, cuts a deal with your office because his attorney is seven times smarter than 'Boomer' and he pleads to reduced charges and doesn't testify, so there's no cross-examination. There's the error I'm singling out. And there are others—" Roger heard his aggrieved voice, and saw the resentful glaze in Calvin Ransom's face, and knew he'd crossed over into a territory foreign to him. To be "involved"—to care passionately about someone, something not yourself—this wasn't Roger Cavanagh's nature; and yet, here he was.

Ransom said, with a smile, "Since when are you a crusader, Cavanagh? It's a little late, isn't it?"

"Fuck you, Ransom."

Roger left the comptroller's office before his half-hour was up. He felt the horror of it, that officers of the court, men like Calvin Ransom, men like himself, would wish to send an innocent man to death. *This is the enemy. They would kill for their profession.* Though afterward, driving back to Salthill, he'd tell himself it was a damned good feeling for once, to acknowledge you hate another's guts, and are hated in turn.

11

"WHAT ARE THESE? Fossils?"

In December, in Naomi Volpe's flat in Jersey City where Roger hadn't been in weeks. In this inelegant setting of thrown-together furnishings, crammed bookshelves, a startlingly large TV on a squat Formica table, unpacked cartons from previous moves. There was a look to the flat as if a strong wind had blown through it. There were odors of cigarette smoke, food, insecticide. (Roaches? Maybe it was a good idea that Roger never stayed the night.) Roger had had to call Volpe several times before she called him back with the excuse she'd been away, in Washington, D.C., on an assignment; Roger happened to know that Volpe hadn't been out of town for so long, but he wasn't going to press the issue. That Volpe should wish to make excuses to him, that she would offer them with a modicum of apology, was enormously flattering.

There was this unexpected side of Naomi Volpe, sometimes: what you might call *feminine*.

Just to be standing in Volpe's flat in Jersey City, in a no-man's-land of rental properties bordering the warehouse district, was sexually arousing to Roger. He had powerful erotic memories of the previous times he'd been in this flat. Then, Volpe had led Roger immediately into her unadorned bedroom; he'd had only a vague awareness of the flat's other rooms. This time he stood in Volpe's narrow rectangular living room as Volpe searched in the kitchen for clean glasses, for drinks; the occasion was far more social, and congenial; still, Roger was excited, and beginning to be impatient. He scrutinized a wall of cheaply framed but striking photographs of what appeared to be the mouths and interiors of caves, and of cuneiform-like shapes in rock. Taken where? The Southwest? Europe? There was a teasing familiarity to these stylized shapes, Roger was certain he recognized.

He didn't intend to betray his irritation with Volpe, that she'd been negligent in returning his calls when he'd wanted so badly to see her. He wasn't going to appear jealous! Not Mr. C.

Volpe hadn't kissed Roger when he stepped into her flat but she hadn't stiff-armed him, either. She'd let him kiss her, and run his hands hungrily over her body. Her mood was unusually subdued, distracted. Even her spiky hair was flattened. The nose ring had vanished from her nostril as if it had never been. Clearly she wasn't picking up on her lover's mood, she had other things on her mind. When Roger told her of visiting that prick Calvin Ransom and of some new developments in the Jackson case she listened with a creased brow but said little. She hadn't shared in Roger's denunciation of Ransom, she'd shrugged as if to say *So? He's the enemy, what can you expect.*

"Female genitalia," Volpe said matter-of-factly, indicating the framed photographs as she gave Roger his drink, "thirty-thousand-year-old cave carvings, in Les Eyzies. Beautiful, aren't they?"

Roger stared at the photographs, a flush rising into his face. Female genitalia! Of course, he could see it now: simple stylized forms, geometrical, Platonic. Pelvic bones, labias and vaginas and vulvae, clitorises. There were hundreds of these. Thousands! Whoever the primitive sculptors were, male or female, they'd been fascinated by their subject as a child might be fascinated by her genitalia. Here was a lost prehistoric world—Neanderthal? Cro-Magnon? Roger's own ancestors, in theory. Volpe was telling Roger that the framed photos had been given to her by "a very special friend, a woman" who'd since died of ovarian cancer. "The carvings tell us that sex is a biological fact, like our elbows, or teeth. It's nothing mystical. Almost, you can reduce it to an equation. Sex as an act, having a baby—these are things the body *does*. New life is created in the female and expelled from the female through these devices. It's no more mystical than the asexual reproduction of amoeba." Volpe spoke as if proclaiming good news, but Roger was feeling mildly depressed. Amoeba! He wanted to protest *But it's more fun!*

They sat. Roger faced the wall of carved cunts. He sipped his drink as they talked. Somehow, he felt foolish. His erection throbbed like an abscessed tooth. Why wasn't Volpe sensing his mood, or did she sense it, and was choosing to ignore it? *What did it symbolize, she'd removed her sexy-glittery little nose ring?* He wondered if she'd removed it for tonight, for him; or whether his visit was totally irrelevant. Volpe was telling him of "profoundly significant" research she'd been doing, partly as background to the Elroy Jackson case, nationwide statistics on blacks, Hispanics, Asians, and Caucasians arrested, indicted, convicted, and sentenced to prison terms since 1980.

Wanting to lighten the mood, Roger said, "Naomi, your research makes me proud of you."

"Proud? Of me?" Volpe was startled, as if Roger had spoken an obscenity. Hurriedly she rose. She disappeared into the kitchen, Roger had the idea she was hiding from him. How unlike Volpe this behavior was! He began to feel uneasy, lifting his eyes to the cuneiform shapes carved in stone, that mocked him with their simplicity.

Homo sapiens: the species that makes too much of biology.

Volpe returned, but didn't sit beside Roger. Her forehead was creased and her skin looked sallow, slightly puffy. She was wearing the jumpsuit she'd worn on their Rahway visit, that fitted her wiry little body loosely as if she'd lost weight. She said, "Roger, I have news for you."

Roger, not Mr. C.!

"Yes?" Roger wasn't sure this was news he wanted to hear.

"I seem to be pregnant."

"Pregnant!"

"I mean—I am pregnant. It's certain."

Roger's first thought was *Now Marina is lost forever.*

His second thought was *Another chance!*

In a daze Roger sat gripping his drink between numbed fingers. He saw rather than heard the spiky-haired young woman speaking to him, and in his astonishment he couldn't have named her, or recalled what their relationship was. Naomi Volpe stood crossing her arms tightly beneath her breasts, as if cold; the fork-prong lines in her forehead deepened; her eyes gleamed with moisture. It was a shock to Roger, that this boy-female could become pregnant. Roger associated pregnancy with vulnerability, and vulnerability with femininity. She said, "I've known for about six weeks. I just haven't known what to do about it. The due date is the first week of July—in theory."

Now Roger's heart had begun to pound, hard. He'd begun to sweat. Six weeks! Due date! He saw himself pleading with Lee Ann to forgive him, and with Robin. Their disgust with him now would be absolute.

Numbly Roger asked what must be asked: why hadn't she told him until now? What did she want to do? And—how had it happened?

"You were on the pill, I thought? Didn't you tell me that?"

Naomi said, with sudden anger, "It can't always be the woman's responsibility, contraception. 'You were on the pill'—*fuck you.*"

"I only meant—"

"I know what you meant, Mr. C. I read you loud and clear."

Roger stammered an apology. Things were moving too swiftly for him to absorb. Pulses beat in his forehead and eyes as if about to burst. Jesus! Afterward he would recall that he hadn't taken Naomi Volpe's hand, he hadn't behaved instinctively as a man would, if he were in love with a woman who'd just told him she was having his baby.

(*His* baby? How could he know?)

(Demand a DNA test? Roger Cavanagh wasn't so crude, or so cruel.)

These matters might have passed through Naomi Volpe's mind, too. She was keeping a distance between herself and Roger. She was speaking quietly, almost formally; her old sexy-feisty manner had vanished, like her nose ring. Roger liked her more, but desired her less. He didn't desire her at all. His erection had wilted, the pit of his belly felt cold. All his blood had rushed to his brain, or had all his blood rushed out of his brain? Roger picked up on part of what Naomi was saying, "—arrangements can be made. Right on East 15th, 'WomanSpace,' it's called."

Roger said, "I'll help you. I mean," Roger's face burned, "—I'll pay for it. And any other expenses."

Naomi looked away with an air of pained acknowledgment. Her left forearm was pressed across her flat abdomen, in an awkward gesture. There was a subtle hurt, and a more subtle acquiescence, in Naomi Volpe, as she listened to Roger. In the past, Volpe would have interrupted him. "Maybe you'd like to take some time off, Naomi? After the—procedure? You've been working very hard. For your paralegal salary. A vacation, over the holidays—?"

"Would you come with me?" Naomi asked, almost wistfully. "I don't want to go alone."

This took Roger by surprise. "I—I could, possibly. That might be a good idea."

"Somewhere in the Caribbean," Naomi said eagerly, "maybe the Dominican Republic? It's beautiful there. You've been working hard, too, Roger. Your two lives!"

Was this Naomi Volpe speaking? So hesitant, and so vulnerable? Roger would swear he'd never met the woman before.

He went to her, and held her. At once she pressed her face against his chest, and he felt the heat of her skin. There was no desire between them, nor even the memory of desire. Roger was thinking *This is what must be done. These are the circumstances.*

In the walk-up flat in Jersey City they stood like that for what seemed like a very long time, spared from looking into each other's face.

12

IN THE END, Roger didn't accompany Naomi Volpe to the Dominican Republic. If that's where Volpe went, Roger wasn't certain. She understood that he had little enthusiasm for being with her, obviously he didn't love her. "I can go alone. I'm a big girl. Thanks for your solicitude!" Feeling generous as well as guilty, for it was Christmas, Roger made out a check to Naomi Volpe for $5,000; seeing the figure, Volpe smiled nervously, and put the check away. "Mr. C.! You're a gentleman."

Roger laughed, embarrassed. Thinking *I'm a prick.*

Volpe was granted a leave of absence from the Project. She disappeared, and Roger didn't hear from her. Weeks passed: it was

January, and finally February. By chance Roger learned that Volpe was back in the States but working temporarily in Washington, D.C., and traveling to Memphis and New Orleans. He called her Jersey City number and left polite, friendly messages—"Naomi? It's Roger. Just checking in. Wondering how you are. Give me a call sometime, will you?" Unexpectedly, Volpe did call Roger, but at such shrewd times when she could assume Roger wouldn't be in. Her recorded messages were brief and guarded. She was "making progress" in her death-penalty research; she was "feeling optimistic, some days." Her voice sounded strained. Roger thought *She has had the abortion, and is in mourning.*

Roger felt the loss, it seemed to him a second, bitter loss. First, there was Robin. And now this wisp of life, unnamed, a fetus of less than two months. *Another chance* and he'd destroyed it.

13

AND THEN VOLPE RETURNED to work in Manhattan, in early March. Roger was surprised and hurt she hadn't informed him: he discovered her in the office one afternoon when he came in. Unmistakable, the paralegal's rapid-fire telephone voice, corrosive as Drano. Roger stood in the doorway of her cubicle, dry-mouthed. There she was: the woman he'd impregnated. She was tanned, and her hair had been dyed a vivid plum-purple, no longer shaved up the back of her head but scissor-cut, covering just the tips of her ears. Both her earlobes glittered with metal and the nose ring was back. She was wearing a black jersey top loose over black wool trousers and, seeing the swell of her breasts, and the ruddy fullness of her face, Roger was stunned. *This woman is pregnant.*

Seeing Roger, Volpe quickly glanced away, and continued her vehement conversation. When at last she hung up the receiver she said, disgusted, "What an asshole! I'd be better off talking to a recorded message."

Roger said, "Naomi, we need to talk, yes?"

Volpe said, "I'm busy now, Roger. I've got weeks of e-mail."

Roger said, "We do have something to talk about—don't we?"

Volpe said, evenly, "Mr. C, how do I know? I can't speak for you. *I* don't have much to say to *you*."

"But—how are you?"

"*I'm* fine, *I've* never felt better."

Roger was staring, in a daze. He heard the most banal words issuing from his mouth. "Yes, you're—looking good, Naomi."

At once Volpe flared up, "Shouldn't I? What'd you prefer, I should look like shit? I should've hemorrhaged to death, or OD'd on barbiturates? That's the preferred scenario?"

"Naomi, let's go somewhere private, we need to talk."

"'Need,' who says? Whose 'need'?"

"For just a few minutes? I only want— "

"I told you, Mr. C., I'm fucking *busy*. I'm overworked, I'm underpaid, I'm a slave to this system, I never got my law degree like you hot-shit fellas, still I'm dedicated to the cause, see, so stop harassing me. Go beat on some other disadvantaged female assistant."

Roger was trembling. He saw the fury in Volpe's ferret-eyes, and knew he'd better back off.

In the office he shared with another lawyer, Roger clicked onto his e-mail and typed out a message for Naomi Volpe—

> Dinner at Union Square Cafe at 8 PM? I'll be the guy with a spike through his groin.
>
> R.

Within minutes Volpe e-mailed him back—

> Mr. C.! You are a gentleman.

Roger knew Naomi Volpe couldn't resist the lure of a first-rate restaurant.

* * *

AND SO ROGER LEARNED, to his astonishment: yes she'd originally intended to have the abortion, no she hadn't planned things quite as they were turning out, yes she "liked" him, "thought well" of him, "respected" him as a lawyer and a man, no she hadn't meant to "deceive" him. But her body was her body after all. Her life was her life. The life of the baby-to-be was her responsibility, not his. "The father's role is minuscule. In nature. It's over in an instant." Volpe snapped her fingers. Her eyes shone, she was sleek with well-being, the most attractive Roger had seen her. And she was certainly enjoying the wine.

Roger knew better than to inflame this woman, he chose his words with care. "Naomi, it's just that I'm shocked. I am the father, after all." He paused, to allow them both to think *But is this so? Without a test, is it a fact?* "I consider this a mutual responsibility. I thought we'd come to a decision back in December. I'm not accusing you of anything, Naomi, but—"

Volpe flared up, "'Not accusing'! I hope not! Who the fuck are you to judge *me?* I'm not your assistant in my private life, Mr. C.! I'm not your sex slave. I'm not some vessel you poured your precious seed into, and walked away and forgot about, like you'd wipe your precious ass and flush a toilet. If maybe I changed my mind and want to bring this baby to term and find a good deserving home for him, or her, what's it to you? This is the twenty-first century, not the first. A woman has autonomy over her own body, I hope!" Volpe's nostrils were dilated, she leaned across the table with such drama that Roger shrank back. In an unnervingly loud voice, which drew the attention of diners at nearby tables, she proclaimed, "I *freely chose* not to kill my baby, which *you'd dictated.*"

Roger protested, "I didn't 'dictate'—I didn't want—"

"'I'll pay for it,' you said. The first words that came from your mouth."

"Naomi, I don't think—"

"By which you didn't mean you'd pay for the kid's college tuition, right?"

"At that point, I thought you wanted—"

"You showed no emotion except shock. Possibly a little

repugnance. No, don't look guilty, don't look 'concerned,' it's too late now. You wouldn't even touch me, for Christ's sake. Like I was a *leper*."

"Naomi, I did touch you. I was very concerned for—"

"The fact is, Mr. C., you didn't want this baby. This baby I'm carrying, four months and one week old, and kicking. Not a fetus but a *baby*. Get it?—*baby*. You surrendered your moral and legal right to this baby when you tried to buy me off, made out a check and considered the hit-job done, and couldn't get out of my life fast enough. You *prick*."

Roger gripped his head in his hands. Was this true? And even if true to a degree, did it bind him? Weakly he tried to explain, "Naomi, I wouldn't have wished for you a pregnancy you wouldn't have wanted. Maybe I misread you. Yes, I was in shock. I didn't know how to respond."

Volpe said, in a voice heavy with sarcasm, "Because you were terrified that having a baby would link us. That I might expect you to 'commit' yourself to me. We might live together, or get married, that terrified you, yes?" Volpe laughed, and swallowed a large mouthful of wine. Clearly she was enjoying this scene. Roger would wonder if she'd rehearsed it beforehand or if—but this was a thought too awful to allow into consciousness—she'd actually played it out before, with another man. Or men.

He remembered the rumor he'd heard about Naomi Volpe: that she'd had a baby, and gave it out for adoption. To a "wealthy" couple.

"If Naomi Volpe comes with the baby, the baby's got to be dumped in the toilet, right? That was precisely what showed in your face, Mr. C. Every low fucking degrading crap emotion you think you're hiding from the world shows in your face and is decipherable by anyone with half a brain. Tell me I'm wrong."

Roger went silent. Well, it was true. Baby or no baby, he'd rather swallow poison than live with, let alone marry, a female like Naomi Volpe.

What lousy luck! If Roger Cavanagh had been fated to impregnate any woman a few months ago, why hadn't that woman been Abigail Des Pres? Abigail was still young enough, if barely.

She was certainly a gorgeous woman. They'd come close to making love more than once. He *had* loved Abigail—to a degree. She was malleable enough, neurotic enough, to love him. By now, they'd be living together, preferably in her house on Wheatsheaf Drive. They'd be married. They'd have this baby. The Salthill circle would have rejoiced in their union as a major social event of any season. A *second chance* for both, and naturally Roger had fucked up.

The remainder of the evening at Union Square Cafe passed in a blur for Roger. He would learn from the woman who meant to bear his baby "to term" that, yes, she'd had this experience before—"It was an accident then, too. But accidents can be profitable." They were on their second bottle of red wine. And it wasn't inexpensive red wine. Volpe devoured her grilled smoked shell steak with a zestful appetite, grease glistened on her thin lips. With the aplomb of a woman undressing in a locker room, not giving a damn who looked on, Volpe informed Roger that, in case he was wondering, she'd had several "successful" abortions, the first at the age of sixteen; but more recently she'd acquired a "radically different perspective" on the reproductive function of the female. "In our capitalist-consumer society, at least." Pregnancy and childbirth were nothing more than physical experiences that had been grotesquely sentimentalized in so-called first-world countries. "I'm not a 'mother' in myself, only in a brief relationship. If the baby is given out immediately for adoption, that is. Through a reputable broker. Adoption is online now, and very efficient. Nobody's 'buying'—that's illegal. True, money changes hands, and we're talking five figures here, but it's elliptical, it's in good taste and nobody's 'selling' per se. It's a charitable act to have a baby for someone desperately wanting a baby, yes?" Volpe put the question to Roger as if this were a subject they'd been discussing, and Roger should know the answer. "These are educated couples, people with money, and a sense of entitlement. They do pro bono work for liberal causes. They're generous with donations. They're politically active. But when they can't have babies as they've planned they get crazy. They need to propagate their own kind. Civilization needs superior genes. So they'd be impressed with a pedigree like Baby's: pure Caucasian on both sides. Smart Caucasians. One of them a hot-shit litigator. The other just a paralegal, but with an IQ measured at 153 when she was tested at age fifteen. (I actually have this document. I carry it in my wallet.) No chance of a crack or AIDS baby. No blind DNA lottery." She laughed, happily.

Roger smiled wanly. "You could take orders, I guess? 'Cavanagh.'"

"That's a cynical remark. I hate cynicism."

"Yes, I can see that. You're an idealist."

"*You* could've used protection, friend. You knew the risk you were taking."

Risk? He'd been dazed with sexual need. And Volpe had seemed to be, too.

(Or had it been a ruse on the woman's part? Shrewdly plotted, executed?)

"I don't know," Roger muttered, meaning *I don't know why I took the risk*. "I assumed you were on the pill. I seem to remember you telling me."

"So? Miscalculations happen."

"*It* happened, improvidently."

How like a young girl Roger sounded, knocked up as a result of naïveté and stupidity. *He* was knocked up as a result of naïveté and stupidity; and maybe, just maybe he wasn't all that surprised that Volpe hadn't had the abortion. Or disconcerted.

"One thing I do know," Roger said, "no baby of mine is going to be marketed."

The lengthy dinner ended with Roger Cavanagh making out, to Naomi Volpe, a check for ten thousand dollars. This was "part-payment" for services rendered, the remainder to be negotiated when the baby was born and delivered to the father. There would be a contract, Roger insisted. "Of course, Mr. C.! Everything up-front and legal," Volpe said. "*I* don't intend to bring up this child." When Roger handed her the check she glanced at the figure, then quickly folded the check and slipped it into her handbag. A small portion of wine remained in the second bottle and Naomi divided it between their glasses. "Mr. C.! Let's drink to our future—the three of us."

14

The shimmering aqua pool floating in twilight. How he yearned to dive into it as if diving into the sky. But he was ashamed: for what if he sank to the bottom? The red-haired woman was in the water at the far end of the pool, unaware of him. Nor could he see her face. And there was his friend Adam Berendt boldly diving into the water, broad shoulders and scarred chest covered in graying bronze hairs, his strong limbs pumping. Roger cried, Adam? Help me? Tell me what to do. His tremulous voice issued from all sides. It was possible to ignore such a voice, as Adam paid it not the slightest heed, swimming the length of the pool. Roger forced himself into the water. Swimming in Adam's wake. Whether he sank to the bottom or managed to keep afloat, he never knew, for the dream ended in a soft silent explosion.

15

"IT'S THE RIGHT THING. For once, I'm doing the right thing."

Not wanting to think *The woman is blackmailing me, I'm helpless.*

Not wanting to think *What if it isn't even my child?*

And yet: how much money Roger would give to Naomi Volpe during the course of their unorthodox friendship, in outright payments and "loans," he would not have wished to calculate. The initial $5,000 for the aborted abortion; $10,000 in March, and eight thousand in June for "miscellaneous interim expenses"; and a final $12,000 when the baby was born and "delivered" to the father in July . . . Unexpectedly, Roger's relationship with Volpe became increasingly paternal. As if Roger himself were the young woman's father. (And what did it matter, finally, who the father of the baby actually *was*? The profound fact was: *the baby*.)

So Roger, in his new infatuation with fatherhood-to-be, told himself.

Rarely now did he and Volpe have sex, and then only when Volpe, aroused from a day of frustrations at the office, initiated it. She was yet more frustrated with Roger's diminished libido, and one evening exploded in a fury of slaps and kicks aimed against him. "God damn you, Cavanagh! You can't be bothered, can you! Like every other fucking male of the fucking species, a healthy pregnant female who wants sex turns you *off*." Roger protested, "Darling, I wouldn't want to hurt you. Or the baby." Volpe laughed, "Hurt me! How the hell are you going to hurt me! With that limp cock? *That?* You couldn't poke that into a bowl of pudding, you asshole. And don't call me 'darling'! You don't love me. You don't even like me. You can't wait to get rid of me, and have Baby all to yourself."

Roger winced, but couldn't deny this. How like a married couple he and Volpe had become, in the final, exhausting stages of combat.

He didn't desire the woman, but he wanted very much to oversee her life, and the life of the baby. (For what if Volpe had a miscarriage? She still smoked, he'd caught her several times. She drank, and was physically careless. What if she fell down in the subway? Climbing out of a taxi? Roger would never forgive himself.) *My second chance. I don't intend to fuck it up*. Those evenings when Volpe was with friends in Manhattan, even when she spent much of the night in a lover's flat, Roger insisted upon driving her home to Jersey City, no matter the hour. They communicated by cell phone: Roger worked late at the office, had dinner alone in the neighborhood, waited uncomplainingly in a bar or in his car parked on a side street until Volpe called. "Roger? You awake? O.K. to come pick me up now." The time might be midnight, one A.M., three-thirty A.M. Roger Cavanagh had become the paralegal's private limo service! Sometimes Volpe took pity on him and told him to go home, she'd spend the night in the city, she could take care of herself, but Roger insisted, he didn't at all mind; he hadn't anything "more worthwhile" to do, anyway. Volpe laughed, "Mr. C.! This is embarrassing."

Roger said gravely, "Not for me."

It was about this time that Roger encountered Lionel Hoffmann on a midtown street, and went with his old Salthill friend for drinks in a Sixth Avenue hotel cigar lounge. What a change in Lionel Hoffmann! Where Lionel had long been one of Salthill's middle-aged husbands, even as a relatively young man, he had now the air of a lone wolf; lean-faced, and vigilant; edgy, anxious, restless; as Roger spoke, Lionel continually glanced up at the scantily clad cocktail waitresses, and was continually sniffing and blowing his nose, which annoyed Roger; though Roger was forthcoming about the extraordinary development in his private life, Lionel was close-mouthed about his private life, until finally Roger told Lionel he was sorry to have heard that Lionel and Camille were separated, and Lionel blew his nose loudly and mumbled what sounded like, "Yes, I'm sorry, too." And the subject was dropped.

Yet: not long afterward, Roger saw his Salthill friend in the company of a young woman, in an expensive Midtown restaurant, and kept his distance to observe, through a mirror, the disparity in their ages and types. The girl was very young, stylish; a light-skinned black, or an East Indian; her hair was braided and scintillant, like a nest of snakes; and her eyes moved restlessly, even as Lionel spoke earnestly to her, clasping both her hands. For some painful minutes Roger watched, fascinated and repelled.

"Poor Lionel! What a sucker."

EAGERLY AND OBSESSIVELY Roger began to read of pregnancy, childbirth, infants. He bought out most of the baby shelf at the Salthill Bookstore. ("Mr. Cavanagh," Molly Ivers said, startled, "what's your sudden interest in babies?" "I'm going to have one, in July.") He began to make inquiries among his Salthill acquaintances into full-time nannies. Except when he was most absorbed in his work there wasn't an hour when Roger didn't brood upon the baby-to-come. On principle Volpe disliked "intrusive medical technology" and refused to have an ultrasound to determine the baby's sex. "You'll just have to be surprised, like daddies through the millennia." As her pregnancy advanced Roger fell into the habit of calling Volpe on her cell phone frequently. Always he was casual, calm. "How are you, Naomi?" "Mr. C., I'm *fine,*" Volpe said, laughing, exasperated. "If I weren't, you'd be the first to be informed." Roger kept a calendar of Volpe's medical appointments and made certain she kept them, for Volpe disliked even female doctors. The "capitalist-consumer enterprise" of childbearing sickened her, she said. "We were meant to squat in the fields and ditches and have our babies, cut the umbilical cord with our teeth, and get on with it."

Get on with what, Roger wondered.

Yet Volpe complained of her pregnancy, once she began to get heavy, seriously heavy, in her sixth month. She complained of bladder trouble and of "everything swollen" and she hinted that maybe she'd made a mistake, agreeing to bring the baby "to term," maybe it wasn't too late (in the final trimester) for an abortion, somewhere? Roger shuddered, hearing such words. He couldn't gauge if Volpe was sincere or testing him, taunting or teasing him, if at such moments her deepest wishes emerged, or whether she was simply playing a role, carelessly improvising. *I must be very careful how I respond. I must not contradict her. Oh, God!* He dreaded calling her one day to be told bluntly that the baby was gone, she'd changed her mind after all.

He drove her to the obstetrician's office and waited for her in the outer room, self-conscious as any expectant father. Under Volpe's influence he'd begun to dress "younger" when he wasn't in a professional setting; true, his hairline was eroding, what remained of his thick, wiry hair was turning an innocuous gray; he'd become somewhat edgy, restless (like his friend Lionel?); yet he was unfailingly optimistic, youthful . . . One afternoon the obstetrician's new receptionist asked Roger where he and his "daughter" lived, and Roger said, stung, "My daughter is a boarder at a prep school in Maine, and I live in Salthill, New York." The young woman stared at him with a puzzled smile, but asked no further questions. When he told Volpe about the exchange, she expressed indignation on Roger's behalf. "Your daughter! That's ridiculous. My father looks old enough to be *your* father. Our ages are nobody's business but our own." She grabbed him, and kissed him fiercely on the mouth. If anyone was going to insult Roger Cavanagh, it would be *her*.

16

"WHEN I FIRST HEARD, I didn't believe it. But of course I believed it. You selfish bastard!"

Had to tell Lee Ann knowing that (of course) Lee Ann would tell Robin. Had to make the dread call and yet guiltily, shamefacedly he delayed long enough, mid-April, Volpe in her sixth month, knowing that by this time Lee Ann would already be informed by mutual Salthill friends. *Roger Cavanagh is having a baby with a woman no one knows. A much younger woman of course. Imagine! At his age*. Roger said, "What's 'selfish' about it, Lee Ann? I didn't get your permission first?" and Lee Ann said angrily, "Do you think of anyone beside yourself, ever? Did you think of Robin, how she'll take this?" "The pregnancy was an accident, Lee Ann. Frankly, I wasn't thinking of Robin at the time." "There you go, your sick sense of humor. You truly are a selfish bastard," and Roger said, trying to remain reasonable, "But what is selfish about bringing a baby that's wanted into the world, a baby that will be provided for, loved—" and Lee Ann cut in, derisively, "'Loved'! What a joke! Ask Robin about your 'love,' you son of a bitch," and hung up the receiver.

Roger was astounded, and hurt, and eventually furious with his ex-wife. What right had she to pass a moral judgment on him? Lee Ann had hated pregnancy. She'd hated the hormonal tyranny as she called it, and she'd hated the changes in her body. Lee Ann's female vanity which she'd managed to hide, or to deny, had emerged, sometimes in outbursts of considerable emotion; it was at this time she'd first begun to be unreasonably jealous of Roger. (When Roger, a devoted young husband and father, was wholly innocent of being attracted to any other woman, he swore!)

And then Robin was in their lives, fully in the center of their lives. A giant infant squeezing their marriage out of shape. They'd talked vaguely of having a second child, they'd hoped for a boy, but Robin was simply too demanding, even as an infant; by the time she was four, she was requiring an extraordinary investment of time and emotional effort, especially on the part of her mother, and any thought of a second child filled Lee Ann with revulsion. Of course, she tried to temper this revulsion with good humor. It became Lee Ann's reiterated marital joke, "One Robin is enough!"

To which Roger sometimes amended, silently *One Robin is more than enough.*

17

IN HIS REASONABLE-LAWYER voice he said, "Naomi? I don't mean to be critical or intrusive— " and Volpe interrupted, "So? Don't be either, Mr. C."—and he persevered, hoping to God not to offend this volatile woman who bore his happiness, his reason-for-being, his very future in her belly—"but pregnant women are advised not to smoke, yes? Your doctor has informed you I'm sure, and there are warnings everywhere, yes?" Volpe exhaled smoke lavishly from both nostrils and fixed her defiant little ferret-eyes on Roger's face. "Look: I smoke possibly two-three cigarettes a week. I don't even finish them." A *week?* A day was more likely. But Roger said, "Still, Naomi, you do smoke. And I think you promised— " "*You* smoke." "I'm not a pregnant woman." "*I* didn't choose to become a 'pregnant woman,'" Volpe said angrily, "it was forced upon me." She made a show of stubbing out her cigarette in an ashtray. "And I don't like to be spied upon, Mr. C. That's grounds for sexual harassment in itself."

Volpe's laughter was high-pitched and sobering to hear.

Roger had fantasies of the baby born deformed, stunted. Brain-damaged. He'd heard of a baby born with its organs exposed, including the brain stem; he'd heard of a baby born without a spine; an aunt of his had had a breakdown when, it was said, she gave birth to a misshapen infant with facial features scrunched together as if melted . . . In the night he woke agitated and moaning. "This is a mistake. Lee Ann is right. What was I thinking of!"

He wished he'd never met Naomi Volpe. He wished he'd never arranged to do pro bono legal work for the Project to Free the Innocent. Somehow, it was Adam Berendt's fault.

He would name the baby after Adam. If there was a baby.

18

SHORTLY AFTER the first of July, Naomi Volpe disappeared.

She left behind a cryptic note for Roger:

> I'm sorry—
> I'm not sure if I can go through
> with this. Giving my baby up
> even to its (biological) father.
> I know, I have signed a contract.
> But you & I know that such a
> contract is not enforceable. Especially if mother & infant
> are *whereabouts unknown*.
>
> N.V.

This was a handwritten note, on the reverse of a printed page; after three hellish days a second message appeared, glimmering on Roger's computer screen:

> Sorry to cause you grief.
> I guess you are regretting you ever met me.
> I wish I could be this baby's true mother.
> You are a good man, Roger. Your faults
> are those of your class which you have
> struggled against.

I know: I promised you I would
bring this baby to term & it would
be yours.
Please cease looking for me.
It's futile, I am not within 1,000
miles of you. But I know of your
efforts, I'm kept informed.
You are making a fool of yourself.

I wish we could have loved each
other don't you?

N.V.

—

Hurriedly Roger typed a reply and sent it to N.V. at her e-mail address (if located in space this address was the flat in Jersey City, but Roger knew no one was there) and there followed several more days of virtually unrelieved panic. Why was Volpe doing this to him? Had she always despised him? Or were her feelings sincere? These days preliminary to the baby's anticipated birth (July eleventh), Roger would recall as indisputably the worst days of his life, though afterward a perverse amnesia would obscure them as (it's said) a woman forgets the agony of childbirth. And on the eve of July eleventh there came this remarkable message out of cyberspace:

The FIRST CONTRACTIONS have begun.
Approximately 15 minutes apart.
Now there is no going back,
this baby will be BORN.
If a man could feel the pain of labor,
would the race EXIST?

* * *

You wanted this baby killed,
do you remember?
Another party has expressed interest
in this baby. You must concede

that a loving & educated & well-to-do
couple (in their 30's) is preferable
to a single male (middle-aged).
If you wish the best for this baby
Roger you will concede this point, yes?
N.V.

"No!" Never would Roger concede this point, Roger was in a state of delirium waiting at his computer, by his telephone, pacing his Salthill town house in which Naomi Volpe had never set foot, and would not; he was drunk, and he was chain-smoking, and he didn't undress to sleep but lay across his rumpled bed wakeful and murderous and in a state of suspension for forty-eight hours, until at last this message appeared on the glassy screen:

Dear Roger Cavangh,
NV has instructed me to inform you—
there is good news. The baby has
been born. The baby is a BOY.
He weighs 8 lbs 11 oz. He is 21"
long & has thick dark hair & blue
eyes. He is nursing well.
NV wishes to say that it is her wish
to do the right thing. PLEASE DO NOT
ATTEMPT TO SEEK HER, SHE WILL CONTACT
YOU WHEN IT'S TIME.

The message was unsigned. Roger knew it was pointless to send a reply to the sender at the e-mail address provided. Like shouting into an abyss. Maybe it was Volpe herself? Testing him, tormenting him? Torturing him? Slyly misspelling his name? *Don't do this to me. God damn you gave your word, is it more money you want, yes, I'll pay more. Only just give me my son!*

IN AN ECSTATIC BLITZ of shopping a few weeks before at Baby-World in the Palisades Mall, Roger had bought furnishings for the nursery. This magical room, white-walled, dominated by a glowing white wicker crib, was next to Roger's room on the second floor of the three-storey townhouse. The nanny Roger had engaged, a Guatemalan-born woman named Herlinda, was to live in a room that opened onto the nursery; when Roger showed Herlinda through these quarters, leading her on a quick tour of the house, the woman had many questions to ask of which the most awkward was: where was Mrs. Cavanagh?

Roger said carefully, "Herlinda, there is no 'Mrs. Cavanagh' at the present time. The mother of the baby-to-be is a friend, and she has gone away to have her baby in private. Maybe," Roger said, inspired by Herlinda's dark attentive eyes and clay-colored face, "she has gone back to her hometown, to be with her own mother? We're temporarily out of touch. But everything is fine, Herlinda! She'll be back soon, I promise. Though you may not meet her. The baby will be here soon, I *promise.*" If Herlinda, a nanny with years of experience and superlative recommendations, was suspicious, or doubtful, she gave no sign. How practiced Herlinda was in the enigmatic ways of the American-Caucasian suburban class! Politely she asked Mr. Cavanagh for a "prepayment"; a check for a considerable amount of "nonrefundable" salary, which Roger eagerly made out for her, his hand badly shaking.

Yes, I'll pay! I'm the man who pays.

Only just—please, God—GIVE ME MY SON.

19

HE WAS PREPARED for an unhappy ending. He was not prepared for a happy ending.

He'd lost his faith in romance. If he never touched another woman again in his lifetime, good!

Still he waited to hear from Naomi Volpe. Rarely did he leave the Salthill town house, fearful of missing a call from her, or an actual visit from her. (Maybe she'd bring his son to him, to "deliver" him in person? Was that too fantastical a hope?) Roger had brought work home with him, and kept in touch with

Abercrombie, Cavanagh, Kruller & Hook by phone and e-mail; he was capable of losing himself in sixteen-hour workdays; he worked on behalf of his rich Salthill clients, and he worked on behalf of the indigent Elroy Jackson, Jr., completing the motion to be presented in federal court the following week. What purity, in work! Impersonality, integrity. You could keep your mind brilliantly focused, and sane. Though afterward Roger would acknowledge, yes he'd been close to the edge, those days. Forcing himself to shower, to shave. Forcing himself to change his clothes. Those long midsummer nights, unable to sleep. Waiting for Naomi Volpe to "contact" him. Waiting to see his infant son. Not daring to think *It's all a ruse. A fucking scam. The baby was never mine. She planned this, she's sold him to strangers.*

On the evening of July thirtieth he fell asleep at his desk, head on his arms. How heavy his head was, like one of Adam Berendt's stone shapes! He was allowed to know by dream-logic that in fact he was one of Adam Berendt's sculpted figures. There came into his presence the elusive baby. The baby weighing eight pounds, eleven ounces, twenty-one inches in length, the baby with thick dark hair and blue eyes, the baby that, when Roger reached for him, seemed to drift away. Where *was* Roger?—in a place of confusion like Penn Station. Crowds of persons with indistinct faces. Trains were being announced yet at the same time there was swampy, spongy soil underfoot. There was Adam Berendt speaking to Roger, consoling him. But the words were lost. Adam, and the baby to be called "Adam." This was dream-logic. If it made no sense elsewhere it made sense here. Roger was stumbling, groping for the baby, but the baby dissolved—where? Roger woke groaning, utterly spent.

He saw that he had a new message waiting for him.

Mr. C.! Call me. I'm back.

N.V.

20

ALWAYS ROGER WILL REMEMBER, as if it were a continuation of his dream.

Hurrying to the street corner where the car is parked. Beneath a street light. She's sitting on the passenger's side, the door open. The car belongs to a stranger, there's a woman behind the wheel but it's Naomi Volpe at whom Roger stares, she's sitting sideways in the passenger's seat with her trousered legs out, crossed. In her lap, a squirming white-bundled shape.

Lightly mocking, laughter in her voice she says, "Look who's here, Buzz. It's Dad-dy."

21

NOW ALL OF SALTHILL was talking of Roger Cavanagh.

"Roger? A *father?* Of a newborn *baby?* And he *has the baby?*"

"But—what of the mother? *Who is the mother?*"

There was a collective sense of panic, anxiety. That Roger Cavanagh, one of their own, had gone outside the tribe to take for himself what seemed, to all who knew him, his greatest happiness.

For here was Roger, who'd rarely confided in others, now answering friends' questions with startling candor. In the recklessness of new fatherhood he seemed hardly to care for privacy. Making the rounds of Salthill houses to show off the infant—"Adam"—and you were invited to drop by his town house for drinks in the early evening, and all day Sunday: there was the smiling Guatemalan nanny in the background, and Roger lifting his baby tenderly in his arms, proud, exhilarated, in a bliss of fatherhood. Yes, Roger changed diapers: sometimes. Yes, Roger helped with feedings and baths: sometimes. He never missed putting the baby to bed. This was a sacred ritual. He hadn't much participated in his daughter's childhood, he acknowledged, he'd been too damned busy with his career, too young, ambitious, callow. "This time, I mean to do things right."

His "lost life" had been restored to him, he said.

To his male friends he confided, "My life was shit. A backed-up toilet. This has changed everything."

It was noted that Roger Cavanagh looked "years younger."

It was noted that Roger spoke with a new, entertaining levity, reminiscent of the late Adam Berendt. He made his friends laugh even as he mildly scandalized them. He was unsparing on himself, describing his "clinical relationship" with the baby's mother, the elusive paralegal whom no one in Salthill had met. How, when she'd handed over the baby to him, she'd said, "Mr. C., here he is. Where's my check?"

This feckless young woman had relocated to San Jose where she would be managing an office of the National Project to Free the Innocent. Roger had recommended her highly for the position, and Roger had paid her moving expenses. She'd granted him full custody of the baby. On the birth certificate *Roger Cavanagh* was designated as *father*. He'd examined this document a dozen times. *Naomi Volpe, Roger Cavanagh*. Out of this mating of strangers had come *Adam Cavanagh*.

Roger had every reason to be confident he'd never see Volpe again.

When Beatrice Archer first saw the infant Adam, and was allowed to hold him in her arms, she burst into tears. Never would she have a baby of her own, again! And this baby was remarkably curious, alive, obviously male, a husky-kicky little boy with blue eyes and something of Adam Berendt's squareness in his jaw—"Though of course little Adam isn't Adam's son. We know this." Beatrice was a woman who thrilled to the happiness of friends as sometimes she thrilled to their disasters; she was a woman who loved a story, an unexpected turn of fortune. She telephoned friends who were away for the summer, some of them as distant as Europe, to tell them of Roger Cavanagh's astonishing news.

Inevitably the question was asked, who's the mother? Beatrice explained, "No one we know."

22

ABIGAIL MURMURED, "How strange to call him 'Adam.' Why did you do that, Roger?"

Roger shrugged. "Why not?"

The two were drifting off from Abigail's guests gathered on the fieldstone terrace at the rear of her large house. It was Labor Day weekend. Abigail and Gerhardt had just returned from several weeks on Nantucket and were giving a dinner party to announce their upcoming wedding. ("Abigail, at last remarried!" her friends marveled. "It's the end of an era.") Happy as he was with his son, now seven weeks old, Roger wasn't altogether happy to learn that Abigail was going to marry a Salthill architect of whom no one in their circle knew much—Gerhardt Ault.

The man was wholly unprepossessing. You wouldn't give him a second glance. Roger had made inquiries, and learned that Ault was a highly respected architect, so possibly he had money, and would be making money, but Abigail Des Pres didn't need money, she needed—what? Not this boyish-gawky-homely character with a thin beaky face and receding chin, cavernous nostrils, a nervous pumping handshake, and an inclination to stammer. Ault was hardly Abigail's height and he gazed at her in awe, clearly in love; clearly devoted; yet, how was it possible, Abigail loved *him?* The two were *lovers?* Roger felt a stab of sexual jealousy, almost anger.

He might have married Abigail Des Pres.

Everywhere Roger was invited that fall in Salthill and environs he'd bring the husky infant Adam, and the capable Guatemalan nanny, and after guests cooed over the infant for a respectable amount of time little Adam was dispatched back to the nursery at Belle Meade Place with Herlinda. Abigail, lifting the baby to embrace him in her bare, slender arms, bringing her lips against the baby's warm brow, burst into tears gratifying to the father. Abigail murmured, "I'm so happy for you, Roger. This is—quite a surprise." Roger said, "I'm so happy for *you,* Abigail. Of course," with as much conviction as if he meant it.

With Gerhardt Ault, Roger was civil, polite. He foresaw having to see a good deal of Ault, socially. He'd work out his attitude toward Ault, in time, as you'd work out a settlement for your client, demanding as much as you dared, giving up as little as you could get away with.

Ault was only a few feet away looking on with his shy, hopeful smile, but Abigail and Roger seemed not to notice him. After the baby was sent home with Herlinda, Abigail downed a glass of champagne and slipped her hand boldly into Roger's. "Come talk to me, Roger! We have so much to catch up on." Abigail asked Roger about his voluntary legal work, and appeared to listen intently (as many of his Salthill friends did not) when he told her; impulsively, Abigail spoke of donating money to the committee—"It was one of Adam's things, I guess?" Roger said. "Yes. One of Adam's things." *From this thing, Volpe. From Volpe, the baby.* Yet he drew back from speaking of the connection so rawly, even to Abigail Des Pres. Now it was Abigail's turn to talk, warmly, with a tremor in her voice, of her new life, not much about Gerhardt Ault but about his thirteen-year-old adopted daughter Tamar, Chinese-born, and very shy. The girl had been adopted as a year-old by Ault and his wife who'd died of cancer when Tamar was a small child. "She was devastated by losing her mother. She doesn't trust anyone, and I don't blame her. I want to love her as a mother, I only need to learn how. The girl is like a newly blossomed flower. The petals have opened, a little—but if the sun is too strong they'll shut again." Abigail astonished Roger by speaking with such passion of how she makes herself "very still, like Zen" around the girl; never enters her room, for instance, unless she's been invited; never speaks to Tamar unless she can sense that Tamar wants her to. "I don't 'waylay' her, I don't 'ambush' her, as Jared was always accusing me of doing, with him. The worst thing you can do is impose your emotions upon a child—I've learned! I take Tamar into the city to the ballet, to museums and shows. She's a promising cellist, and I've become her principal listener. I say little, I restrain my praise. Mostly I just listen. That's how we commune. That's how I will be Tamar's mother. Oh, Roger, do you think it will work? I want so badly for it to work. Tamar loves her father but can't talk to him, nor can Gerhardt talk very easily to her . . ." Abigail's voice quavered with a strange ecstatic emotion. Roger was touched that Abigail was confiding in him, this was an act of true intimacy between them, at last; yet he rather resented Abigail's new, obviously thrilling connection with the Aults, strangers to him. Innocently he said, "And what does Jared think about this, his mother remarrying?" Abigail stiffened, and looked away, with the dignity of one whose heart has been broken, and has been mended, or nearly. She said, "Harry complains that Jared is becoming more difficult—'more adolescent'—all the time. He quarrels with his father and with his stepmother. I never hear from him any longer. And I keep my distance. I have my new life, Roger, just like you."

As inconspicuously as he could manage, Roger had been leading Abigail around the corner of the house, out of sight of the terrace. And Abigail went willingly. Roger knew that Gerhardt Ault would never dare follow them. Nor any of their Salthill friends. In the Salthill imagination, Roger and Abigail were a "romantic couple"—of some undefined sort. Abigail had slipped her hand out of Roger's warm hand but he regained it, gripping the fingers. He said, meanly, "Abigail, you don't really love this 'Gerhardt Ault,' do you? Is there an emotional, sexual rapport between the two of you, really?" Roger spoke in the reproving tone of an elder brother. Abigail said, "I respect and admire Gerhardt, I could only love *you*." She laughed, a sound like rippling water.

Roger turned aside, smiling angrily. Bitch!

But he'd let Abigail Des Pres have the final word on their romance, he was a gentleman.

FOR WHEN, later that evening, he returned home to the town house on Belle Meade Place, there was his baby son—Roger's *son!*—in the nursery beside his bedroom.

"Adam Cavanagh" at the center of the life of Roger Cavanagh who'd had no center to his life, previously.

There was Herlinda who reported to the doting father every minute wondrous transaction between her and little Adam since Roger had seen them last (feeding, "burping," diaper change, bath, pacifier, kicking-thrashing in his bassinet, blanket on, blanket off, squealing, crying, gooing-gurgling, eye-rolling, "listening," and "smiling") to which Roger listened as attentively as if his life depended upon it. Long after Herlinda had gone to bed, and little Adam was sunk in the deepest of sleeps, Roger hung over the white wicker crib, lost in awe. So happy, he was beginning to forget to be afraid.

The Missing

I

At last, in late June, the call came.

The call Owen Cutler had been anticipating with dread since Augusta had vanished from his life eight months before.

"Mr. Cutler? You're sitting down, I hope? Please sit."

It was Elias West, the private investigator Owen had hired to find Augusta. He was in Florida. Here, it seemed, the nude, headless corpse of a middle-aged Caucasian female of about fifty had been found by hikers in Hendry County, north of the Everglades. The unidentified woman had been "sexually assaulted" and her pelvic region "mutilated" and her fingertips "crudely chopped off," in an obvious attempt to thwart police identification. Fortunately the corpse had been found less than forty-eight hours after it was dumped, so decomposition, which ordinarily would have been rapid and devastating in that climate, was minimal.

A missing persons alert had gone out nationally. Elias West believed they should confer, since one of the places West had tracked Augusta to was Florida. (A Gucci handbag containing

Augusta Cutler's identification had been found discarded in Miami Beach, in April.) West put the question frankly to his employer: Did Mr. Cutler think he could make the trip to Florida and bear to view a body in such a condition? Did he think he might be able to identify his wife by bodily markings like moles, freckles, scars, etc. in such—circumstances?

Owen Cutler, who'd answered the phone on the first ring, hesitated but a moment before saying yes. And yes, he was seated. His voice was faint, but calm. Owen dealt with loneliness—and the particular shame of this loneliness—by working in his greenhouse in cool weather, and in his newly established, lavish gardens in warm weather; he was still a partner in the ownership of a number of medical facilities in Rockland County, but no longer an active partner; on this sunny June morning he was seated at a crude worktable in his backyard, beneath a canopy of red climber roses, scanning his usual dozen daily newspapers (among them the *Miami Herald* and *USA Today*) in his ceaseless search for "leads" into Augusta's disappearance.

"If that woman is Augusta, I must claim her. We've been too long apart."

WHAT DID the discovery of Augusta Cutler's handbag, discarded in a construction site in Miami Beach, *mean?*

Elias West could offer only the theory that, it seemed, Augusta had been in Miami Beach, and yes of course her handbag had been taken from her, forcibly; but it had possibly been only stolen, and Augusta herself hadn't been injured . . . "It might be construed as a sign that my wife is alive, then?" Owen Cutler asked anxiously. West had brought the handbag to Salthill for Owen to identify. Owen pressed its scratched and soiled leather against his face, inhaling what he wished might be Augusta's fragrance, but there was no perfume scent, only a scent of . . . rot. And, to be honest, Owen wasn't certain he could have identified the handbag as a possession of his wife's for Augusta owned so many handbags . . .

"Absolutely yes, Mr. Cutler," Elias West said emphatically,

"you can infer that interpretation from the evidence, if you wish."

THE MORNING FOLLOWING West's call, Owen flew to Naples, Florida, where he was met at the small airport by the private investigator and two deeply tanned Hendry County sheriff's deputies who drove him to the Hendry County morgue in Cropsey. It was a blinding-glaring-hot day in the hell of the Florida interior but Owen had no awareness of his surroundings. He was treated by his companions as if he were an invalid, and indeed he'd walked unsteadily, and had needed assistance getting into the unmarked police vehicle. His eyes had an unnatural hopeful glisten. The mood in the vehicle speeding along heat-quivering asphalt highways between acres of empty marshland was subdued, somber. The elder of the deputies informed Owen that a search team hadn't yet located "the missing portion of the deceased's anatomy," and that it might never be located. "Some of these sick individuals would save a head for their own purposes. Or they would take care to thoroughly destroy it to avoid identification." Elias West, who was sitting in the rear of the vehicle with his employer, corroborated these remarks, saying, "A body not identified, Mr. Cutler, is almost impossible to trace to any perpetrator." Owen shifted in his seat as if his clothes were too tight. He murmured, "Yes. I can understand that. I'm sorry."

Owen was informed that the victim he would be viewing had been killed not by stab wounds, nor even the decapitation, but by garroting. "Meaning the victim was dead before the head was severed from the body." (Yes, but what did this *mean?* The anxious husband wondered.) There were "deep, bloody welts" on both her wrists and ankles, meaning she'd been bound, by wire, but the wire had been removed when the body had been dumped, or before, and was nowhere in the vicinity of the body. There were indications that the victim had been wearing several rings, but no jewelry was found on the body, as all clothing was missing. It was repeated that the victim was about fifty years old and in "good, ample physical condition" prior to the trauma; she'd had a baby, or babies . . . Though Owen was listening intently, he'd become physically anxious, and at last asked if they might please stop at the next gas station or rest area where he might use a lavatory. When he reappeared, his face was clammy-pale and there was a smell about him of panic, vomit. The Hendry County deputies and Elias West, who'd been talking quietly together in the vehicle while Owen was absent, fell silent as soon as he returned.

Owen was carrying with him a briefcase filled with personal items, including photographs of Augusta should these be requested, and a paperback anthology titled *The Ethical Life*. Owen had not been a friend of Adam Berendt's (he would admit) and he'd rejoiced (to his shame!) when first he'd heard of Adam's death, but during the months of Augusta's disappearance he'd become interested in philosophy, remembering Berendt's interest, and was particularly drawn to the ancient Greek teachings of Epicurus ("the removal of all pain is the limit of pleasure's magnitude"—"cultivate your garden!") and the Stoics ("nothing that falls outside the human mind is 'good' or bad'"). He believed that he was leading, at last, a philosophical life; a rational life; Gussie would admire him, now; all of Salthill would admire him, if they could but know. Now, he would overcome the terrible weakness that suffused his body by asking the deputies intelligent questions about their work, and by evincing sympathy for their lives which he tried, so far as he was capable, to imagine. "What horror you must see! Most people couldn't bear it." The deputies, for whom such lurid adventures as the headless female corpse, possibly the remains of the wife of a rich businessman from suburban New York City, were welcome diversions from the tedium of routine policework, accepted Owen's praise with murmured thanks.

"Just doin our job, Mr. Cutler. We'll see how this turns out."

The vehicle sped onward into blinding sunshine. Augusta's accusing voice was never far from Owen's thoughts. How she'd mocked him, uttering unforgettable—unforgivable!—words. *Lost all mystery for each other. Corpses embalmed together.*

Had he struck her, silenced her, then? Had he strangled her? (But how had he transported her body to Hendry County, Florida? His brain collapsed, confronted with such a puzzle.)

"They say, in such cases, a disappeared wife, a possibly dead wife, the husband is always the prime suspect," Owen meekly offered, "but I would guess, in this case, you're probably looking—elsewhere?"

The driver of the vehicle regarded Owen in his rearview mirror, and the deputy beside him turned to Owen, with a look of some surprise. Elias West said quickly, "These officers aren't investigating Augusta's disappearance, Mr. Cutler. That's an entirely different case. I should have explained more carefully, I guess. This case, it's an unidentified body, and missing persons fitting the description are being investigated, but not necessarily your wife, Mr. Cutler, d'you see?" West, a former U.S. marshal who'd been urged to take a premature retirement in his late forties, was a lanky slope-shouldered man now in his late fifties with thick grizzled hair around a bald pate, the hair long and curly as in a caricature of a Western lawman. He was humble, and vain; conspicuously well-mannered, and deeply cynical; he wore good white shirts with string ties, vests, and black coats; his belts were studded with metal and rode low on his hips. His face was dark clay brick and his eyes were pale and jumpy. He gave the impression of being "armed"—and willing to use his weapon. He was costing Owen Cutler a small fortune and this fact Owen Cutler supposed to be a sign of the private investigator's expertise. It was clear that West and the Hendry County deputies understood one another; they were of the same species. When West had remarked to the deputies that he'd started out as a U.S. marshal, the deputies were impressed, and asked where he'd been stationed, and why he'd quit, and West said briefly that he'd "stopped some bullets in my gut." Unknown to Owen, the deputies had quizzed West about his employer and West had said respectfully that Mr. Cutler was a man of integrity and honesty who was searching for a wife who had left him, possibly with a lover though there were no "living" candidates of which West was aware. She'd sold some property that was in her name, for a half-million dollars, and vanished. Her handbag had been found in Miami Beach the previous April. He, West, had made extensive inquiries and had come up with no leads. "I don't believe this woman, who is no common housewife, was abducted. Augusta Cutler left home voluntarily. But she may have met with trouble by now, you've seen these photos, she was a damned good-looking, sexy woman. And rich."

OWEN WAS SAYING, in a wondering voice, "A strange prophetic remark Augusta made, the last time she spoke with me—'We're embalmed corpses together, this is our mausoleum.'" He laughed, with a sound like something being crushed beneath the wheels of a speeding vehicle. The Hendry County deputies and the private investigator Elias West listened in what might have been shocked silence.

For this nightmare journey to central Florida, Owen Cutler wore a smart but somewhat rumpled seersucker suit that Augusta had selected for him, for their elder son's wedding years ago. (Was the desperate husband imagining that if the mutilated female corpse was not Augusta's, and Augusta was somehow close by, she would take note of the seersucker suit and recognize it and be moved?) He wore a white sports shirt, open at the throat. He'd shaved hastily and had several times nicked himself, thinking with satisfaction *At least I am alive, here's proof: blood.* Yet his facial skin was pale as soapstone and appeared to be finely pitted. He'd become, over the past eight months, a man of stone. His head, now nearly bald, had a noble, Roman stoniness about it; the bones of his face were jutting. There were curious calligraphic indentations and striations in his skull, like rivulets caused by erosion. His eyes were naked, blinking, exposed. He gave an impression of being severely myopic, and having misplaced his glasses. Of the men traveling in the police vehicle to Cropsey, Florida, Owen was the only one not wearing sunglasses, as he was the only one sitting with his mouth slightly open, as if he were lost, not in thought, but in the humming-buzzing heat of central Florida in June. This mouth, which no woman had kissed in a very long time, had shrunken to the size of a slug.

A dead man. Posthumous. This was how Salthill had come to think of Owen Cutler as they'd come to think of the voluptuous, unpredictable Augusta. To have vanished from Salthill was to have vanished from the earth's face. To some observers, Owen was a figure of pathos, an emblem of their own possible (but not probable!) disgrace whom they avoided when they saw publicly; to others, who'd known the man for years, and admired him more readily than they'd loved him, Owen had attained the stature of suburban tragedy, and they avoided him publicly. Though he made a heroic effort to be well groomed, at those social events to which he was still invited, he let himself go on those slack days when he stayed at home, unshaven, in soiled gardener's clothes and much-worn bedroom slippers. He was seen to be walking now with a slight drag to his left foot, like a regional drawl. It was noted that Owen seemed not to hear most of what was being said to him; at other times, he seemed to hear, very keenly, what wasn't being said to him. The Cutler children, with that acute sense of personal advantage couched in terms of a concern for their elders that has come to characterize their generation, coming of age in the rapacious Wall Street eighties, expressed concern that their father was becoming "clinically depressed"; there was a history of dementia (Alzheimer's?) in the Cutler family, though it hadn't yet manifested itself in any individual younger than eighty-five. Still they worried, Owen Cutler's heirs, that he might do something "reckless"—like give away his money. Already Owen had alarmed the family by shifting his financial responsibilities onto younger associates, and by gradually losing interest in finances. He no longer perused the *Wall Street Journal!* He'd offered a reward of $500,000 for information leading to the recovery of Augusta, which perhaps wasn't excessive, for (of course) the Cutler children wanted their mother returned to them, too, but he was talking of establishing the Augusta Cutler Foundation to give grants to worthy local arts organizations and charities. And there was his entirely new, unprecedented fanaticism about growing orchids, and gardening, and reading philosophy. Owen was uneasily aware of his children's disapproval; his elder son in particular, an aggressive young graduate of the Wharton Business School, expressed "concern" about Owen's health; much was made of the physical and mental collapse of Owen's friend and neighbor Lionel Hoffmann, who'd returned to the house on Old Mill Way as a broken man, an invalid, having relinquished his executive position in his family-owned publishing business. *That's the beginning of the end: a loss of interest in money-making.*

Owen had promised his children that he'd share with them any significant developments in the search for Augusta. But he'd told them nothing of Elias West's call, for there seemed no purpose in their accompanying him on this nightmare trip. If the mutilated female was Augusta, they would be spared a hideous last vision of their mother; if the mutilated female wasn't Augusta, better for them not to have known.

He'd long ago memorized, with a lover's devotion, the constellation of small freckles on Augusta's upper back; the single mole beneath her left breast (unless the mole was beneath the right breast); the mole in her cheek she'd enlarged, in imitation of Marilyn Monroe, with pencil, as a beauty mark; the warm brown aureole of her nipples, and their flushed stubbiness when aroused. And there was Augusta's unmistakable fair soft-creamy skin; a rosiness beneath the skin; the surging warmth, the irresistible energy, that made Augusta so supremely Augusta. Though (he knew!) it was possible that Augusta was dead, and the corpse he was going to view "was" Augusta, yet he couldn't believe (he would not believe!) that, in a more essential way, Augusta was dead.

Even if, somehow, this was her body. Even if . . .

Owen had been chagrined to learn that Augusta had secretly sold several properties she'd inherited, and taken with her, into hiding, the relatively modest sum of a half-million dollars. This transaction she'd obviously made into a new personal bank account, but where? Under what name? No one knew. Elias West had come up with only dead ends . . .

Just once he'd inquired, was it possible that Mrs. Cutler had *run off* with a man, a lover; and Owen laughed angrily and said not likely, her lover was a dead man.

(Though in fact, now that Owen thought of it: *was* Adam Berendt dead? Owen himself had seen no corpse. There'd been no viewing, no funeral. The "body" was bone chunks and grit raked into the soil of Adam's garden, but these remains might have belonged to anyone. A brilliant scheme might have been concocted between Augusta and her lover . . . But the thought of it, the ingenuity of it, was too much for Owen's brain to consider.)

The outskirts of Cropsey, Florida, appeared to Owen's watery squinting vision as a rapid sequence of façades like playing cards interspersed with glaring plate-glass windows. Were they here, so quickly? He'd only left Salthill that morning . . . The elder of the deputies was addressing him in a neutral but kindly voice. "Mr. Cutler? Are you ready? This won't be easy."

A wall of—was it heat? shimmering, radiant heat?—struck Owen as he climbed out of the vehicle, with the force of a blow. Elias West gripped his arm. "Steady, Mr. Cutler." The younger of the deputies held open a door for him, and warned him of steps. Now refrigerated air wafted about him, but it wasn't fresh air; there was an undercurrent of chemicals and something foul beneath it, and Owen's nostrils pinched, in panic. "More steps here, sir. The railing—" (Why the hell were these strangers treating him, Owen Cutler, like an elderly man? He was only fifty-six. In the Cutler family, fifty-six was young. Owen had yet to have his first heart attack, his first problematic prostate, or colon, diagnosis, *all that lay before him!*) Voices murmured. A female voice among them. You could tell you were in a foreign region of the United States: the southern accent. He resented these uniformed strangers escorting him along a corridor. Where? *A froth of bubbles floating upon a void, always you'd known. You must not be surprised, now.* The Stoics had taught (but had they believed?) that the human mind is the measure of all things: "good"—"evil"—"pleasure"—"pain." We create our experiences, our experiences don't "exist." If a man's wife has been taken from him, and his love has been destroyed, he must examine the phenomena of "wife"—"love"—"loss" and not succumb to mere emotion. "Mr. Cutler? Come a little closer, sir." A sheet was being lifted. It was their strategy to reveal to this individual who might well be the victim's next-of-kin only portions of the body. The neck area, and beyond, was not revealed. The stub of the neck, from which the beautiful head had been removed. *For of course this was Augusta, Owen knew at once.* And the pelvic area too was shielded from his gaze, for which he was grateful. The torso was badly discolored, hardly recognizable as human. Large flaccid bruised breasts, a slack rounded belly, fatty thighs. Ugly! *This was not Augusta Cutler, of course.* He was staring at—something wrong?—the hands. The fingers were too short. No fingernails! And Augusta had been fastidious about her hands. Scented hand lotion, and weekly manicures. Saturday mornings in Salthill, while her hair was being "done." Always impeccable nail polish. Her rings, the tastefully large diamond and the gold wedding ring, an heirloom; and the emerald Owen had given her for their twentieth anniversary. Where were Augusta's beautiful rings? Owen felt the special horror of their loss. A vain childish woman but he'd adored her. *Yes, but you never knew her, only Adam Berendt had known her.* "Mr. Cutler?"—they were expecting something of him. He was not playing his role, perhaps. Sections of the body were being displayed like cuts of meat. Almost, you might think this was a provocative work of contemporary art. Pop art, or shock art, an object fashioned to resemble a hideously mutilated female torso, made of lifelike clay. Owen reached out to touch the thing, and was gratified that it was stony cold. *Augusta was burning hot, this could not be Augusta.* That mole on the rib cage, beneath the left breast, Owen recognized, did he?—or had he never seen it before? The big flaccid breasts were not recognizable, were they? Owen was shaking his head, no. His heart was pounding so violently he believed he might faint, and he would not have resisted fainting. *Better to die, to be extinguished. Than to have such knowledge.* "Mr. Cutler? Are you all right?" Brusquely he informed them yes, of course. He'd made this journey of thousands of miles into Hell for the purpose of identifying, or not identifying, his missing wife, it was an insult to him to be continually asked if he was *all right!* Now the thing, the body, was being turned over on the gurney, slowly, with care, so that the back could be examined. Now the sheet covering the mutilated neck slipped just slightly, and Owen saw what was not to be seen: a stump of a neck, and no head. *No head.* He smiled, confused. How could he identify Augusta if Augusta's head was gone? *Where was Augusta's head?* "This is very strange. This is . . ." They seemed not to hear. They were asking him about moles, freckles, scars. As if they hadn't already asked him, and he'd told them what he knew. It angered him that they spoke to him, even the leathery-faced man in his hire, as you'd speak to a brain-damaged person. "Yes," he said. "I see." He was puzzling over the meaning of a cluster of freckles beneath the corpse's left shoulder blade. (Hadn't that cluster of freckles been a smaller cluster of moles, higher up on Augusta's back?) On the lower back, amid the fatty, bruised, discolored middle-aged flesh, there was a large mole, at first glance you'd think it was an insect, and Owen's instinct was to brush it away. How Gussie hated insects! Next, he examined the arms, which were relatively uninjured, the fair skin dotted with myriad small freckles, but not covered in fine pale hairs as he remembered Augusta's arms. (Unless Owen's memory was outdated. Possibly, in middle age, Augusta's arms had become hairless, like her legs she no longer had to shave?) It was at this point that he glanced sidelong at Elias West who was staring at the thing on the table with a look of recognition. *It is Gussie. This man sees.*

"No," Owen said quickly, panting. "I don't believe it is. I—don't think so. Not Augusta. Not this." He'd begun to cry. In an instant, his stony face had cracked, and was dissolving. The examination appeared to be concluded. Owen was led from the refrigerated room. At the threshold he stumbled, but regained his balance, and his dignity. "How am I to blame for this? *I am not to blame.* Why did you do such a thing to me, and to our family, Augusta!"

A tile floor lurched upward, cracking against his cheek. The stricken man was brought to the emergency room of the local hospital and treated for shock, cardiac trauma. He hadn't had a heart attack per se or a stroke but he'd been unconscious for nearly ten minutes which was "worrisome" as the attending physician said, and so he was kept overnight in the hospital for observation and in the morning discharged, with a strong suggestion that he make an appointment to see his personal physician as quickly as possible. A subdued Elias West drove Owen in a rental car back to the Naples airport. Owen Cutler's effort at identifying the female corpse would be indicated in police reports as "inconclusive." He seemed to acknowledge that, yes, the mutilated woman was his wife, or had been his wife; at the same time, no, she was not. Elias West dared not press his employer on the issue for fear of being immediately discharged from his job. During the drive to Naples, the men scarcely spoke. Owen seemed irritated with West, or in any case indifferent. He appeared tired, an aged man. There was a large white bandage on his left cheek, partly obscuring a purple welt. His seersucker suit was badly rumpled as if he'd slept in it and he had not shaved that morning. For most of the drive he looked through items he'd brought in his briefcase, photographs of beautiful Augusta dating back to the late sixties when they'd first met; it may have been that Owen saw how little the woman he'd loved resembled herself from season to season and from photograph to photograph, for at last he gave up, with a sigh, and shut the briefcase. As the rental car sped along the state highway through hazy white sunshine Owen tried to read in *The Ethical Life* but soon grew restless. He said, with the wistful air of a man making a profound discovery, in utter aloneness, "These words. These philosophers. Froth of bubbles over a void, that's all. They tell themselves things not to notice." Shortly afterward he drifted into a light doze and the book slipped from his fingers, onto the floor.

At the small Naples airport, Elias West made travel arrangements for the trip back north. Finally he dared bring up the subject of whether he should continue in his search for Mrs. Cutler or whether—the woman in the Cropsey morgue was, in fact, Mrs. Cutler?

Staring at the floor, with a vacant expression, Owen said after a moment, "It's her. You know it's her. But we won't give up our search, Elias, will we? *Never.*"

2

FARTHER AND FARTHER into the past! It was like being drawn into a whirlpool, seeking out another's secret life. Augusta wondered at times if she would drown. If this was forbidden knowledge she was seeking, and would regret it.

Still, the adventure was exciting to her! It was like nothing Augusta had done before in her sheltered Salthill life. A woman traveling alone, driving rental cars, always in dark glasses, staying in roadside motels and eating her meals in her room, letting her hair grow out laced with silver . . . "In the pursuit of the truth of Adam Berendt."

Except the truth meant little to her, really. She wanted only this intimacy with Adam, now the man had vanished from the earth. She wanted finally to know him as no one else had ever known him, including his other women.

In Miami Beach, before setting out on her journey, Augusta had acquired a new digital camera for the purpose of taking photographs of Brady's/Berendt's backgrounds. She'd acquired a new, temporary name and the identification to accompany it, a simple virtuous-sounding name, "Elizabeth Eastman." (She'd teased Elias West: "How about I call myself 'Liz West'?" Only a joke, of course.) When Augusta had fled Salthill the previous autumn she'd been desperate and had had no plan except to put distance between herself and the puppet-life she'd been leading, by that time a life excruciating to her who was reminded daily in Salthill of Adam Berendt's absence; it wasn't until months later that she woke one morning, to splotches of sunshine on a white latticed window, with the idea of tracing Adam back to his origins.

"I will! I will try."

It would give her unraveled life a meaning. Augusta Cutler's life, that had so little meaning.

Her life she'd many times wanted to toss away, as you'd toss away an empty wrapper. Without sentiment, and without regret.

And there was the dread of growing older: always older. In America, that was the abyss. Adam had chided her, how trivial this was, this age-obsession of Americans, and she'd said angrily, why yes, yes it is trivial, some of us are drowning in it, take pity!

She, Augusta Cutler, now fifty-three years old.

Reason enough, maybe, for leaving Salthill-on-Hudson where everyone knew her.

"But no one knows me! Fuck them all."

ALL THAT AUGUSTA KNEW, or suspected, was that Adam had changed his name to "Adam Berendt" sometime after June 1969. She suspected this because one afternoon going through his filing cabinet out of curiosity (in fact: jealousy of other women friends of Adam's) she'd discovered a much-creased, yellowed high school "equivalency" diploma issued to "Francis Xavier Brady" by the Red Lake, Minnesota, school district, in June 1969.

Rarely did Adam lock the rear door of his house on the river, the door leading into his studio. It was understood that his closest friends were welcome to drop in at any time whether Adam was home or not, and Augusta often did, to await him. And so she'd dropped by that afternoon to discover only Adam's dogs home . . . and these were friendly dogs, who recognized their master's friend Augusta.

Augusta's mind raced. What did the diploma *mean?* Why would Adam have it in his possession? The logic must be: "Francis Xavier Brady" was Adam Berendt's younger self.

Always there'd been the vague idea that, just possibly, Adam Berendt had changed his name. No one seemed to know exactly how old he was, but clearly he was over fifty, and perhaps not fifty-five. Say he'd been born in 1947. In 1969, he'd have been twenty-two years old. Late to be earning a high school diploma, unless something had happened to interrupt his education.

This line of thinking was exciting to Augusta. She so yearned for intimacy with the man, which he'd denied her.

Here was the logic: Adam was the most reticent of men, no one in Salthill seemed to know anything about him before the mid-1970s when he was living in Manhattan, and on Long Island, prior to his move to Rockland County in 1981. If you asked Adam any direct, personal question, Adam would deflect it with a joke: "How do I know? I'm not a historian of my own life." Or, any question involving a date: "How do I know? Let's say—'Once upon a time.'" It seemed to be known that Adam hadn't been a sculptor, or hadn't been known as a sculptor, before moving to Salthill and buying the old Deppe house. What his Salthill friends knew of the years preceding his move they'd pieced together from accounts provided by New Yorkers who claimed to have known Adam Berendt as a man involved in real estate investments and in the stock market. ("But involved in a quiet way. You'd never have guessed how well he was doing.") Augusta once met a couple who'd lived in an apartment building in which Adam had lived in 1974–75, on East 57th Street; Augusta checked out the building and was mildly disappointed, it was only just a high-rise Manhattan apartment building. Beatrice Archer told Augusta that Avery had run into a man who claimed to have been a "poker friend" of Adam Berendt's when Adam lived in Nassau County, Long Island; there, he'd lived in a succession of rentals, bewildering his friends by never buying a house for himself. Nor was Adam linked to any specific woman: he'd had numerous friends, friends devoted to him, including of course women.

In Salthill, it was rumored that Adam and Augusta were having an affair. Augusta alluded to the rumor with lusty good humor—"Only *if*." Adam seemed oblivious of it, or scornful.

Augusta believed, if Adam was involved with anyone, it was the younger woman, the red-haired Marina Troy. "Except, no: what would Adam see in *her*? The woman has no sex."

It made sense that a man so secretive might certainly have changed his name, but, searching through other drawers in the filing cabinet, which was an old, scarified aluminum cabinet

Adam had picked up at a fire sale, Augusta found no document confirming a name change, nor any more paperwork involving "Francis Xavier Brady."

There was a sound of Adam's car at the top of the driveway! Hurriedly, guiltily Augusta put away the diploma and shut up the filing cabinet and left Adam's study as she'd found it. Adam's dogs, that had accompanied her into the study, now trotted out barking with excitement at their master's arrival. Adam would see Augusta's car in the drive; he'd know she was in the house, and waiting for him; often Augusta dropped by his studio to admire his work-in-progress; she was a woman who "took an interest" in art, especially if the artists were friends of hers. There was nothing out of the ordinary here, nothing to stir Adam's suspicion. But how excited Augusta was: in a state like sexual arousal. She knew! She knew a secret of Adam's! There was this intimacy between them, of which the man himself was unaware.

When Adam entered the house with his heavy footfall, there was Augusta innocently in the kitchen, giving the dogs fresh water from the faucet. They'd rushed to Adam, and now trotted back to her, crowding affectionately against her legs. The dogs were Apollo and—a smaller, older yellow dog, a female, whose name Augusta was forgetting. For this was years ago: the little yellow dog, a foundling like Apollo, had long since died.

Augusta recalled her younger, more hopeful self with a tinge of loss: she'd been wearing a poppy-orange cotton chemise with a skirt slit up the sides, mandarin-style, and open-toed cork shoes. How crucial her clothes, her costumes, had seemed to her in that long-ago life! Her shapely, rather pale legs were bare, and her hair was newly burnished, like a helmet. She might have been Adam Berendt's devoted wife awaiting him in this rundown old "historic" house on the river, the ex-debutante wife of the down-at-the-heels sculptor, except that wasn't the scenario. Augusta felt Adam's fingertips touching the back of her head, as she stooped to set the dogs' plastic dishes on the floor, like a blessing, or a playful chastising.

"Gussie! You don't have to wait on my dogs, for Christ's sake."

"But it's so warm today. Their water . . ."

What was she saying? Why was it important? She stared at Adam Berendt thinking *But who are you? Tell me!*

Gaily Augusta kissed Adam on both cheeks, for that was her style. She drew back from him before he drew back from her. Perfume wafted about them. *Noli me tangere!—touch me not!*—was Adam Berendt's sexual peccadillo. The man's fetish. (Did Augusta mind, really? If they'd been lovers, wouldn't their friendship have ended, inevitably?) That afternoon as many times afterward Augusta would come close to asking Adam, "Who is 'Francis Xavier Brady'? It's you, isn't it?" But she had not the courage. She couldn't risk offending him. For there were things you might say to Adam freely, and things you could not. Any challenge of his integrity. Any persistent probing of his past. Adam's face took on a flushed, savage expression, his good eye glared. No, Augusta wasn't going to ask about "Francis Xavier Brady."

But Augusta was clearly excited, elated. It was impossible for her to speak in an ordinary voice. She admired Adam's crude, curious works-in-progress—so much! She yearned to extract from him his most precious wisdom, if she couldn't extract from him his love. Adam listened to her, bemused. "When I see works of art, I want to know: does the artist *believe?*"

"Believe in what, Gussie?"

"Just—*believe*. In God, maybe."

"What kind of 'God'? A personality, or a principle?"

"Just God. The God of tradition."

"Whose tradition?"

"Adam, don't be perverse. Our tradition."

"But what is this 'our'? How can you be so confident we share a tradition? Because we share a language," Adam said playfully, "doesn't mean we share its meanings."

Augusta threw up her hands in exasperation. How stubborn the man was. Everyone knew what "God" meant, why did Adam play games?

He said, "I don't believe in God, no. Not a God with a personality, the petulant self-regarding God of the Bible. But I find it interesting that others believe."

"And what of an afterlife, Adam?"

"Not very likely."

"The wicked aren't punished for their sins?"

Augusta spoke with coquettish wistfulness. She was one who so wanted the wicked to be punished, that she might be warned off from being wicked herself.

"The wicked may be punished, like all of us, but not for their sins."

"We aren't punished for our pasts? Our pasts don't 'catch up with us' as it's said?"

This was a risky thing to say. To Adam whose past was a question. He glanced at Augusta, and away, and squatted before one of his sculpted pieces, running his hands over its clumsy shape as if blindly. Augusta persisted, "If we aren't punished for things we've done in the past, still we want to hide our pasts? Sometimes? Why is that?" She spoke naively, provocatively.

"There is such a thing as regret, after all," Adam said finally. "There is such a thing as shame."

The dogs had come into Adam's studio, toenails clattering against the paint-splattered floorboards. Apollo, the younger and more vigorous, licked Adam's hands, and managed to lie on the floor in such a way that his head was at Adam's feet and his twitchy tail fell across Augusta's cork shoes. It was a quiet, domestic moment, as close to an intimate moment as Adam would allow.

It was time for Augusta to leave. Yet Augusta was reluctant to leave. Adam walked with her outside, to her car. It was a handsome expensive sleeky black new-model European car, rather out of place in Adam's weed-edged cinder drive, and Augusta never slipped into its leathery interior without thinking *All that I've given up, to drive this car, is it worth it? Maybe!* Adam was in a subdued mood, for which Augusta blamed herself. She said, "What do you believe in, then, Adam?" and he said, "I believe in grace." "Grace!" Augusta smiled uncertainly. "I believe in grace, too. Though I've never been certain what it is." Adam said:

"Grace is a moment of insight. A moment of beauty, and purity. Though it could be a moment of supreme ugliness, I suppose. A sudden swift aerial view. We're lifted up out of ourselves, like out of clay pots, and we *see*. In an instant, we *know*."

"But, Adam—what do we know?"

Augusta spoke sincerely, anxiously. Wanting to take Adam's big-knuckled hands in hers and grip them against her heart.

Adam shrugged, and laughed. "We don't. We never know. We make our way by faith, and we never know where in hell we're going."

IT WAS SO, Augusta had flown to Atlanta. But she hadn't taken another plane out of Atlanta. She'd checked into an airport hotel and slept. She was exhausted, she was deeply shaken, confused. She slept late and swam in the hotel pool, in slow measured luxuriant laps. No makeup, her skin glaring pale, and her hair brushed back flat. She exuded no sexual allure, she attracted the attention of no men. It was easy not to be seen: you simply stopped looking at others. It was easy to feel no guilt about leaving your husband and family: you simply stopped thinking of them.

Never had Augusta been so close to a murderous rage as she'd been at the Thwaites' door, and she never wanted to feel such ugly emotion again. "The girl Samantha will grow up without knowing anything of Adam, who saved her life. Of course. The parents won't want to tell her, out of shame. It's only natural. In their place I'd probably behave the same way. Fuck them." She hoped never to think of the Thwaites again.

From Atlanta she moved in a southerly direction; it was November and beginning to be cold in the north. She rented a car and drove through Georgia, avoiding the interstate, staying in roadside motels. She knew that a "missing" person, an adult, would not be the object of a search by police, no matter how badly Owen Cutler wanted his wife back. Yet she half-surmised she might be discovered, if she drove on I-75, and stayed in high-quality hotels of the kind she and Owen normally patronized. But several times she weakened, she came close to revealing herself: she telephoned her sons, her daughter. She did miss them.

(Did she?) She did feel a tinge of guilt, for surely she'd upset them. (And why not? They'd upset her, plenty. Now it was Mother's turn.) With slow fingers she dialed their memorized numbers preparing to say, "Hey, it's me. Your ridiculous mother," but somehow she could not utter these words. For these were false words. She didn't feel ridiculous, she felt *genuine*. She could not say, with an apologetic little laugh, "Hello, darling! It's me. I'm sorry to have worried you," because in fact she wasn't sorry. *She would never apologize to her children again.*

Augusta continued in her southerly direction. There were relatives in Jacksonville, Florida, and in Palm Beach, girl cousins of hers, and her old, beloved college roommate, now divorced, lived in a luxurious residence in St. Petersburg. Vaguely Augusta had been assuming she would stay with one of these, she'd be welcome and her whereabouts kept secret, but she continued south past Jacksonville and the prospect of spending time in Palm Beach among people of the kind one meets in Palm Beach filled her with repugnance, and she showed no inclination to drive across the state to St. Petersburg, where, amid affection and gaiety and a good deal of drinking, she'd have been very welcome, and invited to stay through the winter. *I can't. I can't be Augusta any longer*. In resort towns along the eastern Florida coast she slept, walked on the windblown beach, fasted and "did" yoga, and slept; she was neglecting to shave her underarms, and indifferent to her hair becoming shapeless and streaked with silver at the hairline. At malls she bought cheap, comfortable clothes: stretch-waist polyester slacks, pullovers in bright pastels, cotton knit sweaters. She was surprised to see how attractive she was—not glamorous, not beautiful: attractive—without makeup. Freckles emerged on her fair skin, her eyes without mascara were the eyes of a sane, intelligent woman of youthful middle age. Still, she had relapses: a ravenous sexual appetite swept upon her, in a Fort Pierce cocktail lounge she picked up a forty-year-old pony-tailed guitarist and brought him back to her beachside motel room with a supply of lavender condoms and a picnic basket of smoked salmon, crusty French bread, brie, grapes, and several bottles of good Italian wine. There were similar relapses in Boca Raton, Fort Lauderdale, and Surfside. And then Augusta was in Miami Beach.

Here, her relapse took the form of checking into the luxury Loews on the beach. Openly she dined in the hotel's opulent dining room instead of ordering room service. She had cocktails on the terrace overlooking the ocean. She had her hair "done," a much-needed manicure and pedicure; she bought parrot-green silk trousers and a matching blouse low-cut to show the tops of her creamy breasts. She strolled along the beach, she shopped in boutiques, guilty in her old, absurd pleasures. ("But it won't last, Adam. I swear!") After a week in Miami Beach she began to notice a man covertly watching her, following her. Out of nowhere he'd appeared: in the hotel lobby, at the edge of the pool as she swam laps, in the cocktail lounge, on the beach. The man had a ravaged, but still handsome dark-tanned face and grizzled Indian-fighter hair that spilled from his bald pate onto his shoulders. Like few other men in Miami Beach he wore dark clothes, string ties, belts with oversized silver buckles. *My stalker* Augusta thought him. He was sexy and swaggering even as (Augusta, a woman of contradictions, could appreciate this) he was trying hard not to be noticed. *My stalker* was a few years older than Augusta, with an eye for a woman of her ample figure. More than once, their eyes caught and a frisson of excitement passed between them. Augusta felt a quicksilver pang in her groin, desire like an electric shock. She turned away and would have left the terrace (it was twilight, cocktail hour) but turned back unexpectedly, to catch *my stalker* staring at her. She went to him, in a swath of perfume, furious and trembling and bold demanding, "Are you following me? *Why?*"

In this way Augusta Cutler met Elias West, the private investigator in her husband's hire.

THE LOOK ON West's face! Here was a cunning crafty man who carried a (registered, legal) handgun beneath his left armpit, like a "private eye' in a Hollywood movie of the forties. Here was a man so skilled in subterfuge he could not clearly recall when he'd last uttered a word of unqualified unvarnished truth. And here was a man who'd been "involved" with so many women, for periods of time ranging from eleven years (an early wife) to eleven minutes (name unknown), it was his boast he was "totally immune" to sexual attraction. Yet, staring up astonished at Augusta Cutler, his rich employer's wife, a tremulous rosy-skinned Renoir beauty in luminescent green, with a bosom remarkable in any woman, but extraordinary for a woman of her reputed age, West hadn't been able to disguise his emotion. He, Elias West, actually blushing, stammering—"Mrs. Cutler, I guess I am. You got me there." A gentleman, West held out his hand to shake hers.

THEY GOT ALONG very well, Augusta and Elias. They were of the same indefinable rogue species. And there was the pleasure of the illicit, the betrayal of faith: making love, they were deceiving poor Owen Cutler back in Salthill-on-Hudson, who anxiously awaited news of any "leads" the private investigator could supply him. "He must love you very much, Mrs. Cutler," Elias West said, cupping Augusta's large soft big-nippled breast in his hand with unusual gentleness, "he's been distraught since you left him, and keeps assuring me 'Money is no object.'" Augusta laughed at this, and poked her tongue into West's hot, waxy ear, and West laughed, too, though he was slightly embarrassed: to so openly betray a client, in a situation that could backfire on him (if, for instance, Augusta returned to Owen, and confessed) was worrisome, indeed. But Augusta assured Elias West no, not very likely she'd confess—"This is too much fun." With brusque practiced fingers gripping West's semi-erect, slowly hardening penis. Like a woman shaking hands with a buddy.

The first time they were alone together, in Augusta's room on the top floor of the hotel, still flushed from lovemaking, Augusta slapped down a wad of bills on a table beside Elias West and said, "I'd like to hire you to keep Owen uninformed of where I am. Is it a deal?" West said, "Augusta, I couldn't take money from you under these circumstances. But I give my word, I'll keep your husband uninformed." He paused, frowning. "Though I may have to mislead him at some point, if I don't want to be fired. He'll be expecting to hear something." "Maybe," Augusta said wistfully, "I could be found dead? I mean—a body resembling me. Somewhere." West said, "That might happen, eventually. But probably not for a long time. And even if the body were badly decomposed, dental records can be checked, and identification made." Augusta hid her face, for a moment overcome by emotion. "That's horrible to think! I wish I hadn't said it." West said, taking her hands, "Darling, whoever it is who may be murdered, whenever it happens, and wherever—it will have nothing to do with you." Augusta shuddered. "It was a strange thing to have said, and I wish I hadn't said it." West said, "If we want to throw your husband off the scent, there are easier ways."

They went on to discuss Owen Cutler. Augusta was touched to hear that Owen was offering a $500,000 reward for information leading to her return. "Poor Owen! I do love him, I suppose. But . . ." In an uncharacteristic gesture of remorse, or sentiment, Augusta wiped at her eyes. Elias West frowned. "If you love your husband, Augusta, why have you left him, and made him so miserable? He does seem to love you." Augusta shook her head emphatically. She was naked, and now slipped into a white terrycloth robe, tightly knotting the sash. "Owen loves his idea of 'wife'—he doesn't love *me*. Only one man loved me in my lifetime, in the sense of knowing me, respecting me, and that man has died." Elias West felt a stirring of jealousy, of which he gave no sign. "And who was this man, this paragon of perfection?" he asked ironically, and Augusta said, smiling, ignoring the irony, "Oh, Adam wasn't perfect. Far from it. He wasn't even very attractive. He had an ugly battered face and one blind eye. And you know," Augusta lowered her voice, playfully stroking West's face, "I love handsome men." "He was a fantastic lover, eh?" West asked, annoyed, and Augusta said, "Lover? Yes. I suppose so. I mean, he would have been. Possibly. We weren't lovers . . . exactly." "Yet you loved him?" West asked, surprised. Augusta said, "Of course I did! Adam was the most powerful, the most romantic masculine presence in my life, including even my father. If you asked me to explain, I couldn't. I can't. Adam was just . . . the man he *was*. I left Salthill because I couldn't seem to bear living in that place, without him. But now I think I'll try to trace him. His origins, I mean." An idea had come to Augusta, inspired by the presence of Elias West in her life. Her eyes brightened as she looked up at him. "Maybe you could help me, Elias? For your regular fee, of course."

To this proposal Elias West allowed himself to say yes.

Within days, to Augusta's surprise, West reported to her what he'd been able to discover by way of telephone calls, faxes, and the Internet, about the late Adam Berendt in those years prior to 1973 when he came to New York. "Before he came east your 'Adam Berendt' was living in Detroit, Michigan, where he worked for a multi-millionaire real estate developer; before that he was living in Muskegon, Michigan, on Lake Michigan, where all I could find out was he became acquainted with this real estate developer who was building lakefront properties, and the guy must've liked your 'Adam Berendt' and brought him to Detroit. At some point he seems to have gotten a license to sell real estate. Before that—if we work our way backward in time, contra-chronologically—Berendt was living a much different life in Minneapolis, where he drove a truck and took night courses in the business school at the University of Minnesota. (Yes, I tried to get his transcript faxed to me but the registrar wouldn't release it.) Before that, in 1969, he was living in a place called Red Lake, in northern Minnesota, where he worked odd jobs including seasonal labor across the border in western Ontario. But prior to that," West said, frowning, "the trail is cold."

Augusta thought *Prior to that "Adam Berendt" hadn't existed.*

She would tell West nothing about "Francis Xavier Brady." Only she, Augusta, would know of "Francis Xavier Brady."

Augusta asked West if there was any record of Adam Berendt having been married, and West said, "No. Not that I've discovered." No family? No relatives? West said, "For more detailed information I'd have to go there, of course. Want to hire me? We could go together."

"No! No, thank you. This is all I need to know." Augusta spoke quickly, almost frightened. She didn't want to share Adam Berendt with anyone, certainly not with a stranger. "How much do I owe you?"

West kissed Augusta, and stroked her shoulders through the terrycloth robe. "My fees are always negotiable."

On the eve of Augusta's departure from Miami Beach, Elias West tossed her handbag over the fence of a hotel construction site a few miles from the hotel. Handling the bag, West wore gloves. All that remained in the bag were used tissues and cosmetics and a wallet emptied of everything except a Salthill-on-Hudson, New York public library card issued to Augusta Cutler, 39 Pheasant Run. The bag, Italian-made, of beautiful hand-tooled leather, had been scratched and dirtied so that the individual who found it wouldn't be tempted to keep it; yet, beautiful as it had once been, and obviously expensive, it would strike the finder as worth reporting to police.

Elias West was in contact with Florida police, in particular Dade County police, in his search for the missing Augusta Cutler. When he checked with them the following day, the handbag had been reported, by which time Augusta had begun her long drive north, alone. The scheme had worked! But Elias West felt little satisfaction, telephoning his employer to tell him news of the "lead"—the first solid lead they'd had yet.

He was missing Augusta, he had to admit. He'd never known anyone quite like her in all his years as a professional.

IN A TRANCE of anticipation and apprehension "Elizabeth Eastman" drove north and west through the states of Georgia, Tennessee, Kentucky, Indiana, Illinois, Wisconsin . . . The drive took her a long time. She wanted, and did not want, to arrive at her destination: Red Lake, Minnesota. She wanted, and did not want, to know: the truth of Adam Berendt's life. By the time she arrived in Minnesota, and began her drive through that long northerly state, her hairline glinted with silver like wires, and wiry hair sprouted in her underarms. She was again wearing polyester elastic-waist pants, T-shirts, and pullovers. She'd taken off her rings, and hidden them in the lining of her suitcase. The polish was chipped from her nails. Her rented car was a sparrow-gray Honda Civic. The glamour of Miami Beach was behind her, the romance of Elias West rapidly fading. For the first week she'd missed him—how well matched they were, sexually and temperamentally!—then she began to forget. West had given her his cell-phone number urging her to call him at any time, he'd come to her, but Augusta threw away the number. Loving Elias West would be a betrayal not of Owen Cutler but of Adam Berendt.

Augusta had purchased a camera in Florida, and now took photographs of the approach to Red Lake, Minnesota, as if transcribing Adam's interior life. He'd left this small, not very prosperous place more than thirty years before, but except for a scattering of newer houses and a few fast-food restaurants and mini-malls on the highway, Red Lake didn't seem to have changed much in a long time. The lake itself was enormous, beautiful in the sun. Its wind-rippled surface drew Augusta's eye, and made her shudder. Adam had died, or had begun to die, in such wind-rippled water. Almost, at times, Augusta imagined she'd been a witness.

Not in Red Lake but thirty miles away in Hannecock, the county seat, in a ground-floor township clerk's office, Augusta would discover the document she sought: the legal notice, dated September 9, 1969, stating that Francis Xavier Brady had officially changed his name to "Adam Berendt." (No middle name! Why, Augusta wondered, hadn't Adam wanted a middle name?) Attached to the document was a badly faded copy of Brady's birth certificate, which Augusta could only just decipher. She held it to the light, her fingers shaking. Francis Xavier Brady born March 30, 1947, in Beauchamp, Montana. Son of Morton and Elsie Brady. Her breath caught. This was it! The clerk who'd located the document for her, a middle-aged woman whom Augusta charmingly inveigled into undertaking the search ("I'm checking the background of this 'Adam Berendt' who wants to marry my sister, my sister is newly widowed and very lonely"), asked Augusta if she was all right, and Augusta stammered yes, "I'm just—suddenly—surprised." For a $25 fee Augusta was allowed to photocopy both documents.

Maybe I should stop now. Maybe this is enough?

Yet curiosity pressed her forward. There was the unconscious hope that, seeking Adam Berendt, venturing ever farther into the past, Augusta would somehow be united with the man, in person. *The young Adam. A boy named Francis.*

No one in Red Lake with whom she spoke seemed ever to have heard of "Adam Berendt," which led Augusta to conclude that he'd left the area soon after changing his name. It was as "Adam Berendt" he'd moved to Minneapolis and then to Muskegon, Michigan, and finally to Detroit where, it appeared, he'd become involved in money-making. In Red Lake, he'd been "Francis Xavier Brady," whom a number of people recalled to Augusta. A local librarian, a woman in her sixties, remembered him as "Frankie Brady, a friendly but lonely-seeming young man with one blind eye, he said he'd injured in a hunting accident," who dropped by the library all the time, sometimes in his work clothes, dirty and sweaty-smelling, wanting to take out books and to talk about them; this raw-boned young guy was a loner, said he'd come from Montana, worked at a lumberyard, and drove a truck, and was taking classes at the high school at night, to get his diploma—"Frankie put a lot of emphasis on education. You could tell, the way he chose his words, he was trying to be the smartest he could be. As if he'd come from someplace where people didn't talk, only grunted and shoved one another around." Augusta asked what sort of books did Frankie Brady withdraw from the library, and the librarian said, warmly, he'd been a boy who read "almost everything, anything." For instance, he'd read his way through the shelf of *Reader's Digest* condensed books in a few weeks. Week after week he took out a hefty anthology titled *The World's Greatest Philosophers,* which he joked about, saying he was "working his way through the centuries, but slow." Frankie favored poetry anthologies, and books on popular science, and self-improvement books like Dale

Carnegie, and picture books on art, and histories of the American West. There was a single book in the library on the Korean War, and this book Frankie withdrew often, for, he said, his dad had died in that war, and was an "unknown hero." For a young man of nineteen or twenty he seemed younger than his age sometimes, but other times, when he was in a melancholy mood, and you couldn't get more than a few words out of him, he seemed much older. "One of those young people with an 'old soul.' That was Frankie Brady when we knew him." The librarian provided Augusta with other names to contact in Red Lake, and, before Augusta could ask, gave her directions to one of the places Frankie Brady had lived. It was a boarding house near the railroad yard: a ramshackle old shingled building, still standing, evidently still inhabited, though very derelict, with a sign on the sagging veranda—ROOMS FOR RENT WEEKLEY & MONTHLY—and guinea fowl picking in the grassless front yard. Augusta stared hungrily. *Adam lived here! Long ago.*

She would go to the front door, boldly. She would knock. She would ask to see—what? Which room?

Instead, Augusta kept a discreet distance, and took photographs.

Next day Augusta called upon the wife of the owner of the Red Lake Marina in the part-brick, part-aluminum "ranch" house at the lakeshore, but the hard-faced, dyed-blond woman (of about Augusta's age, but looking older) regarded her suspiciously, and visibly stiffened when Augusta asked her about Frankie Brady, and told Augusta she was sorry, she couldn't talk to her—"See, I'm too busy. I'm bus-sy, see." The woman's voice trembled with anger, her eyes were fierce with dislike. Augusta went away shaken. *She loved him. Like me. We could be sisters.* What had it been, thirty-two years at least, and the dyed-blond woman still felt the hurt, the loss. What this meant for Augusta, she didn't want to think.

Next, Augusta called upon the white-haired wheelchair-bound former principal of Red Lake High, a courtly gentleman in his late seventies who brightened seeing Augusta's face, and was happy to talk at length about Frankie Brady, the young man he'd taught in night school in—was it 1968? '69?—a bad time in the United States, with the war in Vietnam going all to hell, and local boys, Red Lake graduates, dying there, or coming back hurt. "Frankie Brady was one in a thousand. It was like he'd only just discovered reading—books—the 'life of the mind,' where most people don't live, ever. For sure, folks in these parts don't. Frankie was like a young dog that's been starved, grateful for anything you give him." Of Frankie Brady's private life he'd never known much except "he'd had some trouble behind him, in Montana. That was why he showed up in Red Lake, out of nowhere. He felt guilty, he wasn't fighting in Vietnam, couldn't get in any branch of the armed services because of his eye. And then he disappointed some of us, the way he left." "How did he leave?" Augusta asked. "Ma'am, Frankie just *left*. He was managing a lumberyard here, a pretty big responsibility for a kid in his early twenties, but there was pressure on him, maybe from a girl, or maybe he just got bored here and had to leave. Frankie always had a sort of expansive personality, you know. Even when he didn't say much he'd listen hard, and stare at you with that eye of his, like you felt the specialness of the moment, whatever it was. He could make you happy when he wasn't happy himself, which was a lot of the time. So when Frankie left Red Lake, people missed him, and some were hurt. Not that he owed anybody anything, or made any promises that I know of, but a few months after he earned his diploma, which he'd worked hard for, and was proud of, he told just a few people good-bye, I wasn't one of them, and left Red Lake and nobody ever heard of him again. There was some talk he'd changed his name and gone to live in—maybe Michigan." Augusta could see the puzzlement and hurt in the old man's face and wanted to take his hands in hers and comfort him. "Do you have news of him, ma'am? He's dead now, isn't he?"

Quickly Augusta said no, she knew little of Francis Brady, she was making inquiries on behalf of a relative, she'd never herself met the man.

Days passed. "Elizabeth Eastman" in her dreamy fugue-state, underarms sprouting hairs in the luxury of no one knowing her in this place, this left-behind lakeside town of no distinction where memories of Adam Berendt still rankled, after decades. Augusta drifted about the town and its outskirts taking photographs, telling herself *I will make of his lost life art, he'd be proud of me.* She rented a rowboat at the marina, and rowed along the shore of the lake until her soft hands blistered and her face smarted with sunburn though she was wearing a straw hat. Always keeping in sight of the shabby little marina, making her slow, weaving way past rows of cottages and bungalows, she was thinking *Now he will see me, he will come to me.* Augusta knew, yet didn't wish to know, that life isn't a sequence of posed, "brooding" photographs; life isn't a movie in which a scene must come to a dramatic culmination, or any culmination at all. A middle-aged woman awkwardly rowing a boat on a lake in northern Minnesota, at the onset of mosquito season, shocked by how quickly her shapely body has wearied, her arm, shoulder, back and thigh muscles have begun to ache, may simply row the boat until she gives up, and returns wincing to the dock. Outboard motorboats roared past her, rocking her in their wakes. There were no sailboats on this lake. Certainly there were no yachts. On a dock, a boy yelled what sounded like "Gus-sie!"—or was it "Hus-sie!"—at a black retriever splashing in the water.

Yet: that evening Augusta was approached in the Red Lantern Tavern, where she was drinking whiskey before ordering something to eat, and there was the Ogden County sheriff to speak with her. He introduced himself as Rick Hewitt. Augusta put out her blistered hand to be shaken. Hewitt was a white-haired man in his late fifties with a coarse, shrewd face and eyes that reminded her of—whose?—Roger Cavanagh's. Shifty and reptilian but maybe friendly? Hewitt told Augusta he'd been hearing she was asking after his old friend Frank Brady. He offered to buy her another drink but Augusta deftly countered by insisting upon buying him a drink, if he'd talk to her a little about Frank Brady. "Is Brady somebody you're mixed up with, back where you come from? You doing a check on the guy, or what?" Hewitt asked. Augusta said, summoning her Salthill-hostess smile, "You answer the questions here, Sheriff. Not me."

Hewitt laughed. You could see he was impressed with this good-looking, obviously classy woman from somewhere back east who was trying to fit in with the locals.

He sat across from Augusta in her booth. He accepted the drink. He told her he'd known Frank Brady "pretty well"—"as well as anybody got to know Frank" in Red Lake. For a while they worked at the same lumberyard. They were both in their early twenties, unmarried, kicking around, living in town. Hewitt had come back from Vietnam in '67 after a two-year tour and he'd temporarily had enough of guns and being in uniform and he wasn't in a mood to get married, yet. "Frank hadn't any relatives in Minnesota, or maybe anywhere, from the way he never talked about them. He liked women but was shy of getting involved, which I didn't blame him for, at the time. We were together a lot, I mean like four, five nights a week sometimes, from '67 till September '69 when Frank left Red Lake. Though Frank didn't drink, which set him apart from the rest of us." "Did he say why?" Augusta asked. "Ma'am, he said the stuff was 'poison' to him, it drove him 'crazy.' He said he'd had a drinking problem as a kid." "A drinking problem! How young?" "Like maybe junior high. He wasn't in a mood to talk about it, much. He didn't care to talk about himself. He'd ask me about Vietnam. Lots of questions. He didn't think the war was justified but he felt guilty about not going in. He'd have wanted to join the Marines, his dad had been a Marine, but with his blind eye, for sure they didn't want him. Nobody wanted Frank Brady in any kind of uniform." Augusta said, disbelieving, "Frank Brady wanted to fight in Vietnam, though he didn't approve of the war?" Hewitt said, with a smirk, "What I told you, ma'am. Frank felt guilty about not going in. On account of the other guys, like me, going in. And some of us shot up pretty bad. Or worse." Augusta absorbed this revelation in silence. Well, Adam had been a boy at the time. Younger than her own sons were now. There wasn't the retrospective knowledge then, and the moral disgust spawned of that knowledge, of the Vietnam debacle.

Hewitt said, watching Augusta's face, "Another thing Frank confided in me, ma'am, he didn't want it generally known but he had a record, too. He'd been incarcerated in a youth facility out in Montana." Hewitt spoke so matter-of-factly, Augusta had to touch his arm to make him pause. "Excuse me, officer? A what? 'Facility'?" "Helena State, it's called. It's a kind of camp, midway between a state penitentiary for older felons and a juvenile home." "But—why was Frank Brady incarcerated?" "For almost killing somebody, ma'am." "Almost killing somebody! Who—was it?" "His 'foster father,' he said. Frank was a ward of the county. His parents were dead, he was twelve years old when he came into the system. He got shunted around in foster homes and when he was fourteen he didn't get along with the 'foster father,' a drinker and s.o.b. who was said to push kids around, and one night Frank loses it, and pushes the guy back, and they get into a serious fight, and Frank comes close to beating the guy to death with a pickax." Hewitt shook his head, and took a swallow of his whiskey. "And this guy wasn't any runt, either. I did some inquiries, a few years later." Augusta was listening in horror. Adam Berendt? A boy of fourteen wielding a pickax? Nearly killing a man? Hewitt said, "At Helena, some Ojibways ganged up on Frank and beat him, blinded him in one eye. Indians and whites are always fighting in these facilities. Frank was fifteen when he lost the eye. He'd say, 'I'm God-damned lucky to be alive. I don't mind being half-blind if that's the price.'" Hewitt laughed. "It was like Frank in a certain mood, to make the best of a thing. Like losing an eye was a sign of something positive, if you reasoned it out. He always said Helena straightened his head. He had to calm down there, went back to school. He'd had a hard time learning to read and write, he was what d'you call it—dyslexic. 'My brain is wired wrong,' Frank would say. 'I got to work twice as hard as anybody else to make it work right.' They paroled him when he was eighteen. The charge was aggravated assault with a deadly weapon and with intent to kill." Hewitt spoke slowly, as if reluctantly. But there was a cruel, sly purpose to his words.

Augusta was feeling faint. "Thank you. I see."

"Not surprised, are you, ma'am? You look a little white. This was all a long time ago."

"Yes."

"Frank would be—what?—a pretty old guy by now? Mid-fifties?"

When Augusta didn't reply, Hewitt said, leaning across the table, "Frank had a hard time in those foster homes. You can't blame an excitable kid for protecting himself."

"Yes. I mean—no."

"He'd always say he was God-damned lucky, not just the eye, but that the guy he assaulted hadn't died. That makes a big difference in the system, ma'am, let me tell you."

Augusta was frightened of Hewitt now. His maleness, his insinuating tone. His eyes on her, his wish to know her. She thought *You brought this on yourself. You have only yourself to blame.*

"Excuse me, please—I must leave." Augusta slid out of the booth awkwardly, and nearly lost her balance, and Hewitt stood with the agility of a young man. Augusta said, panting, "No! I'm going now. I'm leaving. Please don't follow me." Hewitt followed her out of the noisy tavern and into the parking lot, he was carrying her handbag which she'd left behind—"Say, ma'am? You forgot this." Augusta had no choice but to take the handbag from him, and to thank him, and to fumble inside for the car key as he watched closely. (But which of these cars was her rental? She couldn't remember.) Terror beat in her chest like a trapped, maddened bird. The white-haired, coarse-faced sheriff of Ogden County was saying, in a low, insinuating voice, "Any more questions about my old friend Frank Brady, ma'am, I'd be happy to help you out. You're staying at the Bull's Eye Motel, eh? You're feeling O.K. to drive back there by yourself?"

Augusta managed to locate her car. Hurriedly she checked out of the motel and drove south out of Red Lake and by midnight was checking into a Days Inn, smelling powerfully of disinfectant, outside Bemidji.

"HE WAS a wild kid. Not bad, not mean, but unpredictable. This terrible thing that happened—it was an accident. But Frankie caused it to happen. That was a fact."

Mrs. Maudie Creznik of the Canyon Creek Mobile Home Campground spoke sadly but vehemently. This was all fresh to her, you could see. More than forty years ago and vivid as last night's nightmare.

Now in western Montana. In summer. Augusta in jeans and T-shirt, her ashy-silver hair plaited in a single stiff braid at the nape of her neck, found herself seated in a green plastic lawn chair having coffee with Mrs. Creznik, proprietor of the campground six miles west of Beauchamp, Montana, and approximately twenty-five miles west of the small city of Helena. It was the American West: where everything is oversized except the people. The women were seated on a rectangular strip of cement ("my patio" Mrs. Creznik called it) bordered by blood-red geraniums, in the shadow of Mrs. Creznik's mobile home, which was a bullet-shaped aluminum vehicle the size of a trailer truck, with complicated TV antenna, window boxes and shutters. The mobile home was solidly set upon concrete blocks, there were tall grasses surrounding it, which suggested to Augusta that it had been rooted in this place for a long time, like others she'd noticed in the campground. Why then, she wondered, were these *mobile* homes? Why not cottages, bungalows? Beyond Mrs. Creznik's fussily tended plot of lawn were rows of similar mobile homes, as in a residential housing development. Children were everywhere, and dogs. Young mothers were hanging laundry. In the distance were the densely wooded slopes of the Helena National Forest and several high, ice-capped mountain peaks. This was the legendary Rocky Mountain range, of which in all their years of friendship she'd never heard Adam Berendt speak, though he'd been a boy in literally the shadow of those mountains. At her motel in Beauchamp she'd had pointed out to her the highest peak in the vicinity—Scapegoat Mountain, 9,202 feet.

On her map of Montana, Augusta was intrigued to discover "Berendt Pass," 5,609 feet, north of Scapegoat.

"'Berendt'! That's where he got the name from."

Adam. Berendt. Born here.

Augusta herself was "Elizabeth Eastman." This disguise now coming to an end.

Still, she'd come this far. She would not be discouraged. More than eight hundred miles since Red Lake. What a long time the drive had taken her! Nearly as long, she was thinking, as the voyage out had been for Adam. Her compact car was buffeted by prairie winds. She heard in these winds the plaintive, hurt cries of her abandoned husband, even her children. She heard Adam's reasonable plea *Why? Gussie for God's sake why?* Often she stopped by the side of the interstate, fatigued, a headache behind her eyes. Sometimes she discovered to her horror that she'd been driving without awareness. No memory. Hypnotized by the rushing monotonous pavement and the enormous sky overhead. BIG SKY COUNTRY the Montana license plate boasted. In the east, in Salthill-on-Hudson, there was virtually no sky. The sky was a painted ceiling. You glanced upward and saw mostly trees, buildings. In the West, everything was distant and what appeared near, often was not. It was a place to inspire trance. Augusta supposed she was risking physical danger, a woman driving alone in this part of the country; a fanatic, deranged middle-aged woman driving such distances through the high desolate plains of North Dakota, then southward into the more populated, yet still sparsely populated, mountainous center of Montana. After being rebuffed at Helena she'd driven to Beauchamp, and in Beauchamp, where Adam Berendt had been born on March 30, 1947, in the local hospital, she'd made inquiries, *Morton Brady, Elsie Brady, Frankie Brady* . . . "Some of us would go to visit Frankie at the Helena camp," Mrs. Creznik was saying, "but you could see he was ashamed to see us. He must've been lonely but it was worse to see us, so we stopped going, finally. When? About 1963, I guess. The last time I saw Frankie."

Maudie Creznik had a large, open, florid, and friendly face, like a sunflower. There were myriad lines, cracks, creases in her stained-looking skin and her teeth (or dentures) were startlingly white. She smiled often, nervously. She was not a woman accustomed to visits from strangers. Yet she had a story to tell she had not told in some time, and there was attractive busty "Elizabeth Eastman" to hear it, camera in her lap. The palms of Augusta's hands were perspiring. She swallowed hard, and asked where the

Bradys' trailer had been? Mrs. Creznik laughed and said, chiding, "'Mobile home,' dear. Not 'trailer.' These are not 'trailers' we live in, dear."

"Mobile *home*. Of course, I knew that. Sorry!"

"We'll walk over. Hand me my cane, dear."

Maudie Creznik would have been a robust older woman in her late sixties except she had arthritis in hips and knees. She was cheerful in her complaints as a TV personality. Her hair was a frazzle of gray through which a pale scalp glimmered. She wore a floral pink polyester shift that fitted her lumpy figure like a tent, her pale, hairless legs were marbled with blue-ink varicose veins. Augusta liked her, yet was shy of touching her. She had to help Mrs. Creznik heave herself up out of the lawn chair.

"It was over that way. I remember well."

Mrs. Creznik leaned on Augusta's arm, and on the cane, as she walked. Augusta steeled herself against the woman's pungent smell but found it pleasant, comforting, a warm bisquity odor.

"Canyon Creek Campground used to be smaller. Always it extended back to the creek but wasn't so wide. We're on six acres now. Then, it was about half. There were just twelve lots. The homes, like the Bradys', were smaller then. The Bradys' was secondhand, and not in good repair. One of the camp eyesores. Elsie, Frankie's mom, was a sweet woman but overwhelmed. What happened to her, marrying so young, and her kids. She loved them but couldn't take care of them too well. The little girl, Holly, was born with a hearing impairment. Now, you'd get treatment for it easy, but then, I don't know how it worked out. She was a real cute, sweet, always smiling little girl, very shy, the other kids would tease, 'cause she couldn't always hear them and she didn't talk exactly right. Frankie loved his sister, he was a big clumsy kid for his age, husky, and a good swimmer, and he had something wrong with him, too, real restless in school they said, had trouble reading, which made him quick-tempered. Elsie was on the county rolls after her husband left. (That bastard! He took their car. How'd he think Elsie could live out here without a car?) Him, Morton Brady, I never knew well. Nor did my husband or father-in-law know him. Or trust him. They played cards a few times. He did just odd jobs in Beauchamp. He had a loud, gutsy laugh. You could see how a sweet trusting girl like Elsie could fall in love with him. Frankie would say later, at Helena, that his father had been a Marine killed in action in Korea, but that wasn't so. That bastard was alive as you or me. He just wasn't *here*." Mrs. Creznik paused, shading her eyes. She was panting slightly. Perspiration glistened on her upper lip. "See, where that Winnebago is parked? That was the Bradys' lot, more or less. They moved in sometime in early 1957. They'd been living in Beauchamp, different places. The boy Frankie was ten and the little girl Holly was four. I remember these facts well. Everything from those early years, I remember. Things that happen yesterday, I can't. Like there's nothing important happening now, in my life, eh? That year, 1957, I was only just married in January and we came out here to live with my husband's folks, and it wasn't an easy life, especially in the winter. I got pregnant right away and was sick a lot and then at the time of the fire I almost lost the baby at ten weeks, which turned out to be my son Timmy, now Timmy mostly runs the camp . . . The fire was April 19, 1959. A Saturday night. *I will never forget that date*." Mrs. Creznik spoke vehemently, clutching at Augusta's arm with strong talon fingers. "Like I said, the father was gone. Nor would he return for the funeral. Where he went, nobody knew or would say. He had some cousins in Beauchamp and they claimed not to know. Lowlife bastards. There was a lower class of individual out here in those days . . ." Mrs. Creznik's voice had grown tremulous.

She and Augusta were contemplating the lot where, forty years before, a secondhand mobile home owned by the luckless Bradys had been. They were trying not to be distracted by the bulky mobile home in its place with a dull-bronze aluminum exterior, window boxes and shutters, TV antenna, diapers hanging out to dry.

Augusta asked what had happened, exactly?

"'Exactly'—we never knew. The boy himself did not know. He was drunk! A twelve-year-old, drunk on beer. There were teenaged kids around here, a pack of them, not just boys but a few girls, too, their parents couldn't or wouldn't keep them in line. They'd steal boats on the creek, they'd sic dogs on one another for the hell of it. They drank, when they could get six-packs. They didn't smoke dope like kids today but they smoked cigarettes. Frankie wasn't the worst of them, he was the youngest and what you'd call easy-influenced. Well, basically he was a nice, decent boy, he loved his mother and baby sister but he was weak, he took after the others. Like I said it was a hard time for me. Some of those older kids, fifteen, sixteen years old, I was scared of, frankly. It was a rough life. I was just twenty-two . . ."

"And this boy, Frankie Brady, he'd been drinking that night?"

Augusta spoke carefully, not wanting to agitate Mrs. Creznik.

"He was. Sure. Some of those kids were what you'd actually call alcoholics except you don't think of it, in a kid that young. Eleven, twelve years old! We'd never allow that kind of behavior in this camp, today. But then, it was another time, you couldn't pick and choose your tenants out here. That night, Elsie and the little girl were in bed. It was late. The boy came in late, and he was drunk, and smoking, and he dropped a butt and it rolled under the sofa, and he couldn't find it, or maybe didn't look for it, too drunk to know what he was doing. So he falls asleep! At the kitchen table. And the smoke wakes him, around one A.M., and the curtains catch fire, and the place goes up in flames, and Elsie and the little girl are trapped in the back, there's only the front way out. The mobile home next to them went up in flames, too, but that family got out, lucky for them. But Elsie and the little girl weren't so lucky. Frankie escaped, and then he tried to go back inside to help them, you could hear that poor terrified woman screaming, and the little girl. It was a horrible, hellish thing. I don't want to talk about it anymore, I guess. This has got to be all I can tell you." But Mrs. Creznik gripped Augusta's hand hard and pressed it against her bony chest so that Augusta had no choice but to feel, appalled, the woman's pounding heart.

On their walk back to Maudie Creznik's mobile home, Mrs. Creznik asked if Frankie Brady was still alive?

"No," Augusta said. "He has died."

"Died! It's all over for him, then."
"Yes. It's all over for him."

Now I know. Adam, forgive me!

She took photographs at Canyon Creek. The mobile homes, the creek at the rear in which Frankie Brady must have swum, the mountains in the distance, the enormous sky with its harsh sculpted clouds. She positioned herself near the Brady lot, to take photographs from that site, views that the boy Frankie Brady must have seen. In the small town of Beauchamp, she located the cemetery, and spent forty minutes tramping through the grass, fending off gnats and enormous horseflies, at last finding the small cheap flat marker nearly hidden by moss and weeds. ELSIE BRADY 1927–1959 HOLLY BRADY 1955–1959 Of this she took photographs until her roll of film ran out.

PART III

Ever After

Dream Creatures

Through the opened window she saw him. Her heart leapt!

Who?

What you can't believe yet you will one day come to believe. And how natural it will be, on that day. So Adam Berendt foretold.

And yet. There came an hour in late winter, when the snow was at last melting off the roof of the old stone house in Damascus Crossing, Pennsylvania. Then, several hours in succession. At last, in the March thaw, most of a day. Absorbed in her work, fashioning a sphinx-lynx by gluing together a playful assemblage of metal buttons, shiny knobs, bleached birds' bones, shellacked moths and shellacked strips of newspaper, dolls' hair, dolls' glass eyes and other wayward materials, Marina Troy failed to think of her loss. And when she remembered, she was stricken to the heart.

"Am I forgetting Adam? Is that what will happen, I'll lose Adam a second time?"

Never! I will never forget.
I will never love another man as I have loved Adam.
I will return to Damascus Crossing, to the old stone house.
I will never part with this house Adam deeded to me. Never!

In fact, she couldn't wait to escape Damascus Crossing.

Shutting up the house, and Adam's uncompleted, abandoned work in the rear room, draped in newspaper. Loading the Jeep, and driving back to Salthill on Labor Day. "At last! I've been so lonely."

MARINA WAS SPEAKING with the owner of the Open Eye Gallery near Shaker Square when her attention was drawn through the front window by a dark-haired man she would have sworn she'd never seen before, pushing a baby stroller past the gallery. The Open Eye was set back from the sidewalk; in its front lawn were abstract sculpted pieces and a stone bench. It was a bright September day. The dark-haired man was carrying a sport coat flung over his shoulder, and had rolled up the sleeves of his white shirt to his elbows; the baby in the stroller was protected from the sun by a little fringed canopy. Marina watched fascinated as the man paused to lean over the baby and to adjust its clothing, or to speak to it. Or was he kissing the baby's forehead? Marina felt faint with longing. The dark-haired man was no one she knew—was he?

Marina was being informed that, yes, the gallery would like to exhibit her sculpted Dream Creatures sometime that winter. The owner, a friend of Adam Berendt's who'd frequently exhibited Adam's sculpted pieces, was telling Marina how much he liked her work, and how it had surprised him. There were twenty-two figures, birds and animals, none of them less than life-sized and several larger than life-sized, arranged before them, glittering and bizarre. The lynx in several postures, a seated German shepherd with a high head and pricked-up ears, a young white-tailed buck, a large rabbit, a large rooster composed of actual fowl feathers brightly painted: the creatures were dreamlike and surreal but not nightmarish, rather funny, witty, enigmatic. Recognizable shapes composed of numberless small shapes, *objets trouvés,* "found things." The gallery owner confessed, "I don't know what I was expecting from you, Marina. Tragedy, I guess."

Marina laughed, to disguise her annoyance. "I'm sorry to disappoint you, then."

"No, don't apologize. These are pieces I know I can sell."

He went on to speak with Marina of technical matters. He would draw up a contract for her to sign.

He'd been Adam Berendt's principal dealer and knew of the unfinished, stored pieces of Adam's in the house in Damascus Crossing; Marina had described these pieces to him. He believed it was most practical to leave them in storage for the time being, as Marina had done, since they were unfinished, and Adam clearly hadn't wanted them to be seen, still less exhibited; since Adam's death, there had been an increase in sales of his work, and prices were rising. Adam Berendt was one of those artists liked and admired locally but lacking reputation in art circles, and it would do his posthumous reputation no good to exhibit inferior work, even if, as Marina said, these were "promising." But Marina was disoriented, and kept losing the thread of their conversation. The Dream Creatures surrounded her, vivid, intense, glittering with a mysterious animal vigor. The large, rather burly lynx, a feline thug, though handsome, with erect tufted ears and brass-button eyes that glared, was supine in the classic pose of the sphinx, forepaws tucked beneath its muscular chest. Its jaws were muscular, too, made for tearing and devouring; its glimpsed teeth were rhinestones, with a sinister glitter; yet its stiff, conspicuous wire-whiskers gave it a playful look, you were meant to understand that this big cat wasn't about to spring into life, wasn't a dangerous predator but a work of art: in itself an *objet trouvé*. So with the hawks, the black bear cub, the coyote. The Dream Creatures had turned out a surprise to Marina herself, not figures to provoke the viewer to frown, to step back, to steel himself against feeling, but on the contrary to provoke sympathy, smiles. Adam Berendt's was the heroic mode, in ruins; Marina Troy's the childlike, playful. Marina's, she was being told, would sell.

So strange! Marina Troy back in Salthill after her year in exile, and grateful to be back; Marina Troy at the age of almost-forty, finally an artist, a sculptor, after her years in exile . . . She was smiling at the gallery owner without hearing what he said. All she was wanting was to run impulsively after the dark-haired man pushing the baby stroller.

"I'M HAPPY. *I'm* alive."

WHAT WOULD HE SAY when he saw her. What would he think.

Immediately, she would know. Always, a woman knows.

SHE'D HAD MOST of her heavy hair cut off. Gone! Good riddance!

At the start of summer in the Poconos, one day she decided. Shivering as swaths and clumps fell from her bowed head. The scissors' skilled cutting, snipping. She'd come to intensely dislike the heavy wavy dark-red hair that turned greasy within a day or two of being shampooed, gathering heat at the nape of her neck; getting into her mouth as she slept, falling into her face as she worked. It was associated in her memory with night: with Night: the heavy furry creature climbing onto her chest, straddling her in her sleep. No more. She wore her hair trimmed short now as a boy's. It was feathery-light, and exposed her face. A stylish bobbed cut that skimmed her cheekbones and the tips of her earlobes and would provoke her Salthill friends, when they saw her, and they hadn't yet seen her, to cry, *Marina! We hardly know you, why did you do such a thing, your beautiful hair . . . But how lovely you look, Marina. Really.*

No one would now mistake Marina Troy for the young, white-skinned Elizabeth I.

* * *

IT WAS A REVELATION to Marina, how beautiful Salthill seemed to her after her year away. She had wanted to loathe it, and she had ended missing it.

"Why do affluence, beauty, 'order' seem to us more superficial than poverty, ugliness, disorder; why does the human spirit seem dulled by the one, and enhanced by the other? Surely this is illogical? A delusion?"

Adam Berendt had chosen to live in Salthill, after all.

(But had Marina known Adam, really? Maybe he'd been her supreme delusion.)

In the Jeep, returning home, Marina drove along the River Road preparing herself for the sight of Adam's house, its roof only just visible through a stand of trees, but somehow in her anxiety she failed even to see his driveway, and was past his property line without realizing. In the whitish sun of early autumn the Hudson River was wider than Marina recalled, glittering like the broad, restless back of a gigantic snake.

THE YOUNG COUPLE who'd leased Marina's old Colonial house on North Pearl Street moved out on Labor Day, and on the following day Marina Troy moved in. She entered the house fearful of what she might find and found instead solace. She was home! The young couple had left the house in excellent condition. She'd liked them, and had trusted them, and hadn't charged them nearly so much rent as the real estate agent had wanted, and her trust had not been misplaced. The carpets were worn but freshly vacuumed, the furniture was Marina's familiar old furniture but the cushions had been plumped up and the wood gleamed with polish. Windows had been washed, at least on the inside. That tarry odor and taste *Thwaite Thwaite* had been banished, as with a powerful rug cleaner. On the dining room table was a vase and in it, a handful of blowsy but still gorgeous roses. Seeing these, Marina hid her face. She was terrified of breaking down, even with no one to see.

"I'm happy. I'm alive. I'm *home*."

* * *

SHE HADN'T WANTED to drive the Jeep into the village. She'd bicycled instead. On Pedlar's Lane quickly entering the bookstore, hoping that no one would recognize her. She wore khaki shorts, a green T-shirt, canvas shoes. On her head a white cotton cap. Her legs were long and tanned, her hair unnervingly short. The bell above the door tinkled and there was Molly Ivers in a denim jumper and new stylishly tinted glasses, shelving books in the nearly empty store, staring at her. "Mar*ina?*" The women embraced self-consciously. Never had Marina Troy and Molly Ivers embraced until this moment. Molly had known that Marina was returning to Salthill, but would have assumed that Marina would call before coming into the store. Yet Marina hadn't; Marina hadn't called anyone yet. Molly said, more in surprise than in reproach, "Marina, your hair. You look—younger." Marina laughed. "Younger than what, Molly?" Molly was embarrassed, her cheeks reddening. "Than you used to be."

The women had much to discuss. They would require hours, several days of talking, considering. Marina had been thinking (she confessed) of selling the store; but after stepping inside, seeing it again, she felt the old tug of affection; an almost familial affection as if here, too, in this quaint little crooked-floored shop, she was coming home. For what were books but Marina's earliest friends. Children's picture books, and in time adult books, which were (you might argue, in Adam's Socratic manner) artful variants of children's books in which fantasy has become reconstituted as "realism." Marina did love books, she loved the smell and feel of books, new hardcovers in their glossy jackets, quality paperbacks festooned with enthusiastic snippets of praise like the tiny shouted voices of friends, almost inaudible. Now Marina was an "artist" but—how realistic was it to suppose that she could support herself, or even wish to support herself, on her art; how realistic was it to suppose that she could endure long periods of isolation another time . . . "If I had the money, know what I'd like to do? Buy the place next door. Break through the wall. Expand the store, add a café, like everyone else. Display more books. Children's books. A children's nook. More art books. Display art. Sell art. Bring more people in!" Marina had taken Molly out to dinner in a restaurant a safe distance from Salthill, the women were sharing a bottle of wine and laughing a good deal and discovering to their mutual surprise that they quite liked each other, though, strictly speaking, Marina was Molly's employer. Boldly Molly said, "Marina, you have lots of rich friends. Maybe one of them would like to invest?"

The women laughed together like schoolgirls.

AFTER MARINA GAVE UP on "completing" Adam's sculptures, her life began to change. She'd failed, but there was a surprising relief in failure. Such relief! Marina had not known. Her own work came now spontaneous and uncalculated, fueled by this relief; at times it seemed to spring directly from her fingertips.

The first of her visions was Night. The predator lynx. The creature of the woods, and of her bed. In a rush of emotion Marina created Night in repose, standing, seated, ready to pounce, creeping low against the ground, devouring prey. Night's eyes were widened in cruelty, half-shut in ecstasy. Marina made no effort to suggest Night's thick, beautiful pelt, but composed Night of shiny things, as if perversely. Screws and bolts, nails, keys, metal buttons and zippers; bits of steel wool and glass. In one of the pieces, Night's eyes were two slightly mismatched watch faces, stopped at different times. Like a predator Marina tore apart dolls purchased at yard sales and used hair, glass eyes, face fragments, tiny fingers and toes. She used feathers, bones, the shellacked carcasses of large moths with black markings on their wings. She used Polaroid images of rabbit carcasses, part-devoured, and strips of shellacked newspaper pages smeared with rabbit blood. She used strands of her own winey-red hair. She used mummified mouse remains. These many objects were ingeniously glued upon a wire mesh outline of Night. There was an air of innocence, even cockiness, about Night. Even when holding his mangled prey aloft in his jaws, in triumph. For Night was *he who is*. Comprised of *objets trouvés,* he was the stylized shape of a creature. You stared at Night and smiled. The cruel tearing jaws were but the jaws of romance, made up of screws, nails, bolts, zippers. The mad-glaring eyes were but clock-eyes. You could touch this creature, even pet him, and laugh at the intricacy of his construction. Erect tufted ears fashioned of—mummified mouse hide? A jewel-glisten on—a crimson felt tongue? "This guy, you call 'Night,' is my favorite of all the pieces," the owner of the Open Eye would say, touching the head of the sphinx-lynx, as if familiarly. "There's a lot to this concept, but don't ask me what."

Those winter mornings in the Poconos, Marina worked on Night, and her mounting excitement and pleasure in the curious, unexpected shapes forming beneath her fingers came to obliterate her fear of the nocturnal creature itself. By degrees, Night ceased to crouch on her chest. Night ceased to suck at her mouth. And after Night she created an even larger figure, and a more congenial one: an obediently seated German shepherd, "Apollo," composed of dark shiny things, or shiny things darkened with stain, with flashbulb eyes and a pink plastic tongue lolling from his jaws. She made big roosters of actual fowl feathers, painted extravagant rooster-colors, glued to wire mesh frames. Their eyes were mismatched dolls' eyes, their feet were razors and spikes. She made deer, fawns, bear cubs, twin raccoons, a coyote and cub. In all, she worked on more than thirty Dream Creatures, and of these she was satisfied with twenty-two.

She asked the owner of the Open Eye if he truly thought these things might sell.

"Yes. I do."

"Because they aren't 'art'—exactly?"

"They're 'art.' Don't worry about that."

"But," Marina was thinking rapidly, "do you think—Adam would have liked them?"

"Adam would have loved them, you know Adam."

"I'm not sure that I do. That I did."

"Adam would have loved anything you did, Marina. Adam loved you."

* * *

MARINA SAW: the dark-haired man was Roger Cavanagh.

She stared. She'd stopped dead in her tracks. There was Roger Cavanagh whom she hadn't seen in a very long time, lifting a baby out of its stroller.

Whose baby? There was no one else around. Yet the baby couldn't be Roger's—could it?

Suddenly Marina recalled: Molly had alluded to a rumor about the man she'd called Cavanagh, the rude, pushy lawyer Cavanagh, a mildly scandalous rumor of Cavanagh having become involved with a much younger woman, and having a baby . . . Hurt, Marina had blocked out the rumor immediately.

Now she stared, and stared. Oblivious of her though she was only across the cobblestoned Quaker Street from him, Roger was painstakingly, just slightly clumsily, removing the baby from its stroller preparatory to placing it, in a baby seat, in the rear of his car. Marina saw Roger Cavanagh as she'd never before seen him. He seemed to her young, invigorated; a figure of mystery. How fey and contrived her Dream Creatures, set beside Roger Cavanagh and his baby. *He has a new life, and I have no place in it.* Yet, impulsively, not caring that he might rebuff her, or look with distaste at her wispy hacked-off hair, she came forward, smiling happily. "Roger! Hello."

For a moment Roger Cavanagh squinted at Marina Troy in the bright Salthill sunshine, without seeming to recognize her.

"Marina? *You?*"

FOLLOWING THIS, things happened swiftly between them.

Old Mill Way: The Attack

It would be known as the most horrific fate suffered by any individual in Salthill-on-Hudson since the infamous tar-and-feathering lynchings of the 1770s.

And it would happen on historic Old Mill Way, to the rear of the beautifully restored eighteenth-century Colonial property known as the "Macomb House," or, alternatively, the "Wade House."

On the morning before Lionel Hoffmann's fatal accident, Camille overheard her husband speaking on his cell phone in a low, urgent voice. "Are you certain, Doctor? You're telling me the truth? I can take it." Lionel paused, breathing hoarsely. Over the long, humid Salthill summer his asthma and sinus condition had worsened, despite the numerous medications he was taking. "I'm *not*—infected? My blood is *not*—'positive'?" Another pause, and the harsh angry breathing. "But can I believe you, Doctor? Oh, God. I don't know whether to believe you."

Such anguish in Lionel's voice! Camille was stricken to the heart, hearing. She stood hidden against an exterior wall of the guest house; Lionel stood, leaning on his cane, on the flagstone terrace behind the house, near the pool. Though it was October, the air was warm and sunny; the pool was heated, and Lionel tried to swim in it frequently, for therapeutic reasons. For personal reasons, and to protest the incursion of Camille's dogs into the house, Lionel had moved into the guest house at the start of the summer.

Camille hadn't meant to eavesdrop. Lionel would be furious if he discovered her. He would never believe she'd blundered into the situation in all innocence; he suspected her, she knew, of spying on him generally. In his convalescence he'd become despotic and unpredictable. He must have arranged to take a blood test in secret, given by someone other than the Hoffmanns' Salthill physician, who was an acquaintance. Lionel was now mocking the doctor's voice. "Why would you lie? How the hell would I know why you might lie, doctor?" Lionel said coldly. "I'm not a mind-reader. Everybody lies to me. My wife lies to me. My children lie to me, assuring me they love me—they 'forgive' me. As if I wanted their forgiveness! Doctor, there's a conspiracy here to keep me from knowing the truth, though it's staring me in the face." Lionel threw the phone violently from him to the flagstone terrace, where, judging from the sound Camille heard, it shattered.

Camille stood frozen against the wall of the little house. What had Lionel anticipated? *Infected blood, HIV-positive, AIDS?*

Camille felt a shiver of revulsion, and of relief. At least, there had never been any danger of her being infected. For the Hoffmanns had long since ceased all "marital relations"—as the awkward phrase has it.

She smiled wryly. *That* made her life so much less emotional, and painful, at least.

Camille went away shaken. She'd hurried to the guest house to share with Lionel some extraordinary good news she'd just received, that would surely improve their strained relationship, but—"Now isn't the time. Obviously." One of the dogs, three-legged Shadow, who must have followed after her, limped beside her, eagerly licking her hands. Out of nowhere charged the two most recent dogs, the thick-bodied mastiffs Soot and Hungry, panting, not barking, for they'd been conditioned by a cruel master never to bark under pain of being kicked, tails quivering with unspeakable excitement. "Good dogs! But you must be quiet," Camille warned in a whisper. "This isn't a time for—mirth."

SOMEHOW IT HAD happened, Camille had no idea how, there were now seven dogs under her protection. Seven! These were Apollo, Thor, Shadow, Fancy, Belle, and the two brother mastiffs Soot and Hungry. She tried to love the dogs equally, for they were anxiously aware of their mistress's every nuance of emotion and mood, and inclined to be jealous of one another except that overt jealousy displeased her; they feared and disliked Lionel, who so clearly loathed them, and slunk away when he approached. Apollo remained Camille's favorite, of course. (There were odd, eerie moments when the handsome husky-shepherd mix seemed to embody the spirit of Camille's lost friend Adam. Or maybe it was the case that Apollo bore her unspoken thoughts, her deepest wishes, to Adam, wherever he was. "Apollo! Tell your master for me that I miss him terribly. But I have my new life now, and Adam will always be part of it." At such times Apollo quivered with emotion, licking Camille's hands and face, and fixing her a look that seemed almost human.) Still, Camille loved Thor nearly as much as Apollo, for the Doberman pinscher was clearly devoted to her. And Camille's heart was bound up with Shadow, for she'd singlehandedly saved the misshapen little black dog's life. And there was Fancy, Mrs. Florence Ferris's curly-haired white poodle, the shrewdest of the dogs and yet the most childish and demanding. (Camille laughed, Fancy was so like her own children when they'd been small: "Always needing to be the center of attention, and never satisfied." Though Fancy had long been housebroken you would never have guessed it from the way, out of spite, she sometimes piddled urine on the kitchen floor that

Camille was desperate to quickly mop up, before her housekeeper, or worse yet her husband, discovered it.) Occupying a special place in Camille's heart was the husky, mud-colored Belle, a mongrel mix of bulldog and retriever, the most severely scarred of the dogs; Belle quaked and whimpered if she believed Camille was upset (on the telephone, for instance) or if she believed something had happened to Camille (if Camille was away from the house more than an hour). The thick-bodied, deep-chested oily-black mastiffs Soot and Hungry (as their name tags identified them) were mistreated, abandoned dogs condemned to be put down at the animal shelter because of their nervousness and unpredictable behavior, for no one would ever adopt them, and the attendants were afraid of them. (Yet Soot and Hungry touched Camille's heart, too. She knew to speak very softly to them and to stroke their hard-boned heads at exactly the same time, murmuring identical words to each; she knew to feed them separately from the other dogs, always first, and very generously. "I realize I really have no room at home for two more dogs," Camille said apologetically, "but I can't bear to allow these innocent creatures to be executed. Mastiffs don't choose their nature. None of us chooses his nature. God can't wish to punish us for being what we *are*.")

Camille promised Lionel she would find "decent, deserving homes" for most of her dogs. In the fall, she was to be involved in an ambitious fund-raising campaign to raise money for a new branch of the Rockland County Homeless Animal Shelter—"There'll be kennels for sixty more dogs, we've been assured!" It was Camille's intention that the dogs be confined to a part of the lawn and the garage, bounded by a new, ugly chain-link fence, and if Camille allowed them into the house they were to be confined absolutely to a small part of the downstairs, yet somehow—who knew how?—one or another of the dogs was always slipping free of these constraints, and a number of the expensive antique furnishings had been damaged. Lionel complained with extravagant bitterness, "The air is rife with dog hairs and the lawn is rich with dog dung. I wake in the middle of the night and know from the smell that I'm in Hades, though still alive, and the three-legged Cerberus is guarding my door to keep me captive. On my own property!" Living now in the guest house, about thirty feet to the rear of the main house, Lionel spent much of his time alone, brooding. Camille was often away at the Rockland County Homeless Animal Shelter, doing volunteer work, and rarely prepared meals; had she prepared them, Lionel might not have wished to dine with her; he was permanently furious with her, and deeply hurt by what he believed to be, fairly or unfairly, her preference for her "dog-disciples" over him. "Is it revenge? Because I'd been unfaithful? Or—would it have happened anyway?" He detested all the dogs but harbored a passionate dislike for Apollo, the dog that had "started it all"—"Adam Berendt's damned dog"—and had come to think, in his misery, that his friend Adam had somehow betrayed him, advising him to emerge from his cave-existence into the light. But where *was* the light?

Lionel's physical therapist A. D. Jones, a six-feet-four Haitian-born young man with rippling muscles and a quick, warm, placating smile, came to work with Lionel several times a week, at considerable expense, but Lionel's progress was slow; he'd come to believe he would never walk normally again. This, A. D. Jones rejected as "negative, pessimist" thinking. (When Jones seized and massaged Lionel's slack white flesh with his supple fingers, how desperately Lionel willed himself not to think of *her*. Never, in his waking hours, did he allow himself to weaken, and think of *her*.) For a few weeks in the early summer, Lionel spent hours each day at his new computer, trading stocks, but he had no luck, and grew discouraged after losing $100,000 in a single nightmare week—"It's a young person's world in the machine. Nasty, brutish, and short." He walked cautiously, with his cane. His recovery from surgery was slow, and now his right knee was giving him pain. There were often shooting pains in his neck. If the air smelled even faintly of dog, Lionel coughed, wheezed, sneezed. He blew his nose until his nostrils flamed. He was insomniac by night, and by day groggy and lethargic. Though he refused telephone calls from the Hoffmann family, and never spoke of Hoffmann Publishing, Inc., he seemed to miss the mechanical routine of commuting into the city and to his office.

There was a mysterious emptiness, like a cave, at the core of Lionel's existence. "What was the point of my life?" He was sincerely perplexed, like a man slapping his pockets for something he has mislaid, but damned if he can remember *what*.

CAMILLE REGARDED her troubled husband with a confused, tender love, like a mother regarding a handicapped, difficult child. She knew it was shameful that Lionel Hoffmann should be living in the guest house (though, in fact, the guest house was a handsomely modernized two-bedroom suite overlooking the pool and hillsides) and that all of Salthill was talking of this new, so very perverse "separation" of the Hoffmanns. Camille's women friends strongly advised her to get rid of her dogs, have the house thoroughly cleaned, and invite Lionel back—"Surely you don't want to drive him away a second time, do you?" Marcy was even more adamant—"Mo*ther*. Next time Daddy will get a divorce, and the new wife will take over everything. And you and your precious dogs will wind up somewhere in a *kennel*." Camille agreed, guiltily; of course she didn't want to drive Lionel away a second time, especially when he was unwell and needed her—"But my dogs need me, too. My dogs love me."

How plaintive the claim. *My dogs love me*.

Camille wondered: had the predatory young woman with whom Lionel had been involved contacted him, since he'd returned to Salthill a broken, defeated man? So far as Camille knew, she had not. Lionel had never spoken of her by name; he'd confessed only that he'd made a "hideous, humiliating mistake"; he hoped Camille would "forgive" him. Camille had said without hesitation yes, of course, she forgave him, she loved him, she was so relieved he'd returned . . . But Lionel's return had marked only the end of his adulterous affair in New York City, not the beginning of a new marital romance. Marcy warned her mother that Lionel might be slipping away to see the woman again, or other, even younger women, for "once a man begins, he becomes an addict," but Camille was certain that Lionel's days of slipping away were over. The poor man could scarcely walk! He suffered terribly from asthma and sinus headaches. His head seemed permanently congested, as if with wet cement. Though his pale, handsome face was surprisingly unlined, and his silver-tipped hair hadn't thinned, Lionel had clearly aged. Sometimes without wishing to, Camille caught sight of him grimacing at himself in a mirror: how like a death's-head he'd become! Sometimes he shook his cane at one of the dogs, and it shocked her to see how his shoulder blades protruded through the cloth of his shirt, like malformed wings.

THAT AFTERNOON, the Hoffmanns' physician, a Salthill resident and an old friend, telephoned to speak with Camille about Lionel. Though this doctor apparently knew nothing of Lionel's anxiety about infected blood, he expressed concern for Lionel's mental health, as well as his physical health. He told Camille, "I've been hearing from Lionel's specialists, and they all report the same thing: Lionel calls them frequently, never believes what he's told, expects the worst and thinks we're all lying. Then again, he often doesn't follow instructions. He thinks we're trying to 'dope him up.' He threw away two prescriptions I gave him. His therapist says that Lionel is either despairing and lethargic, or angry and hyperactive. Lionel was always the most reasonable man of my acquaintance, Camille, and now he's becoming a disturbed man. He *is* a disturbed man. It might be advisable for him to see a psychiatrist." Quickly Camille said, "Lionel would never see a psychiatrist! I could never bring the subject up, he'd be furious. He's a man of pride, you know." "He's beginning to be a very disturbed man." Camille, stung as if the insult were lodged against her, made no reply.

Though after the accident she would think *Why didn't I speak with Lionel, as I'd been advised! His life might have been saved.*

THE NEWS CAMILLE had been bringing to Lionel was wholly unexpected: the elderly dowager Florence Ferris had died, and had left \$3 million as a gift "to my dear friend Camille

Hoffmann who has made me so happy, providing a loving home for my beloved Fancy." Camille had received a call from Mrs. Ferris's attorney, and sat down, stunned by the news. Her first reaction was to protest, "Oh, but I can't accept Mrs. Ferris's bequest! It's too much money. Her heirs would be furious with me." The attorney assured Camille that this would not be the case, Mrs. Ferris's estate had been divided into numerous bequests many of which might be characterized as eccentric, and the $3 million to her, as Fancy's keeper, was typical. "But—I love Fancy for her own sake, not for *money*. I never expected to be *paid*." Camille hung up the phone, and sat for some time in a daze, as dogs licked her hands and nudged whimpering against her, sensing the turmoil of her thoughts. "Oh, Shadow! Belle. And Fancy." She stroked the dogs' heads, and allowed the curly-haired white poodle to clamber up into her lap; Fancy was in one of her nervous-quivering moods, hungry for her mistress's assurance she was loved. "You, Fancy, are a very good dog. You've brought us all such a blessing . . ." *Now I am free. If it's freedom I want.*

She could leave Lionel this property, and buy another house, in a more rural area of Rockland County, where she could live with her dogs undisturbed. With so much money she could virtually fund a new wing of the Shelter. She could help enormously in the campaign to make cruelty to animals a felony in New Jersey. Elation filled her heart: at last! But she felt guilty, too. Was she, Camille, now becoming the unfaithful spouse? Was she behaving immorally? *I must do what is right. What is best for all. But—what?*

Camille waited until the following day, when she hoped Lionel might be in a better mood, to tell him the news. But even as she approached the guest house, and the pool in which turquoise water shimmered in autumnal light, she heard Lionel's raised, angry voice.

He'd found dog excrement in the pool. He shouted at Camille, waving his cane, "God damn it, Camille! I've had enough. I want those repulsive beasts *gone*." Camille too was shocked at excrement in the exquisite turquoise water, though there wasn't much of it, a smallish sort of dog turd, clearly not the work of one of the larger dogs; murmuring apologies, Camille awkwardly took up the pool net, and tried to fish out the excrement, while Lionel followed after her limping and cursing. He continued to shout, "Camille, God damn it! God damn those dogs, and God damn *you.*" His face was contorted and not so handsome now. His eyes were a madman's eyes. He lifted the cane, he brought it down on Camille's shoulder, causing her to scream in pain. Camille would afterward claim that Lionel hadn't meant to hit her, he wasn't the sort of man to hit a woman, he'd merely meant to warn her, but in his disturbed state of mind he'd misjudged, and struck her, and she'd overreacted perhaps, by crying out; and there came, snarling and barking, as if he'd been guarding his mistress at a distance and awaiting just such an emergency, Apollo; and close behind Apollo came Thor, barking furiously; and there was Shadow charging on three legs, teeth bared; and there came Belle, wheezing and snarling; and Fancy in a savage mood, teeth bared and slobbering saliva; and, in deadly silence, charging like twin missiles, the thick-bodied deep-chested mastiffs Soot and Hungry. Camille cried for the dogs to stop, but Lionel was shouting and swiping at them with his cane, like a scythe, which provoked them past restraint. "Beasts! Filthy things! Get away! I'll have you put to death!" Thor leapt for Lionel's throat, and Lionel managed to shove him aside, but there was Shadow sinking her teeth into his leg, and there was Apollo leaping in a frenzy, and Thor quickly leapt again, and Lionel slipped to one knee, screaming in pain, and there was Belle with bulldog tenacity sinking her teeth into Lionel's ankle, and the excitable mastiffs Soot and Hungry were crazed, though still silent, tearing at their prey with powerful teeth and jaws . . .

For years to come the Hoffmanns' neighbors on Old Mill Way would tell of hearing human screams on that idyllic October morning in the country, and the frenzied barking and snarling of the dogs, for many minutes— "The most grisly, blood-chilling sound you can imagine. But you would not want to imagine!"

* * *

OF CAMILLE HOFFMANN'S seven dogs, she would insist that only three were "actively" involved in the attack. These were the mastiffs, covered in blood when rescue workers arrived, and the mixed-breed bulldog, which seemed to have gone mad in the attack, her muzzle and chest also covered in blood. Though Camille was in a state of shock, and would be in a state of shock for some time, she was adamant in speaking with authorities. The other four dogs were shut up in the garage, wetted down, still excited, but (as Camille insisted) remorseful. Knowing Mrs. Hoffmann's involvement in the Rockland County Homeless Animal Shelter, authorities decided to take her word, and only three dogs were taken from her and, in the somber parlance of the trade, *put down*.

The Ballet

This gift, this beauty. For you.

On the Sunday following Lionel Hoffmann's tragic accident, as the incident will come to be called, Abigail Des Pres takes Gerhardt Ault's thirteen-year-old daughter Tamar into the city for a matinee performance by the New York City Ballet. Abigail has gone to some trouble to secure excellent seats, in the eighth row, center of the theater; how tense Abigail is, and how hopeful, that this New York outing will go well. She's pleased to see that Tamar is deeply absorbed in the first dance, in the way that Abigail herself would have been thirty years before. There's a new young ballerina dancing, a serenely beautiful girl with long straight dark hair, flamelike, fascinating to watch. The troupe of gifted young dancers, female and male, are all Caucasian with the exception of a young black man and an Asian-American girl of astonishing suppleness and grace. The ballet, revived from the eighties, is lushly romantic, with dissonant "post-modernist" interludes, a jazzy-sexy beat, but at the end romantic again, and resolved. No ambiguity here: this is the triumph of wish-fulfillment.

The night before, Abigail had prepared dinner for Gerhardt and Tamar at Gerhardt's house, as she has several times done, and Tamar helped in the kitchen. Tamar is a vegetarian, and Abigail has recently become a vegetarian, or almost; she no longer eats "red meat," and imagines that Tamar approves of this decision, though Tamar, characteristically, has said nothing. The dinner was vegetarian for Tamar and Abigail, and Abigail prepared a grilled steak for Gerhardt.

Gerhardt, the carnivore! Abigail teases him, his face mottles with pleasure. How long has it been, Abigail wonders, since anyone has teased this poor deprived man?

Tamar eats lightly, you mustn't try to force food upon her. Abigail, who's had her own flirtations with anorexia well into adulthood, knows this. But Tamar will eat some of what Abigail prepares, and always says politely that it's "delicious."

Abigail and Gerhardt Ault are going to be married in January, in a small ceremony in the Salthill Episcopal Church. Abigail's numerous friends are eager to celebrate the couple with parties and dinners, but Abigail has declined, with thanks—"I don't want Gerhardt to be overwhelmed. He isn't very 'social,' by our standards." Abigail is charmed by Gerhardt, who loves her as no other man has ever quite loved her; it's truly flattering to be, at the age of forty-three, unabashedly adored. Abigail wishes she could introduce Gerhardt to Adam Berendt, and nudge Adam in the ribs—"See? This guy has fallen for me hard. Not like you, you selfish bastard." (Only joking!) But Abigail intends never to introduce Gerhardt to Harry Tierney, a genuine bastard capable of murmuring in Abigail's ear, in Gerhardt's very presence, "What a sweet sap! Congratulations at last, Abby."

No, Abigail has no plans for Gerhardt and Harry to meet. She has no plans for Gerhardt and Jared to meet.

You gave me up. Now another has taken me.

The previous Sunday, Gerhardt took Abigail and Tamar to visit one of his renovation projects, a Roman Catholic church built in 1923, in Paterson, New Jersey. The church was massive, ugly, decaying, its exterior walls sooty with grime, its interior damp and dim as a mausoleum. Abigail couldn't keep from shuddering. "Yes, it is ugly," Gerhardt conceded, "but it's of historic significance and should be preserved." Abigail found this cheering—*Nothing is ugly that is of historic significance.*

Gerhardt works long hours, and when he's home talks tirelessly of his work. Abigail, a born listener, knows the right questions to ask. If at dinner Tamar seems receptive, Abigail will ask her gently about school, or her music lesson, and Tamar will reply in carefully chosen words, with a shy, fleeting smile. *She wants to trust me. Maybe, someday!*

My life is saved. At last.

AT INTERMISSION, Abigail tells Tamar, "This next ballet! I first saw it when I was fourteen. I loved it. I wanted so badly to be a dancer. There's such beauty in dance, and a kind of innocence you don't find elsewhere. Of course, for me, it was sheerly romance." Tamar, reading program notes, glances up briefly as Abigail speaks, with a polite, veiled expression; her eyes return to the program as Abigail continues, "I've told you, I guess?—I'd started dance lessons when I was eight. But—" Abigail pauses, embarrassed suddenly that she's confiding, confessing, too much. Tamar would prefer to read the program notes.

During the next ballet, which is less familiar to Abigail than she would have anticipated, Abigail is aware of Tamar's intense involvement in the music. The pulse, beat, throb, soaring of the music. Abigail tries to listen with Tamar, and through Tamar. In this way the ballet is doubly enhanced for her. Abigail has come to love Gerhardt Ault, to a degree—she has even managed to make love with him, tenderly if not very passionately—but Gerhardt is a known, finite quantity to her, while Tamar remains elusive, mysterious. *The girl in the red beret.* Covertly Abigail watches Tamar's small-boned, delicate face, the smooth pale perfect skin, the long-lashed somber eyes. To Abigail, Tamar is like the lead ballerina in this ballet: as male dancers reach for her, she leaps away; always, she eludes them; she isn't to be embraced, or captured; the music signals laughter, effervescence. The stage is bathed in a liquidy golden light. What appear to be fireflies—hundreds of fireflies!—emerge out of shadows as the dancers leap and glide through them. There's a witty, brisk pas de deux as a finale. Abigail takes pleasure in Tamar's rapt attention. She wishes she dared reach over to squeeze Tamar's hand as she might have done with her own daughter. *Lovely, isn't it?* But she's shy of touching Tamar too often, she dreads the first rebuff.

The final dance is a Tchaikovsky suite based on themes from Mozart. Abigail knows the ballet, and finds it consoling in its classic familiarity. Dancers in white, lithe young girls on their toes, the astonishing feet of dancers who never (visibly) tremble or feel pain. Or perspire. Abigail thinks of the ancient Chinese custom of foot-binding for women. Foot-binding! To make of a female, of a certain class, a virtual cripple. For life. The tiny crushed foot. A malformed female genital? There must be some symbolism here, but Abigail doesn't want to pursue it.

Tamar is reported to have been born in a rural area near Canton, on February 11, 1988. Gerhardt has said the date is probably an approximation, Tamar might be older, or younger. Abigail wonders uneasily who Tamar's mother was, or is? How old was she at the time of Tamar's birth? Does this woman ever think of Tamar, her given-away daughter, or was the baby's birth of little consequence to her? The Christian adoption organization surely saved Tamar's life. For female life is notoriously cheap in China, India. Female infanticide is common, pragmatic. Abigail shivers to think how Tamar, whom she adores, would not be adored universally. As a newborn she might have been brutally extinguished, tossed away like garbage.

Life devours life, but man breaks the cycle, man has memory.

Adam was an idealist, for all his earthy good humor and lack of pretense. An idealist, who would not have wished to acknowledge the desperation of mankind, the cruelty. To rise above such desperation, you must rise above poverty. Civilization is this rise, this ascent. Abigail knows she doesn't deserve her privileged white-skinned American life, still less her paradisical Salthill life.

But she means to live it, and to wring every drop of happiness from it, she can.

Abigail has noticed how, when they're in public together, people glance at her and Tamar. You can read their thoughts—*Adopted?* She both resents this and feels a tinge of pride. She hopes that Tamar doesn't notice. (Of course, Tamar notices.) Uneasily Abigail wonders if, one day soon, Tamar will tire of being so seen, identified. *An adopted Chinese orphan?* Maybe, one day, Tamar will repudiate the well-meaning Caucasians who adopted her. Abigail vows that she will support Tamar in whatever Tamar wishes.

Only good for her. Happiness!

What Abigail wishes: she might hide from Tamar the brutality, evil, ugliness of the world. That week she'd hidden from Tamar those local newspapers with photographs of Lionel Hoffmann on their front pages, above lurid headlines—OLD MILL RESIDENT MAULED, KILLED BY DOGS. What a horror! Abigail couldn't bear to read of the attack herself. To think that Lionel Hoffmann died in such a way, and only a few miles from Abigail's house . . . Abigail wonders if Tamar's classmates talked of it. But maybe Tamar didn't hear? Abigail said nothing to Tamar about the appalling incident, and she and Gerhardt haven't had the opportunity to discuss it. Gerhardt asked, "Didn't you know this poor man, Abigail?" and Abigail said quickly, "Yes. But not well, no one did." Feeling then guilty, as if she'd denied Lionel's humanity; in fact, Abigail had always liked Lionel Hoffmann, Lionel was one of the nicer Salthill husbands; she'd danced with him numerous times over the years, and felt the man's stiff, yearning fingers at the small of her back, and his unarticulated desire—as Abigail's was unarticulated—to embrace tightly, in impulsive passion, and push away again. Abigail told Gerhardt, with a shudder, "I knew Camille much better. The poor woman, the dogs were *hers*."

Abigail called Camille several times, and was relieved when no one answered. Beatrice Archer assured her that Camille's family had come to be with her. Had Abigail known that Camille had seven dogs? *Seven?* "Only three were involved in the attack, though." Abigail asked when the funeral would be, and was surprised to learn that there would be none, only just cremation. "Cremation? Where?" Abigail asked. "A private ceremony," Beatrice said, "at that place in Nyack. Remember Mr. Shad?"

THE DANCE! Abigail tries to concentrate. She's dangerously close to tears. *Adam has been dead, has been gone more than a year. Adam has never seen Tamar.*

If not for Adam's death, Abigail would never have seen Tamar.

The girl in the red beret would have been invisible to her.

Where, then, would Abigail be, at this moment?

Trying to concentrate on the dance, the intricate music. The ballet is the very emblem of civilization. Not-real. Sheer beauty. Romance. Tamar is drawn into it, frowning in concentration. As when Tamar practices her cello there's that look in her face of ardent concentration, and when Abigail has glimpsed her at her computer . . . (Tamar's computer! Abigail has vowed never to snoop. Never to enter the girl's room uninvited, when she is Mrs. Gerhardt Ault. Never will she search among Tamar's things, her e-mail and files. Abigail respects Tamar's privacy. And she is fearful of what she might discover that could destroy her idealization of the girl.)

Romance! Not-knowing what you might know.

Unexpectedly in Salthill, it's a season of romance. There is Abigail Des Pres and Gerhardt Ault, and there is Roger Cavanagh and Marina Troy. Roger and Marina are evasive about future plans, and they don't appear to be living together, but everyone is charmed by their romance. First, there was Roger's baby. Now, there's Roger and Marina. The two look lovestruck, dazed by their good fortune. Marina came back from her year of exile, a sculptor. In a bold gesture, she cut off most of her remarkable winy-red hair. (Abigail thinks this hair-cutting was a mistake, now Marina looks almost ordinary.) "Do you love Marina?" Abigail asked Roger point-blank, for Roger had been rude enough once to ask if Abigail loved Gerhardt, as if that were any of Roger's business, and Roger said, "I adore Marina! I always have. And you can see, she adores Adam."

For a moment Abigail was confused. "'Adam' . . ."

"My son."

The dance is ending. The final ballet. So soon! Shamelessly Abigail has been daydreaming. She hopes that Tamar hasn't noticed. *What a hypocrite, my stepmom.* No, surely Tamar hasn't noticed. Abigail claps loudly, claps until her hands ache; she feels a wave of elation, as the dancers take their bows, glancing shyly out into the enthusiastic audience; when the dancers exit the stage for the final time, Abigail feels a sudden loss, a letdown. She's being expelled from paradise, back into life.

But now, in a display of unrestrained enthusiasm, Abigail does squeeze Tamar's hand. "Oh, wasn't it lovely, Tamar?" The girl surprises Abigail by frowning as if, for just a moment, she's considering how to reply. Then she murmurs almost inaudibly, "Ye-es." She hesitates as if she has more to say, but she says nothing more.

Abigail notices, Tamar leaves the program behind, fallen beneath the red plush seat.

EXPELLED FROM PARADISE. Into midtown Manhattan.

Returning to Abigail's car which is parked in a lot on West 66th Street, Abigail and Tamar are abruptly set upon by several belligerent young men, in their late teens or early twenties, loud, drunk, leering—"Hey, lady! Gimme gimme!" Abigail has a blurred impression of grinning mouths, bared teeth, swarthy rough skin, a soiled sweatshirt bearing the likeness of a TV wrestler; instinctively she steps between Tamar and the men. She will afterward recall how pedestrians stare at them, then look quickly away and hurry past. A half-block away on Broadway a uniformed police officer stands, not noticing, or indifferent. Abigail is being pushed, shoved, her handbag pulled from her, but she grips it tighter. "Go away! Leave us alone!" A shaved-head boy shrieks an obscenity into Abigail's face, bounces his fist against the side of her head. Abigail should fall to the sidewalk, the blow makes her ears ring, but God damn she's stubborn, she refuses to fall, or to surrender her handbag, it's expensive leather, Italian-made, she's a wild woman screaming for help, she's going to protect the girl, even trying (in her high-heeled sling-back shoes) to kick her assailants, who surround her, jabbing and poking, laughing, and suddenly they're running across the street, jostling pedestrians, drumming their fists on the hood of a taxi. Like prankish-dangerous dogs they are, as swiftly as they swoop upon their prey, they're gone.

Abigail is light-headed, adrenaline is coursing through her veins like liquid fire. She sees the girl close beside her, the girl who means so much to her, Tamar, her stepdaughter Tamar, staring at her with widened eyes as if seeing Abigail for the first time. "Abigail—?" The girl speaks urgently. She has taken Abigail's badly shaking hand, and Abigail hugs her, hard, sobbing in relief. "Oh, honey."

Abigail and Tamar stand, trembling in their embrace, on the sidewalk on West 66th, and Abigail thinks *I have never been so happy.*

The Lovers, by Night

"... BUT SHOULD WE BE *married!* It seems so ... belated."

" 'Belated'? It's happening at the perfect time."

"We've known each other for years."

"We've never known each other. We'd been misinformed of each other."

"We'd been misinformed for years. Yes. And now to be married, doesn't it seem to you ..."

"Marina, what? This is almost insulting."

"Everyone is married."

"Aren't we 'everyone'? Are we 'no one'?"

"... so conventional, somehow."

"Falling in love is conventional. Caring for another person. Wanting to live with another person?"

"But where should we live, Roger? You don't want to move into my little house, and I don't blame you. But your townhouse is so completely yours."

"We'll buy our own house. Tomorrow."

"Roger! That's not a good idea."

"Why not?"

"It's . . . too abrupt."

"I am abrupt. I believe in abruptness."

"You're . . . an impetuous man."

"Because I inveigled you into committing a trivial crime against the statute?"

"You didn't 'inveigle.' I was willing."

"No. I seduced you. Then I fell in love with you."

". . . was that what happened?"

"That was exactly what happened. You witnessed a forged signature, and I thought *I love her!*"

"I didn't love you. I was afraid of you."

"You were never afraid, Marina. You were disdainful."

"No."

"You're disdainful now."

"Roger, *no*."

"But you can't lie to me, Marina. I know you too well."

"I'm afraid of being married to . . . a lawyer."

"What's that mean?"

"A lawyer perceives the world as an opportunity for manipulation . . ."

"And a sculptress?"

"I am not a sculptress! That's almost insulting."

"Look, you love Adam, don't you?"

"Adam . . ."

"My son. My son Adam."

"Of course I love Adam. I adore Adam."

"Well, Adam needs a woman's presence, immediately. He needs a mother. He'll be confused, thinking the nanny is his mother. You wouldn't want Adam to grow up confused, would you?"

"Roger, don't be silly."

"We'll buy a house, then. Tomorrow. I've made a few calls."

"This is . . . frightening to me."

"On the river. We'll buy a house on the river."

"Is that a good idea? We'll be reminded of . . ."

"He's easy to live with, I think. Wasn't he, in life?"

". . . but can we afford a house, Roger? *I* can't."

"Well, I can."

"And then, am I expected to sell my house? I love this house, Roger."

"It's a charming little place. No matter if the floors are crooked, liquids spill, and glasses fall off tables. No matter if a man of normal height hits his head going through doorways. And every time I come into this room I expect to see the seven dwarves in this bed."

"I suppose you hate the bookstore, too."

"The 'quaint' bookstore! I love it."

"If you think it's so quaint, you could invest in it. Molly and I would like to buy the place next door, and tear down the walls . . . Is something funny?"

"Nothing about this conversation is funny. Our future is being decided."

"Roger, I don't think I can . . . sell this house. If something went wrong . . . between us. I'm not young enough to . . ."

"You're just young enough. Do what you want. Keep this house, or sell it. It's yours."

". . . I could use it as a studio, I suppose. If you don't think that's wasteful . . ."

"'Wasteful'? How?"

"An entire house, for just . . . a studio."

"In whose eyes is it 'wasteful'? Do you give a damn?"

"I'm not sure. I think, yes . . . sometimes. The opinions of other people . . ."

"Fuck other people's opinions."

"Other people are all we *have*."

"No. Each other is all we have."

"You don't even believe that yourself. We must live in the world."

"Is Salthill the world?"

"Well, we must begin somewhere . . ."

"Look, Marina: do you love me?"

"Yes. I think so . . ."

"You 'think so'? What the hell does that mean?"

"Yes. I do love you. I've decided . . . yes."

"Then that's enough. We'll begin there."

The Homecoming

There was a woman who in the middle of her life fled home, in order one day to return home. And, returning home, was astonished at the changes that had taken place in her absence.

At the rear of the house, the landscape was transformed.

"Owen, my God! These gardens! How did you . . . when . . . ? This is beautiful."

"I'd hoped you would see them one day, Augusta. I never gave up believing you were . . . alive."

Like new, young lovers they clasped each other's hand, and dared not look at each other. Not for the moment.

A year and a day, vanished. Where?

No matter, Augusta Cutler was returned.

How strange Salthill-on-Hudson looked to her! After the great spaces of the West, how small, how precious, how privileged, how locked in time, like a smart, fashionable watch ticking with self-importance, yet no true importance. The very streets—the drives, lanes, circles, passes, "ways" and "runs"—were too narrow. The expensive, exquisite houses were too close together, even the "country estates" on their several acres. And the Cutlers' own house! The six-bedroom French Normandy on Pheasant Run, that provoked her to laughter when she saw it. How absurdly large for any single family, let alone a middle-aged couple whose children have long since grown and gone. ("What were we thinking of, when we bought this? Who were we?") Yet Augusta had to acknowledge the beauty of the property. She had to acknowledge its illusory promise of seeming to bestow upon its inhabitants some measure of moral, spiritual worth. And it was her home.

What most astonished Augusta was the change in her husband Owen.

("*Is* this Owen? Or an older Cutler relative . . . ?")

Not just that Owen was older, and now nearly bald, his head covered in a soft pale down, but he'd become soft-spoken, with an appealing hesitancy to his voice: the hesitancy of a man who is no longer absolutely certain what *is,* and what *is not.* Owen's eyes were now the naked eyes of a man who has surrendered all pride, and consequently all shame. There was no vanity here, but perhaps a kind of ancient tortoise-wisdom. The acerbic patrician manner that Augusta had once found sexually stirring, and had come finally to find hateful, had vanished. Smooth as old, worn stone Owen Cutler now appeared.

Gazing at Augusta, and blinking as if she were bathed in an ethereal, blinding light. How many times exclaiming, "Augusta, darling! Welcome home. You've made me so *happy.*"

Happy! And not a word of reproach.

Augusta shook her head, perplexed.

She'd returned to Salthill a tall suntanned rawboned woman. The rosy Renoir-flesh for which she'd been noted, her startling sensuous beauty, had melted away. Now she was handsome, "striking." Her hair was a bristling ashy-gray that fell to her shoulders like a horse's mane. She wore jeans with soiled knees, a pullover sweatshirt purchased in a roadside café. Her soiled canvas shoes were worn without socks. Her fingernails were clipped, and not wholly clean. (Her beautiful rings were too loose on her fingers, and inappropriate for her fingers.) Unconsciously, back in Salthill, Augusta kept glancing skyward, confused by so many trees, dense foliage. No horizon! It was a curious stunted way to live . . . you almost expected inhabitants of this region to be short, anemic, blind-blinking like moles.

Owen led her eagerly, proudly into the garden at the rear of the house, that was really three gardens. Augusta stared, in disbelief.

The first, bordering the flagstone terrace, was a garden of roses, of all hues and combinations of hues: crimson, yellow, mauve, pink, cream, ivory-white. The second, on a hillside, was dahlias, begonias, zinnias, marigolds, gladioli. The third, terraced on a hillside, was a vegetable garden grown lush in autumn: staked tomato plants grown to a height of six feet, squash and zucchini in abundance on the ground, peppers, sweet basil and thyme, honeydews and watermelons.

Augusta realized *It's Adam's garden. Except—*

So much more ambitious, and better tended, than Adam's garden.

Owen said quietly, "For you, Augusta. You see, I never believed you were . . . gone."

Even as Augusta marveled at these sights, cultivated by a businessman of seemingly limited imagination who'd rarely taken time to stroll about his own property, and "exercised," grudgingly, by riding a motorized cart about the Salthill Golf Club course, Owen was leading her, like a bride, into a greenhouse—a *greenhouse*!—in which tropical orchids of surpassing beauty and delicacy seemed to float, luminescent in the steamy air.

"Owen, when did you build *this?* My God."

"Last winter. It came to me in a dream. Or, rather—you came to me in a dream. *You* suggested it." Owen smiled almost shyly. "You held out an orchid to me, and promised you'd return 'when the orchids bloom.' It was a dream that made me so happy, darling, though when I was awake I hadn't much to be happy about."

These words hung in the air, irresolute. Augusta was tempted to say *Owen, I'm sorry!*

But she could not. The words stuck in her throat. She wasn't sorry, and wasn't going to lie.

That was one of the terms Augusta had set for herself, when she'd decided to return to Salthill. No more lies. Even in the service of making others happy.

In Montana, Augusta had seen such older men: men like Owen Cutler: obscurely wounded by life, retired from the fray of life, ex-cattlemen perhaps, seemingly well-to-do, and yet hesitant, uncertain. Like men venturing out onto thin ice. These men were invisible to younger men, and to many women. Their sexual bravado had faded, the masculine air of energy, self-esteem, self-confidence. In the prime of their lives they'd been "successful" and then, perhaps abruptly, unexpectedly, something had happened—illness, accident, financial losses, disappointing children, divorce, death—to break them, and make them doubt everything they'd believed in. Yet somehow they'd mended, and made a decision to live, and to live happily, as long as possible. Seeing Owen in this light, Augusta saw him with a new respect. Here was a man she would not have left . . . at least, not in the way she'd left Owen. Here was a man she would not have wished to hurt, or to bring to his knees.

Owen was saying, with the air of one confessing a weakness, "A private detective I'd hired to find you, a man named Elias West, who came highly recommended, led me to believe, initially . . . gave me hope . . . he'd found a handbag of yours, in Miami . . . stolen? . . . and later . . . oh, God, Gussie, this is terrible, I don't think I can tell you . . ." Owen paused, wiping his forehead with a tissue. "Maybe another time, dear. For I'd had to identify a . . . a woman's body . . . in Florida. And . . ." Owen was so moved, Augusta felt a stab of panic. Elias West had come up with a possible corpse, then? Augusta didn't want to know.

Augusta said tersely, "Yes. A handbag of mine was stolen. In April."

"And that led us to believe you were in Miami, of course. Just to know that you were somewhere, and alive . . . gave me hope."

Owen continued to show Augusta through the greenhouse, identifying orchids. Yes, they were beautiful, orchids. Useless, beautiful. Vaguely Augusta recalled her first orchid corsage, at least forty years ago. Forty years! Pinning it on her prom dress, she'd managed to stick herself practically in the left breast.

Augusta was thinking she would resume taking photographs that very week. She would take a course in the city, at the New School. She would convert a room in the house, to a studio, with a darkroom. She foresaw photography trips in the future. She might photograph the places of her long-ago past, as she'd photographed those of Adam Berendt. She might return to Florida, and to the West. And there was the Southwest. These would be solitary trips. Though always she would return to Salthill.

Elias West. Augusta had to admit, the mere sound of that man's name stirred her interest. What a character! What a man.

And quite a lover.

Possibly they might meet again?

No. Augusta had discarded West's number. There was something duplicitous and cagey about West, no woman could trust him. In a gesture of good sense and self-abnegation Augusta had discarded his number.

Except: West, a private investigator, could hardly be difficult to locate. No doubt he was listed on the Internet. And his number would be somewhere in Owen's files.

IT HAD BEEN a bright September morning when Augusta telephoned Owen. She was staying in a rented cabin in Montana, with a view of snowcapped Scapegoat Peak. Why exactly at that moment, why had she made her decision, Augusta didn't know. Except the season was changing, she'd been away long enough. She was lonely at last. She did miss Salthill.

The receiver was picked up on the first ring.

"Owen? It's me."

". . . Augusta?"

There was a pause. Augusta might even then have replaced the receiver. "Yes. I suppose."

"Augusta! Darling! Will you be . . . coming home?"

How warm, Owen's voice. How entirely without reproach or the slightest hint of anger. The old Owen, Augusta was thinking, would have been furious, and slammed the receiver down as soon as he heard her voice. The old Owen would have long since ceased loving her, and filed for divorce.

"Yes."

She began to cry. But Owen would not hear.

Augusta would offer Owen no explanation for her behavior. Her final caprice (as her children saw it) was to arrive home days after she'd been expected, and without having telephoned in the interim. *A year and a day absent. Just long enough.* Owen was waiting at the foot of the driveway when at last Augusta's rented car turned into the drive, and he hurried to greet her, kissing her hands, and her face where she allowed him, laughing, breathless, his face dangerously flushed. Augusta blinked away tears, and refused to become emotional. She'd spent a year mourning—what?—emotion, maybe. The passing of, not youth, for her youth had long since passed, but the passing of the attitude, the expectation, of youth. "Yes. Here I am."

Owen was grateful for Augusta's return as a man dying of thirst would be grateful for a mere wadded cloth soaked in water, he demanded no explanation from her. "All that matters, darling, is . . . this."

To Augusta's adult children, to her numerous relatives and friends, she would provide not a hint of where she'd gone, or why. Had she been traveling with a lover? Had she hidden away, with relatives, or friends, who'd kept her secret? *Where* had she been? And why such a radical change in her appearance, and even in her voice? (Augusta noticed no change in her voice. Was it flatter now, less nuanced? Did she speak more abruptly? And with fewer smiles?) Seeing her look of bemused defiance, no one wished to confront her. When her eldest son Mark stared at her disapproving, and began to say reproachfully, "Mot*her*. We were desperate about you. For God's sake how could you do such a—" Augusta raised a warning forefinger, like one raising the barrel of a gun, and the indignant young man ceased speaking.

(To others in the family Mark complained: "Mother is totally changed. Not that she's selfish and stubborn, she'd always been selfish and stubborn. But now she's a woman I don't know. No makeup, and that ugly wild hair, and her legs are *muscled*. Jesus! She looks like she's been living with Indians on a reservation out west.")

Eventually, because she was proud of it, Augusta would show Owen and a few Salthill friends her portfolio of photographs. *Red Lake, Minnesota & Beauchamp, Montana* was the mysterious title. They would remark upon the singular, strong images, as many as fifty or sixty prints, all black-and-white, without knowing what to make of them. (Why Minnesota and Montana? Why had Augusta felt the need to go so *far*?) But Augusta, though clearly fascinated by her own photographs, would volunteer no information about them other than identifying their locale. "This? A prison?" Beatrice Archer asked, mystified. "So ugly! And this grave marker, 'Elsie Brady. Holly Brady.' Where was this taken?"

"Beauchamp, Montana."

"But why? I mean—why did you take so many pictures of this one grave, Augusta, and not any others?"

Augusta said, matter-of-factly, "Because I wanted to." She closed the portfolio, and the discussion.

AUGUSTA WOULD TELL no one what she'd learned of Francis Xavier Brady. She would keep Adam Berendt's secret as if it were her own.

MARRIED FOR THIRTY YEARS yet they were shy and self-conscious as newlyweds, alone together.

And how like a bridegroom Owen Cutler came, bearing a large ripe honeydew melon from his garden, for Augusta.

The honeydew smelled of autumnal sunshine, and rich warm earth, and a sweetly pungent rind-odor. With a long-handled knife Owen cut thin crescent-slices out of the melon, to be eaten by hand. "Owen, how beautiful your melon is. And how delicious." Augusta bit into the fleshy pale-green fruit that was just slightly overripe, and made her mouth water alarmingly though honeydews were not her favorite melons. Juice ran down her fingers, and down her bare forearm.

Owen said, pleased, "It is delicious, isn't it?"

In a patch of fading, though still warm autumn sunshine they were sitting together on the flagstone terrace, at a white wrought-iron table they'd had a very long time. Augusta was surprised at her appetite, and quickly devoured several melon slices. Owen watched her with an adoring look that made her want to laugh at him, and hide her face. "This is like my dream, Augusta. That I would plant my garden, and harvest it, and you would return. 'A year and a day'—somehow, I knew this. Though I didn't dare hope it would actually happen."

Augusta smiled hesitantly. "You didn't give up on me, Owen." It was a question in the form of a statement, she would not have wished to ask directly.

"Never!"

Then, amending: "Well, yes. In weak moments. I had faith that you would return, but I had to acknowledge that you might not. That something might have happened to you."

Augusta said slowly, "Much has happened to me, Owen. But I'm back."

Owen cut another melon slice, and held it for Augusta to eat; Augusta cupped his hand in hers, and ate. Their mood was suddenly playful, flirtatious. "Owen, you amaze me. I mean that sincerely."

"You amaze me, Augusta. Those photographs! You've become a woman with secrets."

Augusta had always been a woman with secrets. But by her silence she acknowledged, what Owen said was so.

"And will you never tell me . . . your secrets?"

Owen spoke lightly, yet wistfully. His stony-smooth face was softened about the jaws, he'd freshly shaved. His eyes seemed to Augusta strangely raw, lashless. You looked into them, and not at them. (And her own eyes? Without makeup? Naked and raw, too, she supposed.) With the edge of the knife Owen scooped sticky, fibrous seeds out of the honeydew's interior. His hand holding the knife trembled just slightly.

Augusta smiled. "Never, Owen."

"You were with a . . . man? Were you?"

Augusta laughed, heat rising into her face. She was eating a thin slice of melon, juicy melon, biting into it with her strong teeth as, ardently, Owen watched. His breath was quickened, his fingers nervously rubbed against one another.

He said, "But I hope, at least, you did love him. That it was . . ." Owen's smile was brave, wavering. " . . . a profound experience."

Augusta stroked her husband's hand, running her fingertips over his bony knuckles. How surprised she'd been to discover that, yes, the palms of his hands were callused. It was nearly dusk. A warm, secretive sort of darkness rose from the gardens, their vivid colors and particularities now obscured by shadow. In a while, the Cutlers would go inside their house; they would light lamps, and prepare a meal in the kitchen; later, they would retire upstairs to their bedroom. How long it had been since they'd shared the same bed, let alone lay in each other's arms! Their kisses would be shy, and hopeful. Their lovemaking would be tender and forgiving. Augusta's eyes filled lavishly with tears, but these were not tears of pain.

"But I came back to you, Owen. And I will never leave again."

Blonde

Joyce Carol Oates

A sweeping, mesmerising novel of the most enduring and evocative cultural icon of the 20th century.

Joyce Carol Oates' masterpiece is a brilliant and deeply moving portrait of a culture hypnotised by its own myths, as well as a deeply moving exploration of the woman who became Marilyn Monroe.

'Nobody has ever caught Marilyn more brilliantly in words than Oates.' *Sunday Times*

'Blonde is an epic achievement, a masterpiece, a piece of art so shatteringly well-conceived and lavishly-wrought that at times it almost does not seem like a mere book.' *Independent on Sunday*

'A torrentially imaginative, compulsively readable *tour de force*… Blonde brings this nearly mythic tale triumphantly and terribly to psychological life.' *Sunday Telegraph*

£ 7.99
1-84115-372-9

We Were the Mulvaneys

Joyce Carol Oates

The Mulvaney family is seemingly blessed by everything that makes life sweet until, in 1976, something terrible happens to Marianne Mulvaney, the pretty sixteen-year-old daughter.

The incident is hushed up in the town and never discussed within the family but its impact reverberates throughout their lives forever.

'I read this book over a year ago, but this family still haunts me.' Oprah Winfrey

'It is a book that will break your heart, heal it, then break it again every time you think about it.' *Los Angeles Times*

'A brilliantly detailed and varied picture of family life… These are people we recognise, and she makes us care deeply about them.' *Kirkus*

'Novelists such as John Updike, Philip Roth, Tom Wolfe and Norman Mailer slug it out for the title of the Great American Novelist. But maybe they're wrong. Maybe, just maybe, the Great American Novelist is a woman.' *The Herald*

£ 6.99
1-84115-699-X

London · New York